Analog

The Best of Science Fiction

Analog

The Best of Science Fiction

Galahad Books   New York

Published by
Galahad Books
149 Madison Avenue
New York, NY 10016

Published by arrangement with Davis Publications, Inc.
Manufactured in U.S.A.
Designed by Jennie Nichols/Levavi & Levavi

10 9 8 7 6 5 4 3 2

Library of Congress Catalog Card Number 82-83238

ISBN 0-88365-671-x

Acknowledgments

The editor makes grateful acknowledgment to the following authors and authors' representatives for granting permission to reprint the stories in this anthology:

Isaac Asimov for *Belief* by Isaac Asimov, © 1953 by Street & Smith Publications, Inc.; renewed 1981 by Davis Publications, Inc.

Blackstone Literary Agency for *Thin Edge* by Jonathan Blake MacKenzie, © 1963 by The Condé Nast Publications, Inc.; and for *A Case of Identity* by Randall Garrett, © 1964 by The Condé Nast Publications, Inc.

Davis Publications, Inc. for *Berom* by John Berryman, © 1950 by Street & Smith Publications, Inc.; renewed 1977 by The Condé Nast Publications, Inc.; for *Adam and No Eve* by Alfred Bester, © 1941 by Street & Smith Publications, Inc.; renewed 1968 by The Condé Nast Publications, Inc.; for *Tiger Ride* by James Blish & Damon Knight, © 1948 by Street & Smith Publications, Inc.; renewed 1975 by The Condé Nast Publications, Inc.; for *The Chonokinesis of Jonathan Hull* by Anthony Boucher, © 1946 by Street & Smith Publications, Inc.; renewed 1973 by The Condé Nast Publications, Inc.; for *Rescue Party* by Arthur C. Clarke, © 1946 by Street & Smith Publications, Inc.; renewed 1973 by The Condé Nast Publications, Inc.; for *The Day Is Done* by Lester del Rey, © 1939 by Street & Smith Publications, Inc.; renewed 1966 by The Condé Nast Publications, Inc.; for *Over the Top* by Lester del Rey, © 1949 by Street & Smith Publications, Inc.; renewed 1976 by The Condé Nast Publications, Inc.; for *"The Years Draw Nigh"* by Lester del Rey, © 1951 by Street & Smith Publications, Inc.; renewed 1978 by The Condé Nast Publications, Inc.; for *Protected Species* by H. B. Fyfe, © 1951 by Street & Smith Publications, Inc.; renewed 1978 by The Condé Nast Publications, Inc.; for *Thinking Machine* by H. B. Fyfe, © 1951 by Street & Smith Publications, Inc.; renewed 1978 by The Condé Nast Publications, Inc.; for *Implode and Peddle* by H. B. Fyfe, © 1951 by Street & Smith Publications, Inc.; renewed 1978 by The Condé Nast Publications, Inc.; for *The Waiting Game* by Randall Garrett, © 1950 by Street & Smith Publications, Inc.; renewed 1977 by The Condé Nast Publications, Inc.; for *The Little Black Bag* by C. M. Kornbluth, © 1950 by Street & Smith Publications, Inc.; renewed 1977 by The Condé Nast Publications, Inc.; for *Incommunicado* by Katherine MacLean, © 1950 by Street & Smith Publications, Inc.; renewed 1977 by The Condé Nast Publications, Inc.; for *Invariant* by John Pierce, © 1944 by Street & Smith Publications, Inc.; renewed 1971 by The Condé Nast Publications, Inc.; for *Police Operation* by H. Beam Piper, © 1948 by Street & Smith Publications, Inc.; renewed 1975 by The Condé Nast Publications, Inc.; for *Ogre* by Clifford D. Simak, © 1943 by Street & Smith Publications, Inc.; renewed 1970 by The Condé Nast Publications, Inc.; and for *Desertion* by Clifford D. Simak, © 1944 by Street & Smith Publications, Inc.; renewed 1971 by The Condé Nast Publications, Inc.

Joe W. Haldeman for *Hero* by Joe W. Haldeman, © 1972 by The Condé Nast Publications, Inc.

Harry Harrison for *The Powers of Observation* by Harry Harrison, © 1968 by The Condé Nast Publications, Inc.

Allen Lang for *Blind Man's Lantern* by Allen Lang, © 1962 by The Condé Nast Publications, Inc.

Kirby McCauley, Ltd. for *Monument* by Lloyd Biggle, Jr., © 1961 by Lloyd Biggle, Jr.

Dean McLaughlin for *The Permanent Implosion* by Dean McLaughlin, © 1964 by Dean McLaughlin.

Scott Meredith Literary Agency, Inc. for *Minor Ingredient* by Eric Frank Russell, © 1956 by Street & Smith Publications, Inc.; for *Balanced Ecology* by James H. Schmitz, © 1965 by The Condé Nast

Publications, Inc.; and for *The Easy Way Out* by Lee Correy, © 1966 by The Condé Nast Publications, Inc.

Robert D. Mills, Ltd. for *The Last Command* by Keith Laumer, © 1966 by The Condé Nast Publications, Inc.

Frederik Pohl for *The Gold at the Starbow's End* by Frederik Pohl, © 1972 by The Condé Nast Publications, Inc.

Winston P. Sanders for *Barnacle Bull* by Winston P. Sanders, © 1960 by Street & Smith Publications, Inc.

Contents

Analog

The Best of Science Fiction

The Day Is Done

Hwoogh scratched the hair on his stomach and watched the sun climb up over the hill.   He beat listlessly on his chest and yelled at it timidly, then grumbled and stopped.   In his youth, he had roared and stumped around to help the god up, but now it wasn't worth the effort.   Nothing was.   He found a fine flake of sweaty salt under his hair, licked it off his fingers, and turned over to sleep again.

But sleep wouldn't come.   On the other side of the hill there was a hue and cry, and somebody was beating a drum in a throbbing chant.   The old Neanderthaler grunted and held his hands over his ears, but the Sun-Warmer's chant couldn't be silenced.   More ideas of the Talkers.

In his day, it had been a lovely world, full of hairy grumbling people; people a man could understand.   There had been game on all sides, and the caves about had been filled with the smoke of cooking fires.   He had played with the few young that were born—though each year fewer children had come into the tribe— and had grown to young manhood with the pride of achievement.   But that was before the Talkers had made this valley one of their hunting grounds.

Old traditions, half told, half understood, spoke of the land in the days of old, when only his people roamed over the broad tundra.   They had filled the caves and gone out in packs too large for any animal to withstand.   And the animals swarmed into the land, driven south by the Fourth Glaciation.   Then the great cold had come again, and times had been hard.   Many of his people had died.

But many had lived, and with the coming of the warmer, drier climate again, they had begun to expand before the Talkers arrived.   After that—Hwoogh stirred uneasily—for no good reason he could see, the Talkers took more and more of the land, and his people retreated and diminished before them.   Hwoogh's father had made it understood that their little band in the valley were all that were left, and that this was the only place on the great flat earth where Talkers seldom came.

Hwoogh had been twenty when he first saw them, great long-legged men, swift of foot and eye, stalking along as if they owned the earth, with their incessant mouth noises.   In the summer that year, they pitched their skin-and-wattle tents at the back of the hill, away from the caves, and made magic to their gods.   There was magic on their weapons, and the beasts fell theirprey.   Hwoogh's people had settled back, watching fearfully, hating numbly, finally resorting to begging and stealing.   Once a young buck had killed the child of a Talker, and been flayed and sent out to die for it.   Thereafter, there had been a truce between Cro-Magnon and Neanderthaler.

Now the last of Hwoogh's people were gone, save only himself, leaving no children.   Seven years it had been since Hwoogh's brother had curled up in the cave and sent his breath forth on the long journey to his ancestors.   He had always been dispirited and weak of will, but he had been the only friend left to Hwoogh.

The old man tossed about and wished that Keyoda would return.   Maybe she would bring food from the Talkers.   There was no use hunting now, when the Talkers had already been up and killed all the easy game.   Better that a man should sleep all the time, for sleep was the only satisfying thing left in the topsy-turvy world; even the drink the tall Cro-Magnons made from mashed roots left a headache the next day.

He twisted and turned in his bed of leaves at the edge of the cave, grunting surlily.   A fly buzzed over his head provocatively, and he lunged at it.   Surprise lighted his features as his fingers closed on the insect, and he swallowed it with a momentary flash of pleasure.   It wasn't as good as the grub in the forest, but it made a tasty appetizer.

The sleep god had left, and no amount of lying still and snoring would lure him back.   Hwoogh gave up and squatted down on his haunches.   He had been meaning to make a new head for his crude spear for weeks, and he rummaged around in the cave for materials.   But the idea grew farther away the closer he approached work, and he let his eyes roam idly over the little creek below him and the fleecy clouds in the sky.   It was a warm spring, and the sun made idleness pleasant.

The sun god was growing stronger again, chasing the old fog and mist away. For years, he had worshipped the sun god as his, and now it seemed to grow strong again only for the Talkers.   While the god was weak, Hwoogh's people had been mighty; now that its long sickness was over, the Cro-Magnons spread out over the country like fleas on his belly.

Keyoda crept around the boulder in front of the cave, interrupting his brooding. She brought scraps of food from the tent village and the half-chewed leg of a horse, which Hwoogh seized on and ripped at with his strong teeth.   Evidently the Talkers had make a big kill the day before, for they were lavish with their gifts.   He grunted at Keyoda, who sat under the cave entrance in the sun, rubbing her back.

Keyoda was as hideous as most of the Talkers were to Hwoogh, with her long dangling legs and short arms, and the ungainly straightness of her carriage.   Hwoogh remembered the young girls of his own day with a sigh; they had been beautiful, short and squat, with forward-jutting necks and nice low foreheads.   How the flat-faced Cro-Magnon women could get mates had been a puzzle to Hwoogh, but they seemed to succeed.

Keyoda had failed, however, and in her he felt justified in his judgment.   There were times when he felt almost in sympathy with her, and in his own way he was fond of her.   As a child, she had been injured, her back made useless for the work of a mate.   Kicked around by the others of her tribe, she had gradually drifted away from them, and when she stumbled on Hwoogh, his hospitality had been welcome to her.   The Talkers were nomads who followed the herds north in the summer, south in the winter, coming and going with the seasons, but Keyoda stayed with Hwoogh in his cave and did the few desultory tasks that were necessary. Even such a half-man as the Neanderthaler was preferable to the scornful pity of her own people, and Hwoogh was not unkind.

"Hwunkh?" asked Hwoogh.   With his stomach partly filled, he felt more kindly toward the world.

"Oh, they come out and let me pick up their scraps—me, who was once a chief's daughter!—same as they always do."   Her voice had been shrewish, but the weariness of failure and age had taken the edge from it.   " 'Poor, poor Keyoda,' thinks they, 'let her have what she wants, just so it don't mean nothin' we like.' Here."   She handed him a roughly made spear, flaked on both sides of the point, but with only a rudimentary barb, unevenly made.   "One of 'em give me this— it ain't the like of what they'd use, I guess, but it's good as you could make.   One of the kids is practicing."

Hwoogh examined it; good, he admitted, very good, and the point was fixed nicely in the shaft.   Even the boys, with their long limber thumbs that could twist any which way, make better weapons than he; yet once, he had been famous among his small tribe for the nicety of his flint work.

Making a horse gesture, he got slowly to his feet.   The shape of his jaw and the attachment of his tongue, together with a poorly developed left frontal lobe of his brain, made speech rudimentary, and he supplemented his glottals and labials with motions that Keyoda understood well enough.   She shrugged and waved him out, gnawing on one of the bones.

Hwoogh wandered about without much spirit, conscious that he was growing old.   And vaguely, he knew that age should not have fallen upon him for many snows; it was not the number of seasons, but something else, something that he could feel but not understand.   He struck out for the hunting fields, hoping that he might find some game for himself that would require little effort to kill.   The scornful gifts of the Talkers had become bitter in his mouth.

But the sun god climbed up to the top of the blue cave without Hwoogh's stumbling on anything.   He swung about to return, and ran into a party of Cro-Magnons returning with the carcass of a reindeer strapped to a pole on their shoulders. They stopped to yell at him.

"No use, Hairy One!" they boasted, their voices light and gay.   "We caught all the game this way.   Turn back to your cave and sleep."

Hwoogh dropped his shoulders and veered away, his spear dragging limply on the ground.   One of the party trotted over to him lightly.   Sometimes Legoda, the tribal magic man and artist, seemed almost friendly, and this was one of the times.

"It was my kill, Hairy One," he said tolerantly.   "Last night I drew strong reindeer magic, and the beast fell with my first throw.   Come to my tent and I'll save a leg for you.   Keyoda taught me a new song that she got from her father, and I would repay her."

Legs, ribs, bones! Hwoogh was tired of the outer meat. His body demanded the finer food of the entrails and liver. Already his skin was itching with a rash, and he felt that he must have the succulent inner parts to make him well; always, before, that had cured him. He grunted between appreciation and annoyance, and turned off. Legoda pulled him back.

"Nay, stay, Hairy One. Sometimes you bring good fortune to me, as when I found the bright ocher for my drawing. There is meat enough in the camp for all. Why hunt today?" As Hwoogh still hesitated, he grew more insistent, not from kindness, but more from a wish to have his own way. "The wolves are running near today, and one is not enough against them. We crave the reindeer at the camp as soon as it comes from the poles. I'll give you first choice of the meat!"

Hwoogh grunted a surly acquiescence and waddled after the party. The dole of the Talkers had become gall to him, but liver was liver—if Legoda kept his bargain. They were chanting a rough marching song, trotting easily under the load of the reindeer, and he lumbered along behind, breathing hard at the pace they set.

As they neared the village of the nomads, its rough skin tents and burning fires threw out a pungent odor that irritated Hwoogh's nostrils. The smell of the long-limbed Cro-Magnons was bad enough without the dirty smell of a camp and the stink of their dung-fed fires. He preferred the accustomed moldy stench of his own musty cave.

Youths came swarming out at them, yelling with disgust at being left behind on this easy hunt. Catching sight of the Neanderthaler, they set up a howl of glee and charged at him, throwing sticks and rocks and jumping at him with play fury. Hwoogh shivered and crouched over, menacing them with his spear, and giving voice to throaty growls. Legoda laughed.

"In truth, O Hairy Chokanga, your voice should drive them from you. But see, they fear it not. Kuck, you two-legged pests! Out and away. Kuck, I say!" They leaped back at his voice and dropped behind, still yelling. Hwoogh eyed them warily, but so long as it suited the pleasure of Legoda, he was safe from their pranks.

Legoda was in a good mood, laughing and joking, tossing his quips at the women until his young wife came out and silenced it. She sprang at the reindeer with her flint knife, and the other women joined her.

"Heya," called Legoda. "First choice goes to Chokanga, the Hairy One. By my word, it is his."

"Oh, fool!" There was scorn in her voice and in the look she gave Hwoogh. "Since when do we feed the beasts of the caves and the fish of the river? Art mad, Legoda. Let him hunt for himself."

Legoda tweaked her back with the point of his spear, grinning. "Aye, I knew thou'dst cry at that. But then, we owe his kind some pay—this was his hunting ground when we were but pups, straggling into this far land. What harm to give to an old man?" He swung to Hwoogh and gestured. "See, Chokanga, my word is good. Take what you want, but see that it is not more than your belly and that of Keyoda can hold this night."

Hwoogh darted in and came out with the liver and the fine sweet fat from the entrails.   With a shrill cry of rage, Legoda's mate sprang for him, but the magic man pushed her back.

"Nay, he did right!   Only a fool would choose the haunch when the heart of the meat was at hand.   By the gods of my father, and I expected to eat of that myself!   O Hairy One, you steal the meat from my mouth, and I like you for it. Go, before Heya gets free."

Tomorrow, Hwoogh knew, Legoda might set the brats on him for this day's act, but tomorrow was in another cave of the sun.   He drew his legs under him and scuttled off to the left and around the hill, while the shrill yells of Heya and the lazy good humor of Legoda followed.   A piece of liver dangled loose, and Hwoogh sucked on it as he went.   Keyoda would be pleased, since she usually had to do the begging for both of them.

And a little of Hwoogh's self-respect returned.   Hadn't he outsmarted Legoda and escaped with the choicest meat?   And had Keyoda ever done as well when she went to the village of the Talkers?   Ayeee, they had a thing yet to learn from the cunning brain of old Hwoogh!

Of course the Talkers were crazy; only fools would act as Legoda had done. But that was none of his business.   He patted the liver and fat fondly and grinned with a slight return of good humor.   Hwoogh was not one to look a gift horse in the mouth.

The fire had shrunk to a red bed of coals when he reached the cave, and Keyoda was curled up on his bed, snoring loudly, her face flushed.   Hwoogh smelled her breath, and his suspicions were confirmed.   Somehow, she had drunk of the devil brew of the Talkers, and her sleep was dulled with its stupor.   He prodded her with his toe, and she sat up bleary-eyed.

"Oh, so you're back.   Ayeee, and with liver and fat!   But that never came from your spear throw; you been to the village and stole it.   Oh, but you'll catch it!" She grabbed at the meat greedily and stirred up the fire, spitting the liver over it.

Hwoogh explained as best he could, and she got the drift of it.   "So?   Eh, that Legoda, what a prankster he is, and my own nephew, too."   She tore the liver away, half raw, and they fell to eagerly, while she chuckled and cursed by turns. Hwoogh touched her nose and wrinkled his face up.

"Well, so what if I did?"   Liquor had sharpened her tongue.   "That no-good son of the chief come here, after me to be telling him stories.   And to make my old tongue free, he brings me the root brew.   Ah, what stories I'm telling—and some of 'em true, too!"   She gestured toward a crude pot.   "I reckon he steals it, but what's that to us?   Help yourself, Hairy One.   It ain't ever' day we're getting the brew."

Hwoogh remembered the headaches of former experiments, but he smelled it curiously and the lure of the magic water caught at him.   It was the very essence of youth, the fire that brought life to his legs and memories to his mind.   He held it up to his mouth, gasping as the beery liquid ran down his throat.   Keyoda caught it before he could finish and drained the last quart.

"Ah, it strengthens my back and puts the blood a-running hot through me again."
She swayed on her feet and sputtered out the fragments of an old skin-scraping
song. "Now, there you go—can't you never learn not to drink it all to once?
That way, it don't last as long, and you're out before you get to feeling good."

Hwoogh staggered as the brew took hold of him, and his knees bent even farther
under him. The bed came up in his face, his head was full of bees buzzing merrily,
and the cave spun around him. He roared at the cave, while Keyoda laughed.

"Heh! To hear you a-yelling, a body might think you was the only Chokanga
left on earth. But you ain't—no, you ain't!"

"Hwunkh?" That struck home. To the best of Hwoogh's knowledge, there
were no others of his kind left on earth. He grabbed at her and missed, but she
fell and rolled against him, her breath against his face.

"So? Well, it's the truth. The kid up and told me. Legoda found three of
'em, just like you, he says, up the land to the east, three springs ago. You'll have
to ask him—I dunno nothing about it." She rolled over against him, grunting
half-formed words, and he tried to think of this new information. But the brew
was too strong for his head, and he was soon snoring beside her.

Keyoda was gone to the village when he awoke, and the sun was a spear length
high on the horizon. He rummaged around for a piece of the liver, but the flavor
was not as good as it had been, and his stomach protested lustily at going to work
again. He leaned back until his head got control of itself, then swung down to
the creek to quench a thirst devil that had seized on him in the night.

But there was something he should do, something he half remembered from last
night. Hadn't Keyoda said something about others of his people? Yes, three of
them, and Legoda knew. Hwoogh hestitated, remembering that he had bested
Legoda the day before; the young man might resent it today. But he was filled
with an overwhelming curiosity, and there was a strange yearning in his heart.
Legoda must tell him.

Reluctantly, he went back to the cave and fished around in a hole that was a
secret even from Keyoda. He drew out his treasures, fingering them reverently,
and selecting the best. There were bright shells and colored pebbles, a roughly
drilled necklace that had belonged to his father, a sign of completed manhood, bits
of this and that with which he had intended to make himself ornaments. But the
quest for knowledge was stronger than the pride of possession; he dumped them
out into his fist and struck out for the village.

Keyoda was talking with the women, whining the stock formula that she had
developed, and Hwoogh skirted around the camp, looking for the young artist.
Finally he spotted the Talker out behind the camp, making odd motions with two
sticks. He drew near cautiously, and Legoda heard him coming.

"Come near, Chokanga, and see my new magic." The young man's voice was
filled with pride, and there was no threat to it. Hwoogh sighed with relief, but
sidled up slowly. "Come nearer, don't fear me. Do you think I'm sorry of the
gift I made? Nay, that was my own stupidity. See."

He held out the sticks and Hwoogh fingered them carefully. One was long and springy, tied end to end with a leather thong, and the other was a little spear with a tuft of feather on the blunt end. He grunted a question.

"A magic spear, Hairy One, that flies from the hand with wings, and kills beyond the reach of other spears."

Hwoogh snorted. The spear was too tiny to kill more than rodents, and the big stick had not even a point. But he watched as the young man placed the sharp stick to the tied one, and drew back on it. There was a sharp twang, and the little spear sailed out and away, burying its point in the soft bark of a tree more than two spear throws away. Hwoogh was impressed.

"Aye, Chokanga, a new magic that I learned in the south last year. There are many there who use it, and with it they can throw the point farther and better than a full-sized spear. One man may kill as much as three!"

Hwoogh grumbled; already they killed all the good game, and yet they must find new magic to increase their power. He held out his hand curiously, and Legoda gave him the long stick and another spear, showing him how it was held. Again there was a twang, and the leather thong struck at his wrist, but the weapon sailed off erratically, missing the tree by yards. Hwoogh handed it back glumly—such magic was not for his kind. His thumbs made the handling of it even more difficult.

Now, while the magic man was pleased with his superiority, was a good time to show the treasure. Hwoogh spread it out on the bare earth and gestured at Legoda, who looked down thoughtfully.

"Yes," the Talker conceded. "Some of it is good, and some would make nice trinkets for the women. What is it you want—more meat, or one of the new weapons? Your belly was filled yesterday; and with my beer, that was stolen, I think, though for that I blame you not. The boy has been punished already. And this weapon is not for you."

Hwoogh snorted, wriggled and fought for expression, while the young man stared. Little by little, his wants were made known, partly by signs, partly by the questions of the Cro-Magnon. Legoda laughed.

"So, there is a call of the kind in you, Old Man?" He pushed the treasure back to Hwoogh, except one gleaming bauble. "I would not cheat you, Chokanga, but this I take for the love I bear you, as a sign of our friendship." His grin was mocking as he stuck the valuable in a flap of his clout.

Hwoogh squatted down on his heels, and Legoda sat on a rock as he began. "There is but little to tell you, Hairy One. Three years ago I did run onto a family of your kind—a male and his mate, with one child. They ran from us, but we were near their cave, and they had to return. We harmed them not, and sometimes gave them food, letting them accompany us on the chase. But they were thin and scrawny, too lazy to hunt. When we returned next year, they were dead, and so far as I know, you are the last of your kind."

He scratched his head thoughtfully. "Your people die too easily, Chokanga; no sooner do we find them and try to help them than they cease hunting and become beggars. And then they lose interest in life, sicken and die: I think your gods must be killed off by our stronger ones."

Hwoogh grunted a half assent, and Legoda gathered up his bow and arrows, turning back toward camp.   But there was a strange look on the Neanderthaler's face that did not escape the young man's eyes.   Recognizing the misery in Hwoogh's expression, he laid a hand on the old man's shoulder and spoke more kindly.

"That is why I would see to your well-being, Hairy One.   When you are gone, there will be no more, and my children will laugh at me and say I lie when I spin the tale of your race at the feast fire.   Each time that I kill, you shall not lack for food."

He swung down the single street toward the tent of his family, and Hwoogh turned slowly back toward his cave.   The assurance of food should have cheered him, but it only added to his gloom.   Dully, he realized that Legoda treated him as a small child, or as one whom the sun god had touched with madness.

Hwoogh heard the cries and laughter of children as he rounded the hill, and for a minute he hesitated before going on.   But the sense of property was well developed in him, and he leaped forward grimly.   They had no business near his cave.

They were of all ages and sizes, shouting and chasing each other about in a crazy disorder.   Having been forbidden to come on Hwoogh's side of the hill, and having broken the rule in a bunch, they were making the most of their revolt.   Hwoogh's fire was scattered down the side of the hill into the creek, and they were busily sorting through the small store of his skins and weapons.

Hwoogh let out a savage yell and ran forward, his spear held out in jabbing position.   Hearing him, they turned and jumped back from the cave entrance, clustering up into a tight group.   "Go on away, Ugly Face," one yelled.   "Go scare the wolves!   Ugly Face, Ugly Face, waaaah!"

He dashed in among them, brandishing his spear, but they darted back on their nimble legs, slipping easily from in front of him.   One of the older boys thrust out a leg and caught him, tripping him down on the rocky ground.   Another dashed in madly and caught his spear away, hitting him roughly with it.   From the time of the first primate, the innate cruelty of thoughtlessness had changed little in children.

Hwoogh let out a whooping bellow, scrambled up clumsily and was in among them.   But they slipped nimbly out of his clutching hands.   The little girls were dancing around gleefully, chanting: "Ugly Face ain't got no mother, Ugly Face ain't got no wife, waaah on Ugly Face!"   Frantically he caught at one of the boys, swung him about savagely, and tossed him to the ground, where the youth lay white and silent.   Hwoogh felt a momentary glow of elation at his strength.   Then somebody threw a rock.

The old Neanderthaler was tied down crudely when he swam back to consciousness, and three of the boys sat on his chest, beating the ground with their heels in time to a victory chant.   There was a dull ache in his head, and bruises were swelling on his arms and chest where they had handled him roughly.   He growled savagely, heaving up, and tumbled them off, but the cords were too strong for him.   As surely as if grown men had done it, he was captured.

For years they had been his enemies, ever since they had found that Hwoogh-baiting was one of the pleasant occupations that might relieve the tedium of camp life. Now that the old feud was about finished, they went at the business of subduing him with method and ingenuity.

While the girls rubbed his face with soft mud from the creek, the boys ransacked the cave and tore at his clothes. The rough bag in which he had put his valuables came away in their hands, and they paused to distribute this new wealth. Hwoogh howled madly.

But a measure of sanity was returning to them, now that the first fury of the fight was over, and Kechaka, the chief's eldest son, stared at Hwoogh doubtfully. "If the elders hear of this," he muttered unhappily, "there will be trouble. They'd not like our bothering Ugly Face."

Another grinned. "Why tell them? He isn't a man, anyway, but an animal; see the hair on his body! Toss old Ugly Face in the river, clean up his cave, and hide these treasures. Who's to know?"

There were half-hearted protests, but the thought of the beating waiting for them added weight to the idea. Kechaka nodded finally, and set them to straightening up the mess they had made. With broken branches, they eliminated the marks of their feet, leaving only the trail to the creek.

Hwoogh tossed and pitched in their arms as four of them picked him up; the bindings loosened somewhat, but not enough to free him. With some satisfaction, he noted that the boy he had caught was still retching and moaning, but that was no help to his present position. They waded relentlessly into the water, laid him on it belly down, and gave him a strong push that sent him gliding out through the rushing stream. Foaming and gasping, he fought the current, struggling against his bonds. His lungs ached for air, and the current buffeted him about; blackness was creeping up on his mind.

With a last desperate effort he tore loose the bonds and pushed up madly for the surface, gulping in air greedily. Water was unpleasant to him, but he could swim, and struck out for the bank. The children were disappearing down the trail, and were out of sight as he climbed from the water, bemoaning his lost fire that would have warmed him. He lumbered back to his cave and sank soddenly on the bed.

He, who had been a mighty warrior, bested by a snarling pack of Cro-Magnon brats! He clenched his fists savagely and growled, but there was nothing he could do. Nothing! The futility of his own effort struck down on him like a burning knife. Hwoogh was an old man, and the tears that ran from his eyes were the bitter, aching tears that only age can shed.

Keyoda returned late, cursing when she found the fire gone, but her voice softened as she spied him huddled in his bed, staring dully at the wall of the cave. Her old eyes spotted the few footprints the boys had missed, and she swore with a vigor that was almost youthful before she turned back to Hwoogh.

"Come, Hairy One, get out of that cold, wet fur!" Her hands were gentle on the straps, but Hwoogh shook her aside. "You'll be sick, lying there on them few leaves, all wet like that. Get off the fur, and I'll go back to the village for fire. Them kids! Wait'll I tell Legoda!"

Seeing there was nothing he would let her do for him, she turned away down

the trail.   Hwoogh sat up to change his furs, then lay back.   What was the use?
He grumbled a little when Keyoda returned with fire, but refused the delicacies she
had wheedled at the village, and tumbled over into a fitful sleep.

The sun was long up when he awoke to find Legoda and Keyoda fussing over
him.   There was an unhappy feeling in his head, and he coughed.   Legoda patted
his back.   "Rest, Hairy One.   You have the sickness devil that burns the throat
and runs at the nose, but that a man can overcome.   Ayeee, how the boys were
whipped!   I, personally, attended to that, and this morning not one is less sore
than you.   Before they bother you again, the moon will eat up the sun."

Keyoda pushed a stew of boiled liver and kidneys at him, but he shoved it away.
Though the ache in his head had gone down, a dull weight seemed to rest on his
stomach, and he could not eat.   It felt as though all the boys he had fought were
sitting on his chest and choking him.

Legoda drew out a small painted drum and made heavy magic for his recovery,
dancing before the old man and shaking the magic gourd that drove out all sickness
devils.   But this was a stronger devil.   Finally the young man stopped and left
for the village, while Keyoda perched on a stone to watch over the sick man.
Hwoogh's mind was heavy and numb, and his heart was leaden in his breast.   She
fanned the flies away, covering his eyes with a bit of skin, singing him some song
that the mothers lulled their children with.

He slept again, stirring about in a nightmare of Talker mockery, with a fever
flushing his face.   But when Legoda came back at night, the magic man swore he
should be well in three days.   "Let him sleep and feed him.   The devil will leave
him soon.   See, there is scarce a mark where the stone hit."

Keyoda fed him, as best she could, forcing the food that she begged at the village
down his throat.   She lugged water from the creek as often as he cried for it, and
bathed his head and chest when he slept.   But the three days came and went, and
still he was not well.   The fever was little higher, and the cold little worse, than
he had gone through many times before.   But he did not throw it off as he should
have done.

Legoda came again, bringing magic and food, but they were of little help.   As
the day drew to a close, he shook his head and spoke low words to Keyoda.
Hwoogh came out of a half stupor and listened dully.

"He tires of life, Keyoda, my father's sister."   The young man shrugged.
"See, he lies there not fighting.   When a man will not try to live, he cannot."

"Ayyeah!"   Her voice shrilled dolefully.   "What man will not live if he can?
Thou art foolish, Legoda."

"Nay.   His people tire easily of life, O Keyoda.   Why, I know not.   But it
takes little to make him die."   Seeing that Hwoogh had heard, he drew closer to
the Neanderthaler.   "O Chokanga, put away your troubles, and take another bite
out of life.   It can still be good, if you choose.   I have taken your gift as a sign
of friendship, and I would keep my word.   Come to my fire, and hunt no more;
I will tend you as I would my father."

Hwoogh grunted.   Follow the camps, eat from Legoda's hunting, be paraded
as a freak and a half-man!   Legoda was kind, sudden and warm in his sympathy,

but the others were scornful.   And if Hwoogh should die, who was to mourn him?
Keyoda would go back to her people, Legoda would forget him, and not one
Chokanga would be there to show them the ritual for burial.

Hwoogh's old friends had come back to him in his dreams, visiting him and
showing the hunting grounds of his youth.   He had heard the grunts and grumblings
of the girls of his race, and they were awaiting him.   That world was still empty
of the Talkers, where a man could do great things and make his own kills, without
hearing the laughter of the Cro-Magnons.   Hwoogh sighed softly.   He was tired,
too tired to care what happened.

The sun sank low, and the clouds were painted a harsh red.   Keyoda was wailing
somewhere, far off, and Legoda beat on his drum and muttered his magic.   But
life was empty, barren of pride.

The sun dropped from sight, and Hwoogh sighed again, sending his last breath
out to join the ghosts of his people.

ALFRED BESTER

Adam and No Eve

Krane knew this must be the seacoast. Instinct told him; but more than instinct, the few shreds of knowledge that clung to his torn brain told him; the stars that had shown at night through the rare breaks in the clouds, and his compass that still pointed a trembling finger north. That was strangest of all, Krane thought. The rubbled Earth still retained its polarity.

It was no longer a coast; there was no longer any sea. Only the faint line of what had been a cliff stretched north and south for endless miles. It was a line of grey ash; the same grey ash and cinders that lay behind him and stretched before him. . . . Fine silt, knee-deep, that swirled up at every motion and choked him; cinders that scudded in dense night clouds when the mad winds blew; black dust that was churned to mud when the frequent rains fell.

The sky was jet overhead. The heavy clouds rode high and were pierced with shafts of sunlight that marched swiftly over the Earth. Where the light struck a cinder-storm, it was filled with gusts of dancing, gleaming particles. Where it played through rain it brought the arches of rainbows into being. Rain fell; cinder-storms blew; light thrust down—together, alternately and continually in a jigsaw of black and white violence. So it had been for months. So it was over every mile of the broad Earth.

Krane passed the edge of the ashen cliffs and began crawling down the even slope that had once been the ocean bed. He had been traveling so long that pain had become part of him. He braced elbows and dragged his body forward. Then he brought his right knee under him and reached forward with elbows again. Elbows, knee, elbows, knee—He had forgotten what it was to walk.

Life, he thought dazedly, is miraculous. It adapts itself to anything. If it must crawl, it crawls. Callus forms on the elbows and knees. The neck and shoulders toughen. The nostrils learn to snort away the ashes before they breathe. The bad leg swells and festers. It numbs, and presently it will rot and fall off.

"I beg pardon?" Krane said, "I didn't quite get that—"

He peered up at the tall figure before him and tried to understand the words. It was Hallmyer. He wore his stained lab coat and his grey hair was awry. Hallmyer stood delicately on top of the ashes and Krane wondered why he could see the scudding cinder clouds through his body.

"How do you like your world, Steven?" Hallmyer asked.

Krane shook his head miserably.

"Not very pretty, eh?" said Hallmyer. "Look around you. Dust, that's all; dust and ashes. Crawl, Steven, crawl. You'll find nothing but dust and ashes—"

Hallmyer produced a goblet of water from nowhere. It was clear and cold. Krane could see the fine mist of dew on its surface and his mouth was suddenly coated with grit.

"Hallmyer!" he cried. He tried to get to his feet and reach for the water, but the jolt of pain in his right leg warned him. He crouched back.

Hallmyer sipped and then spat in his face. The water felt warm.

"Keep crawling," said Hallmyer bitterly. "Crawl round and round the face of the Earth. You'll find nothing but dust and ashes—" He emptied the goblet on the ground before Krane. "Keep crawling. How many miles? Figure it out for yourself. Pi times D. The diameter is eight thousand or so—"

He was gone, coat and goblet. Krane realized that rain was falling again. He pressed his face into the warm cinder mud, opened his mouth and tried to suck the moisture. Presently he began crawling again.

There was an instinct that drove him on. He had to get somewhere. It was associated, he knew, with the sea—with the edge of the sea. At the shore of the sea something waited for him. Something that would help him understand all this. He had to get to the sea—that is, if there was a sea any more.

The thundering rain beat his back like heavy planks. Krane paused and yanked the knapsack around to his side where he probed in it with one hand. It contained exactly three things. A gun, a bar of chocolate, and a can of peaches. All that was left of two months' supplies. The chocolate was pulpy and spoiled. Krane knew he had best eat it before all value rotted away. But in another day he would lack the strength to open the can. He pulled it out and attacked it with the opener. By the time he had pierced and pried away a flap of tin, the rain had passed.

As he munched the fruit and sipped the juice, he watched the wall of rain marching before him down the slope of the ocean bed. Torrents of water were gushing through the mud. Small channels had already been cut—channels that would be new rivers some day; a day he would never see; a day that no living thing would ever see. As he flipped the empty can aside, Krane thought: The last living thing on Earth eats its last meal. Metabolism begins the last act.

Wind would follow the rain. In the endless weeks that he had been crawling, he had learned that. Wind would come in a few minutes and flog him with its clouds of cinders and ashes. He crawled forward, bleary eyes searching the flat grey miles for cover.

Evelyn tapped his shoulder.

Krane knew it was she before he turned his head. She stood alongside, fresh and gay in her bright dress, but her lovely face was puckered with alarm.

"Steven," she said, "you've got to hurry!"

He could only admire the way her smooth hair waved to her shoulders.

"Oh, darling!" she said, "you've been hurt!" Her quick gentle hands touched his legs and back. Krane nodded.

"Got it landing," he said. "I wasn't used to a parachute. I always thought you came down gently—like plumping onto a bed. But the earth came up at me like a fist—And Umber was fighting around in my arms. I couldn't let him drop, could I?"

"Of course not, dear," Evelyn said.

"So I just held on to him and tried to get my legs under me," Krane said. "And then something smashed my legs and side—"

He hesitated, wondering how much she knew of what really had happened. He didn't want to frighten her.

"Evelyn, darling—" he said, trying to reach up his arms.

"No, dear," she said. She looked back in fright. "You've got to hurry. You've got to watch out behind!"

"The cinder-storms?" He grimaced. "I've been through them before."

"Not the storms!" Evelyn cried. "Something else. Oh, Steven—"

Then she was gone, but Krane knew she had spoken the truth. There was something behind—something that had been following him. In the back of his mind he had sensed the menace. It was closing in on him like a shroud. He shook his head. Somehow that was impossible. He was the last living thing on Earth. How could there be a menace?

The wind roared behind him, and an instant later came the heavy clouds of cinders and ashes. They lashed over him, biting his skin. With dimming eyes, he saw the way they coated the mud and covered it with a fine dry carpet. Krane drew his knees under him and covered his head with his arms. With the knapsack as a pillow, he prepared to wait out the storm. It would pass as quickly as the rain.

The storm whipped up a great bewilderment in his sick head. Like a child he pushed at the pieces of his memory, trying to fit them together. Why was Hallmyer so bitter toward him? It couldn't have been that argument, could it?

What argument?

Why, that one before all this happened.

Oh, that!

Abruptly, the pieces locked together.

Krane stood alongside the sleek lines of his ship and admired it tremendously. The roof of the shed had been removed and the nose of the ship hoisted so that it rested on a cradle pointed toward the sky. A workman was carefully burnishing the inner surfaces of the rocket jets.

The muffled sounds of swearing came from within the ship and then a heavy clanking. Krane ran up the short iron ladder to the port and thrust his head inside. A few feet beneath him, two men were clamping the long tanks of ferrous solution into place.

"Easy there," Krane called. "Want to knock the ship apart?"

One looked up and grinned.   Krane knew what he was thinking.   That the ship would tear itself apart.   Everyone said that.   Everyone except Evelyn.   She had faith in him.   Hallmyer never said it either, but Hallmyer thought he was crazy in another way.   As he descended the ladder, Krane saw Hallmyer come into the shed, lab coat flying.

"Speak of the devil!" Krane muttered.

Hallmyer began shouting as soon as he saw Krane.   "Now, listen—"

"Not all over again," Krane said.

Hallmyer dug a sheaf of papers out of his pocket and waved it under Krane's nose.

"I've been up half the night," he said, "working it through again.   I tell you I'm right.   I'm absolutely right—"

Krane looked at the tight-written equations and then at Hallmyer's bloodshot eyes.   The man was half-mad with fear.

"For the last time," Hallmyer went on.   "You're using your new catalyst on iron solution.   All right.   I grant that it's a miraculous discovery.   I give you credit for that."

Miraculous was hardly the word for it.   Krane knew that without conceit, for he realized he'd only stumbled on it.   You had to stumble on a catalyst that would induce atomic disintegration of iron and give 10×10^{10} foot-pounds of energy for every gram of fuel.   No man was smart enough to think all that up by himself.

"You don't think I'll make it?" Krane asked.

"To the Moon?   Around the Moon?   Maybe.   You've got a fifty-fifty chance." Hallmyer ran fingers through his lank hair.   "But for God's sake, Steven, I'm not worried about you.   If you want to kill yourself, that's your own affair.   It's the Earth I'm worried about—"

"Nonsense.   Go home and sleep it off."

"Look—"   Hallmyer pointed to the sheets of paper with a shaky hand—"No matter how you work the feed and mixing system, you can't get one hundred percent efficiency in the mixing and discharge."

"That's what makes it a fifty-fifty chance," Krane said.   "So what's bothering you?"

"The catalyst that will escape through the rocket tubes.   Do you realize what it'll do if a drop hits the Earth?   It'll start a chain of disintegration that'll envelop the globe.   It'll reach out to every iron atom—and there's iron everywhere.   There won't be any Earth left for you to return to—"

"Listen," Krane said wearily, "we've been through all this before."

He took Hallmyer to the base of the rocket cradle.   Beneath the iron framework was a two-hundred-foot pit, fifty feet wide and lined with firebrick.

"That's for the initial discharge flames.   If any of the catalyst goes through, it'll be trapped in this pit and taken care of by the secondary reactions.   Satisfied now?"

"But while you're in flight," Hallmyer persisted, "you'll be endangering the Earth until you're beyond Roche's limit.   Every drop of nonactivated catalyst will eventually sink back to the ground and—"

"For the very last time," Krane said grimly, "the flame of the rocket discharge takes care of that. It will envelop any escaped particles and destroy them. Now get out. I've got work to do."

As Krane pushed him to the door, Hallmyer screamed and waved his arms. "I won't let you do it!" he repeated over and over. "I won't let you risk it—"

Work? No, it was sheer intoxication to labor over the ship. It had the fine beauty of a well-made thing. The beauty of polished armor, of a balanced swept-hilt rapier, of a pair of matched guns. There was no thought of danger and death in Krane's mind as he wiped his hands with waste after the last touches were finished.

She lay in the cradle ready to pierce the skies. Fifty feet of slender steel, the rivet heads gleaming like jewels. Thirty feet were given over to fuel and catalyst. Most of the forward compartment contained the spring hammock Krane had devised to absorb the acceleration strain. The ship's nose was a porthole of natural crystal that stared upward like a cyclopean eye.

Krane thought: She'll die after this trip. She'll return to the Earth and smash in a blaze of fire and thunder, for there's no way yet of devising a safe landing for a rocket ship. But it's worth it. She'll have had her one great flight, and that's all any of us should want. One great beautiful flight into the unknown—

As he locked the workshop door, Krane heard Hallmyer shouting from the cottage across the fields. Through the evening gloom he could see him waving urgently. He trotted through the crisp stubble, breathing the sharp air deeply, grateful to be alive.

"It's Evelyn on the phone," Hallmyer said.

Krane stared at him. Hallmyer refused to meet his eyes.

"What's the idea?" Krane asked. "I thought we agreed that she wasn't to call—wasn't to get in touch with me until I was ready to start? You been putting ideas into her head? Is this the way you're going to stop me?"

Hallmyer said, "No—" and studiously examined the darkening horizon.

Krane went into his study and picked up the phone.

"Now listen, darling," he said without preamble, "there's no sense getting alarmed now. I explained everything very carefully. Just before the ship crashes, I take to a parachute. I love you very much and I'll see you Wednesday when I start. So long—"

"Good-bye, sweetheart," Evelyn's clear voice said, "and is that what you called me for?"

"Called you!"

A brown hulk disengaged itself from the hearth rug and lifted itself to strong legs. Umber, Krane's mastiff, sniffed and cocked an ear. Then he whined.

"Did you say I called you?" Krane repeated

Umber's throat suddenly poured forth a bellow. He reached Krane in a single bound, looked up into his face and whined and roared all at once.

"Shut up, you monster!" Krane said. He pushed Umber away with his foot.

"Give Umber a kick for me," Evelyn laughed. "Yes, dear. Someone called and said you wanted to speak to me."

"They did, eh? Look, honey, I'll call you back—"

Krane hung up. He arose doubtfully and watched Umber's uneasy actions. Through the windows, the late evening glow sent flickering shadows of orange light. Umber gazed at the light, sniffed and bellowed again. Suddenly struck, Krane leaped to the window.

Across the fields a mass of flame thrust high into the air, and within it were the crumbling walls of the workshop. Silhouetted against the blaze, the figures of half a dozen men darted and ran.

Krane shot out of the cottage and with Umber hard at his heels, sprinted toward the shed. As he ran he could see the graceful nose of the spaceship within the fire, still looking cool and untouched. If only he could reach it before the flames softened its metal and started the rivets.

The workmen trotted up to him, grimy and panting. Krane gaped at them in a mixture of fury and bewilderment.

"Hallmyer!" he shouted. "Hallmyer!"

Hallmyer pushed through the crowd. His eyes gleamed with triumph.

"Too bad," he said, "I'm sorry, Steven—"

"You bastard!" Krane shouted. He grasped Hallmyer by the lapels and shook him once. Then he dropped him and started into the shed.

Hallmyer snapped orders to the workmen and an instant later a body hurtled against Krane's calves and spilled him to the ground. He lurched to his feet, fists swinging. Umber was alongside, growling over the roar of the flames. Krane battered a man in the face, and saw him stagger back against a second. He lifted a knee in a vicious drive that sent the last workman crumpling to the ground. Then he ducked his head and plunged into the shop.

The scorch felt cool at first, but when he reached the ladder and began mounting to the port, he screamed with the agony of his burns. Umber was howling at the foot of the ladder, and Krane realized that the dog could never escape from the rocket blasts. He reached down and hauled Umber into the ship.

Krane was reeling as he closed and locked the port. He retained consciousness barely long enough to settle himself in the spring hammock. Then instinct alone prompted his hands to reach out toward the control board; instinct and the frenzied refusal to let his beautiful ship waste itself in the flames. He would fail—yes. But he would fail trying.

His fingers tripped the switches. The ship shuddered and roared. And blackness descended over him.

How long was he unconscious? There was no telling. Krane awoke with cold pressing against his face and body, and the sound of frightened yelps in his ears. Krane looked up and saw Umber tangled in the springs and straps of the hammock. His first impulse was to laugh, then suddenly he realized; he had looked *up!* He had looked up at the hammock.

He was lying curled in the cup of the crystal nose. The ship had risen high—perhaps almost to Roche's zone, to the limit of the Earth's gravitational attraction, but then without guiding hands at the controls to continue its flight, had turned and was dropping back toward Earth. Krane peered through the crystal and gasped.

Below him was the ball of the Earth. It looked three times the size of the Moon. And it was no longer his Earth. It was a globe of fire mottled with black clouds. At the northernmost pole there was a tiny patch of white, and even as Krane watched, it was suddenly blotted over with hazy tones of red, scarlet and crimson. Hallmyer had been right.

Krane lay frozen in the cup of the nose as the ship descended, watching the flames gradually fade away to leave nothing but the dense blanket of black around the Earth. He lay numb with horror, unable to understand—unable to reckon up a people snuffed out, a green, fair planet reduced to ashes and cinders. Everything that was once dear and close to him—gone. He could not think of Evelyn.

Air whistling outside awoke some instinct in him. The few shreds of reason left told him to go down with his ship and forget everything in the thunder and destruction, but the instinct of life forced him to action. He climbed up to the store chest and prepared for the landing. Parachute, a small oxygen tank—a knapsack of supplies. Only half-aware of what he was doing he dressed for the descent, buckled on the 'chute and opened the port. Umber whined pathetically, and he took the heavy dog in his arms and stepped out into space.

But space hadn't been so clogged, the way it was now. Then it had been difficult to breathe. But that was because the air had been rare—not filled with clogging grit like now.

Every breath was a lungful of ground glass—or ashes—or cinders— He had returned to a suffocating black present that hugged him with soft weight and made him fight for breath. Krane struggled in panic, and then relaxed.

It had happened before. A long time past he'd been buried deep under ashes when he'd stopped to remember. Weeks ago—or days—or months. Krane clawed with his hands, inching out of the mound of cinders that the wind had thrown over him. Presently he emerged into the light again. The wind had died away. It was time to begin his crawl to the sea once more.

The vivid pictures of his memory scattered again before the grim vista that stretched out ahead. Krane scowled. He remembered too much, and too often. He had the vague hope that if he remembered hard enough, he might change one of the things he had done—just a very little thing—and then all this would become untrue. He thought: It might help if everyone remembered and wished at the same time—but there isn't any everyone. I'm the only one. I'm the last memory on Earth. I'm the last life.

He crawled. Elbows, knee, elbows, knee—And then Hallmyer was crawling alongside and making a great game of it. He chortled and plunged in the cinders like a happy sea lion.

Krane said: "But why do we have to get to the sea?"

Hallmyer blew a spume of ashes.

"Ask her," he said, pointing to Krane's other side.

Evelyn was there, crawling seriously, intently, mimicking Krane's smallest action.

"It's because of our house," she said.   "You remember our house, darling? High on the cliff.   We were going to live there forever and ever.   I was there when you left.   Now you're coming back to the house at the edge of the sea. Your beautiful flight is over, dear, and you're coming back to me.   We'll live together, just we two, like Adam and Eve—"

Krane said, "That's nice."

Then Evelyn turned her head and screamed, "Oh, Steven!   Watch out!" and Krane felt the menace closing in on him again.   Still crawling, he stared back at the vast grey plains of ash, and saw nothing.   When he looked at Evelyn again he saw only his shadow, sharp and black.   Presently, it too, faded away as the marching shaft of sunlight passed.

But the dread remained.   Evelyn had warned him twice, and she was always right.   Krane stopped and turned, and settled himself to watch.   If he was really being followed, he would see whatever it was, coming along his tracks.

There was a painful moment of lucidity.   It cleaved through his fever and bewilderment, bringing with it the sharpness and strength of a knife.

I'm mad, he thought.   The corruption in my leg has spread to my brain.   There is no Evelyn, no Hallmyer, no menace.   In all this land there is no life but mine— and even ghosts and spirits of the underworld must have perished in the inferno that girdled the planet.   No—there is nothing, but me and my sickness. I'm dying—and when I perish, everything will perish.   Only a mass of lifeless cinders will go on.

But there was a movement.

Instinct again—Krane dropped his head and lay still.   Through slitted eyes he watched the ashen plains, wondering if death was playing tricks with his eyes. Another facade of rain was beating down toward him, and he hoped he could make sure before all vision was obliterated.

Yes.   There.

A quarter mile back, a grey-brown shape was flitting along the grey surface. Despite the drone of the distant rain, Krane could hear the whisper of trodden cinders and see the little clouds kicking up.   Stealthily he groped for the revolver in the knapsack as his mind reached feebly for explanations and recoiled from fear.

The thing approached, and suddenly Krane squinted and understood.   He recalled Umber kicking with fear and springing away from him when the 'chute landed them on the ashen face of the Earth.

"Why, it's Umber," he murmured.   He raised himself.   The dog halted. "Here, boy!"   Krane croaked gaily.   "Here, boy!"

He was overcome with joy.   He realized that loneliness had hung over him, a horrible sensation of oneness in emptiness.   Now his was not the only life.   There was another.   A friendly life that could offer love and companionship.   Hope kindled again.

"Here, boy!" he repeated.   "Come on, boy—"

After a while he stopped trying to snap his fingers. The mastiff hung back, showing fangs and a lolling tongue. The dog was emaciated and its eyes gleamed red in the dusk. As Krane called once more, the dog snarled. Puffs of ash leaped beneath its nostrils.

He's hungry, Krane thought, that's all. He reached into the knapsack and at the gesture the dog snarled again. Krane withdrew the chocolate bar and laboriously peeled off the paper and silver foil. Weakly he tossed it toward Umber. It fell far short. After a minute of savage uncertainty, the dog advanced slowly and snapped up the food. Ashes powdered its muzzle. It licked its chops ceaselessly and continued to advance on Krane.

Panic jerked within him. A voice persisted: This is no friend. He has no love or companionship for you. Love and companionship have vanished from the land along with life. Now there is nothing left but hunger.

"No—" Krane whispered. "That isn't right that we should tear at each other and seek to devour—"

But Umber was advancing with a slinking sidle, and his teeth showed sharp and white. And even as Krane stared at him, the dog snarled and lunged.

Krane thrust up an arm under the dog's muzzle, but the weight of the charge carried him backward. He cried out in agony as his broken, swollen leg was struck by the weight of the dog. With his free hand he struck weakly, again and again, scarcely feeling the grind of teeth on his left arm. Then something metallic was pressed under him and he realized he was lying on the revolver he had let fall.

He groped for it and prayed the cinders had not clogged it. As Umber let go his arm and tore at his throat, Krane brought the gun up and jabbed the muzzle blindly against the dog's body. He pulled and pulled the trigger until the roars died away and only empty clicks sounded. Umber shuddered in the ashes before him, his body nearly shot in two. Thick scarlet stained the grey.

Evelyn and Hallmyer looked down sadly at the broken animal. Evelyn was crying, and Hallmyer reached nervous fingers through his hair in the same old gesture.

"This is the finish, Steven," he said. "You've killed part of yourself. Oh— you'll go on living, but not all of you. You'd best bury that body, Steven. It's the corpse of your soul."

"I can't," Krane said. "The wind will blow the cinders away."

"Then burn it," Hallmyer ordered with dream-logic.

It seemed that they helped him thrust the dead dog into his knapsack. They helped him take off his clothes and packed them underneath. They cupped their hands around the matches until the cloth caught fire, and blew on the weak flame until it sputtered and burned limply. Krane crouched by the fire and nursed it. Then he turned and once again began crawling down the ocean bed. He was naked now. There was nothing left of what-had-been but his flickering little life.

He was too heavy with sorrow to notice the furious rain that slammed and buffeted him, or the searing pains that were searing through his blackened leg and up his hip. He crawled. Elbows, knee, elbows, knee— Woodenly, mechanically, apathetic to everything . . . to the latticed skies, the dreary ashen plains and even the dull glint of water that lay far ahead.

He knew it was the sea—what was left of the old, or a new one in the making. But it would be an empty, lifeless sea that someday would lap against a dry, lifeless shore.   This would be a planet of stone and dust, of metal and snow and ice and water, but that would be all.   No more life.   He, alone, was useless.   He was Adam, but there was no Eve.

Evelyn waved gaily to him from the shore.   She was standing alongside the white cottage with the wind snapping her dress to show the slender lines of her figure.   And when he came a little closer, she ran out to him and helped him. She said nothing—only placed her hands under his shoulders and helped him lift the weight of his heavy, pain-ridden body.   And so at last he reached the sea.

It was real.   He understood that.   For even after Evelyn and the cottage had vanished, he felt the cool waters bathe his face.

Here's the sea, Krane thought, and here am I.   Adam and no Eve.   It's hopeless.

He rolled a little farther into the waters.   They laved his torn body.   He lay with face to the sky, peering at the high menacing heavens, and the bitterness within him welled up.

"It's not right!" he cried.   "It's not right that all this should pass away.   Life is too beautiful to perish at the mad act of one mad creature—"

Quietly the waters laved him.   Quietly . . . Calmly . . .

The sea rocked him gently, and even the death that was reaching up toward his heart was no more than a gloved hand.   Suddenly the skies split apart—for the first time in all those months—and Krane stared up at the stars.

Then he knew.   This was not the end of life.   There could never be an end to life.   Within his body, within the rotting tissues rocking gently in the sea was the source of ten million-million lives.   Cells—tissues—bacteria—amoeba—Countless infinities of life that would take new root in the waters and live long after he was gone.

They would live on his rotting remains.   They would feed on each other.   They would adapt themselves to the new environment and feed on the minerals and sediments washed into this new sea.   They would grow, burgeon, evolve.   Life would reach out to the lands once more.   It would begin again the same old repeated cycle that had begun perhaps with the rotting corpse of some last survivor of interstellar travel.   It would happen over and over in the future ages.

And then he knew what had brought him back to the sea.   There need be no Adam—no Eve.   Only the sea, the great mother of life was needed.   The sea had called him back to her depths that presently life might emerge once more, and he was content.

Quietly the waters comforted him.   Quietly . . . Calmly . . .   The mother of life rocked the last-born of the old cycle who would become the first-born of the new.   And with glazing eyes Steven Krane smiled up at the stars, stars that were sprinkled evenly across the sky.   Stars that had not yet formed into the familiar constellations, and would not for another hundred million centuries.

Ogre

The moss brought the news. Hundreds of miles the word had gossiped its way along, through many devious ways. For the moss did not grow everywhere. It grew only where the soil was sparse and niggardly, where the larger, lustier, more vicious plant things could not grow to rob it of light or uproot it, or crowd it out, or do it other harm.

The moss told the story to Nicodemus, life blanket of Don Mackenzie, and it all came about because Mackenzie took a bath.

Mackenzie took his time in the bathroom, wallowing around in the tub and braying out a song, while Nicodemus, feeling only half a thing, moped outside the door. Without Mackenzie Nicodemus was, in fact, even less than half a thing. Accepted as intelligent life, Nicodemus and others of his tribe were intelligent only when they were wrapped about their humans. Their intelligence and emotions were borrowed from the things that wore them.

For the aeons before the human beings came to this twilight world, the life blankets had dragged out a humdrum existence. Occasionally one of them allied itself with a higher form of plant life, but not often. After all, such an arrangement was very little better than staying as they were.

When the humans came, however, the blankets finally clicked. Between them and the men of Earth grew up a perfect mutual agreement, a highly profitable and agreeable instance of symbiosis. Overnight, the blankets became one of the greatest single factors in galactic exploration.

For the man who wore one of them, like a cloak around his shoulders, need never worry where a meal was coming from; knew, furthermore, that he would be fed correctly, with a scientific precision that automatically counterbalanced any upset of metabolism that might be brought by alien conditions. For the curious plants had the ability to gather energy and convert it into food for the human body, had an uncanny instinct as to the exact needs of the body, extending, to a limited extent, to certain basic medical requirements.

But if the life blankets gave men food and warmth, served as a family doctor, man lent them something that was even more precious—the consciousness of life. The moment one of the plants wrapped itself around a man it became, in a sense, the double of that man. It shared his intelligence and emotions, was whisked from the dreary round of its own existence into a more exalted pseudo-life.

Nicodemus, at first moping outside the bathroom door, gradually grew peeved. He felt his thin veneer of human life slowly ebbing from him and he was filled with a baffling resentment.

Finally, feeling very put upon, he waddled out of the trading post upon his own high lonesome, flapping awkwardly along, like a sheet billowing in the breeze.

The dull brick-red sun that was Sigma Draco shone down upon a world that even at high noon appeared to be in twilight and Nicodemus' bobbling shape cast squirming, unsubstantial purple shadows upon the green and crimson ground. A rifle tree took a shot at Nicodemus but missed him by a yard at least. That tree had been off the beam for weeks. It had missed everything it shot at. Its best effort had been scaring the life out of Nellie, the bookkeeping robot that never told a lie, when it banked one of its bulletlike seeds against the steel-sheeted post.

But no one had felt very badly about that, for no one cared for Nellie. With Nellie around, no one could chisel a red cent off the company. That, incidentally, was the reason she was at the post.

But for a couple of weeks now, Nellie hadn't bothered anybody. She had taken to chumming around with Encyclopedia, who more than likely was slowly going insane trying to figure out her thoughts.

Nicodemus told the rifle tree what he thought of it, shooting at its own flesh and blood, as it were, and kept shuffling along. The tree, knowing Nicodemus for a traitor to his own, a vegetable renegade, took another shot at him, missed by two yards and gave up in disgust.

That is how he heard that Alder, a minor musician out in Melody Bowl, finally had achieved a masterpiece. Nicodemus knew it might have happened weeks before, for Melody Bowl was half a world away and the news sometimes had to travel the long way around, but just the same he scampered as fast as he could hump back toward the post.

For this was news that couldn't wait. This was news Mackenzie had to know at once. He managed to kick up quite a cloud of dust coming down the home stretch and flapped triumphantly through the door, above which hung the crudely lettered sign:

GALACTIC TRADING CO.

Just what good the sign did, no one yet had figured out. The humans were the only living things on the planet that could read it.

Before the bathroom door, Nicodemus reared up and beat his fluttering self against it with tempetuous urgency.

"All right," yelled Mackenzie. "All right. I know I took too long again. Just calm yourself. I'll be right out."

Nicodemus settled down but, still wriggling with the news he had to tell, heard Mackenzie swabbing out the tub.

*   *   *

With Nicodemus wrapped happily about him, Mackenzie strode into the office and found Nelson Harper, the factor, with his feet up on the desk, smoking his pipe and studying the ceiling.

"Howdy, lad," said the factor.   He pointed at a bottle with his pipestem.   "Grab yourself a snort."

Mackenzie grabbed one.

"Nicodemus has been out chewing fat with the moss," he said.   "Tells me a conductor by the name of Alder has composed a symphony.   Moss says it's a masterpiece."

Harper took his feet off the desk.   Never heard of this chap, Alder," he said.

"Never heard of Kadmar, either," Mackenzie reminded him, "until he produced the Red Sun symphony.   Now everyone is batty over him.

"If Alder has anything at all, we ought to get it down.   Even a mediocre piece pays out.   People back on Earth are plain wacky over this tree music of ours. Like that one fellow . . . that composer—"

"Wade," Harper filled in.   "J.   Edgerton Wade.   One of the greatest composers Earth had ever known.   Quit in mortification after he heard the Red Sun piece.   Later disappeared.   No one knows where he went."

The factor nursed his pipe between his palms.   "Funny thing.   Came out here figuring our best-grading bet would be new drugs or maybe some new kind of food. Something for the high-class restaurants to feature, charge ten bucks a plate for. Maybe even a new mineral.   Like out on Eta Cassiop.   But it wasn't any of those things.   It was music.   Symphony stuff.   High-brow racket."

Mackenzie took another shot at the bottle, put it back and wiped his mouth. "I'm not so sure I like this music angle," he declared.   "I don't know much about music.   But it sounds funny to me, what I've heard of it.   Brain-twisting stuff."

Harper grunted.   "You're O.K. as long as you have plenty of serum along. If you can't take the music, just keep yourself shot full of serum.   That way it can't touch you."

Mackenzie nodded.   "It almost got Alexander that time, remember?   Ran short on serum while he was down in the Bowl trying to dicker with the trees.   Music seemed to have a hold on him.   He didn't want to leave.   He fought and screeched and yelled around . . . I felt like a heel, taking him away.   He never has quite been the same since then.   Doctors back on Earth finally were able to get him straightened out, but warned him never to come back."

"He's back again," said Harper, quietly.   "Grant spotted him over at the Groombridge post.   Throwing in with the Groomies, I guess.   Just a yellow-bellied renegade.   Going against his own race.   You boys shouldn't have saved him that time.   Should have let the music get him."

"What are you going to do about it?"   demanded Mackenzie.

Harper shrugged his shoulders.   "What can I do about it?   Unless I want to declare war on the Groombridge post.   And that is out.   Haven't you heard it's all sweetness and light between Earth and Groombridge 34?   That's the reason the two posts are stuck away from Melody Bowl.   So each one of us will have a fair shot at the music.   All according to some pact the two companies rigged up. Galactic's got so pure they wouldn't even like it if they knew we had a spy planted on the Groomie post.''

"But they got one planted on us," declared Mackenzie.   "We haven't been able to find him, of course, but we know there is one.   He's out there in the woods somewhere, watching every move we make.''

Harper nodded his head.   "You can't trust a Groomie.   The lousy little insects will stoop to anything.   They don't want that music, can't use it.   Probably don't even know what music is.   Haven't any hearing.   But they know Earth wants it, will pay any price to get it, so they are out here to beat us to it.   They work through birds like Alexander.   They get the stuff, Alexander peddles it.''

"What if we run across Alexander, chief?''

Harper clicked his pipestem across his teeth.   "Depends on circumstances.   Try to hire him, maybe.   Get him away from the Groomies.   He's a good trader. The company would do right by him.''

Mackenzie shook his head.   "No soap.   He hates Galactic.   Something that happened years ago.   He'd rather make us trouble than turn a good deal for himself.''

"Maybe he's changed," suggested Harper.   "Maybe you boys saving him changed his mind.''

"I don't think it did," persisted Mackenzie.

The factor reached across the desk and drew a humidor in front of him, began to refill his pipe.

"Been trying to study out something else, too," he said.   "Wondering what to do with the Encyclopedia.   He wants to go to Earth.   Seems he's found out just enough from us to whet his appetite for knowledge.   Says he wants to go to Earth and study our civilization.''

Mackenzie grimaced.   "That baby's gone through our minds with a fine-toothed comb.   He knows some of the things we've forgotten we ever knew.   I guess it's just the nature of him, but it gets my wind up when I think of it.''

"He's after Nellie now," said Harper.   "Trying to untangle what she knows.''

"It would serve him right if he found out.''

"I've been trying to figure it out," said Harper.   "I don't like this brain-picking of his any more than you do, but if we took him to Earth, away from his own stamping grounds, we might be able to soften him up.   He certainly knows a lot about this planet that would be of value to us.   He's told me a little—''

"Don't fool yourself," said Mackenzie.   "He hasn't told you a thing more than he's had to tell to make you believe it wasn't a one-way deal.   Whatever he has told you has no vital significance.   Don't kid yourself, he'll exchange information for information.   That cookie's out to get everything he can get for nothing.''

The factor regarded Mackenzie narrowly.   "I'm not sure but I should put you in for an Earth vacation," he declared.   "You're letting things upset you.   You're losing your perspective.   Alien planets aren't Earth, you know.   You have to expect wacky things, get along with them, accept them on the basis of the logic that makes them the way they are.''

"I know all that," agreed Mackenzie, "but honest, chief, this place gets in my hair at times.   Trees that shoot at you, moss that talks, vines that heave thunderbolts at you—and now, the Encyclopedia."

"The Encyclopedia is logical," insisted Harper.   "He's a repository for knowledge.   We have parallels on Earth.   Men who study merely for the sake of learning, never expect to use the knowledge they amass.   They derive a strange, smug satisfaction from being well informed.   Combine that yearning for knowledge with a phenomenal ability to memorize and co-ordinate that knowledge and you have the Encyclopedia."

"But there must be a purpose to him," insisted Mackenzie.   "There must be some reason back of this thirst for knowledge.   Just soaking up facts doesn't add up to anything unless you use those facts."

Harper puffed stolidly at his pipe.   "There may be a purpose in it, but a purpose so deep, so different, we could not recognize it.   This planet is a vegetable world and a vegetable civilization.   Back on earth the animals got the head start and plants never had a chance to learn or to evolve.   But here it's a different story. The plants were the ones that evolved, became masters of the situation."

"If there is a purpose, we should know it," Mackenzie declared, stubbornly. "We can't afford to go blind on a thing like this.   If the Encyclopedia has a game, we should know it.   Is he acting on his own, a free lance?   Or is he the representative of the world, a sort of prime minister, a state department?   Or is he something that was left over by another civilization, a civilization that is gone? A kind of living archive of knowledge, still working at his old trade even if the need of it is gone?"

"You worry too much," Harper told him.

"We have to worry, chief.   We can't afford to let anything get ahead of us. We have taken the attitude we're superior to this vegetable civilization, if you can call it a civilization, that has developed here.   It's the logical attitude to take because nettles and dandelions and trees aren't anything to be afraid of back home. But what holds on Earth doesn't hold here.   We have to ask ourselves what a vegetable civilization would be like.   What would it want?   What would be its aspirations and how would it go about realizing them?"

"We're getting off the subject," said Harper, curtly.   "You came in here to tell me about some new symphony."

Mackenzie flipped his hands.   "O. K. if that's the way you feel about it."

"Maybe we better figure on grabbing up this symphony soon as we can," said Harper.   "We haven't had a really good one since the Red Sun.   And if we mess around, the Groomies will beat us to it."

"Maybe they have already," said Mackenzie.

Harper puffed complacently at his pipe.   "They haven't done it yet.   Grant keeps me posted on every move they make.   He doesn't miss a thing that happens at the Groombridge post."

"Just the same," declared Mackenzie, "we can't go rushing off and tip our hand.   The Groomie spy isn't asleep, either."

"Got any ideas?" asked the factor.

"We could take the ground car," suggested Mackenzie. "It's slower than the flier, but if we took the flier the Groomie would know there was something up. We use the car a dozen times a day. He'd think nothing of it."

Harper considered. "The idea has merit, lad. Who would you take?"

"Let me have Brad Smith," said Mackenzie. "We'll get along all right, just the two of us. He's an old-timer out here. Knows his way around."

Harper nodded. "Better take Nellie, too."

"Not on your life!" yelped Mackenzie. "What do you want to do? Get rid of her so you can make a cleaning?"

Harper wagged his grizzled head sadly. "Good idea, but it can't be did. One cent off and she's on your trail. Use to be a little graft a fellow could pick up here and there, but not any more. Not since they got those robot bookkeepers indoctrinated with truth and honesty."

"I won't take her," Mackenzie declared, flatly. "So help me, I won't. She'll spout company law all the way there and back. With the crush she has on this Encyclopedia, she'll probably want to drag him along, too. We'll have trouble enough with rifle trees and electro vines and all the other crazy vegetables without having an educated cabbage and a tin-can lawyer underfoot."

"You've got to take her," insisted Harper, mildly. "New ruling. Got to have one of the things along on every deal you make to prove you did right by the natives. Come right down to it, the ruling probably is your own fault. If you hadn't been so foxy on that Red Sun deal, the company never would have thought of it."

"All I did was to save the company some money," protested Mackenzie.

"You knew," Harper reminded him crisply, "that the standard price for a symphony is two bushels of fertilizer. Why did you have to chisel half a bushel on Kadmar?"

"Cripes," said Mackenzie, "Kadmar didn't know the difference. He practically kissed me for a bushel and a half."

"That's not the point," declared Harper. "The company's got the idea we got to shoot square with everything we trade with, even if it's nothing but a tree."

"I know," said Mackenzie, dryly. "I've read the manual."

"Just the same," said Harper, "Nellie goes along."

He studied Mackenzie over the bowl of his pipe.

"Just to be sure you don't forget again," he said.

The man who back on Earth had been known as J. Edgerton Wade, crouched on the low cliff that dropped away into Melody Bowl. The dull red sun was slipping toward the purple horizon and soon, Wade knew, the trees would play their regular evening concert. He hoped that once again it would be the wondrous new symphony Alder had composed. Thinking about it, he shuddered in ecstasy— shuddered again when he thought about the setting sun. The evening chill would be coming soon.

Wade had no life blanket. His food, cached back in the tiny cave in the cliff, was nearly gone.   His ship, smashed in his inexpert landing on the planet almost a year before, was a rusty hulk.   J. Edgerton Wade was near the end of his rope— and knew it.   Strangely, he didn't care.   In that year since he'd come here to the cliffs, he'd lived in a world of beauty.   Evening after evening he had listened to the concerts.   That was enough, he told himself.   After a year of music such as that any man could afford to die.

He swept his eyes up and down the little valley that made up the Bowl, saw the trees set in orderly rows, almost as if someone had planted them.   Some intelligence that may at one time, long ago, have squatted on this very cliff edge, even as he squatted now, and listened to the music.

But there was no evidence, he knew, to support such a hypothesis.   No ruins of cities had been found upon this world.   No evidence that any civilization, in the sense that Earth had built a civilization, ever had existed here.   Nothing at all that suggested a civilized race had ever laid eyes upon this valley, had ever had a thing to do with the planning of the bowl.

Nothing, that was, except the cryptic messages on the face of the cliff above the cave where he cached his food and slept.   Scrawlings that bore no resemblance to any other writing Wade had ever seen.   Perhaps, he speculated, they might have been made by other aliens who, like himself, had come to listen to the music until death had come for them.

Still crouching, Wade rocked slowly on the balls of his feet.   Perhaps he should scrawl his own name there with the other scrawlings.   Like one would sign a hotel register.   A lonely name scratched upon the face of a lonely rock.   A grave name, a brief memorial—and yet it would be the only tombstone he would ever have.

The music would be starting soon and then he would forget about the cave, about the food that was almost gone, about the rusting ship that never could carry him back to Earth again—even had he wanted to go back.   And he didn't—he couldn't have gone back.   The Bowl had trapped him, the music had spun a web about him.   Without it, he knew, he could not live.   It had become a part of him.   Take it from him and he would be a shell, for it was now a part of the life force that surged within his body, part of his brain and blood, a silvery thread of meaning that ran through his thoughts and purpose.

The trees stood in quiet, orderly ranks and beside each tree was a tiny mound, podia for the conductors, and beside each mound the dark mouths of burrows. The conductors, Wade knew, were in those burrows resting for the concert.   Being animals, the conductors had to get their rest.

But the trees never needed rest.   They never slept.   They never tired, these gray, drab music trees, the trees that sang to the empty sky, sang of forgotten days and days that had not come, of days when Sigma Draco had been a mighty sun and of the later days when it would be a cinder circling in space.   And of other things an Earthman could never know, could only sense and strain toward and wish he knew.   Things that stirred strange thoughts within one's brain and choked one with alien emotion an Earthman was never meant to feel.   Emotion and thought that one could not even recognize, yet emotion and thought that one yearned toward and knew never could be caught.

Technically, of course, it wasn't the trees that sang.   Wade knew that, but he did not think about it often.   He would rather it had been the trees alone.   He seldom thought of the music other than belonging to the trees and disregarded the little entities inside the trees that really made the music, using the trees for their sounding boards.   Entities?   That was all he knew.   Insects, perhaps, a colony of insects to each tree—or maybe even nymphs or sprites or some of the other little folks that run on skipping feet through the pages of children's fairy books.   Although that was foolish, he told himself—there were no sprites.

Each insect, each sprite contributing its own small part to the orchestration, compliant to the thought-vibrations of the conductors.   The conductors thought the music, held it in their brains and the things in the trees responded.

It didn't sound so pretty that way, Wade told himself.   Thinking it out spoiled the beauty of it.   Better to simply accept it and enjoy it without explanation.

Men came at times—not often—men of his own flesh and blood, men from the trading post somewhere on the planet.   They came to record the music and then they went away.   How anyone could go away once they had heard the music, Wade could not understand.   Faintly he remembered there was a way one could immunize one's self against the music's spell, condition one's self so he could leave after he had heard it, dull his senses to a point where it could not hold him.   Wade shivered at the thought.   That was sacrilege.   But still no worse than recording the music so Earth orchestras might play it.   For what Earth orchestra could play it as he heard it here, evening after evening?   If Earth music lovers only could hear it as it was played here in this ancient bowl!

When the Earthmen came, Wade always hid.   It would be just like them to try to take him back with them, away from the music of the trees.

Faintly the evening breeze brought the foreign sound to him, the sound that should not have been heard there in the Bowl—the clank of steel on stone.

Rising from his squatting place, he tried to locate the origin of the sound.   It came again, from the far edge of the Bowl.   He shielded his eyes with a hand against the setting sun, stared across the Bowl at the moving figures.

There were three of them and one, he saw at once, was an Earthman.   The other two were strange creatures that looked remotely like monster bugs, chitinous armor glinting in the last rays of Sigma Draco.   Their heads, he saw, resembled grinning skulls and they wore dark harnesses, apparently for the carrying of tools or weapons.

Groombridgians!   But what would Groombridgians be doing with an Earthman?   The two were deadly trade rivals, were not above waging intermittent warfare when their interests collided.

Something flashed in the sun—a gleaming tool that stabbed and probed, stabbed and lifted.

J. Edgerton Wade froze in horror.

Such a thing, he told himself, simply couldn't happen!

The three across the Bowl were digging up a music tree!

The vine sneaked through the rustling sea of grass, cautious tendrils raised to keep tab on its prey, the queer, clanking thing that still rolled on unswervingly.

Came on without stopping to smell out the ground ahead, without zigzagging to throw off possible attack.

Its action was puzzling; that was no way for anything to travel on this planet. For a moment a sense of doubt trilled along the length of vine, doubt of the wisdom of attacking anything that seemed so sure.   But the doubt was short lived, driven out by the slavering anticipation that had sent the vicious vegetable from its lair among the grove of rifle trees.   The vine trembled a little—slightly drunk with the vibration that pulsed through its tendrils.

The queer thing rumbled on and the vine tensed itself, every fiber alert for struggle.   Just let it get so much as one slight grip upon the thing—

The prey came closer and for one sense-shattering moment it seemed it would be out of reach.   Then it lurched slightly to one side as it struck a hump in the ground and the vine's tip reached out and grasped, secured a hold, would itself in a maddened grip and hauled, hauled with all the might of almost a quarter mile of trailing power.

Inside the ground car, Don Mackenzie felt the machine lurch sickeningly, kicked up the power and spun the tractor on its churning treads in an effort to break loose.

Back of him Bradford Smith uttered a startled whoop and dived for an energy gun that had broken from its rack and was skidding across the floor.   Nellie, upset by the lurch, was flat on her back, jammed into a corner.   The Encyclopedia, at the moment of shock, had whipped out its coiled-up taproot and tied up to a pipe. Now, like an anchored turtle, it swayed pendulum-wise across the floor.

Glass tinkled and metal screeched on metal as Nellie thrashed to regain her feet. The ground car reared and seemed to paw the air, slid about and plowed great furrows in the ground.

"It's a vine!" shrieked Smith.

Mackenzie nodded, grim-lipped, fighting the wheel.   As the car slewed around, he saw the arcing loops of the attacker, reaching from the grove of rifle trees. Something pinged against the vision plate, shattered into a puff of dust.   The rifle trees were limbering up.

Mackenzie tramped on the power, swung the car in a wide circle, giving the vine some slack, then quartered and charged across the prairie while the vine twisted and flailed the air in looping madness.   If only he could build up speed, slap into the stretched-out vine full tilt, Mackenzie was sure he could break its hold.   In a straight pull, escape would have been hopeless, for the vine, once fastened on the thing, was no less than a steel cable of strength and determination.

Smith had managed to get a port open, was trying to shoot, the energy gun crackling weirdly.   The car rocked from side to side, gaining speed while bulletlike seeds from the rifle trees pinged and whined against it.

Mackenzie braced himself and yelled at Smith.   They must be nearing the end of their run.   Any minute now would come the jolt as they rammed into the tension of the outstretched vine.

It came with terrifying suddenness, a rending thud.   Instinctively, Mackenzie threw up his arms to protect himself, for one startled moment knew he was being hurled into the vision plate.   A gigantic burst of flame flared in his head and filled the universe.   Then he was floating through darkness that was cool and soft and he found himself thinking that everything would be all right, everything would be . . . everything—

But everything wasn't all right.   He knew that, the moment he opened his eyes and stared up into the mass of tangled wreckage that hung above him.   For many seconds he did not move, did not even wonder where he was.   Then he stirred and a piece of steel bit into his leg.   Carefully he slid his leg upward, clearing it of the steel.   Cloth ripped with an angry snarl, but his leg came free.

"Lie still, you lug," something said, almost as if it were a voice from inside him.

Mackenzie chuckled.   "So you're all right," he said.

"Sure.   I'm all right," said Nicodemus.   "But you got some bruises and a scratch or two and you're liable to have a headache if you—"

The voice trailed off and stopped.   Nicodemus was busy.   At the moment, he was the medicine cabinet, fashioning from pure energy those things that a man needed when he had a bruise or two and was scratched-up and might have a headache later.

Mackenzie lay on his back and stared up at the mass of tangled wreckage.

"Wonder how we'll get out of here," he said.

The wreckage above him stirred.   A gadget of some sort fell away from the twisted mass and gashed his cheek.   He swore—unenthusiastically.

Someone was calling his name and he answered.

The wreckage was jerked about violently, literally torn apart.   Long metal arms reached down, gripped him by the shoulders and yanked him out, none too gently.

"Thanks, Nellie," he said.

"Shut up," said Nellie, tartly.

His knees were a bit wobbly and he sat down, staring at the ground car.   It didn't look much like a ground car any more.   It had smashed full tilt into a boulder and was a mess.

To his left Smith also was sitting on the ground and he was chuckling.

"What's the matter with you," snapped Mackenzie.

"Jerked her right up by the roots," exulted Smith.   "So help me, right smack out of the ground.   That's one vine that'll never bother anyone again."

Mackenzie stared in amazement.   The vine lay coiled on the ground, stretching back toward the grove, limp and dead.   Its smaller tendrils still were entwined in the tangled wreckage of the car.

"It hung on," gasped Mackenzie.   "We didn't break its hold!"

"Nope," agreed Smith, "we didn't break its hold, but we sure ruined it."

"Lucky thing it wasn't an electro," said Mackenzie, "or it would have fried us."

Smith nodded glumly.   "As it is it's loused us up enough.   That car will never run again.   And us a couple thousand miles from home."

Nellie emerged from a hole in the wreckage, with the Encyclopedia under one arm and a mangled radio under the other.   She dumped them both on the ground. The Encyclopedia scuttled off a few feet, drilled his taproot into the soil and was at home.

Nellie glowered at Mackenzie. "I'll report you for this," she declared, vengefully. "The idea of breaking up a nice new car! Do you know what a car costs the company? No, of course, you don't. And you don't care. Just go ahead and break it up. Just like that. Nothing to it. The company's got a lot more money to buy another one. I wonder sometimes if you ever wonder where your pay is coming from. If I was the company, I'd take it out of your salary. Every cent of it, until it was paid for."

Smith eyed Nellie speculatively. "Some day," he said, "I'm going to take a sledge and play tin shinny with you."

"Maybe you got something there," agreed Mackenzie. "There are times when I'm inclined to think the company went just a bit too far in making those robots cost conscious."

"You don't need to talk like that," shrilled Nellie. "Like I was just a machine you didn't need to pay no attention to. I suppose next thing you will be saying it wasn't your fault, that you couldn't help it."

"I kept a good quarter mile from all the groves," growled Mackenzie. "Who ever heard of a vine that could stretch that far?"

"And that ain't all, neither," yelped Nellie. "Smith hit some of the rifle trees."

The two men looked toward the grove. What Nellie said was true. Pale wisps of smoke still rose above the grove and what trees were left looked the worse for wear.

Smith clucked his tongue in mock concern.

"The trees were shooting at us," retorted Mackenzie.

"That don't make any difference," Nellie yelled. "The rule book says—"

Mackenzie waved her into silence. "Yes, I know. Section 17 of the Chapter on Relations with Extraterrestrial Life: *'No employee of this company may employ weapons against or otherwise injure or attempt to injure or threaten with injury an inhabitant of any other planet except in self-defense and then only if every means of escape or settlement has failed.'* "

"And now we got to go back to the post," Nellie shrieked. "When we were almost there, we got to turn back. News of what we did will get around. The moss probably has started already. The idea of ripping a vine up by the roots and shooting trees. If we don't start back right now, we won't get back. Every living thing along the way will be laying for us."

"It was the vine's fault," yelled Smith. "It tried to trap us. It tried to steal our car, probably would have killed us, just for the few lousy ounces of radium we have in the motors. That radium was ours. Not the vine's. It belonged to your beloved company."

"For the love of gosh, don't tell her that," Mackenzie warned, "or she'll go out on a one-robot expedition, yanking vines up left and right."

"Good idea," insisted Smith. "She might tie into an electro. It would peel her paint."

"How about the radio!" Mackenzie asked Nellie.

"Busted," said Nellie, crustily.

"And the recording equipment?"

"The tape's all right and I can fix the recorder."

"Serum jugs busted?"

"One of them ain't," said Nellie.

"O.K., then," said Mackenzie, "get back in there and dig out two bags of fertilizer. We're going on. Melody Bowl is only about fifty miles away."

"We can't do that," protested Nellie. "Every tree will be waiting for us, every vine—"

"It's safer to go ahead than back," said Mackenzie. "Even if we have no radio, Harper will send someone out with the flier to look us up when we are overdue."

He rose slowly and unholstered his pistol.

"Get in there and get that stuff," he ordered. "If you don't, I'll melt you down into a puddle."

"All right," screamed Nellie in sudden terror. "All right. You needn't get so tough about it."

"Any more back talk out of you," Mackenzie warned, "and I'll kick you so full of dents you'll walk stooped over."

They stayed in the open, well away from the groves, keeping a close watch. Mackenzie went ahead and behind him came the Encyclopedia, humping along to keep pace with them. Back of the Encyclopedia was Nellie, loaded down with the bags of fertilizer and equipment. Smith brought up the rear.

A rifle tree took a shot at them, but the range was too far for accurate shooting. Back a way, an electro vine had come closer with a thunderbolt.

Walking was grueling. The grass was thick and matted and one had to plow through it, as if one were walking in water.

"I'll make you sorry for this," seethed Nellie. "I'll make—"

"Shut up," snapped Smith. "For once you're doing a robot's work instead of gumshoeing around to see if you can't catch a nickel out of place."

They breasted a hill and started to climb the long grassy slope.

Suddenly a sound like the savage ripping of a piece of cloth struck across the silence.

They halted, tensed, listening. The sound came again and then again.

"Guns!" yelped Smith.

Swiftly the two men loped up the slope, Nellie galloping awkwardly behind, the bags of fertilizer bouncing on her shoulders.

From the hilltop, Mackenzie took in the situation at a glance.

On the hillside below a man was huddled behind a boulder, working a gun with fumbling desperation, while farther down the hill a ground car had toppled over. Behind the car were three figures—one man and two insect creatures.

"Groomies!" whooped Smith.

A well-directed shot from the car took the top off the boulder and the man behind it hugged the ground.

Smith was racing quarterly down the hill, heading toward another boulder that would outflank the trio at the car.

A yell of human rage came from the car and a bolt from one of the three guns snapped at Smith, plowing a smoking furrow no more than ten feet behind him.

Another shot flared toward Mackenzie and he plunged behind a hummock. A second shot whizzed just above his head and he hunkered down trying to push himself into the ground.

From the slope below came the high-pitched, angry chittering of the Groombridgians.

The car, Mackenzie saw, was not the only vehicle on the hillside. Apparently it had been pulling a trailer to which was lashed a tree. Mackenzie squinted against the setting sun, trying to make out what it was all about. The tree, he saw, had been expertly dug, its roots balled in earth and wrapped in sacking that shone wetly. The trailer was canted at an awkward angle, the treetop sweeping the ground, the balled roots high in the air.

Smith was pouring a deadly fire into the hostile camp and the three below were replying with a sheet of blasting bolts, plowing up the soil around the boulder. In a minute or two, Mackenzie knew, they would literally cut the ground out from under Smith. Cursing under his breath, he edged around the hummock, pushing his pistol before him, wishing he had a rifle.

The third man was slinging an occasional, inexpert shot at the three below, but wasn't doing much to help the cause along. The battle, Mackenzie knew, was up to him and Smith.

He wondered abstractedly where Nellie was.

"Probably halfway back to the post by now," he told himself, drawing a bead on the point from which came the most devastating blaze of firing.

But even as he depressed the firing button, the firing from below broke off in a chorus of sudden screams. The two Groombridgians leaped up and started to run, but before they made their second stride, something came whizzing through the air from the slope below and crumpled one of them.

The other hesitated, like a startled hare, uncertain where to go, and a second thing came whishing up from the bottom of the slope and smacked against his breastplate with a thud that could be heard from where Mackenzie lay.

Then, for the first time Mackenzie saw Nellie. She was striding up the hill, her left arm holding an armful of stones hugged tight against her metal chest, her right arm working like a piston. The ringing clang of stone against metal came as one of the stones missed its mark and struck the ground car.

The human was running wildly, twisting and ducking, while Nellie pegged rock after rock at him. Trying to get set for a shot at her, the barrage of whizzing stones kept him on the dodge. Angling down the hill, he finally lost his rifle when he tripped and fell. With a howl of terror, he bolted up the hillside, his life blanket standing out almost straight behind him. Nellie pegged her last stone at him, then set out, doggedly loping in his wake.

Mackenzie screamed hoarsely at her, but she did not stop. She passed out of sight over the hill, closely behind the fleeing man.

Smith whooped with delight. "Look at our Nellie go for him," he yelled. "She'll give him a working over when she nails him."

Mackenzie rubbed his eyes. "Who was he?" he asked.

"Jack Alexander," said Smith. "Grant said he was around again."

The third man got up stiffly from behind his boulder and advanced toward them. He wore no life blanket, his clothing was in tatters, his face was bearded to the eyes.

He jerked a thumb toward the hill over which Nellie had disappeared. "A masterly military maneuver," he declared. "Your robot sneaked around and took them from behind."

"If she lost the recording stuff and the fertilizer, I'll melt her down," said Mackenzie, savagely.

The man stared at them. "You are the gentlemen from the trading post?" he asked.

They nodded, returning his stare.

"I am Wade," he said. "J. Edgerton Wade—"

"Wait a second," shouted Smith. "Not *the* J. Edgerton Wade? The lost composer?"

The man bowed, whiskers and all. "The same," he said. "Although I had not been aware that I was lost. I merely came out here to spend a year, a year of music such as man has never heard before."

He glared at them. "I am a man of peace," he declared, almost as if daring them to argue that he wasn't, "but when those three dug up Delbert, I knew what I must do."

"Delbert?" asked Mackenzie.

"The tree," said Wade. "One of the music trees."

"Those lousy planet-runners," said Smith, "figured they'd take that tree and sell it to someone back on Earth. I can think of a lot of big shots who'd pay plenty to have one of those trees in their back yard."

"It's a lucky thing we came along," said Mackenzie, soberly. "If we hadn't, if they'd got away with it, the whole planet would have gone on the warpath. We could have closed up shop. It might have been years before we dared come back again."

Smith rubbed his hands together, smirking. "We'll take back their precious tree," he declared, "and will that put us in solid! They'll give us their tunes from now on, free for nothing, just out of pure gratitude."

"You gentlemen," said Wade, "are motivated by mercenary factors but you have the right idea."

A heavy tread sounded behind them and when they turned they saw Nellie striding down the hill. She clutched a life blanket in her hand.

"He got away," she said, "but I got his blanket. Now I got a blanket, too, just like you fellows."

"What do you need with a life blanket?" yelled Smith. "You give that blanket to Mr. Wade. Right away. You hear me."

Nellie pouted. "You won't let me have anything. You never act like I'm human—"

"You aren't," said Smith.

"If you give that blanket to Mr. Wade," wheedled Mackenzie, "I'll let you drive the car."

"You would?" asked Nellie, eagerly.

"Really," said Wade, shifting from one foot to the other, embarrassed.

"You take that blanket," said Mackenzie. "You need it. Looks like you haven't eaten for a day or two."

"I haven't," Wade confessed.

"Shuck into it then and get yourself a meal," said Smith.

Nellie handed it over.

"How come you were so good pegging those rocks?" asked Smith.

Nellie's eyes gleamed with pride. "Back on Earth I was on a baseball team," she said. "I was the pitcher."

Alexander's car was undamaged except for a few dents and a smashed vision plate where Wade's first bolt had caught it, blasting the glass and startling the operator so that he swerved sharply, spinning the treads across a boulder and upsetting it.

The music tree was unharmed, its roots still well moistened in the burlap-wrapped, water-soaked ball of earth. Inside the tractor, curled in a tight ball in the darkest corner, unperturbed by the uproar that had been going on outside, they found Delbert, the two-foot high, roly-poly conductor that resembled nothing more than a poodle dog walking on its hind legs.

The Groombridgians were dead, their crushed chitinous armor proving the steam behind Nellie's delivery.

Smith and Wade were inside the tractor, settled down for the night. Nellie and the Encyclopedia were out in the night, hunting for the gun Alexander had dropped when he fled. Mackenzie, sitting on the ground, Nicodemus pulled snugly about him, leaned back against the car and smoked a last pipe before turning in.

The grass behind the tractor rustled.

"That you, Nellie?" Mackenzie called, softly.

Nellie clumped hesitantly around the corner of the car.

"You ain't sore at me?" she asked.

"No, I'm not sore at you. You can't help the way you are."

"I didn't find the gun," said Nellie.

"You knew where Alexander dropped it?"

"Yes," said Nellie. "It wasn't there."

Mackenzie frowned in the darkness. "That means Alexander managed to come back and get it. I don't like that. He'll be out gunning for us. He didn't like the company before. He'll really be out for blood after what we did today."

He looked round. "Where's the Encyclopedia?"

"I sneaked away from him. I wanted to talk to you about him."

"O.K.," said Mackenzie. "Fire away."

"He's been trying to read my brain," said Nellie.

"I know. He read the rest of ours. Did a good job of it."

"He's been having trouble," declared Nellie.

"Trouble reading your brain? I wouldn't doubt it."

"You don't need to talk as if my brain—" Nellie began, but Mackenzie stopped her.

"I don't mean it that way, Nellie. Your brain is all right, far as I know. Maybe even better than ours.   But the point is that it's different.   Ours are natural brains, the orthodox way for things to think and reason and remember.   The Encyclopedia knows about those kinds of brains and the minds that go with them.   Yours isn't that kind.   It's artificial.   Part mechanical, part chemical, part electrical, Lord knows what else; I'm not a robot technician.   He's never run up against that kind of brain before.   It probably has him down.   Matter of fact, our civilization probably has him down.   If this planet ever had a real civilization, it wasn't a mechanical one.   There's no sign of mechanization here.   None of the scars machines inflict on planets.''

"I been fooling him,'' said Nellie quietly.   "He's been trying to read my mind, but I been reading his.''

Mackenzie started forward.   "Well, I'll be—'' he began.   Then he settled back against the car, dead pipe hanging from between his teeth.   "Why didn't you ever let us know you could read minds?'' he demanded.   "I suppose you been sneaking around all this time, reading our minds, making fun of us, laughing behind our backs.''

"Honest, I ain't,'' said Nellie.   "Cross my heart, I ain't.   I didn't even know I could.   But, when I felt the Encyclopedia prying around inside my head the way he does, it kind of got my dander up.   I almost hauled off and smacked him one. And then I figured maybe I better be more subtle.   I figured that if he could pry around in my mind, I could pry around in his.   I tried it and it worked.''

"Just like that,'' said Mackenzie.

"It wasn't hard,'' said Nellie.   "It come natural.   I seemed to just know how to do it.''

"If the guy that made you knew what he'd let slip through his fingers, he'd cut his throat,'' Mackenzie told her.

Nellie sidled closer.   "It scares me,'' she said.

"What's scaring you now?''

"That Encyclopedia knows too much.''

"Alien stuff,'' said Mackenzie.   "You should have expected that.   Don't go messing around with an alien mentality unless you're ready for some shocks.''

"It ain't that,'' said Nellie.   "I knew I'd find alien stuff.   But he knows other things.   Things he shouldn't know.''

"About us?''

"No, about other places.   Places other than the Earth and this planet here. Places Earthmen ain't been to yet.   The kind of things no Earthman could know by himself or that no Encyclopedia could know by himself, either.''

"Like what?''

"Like knowing mathematical equations that don't sound like anything we know about,'' said Nellie.   "Nor like he'd know about if he'd stayed here all his life. Equations you couldn't know unless you knew a lot more about space and time than even Earthmen know.

"Philosophy, too.   Ideas that make sense in a funny sort of way, but make your head swim when you try to figure out the kind of people that would develop them.''

Mackenzie got out his pouch and refilled his pipe, got it going.

"Nellie, you think maybe this Encyclopedia has been at other minds?   Minds of other people who may have come here?"

"Could be," agreed Nellie.   "Maybe a long time ago.   He's awful old.   Lets on he could be immortal if he wanted to be.   Said he wouldn't die until there was nothing more in the universe to know.   Said when the time came there'd be nothing more to live for."

Mackenzie clicked his pipestem against his teeth.   "He could be, too," he said. "Immortal, I mean.   Plants haven't got all the physiological complications animals have.   Given any sort of care, they theoretically could live forever."

Grass rustled on the hillside above them and Mackenzie settled back against the car, kept on smoking.   Nellie hunkered down a few feet away.

The Encyclopedia waddled down the hill, starlight glinting from his shell-like back.   Ponderously he lined up with them beside the car, pushing his taproot into the ground for an evening snack.

"Understand you may be going back to Earth with us," said Mackenzie, conversationally.

The answer came, measured in sharp and concise thought that seemed to drill deep into Mackenzie's mind.   "I should like to.   Your race is interesting."

It was hard to talk to a thing like that, Mackenzie told himself.   Hard to keep the chatter casual when you knew all the time it was hunting around in the corners of your mind.   Hard to match one's voice against the brittle thought with which it talked.

"What do you think of us?" he asked and knew, as soon as he had asked it, that it was asinine.

"I know very little of you," the Encyclopedia declared.   "You have created artificial lives, while we on this planet have lived natural lives.   You have bent every force that you can master to your will.   You have made things work for you.   First impression is that, potentially, you are dangerous."

"I guess I asked for it," Mackenzie said.

"I do not follow you."

"Skip it," said Mackenzie.

"The only trouble," said the Encyclopedia, "is that you don't know where you're going."

"That's what makes it so much fun," Mackenzie told him.   "Cripes, if we knew where we were going there'd be no adventure.   We'd know what was coming next.   As it is, every corner that we turn brings a new surprise."

"Knowing where you're going has its advantages," insisted the Encyclopedia.

Mackenzie knocked the pipe bowl out on his boot heel, tramped on the glowing ash.

"So you have us pegged," he said.

"No," said the Encyclopedia.   "Just first impressions."

The music trees were twisted gray ghosts in the murky dawn.   The conductors, except for the few who refused to let even a visit from the Earthmen rouse them from their daylight slumber, squatted like black imps on their podia.

Delbert rode on Smith's shoulder, one clawlike hand entwined in Smith's hair to keep from falling off.   The Encyclopedia waddled along in the wake of the Earthman party.   Wade led the way toward Alder's podium.

The Bowl buzzed with the hum of distorted thought, the thought of many little folk squatting on their mounds—an alien thing that made Mackenzie's neck hairs bristle just a little as it beat into his mind.   There were no really separate thoughts, no one commanding thought, just the chitterchatter of hundreds of little thoughts, as if the conductors might be gossiping.

The yellow cliffs stood like a sentinel wall and above the path that led to the escarpment, the tractor loomed like a straddled beetle against the early dawn.

Alder rose from the podium to greet them, a disreptuable-looking gnome on gnarly legs.

The Earth delegation squatted on the ground.   Delbert, from his perch on Smith's shoulder, made a face at Alder.

Silence held for a moment and then Mackenzie, dispensing with formalities, spoke to Alder.   "We rescued Delbert for you," he told the gnome.   "We brought him back."

Alder scowled and his thoughts were fuzzy with disgust.   "We do not want him back," he said.

Mackenzie taken aback, stammered.   "Why, we thought . . . that is, he's one of you . . . we went to a lot of trouble to rescue him—"

"He's a nuisance," declared Alder.   "He's a disgrace.   He's a no-good.   He's always trying things."

"You're not so hot yourself," piped Delbert's thought.   "Just a bunch of fuddy-duddies.   A crowd of corn peddlers.   You're sore at me because I want to be different.   Because I dust it off—"

"You see," said Alder to Mackenzie, "what he is like."

"Why, yes," agreed Mackenzie, "but there are times when new ideas have some values.   Perhaps he may be—"

Alder leveled an accusing finger at Wade.   "He was all right until you took to hanging around," he screamed.   "Then he picked up some of your ideas.   You contaminated him.   Your silly notions about music—"   Alder's thoughts gulped in sheer exasperation, then took up again.   "Why did you come?   No one asked you to.   Why don't you mind your own business?"

Wade, red faced behind his beard, seemed close to apoplexy.

"I've never been so insulted in all my life," he howled.   He thumped his chest with a doubled fist.   "Back on Earth I wrote great symphonies myself.   I never held with frivolous music.   I never—"

"Crawl back into your hole," Delbert shrilled at Alder.   "You guys don't know what music is.   You saw out the same stuff day after day.   You never lay it in the groove.   You never get gated up.   You all got long underwear."

Alder waved knotted fists above his head and hopped up and down in rage.   "Such language!" he shrieked.   "Never was the like heard here before."

The whole Bowl was yammering.   Yammering with clashing thoughts of rage and insult.

"Wait," Mackenzie shouted. "All of you, quiet down!"

Wade puffed out his breath, turned a shade less purple. Alder squatted back on his haunches, unknotted his fists, tried his best to look composed. The clamor of thought subsided to a murmur.

"You're sure about this?" Mackenzie asked Alder. "Sure you don't want Delbert back."

"Mister," said Alder, "there never was a happier day in Melody Bowl than the day we found him gone."

A rising murmur of assent from the other conductors underscored his words.

"We have some others we'd like to get rid of, too," said Alder.

From far across the Bowl came a yelping thought of derision.

"You see," said Alder, looking owlishly at Mackenzie, "what it is like. What we have to contend with. All because this . . . this . . . this—"

Glaring at Wade, thoughts failed him. Carefully he settled back upon his haunches, composed his face again.

"If the rest were gone," he said, "we could settle down. But as it is, these few keep us in an uproar all the time. We can't concentrate, we can't really work. We can't do the things we want to do."

Mackenzie pushed back his hat and scratched his head.

"Alder, he declared, "you sure are in a mess."

"I was hoping," Alder said, "that you might be able to take them off our hands."

"Take them off your hands!" yelled Smith. "I'll say we'll take them! We'll take as many—"

Mackenzie nudged Smith in the ribs with his elbow, viciously. Smith gulped into silence. Mackenzie tried to keep his face straight.

"You can't take them trees," said Nellie, icily. "It's against the law."

Mackenzie gasped. "The law?"

"Sure, the regulations. The company's got regulations. Or don't you know that? Never bothered to read them, probably. Just like you. Never pay no attention to the things you should."

"Nellie," said Smith savagely, "you keep out of this. I guess if we want to do a little favor for Alder here—"

"But it's against the law!" screeched Nellie.

"I know," said Mackenzie. "Section 34 of the chapter on Relations with Extraterrestrial Life. *'No member of this company shall interfere in any phase of the internal affairs of another race.'* "

"That's it," said Nellie, pleased with herself. "And if you take some of these trees, you'll be meddling in a quarrel that you have no business having anything to do with."

Mackenzie flipped his hands. "You see," he said to Alder.

"We'll give you a monopoly on our music," tempted Alder. "We'll let you know when we have anything. We won't let the Groomies have it and we'll keep our prices right."

Nellie shook her head. "No," she said.

Alder bargained. "Bushel and a half instead of two bushels."

"No," said Nellie.

"It's a deal," declared Mackenzie. "Just point out your duds and we'll haul them away."

"But Nellie said no," Alder pointed out. "And you say yes. I don't understand."

"We'll take care of Nellie," Smith told him, soberly.

"You won't take them trees," said Nellie. "I won't let you take them. I'll see to that."

"Don't pay any attention to her," Mackenzie said. "Just point out the ones you want to get rid of."

Alder said primly: "You've made us very happy."

Mackenzie got up and looked around. "Where's the Encyclopedia?" he asked.

"He cleared out a minute ago," said Smith. "Headed back for the car."

Mackenzie saw him, scuttling swiftly up the path toward the cliff top.

It was topsy-turvy and utterly crazy, like something out of that old book for children written by a man named Carroll. There was no sense to it. It was like taking candy from a baby.

Walking up the cliff path back to the tractor, Mackenzie knew it was, felt that he should pinch himself to know it was no dream.

He had hoped—just hoped—to avert relentless, merciless war against Earthmen throughout the planet by bringing back the stolen music tree. And here he was, with other music trees for his own, and a bargain thrown in to boot.

There was something wrong, Mackenzie told himself, something utterly and nonsensically wrong. But he couldn't put his finger on it.

There was no need to worry, he told himself. The thing to do was to get those trees and get out of there before Alder and the others changed their minds.

"It's funny," Wade said behind him.

"It is," agreed Mackenzie. "Everything is funny here."

"I mean about those trees," said Wade. "I'd swear Delbert was all right. So were all the others. They played the same music the others played. If there had been any faulty orchestration, any digression from form, I am sure I would have noticed it."

Mackenzie spun around and grasped Wade by the arm. "You mean they weren't lousing up the concerts? That Delbert, here, played just like the rest?"

Wade nodded.

"That ain't so," shrilled Delbert from his perch on Smith's shoulder. "I wouldn't play like the rest of them. I want to kick the stuff around. I always dig it up and hang it out the window. I dream it up and send it away out wide."

"Where'd you pick up that lingo?" Mackenzie snapped. "I never heard anything like it before."

"I learned it from him," declared Delbert, pointing at Wade.

Wade's face was purple and his eyes were glassy.

"It's practically prehistoric," he gulped. "It's terms that were used back in the twentieth century to describe a certain kind of popular rendition. I read about it in a history covering the origins of music. There was a glossary of terms. They were so fantastic they stuck in my mind.''

Smith puckered his lips, whistling soundlessly. ''So that's how he picked it up. He caught it from your thoughts. Same principle that Encyclopedia uses, although not so advanced.''

''He lacks the Encyclopedia's distinction,'' explained Mackenzie. ''He didn't know the stuff he was picking up was something that had happened long ago.''

''I have a notion to wring his neck,'' Wade threatened.

''You'll keep your hands off him,'' grated Mackenzie. ''This deal stinks to the high heavens, but seven music trees are seven music trees. Screwy deal or not, I'm going through with it.''

''Look fellows,'' said Nellie, ''I wish you wouldn't do it.''

Mackenzie puckered his brow. ''What's the matter with you, Nellie? Why did you make that uproar about the law down there? There's a rule, sure, but in a thing like this it's different. The company can afford to have a rule or two broken for seven music trees. You know what will happen, don't you, when we get those trees back home. We can charge a thousand bucks a throw to hear them and have to use a club to keep the crowds away.''

''And the best of it is,'' Smith pointed out, ''that once they hear them, they'll have to come again. They'll never get tired of them. Instead of that, every time they hear them, they'll want to hear them all the more. It'll get to be an obsession, a part of the people's life. They'll steal, murder, do anything so they can hear the trees.''

''That,'' said Mackenzie, soberly, ''is the one thing I'm afraid of.''

''I only tried to stop you,'' Nellie said. ''I know as well as you do that the law won't hold in a thing like this. But there was something else. The way the conductors sounded. Almost as if they were jeering at us. Like a gang of boys out in the street hooting at someone they just pulled a fast one on.''

''You're batty,'' Smith declared.

''We have to go through with it,'' Mackenzie announced, flatly. ''If anyone ever found we'd let a chance like this slip through our fingers, they'd crucify us for it.''

''You're going to get in touch with Harper?'' Smith asked.

Mackenzie nodded. ''We have to get hold of Earth, have them send out a ship right away to take back the trees.''

''I still think,'' said Nellie, ''there's a nigger in the woodpile.''

Mackenzie flipped the toggle and the visiphone went dead.

Harper had been hard to convince. Mackenzie, thinking about it, couldn't blame him much. After all, it did sound incredible. But then, this whole planet was incredible.

Mackenzie reached into his pocket and hauled forth his pipe and pouch. Nellie probably would raise hell about helping to dig up those other six trees, but she'd have to get over it. They'd have to work as fast as they could. They couldn't spend more than one night up here on the rim.   There wasn't enough serum for longer than that.   One jug of the stuff wouldn't go too far.

Suddenly excited shouts came from outside the car, shouts of consternation.

With a single leap, Mackenzie left the chair and jumped for the door.   Outside, he almost bumped into Smith, who came running around the corner of the tractor. Wade, who had been down at the cliff's edge, was racing toward them.

"It's Nellie," shouted Smith.   "Look at that robot!"

Nellie was marching toward them, dragging in her wake a thing that bounced and struggled.   A rifle-tree grove fired a volley and one of the pellets caught Nellie in the shoulder, puffing into dust, staggering her a little.

The bouncing thing was the Encyclopedia.   Nellie had hold of his taproot, was hauling him unceremoniously across the bumpy ground.

"Put him down!" Mackenzie yelled at her.   "Let him go!"

"He stole the serum," howled Nellie.   "He stole the serum and broke it on a rock!"

She swung the Encyclopedia toward them in a looping heave.   The intelligent vegetable bounced a couple of times, struggled to get right side up, then scurried off a few feet, root coiled tightly against its underside.

Smith moved toward it threateningly.   "I ought to kick the living innards out of you," he yelled.   "We need that serum.   You knew why we needed it."

"You threaten me with force," said the Encyclopedia.   "The most primitive method of compulsion."

"It works," Smith told him shortly.

The Encyclopedia's thoughts were unruffled, almost serene, as clear and concise as ever.   "You have a law that forbids your threatening or harming any alien thing."

"Chum," declared Smith, "you better get wised up on laws.   There are times when certain laws don't hold.   And this is one of them."

"Just a minute," said Mackenzie.   He spoke to the Encyclopedia.   "What is your understanding of a law?"

"It is a rule you live by," the Encyclopedia said.   "It is something that is necessary.   You cannot violate it."

"He got that from Nellie," said Smith.

"You think because there is a law against it, we won't take the trees?"

"There is a law against it," said the Encyclopedia.   "You cannot take the trees."

"So as soon as you found that out, you lammed up here and stole the serum, eh!"

"He's figuring on indoctrinating us," Nellie explained.   "Maybe that word ain't so good.   Maybe conditioning is better.   It's sort of mixed up.   I don't know if I've got it straight.   He took the serum so we would hear the trees without being able to defend ourselves against them.   He figured when we heard the music, we'd go ahead and take the trees."

"Law or no law?"

"That's it," Nellie said. "Law or no law."

Smith whirled on the robot. "What kind of jabber is this? How do you know what he was planning?"

"I read his mind," said Nellie. "Hard to get at, the thing that he was planning, because he kept it deep. But some of it jarred up where I could reach it when you threatened him."

"You can't do that!" shrieked the Encyclopedia. "Not you! Not a machine!"

Mackenzie laughed shortly. "Too bad, big boy, but she can. She's been doing it."

Smith stared at Mackenzie.

"It's all right," Mackenzie said. "It isn't any bluff. She told me about it last night."

"You are unduly alarmed," the Encyclopedia said. "You are putting a wrong interpretation—"

A quiet voice spoke, almost as if it were a voice inside Mackenzie's mind.

"Don't believe a thing he tells you, pal. Don't fall for any of his lies."

"Nicodemus! You know something about this?"

"It's the trees," said Nicodemus. "The music does something to you. It changes you. Makes you different than you were before. Wade is different. He doesn't know it, but he is."

"If you mean the music chains one to it, that is true," said Wade. "I may as well admit it. I could not live without the music. I could not leave the Bowl. Perhaps you gentlemen thought that I would go back with you. But I cannot go. I cannot leave. It will work the same with anyone. Alexander was here for a while when he ran short of serum. Doctors treated him and he was all right, but he came back. He had to come back. He couldn't stay away."

"It isn't only that," declared Nicodemus. "It changes you, too, in other ways. It can change you any way it wants to. Change your way of thinking. Change your viewpoints."

Wade strode forward. "It isn't true," he yelled. "I'm the same as when I came here."

"You heard things," said Nicodemus, "felt things in the music you couldn't understand. Things you wanted to understand, but couldn't. Strange emotions that you yearned to share, but could never reach. Strange thoughts that tantalized you for days."

Wade sobered, stared at them with haunted eyes.

"That was the way it was," he whispered. "That was just the way it was."

He glanced around, like a trapped animal seeking escape.

"But I don't feel any different," he mumbled. "I still am human. I think like a man, act like a man."

"Of course you do," said Nicodemus. "Otherwise you would have been scared away. If you had known what was happening to you, you wouldn't let it happen. And you have had less than a year of it. Less than a year of this conditioning.

Five years and you would be less human.   Ten years and you would be beginning to be the kind of thing the trees want you to be.''

"And we were going to take some of those trees to Earth!'' Smith shouted. "Seven of them!   So the people of Earth could hear them.   Listen to them, night after night.   The whole world listening to them on the radio.   A whole world being conditioned, being changed by seven music trees.''

"But why?'' asked Wade, bewildered.

"Why did men domesticate animals?'' Mackenzie asked.   "You wouldn't find out by asking the animals, for they don't know.   There is just as much point asking a dog why he was domesticated as there is in asking us why the trees want to condition us.   For some purpose of their own, undoubtedly, that is perfectly clear and logical to them.   A purpose that undoubtedly never can be clear and logical to us.''

"Nicodemus,'' said the Encyclopedia and this thought was deathly cold, "you have betrayed your own.''

Mackenzie laughed harshly.   "You're wrong there,'' he told the vegetable, "because Nicodemus isn't a plant, any more.   He's a human.   The same thing has happened to him as you want to have happen to us.   He has become a human in everything but physical make-up.   He thinks as a man does.   His viewpoints are ours, not yours.''

"That is right,'' said Nicodemus.   "I am a man.''

A piece of cloth ripped savagely and for an instant the group was blinded by a surge of energy that leaped from the thicket a hundred yards away.   Smith gurgled once in sudden agony and the energy was gone.

Frozen momentarily by surprise, Mackenzie watched Smith stagger, face tight with pain, hand clapped to his side.   Slowly the man wilted, sagged in the middle and went down.

Silently, Nellie leaped forward, was sprinting for the thicket.   With a hoarse cry, Mackenzie bent over Smith.

Smith grinned at him, a twisted grin.   His mouth worked, but no words came. His hand slid away from his side and he went limp, but his chest rose and fell with a slightly slower breath.   His life blanket had shifted its position to cover the wounded side.

Mackenzie straightened up, hauling the pistol from his belt.   A man had risen from the thicket, was leveling a gun at the charging Nellie.   With a wild yell, Mackenzie shot from the hip.   The lashing charge missed the man but half the thicket disappeared in a blinding sheet of flame.

The man with the gun ducked as the flame puffed out at him and in that instant Nellie closed in.   The man yelled once, a long-drawn howl of terror as Nellie swung him above her head and dashed him down.   The smoking thicket hid the rest of it.   Mackenzie, pistol hanging limply by his side, watched Nellie's fist lift and fall with brutal precision, heard the thud of life being beaten from a human body.

Sickened, he turned back to Smith.   Wade was kneeling beside the wounded man.   He looked up.

"He seems to be unconscious."

Mackenzie nodded.   "The blanket put him out.   Gave him an anaesthesia. It'll take care of him."

Mackenzie glanced up sharply at a scurry in the grass.   The Encyclopedia, taking advantage of the moment, was almost out of sight, scuttling toward a grove of rifle trees.

A step grated behind him.

"It was Alexander," Nellie said.   "He won't bother us no more."

Nelson Harper, factor at the post, was lighting up his pipe when the visiphone signal buzzed and the light flashed on.

Startled, Harper reached out and snapped on the set.   Mackenzie's face came in, a face streaked with dirt and perspiration, stark with fear.   He waited for no greeting.   His lips were already moving even as the plate flickered and cleared.

"It's all off, chief," he said.   "The deal is off.   I can't bring in those trees."

"You got to bring them in," yelled Harper.   "I've already called Earth.   I got them turning handsprings.   They say it's the greatest thing that ever happened. They're sending out a ship within an hour."

"Call them back and tell them not to bother," Mackenzie snapped.

"But you told me everthing was set," yelped Harper.   "You told me nothing could happen.   You said you'd bring them in if you had to crawl on hands and knees and pack them on your back."

"I told you every word of that," agreed Mackenzie.   "Probably even more. But I didn't know what I know now."

Harper groaned.   "Galactic is plastering every front page in the Solar System with the news.   Earth radios right now are bellowing it out from Mercury to Pluto. Before another hour is gone every man, woman and child will know those trees are coming to Earth.   And once they know that, there's nothing we can do.   Do you understand that, Mackenzie?   We have to get them there!"

"I can't do it, chief," Mackenzie insisted, stubbornly.

"Why can't you?" screamed Harper.   "So help me Hannah, if you don't—"

"I can't bring them in because Nellie's burning them.   She's down in the Bowl right now with a flamer.   When she's through, there won't be any music trees."

"Go out and stop her!" shrieked Harper.   "What are you sitting there for!   Go out and stop her!   Blast her if you have to.   Do anything, but stop her!   That crazy robot—"

"I told her to," snapped Mackenzie.   "I ordered her to do it.   When I get through here, I'm going down to help her."

"You're crazy, man!" yelled Harper.   "Stark, staring crazy.   They'll throw the book at you for this.   You'll be lucky if you just get life—"

Two darting hands loomed in the plate, hands that snapped down and closed around Mackenzie's throat, hands that dragged him away and left the screen blank, but with a certain blurring motion, as if two men might be fighting for their lives just in front of it.

"Mackenzie!" screamed Harper.   "Mackenzie!"

Something smashed into the screen and shattered it, leaving the broken glass gaping in jagged shards.

Harper clawed at the visiphone.   "Mackenzie!   Mackenzie, what's happening!"

In answer the screen exploded in a flash of violent flame, howled like a screeching banshee and then went dead.

Harper stood frozen in the room, listening to the faint purring of the radio.   His pipe fell from his hand and bounced along the floor spilling burned tobacco.

Cold, clammy fear closed down upon him, squeezing his heart.   A fear that twisted him and mocked him.   Galactic would break him for this, he knew.   Send him out to some of the jungle planets as the rankest subordinate.   He would be marked for life, a man not to be trusted, a man who had failed to uphold the prestige of the company.

Suddenly a faint spark of hope stirred deep within him.   If he could get there soon enough!   If he could get to Melody Bowl in time, he might stop this madness. Might at least save something, save a few of the precious trees.

The flier was in the compound, waiting.   Within half an hour he could be above the Bowl.

He leaped for the door, shoved it open and even as he did a pellet whistled past his cheek and exploded into a puff of dust against the door frame.   Instinctively, he ducked and another pellet brushed his hair.   A third caught him in the leg with stinging force and brought him down.   A fourth puffed dust into his face.

He fought his way to his knees, was staggered by another shot that slammed into his side.   He raised his right arm to protect his face and a sledge-hammer blow slapped his wrist.   Pain flowed along his arm and in sheer panic he turned and scrambled on hands and knees across the threshold and kicked the door shut with his foot.

Sitting flat on the floor, he held his right wrist in his left hand.   He tried to make his fingers wiggle and they wouldn't.   The wrist, he knew, was broken.

After weeks of being off the beam, the rifle tree outside the compound suddenly had regained its aim and gone on a rampage.

Mackenzie raised himself off the floor and braced himself with one elbow, while with the other hand he fumbled at his throbbing throat.   The interior of the tractor danced with wavy motion and his head thumped and pounded with pain.

Slowly, carefully, he inched himself back so he could lean against the wall. Gradually the room stopped rocking, but the pounding in his head went on.

Someone was standing in the doorway of the tractor and he fought to focus his eyes, trying to make out who it was.

A voice screeched across his nerves.

"I'm taking your blankets.   You'll get them back when you decide to leave the trees alone."

Mackenzie tried to fashion words, but all he accomplished was a croak.   He tried again.

"Wade?" he asked.

It was Wade, he saw.

The man stood within the doorway, one hand clutching a pair of blankets, the other holding a gun.

"You're crazy, Wade," he whispered. "We have to burn the trees. The human race never would be safe. Even if they fail this time, they'll try again. And again—and yet again. And some day they will get us. Even without going to Earth they can get us. They can twist us to their purpose with recordings alone: Long distance propaganda. Take a bit longer, but it will do the job as well."

"They are beautiful," said Wade. "The most beautiful things in all the universe. I can't let you destroy them. You must not destroy them."

"But can't you see," croaked Mackenzie, "that's the thing that makes them so dangerous. Their beauty, the beauty of their music, is fatal. No one can resist it."

"It was the thing I lived by," Wade told him, soberly. "You say it made me something that was not quite human. But what difference does that make. Must racial purity, in thought and action, be a fetish that would chain us to a drab existence when something better, something greater, is offered. And we never would have known. That is the best of it all, we never would have known. They would have changed us, yes, but so slowly, so gradually, that we would not have suspected. Our decisions and our actions and our way of thought would still have seemed to be our own. The trees never would have been anything more than something cultural."

"They want our mechanization," said Mackenzie. "Plants can't develop machines. Given that, they might have taken us along a road we, in our rightful heritage, never would have taken."

"How can we be sure," asked Wade, "that our heritage would have guided us aright?"

Mackenzie slid straighter against the wall. His head still throbbed and his throat still ached.

"You've been thinking about this?" he asked.

Wade nodded. "At first there was the natural reaction of horror. But, logically, that reaction is erroneous. Our schools teach our children a way of life. Our press strives to formulate our adult opinion and belief. The trees were doing no more to us than we do to ourselves. And perhaps, for a purpose no more selfish."

Mackenzie shook his head. "We must live our own life. We must follow the path the attributes of humanity decree that we should follow. And anyway, you're wasting your time."

"I don't understand," said Wade.

"Nellie already is burning the trees," Mackenzie told him. "I sent her out before I made the call to Harper."

"No, she's not," said Wade.

Mackenzie sat bolt upright. "What do you mean?"

Wade flipped the pistol as Mackenzie moved as if to regain his feet.

"It doesn't matter what I mean," he snapped.   "Nellie isn't burning any trees. She isn't in a position to burn any trees.   And neither are you, for I've taken both your flamers.   And the tractor won't run, either.   I've seen to that.   So the only thing that you can do is stay right here."

Mackenzie motioned toward Smith, lying on the floor.   "You're taking his blanket, too?"

Wade nodded.

"But you can't.   Smith will die.   Without that blanket he doesn't have a chance. The blanket could have healed the wound, kept him fed correctly, kept him warm—"

"That," said Wade, "is all the more reason that you come to terms directly."

"Your terms," said Mackenzie, "are that we leave the trees unharmed."

"Those are my terms."

Mackenzie shook his head.   "I can't take the chance," he said.

"When you decide, just step out and shout," Wade told him.   "I'll stay in calling distance."

He backed slowly from the door.

Smith needed warmth and food.   In the hour since his blanket had been taken from him he had regained consciousness, had mumbled feverishly and tossed about, his hand clawing at his wounded side.

Squatting beside him, Mackenzie had tried to quiet him, had felt a wave of slow terror as he thought of the hours ahead.

There was no food in the tractor, no means for making heat.   There was no need for such provision so long as they had had their life blankets—but now the blankets were gone.   There was a first-aid cabinet and with the materials that he found there, Mackenzie did his fumbling best, but there was nothing to relieve Smith's pain, nothing to control his fever.   For treatment such as that they had relied upon the blankets.

The atomic motor might have been rigged up to furnish heat, but Wade had taken the firing mechanism control.

Night was falling and that meant the air would grow colder.   Not too cold to live, of course, but cold enough to spell doom to a man in Smith's condition.

Mackenzie squatted on his heels and stared at Smith.

"If I could only find Nellie," he thought.

He had tried to find her—briefly.   He had raced along the rim of the Bowl for a mile or so, but had seen no sign of her.   He had been afraid to go farther, afraid to stay too long from the man back in the tractor.

Smith mumbled and Mackenzie bent low to try to catch the words.   But there were no words.

Slowly he rose and headed for the door.   First of all, he needed heat.   Then food.   The heat came first.   An open fire wasn't the best way to make heat, of course, but it was better than nothing.

The uprooted music tree, balled roots silhouetted against the sky, loomed before him in the dusk.   He found a few dead branches and tore them off.   They would do to start the fire.   After that he would have to rely on green wood to keep it going.   Tomorrow he could forage about for suitable fuel.

In the Bowl below, the music trees were tuning up for the evening concert.

Back in the tractor, he found a knife, carefully slivered several of the branches for easy lighting, piled them ready for his pocket lighter.

The lighter flared and a tiny figure hopped up on the threshold of the tractor, squatting there, blinking at the light.

Startled, Mackenzie held the lighter without touching it to the wood, stared at the thing that perched in the doorway.

Delbert's squeaky thought drilled into his brain.

"What you doing?"

"Building a fire," Mackenzie told him.

"What's a fire?"

"It's a . . . it's a . . . say, don't you know what a fire is?"

"Nope," said Delbert.

"It's a chemical action," Mackenzie said.   "It breaks up matter and releases energy in the form of heat."

"What you building a fire with?" asked Delbert, blinking in the flare of the lighter.

"With branches from a tree."

Delbert's eyes widened and his thought was jittery.

"A tree?"

"Sure, a tree.   Wood.   It burns.   It gives off heat.   I need heat."

"What tree?"

"Why—"   And then Mackenzie stopped with sudden realization.   His thumb relaxed and the flame went out.

Delbert shrieked at him in sudden terror and anger.   "It's my tree!   You're building a fire with my tree!"

Mackenzie sat in silence.

"When you burn my tree, it's gone," yelled Delbert.   "Isn't that right?   When you burn my tree, it's gone?"

Mackenzie nodded.

"But why do you do it?" shrilled Delbert.

"I need heat," said Mackenzie, doggedly.   "If I don't have heat, my friend will die.   It's the only way I can get heat."

"But my tree!"

Mackenzie shrugged.   "I need a fire, see?   And I'm getting it any way I can."

He flipped his thumb again and the lighter flared.

"But I never did anything to you," Delbert howled, rocking on the metal door sill.   "I'm your friend, I am.   I never did a thing to hurt you."

"No?" asked Mackenzie.

"No," yelled Delbert.

"What about that scheme of yours?" asked Mackenzie.   "Trying to trick me into taking trees to Earth?"

"That wasn't my idea," yipped Delbert.   "It wasn't any of the trees' ideas.
The Encyclopedia thought it up."

A bulky form loomed outside the door.   "Someone talking about me?" it asked.
The Encyclopedia was back again.
Arrogantly, he shouldered Delbert aside, stepped into the tractor.
"I saw Wade," he said.
Mackenzie glared at him.   "So you figured it would be safe to come."
"Certainly," said the Encyclopedia.   "Your formula of force counts for nothing
now.   You have no means to enforce it."
Mackenzie's hand shot out and grasped the Encyclopedia with a vicious grip,
hurled him into the interor of the tractor.
"Just try to get out this door," he snarled.   "You'll soon find out if the formula
of force amounts to anything."
The Encyclopedia picked himself up, shook himself like a ruffled hen.   But his
thought was cool and calm.
"I can't see what this avails you."
"It gives us soup," Mackenzie snapped.
He sized the Encyclopedia up.   "Good vegetable soup.   Something like cab-
bage.   Never cared much for cabbage soup, myself, but—"
"Soup?"
"Yeah, soup.   Stuff to eat.   Food."
"Food!"   The Encyclopedia's thought held a tremor of anxiety.   "You would
use me as food."
"Why not?" Mackenzie asked him.   "You're nothing but a vegetable.   An
intelligent vegetable, granted, but still a vegetable."
He felt the Encyclopedia's groping thought-fingers prying into his mind.
"Go ahead," he told him, "but you won't like what you find."
The Encyclopedia's thoughts almost gasped.   "You withheld this from me!"
he charged.
"We withheld nothing from you," Mackenzie declared.   "We never had occasion to think of it . . . to remember to what use Men at one time put plants, to
what use we still put plants in certain cases.   The only reason we don't use them
so extensively now is that we have advanced beyond the need of them.   Let that
need exist again and—"
"You ate us," strummed the Encyclopedia.   "You used us to build your shelters!
You destroyed us to create heat for your selfish purposes!"
"Pipe down," Mackenzie told him.   "It's the way we did it that gets you.   The
idea that we thought we had a right to.   That we went out and took, without even
asking, never wondering what the plant might think about it.   That hurts your
racial dignity."
He stopped, then moved closer to the doorway.   From the Bowl below came
the first strains of the music.   The tuning up, the preliminary to the concert was
over.

"O.K.," Mackenzie said, "I'll hurt it some more.   Even you are nothing but a plant to me.   Just because you've learned some civilized tricks doesn't make you my equal.   It never did.   We humans can't slur off the experiences of the past so easily.   It would take thousands of years of association with things like you before we even began to regard you as anything other than a plant, a thing that we used in the past and might use again."

"Still cabbage soup," said the Encyclopedia.

"Still cabbage soup," Mackenzie told him.

The music stopped.   Stopped dead still, in the middle of a note.

"See," said Mackenzie, "even the music fails you."

Silence rolled at them in engulfing waves and through the stillness came another sound, the *clop, clop* of heavy, plodding feet.

"Nellie!" yelled Mackenzie.

A bulky shadow loomed in the darkness.

"Yeah, chief, it's me," said Nellie.   "I brung you something."

She dumped Wade across the doorway.

Wade rolled over and groaned.   There were skittering, flapping sounds as two fluttering shapes detached themselves from Wade's shoulders.

"Nellie," said Mackenzie, harshly, "there was no need to beat him up.   You should have brought him back just as he was and let me take care of him."

"Gee, boss," protested Nellie.   "I didn't beat him up.   He was like that when I found him."

Nicodemus was clawing his way to Mackenzie's shoulder, while Smith's life blanket scuttled for the corner where his master lay.

"It was us, boss," piped Nicodemus.   "We laid him out."

"You laid him out?"

"Sure, there was two of us and only one of him.   We fed him poison."

Nicodemus settled into place on Mackenzie's shoulders.

"I didn't like him," he declared.   "He wasn't nothing like you, boss.   I didn't want to change like him.   I wanted to stay like you."

"This poison?" asked Mackenzie.   "Nothing fatal, I hope."

"Sure not, pal," Nicodemus told him.   "We only made him sick.   He didn't know what was happening until it was too late to do anything about it.   We bargained with him, we did.   We told him we'd quit feeding it to him if he took us back.   He was on his way here, too, but he'd never made it if it hadn't been for Nellie."

"Chief," pleaded Nellie, "when he gets so he knows what it's all about, won't you let me have him for about five minutes?"

"No," said Mackenzie.

"He strung me up," wailed Nellie.   "He hid in the cliff and lassoed me and left me hanging there.   It took me hours to get loose.   Honest, I wouldn't hurt him much.   I'd just kick him around a little, gentlelike."

From the cliff top came the rustling of grass as if hundreds of little feet were advancing upon them.

"We got visitors," said Nicodemus.

The visitors, Mackenzie saw, were the conductors, dozens of little gnomelike figures that moved up and squatted on their haunches, faintly luminous eyes blinking at them.

One of them shambled forward.   As he came closer, Mackenzie saw that it was Alder.

"Well?" Mackenzie demanded.

"We came to tell you the deal is off," Alder squeaked.   "Delbert came and told us."

"Told you what?"

"About what you do to trees."

"Oh, that."

"Yes, that."

"But you made the deal," Mackenzie told him.   "You can't back out now. Why, Earth is waiting breathless—"

"Don't try to kid me," snapped Alder.   "You don't want us any more than we want you.   It was a dirty trick to start with, but it wasn't any of our doing.   The Encyclopedia talked us into it.   He told us we had a duty.   A duty to our race. To act as missionaries to the inferior races of the Galaxy.

"We didn't take to it at first.   Music, you see, is our life.   We have been creating music for so long that our origin is lost in the dim antiquity of a planet that long ago has passed its zenith of existence.   We will be creating music in that far day when the planet falls apart beneath our feet.   You live by a code of accomplishment by action.   We live by a code of accomplishment by music. Kadmar's Red Sun symphony was a greater triumph for us than the discovery of a new planetary system is for you.   It pleased us when you liked our music.   It will please us if you still like our music, even after what has happened.   But we will not allow you to take any of us to Earth."

"The monopoly on the music still stands?" asked Mackenzie.

"It still stands.   Come whenever you want to and record my symphony.   When there are others we will let you know."

"And the propaganda in the music?"

"From now on," Alder promised, "the propaganda is out.   If, from now on, our music changes you, it will change you through its own power.   It may do that, but we will not try to shape your lives."

"How can we depend on that?"

"Certainly," said Alder.   "There are certain tests you could devise.   Not that they will be necessary."

"We'll devise the tests," declared Mackenzie.   "Sorry, but we can't trust you."

"I'm sorry that you can't," said Alder, and he sounded as if he were.

"I was going to burn you," Mackenzie said, snapping his words off brutally. "Destroy you.   Wipe you out.   There was nothing you could have done about it.   Nothing you could have done to stop me."

"You're still barbarians," Alder told him.   "You have conquered the distances between the stars, you have built a great civilization, but your methods are still ruthless and degenerate.''

''The Encyclopedia calls it a formula of force,'' Mackenzie said.   ''No matter what you call it, it still works.   It's the thing that took us up.   I warn you.   If you ever again try to trick the human race, there will be hell to pay.   A human being will destroy anything to save himself.   Remember that—we destroy anything that threatens us.''

Something swished out of the tractor door and Mackenzie whirled about.

''It's the Encyclopedia!'' he yelled.   ''He's trying to get away!   Nellie!''

There was a thrashing rustle.   ''Got him, boss,'' said Nellie.

The robot came out of the darkness, dragging the Encyclopedia along by his leafy topknot.

Mackenzie turned back to the composers, but the composers were gone.   The grass rustled eerily toward the cliff edge as dozens of tiny feet scurried through it.

''What now?'' asked Nellie.   ''Do we burn the trees?''

Mackenzie shook his head.   ''No, Nellie.   We won't burn them.''

''We got them scared,'' said Nellie.   ''Scared pink with purple spots.''

''Perhaps we have,'' said Mackenzie.   ''Let's hope so, at least.   But it isn't only that they're scared.   They probably loathe us and that is better yet.   Like we'd loathe some form of life that bred and reared men for food—that thought of Man as nothing else than food.   All the time they've thought of themselves as the greatest intellectual force in the universe.   We've given them a jolt.   We've scared them and hurt their pride and shook their confidence.   They've run up against something that is more than a match for them.   Maybe they'll think twice again before they try any more shenanigans.''

Down in the Bowl the music began again.

Mackenzie went in to look at Smith.   The man was sleeping peacefully, his blanket wrapped around him.   Wade sat in a corner, head held in his hands.

Outside, a rocket murmured and Nellie yelled.   Mackenzie spun on his heel and dashed through the door.   A ship was swinging over the Bowl, lighting up the area with floods.   Swiftly it swooped down, came to ground a hundred yards away.

Harper, right arm in a sling, tumbled out and raced toward them.

''You didn't burn them!'' he was yelling.   ''You didn't burn them!''

Mackenzie shook his head.

Harper pounded him on the back with his good hand.   ''Knew you wouldn't. Knew you wouldn't all the time.   Just kidding the chief, eh?   Having a little fun.''

''Not exactly fun.''

''About them trees,'' said Harper.   ''We can't take them back to Earth, after all.''

''I told you that,'' Mackenzie said.

''Earth just called me, half an hour ago,'' said Harper.   ''Seems there's a law, passed centuries ago.   Against bringing alien plants to Earth.   Some lunkhead once brought a bunch of stuff from Mars that just about ruined Earth, so they passed the law.   Been there all the time, forgotten.''

Mackenzie nodded.   ''Someone dug it up.''

"That's right," said Harper.   "And slapped an injunction on Galactic.   We can't touch those trees."

"You wouldn't have anyhow," said Mackenzie.   "They wouldn't go."

"But you made the deal!   They were anxious to go—"

"That," Mackenzie told him, "was before they found out we used plants for food—and other things."

"But . . . but—"

"To them," said Mackenzie, "we're just a gang of ogres.   Something they'll scare the little plants with.   Tell them if they don't be quiet the humans will get 'em."

Nellie came around the corner of the tractor, still hauling the Encyclopedia by his topknot.

"Hey," yelled Harper, "what goes on here?"

"We'll have to build a concentration camp," said Mackenzie.   "Big high fence."   He motioned with his thumb towards the Encyclopedia.

Harper stared.   "But he hasn't done anything!"

"Nothing but try to take over the human race," Mackenzie said.

Harper sighed.   "That makes two fences we got to build.   That rifle tree back at the post is shooting up the place."

Mackenzie grinned.   "Maybe the one fence will do for the both of them."

JOHN PIERCE

Invariant

Y ou know the general facts concerning Homer Green, so I don't need to describe him or his surroundings.   I knew as much and more, yet it was an odd sensation, which you don't get through reading, actually to dress in that primitive fashion, to go among strange surroundings, and to see him.

The house is no more odd than the pictures.   Hemmed in by other twentieth century buildings, it must be indistinguishable from the original structure and its surroundings.   To enter it, to tread on rugs, to see chairs covered in cloth with a nap, to see instruments for smoking, to see and hear a primitive radio, even though operating really from a variety of authentic transcriptions, and above all, to see an open fire; all this gave me a sense of unreality, prepared though I was.   Green sat by the fire in a chair, as we almost invariably find him, with a dog at his feet.   He is perhaps the most valuable man in the world, I thought.   But I could not shake off the sense of unreality concerning the substantial surroundings.   He, too, seemed unreal, and I pitied him.

The sense of unreality continued through the form of self-introduction.   How many have there been!   I could, of course, examine the records.

"I'm Carew, for the Institute," I said.   "We haven't met before, but they told me you'd be glad to see me."

Green rose and extended his hand.   I took it obediently, making the unfamiliar gesture.

"Glad to see you," he said.   "I've been dozing here.   It's a little of a shock, the treatment, and I thought I'd rest a few days.   I hope it's really permanent.

"Won't you sit down?" he added.

We seated ourselves before the fire.   The dog, which had risen, lay down, pressed against his master's feet.

"I suppose you want to test my reactions?" Green asked.

"Later," I replied.   "There's no hurry.   And it's so very comfortable here."

Green was easily distracted.   He relaxed, staring at the fire.   This was an opportunity, and I spoke in a somewhat purposeful voice.

"It seems more a time for politics, here," I said.   "What the Swede intends, and what the French—"

"Drench our thoughts in mirth—" Green replied.

I had thought from the records the quotation would have some effect.

"But one doesn't leave politics to drench his thoughts in mirth," he continued. "One studies them—"

I won't go into the conversation. You've seen it in Appendix A of my thesis, "An Aspect of Twentieth Century Politics and Speech." It was brief, as you know. I had been very lucky to get to see Green. I was more lucky to hit on the right thread directly. Somehow, it had never occurred to me before that twentieth century politicians had meant, or had thought that they meant, what they said; that indeed, they had in their own minds attached a sense of meaning or relevancy to what seem to us meaningless or irrelevant phrases. It's hard to explain so foreign an idea; perhaps an example would help.

For instance, would you believe that a man accused of making a certain statement would seriously reply, "I'm not in the habit of making such statements?" Would you believe that this might even mean that he had not made the statement? Or would you further believe that even if he had made the statement, this would seem to him to classify it as some sort of special instance, and his reply as not truly evasive? I think these conjectures plausible, that is, when I struggle to immerse myself in the twentieth century. But I would never have dreamed them before talking with Green. How truly invaluable the man is!

I have said that the conversation recorded in Appendix A is very short. There was no need to continue along political lines after I had grasped the basic idea. Twentieth century records are much more complete than Green's memory, and that itself has been thoroughly catalogued. It is not the airy bones of information, but the personal contact, the infinite variation in combinations, the stimulation of the warm human touch, that are helpful and suggestive.

So I was with Green, and most of a morning was still before me. You know that he is given meal times free, and only one appointment between meals, so that there will be no overlapping. I was grateful to the man, and sympathetic, and I was somewhat upset in his presence. I wanted to talk to him of the thing nearest his heart. There was no reason I shouldn't. I've recorded the rest of the conversation, but not published it. It's not new. Perhaps it is trivial, but it means a great deal to me. Maybe it's only my very personal memory of it. But I thought you might like to know.

"What led to your discovery?" I asked him.

"Salamanders," he replied with hesitation. "Salamanders."

The account I got of his perfect regeneration experiments was, of course, the published story. How many thousands of times has it been told? Yet, I swear I detected variations from the records. How nearly infinite the possible combinations are! But the chief points came in the usual order. How the regeneration of limbs in salamanders led to the idea of perfect regeneration of human parts. How, say, a cut heals, leaving not a scar, but a perfect replica of the damaged tissue. How in normal metabolism tissue can be replaced not imperfectly, as in an aging organism, but perfectly, indefinitely. You've seen it in animals, in compulsory biology. The chick whose metabolism replaces its tissues, but always in an exact, invariant form, never changing. It's disturbing to think of it in a man. Green looked so young, as young as I. Since the twentieth century—

*   *   *

When Green had concluded his description, including that of his own inoculation in the evening, he ventured to prophesy.

"I feel confident," he said, "that it will work, indefinitely."

"It does work, Dr. Green," I assured him.   "Indefinitely."

"We mustn't be premature," he said.   "After all, a short time—"

"Do you recall the date, Dr. Green?" I asked.

"September, 11th," he said.   "1943."

"Dr. Green, today is August 4, 2170," I told him earnestly.

"Look here," Green said.   "If it were, I wouldn't be here dressed this way, and you wouldn't be there dressed that way."

The impasse could have continued indefinitely.   I took my communicator from my pocket and showed it to him.   He watched with growing wonder and delight as I demonstrated, finally with projection, binaural and stereo.   Not simple, but exactly the sort of electronic development which a man of Green's era associated with the future.   Green seemed to have lost all thought of the conversation which had led to my production of the communicator.

"Dr. Green," I said, "the year is 2170.   This is the twenty-second century."

He looked at me baffled, but this time not with disbelief.   A strange sort of terror was spread over his features.

"An accident?" he asked.   "My memory?"

"There has been no accident," I said.   "Your memory is intact, as far as it goes.   Listen to me.   Concentrate."

Then I told him, simply and briefly, so that his thought processes would not lag. As I spoke to him he stared at me apprehensively, his mind apparently racing. This is what I said:

"Your experiment succeeded, beyond anything you had reason to hope.   Your tissues took on the ability to reform themselves in exactly the same pattern year after year.   Their form became invariant.

"Photographs and careful measurements show this, from year to year, yes, from century to century.   You are just as you were over two hundred years ago.

"Your life has not been devoid of accident.   Minor, even major wounds have left no trace of healing.   Your tissues are invariant.

"Your brain is invariant, too; that is as far as the cell patterns are concerned. A brain may be likened to an electrical network.   Memory is the network, the coils and condensers, and their interconnections.   Conscious thought is the pattern of voltage across them and currents flowing through them.   The pattern is complicated, but transitory—transient.   Memory is changing the network of the brain, affecting all subsequent thoughts, or patterns in the network.   The network of your brain never changes.   It is invariant.

"Or thought is like the complicated operation of the relays and switches of a telephone exchange of your century, but memory is the interconnections of elements. The interconnections on other people's brains change in the process of thought, breaking down, building up, giving them new memories.   The pattern of connections in your brain never changes.   It is invariant.

"Other people can adapt themselves to new surroundings, learning where objects of necessity are, the pattern of rooms, adapting themselves unconsciously, without friction. You cannot; your brain is invariant. Your habits are keyed to a house, your house as it was the day before you treated yourself. It has been preserved, replaced through two hundred years so that you could live without friction. In it, you live, day after day, the day after the treatment which made your brain invariant.

"Do not think you give no return for this care. You are perhaps the most valuable man in the world. Morning, afternoon, evening; you have three appointments a day, when the lucky few who are judged to merit or need your help are allowed to seek it.

"I am a student of history. I came to see the twentieth century through the eyes of an intelligent man of that century. You are a very intelligent, brilliant man. Your mind has been analyzed in a detail greater than that of any other. Few brains are better. I came to learn from this powerful observant brain what politics meant to a man of your period. I learned from a fresh new source, your brain, which is not overlaid, not changed by the intervening years, but is just as it was in 1943.

"But I am not very important. Important workers: psychologists, come to see you. They ask you questions, then repeat them a little differently, and observe your reactions. One experiment is not vitiated by your memory of an earlier experiment. When your train of thought is interrupted, it leaves no memory behind. Your brain remains invariant. And these men, who otherwise could draw only general conclusions from simple experiments on multitudes of different, differently constituted and differently prepared individuals, can observe undisputable differences of response due to the slightest changes in stimulus. Some of these men have driven you to a frenzy. You do not go mad. Your brain cannot change; it is invariant.

"You are so valuable it seems that the world could scarcely progress without your invariant brain. And yet, we have not asked another to do as you did. With animals, yes. Your dog is an example. What you did was willingly, and you did not know the consequences. You did the world this greatest service unknowingly. But we know."

Green's head had sunk to his chest. His face was troubled, and he seemed to seek solace in the warmth of the fire. The dog at his feet stirred, and he looked down, a sudden smile on his face. I knew that his train of thought had been interrupted. The transients had died from his brain. Our whole meeting was gone from his processes of thought.

I rose and stole away before he looked up. Perhaps I wasted the remaining hour of the morning.

CLIFFORD D. SIMAK

Desertion

Four men, two by two, had gone into the howling maelstrom that was Jupiter and had not returned. They had walked into the keening gale—or rather, they had loped, bellies low against the ground, wet sides gleaming in the rain.

For they did not go in the shape of men.

Now the fifth man stood before the desk of Kent Fowler, head of Dome No. 3, Jovian Survey Commission.

Under Fowler's desk, old Towser scratched a flea, then settled down to sleep again.

Harold Allen, Fowler saw with a sudden pang, was young—too young. He had the easy confidence of youth, the face of one who never had known fear. And that was strange. For men in the domes of Jupiter did know fear—fear and humility. It was hard for Man to reconcile his puny self with the mighty forces of the monstrous planet.

"You understand," said Fowler, "that you need not do this. You understand that you need not go."

It was formula, of course. The other four had been told the same thing, but they had gone. This fifth one, Fowler knew, would go as well. But suddenly he felt a dull hope stir within him that Allen wouldn't go.

"When do I start?" asked Allen.

There had been a time when Fowler might have taken quiet pride in that answer, but not now. He frowned briefly.

"Within the hour," he said.

Allen stood waiting, quietly.

"Four other men have gone out and have not returned," said Fowler. "You know that, of course. We want you to return. We don't want you going off on any heroic rescue expedition. The main thing, the only thing, is that you come back, that you prove man can live in a Jovian form. Go to the first survey stake, no farther, then come back. Don't take any chances. Don't investigate anything. Just come back."

Allen nodded. "I understand all that."

"Miss Stanley will operate the converter," Fowler went on. "You need have no fear on that particular score. The other men were converted without mishap. They left the converter in apparently perfect condition. You will be in thoroughly competent hands. Miss Stanley is the best qualified conversion operator in the Solar System. She has had experience on most of the other planets. That is why she's here.''

Allen grinned at the woman and Fowler saw something flicker across Miss Stanley's face—something that might have been pity, or rage—or just plain fear. But it was gone again and she was smiling back at the youth who stood before the desk. Smiling in that prim, school-teacherish way she had of smiling, almost as if she hated herself for doing it.

"I shall be looking forward," said Allen, "to my conversion."

And the way he said it, he made it all a joke, a vast, ironic joke.

But it was no joke.

It was serious business, deadly serious. Upon these tests, Fowler knew, depended the fate of men on Jupiter. If the tests succeeded, the resources of the giant planet would be thrown open. Man would take over Jupiter as he already had taken over the smaller planets. And if they failed—

If they failed, Man would continue to be chained and hampered by the terrific pressure, the greater force of gravity, the weird chemistry of the planet. He would continue to be shut within the domes, unable to set actual foot upon the planet, unable to see it with direct, unaided vision, forced to rely upon the awkward tractors and the televisor, forced to work with clumsy tools and mechanisms or through the medium of robots that themselves were clumsy.

For Man, unprotected and in his natural form, would be blotted out by Jupiter's terrific pressure of fifteen thousand pounds per square inch, pressure that made terrestrial sea bottoms seem a vacuum by comparison.

Even the strongest metal Earthmen could devise couldn't exist under pressure such as that, under the pressure and the alkaline rains that forever swept the planet. It grew brittle and flaky, crumbling like clay, or it ran away in little streams and puddles of ammonia salts. Only by stepping up the toughness and strength of that metal, by increasing its electronic tension, could it be made to withstand the weight of thousands of miles of swirling, choking gases that made up the atmosphere. And even when that was done, everything had to be coated with tough quartz to keep away the rain—the liquid ammonia that fell as bitter rain.

Fowler sat listening to the engines in the sub-floor of the dome—engines that ran on endlessly, the dome never quiet of them. They had to run and keep on running, for if they stopped the power flowing into the metal walls of the dome would stop, the electronic tension would ease up and that would be the end of everything.

Towser roused himself under Fowler's desk and scratched another flea, his leg thumping hard against the floor.

"Is there anything else?" asked Allen.

Fowler shook his head. "Perhaps there's something you want to do," he said. "Perhaps you—"

He had meant to say write a letter and he was glad he caught himself quick enough so he didn't say it.

Allen looked at his watch.   "I'll be there on time," he said.   He swung around and headed for the door.

Fowler knew Miss Stanley was watching him and he didn't want to turn and meet her eyes.   He fumbled with a sheaf of papers on the desk before him.

"How long are you going to keep this up?" asked Miss Stanley and she bit off each word with a vicious snap.

He swung around in his chair and faced her then.   Her lips were drawn into a straight, thin line; her hair seemed skinned back from her forehead tighter than ever, giving her face that queer, almost startling death-mask quality.

He tried to make his voice cool and level.   "As long as there's any need of it," he said.   "As long as there's any hope."

"You're going to keep on sentencing them to death," she said.   "You're going to keep marching them out face to face with Jupiter.   You're going to sit in here safe and comfortable and send them out to die."

"There is no room for sentimentality, Miss Stanley," Fowler said, trying to keep the note of anger from his voice.   "You know as well as I do why we're doing this.   You realize that Man in his own form simply cannot cope with Jupiter.   The only answer is to turn men into the sort of things that can cope with it.   We've done it on the other planets.

"If a few men die, but we finally succeed, the price is small.   Through the ages men have thrown away their lives on foolish things, for foolish reasons.   Why should we hesitate, then, at a little death in a thing as great as this?"

Miss Stanley sat stiff and straight, hands folded in her lap, the lights shining on her graying hair and Fowler, watching her, tried to imagine what she might feel, what she might be thinking.   He wasn't exactly afraid of her, but he didn't feel quite comfortable when she was around.   Those sharp blue eyes saw too much, her hands looked far too competent.   She should be somebody's Aunt sitting in a rocking chair with her knitting needles.   But she wasn't.   She was the top-notch conversion unit operator in the Solar System and she didn't like the way he was doing things.

"There is something wrong, Mr. Fowler," she declared.

"Precisely," agreed Fowler.   "That's why I'm sending young Allen out alone. He may find out what it is."

"And if he doesn't?"

"I'll send someone else."

She rose slowly from her chair, started toward the door, then stopped before his desk.

"Some day," she said, "you will be a great man.   You never let a chance go by.   This is your chance.   You knew it was when this dome was picked for the tests.   If you put it through, you'll go up a notch or two.   No matter how many men may die, you'll go up a notch or two."

"Miss Stanley," he said and his voice was curt, "young Allen is going out soon. Please be sure that your machine—"

"My machine," she told him, icily, "is not to blame. It operates along the co-ordinates the biologists set up."

He sat hunched at his desk, listening to her footsteps go down the corridor.

What she said was true, of course. The biologists had set up the co-ordinates. But the biologists could be wrong. Just a hairbreadth of difference, one iota of digression and the converter would be sending out something that wasn't the thing they meant to send. A mutant that might crack up, go haywire, come unstuck under some condition or stress of circumstance wholly unsuspected.

For Man didn't know much about what was going on outside. Only what his instruments told him was going on. And the samplings of those happenings furnished by those instruments and mechanisms had been no more than samplings, for Jupiter was unbelievably large and the domes were very few.

Even the work of the biologists in getting the data on the Lopers, apparently the highest form of Jovian life, had involved more than three years of intensive study and after that two years of checking to make sure. Work that could have been done on Earth in a week or two. But work that, in this case, couldn't be done on Earth at all, for one couldn't take a Jovian life form to Earth. The pressure here on Jupiter couldn't be duplicated outside of Jupiter and at Earth pressure and temperature the Lopers would simply have disappeared in a puff of gas.

Yet it was work that had to be done if Man ever hoped to go about Jupiter in the life form of the Lopers. For before the converter could change a man to another life form, every detailed physical characteristic of that life form must be known— surely and positively, with no chance of mistake.

Allen did not come back.

The tractors, combing the nearby terrain, found no trace of him, unless the skulking thing reported by one of the drivers had been the missing Earthman in Loper form.

The biologists sneered their most accomplished academic sneers when Fowler suggested the co-ordinates might be wrong. Carefully they pointed out, the co-ordinates worked. When a man was put into the converter and the switch was thrown, the man became a Loper. He left the machine and moved away, out of sight, into the soupy atmosphere.

Some quirk, Fowler suggested; some tiny deviation from the thing a Loper should be, some minor defect. If there were, the biologists said, it would take years to find it.

And Fowler knew that they were right.

So there were five men now instead of four and Harold Allen had walked out into Jupiter for nothing at all. It was as if he'd never gone so far as knowledge was concerned.

Fowler reached across his desk and picked up the personnel file, a thin sheaf of paper neatly clipped together. It was a thing he dreaded but a thing he had to do. Somehow the reason for these strange disappearances must be found. And there was no other way than to send out more men.

He sat for a moment listening to the howling of the wind above the dome, the everlasting thundering gale that swept across the planet in boiling, twisting wrath.

Was there some threat out there, he asked himself? Some danger they did not know about? Something that lay in wait and gobbled up the Lopers, making no distinction between Lopers that were *bona fide* and Lopers that were men? To the gobblers, of course, it would make no difference.

Or had there been a basic fault in selecting the Lopers as the type of life best fitted for existence on the surface of the planet? The evident intelligence of the Lopers, he knew, had been one factor in that determination. For if the thing Man became did not have capacity for intelligence, Man could not for long retain his own intelligence in such a guise.

Had the biologists let that one factor weigh too heavily, using it to offset some other factor that might be unsatisfactory, even disastrous? It didn't seem likely. Stiff-necked as they might be, the biologists knew their business.

Or was the whole thing impossible, doomed from the very start? Conversion to other life forms had worked on other planets, but that did not necessarily mean it would work on Jupiter. Perhaps Man's intelligence could not function correctly through the sensory apparatus provided Jovian life. Perhaps the Lopers were so alien there was no common ground for human knowledge and the Jovian conception of existence to meet and work together.

Or the fault might lie with Man, be inherent with the race. Some mental aberration which, coupled with what they found outside, wouldn't let them come back. Although it might not be an aberration, not in the human sense. Perhaps just one ordinary human mental trait, accepted as commonplace on Earth, would be so violently at odds with Jovian existence that it would blast human sanity.

Claws rattled and clicked down the corridor. Listening to them, Fowler smiled wanly. It was Towser coming back from the kitchen, where he had gone to see his friend, the cook.

Towser came into the room, carrying a bone. He wagged his tail at Fowler and flopped down beside the desk, bone between his paws. For a long moment his rheumy old eyes regarded his master and Fowler reached down a hand to ruffle a ragged ear.

"You still like me, Towser?" Fowler asked and Towser thumped his tail.

"You're the only one," said Fowler.

He straightened and swung back to the desk. His hand reached out and picked up the file.

Bennett? Bennett had a girl waiting for him back on Earth.

Andrews? Andrews was planning on going back to Mars Tech just as soon as he earned enough to see him through a year.

Olson? Olson was nearing pension age. All the time telling the boys how he was going to settle down and grow roses.

Carefully, Fowler laid the file back on the desk.

Sentencing men to death. Miss Stanley had said that, her pale lips scarcely moving in her parchment face.   Marching men out to die while he, Fowler, sat here safe and comfortable.

They were saying it all through the dome, no doubt, especially since Allen had failed to return.   They wouldn't say it to his face, of course.   Even the man or men he called before his desk and told they were the next to go, wouldn't say it to him.

But he would see it in their eyes.

He picked up the file again.   Bennett, Andrews, Olson.   There were others, but there was no use in going on.

Kent Fowler knew that he couldn't do it, couldn't face them, couldn't send more men out to die.

He leaned forward and flipped up the toggle on the intercommunicator.

"Yes, Mr. Fowler."

"Miss Stanley, please."

He waited for Miss Stanley, listening to Towser chewing halfheartedly on the bone.   Tower's teeth were getting bad.

"Miss Stanley," said Miss Stanley's voice.

"Just wanted to tell you, Miss Stanley, to get ready for two more."

"Aren't you afraid," asked Miss Stanley, "that you'll run out of them?   Sending out one at a time, they'd last longer, give you twice the satisfaction."

"One of them," said Fowler, "will be a dog."

"A dog!"

"Yes, Towser."

He heard the quick, cold rage that iced her voice.   "Your own dog!   He's been with you all these years—"

"That's the point," said Fowler.   "Towser would be unhappy if I left him behind."

It was not the Jupiter he had known through the televisor.   He had expected it to be different, but not like this.   He had expected a hell of ammonia rain and stinking fumes and the deafening, thundering tumult of the storm.   He had expected swirling clouds and fog and the snarling flicker of monstrous thunderbolts.

He had not expected the lashing downpour would be reduced to drifting purple mist that moved like fleeing shadows over a red and purple sward.   He had not even guessed the snaking bolts of lightning would be flares of pure ecstasy across a painted sky.

Waiting for Towser, Fowler flexed the muscles of his body, amazed at the smooth, sleek strength he found.   Not a bad body, he decided, and grimaced at remembering how he had pitied the Lopers when he glimpsed them through the television screen.

For it had been hard to imagine a living organism based upon ammonia and hydrogen rather than upon water and oxygen, hard to believe that such a form of life could know the same quick thrill of life that humankind could know.   Hard to conceive of life out in the soupy maelstrom that was Jupiter, not knowing, of course, that through Jovian eyes it was no soupy maelstrom at all.

The wind brushed against him with what seemed gentle fingers and he remembered with a start that by Earth standards the wind was a roaring gale, a two-hundred-mile an hour howler laden with deadly gases.

Pleasant scents seeped into his body. And yet scarcely scents, for it was not the sense of smell as he remembered it. It was as if his whole being was soaking up the sensation of lavender—and yet not lavender. It was something, he knew, for which he had no word, undoubtedly the first of many enigmas in terminology. For the words he knew, the thought symbols that served him as an Earthman would not serve him as a Jovian.

The lock in the side of the dome opened and Towser came tumbling out—at least he thought it must be Towser.

He started to call to the dog, his mind shaping the words he meant to say. But he couldn't say them. There was no way to say them. He had nothing to say them with.

For a moment his mind swirled in muddy terror, a blind fear that eddied in little puffs of panic through his brain.

How did Jovians talk? How—

Suddenly he was aware of Towser, intensely aware of the bumbling, eager friendliness of the shaggy animal that had followed him from Earth to many planets. As if the thing that was Towser had reached out and for a moment sat within his brain.

And out of the bubbling welcome that he sensed, came words.

"Hiya, pal."

Not words really, better than words. Thought symbols in his brain, communicated thought symbols that had shades of meaning words could never have.

"Hiya, Towser," he said.

"I feel good," said Towser. "Like I was a pup. Lately I've been feeling pretty punk. Legs stiffening up on me and teeth wearing down to almost nothing. Hard to mumble a bone with teeth like that. Besides, the fleas give me hell. Used to be I never paid much attention to them. A couple of fleas more or less never meant much in my early days."

"But . . . but—" Fowler's thoughts tumbled awkwardly. "You're talking to me!"

"Sure thing," said Towser. "I always talked to you, but you couldn't hear me. I tried to say things to you, but I couldn't make the grade."

"I understood you sometimes," Fowler said.

"Not very well," said Towser. "You knew when I wanted food and when I wanted a drink and when I wanted out, but that's about all you ever managed."

"I'm sorry," Fowler said.

"Forget it," Towser told him. "I'll race you to the cliff."

For the first time, Fowler saw the cliff, apparently many miles away, but with a strange crystalline beauty that sparkled in the shadow of the many-colored clouds.

Fowler hesitated. "It's a long way—"

"Ah, come on," said Towser and even as he said it he started for the cliff.

*   *   *

Fowler followed, testing his legs, testing the strength in that new body of his, a bit doubtful at first, amazed a moment later, then running with a sheer joyousness that was one with the red and purple sward, with the drifting smoke of the rain across the land.

As he ran the consciousness of music came to him, a music that beat into his body, that surged throughout his being, that lifted him on wings of silver speed. Music like bells might make from some steeple on a sunny, springtime hill.

As the cliff drew nearer the music deepened and filled the universe with a spray of magic sound. And he knew the music came from the tumbling waterfall that feathered down the face of the shining cliff.

Only, he knew, it was no waterfall, but an ammonia-fall and the cliff was white because it was oxygen, solidified.

He skidded to a stop beside Towser where the waterfall broke into a glittering rainbow of many hundred colors. Literally many hundred, for here, he saw, was no shading of one primary to another as human beings saw, but a clearcut selectivity that broke the prism down to its last ultimate classification.

"The music," said Towser.

"Yes, what about it?"

"The music," said Towser, "is vibrations. Vibrations of water falling."

"But Towser, you don't know about vibrations."

"Yes, I do," contended Towser. "It just popped into my head."

Fowler gulped mentally. "Just popped!"

And suddenly, within his own head, he held a formula—the formula for a process that would make metal to withstand the pressure of Jupiter.

He stared, astounded, at the waterfall and swiftly his mind took the many colors and placed them in their exact sequence in the spectrum. Just like that. Just out of blue sky. Out of nothing, for he knew nothing either of metals or of colors.

"Towser," he cried. "Towser, something's happening to us!"

"Yeah, I know," said Towser.

"It's our brains," said Fowler. "We're using them, all of them, down to the last hidden corner. Using them to figure out things we should have known all the time. Maybe the brains of Earth things naturally are slow and foggy. Maybe we are the morons of the universe. Maybe we are fixed so we have to do things the hard way."

And, in the new sharp clarity of thought that seemed to grip him, he knew that it would not only be the matter of colors in a waterfall or metals that would resist the pressure of Jupiter. He sensed other things, things not yet quite clear. A vague whispering that hinted of greater things, of mysteries beyong the pale of human thought, beyond even the pale of human imagination. Mysteries, fact, logic built on reasoning. Things that any brain should know if it used all its reasoning power.

"We're still mostly Earth," he said. "We're just beginning to learn a few of the things we are to know—a few of the things that were kept from us as human beings, perhaps because we were human beings. Because our human bodies were poor bodies. Poorly equipped in certain senses that one has to have to know. Perhaps even lacking in certain senses that are necessary to true knowledge.''

He stared back at the dome, a tiny black thing dwarfed by the distance.

Back there were men who couldn't see the beauty that was Jupiter. Men who thought that swirling clouds and lashing rain obscured the planet's face. Unseeing human eyes. Poor eyes. Eyes that could not see the beauty in the clouds, that could not see through the storm. Bodies that could not feel the thrill of trilling music stemming from the rush of broken water.

Men who walked alone, in terrible loneliness, talking with their tongue like Boy Scouts wigwagging out their messages, unable to reach out and touch one another's mind as he could reach out and touch Towser's mind. Shut off forever from that personal, intimate contact with other living things.

He, Fowler, had expected terror inspired by alien things out here on the surface, had expected to cower before the threat of unknown things, had steeled himself against disgust of a situation that was not of Earth.

But instead he had found something greater than Man had ever known. A swifter, surer body. A sense of exhilaration, a deeper sense of life. A sharper mind. A world of beauty that even the dreamers of the Earth had not yet imagined.

"Let's get going," Towser urged.

"Where do you want to go?''

"Anywhere," said Towser. "Just start going and see where we end up. I have a feeling . . . well, a feeling—''

"Yes, I know," said Fowler.

For he had the feeling, too. The feeling of high destiny. A certain sense of greatness. A knowledge that somewhere off beyond the horizons lay adventure and things greater than adventure.

Those other five had felt it, too. Had felt the urge to go and see, the compelling sense that here lay a life of fullness and of knowledge.

That, he knew, was why they had not returned.

"I won't go back," said Towser.

"We can't let them down," said Fowler.

Fowler took a step or two, back toward the dome, then stopped.

Back to the dome. Back to that aching, poison-laden body he had left. It hadn't seemed aching before, but now he knew it was.

Back to the fuzzy brain. Back to muddled thinking. Back to the flapping mouths that formed signals others understood. Back to eyes that now would be worse than no sight at all. Back to squalor, back to crawling, back to ignorance.

"Perhaps some day," he said, muttering to himself.

"We got a lot to do and a lot to see," said Towser. "We got a lot to learn. We'll find things—''

Yes, they could find things. Civilizations, perhaps. Civilizations that would make the civilization of Man seem puny by comparison. Beauty and, more important, an understanding of that beauty. And a comradeship no one had ever known before—that no man, no dog had ever known before.

And life.   The quickness of life after what seemed a drugged existence.

"I can't go back," said Towser.

"Nor I," said Fowler.

"They would turn me back into a dog," said Towser.

"And me," said Fowler, "back into a man."

ARTHUR C. CLARKE

Rescue Party

Who was to blame? For three days Alveron's thoughts had come back to that question, and still he had found no answer. A creature of a less civilized or a less sensitive race would never have let it torture his mind and would have satisfied himself with the assurance that no one could be responsible for the working of fate. But Alveron and his kind had been lords of the universe since the dawn of history, since that far distant age when the time barrier had been folded around the cosmos by the unknown powers that lay beyond the beginning. To them had been given all knowledge—and with infinite knowledge went infinite responsibility. If there were mistakes and errors in the administration of the galaxy, the fault lay on the heads of Alveron and his people. And this was no mere mistake: it was one of the greatest tragedies in history.

The crew still knew nothing. Even Rugon, his closest friend and the ship's deputy captain, had been told only part of the truth. But now the doomed worlds lay less than a billion miles ahead. In a few hours, they would be landing on the third planet.

Once again Alveron read the message from base; then, with a flick of a tentacle that no human eye could have followed, he pressed the "general attention" button. Throughout the mile-long cylinder that was the galactic survey ship S9000, creatures of many races laid down their work to listen to the words of their captain.

"I know you have all been wondering," began Alveron, "why we were ordered to abandon our survey and to proceed at such an acceleration to this region of space. Some of you may realize what this acceleration means. Our ship is on its last voyage: the generators have already been running for sixty hours at ultimate overload. We will be very lucky if we return to base under our own power.

"We are approaching a sun which is about to become a nova. Detonation will occur in seven hours, with an uncertainty of one hour, leaving us a maximum of only four hours for exploration. There are ten planets in the system about to be destroyed—and there is a civilization on the third. That fact was discovered only a few days ago. It is our tragic mission to contact that doomed race and if possible to save some of its members. I know that there is little we can do in so short a time with this single ship. No other machine can possibly reach the system before detonation occurs."

There was a long pause during which there could have been no sound or movement in the whole of the mighty ship as it sped silently toward the worlds ahead. Alveron knew what his companions were thinking and he tried to answer their unspoken question.

"You will wonder how such a disaster, the greatest of which we have any record, has been allowed to occur. On one point I can reassure you. The fault does not lie with the survey.

"As you know, with our present fleet of under twelve thousand ships, it is possible to reexamine each of the eight thousand million solar systems in the galaxy at intervals of about a million years. Most worlds change very little in so short a time as that.

"Less than four hundred thousand years ago, the survey ship S5060 examined the planets of the system we are approaching. It found intelligence on none of them, though the third planet was teeming with animal life and two other worlds had once been inhabited. The usual report was submitted and the system is due for its next examination in six hundred thousand years.

"It now appears that in the incredibly short period since the last survey, intelligent life has appeared in the system. The first intimation of this occurred when unknown radio signals were detected on the planet Kulath in the system X29.35, Y34.76, Z27.93. Bearings were taken on them; they were coming from the system ahead.

"Kulath is two hundred light-years from here, so those radio waves had been on their way for two centuries. Thus for at least that period of time a civilization has existed on one of these worlds—a civilization that can generate electromagnetic waves and all that that implies.

"An immediate telescopic examination of the system was made and it was then found that the sun was in the unstable pre-nova stage. Detonation might occur at any moment, and indeed might have done so while the light waves were on their way to Kulath.

"There was a slight delay while the supervelocity scanners on Kulath II were focused on the system. They showed that the explosion had not yet occurred but was only a few hours away. If Kulath had been a fraction of a light-year farther from this sun, we should never have known of its civilization until it had ceased to exist.

"The administrator of Kulath contacted sector base immediately, and I was ordered to proceed to the system at once. Our object is to save what members we can of the doomed race, if indeed there are any left. But we have assumed that a civilization possessing radio could have protected itself against any rise of temperature that may have already occurred.

"This ship and the two tenders will each explore a section of the planet. Commander Torkalee will take Number One, Commander Orostron Number Two. They will have just under four hours in which to explore this world. At the end of that time, they must be back in the ship. It will be leaving then, with or without them. I will give the two commanders detailed instructions in the control room immediately.

"That is all. We enter atmosphere in two hours."

*   *   *

On the world once known as Earth the fires were dying out: there was nothing left to burn.   The great forests that had swept across the planet like a tidal wave with the passing of the cities were now no more than glowing charcoal and the smoke of their funeral pyres still stained the sky.   But the last hours were still to come, for the surface rocks had not yet begun to flow.   The continents were dimly visible through the haze, but their outlines meant nothing to the watchers in the approaching ship.   The charts they possessed were out of date by a dozen Ice Ages and more deluges than one.

The S9000 had driven past Jupiter and seen at once that no life could exist in those half-gaseous oceans of compressed hydrocarbons, now erupting furiously under the sun's abnormal heat.   Mars and the outer planets they had missed, and Alveron realized that the worlds nearer the sun than Earth would be already melting. It was more than likely, he thought sadly, that the tragedy of this unknown race was already finished.   Deep in his heart, he thought it might be better so.   The ship could only have carried a few hundred survivors, and the problem of selection had been haunting his mind.

Rugon, chief of communications and deputy captain, came into the control room.   For the last hour he had been striving to detect radiation from Earth, but in vain.

"We're too late," he announced gloomily.   "I've monitored the whole spectrum and the ether's dead except for our own stations and some two-hundred-year-old programs from Kulath.   Nothing in this system is radiating any more."

He moved toward the giant vision screen with a graceful flowing motion that no mere biped could ever hope to imitate.   Alveron said nothing; he had been expecting this news.

One entire wall of the control room was taken up by the screen, a great black rectangle that gave an impression of almost infinite depth.   Three of Rugon's slender control tentacles, useless for heavy work but incredibly swift at all manipulation, flickered over the selector dials and the screen lit up with a thousand points of light.   The star field flowed swiftly past as Rugon adjusted the controls, bringing the projector to bear upon the sun itself.

No man of Earth would have recognized the monstrous shape that filled the screen.   The sun's light was white no longer: great violet blue clouds covered half its surface and from them long streamers of flame were erupting into space.   At one point an enormous prominence had reared itself out of the photosphere, far out even into the flickering veils of the corona.   It was as though a tree of fire had taken root in the surface of the sun—a tree that stood half a million miles high and whose branches were rivers of flame sweeping through space at hundreds of miles a second.

"I suppose," said Rugon presently, "that you are quite satisfied about the astronomers' calculations.   After all . . ."

"Oh, we're perfectly safe," said Alveron confidently.   "I've spoken to Kulath Observatory and they have been making some additional checks through our own instruments.   That uncertainty of an hour includes a private safety margin which they won't tell me in case I feel tempted to stay any longer."

He glanced at the instrument board.

"The pilot should have brought us to the atmosphere now. Switch the screen back to the planet, please. Ah, there they go!"

There was a sudden tremor underfoot and a raucous clanging of alarms, instantly stilled. Across the vision screen two slim projectiles dived toward the looming mass of Earth. For a few miles they traveled together, then they separated, one vanishing abruptly as it entered the shadow of the planet.

Slowly the huge mother ship, with its thousand times greater mass, descended after them into the raging storms that already were tearing down the deserted cities of man.

It was night in the hemisphere over which Orostron drove his tiny command. Like Torkalee, his mission was to photograph and record and to report progress to the mother ship. The little scout had no room for specimens or passengers. If contact was made with the inhabitants of this world, the S9000 would come at once. There would be no time for parleying. If there was any trouble the rescue would be by force and the explanations could come later.

The ruined land beneath was bathed with an eerie, flickering light, for a great auroral display was raging over half the world. But the image on the vision screen was independent of external light, and it showed clearly a waste of barren rock that seemed never to have known any form of life. Presumably this desert land must come to an end somewhere. Orostron increased his speed to the highest value he dared risk in so dense an atmosphere.

The machine fled on through the storm, and presently the desert of rock began to climb toward the sky. A great mountain range lay ahead, its peaks lost in the smoke-laden clouds. Orostron directed the scanners toward the horizon, and on the vision screen the line of mountains seemed suddenly very close and menacing. He started to climb rapidly. It was difficult to imagine a more unpromising land in which to find civilization and he wondered if it would be wise to change course. He decided against it. Five minutes later, he had his reward.

Miles below lay a decapitated mountain, the whole of its summit sheared away by some tremendous feat of engineering. Rising out of the rock and straddling the artificial plateau was an intricate structure of metal girders, supporting masses of machinery. Orostron brought his ship to a halt and spiraled down toward the mountain.

The slight Doppler blur had now vanished, and the picture on the screen was clear-cut. The latticework was supporting some scores of great metal mirrors, pointing skyward at an angle of forty-five degrees to the horizontal. They were slightly concave, and each had some complicated mechanism at its focus. There seemed something impressive and purposeful about the great array; every mirror was aimed at precisely the same spot in the sky—or beyond.

Orostron turned to his colleagues.

"It looks like some kind of observatory to me," he said. "Have you ever seen anything like it before?"

Klarten, a multitentacled, tripedal creature from a globular cluster at the edge of the Milky Way, had a different theory.

"That's communication equipment. Those reflectors are for focusing electromagnetic beams. I've seen the same kind of installation on a hundred worlds before. It may even be the station that Kulath picked up—though that's rather unlikely, for the beams would be very narrow from mirrors that size."

"That would explain why Rugon could detect no radiation before we landed," added Hansur II, one of the twin beings from the planet Thargon.

Orostron did not agree at all.

"If that is a radio station, it must be built for interplanetary communication. Look at the way the mirrors are pointed. I don't believe that a race which has only had radio for two centuries can have crossed space. It took my people six thousand years to do it."

"We managed it in three," said Hansur II mildly, speaking a few seconds ahead of his twin. Before the inevitable argument could develop, Klarten began to wave his tentacles with excitement. While the others had been talking, he had started the automatic monitor.

"Here it is! Listen!"

He threw a switch, and the little room was filled with a raucous whining sound, continually changing in pitch but nevertheless retaining certain characteristics that were difficult to define.

The four explorers listened intently for a minute; then Orostron said, "Surely that can't be any form of speech! No creature could produce sounds as quickly as that!"

Hansur I had come to the same conclusion. "That's a television program. Don't you think so, Klarten?"

The other agreed.

"Yes, and each of those mirrors seems to be radiating a different program. I wonder where they're going? If I'm correct, one of the other planets in the system must lie along those beams. We can soon check that."

Orostron called the S9000 and reported the discovery. Both Rugon and Alveron were greatly excited and made a quick check of the astronomical records.

The result was surprising—and disappointing. None of the other nine planets lay anywhere near the line of transmission. The great mirrors appeared to be pointing blindly into space.

There seemed only one conclusion to be drawn, and Klarten was the first to voice it.

"They had interplanetary communication," he said. "But the station must be deserted now and the transmitters no longer controlled. They haven't been switched off and are just pointing where they were left."

"Well, we'll soon find out," said Orostron. "I'm going to land."

He brought the machine slowly down to the level of the great metal mirrors and past them until it came to rest on the mountain rock. A hundred yards away, a white stone building crouched beneath the maze of steel girders. It was windowless, but there were several doors in the wall facing them.

Orostron watched his companions climb into their protective suits and wished he could follow. But someone had to stay in the machine to keep in touch with the mother ship.   Those were Alveron's instructions, and they were very wise. One never knew what would happen on a world that was being explored for the first time, especially under conditions such as these.

Very cautiously, the three explorers stepped out of the airlock and adjusted the antigravity field of their suits.   Then, each with the mode of locomotion peculiar to his race, the little party went toward the building, the Hansur twins leading and Klarten following close behind.   His gravity control was apparently giving trouble, for he suddenly fell to the ground, rather to the amusement of his colleagues. Orostron saw them pause for a moment at the nearest door—then it opened slowly and they disappeared from sight.

So Orostron waited with what patience he could while the storm rose around him and the light of the aurora grew even brighter in the sky.   At the agreed times he called the mother ship and received brief acknowledgments from Rugon.   He wondered how Torkalee was faring, halfway round the planet, but he could not contact him through the crash and thunder of solar interference.

It did not take Klarten and the Hansurs long to discover that their theories were largely correct.   The building was a radio station, and it was utterly deserted.   It consisted of one tremendous room with a few small offices leading from it.   In the main chamber, row after row of electrical equipment stretched into the distance; lights flickered and winked on hundreds of control panels, and a dull glow came from the elements in a great avenue of vacuum tubes.

But Klarten was not impressed.   The first radio sets his race had built were now fossilized in strata a thousand million years old.   Man, who had possessed electrical machines for only a few centuries, could not compete with those who had known them for half the lifetime of the Earth.

Nevertheless, the party kept their recorders running as they explored the building. There was still one problem to be solved.   The deserted station was broadcasting programs, but where were they coming from?   The central switchboard had been quickly located.   It was designed to handle scores of programs simultaneously, but the source of those programs was lost in a maze of cables that vanished underground.   Back in the S9000, Rugon was trying to analyze the broadcasts and perhaps his researches would reveal their origin.   It was impossible to trace cables that might lead across continents.

The party wasted little time at the deserted station.   There was nothing they could learn from it, and they were seeking life rather than scientific information. A few minutes later the little ship rose swiftly from the plateau and headed toward the plains that must lie beyond the mountains.   Less than three hours were still left to them.

As the array of enigmatic mirrors dropped out of sight, Orostron was struck by a sudden thought.   Was it imagination, or had they all moved through a small angle while he had been waiting, as if they were still compensating for the rotation of the Earth?   He could not be sure, and he dismissed the matter as unimportant. It would only mean that the directing mechanism was still working, after a fashion.

They discovered the city fifteen minutes later.   It was a great, sprawling metropolis, built around a river that had disappeared, leaving an ugly scar winding its way among the great buildings and beneath bridges that looked very incongruous now.

Even from the air, the city looked deserted.   But only two and a half hours were left—there was no time for further exploration.   Orostron made his decision and landed near the largest structure he could see.   It seemed reasonable to suppose that some creatures would have sought shelter in the strongest buildings, where they would be safe until the very end.

The deepest caves—the heart of the planet itself—would give no protection when the final cataclysm came.   Even if this race had reached the outer planets, its doom would only be delayed by the few hours it would take for the ravening wavefronts to cross the solar system.

Orostron could not know that the city had been deserted not for a few days or weeks, but for over a century.   For the culture of cities, which had outlasted so many civilizations had been doomed at last when the helicopter brought universal transportation.   Within a few generations the great masses of mankind, knowing that they could reach any part of the globe in a matter of hours, had gone back to the fields and forests for which they had always longed.   The new civilization had machines and resources of which earlier ages had never dreamed, but it was essentially rural and no longer bound to the steel and concrete warrens that had dominated the centuries before.   Such cities as still remained were specialized centers of research, administration or entertainment; the others had been allowed to decay, where it was too much trouble to destroy them.   The dozen or so greatest of all cities, and the ancient university towns, had scarcely changed and would have lasted for many generations to come.   But the cities that had been founded on steam and iron and surface transportation had passed with the industries that had nourished them.

And so while Orostron waited in the tender, his colleagues raced through endless empty corridors and deserted halls, taking innumerable photographs but learning nothing of the creatures who had used these buildings.   There were libraries, meeting places, council rooms, thousands of offices—all were empty and deep with dust.   If they had not seen the radio station on its mountain aerie, the explorers could well have believed that this world had known no life for centuries.

Through the long minutes of waiting, Orostron tried to imagine where this race could have vanished.   Perhaps they had killed themselves knowing that escape was impossible; perhaps they had built great shelters in the bowels of the planet and even now were cowering in their millions beneath his feet, waiting for the end. He began to fear that he would never know.

It was almost a relief when at last he had to give the order for the return.   Soon he would know if Torkalee's party had been more fortunate.   And he was anxious to get back to the mother ship, for as the minutes passed the suspense had become more and more acute.   There had always been the thought in his mind: what if the astronomers of Kulath have made a mistake?   He would begin to feel happy when the walls of the S9000 were around him.   He would be happier still when they were out in space and this ominous sun was shrinking far astern.

As soon as his colleagues had entered the airlock, Orostron hurled his tiny machine into the sky and set the controls to home on the S9000.   Then he turned to his friends.

"Well, what have you found?" he asked.

Klarten produced a large roll of canvas and spread it out on the floor.

"This is what they were like," he said quietly.   "Bipeds, with only two arms. They seem to have managed well, in spite of that handicap.   Only two eyes as well, unless there are others in the back.   We were lucky to find this; it's about the only thing they left behind."

The ancient oil paintings stared stonily back at the three creatures regarding it so intently.   By the irony of fate, its complete worthlessness had saved it from oblivion.   When the city had been evacuated, no one had bothered to move Alderman John Richards, 1909–1974.   For a century and a half he had been gathering dust while far away from the old cities the new civilization had been rising to heights no earlier culture had ever known.

"That was almost all we found," said Klarten.   "The city must have been deserted for years.   I'm afraid our expedition has been a failure.   If there are any living beings on this world, they've hidden themselves too well for us to find them."

His commander was forced to agree.

"It was an almost impossible task," he said.   "If we'd had weeks instead of hours we might have succeeded.   For all we know, they may even have built shelters under the sea.   No one seems to have thought of that."

He glanced quickly at the indicators and corrected the course.

"We'll be there in five minutes.   Alveron seems to be moving rather quickly. I wonder if Torkalee has found anything."

The S9000 was hanging a few miles above the seaboard of a glazing continent when Orostron homed upon it.   The danger line was thirty minutes away and there was no time to lose.   Skillfully, he maneuvered the little ship into its launching tube and the party stepped out of the airlock.

There was a small crowd waiting for them.   That was to be expected, but Orostron could see at once that something more than curiosity had brought his friends here. Even before a word was spoken, he knew that something was wrong.

"Torkalee hasn't returned.   He's lost his party and we're going to the rescue. Come along to the control room at once."

From the beginning, Torkalee had been luckier than Orostron.   He had followed the zone of twilight, keeping away from the intolerable glare of the sun, until he came to the shores of an inland sea.   It was a very recent sea, one of the latest of man's works, for the land it covered had been desert less than a century before. In a few hours it would be desert again, for the water was boiling and clouds of steam were rising to the skies.   But they could not veil the loveliness of the great white city that overlooked the tideless sea.

Flying machines were still parked neatly round the square in which Torkalee landed.   They were disappointingly primitive, though beautifully finished, and depended on rotating airfoils for support.   Nowhere was there any sign of life, but the place gave the impression that its inhabitants were not very far away.   Lights were still shining from some of the windows.

Torkalee's three companions lost no time in leaving the machine.   Leader of the party, by seniority of rank and race was T'sinadree, who like Alveron himself had been born on one of the ancient planets of the Central Suns.   Next came Alarkane, from a race which was one of the youngest in the universe and took a perverse pride in the fact.   Last came one of the strange beings from the system of Palador.   It was nameless, like all its kind, for it possessed no identity of its own, being merely a mobile but still dependent cell in the consciousness of its race. Though it and its fellows had long been scattered over the galaxy in the exploration of countless worlds, some unknown link still bound them together as inexorably as the living cells in a human body.

When a creature of Palador spoke, the pronoun it used was always "we."   There was not, nor could there ever be, any first person singular in the language of Palador.

The great doors of the splendid building baffled the explorers, though any human child would have known their secret.   T'sinadree wasted no time on them but called Torkalee on his personal transmitter.   Then the three hurried aside while their commander maneuvered his machine into the best position.   There was a brief burst of intolerable flame; the massive steelwork flickered once at the edge of the visible spectrum and was gone.   The stones were still glowing when the eager party hurried into the building, the beams of their light projectors fanning before them.

The torches were not needed.   Before them lay a great hall, flowing with light from lines of tubes along the ceiling.   On either side, the hall opened out into long corridors, while straight ahead a massive stairway swept majestically toward the upper floors.

For a moment T'sinadree hesitated.   Then, since one way was as good as another, he led his companions down the first corridor.

The feeling that life was near had now become very strong.   At any moment, it seemed, they might be confronted by the creatures of this world.   If they showed hostility—and they could scarcely be blamed if they did—the paralyzers would be used at once.

The tension was very great as the party entered the first room and only relaxed when they saw that it held nothing but machines—row after row of them, now stilled and silent.   Lining the enormous room were thousands of metal filing cabinets, forming a continuous wall as far as the eye could reach.   And that was all; there was no furniture, nothing but the cabinets and the mysterious machines.

Alarkane, always the quickest of the three, was already examining the cabinets. Each held many thousand sheets of tough, thin material, perforated with innumerable holes and slots.   The Paladorian appropriated one of the cards and Alarkane recorded the scene together with some close-ups of the machines.   Then they left. The great room, which had been one of the marvels of the world, meant nothing to them.   No living eye would ever again see that wonderful battery of almost human Hollerith analyzers and the five thousand million punched cards holding all that could be recorded of each man, woman and child on the planet.

It was clear that this building had been used very recently. With growing excitement, the explorers hurried on to the next room. This they found to be an enormous library, for millions of books lay all around them on miles and miles of shelving. Here, though the explorers could not know it, were the records of all the laws that man had ever passed and all the speeches that had ever been made in his council chambers.

T'sinadree was deciding his plan of action, when Alarkane drew his attention to one of the racks a hundred yards away. It was half empty, unlike all the others. Around it books lay in a tumbled heap on the floor, as if knocked down by someone in frantic haste. The signs were unmistakable. Not long ago, other creatures had been this way. Faint wheel marks were clearly visible on the floor to the acute sense of Alarkane, though the others could see nothing. Alarkane could even detect footprints, but knowing nothing of the creatures that had formed them he could not say which way they led.

The sense of nearness was stronger than ever now, but it was nearness in time, not in space. Alarkane voiced the thoughts of the party.

"Those books must have been valuable, and someone has come to rescue them—rather as an afterthought, I should say. That means there must be a place of refuge, possibly not very far away. Perhaps we may be able to find some other clues that will lead us to it."

T'sinadree agreed; the Paladorian wasn't enthusiastic.

"That may be so," it said, "but the refuge may be anywhere on the planet, and we have just two hours left. Let us waste no more time if we hope to rescue these people."

The party hurried forward once more, pausing only to collect a few books that might be useful to the scientists at base—though it was doubtful if they could ever be translated. They soon found that the great building was composed largely of small rooms, all showing signs of recent occupation. Most of them were in a neat and tidy condition, but one or two were very much the reverse. The explorers were particularly puzzled by one room—clearly an office of some kind—that appeared to have been completely wrecked. The floor was littered with papers, the furniture had been smashed and smoke was pouring through the broken windows from the fires outside.

T'sinadree was rather alarmed.

"Surely no dangerous animal could have got into a place like this!" he exclaimed, fingering his paralyzer nervously.

Alarkane did not answer. He began to make that annoying sound which his race called "laughter." It was several minutes before he would explain what had amused him.

"I don't think any animal has done it," he said. "In fact, the explanation is very simple. Suppose *you* had been working all your life in this room, dealing with endless papers, year after year. And suddenly, you are told that you will never see it again, that your work is finished and that you can leave it forever. More than that—no one will come after you. Everything is finished. How would you make your exit, T'sinadree?''

The other thought for a moment.

"Well, I suppose I'd just tidy things up and leave. That's what seems to have happened in all the other rooms.''

Alarkane laughed again.

"I'm quite sure you would. But some individuals have a different psychology. I think I should have liked the creature that used this room.''

He did not explain himself further, and his two colleagues puzzled over his words for quite a while before they gave it up.

It came as something of a shock when Torkalee gave the order to return. They had gathered a great deal of information, but had found no clue that might lead them to the missing inhabitants of this world. That problem was as baffling as ever, and now it seemed that it would never be solved. There were only forty minutes left before the S9000 would be departing.

They were halfway back to the tender when they saw the semi-circular passage leading down into the depths of the building. Its architectural style was quite different from that used elsewhere, and the gently sloping floor was an irresistible attraction to creatures whose many legs had grown weary of the marble staircases which only bipeds could have built in such profusion. T'sinadree had been the worst sufferer, for he normally employed twelve legs and could use twenty when he was in a hurry, though no one had ever seen him perform this feat.

The party stopped dead and looked down the passageway with a single thought. A tunnel, leading down into the depths of Earth! At its end, they might yet find the people of this world and rescue some of them from their fate. For there was still time to call the mother ship if the need arose.

T'sinadree signaled to his commander and Torkalee brought the little machine immediately overhead. There might not be time for the party to retrace its footsteps through the maze of passages, so meticulously recorded in the Paladorian mind that there was no possibility of going astray. If speed was necessary, Torkalee could blast his way through the dozen floors above their head. In any case, it should not take long to find what lay at the end of the passage.

It took only thirty seconds. The tunnel ended quite abruptly in a very curious cylindrical room with magnificently padded seats along the walls. There was no way out save that by which they had come and it was several seconds before the purpose of the chamber dawned on Alarkane's mind. It was a pity, he thought, that they would never have time to use this. The thought was suddenly interrupted by a cry from T'sinadree. Alarkane wheeled around and saw that the entrance had closed silently behind them.

Even in that first moment of panic, Alarkane found himself thinking with some admiration: whoever they were, they knew how to build automatic machinery!

The Paladorian was the first to speak. It waved one of its tentacles toward the seats.

"We think it would be best to be seated," it said. The multiplex mind of Palador had already analyzed the situation and knew what was coming.

They did not have long to wait before a low-pitched hum came from a grill overhead, and for the very last time in history a human, even if lifeless, voice was heard on Earth. The words were meaningless, though the trapped explorers could guess their message clearly enough.

"Choose your stations, please, and be seated."

Simultaneously, a wall panel at one end of the compartment glowed with light. On it was a simple map, consisting of a series of a dozen circles connected by a line. Each of the circles had writing alongside it, and beside the writing were two buttons of different colors.

Alarkane looked questioningly at his leader.

"Don't touch them," said T'sinadree. "If we leave the controls alone, the doors may open again."

He was wrong. The engineers who had designed the automatic subway had assumed that anyone who entered it would naturally wish to go somewhere. If they selected no intermediate station, their destination could only be the end of the line.

There was another pause while the relays and thyratrons waited for their orders. In those thirty seconds, if they had known what to do, the party could have opened the doors and left the subway. But they did not know, and the machines geared to a human psychology acted for them.

The surge of acceleration was not very great; the lavish upholstery was a luxury, not a necessity. Only an almost imperceptible vibration told of the speed at which they were traveling through the bowels of the earth, on a journey the duration of which they could not even guess. And in thirty minutes, the S9000 would be leaving the solar system.

There was a long silence in the speeding machine. T'sinadree and Alarkane were thinking rapidly. So was the Paladorian, though in a different fashion. The conception of personal death was meaningless to it, for the destruction of a single unit meant no more to the group mind than the loss of a nail-paring to a man. But it could, though with great difficulty, appreciate the plight of individual intelligences such as Alarkane and T'sinadree, and it was anxious to help them if it could.

Alarkane had managed to contact Torkalee with his personal transmitter, though the signal was very weak and seemed to be fading quickly. Rapidly he explained the situation, and almost at once the signals became clearer. Torkalee was following the path of the machine, flying above the ground under which they were speeding to their unknown destination. That was the first indication they had of the fact that they were traveling at nearly a thousand miles an hour, and very soon after that Torkalee was able to give the still more disturbing news that they were rapidly approaching the sea. While they were beneath the land, there was a hope, though a slender one, that they might stop the machine and escape. But under the ocean—not all the brains and the machinery in the great mother ship could save them. No one could have devised a more perfect trap.

T'sinadree had been examining the wall map with great attention.   Its meaning was obvious, and along the line connecting the circles a tiny spot of light was crawling.   It was already halfway to the first of the stations marked.

"I'm going to press one of those buttons," said T'sinadree at last.   "It won't do any harm, and we may learn something."

"I agree.   Which will you try first?"

"There are only two kinds, and it won't matter if we try the wrong one first. I suppose one is to start the machine and the other is to stop it."

Alarkane was not very hopeful.

"It started without any button pressing," he said.   "I think it's completely automatic and we can't control it from here at all."

T'sinadree could not agree.

"These buttons are clearly associated with the stations, and there's no point in having them unless you can use them to stop yourself.   The only question is, which is the right one?"

His analysis was perfectly correct.   The machine could be stopped at any intermediate station.   They had only been on their way ten minutes, and if they could leave now, no harm would have been done.   It was just bad luck that T'sinadree's first choice was the wrong button.

The little light on the map crawled slowly through the illuminated circle without checking its speed.   And at the same time Torkalee called from the ship overhead.

"You have just passed underneath a city and are heading out to sea.   There cannot be another stop for nearly a thousand miles."

Alveron had given up all hope of finding life on this world.   The S9000 had roamed over half the planet, never staying long in one place, descending ever and again in an effort to attract attention.   There had been no response; Earth seemed utterly dead.   If any of its inhabitants were still alive, thought Alveron, they must have hidden themselves in its depths where no help could reach them, though their doom would be nonetheless certain.

Rugon brought news of the disaster.   The great ship ceased its fruitless searching and fled back through the storm to the ocean above which Torkalee's little tender was still following the track of the buried machine.

The scene was truly terrifying.   Not since the days when Earth was born had there been such seas as this.   Mountains of water were racing before the storm which had now reached velocities of many hundred miles an hour.   Even at this distance from the mainland the air was full of flying debris—trees, fragments of houses, sheets of metal, anything that had not been anchored to the ground.   No airborne machine could have lived for a moment in such a gale.   And ever and again even the roar of the wind was drowned as the vast water-mountains met head-on with a crash that seemed to shake the sky.

Fortunately, there had been no serious earthquakes yet.   Far beneath the bed of the ocean, the wonderful piece of engineering which had been the World President's private vacuum-subway was still working perfectly, unaffected by the tumult and destruction above. It would continue to work until the last minute of the Earth's existence, which, if the astronomers were right, was not much more than fifteen minutes away—though precisely how much more Alveron would have given a great deal to know. It would be nearly an hour before the trapped party could reach land and even the slightest hope of rescue.

Alveron's instructions had been precise, though even without them he would never have dreamed of taking any risks with the great machine that had been entrusted to his care. Had he been human, the decision to abandon the trapped members of his crew would have been desperately hard to make. But he came of a race far more sensitive than man, a race that so loved the things of the spirit that long ago, and with infinite reluctance, it had taken over control of the universe since only thus could it be sure that justice was being done. Alveron would need all his superhuman gifts to carry him through the next few hours.

Meanwhile, a mile below the bed of the ocean Alarkane and T'sinadree were very busy indeed with their private communicators. Fifteen minutes is not a long time in which to wind up the affairs of a lifetime. It is indeed, scarcely long enough to dictate more than a few of those farewell messages which at such moments are so much more important than all other matters.

All the while the Paladorian had remained silent and motionless, saying not a word. The other two, resigned to their fate and engrossed in their personal affairs, had given it no thought. They were startled when suddenly it began to address them in its peculiarly passionless voice.

"We perceive that you are making certain arrangements concerning your anticipated destruction. That will probably be unnecessary. Captain Alveron hopes to rescue us if we can stop this machine when we reach land again."

Both T'sinadree and Alarkane were too surprised to say anything for a moment. Then the latter gasped, "How do you know?"

It was a foolish question, for he remembered at once that there were several Paladorians—if one could use the phrase—in the S9000, and consequently their companion knew everything that was happening in the mother ship. So he did not wait for an answer but continued. "Alveron can't do that! He daren't take such a risk!"

"There will be no risk," said the Paladorian. "We have told him what to do. It is really very simple."

Alarkane and T'sinadree looked at their companion with something approaching awe, realizing now what must have happened. In moments of crisis, the single units comprising the Paladorian mind could link together in an organization no less close than that of any physical brain. At such moments they formed an intellect more powerful than any other in the universe. All ordinary problems could be solved by a few hundred or thousand units. Very rarely, millions would be needed, and on two historic occasions the billions of cells of the entire Paladorian consciousness had been welded together to deal with emergencies that threatened the race. The mind of Palador was one of the greatest mental resources of the universe; its full force was seldom required, but the knowledge that it was available was supremely comforting to other races. Alarkane wondered how many cells had coordinated to deal with this particular emergency. He also wondered how so trivial an incident had ever come to its attention.

To that question he was never to know the answer, though he might have guessed it had he known that the chillingly remote Paladorian mind possessed an almost human streak of vanity. Long ago, Alarkane had written a book trying to prove that eventually all intelligent races would sacrifice individual consciousness and that one day only group-minds would remain in the universe. Palador, he had said, was the first of those ultimate intellects, and the vast, dispersed mind had not been displeased.

They had no time to ask any further questions before Alveron himself began to speak through their communicators.

"Alveron calling! We're staying on this planet until the detonation waves reach it, so we may be able to rescue you. You're heading toward a city on the coast which you'll reach in forty minutes at your present speed. If you cannot stop yourselves then, we're going to blast the tunnel behind and ahead of you to cut off your power. Then we'll sink a shaft to get you out—the chief engineer says he can do it in five minutes with the main projectors. So you should be safe within an hour, unless the sun blows up before."

"And if that happens, you'll be destroyed as well! You mustn't take such a risk!"

"Don't let that worry you; we're perfectly safe. When the sun detonates, the explosion wave will take several minutes to rise to its maximum. But apart from that, we're on the night side of the planet, behind an eight-thousand-mile screen of rock. When the first warning of the explosion comes, we will accelerate out of the solar system, keeping in the shadow of the planet. Under our maximum drive, we will reach the velocity of light before leaving the cone of shadow, and the sun cannot harm us then."

T'sinadree was still afraid to hope. Another objection came at once into his mind.

"Yes, but how will you get any warning, here on the night side of the planet?"

"Very easily," replied Alveron. "This world has a moon which is now visible from this hemisphere. We have telescopes trained on it. If it shows any sudden increase in brilliance, our main drive goes on automatically and we'll be thrown out of the system."

The logic was flawless. Alveron, cautious as ever, was taking no chances. It would be many minutes before the eight-thousand-mile shield of rock and metal could be destroyed by the fires of the exploding sun. In that time, the S9000 could have reached the safety of the velocity of light.

Alarkane pressed the second button when they were still several miles from the coast. He did not expect anything to happen then, assuming that the machine could not stop between stations. It seemed too good to be true when, a few minutes later, the machine's slight vibration died away and they came to a halt.

The doors slid silently apart. Even before they were fully open, the three had left the compartment. They were taking no more chances. Before them a long tunnel stretched into the distance, rising slowly out of sight.   They were starting along it when suddenly Alveron's voice called from the communicators.

"Stay where you are!   We're going to blast!"

The ground shuddered once, and far ahead there came the rumble of falling rock. Again the earth shook—and a hundred yards ahead the passageway vanished abruptly.A tremendous vertical shaft had been cut clean through it.

The party hurried forward again until they came to the end of the corridor and stood waiting on its lip.   The shaft in which it ended was a full thousand feet across and descended into the earth as far as the torches could throw their beams. Overhead, the storm clouds fled beneath a moon that no man would have recognized, so luridly brilliant was its disk.   And, most glorious of all sights, the S9000 floated high above, the great projectors that had drilled this enormous pit still glowing cherry red.

A dark shape detached itself from the mother ship and dropped swiftly toward the ground.   Torkalee was returning to collect his friends.   A little later, Alveron greeted them in the control room.   He waved to the great vision screen and said quietly, "See, we were barely in time."

The continent below them was slowly settling beneath the mile-high waves that were attacking its coasts.   The last that anyone was ever to see of Earth was a great plain, bathed with the silver light of the abnormally brilliant moon.   Across its face the waters were pouring in a glittering flood toward a distant range of mountains.   The sea had won its final victory, but its triumph would be short-lived for soon sea and land would be no more.   Even as the silent party in the control room watched the destruction below, the infinitely greater catastrophe to which this was only the prelude came swiftly upon them.

It was as though dawn had broken suddenly over this moonlit landscape.   But it was not dawn: it was only the moon, shining with the brilliance of a second sun. For perhaps thirty seconds that awesome, unnatural light burned fiercely on the doomed land beneath.   Then there came a sudden flashing of indicator lights across the control board.   The main drive was on.   For a second Alveron glanced at the indicators and checked their information.   When he looked again at the screen, Earth was gone.

The magnificent, desperately overstrained generators quietly died when the S9000 was passing the orbit of Persephone.   It did not matter; the sun could never harm them now, and although the ship was speeding helplessly out into the lonely night of interstellar space, it would only be a matter of days before rescue came.

There was irony in that.   A day ago, they had been the rescuers going to the aid of a race that now no longer existed.   Not for the first time Alveron wondered about the world that had just perished.   He tried in vain to picture it as it had been in its glory, the streets of its cities thronged with life.   Primitive though its people had been, they might have offered much to the universe.   If only they could have made contact!   Regret was useless; long before their coming, the people of this world must have buried themselves in its iron heart.   And now they and their civilization would remain a mystery for the rest of time.

Alveron was glad when his thoughts were interrupted by Rugon's entrance.   The chief of communications had been very busy ever since the takeoff, trying to analyze the programs radiated by the transmitter Orostron had discovered. The problem was not a difficult one, but it demanded the construction of special equipment, and that had taken time.

"Well, what have you found?" asked Alveron.

"Quite a lot," replied his friend. "There's something mysterious here, and I don't understand it.

"It didn't take long to find how the vision transmissions were built up, and we've been able to convert them to suit our own equipment. It seems that there were cameras all over the planet, surveying points of interest. Some of them were apparently in cities, on the tops of very high buildings. The cameras were rotating continuously to give panoramic views. In the programs we've recorded there are about twenty different scenes.

"In addition, there are a number of transmissions of a different kind, neither sound nor vision. They seem to be purely scientific—possibly instrument readings or something of that sort. All these programs were going out simultaneously on different frequency bands.

"Now there must be a reason for all this. Orostron still thinks that the station simply wasn't switched off when it was deserted. But these aren't the sort of programs such a station would normally radiate at all. It was certainly used for interplanetary relaying—Klarten was quite right there. So these people must have crossed space, since none of the other planets had any life at the time of the last survey. Don't you agree?"

Alveron was following intently.

"Yes, that seems reasonable enough. But it's also certain that the beam was pointing to none of the other planets. I checked that myself."

"I know," said Rugon. "What I want to discover is why a giant interplanetary relay station is busily transmitting pictures of a world about to be destroyed— pictures that would be of immense interest to scientists and astronomers. Someone had gone to a lot of trouble to arrange all those panoramic cameras. I am convinced that those beams were going somewhere."

Alveron started up.

"Do you imagine that there might be an outer planet that hasn't been reported?" he asked. "If so, your theory's certainly wrong. The beam wasn't even pointing in the plane of the solar system. And even if it were—just look at this."

He switched on the vision screen and adjusted the controls. Against the velvet curtain of space was hanging a blue-white sphere, apparently composed of many concentric shells of incandescent gas. Even though its immense distance made all movement invisible, it was clearly expanding at an enormous rate. At its center was a blinding point of light—the white dwarf star that the sun had now become.

"You probably don't realize just how big that sphere is," said Alveron. "Look at this."

He increased the magnification until only the center portion of the nova was visible. Close to its heart were two minute condensations, one on either side of the nucleus.

"Those are the two giant planets of the system.   They have still managed to retain their existence—after a fashion.   And they were several hundred million miles from the sun.   The nova is still expanding—but it's already twice the size of the solar system."

Rugon was silent for a moment.

"Perhaps you're right," he said, rather grudgingly.   "You've disposed of my first theory.   But you still haven't satisfied me."

He made several swift circuits of the room before speaking again.   Alveron waited patiently.   He knew the almost intuitive powers of his friend, who could often solve a problem when mere logic seemed insufficient.

Then rather slowly, Rugon began to speak again.

"What do you think of this?" he said.   "Suppose we've completely under-estimated this people?   Orostron did it once—he thought they could never have crossed space, since they'd only known radio for two centuries.   Hansur II told me that.   Well, Orostron was quite wrong.   Perhaps we're all wrong.   I've had a look at the material that Klarten brought back from the transmitter.   He wasn't impressed by what he found, but it's a marvelous achievement for so short a time.   There were devices in that station that belonged to civilizations thousands of years older.   Alveron, can we follow that beam to see where it leads?"

Alveron said nothing for a full minute.   He had been more than half expecting the question, but it was not an easy one to answer.   The main generators had gone completely.   There was no point in trying to repair them.   But there was still power available, and while there was power, anything could be done in time.   It would mean a lot of improvisation, and some difficult maneuvers, for the ship still had its enormous initial velocity.   Yes, it could be done, and the activity would keep the crew from becoming further depressed, now that the reaction caused by the mission's failure had started to set in.   The news that the nearest heavy repair ship could not reach them for three weeks had also caused a slump in morale.

The engineers, as usual, made a tremendous fuss.   Again as usual, they did the job in half the time they had dismissed as being absolutely impossible.   Very slowly, over many hours, the great ship began to discard the speed its main drive had given it in as many minutes.   In a tremendous curve, millions of miles in radius, the S9000 changed its course and the star fields shifted around it.

The maneuver took three days, but at the end of that time the ship was limping along a course parallel to the beam that had once come from Earth.   They were heading out into emptiness, the blazing sphere that had been the sun dwindling slowly behind them.   By the standards of interstellar flight, they were almost stationary.

For hours Rugon strained over his instruments, driving his detector beams far ahead into space.   There were certainly no planets within many light-years; there was no doubt of that.   From time to time Alveron came to see him and always he had to give the same reply: "Nothing to report."   About a fifth of the time Rugon's intuition let him down badly; he began to wonder if this was such an occasion.

Not until a week later did the needles of the mass-detectors quiver feebly at the ends of their scales.   But Rugon said nothing, not even to his captain.   He waited until he was sure, and he went on waiting until even the short-range scanners began to react and to build up the first faint pictures on the vision screen.   Still he waited patiently until he could interpret the images.   Then, when he knew that his wildest fancy was even less than the truth, he called his colleagues into the control room.

The picture on the vision screen was the familiar one of endless star fields, sun beyond sun to the very limits of the universe.   Near the center of the screen a distant nebula made a patch of haze that was difficult for the eye to grasp.

Rugon increased the magnification.   The stars flowed out of the field; the little nebula expanded until it filled the screen and then—it was a nebula no longer.   A simultaneous gasp of amazement came from all the company at the sight that lay before them.

Lying across league after league of space, ranged in a vast three-dimensional array of rows and columns with the precision of a marching army, were thousands of tiny pencils of light.   They were moving swiftly, the whole immense lattice holding its shape as a single unit.   Even as Alveron and his comrades watched, the formation began to drift off the screen and Rugon had to recenter the controls.

After a long pause, Rugon started to speak.

"This is the race," he said softly, "that has known radio for only two centuries— the race that we believed had crept to die in the heart of its planet.   I have examined those images under the highest possible magnification.

"That is the greatest fleet of which there has ever been a record.   Each of those points of light represents a ship larger than our own.   Of course, they are very primitive—what you see on the screen are the jets of their rockets.   Yes, they dared to use rockets to bridge interstellar space!   You realize what that means. It would take them centuries to reach the nearest star.   The whole race must have embarked on this journey in the hope that its descendants would complete it, generations later.

"To measure the extent of their accomplishment, think of the ages it took us to conquer space and the longer ages still before we attempted to reach the stars. Even if we were threatened with annihilation, could we have done so much in so short a time?   Remember, this is the youngest civilization in the universe.   Four hundred thousand years ago it did not even exist.   What will it be a million years from now?"

An hour later, Orostron left the crippled mother ship to make contact with the great fleet ahead.   As the little torpedo disappeared among the stars, Alveron turned to his friend and made a remark that Rugon was often to remember in the years ahead.

"I wonder what they'll be like?" he mused.   "Will they be nothing but wonderful engineers, with no art or philosophy?   They're going to have such a surprise when Orostron reaches them—I expect it will be rather a blow to their pride.   It's funny how all isolated races think they're the only people in the universe. But they should be grateful to us; we're going to save them a good many hundred years of travel."

Alveron glanced at the Milky Way, lying like a veil of silver mist across the vision screen.   He waved toward it with a sweep of a tentacle that embraced the whole circle of the galaxy, from the Central Planets to the lonely suns of the Rim.

"You know," he said to Rugon, "I feel rather afraid of these people.   Suppose they don't like our little federation?"   He waved once more toward the starclouds that lay massed across the screen, glowing with the light of their countless suns.

"Something tells me they'll be very determined people," he added.   "We had better be polite to them.   After all, we only outnumber them about a thousand million to one."

Rugon laughed at his captain's little joke.

Twenty years afterward, the remark didn't seem funny.

ANTHONY BOUCHER

The Chronokinesis of Jonathan Hull

T his isn't, properly speaking, Fergus O'Breen's story, though it starts with him. Fergus is a private detective, but he didn't function as a detective in the Jonathan Hull episode. It was no fault of his Irish ingenuity that he provided the answer to the mystery; he simply found it, all neatly typed out for him. Typed, in fact, before there ever was any mystery.

In a way, though, it's a typical O'Breen anecdote. "I'm a private eye," Fergus used to say, "and what happens to me shouldn't happen to a Seeing Eye. I'm a catalyst for the unbelievable." As in the case of Mr. Harrison Partridge, who found that the only practical use for a short-range time machine was to provide the perfect alibi for murder. But the Partridge case was simplicity itself compared to the Hull business.

It began—at least according to one means of reckoning a time sequence—on the morning after Fergus had trapped the murderer in the Dubrovsky case—a relatively simple affair involving only such prosaic matters as an unbreakable alibi and a hermetically sealed room.

None the less it was a triumph that deserved, and received, whole-hearted celebration, and it was three o'clock before Fergus wound up in bed. It was eight when he unwound upon hearing a thud in the corner of the room. He sat up and stared into the gloom and saw a tall, thin figure rising from the floor. The figure moved over to his typewriter and switched on the light. He saw a man of about sixty, clean-shaven, but with long, untrimmed gray hair. An odd face—not unkindly, but slightly inhuman, as though he had gone through some experience so unspeakable as to set him a little apart from the rest of his race.

Fergus watched curiously as the old man took an envelope out of a drawer in the desk, opened it, unfolded the papers it contained, set them in a pile beside the typewriter, took the topmost sheet, inserted it in the machine, and began typing furiously.

It seemed a curious procedure, but Fergus' mind was none too clear and the outlines of the room and of the typist still tended to waver. *Oh well,* Fergus thought, *long-haired old men at typewriters is pretty mild in view of those boiler-makers.* And he rolled over and back to sleep.

It was about an hour later that he opened his eyes again, much surprised to find Curly Locks still there. He was typing with his right hand, while his left rested on a pile of paper beside him. As Fergus watched, the old man pulled a sheet from the typewriter and added it to the pile at his left. Then he put the pile in the side section of the desk which housed unused paper, rose from the machine, switched off the light, and walked out the door, with a curious awkward walk, as though he had been paralyzed for years and had had to learn the technique all over again.

The dominant O'Breen trait, the one that has solved more cases than any amount of ingenuity and persistence, is curiosity. A phantasm that stays right there while you sleep is worth investigating. So Fergus was instantly out of bed, without even bothering to pull on a robe, and examining the unused paper compartment.

He sighed with disgust. All the sheets were virginally white. It must have been a delusion after all, though of a singular sort. He turned back to bed. But as he did so, his eye glanced at the corner where he had heard that first thud. He executed a fabulous double take and looked again. There was no doubt about it.

In that corner lay the body of a tall thin man of about sixty, clean-shaven, but with long untrimmed gray hair.

The average man might find some difficulty in explaining to the police how an unidentified corpse happened to turn up in his bedroom. But Detective Lieutenant A. Jackson had reached the point where he was surprised at nothing that involved O'Breen.

He heard the story through and then said judiciously, "I think we'll leave your typewriter out of the report, Fergus. If your Irish blood wants to go fey on you, it's O. K. with me; but I think the Psychical Research Society would be more interested in a report on it than the L. A. Police Department. He died when you heard that thud, so his actions thereafter are pretty irrelevant."

"Cyanide?" Fergus asked.

"Smell it from here, can't you? And the vial still clenched in his hand, so there's no doubt of a verdict of suicide. To try a little reconstruction: Say he came to see you professionally about whatever was preying on him. Found you asleep and decided to wait, but finally got restless and finished the job without seeing you."

"I guess so," said Fergus, taking another gulp of tomato juice. "This and the coffee make the typewriter episode seem pretty unlikely. But no O'Breen's gone in for second sight since great-great-grandfather Seamus. I'll expect the family leprechaun next."

"Tell him these shoes need resoling," said Lieutenant Jackson.

For twenty-four hours the affair rested at that. Suicide of Unknown. Nothing to identify him, not even laundry marks. Check-up on fingerprints fruitless. One odd thing that bothered Jackson a little: the man's trousers had no cuffs.

Sergeant Marcus, whose uncle was in cloaks and suits, had an idea on that. "If we get into this war and run into a shortage of material, we'll all be wearing 'em like that. Maybe he's setting next year's styles."

When Fergus heard this, he laughed. And then he stopped laughing and sat down and began thinking. He thought through half a pack of Camels in a chain before he gave up. There was a hint there. Something that was teasing him. Something that reminded him of the Partridge case and yet not quite.

The notion was still nibbling at the back of his mind when Jackson called him the next day. "Something might interest you, Fergus. Either a pretty far-fetched coincidence or part of a pattern."

"My pattern?"

"Your pattern maybe. Another old man with long hair and no identification. Found in a rooming house out on Adams in a room that was supposed to be vacant. But this one was shot."

Fergus frowned. "Could be. But is long hair enough to make it a coincidence?"

"Not by itself. But he hasn't any cuffs on his pants either."

Fergus lost no time in getting to the West Adams address. Onetime mansion fallen on evil days, reduced to transient cubicles. The landlady was still incoherently horrified.

"I went into the room to fix it up like I always do between tenants and there on the bed . . ."

Jackson shooed her out. The photographing and fingerprinting squads had come and gone, but the basket hadn't arrived yet. He and Fergus stood alone and looked at the man. He was even older than the other—somewhere in his late seventies, at a guess. A hard, cruel face, with a dark hole centered in its forehead.

"Shot at close range," Jackson was commenting. "Powder burns. Gun left here—clear prints on it." There was a knock on the door. "That'll be the basket."

Fergus looked at the trousers. The cuffs hadn't been taken off. They were clearly tailored without cuffs. Two old men with cuffless trousers . . .

Jackson had gone to open the door. Now he started back with a gasp. Fergus turned. Gasps aren't easily extorted from a police lieutenant, but this one was justified. Coming in the door was the exact twin of Fergus' typing corpse, and walking with that same carefully learned awkwardness.

He seemed not to notice the corpse on the bed, but he turned to Jackson when the officer demanded, "And who are you?" To be exact, he seemed to turn a moment before Jackson spoke.

He said something. Or at least he made vocal noises. It was a gibberish not remotely approximating any language that either detective had ever heard. And there followed a minute of complete cross-purposes, a cross-examination in which neither party understood a syllable of the other's speech.

Then Fergus had an idea. He took out his notebook and pencil and handed them over. The old man wrote rapidly and most peculiarly. He began in the lower right hand corner of the page and wrote straight on to the upper left. But the message, when he handed it back, was in normal order.

Fergus whistled. "With that act on a blackboard, you could pack 'em in." Then he read the message:

I see that I will have succeeded, and because of the idea that has just come to my mind I imagine that you already understand this hell as much as it is possible for one to understand who has not gone through it and know that it is impossible to arrest me. But if it will simplify your files, you may consider this a confession.

Jonathan Hull

Jackson drew his automatic and moved toward the door. Fergus took out one of his cards with business and home address and penciled on it:

Look me up if you need help straightening this out.

An idea seemed to strike the man as he accepted the card. Then his features widened in a sort of astonished gratification and he looked at the bed. Then with that same rapid awkwardness he was walking out of the room.

Detective Lieutenant Jackson called a warning to him. He tried to grab him. But the man went right on past him. It isn't easy to fire a close-range bullet into a gray-haired old man. He was out of the room and on the stairs before Jackson's finger could move, and then the bullet went wild.

Jackson was starting out of the room when he felt Fergus' restraining hand on his arm. He tried to shake it off, but it was firm. "You'll never catch him, Andy," said Fergus gently. "Never in God's green eternity. Because you see you can't have caught him or he couldn't have typed . . ."

Jackson exploded. "Fergus! You don't think this trick-writing expert is another wraith for your second sight, do you? I saw him, too. He's real. And he must be your corpse's twin. If we find him, we can have the answer to both deaths. We can . . ."

"Telephone for you, Lieutenant," the landlady called.

When Jackson returned, his chagrin over Jonathan Hull's escape was forgotten. "All right," he said wearily. "Have it your way, Fergus. Ghosts we have yet. Do I care?"

"What happened?"

"Anything can happen. Everything probably will. There's no more sense and order in the world. Nothing a man can trust."

"But what is it?"

"Fingerprints. They don't mean a thing any more."

"The prints on the gun?" Fergus said eagerly. "They belong to my corpse?"

Jackson nodded shamefacedly. "So a cuffless ghost came back and . . . But it's worse than that. Much worse. This stiff's prints—they belong to a seventeen-year-old kid working out at Lockheed." With these words the lanky lieutenant seemed to reach the depth of despair.

But they brought new hope to Fergus' face and a triumphant glint to his green eyes. "Perfect, Andy! I couldn't have asked for better. That rounds it off."

Jackson looked up wide-eyed. "You mean it makes sense? O. K., maestro; what's the answer?"

"I don't know," said Fergus coolly. "But I know *where* the answer is: in the drawer of my desk."

He stubbornly refused to say a word until they were in his room. Then he said, "Look at all the little things we saw: How Hull turned to you just *before* you spoke to him; how he registered amazement, and *then* looked at the corpse; above all, how he wrote that note. And the wording of the note too: 'I *will have* succeeded,' and how we must *already* understand because of something he just thought of. There's only one answer to it all:

"*Jonathan Hull is living backwards.*"

Jackson burst out with a loud, "Nonsense!"

"It even explains the absence of the cuffs. They're trousers from next year, when we'll be in the war and Sergeant Marcus' prophecy will come true."

"Then you mean that the other stiff too . . .?"

"Both of 'em."

"O. K. Grant you that much, and I suppose in some cockeyed way it explains the prints of a corpse on a murder weapon. But that kid out at Lockheed . . ."

". . . *is* your second stiff. But don't trust me: Let's see what Hull himself has to say." Fergus reached for the drawer.

"Hull left a message before he bumped himself off?"

"Don't you see? If he's living backwards, he came into my room, sat at the typewriter, wrote a message, and then killed himself. I just saw it being reeled off hindsideto. So when I 'saw' him taking an envelope out of this drawer, he was actually, in his own time-sequence, *putting it in*."

"I'll believe you," said Jackson, "when I see . . ."

Fergus had pulled the drawer open. There lay a fat envelope, inscribed:

FOR FERGUS O'BREEN FROM JONATHAN HULL.

"All right," said the Lieutenant, "so your conclusion is correct. That still doesn't mean your reasoning is. How can a man live backwards? You might as well ask the universe to run in reverse entropy."

"Maybe it does," said Fergus. "Maybe Hull just found out how to go forwards."

Jackson snorted. "Well, let's see what he says."

Fergus read, " 'The first indication of my strange destiny was that I could see ghosts, or so I then interpreted the phenomena.' "

Jackson groaned. "Ghosts we have again! Fergus, I will not have the supernatural. The parascientific is bad enough, but the supernatural—*no!*"

"Is there necessarily any difference?" Fergus asked. "What we haven't found the answer to, we call supernatural. Maybe Jonathan Hull found an answer or two. Subside, Andy, and let's settle down to this."

They settled.

THE NARRATIVE OF JONATHAN HULL

The first indication of my strange destiny was that I could see ghosts, or so I then interpreted the phenomena. The first such episode occurred when I was five years old and came in from the yard to tell the family that I had been playing with Gramps. Since my grandfather had died the previous year in that mysterious postwar epidemic, the family was not a little concerned as to my veracity; but no amount of spanking shook me from my conviction.

Again in my twentieth year, I was visited in my lodgings near the Institute by my father, who had died when I was fifteen. The two visitations were curiously similar. Both apparitions spoke unintelligible gibberish and walked with awkwardly careful movements.

If not already, you will soon recognize these two traits, Mr. O'Breen. When I add that the Hulls are noted for the marked physical resemblance between generations, you will readily understand the nature of these apparent ghosts.

On neither of these occasions did I feel any of the conventional terror of revenants. In the first case, because I was too young to realize the implications of the visit; in the second, because I had by my twentieth year already reached the conclusion that my chief interest in life lay in the fringes of normal existence.

Too much of scientific work, by the time I reached the Institute, was being devoted to further minute exploration of the already known, and too little to any serious consideration of the unknown or half known, the shadowy blurs on the edges of our field of vision. To pursue the work as mathematical physicist for which I was training myself meant, I feared, a blind alley of infinite refinement and elaboration.

To be sure, there was the sudden blossoming of atomic power which had begun after the war, when peacetime allowed the scientists of the world to pool their recent discoveries with no fear lest they be revealing a possible secret weapon. But the work that needed doing now in that field was that of the mechanic, the technician. Theory was becoming fixed and settled, and it was upon my skill in theoretical matters that I prided myself.

Yes, I was the bright young lad then. There were no limits to my aspirations. The world should glow with the name of Hull. And behold me now: a ghost even to myself, a murderer, and soon a suicide. Already, if my understanding of the reversal is correct, my body lies in that corner; but I cannot turn my eyes to it to verify my assumption. And I was always more satisfied with the theory than with the fact.

I was the prodigy of the Institute. I was the shining star. And Lucifer was a shining star, too.

When the United Nations established the World Institute for Paranormal Research at Basle, I recognized my niche. My record at the local institute and my phenomenal score in the aptitude test made my admission a matter of course. And once surrounded by the magnificent facilities of the WIPR, I began to bestow upon the name of Hull certain small immortalities.

Yes, there is that consolation. The name of Hull will never quite die while extra-sensory perception is still measured in terms of the H. Q., the Hull quotient, or while Hull's "Co-ordinating Concordance to the Data of Charles Fort" still serves as a standard reference work. Nor, I suppose, while mystery-mongers probe the disappearance of Jonathan Hull and couple his name with those of Sir Benjamin Bathurst and the captain of the *Mary Celeste*—a fate that shall be averted, Mr. O'Breen, if you follow carefully the instructions which I shall give you later.

But more and more one aspect of the paranormal began to absorb me. I concentrated on it, devouring everything I could obtain in fact or fiction, until I was recognized as the WIPR's outstanding authority upon the possibilities of chronokinesis, or time travel.

It was a happy day when I hit upon that word *chronokinesis*. Its learned sound seemed to remove the concept from the vulgar realm of the time machines cheapened by fiction fantasists. But even with this semantic advantage, I still had many prejudices to battle, both among the populace and among my own colleagues. For even the very men who had established extra-sensory perception upon a scientific basis could still sneer at time travel.

I knew, of course, of earlier attempts. And now, I realize, Mr. O'Breen, why I was inclined to trust you the moment I saw your card. It was through a fortunately preserved letter of your sister's, which found its way into our archives, that we knew of the early fiasco of Harrison Partridge and your part therein. We knew, too, of the researches of Dr. Derringer, and how he gave up in despair after his time traveler failed to return, having encountered who knows what unimaginable future barrier.

We learned of no totally successful chronokinetic experiment. But from what we did know of the failures, I was able to piece together a little of what I felt must be the truth. Surely the method must involve the rotation of a temporomagnetic field against the "natural" time stream, and Hackendorf's current researches would make the establishment of such a field a simple matter.

It was then that I hit upon my concept of reversed individual entropy—setting, so to speak, the machinery of the individual running in an order opposite to the normal, so that movement along the "contrary" direction of the time stream would be for him natural and feasible.

This was what brought about the break. There were some among my colleagues who thought the notion ridiculous. There were others, those hyperserious scientists who take upon themselves the airs of hierophants, who found it even sacrilegious and evil. There were a few practical souls who simply feared it to be impossibly dangerous.

There was not one who would tolerate my experiments. And that is why, Lucifer-like, I severed my connection with the WIPR and retired to America, to pursue by myself the chronokinetic researches which would, I was sure, make Hull a name to rank with the greatest in all the history of science.

It was at this time that Tim Givens enters into the story. My own character I think you will have gathered sufficiently from these pages, but of Givens I must give a more explicit picture.

He was almost twenty years older than I, and I was then thirty. This was in 1971, which meant that he was just a boy fresh out of high school at the time of the war. His first experience of life was to find himself in an aircraft factory earning highly impressive sums. He had no sooner adjusted himself to a wonderful and extravagant life than he was drafted and shortly engaged in slaughtering Japanese in the Second Malayan Campaign.

He came back from the war pitiably maladjusted. It was difficult enough for most young men to return to civilian life; it was impossible for Tim Givens, because the only civilian life he had known, the lavish boom of war industry, was no more. We skillfully avoided a postwar depression, true, but we did not return to the days when untrained boys in their teens could earn more in a week than their fathers had hoped to see in a month.

Givens felt that he had saved the world, and that the world in return owed him the best.   He took part payment on that debt when and where he could.   He was not a criminal; he was simply a man who took short cuts whenever possible.

I cannot say that I liked him.   But he was recommended to me through remote family connections; he had a shiftily alert mind; and he had picked up, in the course of his many brief jobs, a surprising mechanical dexterity and ingenuity.   The deciding factor, of course, was that the skilled technicians I should have wished to employ were reluctant to work with a man who had left the WIPR under something of a cloud.

So I took Givens on as my handyman and assistant.   Personal relationships had never formed a major element in my life.   I thought that I could tolerate his narrow selfishness, his occasional banal humor, his basic crassness.   I did not realize how lasting some personal relationships may be.

And I went on working on the theory of reversed entropy.   My calculations will be found in my laboratory.   It would be useless to give them here.   They would be meaningless in 1941; so much depends upon the variable significance of the Tamirovich factor—discovered 1958—and the peculiar proportions of the alloy duralin—developed in the 1960's—and my own improvement on it which I had intended to christen chronalin.

The large stationary machine—stationary both in space and in time—was to furnish the field which would make it possible for us to free ourselves from the "normal" flow of time.   The small handsets were to enable us to accelerate and decelerate and eventually, I trusted, to reverse our temporal motion.

This, I say, was the plan.   As to what ultimately happened . . .

I am sure that Tim Givens substituted a cheaper grade of duralin for the grade which had met my tests.   He could have netted a sizable profit on the substitution, and it would have been typical of his petty opportunism.   He never admitted as much, but I remain convinced.

And so what happened was this:

We entered the large machine.   For a moment I had been worried.   I thought I had seen two suspicious-looking figures backing into the room by the rear door, and I feared vandalism.   But a check-up indicated nothing wrong and no sign of intruders; and I pressed the control.

I cannot describe that sensation to anyone who has not experienced it.   A sudden wrenching that seems to take all your vitals, carefully turn them inside out in some fourth dimension, and replace them neatly in your shaken body.   A horrible sensation?   I suppose so; but at the moment it was beautiful to me.   It meant that something had happened.

Even Tim Givens looked beautiful to me, too.   He was my partner on the greatest enterprise of the century—of the centuries.   I had insisted on his presence because

I wanted a witness for my assertions later; and he had assented because, I think, he foresaw a mint of money to be earned in television lectures by "The Man Who Traveled in Time."

I adjusted the handset to a high acceleration so that we might rapidly reach a point sufficiently past to be striking. (Givens' handset was tele-synchronized with mine; I did not trust his own erratic impulse.) At the end of ten minutes I was frowning perplexedly. We were still in the stationary machine and we should by now have passed the point at which I constructed it.

Givens did not notice my concern, but casually asked, "O. K. yet, M. S.?" He thought it humorous to call me "M. S.," which was, indeed, one of my degrees but which he insisted stood for Mad Scientist.

Whatever was wrong I would not find it out by staying there. Perhaps nothing whatsoever had happened. And yet that curious wrenching sensation surely indicated that the temporomagnetic field had had some effect.

I beckoned to Givens to follow me, and we stepped out of the machine. Two men were backing away from it in the distance. Their presence and their crablike retrograde motion worried me, and reminded me of those other two whom we had only glimpsed. To avoid them, we hastily slipped out the rear door, and into a world gone mad.

For a moment I had the absurd notion that some inconceivable error had catapulted us into the far distant future. Surely nothing else could account for a world in which men walked rapidly backwards along sidewalks and conversed in an unheard of gibberish.

But the buildings were those of 1971. The sleek atomic motorcars, despite their fantastic reverse motion, were the familiar 1972 models. I realized the enormity of our plight just as Tim Givens ejaculated, "M. S., everything's going backwards."

"Not everything," I said succinctly, and added none too grammatically, "Just us."

I knew now who the two crab-backing men were that we had seen in the laboratory: ourselves. And I recognized, too, what conspicuous figures we must now be, walking backwards along the sidewalk. Already we were receiving curious stares, which seemed to us, of course, to come just before the starers noticed us.

"Stand still," I said. "We're attracting attention. We don't want to advertise our situation, whatever it is."

We stood there for an hour, while I alternately experimented with the handsets and wrestled with the problem of our existence. The former pursuit I soon found completely fruitless. Obviously the handsets exerted no effect whatsoever upon our status. The latter was more rewarding, for in that hour I had fixed several of the rules necessary to our reversed existence.

It had been early morning when we entered the stationary machine, and by now the sun was already setting in the east—a phenomenon to which I found perhaps more difficulty in adjusting myself than anything else that befell us. "As I recall," I said, "last night, which we are now reapproaching, was exceedingly cold. We need shelter. The laboratory was unoccupied last night. Come."

Followed, or rather preceded, by the stares of passersby we returned to the laboratory, and there for a moment found peace.   The disturbingly arsy—versy normal world was shut off from us, and nothing reminded us of our perverse condition save the clock which persistently told off the minutes counterclockwise.

"We shall have to face the fact," I said, "that we are living backwards."

"I don't get it," Givens objected.   "I thought we were going to go time-traveling."

"We are," I smiled ruefully, and yet not without a certain pride.   "We are traveling backwards in time, something that no one in the history of our race has hitherto accomplished.   But we are doing so at the rate, if I may put it somewhat paradoxically, of exactly one second per second; so that the apparent result is not noticeable travel, but simply reverse living."

"O. K.," he grunted.   "Spread on the words any way you want.   But this is what's bothering me the most: When are we going to eat?"

I confess that I myself was feeling a certain nervous hunger by now.   "There's always food in this small icebox here," I said.   I was exceedingly fond of scrambled eggs at midnight when working on a problem.   "What would you say to beer and eggs?"

I took out a plastic beer-tainer, pressed down the self-opener, and handed it to Givens as it began to foam.   I took another for myself.   It felt good and reassuringly normal as it went down.

Then I set down the beer-tainer, found a frying pan, and put it on the small electric range.   I fetched four eggs from the icebox and returned to the stove to find no frying pan.   I reached out another—it looked like the same one—but handling frying pans while holding four eggs is difficult.   Both eggs and pan escaped my grip and went rolling off to a corner of the lab.   I hastened after them, cloth in hand to clean up the mess.

There was no mess.   There was no frying pan either, and no eggs.

Dazed, I returned to my beer.   And there was no beer.

I got another beer-tainer out of the icebox, and sipping from it I drew a most important conclusion.   Physical objects which we wore or held were affected by our fields and remained with us.   Anything which we set down went on its normal course—away from us forever.

This meant that cooking was impossible for us.   So we would be eating in a restaurant, for we and the waiter would be going in temporally opposite directions. I explained this to Givens while we ate cheese.

"It's just a sample," I said, "of the problems we have ahead of us.   If it weren't for the bare chance of achieving a reversal sometime, I should be tempted to shuffle off this coil now."

It took him a moment to gather my meaning.   Then he guffawed and said, "Uh uh, M. S.   Not for little Timmy.   Life's the one thing to hold on to—the one thing worth living.   And even if it's a screwy wrongwayround life, I'm holding on."

Authors of your time, Mr. O'Breen, have occasionally written of time in reverse; but have they ever realized the petty details that such a life involves?   All contact with other humanity is impossible.   I have, through thirty years of practice, developed a certain ability to understand reverse speech, but no one can understand me in return.   And even by written messages, how can an exchange be carried on if you ask me a question at 12:00 o'clock and I answer it at 11:59?

Then there is the problem of food.   Not only this question of cooking; but how is one to buy food?   How, as one's own clothes wear out, is one to replace them? Imagine yourself speeding along on an empty train, while another train laden with all the necessities of life passes on the parallel track in the opposite direction.

The torture of Tantalus was nothing to this.

I owe my life, such as it is, to Tim Givens, for it was his snide ingenuity which solved this problem.   "It's a cinch," he said, "we just steal it."

We had by now learned to walk backwards, so that we could move along the streets without exciting too much comment.   Visualize this, and you will see that a man walking backwards from 12:00 to 11:55 looks like a man walking forwards from 11:55 to 12:00.

Visualize it further: A man moving in this wise who enters a store empty-handed at 12:00 and leaves loaded with food at 11:50 looks like a normal man who comes in with a full shopping bag at 11:50 and leaves without it at 12:00—a peculiar procedure, but not one to raise a cry of "Stop thief!"

My conscience rebelled, but necessity is proverbially not cognizant of laws.   So we could live.   We could have whatever we wanted, so long as we kept it on our persons.   There was a period when Givens ran amok with this power.   He plundered the city.   For a time he possessed an untold fortune in banknotes and gold and precious gems.   But their weight tired him in the end; crime has no zest when it is neither punishable nor profitable.

Work was impossible.   I tried to do the necessary research and experiment to reverse our courses, but nothing could be achieved when all inanimate objects departed on another time stream as soon as I ceased to hold them.   I could read, and did read inordinately, plundering libraries as eagerly as food stores.   Sometimes I thought I saw a glimmering of hope, but it was the false daylight at the mouth of an endless and self-extending tunnel.

I missed music, although after some twenty years I did succeed in cultivating a taste for the unthinkable progressions of music heard in reverse.   Givens, I think, missed knavery; at last the world was giving him gratis the living which it owed him, and he was bored.

So we took to travel—which was accomplished, of course, by climbing backwards onto a boat or train at its destination and traveling back with it to its origin.   In strange foreign lands the strangeness of reversal is less marked.   And a magnificent mountain, a glinting glacier is free from time.

The best part of travel was waterfalls—perhaps the one advantage of our perverse state.   You cannot conceive the awesome stateliness of a river leaping hundreds of meters in the air.   We even made a special trip to British Guiana to see Kukenaam; and beholding it, I felt almost reconciled to my life.

I was most tormented when I despairingly abandoned any scientific research and took to reading novels.   Human relationships, which had seemed so unnecessary to my self-absorbed life, now loomed all-significant.   I wanted companionship, friendship, perhaps even love, as I had never wanted fame and glory.

And what did I have?   Givens.

The only man with whom I could communicate in all the universe.

We tried separation occasionally, but never without appointing a meeting place and time for which we were always both early.   Loneliness is a terrible thing, as no one else of my race can fully know.

We were inseparable.   We needed each other.   And we hated each other.

I hated Givens for his banal humor, his cheap self-interest.

He hated me for my intellect, my pride.

And each laid on the other the blame for our present fate.

And so, a few days ago, I realized that Givens was planning to kill me.   In a way, I think it was not so much from hatred of me as because he had missed for thirty years the petty conniving of his old life and now at last saw that a grand crime was possible for him.

He thought that he was hiding it from me.   Of course he could not.   I knew every bulge of the possessions that he wore, and easily recognized the revolver when he stole it and added it to his gear.

We were in Los Angeles because I had come to look at myself.   I found an odd pleasure in doing that occasionally, as you will have realized from my "ghosts," a bitter sort of joy.   So now I stood in the Queen of the Angels Hospital peering through glass at my red-faced yowling two-day-old self.   A nurse smiled at me with recognition, and I saw she thought I was Gramps.   There, looking at my beginning life, I resolved to save my life, however tortured and reversed it was.

We were then living in the room you know on West Adams.   For some time we had developed the technique of watching for people moving into a place.   After that—before, from the normal viewpoint—the place is untenanted and safe for our abode for a while.

I returned to the room to find Tim Givens' body on the bed.   Then I knew that death had the power to stop our wanderings, that the dead body resumed its normal movement in time.   And I knew what else I must do.

The rest of that scene you know.   How I took your card, gave your official-looking friend my confession, and backed out—when you thought me entering.

When I next visited the room, Givens was there alive.   It was surprisingly simple.   Underestimating me in practical matters, he was not on his guard.   I secured the revolver with no trouble.   Just before I pressed the trigger—for the bullet, freed from my field, moved for a moment in normal time—I saw the bullet strike.

I pressed hard, and gave him release.

Now I seek it for myself.   Only death can end this Odyssey, this voyage of loneliness and pain compared to which *The Flying Dutchman* sailed on a luxury cruise.   And when this manuscript is typed, I shall swallow the cyanide I stole yesterday.

This manuscript must reach the World Institute for Paranormal Research. They will find my notes in my laboratory. They must know that those who foretold danger were right, that my method must not be used again save with serious revision.

And yet this cannot reach them before the experiment: for they would stop me and I was not stopped. Seal it, then, place it in the hands of some trustworthy institution. And inscribe on it:

To be delivered to the World Institute for Paranormal Research, Basle, Switzerland, F.E.D. Feb. 3, 1971.

Perhaps the name of Hull may yet not be forgotten.

Fergus O'Breen swore comprehensively for a matter of minutes. "The egoist! The low-down egocentric idiot! Think what he could have told us! How the war came out, how the peace was settled, how atomic power was finally developed! And what does he give us? Nothing that doesn't touch him!"

"I wish that was all I had to worry about," said Detective Lieutenant A. Jackson morosely.

"There are hints, of course. Obviously a United Nations victory or he wouldn't have been living in such a free world in 1971. And that F.E.D. in the address . . ."

"What would that mean?"

"Maybe Federated European Democracies—I hope. But at least we've learned a wonderful new word. Chronokinesis . . ." He savored it.

Jackson rose gloomily. "And I've got to get down to the office and try to write a report on this. I'll take this manuscript."

"Uh-uh. This was given me in trust, Andy. And somehow it's going to get to the WIRP on the appointed date."

"O. K. I'm just as glad. If the Inspector saw *that* in the files . . . Want to come down with me and see what we can cook up?"

"Thanks no, Andy. I'm headed for the Queen of the Angels."

"The hospital? Why?"

"Because," Fergus grinned, "I want to see what a two-day-old murderer looks like."

H. BEAM PIPER

Police Operation

. . . there may be something in the nature of an occult police force, which operates to divert human suspicions, and to supply explanations that are good enough for whatever, somewhat in the nature of minds, human beings have—or that, if there be occult mischief makers and occult ravagers, they may be of a world also of other beings that are acting to check them, and to explain them, not benevolently, but to divert suspicion from themselves, because they, too, may be exploiting life upon this earth, but in ways more subtle, and in orderly, or organized, fashion.

Charles Fort: *"LO!"*

John Strawmyer stood, an irate figure in faded overalls and sweatwhitened black shirt, apart from the others, his back to the weathered farm-buildings and the line of yellowing woods and the cirrus-streaked blue October sky. He thrust out a work-gnarled hand accusingly.

"That there heifer was worth two hund'red, two hund'red an' fifty dollars!" he clamored. "An' that there dog was just one uh the fam'ly. An' now look at'm! I don't like t' use profane language, but you'ns gotta *do* some'n about this!"

Steve Parker, the district game protector, aimed his Leica at the carcass of the dog and snapped the shutter. "We're doing something about it," he said shortly. Then he stepped ten feet to the left and edged around the mangled heifer, choosing an angle for his camera shot.

The two men in the gray whipcords of the State police, seeing that Parker was through with the dog, moved in and squatted to examine it. The one with the triple chevrons on his sleeves took it by both forefeet and flipped it over on its back. It had been a big brute, of nondescript breed, with a rough black-and-brown coat. Something had clawed it deeply about the head, its throat was slashed transversely several times, and it had been disemboweled by a single slash that had opened its belly from breastbone to tail. They looked at it carefully, and then went to stand beside Parker while he photographed the dead heifer. Like the dog, it had been talon-raked on either side of the head, and its throat had been slashed deeply several times. In addition, flesh had been torn from one flank in great strips.

113

"I can't kill a bear outa season, no!" Strawmyer continued his plaint. "But a bear comes an' kills my stock an' my dog; that there's all right! That's the kinda deal a farmer always gits, in this state! I don't like t' use profane language—"

"Then don't!" Parker barked at him, impatiently. "Don't use any kind of language. Just put in your claim and shut up!" He turned to the men in whipcords and gray Stetsons. "You boys seen everything?" he asked. "Then let's go."

They walked briskly back to the barnyard, Strawmyer following them, still vociferating about the wrongs of the farmer at the hands of a cynical and corrupt State government. They climbed into the State police car, the sergeant and the private in front and Parker into the rear, laying his camera on the seat beside a Winchester carbine.

"Weren't you pretty short with that fellow back there, Steve?" the sergeant asked as the private started the car.

"Not too short. 'I don't like t' use profane language'," Parker mimicked the bereaved heifer owner, and then he went on to specify: "I'm morally certain that he's shot at least four illegal deer in the last year. When and if I ever get anything on him, he's going to be sorrier for himself then he is now."

"They're the characters that always beef their heads off," the sergeant agreed. "You think that whatever did this was the same as the others?"

"Yes. The dog must have jumped it while it was eating at the heifer. Same superficial scratches about the head, and deep cuts on the throat or belly. The bigger the animal, the farther front the big slashes occur. Evidently something grabs them by the head with front claws, and slashes with hind claws; that's why I think it's a bobcat."

"You know," the private said, "I saw a lot of wounds like that during the war. My outfit landed on Mindanao, where the guerrillas had been active. And this looks like bolo-work to me."

"The surplus-stores are full of machetes and jungle knives," the sergeant considered. "I think I'll call up Doc Winters, at the County Hospital, and see if all his squirrel-fodder is present and accounted for."

"But most of the livestock was eaten at, like the heifer," Parker objected.

"By definition, nuts have abnormal tastes," the sergeant replied. "Or the eating might have been done later, by foxes."

"I hope so; that'd let me out," Parker said.

"Ha, listen to the man!" the private howled, stopping the car at the end of the lane. "He thinks a nut with a machete and a Tarzan complex is just good clean fun. Which way, now?"

"Well, let's see." The sergeant had unfolded a quadrangle sheet; the game protector leaned forward to look at it over his shoulder. The sergeant ran a finger from one to another of a series of variously colored crosses which had been marked on the map.

"Monday night, over here on Copperhead Mountain, that cow was killed," he said. "The next night, about ten o'clock, that sheep-flock was hit, on this side of Copperhead, right about here. Early Wednesday night, that mule got slashed up in the woods back of the Weston farm.   It was only slightly injured; must have kicked the whatzit and got away, but the whatzit wasn't too badly hurt, because a few hours later, it hit that turkey-flock on the Rhymer farm.   And last night, it did that.''   He jerked a thumb over his shoulder at the Strawmyer farm.   ''See, following the ridges, working toward the southeast, avoiding open ground, killing only at night.   Could be a bobcat, at that.''

''Or Jink's maniac with the machete,'' Parker agreed.   ''Let's go up by Hindman's gap and see if we can see anything.''

They turned, after a while, into a rutted dirt road, which deteriorated steadily into a grass-grown track through the woods.   Finally, they stopped, and the private backed off the road.   The three men got out; Parker with his Winchester, the sergeant checking the drum of a Thompson, and the private pumping a buckshot shell into the chamber of a riot gun.   For half an hour, they followed the brush-grown trail beside the little stream; once, they passed a dark gray commercial-model jeep, backed to one side.   Then they came to the head of the gap.

A man wearing a tweed coat, tan field boots, and khaki breeches, was sitting on a log, smoking a pipe; he had a bolt-action rifle across his knees, and a pair of binoculars hung from his neck.   He seemed about thirty years old, and any bobby-soxer's idol of the screen would have envied him the handsome regularity of his strangely immobile features.   As Parker and the two State policemen approached, he rose, slinging his rifle, and greeted them.

''Sergeant Haines, isn't it?'' he asked pleasantly.   ''Are you gentlemen out hunting the critter, too?''

''Good afternoon, Mr. Lee.   I thought that was your jeep I saw, down the road a little.''   The sergeant turned to the others.   ''Mr. Richard Lee; staying at the old Kinchwalter place, the other side of Rutter's Fort.   This is Mr. Parker, the district game protector.   And Private Zinkowski.''   He glanced at the rifle. ''Are you out hunting for it, too?''

''Yes, I thought I might find something, up here.   What do you think it is?''

''I don't know,'' the sergeant admitted.   ''It could be a bobcat.   Canada lynx. Jinx, here, has a theory that it's some escapee from the paper-doll factory, with a machete.   Me, I hope not, but I'm not ignoring the possibility.''

The man with the matinee-idol's face nodded.   ''It could be a lynx.   I understand they're not unknown, in this section.''

''We paid bounties on two in this county, in the last year,'' Parker said.   ''Odd rifle you have there; mind if I look at it?''

''Not at all.''   The man who had been introduced as Richard Lee unslung and handed it over.   ''The chamber's loaded,'' he cautioned.

''I never saw one like this,'' Parker said.   ''Foreign?''

''I think so.   I don't know anything about it; it belongs to a friend of mine, who loaned it to me.   I think the action's German, or Czech; the rest of it's a custom job, by some West Coast gunmaker.   It's chambered for some ultra-velocity wildcat load.''

The rifle passed from hand to hand; the three men examined it in turn, commenting admiringly.

"You find anything, Mr. Lee?" the sergeant asked, handing it back.

"Not a trace." The man called Lee slung the rifle and began to dump the ashes from his pipe. "I was along the top of this ridge for about a mile on either side of the gap, and down the other side as far as Hindman's Run; I didn't find any tracks, or any indication of where it had made a kill."

The game protector nodded, turning to Sergeant Haines.

"There's no use us going any farther," he said. "Ten to one, it followed that line of woods back of Strawmyer's, and crossed over to the other ridge. I think our best bet would be the hollow at the head of Lowrie's Run. What do you think?"

The sergeant agreed. The man called Richard Lee began to refill his pipe methodically.

"I think I shall stay here for a while, but I believe you're right. Lowrie's Run, or across Lowrie's Gap into Coon Valley," he said.

After Parker and the State policemen had gone, the man whom they had addressed as Richard Lee returned to his log and sat smoking, his rifle across his knees. From time to time, he glanced at his wrist watch and raised his head to listen. At length, faint in the distance, he heard the sound of a motor starting.

Instantly, he was on his feet. From the end of the hollow log on which he had been sitting, he produced a canvas musette-bag. Walking briskly to a patch of damp ground beside the little stream, he leaned the rifle against a tree and opened the bag. First, he took out a pair of gloves of some greenish, rubberlike substance, and put them on, drawing the long gauntlets up over his coat sleeves. Then he produced a bottle and unscrewed the cap. Being careful to avoid splashing his clothes, he went about, pouring a clear liquid upon the ground in several places. Where he poured, white vapors rose, and twigs and grass grumbled into brownish dust. After he had replaced the cap and returned the bottle to the bag, he waited for a few minutes, then took a spatula from the musette and dug where he had poured the fluid, prying loose four black, irregular-shaped lumps of matter, which he carried to the running water and washed carefully, before wrapping them and putting them in the bag, along with the gloves. Then he slung bag and rifle and started down the trail to where he had parked the jeep.

Half an hour later, after driving through the little farming village of Rutter's Fort, he pulled into the barnyard of a rundown farm and backed through the open doors of the barn. He closed the double doors behind him, and barred them from within. Then he went to the rear wall of the barn, which was much closer to the front than the outside dimensions of the barn would have indicated.

He took from his pocket a black object like an automatic pencil. Hunting over the rough plank wall, he found a small hole and inserted the pointed end of the pseudo-pencil, pressing on the other end. For an instant, nothing happened. Then a ten-foot-square section of the wall receded two feet and slid noiselessly to one side. The section which had slid inward had been built of three-inch steel, masked by a thin covering of boards; the wall around it was two-foot concrete, similarly camouflaged. He stepped quickly inside.

Fumbling at the right side of the opening, he found a switch and flicked it. Instantly, the massive steel plate slid back into place with a soft, oily click. As it did, lights came on within the hidden room, disclosing a great semiglobe of some fine metallic mesh, thirty feet in diameter and fifteen in height. There was a sliding door at one side of this; the man called Richard Lee opened and entered through it, closing it behind him. Then he turned to the center of the hollow dome, where an armchair was placed in front of a small desk below a large instrument panel. The gauges and dials on the panel, and the levers and switches and buttons on the desk control board, were all lettered and numbered with characters not of the Roman alphabet or the Arabic notation, and, within instant reach of the occupant of the chair, a pistol-like weapon lay on the desk. It had a conventional index-finger trigger and a hand-fit grip, but, instead of a tubular barrel, two slender parallel metal rods extended about four inches forward of the receiver, joined together at what would correspond to the muzzle by a streamlined knob of some light blue ceramic or plastic substance.

The man with the handsome immobile face deposited his rifle and musette on the floor beside the chair and sat down. First, he picked up the pistol-like weapon and checked it, and then he examined the many instruments on the panel in front of him. Finally, he flicked a switch on the control board.

At once, a small humming began, from some point overhead. It wavered and shrilled and mounted in intensity, and then fell to a steady monotone. The dome about him flickered with a queer, cold iridescence, and slowly vanished. The hidden room vanished, and he was looking into the shadowy interior of a deserted barn. The barn vanished; blue sky appeared above, streaked with wisps of high cirrus cloud. The autumn landscape flickered unreally. Buildings appeared and vanished, and other buildings came and went in a twinkling. All around him, half-seen shapes moved briefly and disappeared.

Once, the figure of a man appeared, inside the circle of the dome. He had an angry, brutal face, and he wore a black tunic piped with silver, and black breeches, and polished black boots, and there was an insignia, composed of a cross and thunderbolt, on his cap. He held an automatic pistol in his hand.

Instantly, the man at the desk snatched up his own weapon and thumbed off the safety, but before he could lift and aim it, the intruder stumbled and passed outside the force-field which surrounded the chair and instruments.

For a while, there were fires raging outside, and for a while, the man at the desk was surrounded by a great hall, with a high, vaulted ceiling, through which figures flitted and vanished. For a while, there were vistas of deep forests, always set in the same background of mountains and always under the same blue cirrus-laced sky. There was an interval of flickering blue-white light, of unbearable intensity. Then the man at the desk was surrounded by the interior of vast industrial works. The moving figures around him slowed, and became more distinct. For an instant, the man in the chair grinned as he found himself looking into a big washroom, where a tall blond girl was taking a shower bath, and a pert little redhead was vigorously drying herself with a towel. The dome grew visible, coruscating with many-colored lights and then the humming died and the dome became a cold and inert mesh of fine white metal.   A green light above flashed on and off slowly.

He stabbed a button and flipped a switch, then got to his feet, picking up his rifle and musette and fumbling under his shirt for a small mesh bag, from which he took an inch-wide disk of blue plastic.   Unlocking a container on the instrument panel, he removed a small roll of solidograph-film, which he stowed in his bag. Then he slid open the door and emerged into his own dimension of space-time.

Outside was a wide hallway, with a pale green floor, paler green walls, and a ceiling of greenish off-white.   A big hole had been cut to accommodate the dome, and across the hallway a desk had been set up, and at it sat a clerk in a pale blue tunic, who was just taking the audio-plugs of a music-box out of his ears.   A couple of policemen in green uniforms, with ultrasonic paralyzers dangling by thongs from their left wrists and holstered sigma-ray needlers like the one on the desk inside the dome, were kidding with some girls in vivid orange and scarlet and green smocks.   One of these, in bright green, was a duplicate of the one he had seen rubbing herself down with a towel.

"Here comes your boss-man," one of the girls told the cops, as he approached. They both turned and saluted casually.   The man who had lately been using the name of Richard Lee responded to their greeting and went to the desk.   The policemen grasped their paralyzers, drew their needlers, and hurried into the dome.

Taking the disk of blue plastic from his packet, he handed it to the clerk at the desk, who dropped it into a slot in the voder in front of him.   Instantly, a mechanical voice responded:

"Verkan Vall, blue-seal noble, hereditary Mavrad of Nerros.   Special Chief's Assistant, Paratime Police, special assignment.   Subject to no orders below those of Tortha Karf, Chief of Paratime Police.   To be given all courtesies and cooperation within the Paratime Transposition Code and the Police Powers Code.   Further particulars?"

The clerk pressed the "no" button.   The blue sigil fell out the release-slot and was handed back to its bearer, who was drawing up his left sleeve.

"You'll want to be sure I'm *your* Verkan Vall, I suppose?" he said, extending his arm.

"Yes, quite, sir."

The clerk touched his arm with a small instrument which swabbed it with antiseptic, drew a minute blood-sample, and medicated the needle prick, all in one almost painless operation.   He put the blood-drop on a slide and inserted it at one side of a comparison microscope, nodding.   It showed the same distinctive permanent colloid pattern as the sample he had ready for comparison; the colloid pattern given in infancy by injection to the man in front of him, to set him apart from all the myriad other Verkan Valls on every other probability-line of paratime.

"Right, sir," the clerk nodded.

The two policemen came out of the dome, their needlers holstered and their vigilance relaxed.   They were lighting cigarettes as they emerged.

"It's all right, sir," one of them said.   "You didn't bring anything in with you, this trip."

The other cop chuckled.   "Remember that Fifth Level wild-man who came in on the freight conveyor at Jandar, last month?" he asked.

If he was hoping that some of the girls would want to know what wild-man, it was a vain hope.   With a blue-seal mavrad around, what chance did a couple of ordinary coppers have?   The girls were already converging on Verkan Vall.

"When are you going to get that monstrosity out of our rest room," the little redhead in green coveralls was demanding.   "If it wasn't for that thing, I'd be taking a shower, right now."

"You were just finishing one, about fifty paraseconds off, when I came through," Verkan Vall told her.

The girl looked at him in obviously feigned indignation.

"Why, you— You *parapeeper!*"

Verkan Vall chuckled and turned to the clerk.   "I want a strato-rocket and pilot, for Dhergabar, right away.   Call Dhergabar Paratime Police Field and give them my ETA; have an air-taxi meet me, and have the chief notified that I'm coming in.   Extraordinary report.   Keep a guard over the conveyor; I think I'm going to need it, again, soon."   He turned to the little redhead.   "Want to show me the way out of here, to the rocket field?" he asked.

Outside, on the open landing field, Verkan Vall glanced up at the sky, then looked at his watch.   It had been twenty minutes since he had backed the jeep into the barn on that distant other time-line; the same delicate lines of white cirrus were etched across the blue above.   The constancy of the weather, even across two hundred thousand parayears of perpendicular time, never failed to impress him. The long curve of the mountains was the same, and they were mottled with the same autumn colors, but where the little village of Rutter's Fort stood on that other line of probability, the white towers of an apartment-city rose—the living quarters of the plant personnel.

The rocket that was to take him to headquarters was being hoisted with a crane and lowered into the firing-stand, and he walked briskly toward it, his rifle and musette slung.   A boyish-looking pilot was on the platform, opening the door of the rocket; he stood aside for Verkan Vall to enter, then followed and closed it, dogging it shut while his passenger stowed his bag and rifle and strapped himself into a seat.

"Dhergabar Commercial Terminal, sir?" the pilot asked, taking the adjoining seat at the controls.

"Paratime Police Field, back of the Paratime Administration Building."

"Right, sir.   Twenty seconds to blast, when you're ready."

"Ready now."   Verkan Vall relaxed, counting seconds subconsciously.

The rocket trembled, and Verkan Vall felt himself being pushed gently back against the upholstery.   The seats, and the pilot's instrument panel in front of them, swung on gimbals, and the finger of the indicator swept slowly over a ninety-degree arc as the rocket rose and leveled.   By then, the high cirrus clouds Verkan Vall had watched from the field were far below; they were well into the stratosphere.

There would be nothing to do, now, for the three hours in which the rocket sped northward across the pole and southward to Dhergabar; the navigation was entirely in the electronic hands of the robot controls.   Verkan Vall got out his pipe and lit it; the pilot lit a cigarette.

"That's an odd pipe, sir," the pilot said.   "Out-time item?"

"Yes, Fourth Probability Level; typical of the whole paratime belt I was working in."   Verkan Vall handed it over for inspection.   "The bowl's natural brier-root; the stem's a sort of plastic made from the sap of certain tropical trees.   The little white dot is the maker's trademark; it's made of elephant tusk."

"Sounds pretty crude to me, sir."   The pilot handed it back.   "Nice workmanship, though.   Looks like good machine production."

"Yes.   The sector I was on is really quite advanced, for an electro-chemical civilization.   That weapon I brought back with me—that solid-missile projector— is typical of most Fourth Level culture.   Moving parts machined to the closest tolerances, and interchangeable with similar parts of all similar weapons.   The missile is a small bolt of cupro-alloy coated lead, propelled by expanding gases from the ignition of some nitro-cellulose compound.   Most of their scientific advance occurred within the past century, and most of that in the past forty years. Of course, the life-expectancy on that level is only about seventy years."

"Humph!   I'm seventy-eight, last birthday," the boyish-looking pilot snorted. "Their medical science must be mostly witchcraft!"

"Until quite recently, it was," Verkan Vall agreed.   "Same story there as in everything else—rapid advancement in the past few decades, after thousands of years of cultural inertia."

"You know, sir, I don't really understand this paratime stuff," the pilot confessed.   "I know that all time is totally present, and that every moment has its own past-future line of event-sequence, and that all events in space-time occur according to maximum probability, but I just don't get this alternate probability stuff, at all.   If something exists, it's because it's the maximum-probability effect of prior causes; why does anything else exist on any other time-line?"

Verkan Vall blew smoke at the air-renovator.   A lecture on paratime theory would nicely fill in the three-hour interval until the landing at Dhergabar.   At least, this kid was asking intelligent questions.

"Well, you know the principle of time-passage, I suppose?" he began.

"Yes, of course; Rhogom's Doctrine.   The basis of most of our psychical science.   We exist perpetually at all moments within our life-span; our extraphysical ego component passes from the ego existing at one moment to the ego existing at the next.   During unconsciousness, the EPC is 'time-free'; it may detach, and connect at some other moment, with the ego existing at that time-point.   That's how we precog.   We take an autohypno and recover memories brought back from the future moment and buried in the subconscious mind."

"That's right," Verkan Vall told him.   "And even without the autohypno, a lot of precognitive matter leaks out of the subconscious and into the conscious mind, usually in distorted forms, or else inspires 'instinctive' acts, the motivation for which is not brought to the level of consciousness.   For instance, suppose, you're walking along North Promenade, in Dhergabar, and you come to the Martian

Palace Cafe, and you go in for a drink, and meet some girl, and strike up an acquaintance with her.   This chance acquaintance develops into a love affair, and a year later, out of jealousy, she rays you half a dozen times with a needler.''

"Just about that happened to a friend of mine, not long ago," the pilot said. "Go on, sir."

"Well, in the microsecond or so before you die—or afterward, for that matter, because we know that the extraphysical component survives physical destruction— your EPC slips back a couple of years and re-connects at some point pastward of your first meeting with this girl, and carries with it memories of everything up to the moment of detachment, all of which are indelibly recorded in your subconscious mind.   So, when you re-experience the event of standing outside the Martian Palace with a thirst, you go on to the Starway, or Nhergal's, or some other bar.   In both cases, on both time-lines, you follow the line of maximum probability; in the second case, your subconscious future memories are an added causal factor.''

"And when I back-slip, after I've been needled, I generate a new time-line?   Is that it?''

Verkan Vall made a small sound of impatience.   "No such thing!" he exclaimed. "It's semantically inadmissible to talk about the total presence of time with one breath and about generating new time-lines with the next.   *All* time-lines are totally present, in perpetual co-existence.   The theory is that the EPC passes from one moment, on one time-line, to the next moment on the next line, so that the true passage of the EPC from moment to moment is a two-dimensional diagonal. So, in the case we're using, the event of your going into the Martian Palace exists on one time-line, and the event of your passing along to the Starway exists on another, but both are events in real existence.

"Now, what we do, in paratime transposition, is to build up a hypertemporal field to include the time-line we want to reach, and then shift over to it.   Same point in the plenum; same point in primary time—plus primary time elapsed during mechanical and electronic lag in the relays—but a different line of secondary time.''

"Then why don't we have past-future time travel on our own time-line?" the pilot wanted to know.

That was a question every paratimer has to answer, every time he talks paratime to the laity.   Verkan Vall had been expecting it; he answered patiently.

"The Ghaldron-Hesthor field-generator is like every other mechanism; it can operate in the area of primary time in which it exists.   It can transpose to any other time-line, and carry with it anything inside its field, but it can't go outside its own temporal area of existence, any more than a bullet from that rifle can hit the target a week before it's fired," Verkan Vall pointed out.   "Anything inside the field is supposed to be unaffected by anything outside.   *Supposed to be* is the way to put it; it doesn't always work.   Once in a while, something pretty nasty gets picked up in transit."   He thought, briefly, of the man in the black tunic. "That's why we have armed guards at terminals.''

"Suppose you pick up a blast from a nucleonic bomb," the pilot asked, "or something red-hot, or radioactive?''

"We have a monument, at Paratime Police Headquarters, in Dhergabar, bearing the names of our own personnel who didn't make it back. It's a large monument; over the past ten thousand years, it's been inscribed with quite a few names.''

"You can have it; I'll stick to rockets!" the pilot replied. "Tell me another thing, though: What's all this about levels, and sectors, and belts? What's the difference?

"Purely arbitrary terms. There are five main probability levels, derived from the five possible outcomes of the attempt to colonize this planet, seventy-five thousand years ago. We're on the First Level—complete success, and colony fully established. The Fifth Level is the probability of complete failure—no human population established on this planet, and indigenous quasi-human life evolved indigenously. On the Fourth Level, the colonists evidently met with some disaster and lost all memory of their extraterrestrial origin, as well as all extraterrestrial culture. As far as they know, they are an indigenous race; they have a long pre-history of stone-age savagery.''

"Sectors are areas of paratime on any level in which the prevalent culture has a common origin and common characteristics. They are divided more or less arbitrarily into sub-sectors. Belts are areas within sub-sectors where conditions are the result of recent alternate probabilities. For instance, I've just come from the Europo-American Sector of the Fourth Level, an area of about ten thousand parayears in depth, in which the dominant civilization developed on the North-West Continent of the Major Land Mass, and spread from there to the Minor Land Mass. The line on which I was operating is also part of a sub-sector of about three thousand parayears' depth, and a belt developing from one of several probable outcomes of a war concluded about three elapsed years ago. On that time-line, the field at the Hagraban Synthetics Works, where we took off, is part of an abandoned farm; on the site of Hagraban City is a little farming village. Those things are there, right now, both in primary time and in the plenum. They are about two hundred and fifty thousand parayears perpendicular to each other, and each is of the same general order of reality.''

The red light overhead flashed on. The pilot looked into his visor and put his hands to the manual controls, in case of failure of the robot controls. The rocket landed smoothly, however; there was a slight jar as it was grappled by the crane and hoisted upright, the seats turning in their gimbals. Pilot and passenger un-strapped themselves and hurried through the refrigerated outlet and away from the glowing-hot rocket.

An air-taxi, emblazoned with the device of the Paratime Police, was waiting. Verkan Vall said goodby to the rocket-pilot and took his seat beside the pilot of the aircab; the latter lifted his vehicle above the building level and then set it down on the landing-stage of the Paratime Police Building in a long, side-swooping glide. An express elevator took Verkan Vall down to one of the middle stages, where he showed his sigil to the guard outside the door of Tortha Karf's office and was admitted at once.

The Paratime Police chief rose from behind his semicircular desk, with its array of keyboards and viewing-screens and communicators. He was a big man, well past his two hundredth year; his hair was iron-gray and thinning in front, he had begun to grow thick at the waist, and his calm features bore the lines of middle age.   He wore the dark-green uniform of the Paratime Police.

"Well, Vall," he greeted.   "Everything secure?"

"Not exactly, sir."   Verkan Vall came around the desk, deposited his rifle and bag on the floor, and sat down in one of the spare chairs.   "I'll have to go back again."

"So?"   His chief lit a cigarette and waited.

"I traced Gavran Sarn."   Verkan Vall got out his pipe and began to fill it. "But that's only the beginning.   I have to trace something else.   Gavran Sarn exceeded his Paratime permit, and took one of his pets along.   A Venusian nighthound."

Tortha Karf's expression did not alter; it merely grew more intense.   He used one of the short, semantically ugly terms which serve, in place of profanity, as the emotional release of a race that has forgotten all the taboos and terminologies of supernaturalistic religion and sex inhibition.

"You're sure of this, of course."   It was less a question than a statement.

Verkan Vall bent and took cloth-wrapped objects from his bag, unwrapping them and laying them on the desk.   They were casts, in hard black plastic, of the footprints of some large three-toed animal.

"What do these look like, sir?" he asked.

Tortha Karf fingered them and nodded.   Then he became as visibly angry as a man of his civilization and culture-level ever permitted himself.

"What does that fool think we have a Paratime Code for?" he demanded. "It's entirely illegal to transpose any extraterrestrial animal or object to any time-line on which space-travel is unknown.   I don't care if he is a green-seal thavrad; he'll face charges, when he gets back, for this!"

"He *was* a green-seal thavrad," Verkan Vall corrected.   "And he won't be coming back."

"I hope you didn't have to deal summarily with him," Tortha Karf said.   "With his title, and social position, and his family's political importance, that might make difficulties.   Not that it wouldn't be all right with me, of course, but we never seem to be able to make either the Management or the public realize the extremities to which we are forced, at times."   He sighed.   "We probably never shall."

Verkan Vall smiled faintly.   "Oh, no, sir; nothing like that.   He was dead before I transposed to that time-line.   He was killed when he wrecked a self-propelled vehicle he was using.   One of those Fourth Level automobiles.   I posed as a relative and tried to claim his body for the burial-ceremony observed on that cultural level, but was told that it had been completely destroyed by fire when the fuel tank of this automobile burned.   I was given certain of his effects which had passed through the fire; I found his sigil concealed inside what appeared to be a cigarette case."   He took a green disk from the bag and laid it on the desk. "There's no question; Gavran Sarn died in the wreck of that automobile."

"And the nighthound?"

"It was in the car with him, but it escaped.   You know how fast those things are. I found that track''—he indicated one of the black casts—''in some dried mud near the scene of the wreck. As you see, the cast is slightly defective. The others were fresh this morning, when I made them.''

''And what have you done so far?''

''I rented an old farm near the scene of the wreck, and installed my field-generator there. It runs through to the Hagraban Synthetics Works, about a hundred miles east of Thalna-Jarvizar. I have my this-line terminal in the girls' rest room at the durable plastics factory; handled that on a local police-power writ. Since then, I've been hunting for the nighthound. I think I can find it, but I'll need some special equipment, and a hypno-mech indoctrination. That's why I came back.''

''Has it been attracting any attention?'' Tortha Karf asked anxiously.

''Killing cattle in the locality; causing considerable excitement. Fortunately, it's a locality of forested mountains and valley farms, rather than a built-up industrial district. Local police and wild game protection officers are concerned; all the farmers excited and going armed. The theory is that it's either a wildcat of some sort, or a maniac armed with a cutlass. Either theory would conform, more or less, to the nature of its depredations. Nobody has actually seen it.''

''That's good!'' Tortha Karf was relieved. ''Well, you'll have to go and bring it out, or kill it and obliterate the body. You know why, as well as I do.''

''Certainly, sir,'' Verkan Vall replied. ''In a primitive culture, things like this would be assigned supernatural explanations, and imbedded in the locally accepted religion. But this culture, while nominally religious, is highly rationalistic in practice. Typical lag-effect, characteristic of all expanding cultures. And this Europo-American Sector really has an expanding culture. A hundred and fifty years ago, the inhabitants of this particular time-line didn't even know how to apply steam power; now they've begun to release nuclear energy, in a few crude forms.''

Tortha Karf whistled, softly. ''That's quite a jump. There's a sector that'll be in for trouble in the next few centuries.''

''That is realized, locally, sir.'' Verkan Vall concentrated on relighting his pipe, for a moment, then continued: ''I would predict space-travel on that sector within the next century. Maybe the next half-century, at least to the Moon. And the art of taxidermy is very highly developed. Now, suppose some farmer shoots that thing; what would he do with it, sir?''

Tortha Karf grunted. ''Nice logic, Vall. On a most uncomfortable possibility. He'd have it mounted, and it'd be put in a museum, somewhere. And as soon as the first spaceship reaches Venus, and they find those things in a wild state, they'll have the mounted specimen identified.''

''Exactly. And then, instead of beating their brains about *where* their specimen came from, they'll begin asking *when* it came from. They're quite capable of such reasoning, even now.''

''A hundred years isn't a particularly long time,'' Tortha Karf considered. ''I'll be retired, then, but you'll have my job, and it'll be your headache. You'd better get this cleaned up, now, while it can be handled. What are you going to do?''

"I'm not sure, now, sir. I want a hypno-mech indoctrination, first." Verkan Vall gestured toward the communicator on the desk. "May I?" he asked.

"Certainly." Tortha Karf slid the instrument across the desk. "Anything you want."

"Thank you, sir." Verkan Vall snapped on the code-index, found the symbol he wanted, and then punched it on the keyboard. "Special Chief's Assistant Verkan Vall," he identified himself. "Speaking from office of Tortha Karf, Chief Paratime Police. I want a complete hypno-mech on Venusian nighthounds, emphasis on wild state, special emphasis domesticated nighthounds reverted to wild state in terrestrial surroundings, extra-special emphasis hunting techniques applicable to same. The word 'nighthound' will do for trigger-symbol." He turned to Tortha Karf. "Can I take it here?"

Tortha Karf nodded, pointing to a row of booths along the far wall of the office. "Make set-up for wired transmission; I'll take it here."

"Very well, sir; in fifteen minutes," a voice replied out of the communicator.

Verkan Vall slid the communicator back. "By the way, sir; I had a hitchhiker, on the way back. Carried him about a hundred or so parayears; picked him up about three hundred parayears after leaving my other-line terminal. Nasty-looking fellow, in a black uniform; looked like one of those private army storm troopers you find all through that sector. Armed, and hostile. I thought I'd have to ray him, but he blundered outside the field almost at once. I have a record, if you'd care to see it."

"Yes, put it on." Tortha Karf gestured toward the solidograph-projector. "It's set for miniature reproduction here on the desk; that be all right?"

Verkan Vall nodded, getting out the film and loading it into the projector. When he pressed a button, a dome of radiance appeared on the desk top, two feet in width and a foot in height. In the middle of this appeared a small solidograph-image of the interior of the conveyor, showing the desk, and the control board, and the figure of Verkan Vall seated at it. The little figure of the storm trooper appeared, pistol in hand. The little Verkan Vall snatched up his tiny needler; the storm trooper moved into one side of the dome and vanished.

Verkan Vall flipped a switch and cut out the image.

"Yes. I don't know what causes that, but it happens, now and then," Tortha Karf said. "Usually at the beginning of a transposition. I remember, when I was just a kid, about a hundred and fifty years ago—a hundred and thirty-nine, to be exact—I picked up a fellow on the Fourth Level, just about where you're operating, and dragged him a couple of hundred parayears. I went back to find him and return him to his own time-line, but before I could locate him, he'd been arrested by the local authorities as a suspicious character, and got himself shot trying to escape. I felt badly about that, but—" Tortha Karf shrugged. "Anything else happen on the trip?"

"I ran through a belt of intermittent nucleonic bombing on the Second Level." Verkan Vall mentioned an approximate paratime location.

"Aaagh! That Khiftan civilization—by courtesy so called!" Tortha Karf pulled a wry face. "I suppose the intra-family enmities of the Hvadka Dynasty have reached critical mass again. They'll fool around till they blast themselves back to the stone age."

"Intellectually, they're about there, now. I had to operate in that sector once— Oh, yes, another thing, sir. This rifle." Verkan Vall picked it up, emptied the magazine and handed it to his superior. "The supplies office slipped up on this; it's not appropriate to my line of operation. It's a lovely rifle, but it's about two hundred percent in advance of existing arms design on my line. It excited the curiosity of a couple of police officers and a game-protector, who should be familiar with the weapons of their own time-line. I evaded by disclaiming ownership or intimate knowledge, and they seemed satisfied, but it worried me."

"Yes. That was made in our duplicating shops here in Dhergabar." Tortha Karf carried it to a photographic bench, behind his desk. "I'll have it checked, while you're taking your hypno-mech. Want to exchange it for something authentic?"

"Why, no, sir. It's been identified to me, and I'd excite less suspicion with it than I would if I abandoned it and mysteriously acquired another rifle. I just wanted a check, and Supplies warned to be more careful in future."

Tortha Karf nodded approvingly. The young Mavrad of Nerros was thinking as a paratimer should.

"What's the designation of your line again?"

Verkan Vall told him. It was a short numerical term of six places, but it expressed a number of the order of ten to the fortieth power, exact to the last digit. Tortha Karf repeated it into his stenomemograph, with explanatory comment.

"There seems to be quite a few things going wrong, in that area," he said. "Let's see now."

He punched the designation on a keyboard; instantly, it appeared on a translucent screen in front of him. He punched another combination, and, at the top of the screen under the number, there appeared: EVENTS, PAST ELAPSED FIVE YEARS.

He punched again; below this line appeared the subheading: EVENTS INVOLVING PARATIME TRANSPOSITION.

Another code-combination added a third line: (ATTRACTING PUBLIC NOTICE AMONG INHABITANTS.)

He pressed the "start" button; the headings vanished, to be replaced by page after page of print, succeeding one another on the screen as the two men read. They told strange and apparently disconnected stories—of unexplained fires and explosions; of people vanishing without trace; of unaccountable disasters to aircraft. There were many stories of an epidemic of mysterious disk-shaped objects seen in the sky, singly or in numbers. To each account was appended one or more reference-numbers. Sometimes Tortha Karf or Verkan Vall would punch one of these, and read, on an adjoining screen, the explanatory matter referred to.

Finally Tortha Karf leaned back and lit a fresh cigarette.

"Yes, indeed, Vall; very definitely we will have to take action in the matter of the runaway nighthound of the late Gavran Sarn," he said. "I'd forgotten that

that was the time-line onto which the *Ardrath* expedition launched those antigrav disks.   If this extraterrestrial monstrosity turns up, on the heels of that 'Flying Saucer' business, everybody above the order of intelligence of a cretin will suspect some connection.''

"What really happened, in the *Ardrath* matter?'' Verkan Vall inquired.   "I was on the Third Level, on that Luvarian Empire operation, at the time.''

"That's right; you missed that.   Well, it was one of these joint operation things. The Paratime Commission and the Space Patrol were experimenting with a new technique for throwing a spaceship into paratime.   They used the cruiser *Ardrath*, Kalzarn Jann commanding.   Went into space about halfway to the Moon and took up orbit, keeping on the sunlit side of the planet to avoid being observed.   That was all right.   But then, Captain Kalzarn ordered away a flight of antigrav disks, fully manned, to take pictures, and finally authorized a landing in the western mountain range, Northern Continent, Minor Land-Mass.   That's when the trouble started.''

He flipped the run-back switch, till he had recovered the page he wanted.   Verkan Vall read of a Fourth Level aviator, in his little airscrew-drive craft, sighting nine high-flying saucerlike objects.

"That was how it began,'' Tortha Karf told him.   "Before long, as other incidents of the same sort occurred, our people on that line began sending back to know what was going on.   Naturally, from the different descriptions of these 'saucers,' they recognized the objects as antigrav landing-disks from a spaceship. So I went to the Commission and raised atomic blazes about it, and the *Ardrath* was ordered to confine operations to the lower areas of the Fifth Level.   Then our people on that time-line went to work with corrective action.   Here.''

He wiped the screen and then began punching combinations.   Page after page appeared, bearing accounts of people who had claimed to have seen the mysterious disks, and each report was more fantastic than the last.

"The standard smother-out technique,'' Verkan Vall grinned.   "I only heard a little talk about the 'Flying Saucers,' and all of that was in joke.   In that order of culture, you can always discredit one true story by setting up ten others, palpably false, parallel to it—   Wasn't that the time-line the Tharmax Trading Corporation almost lost their paratime license on?''

"That's right; it was!   They bought up all the cigarettes, and caused a con- spicuous shortage, after Fourth Level cigarettes had been introduced on this line and had become popular.   They should have spread their purchases over a number of lines, and kept them within the local supply-demand frame.   And they also got into trouble with the local government for selling unrationed petrol and automobile tires.   We had to send in a special-operations group, and they came closer to having to engage in out-time local politics than I care to think of.''   Tortha Karf quoted a line from a currently popular song about the sorrows of a policeman's life. "We're jugglers, Vall; trying to keep our traders and sociological observers and tourists and plain idiots like the late Gavran Sarn out of trouble; trying to prevent panics and disturbances and dislocations of local economy as a result of our op- erations; trying to keep out of out-time politics—and, at all times, at all costs and hazards, by all means, guarding the secret of paratime transposition.   Sometimes I wish Ghaldron Karf and Hesthor Ghrom had strangled in their cradles!''

Verkan Vall shook his head.   ''No, chief,'' he said.   ''You don't mean that; not really,'' he said.   ''We've been paratiming for the past ten thousand years. When the Ghaldron-Hesthor trans-temporal field was discovered, our ancestors had pretty well exhausted the resources of this planet.   We had a world population of half a billion, and it was all they could do to keep alive.   After we began paratime transposition, our population climbed to ten billion, and there it stayed for the last eight thousand years.   Just enough of us to enjoy our planet and the other planets of the system to the fullest; enough of everything for everybody that nobody needs fight anybody for anything.   We've tapped the resources of those other worlds on other time-lines, a little here, a little there, and not enough to really hurt anybody. We've left our mark in a few places—the Dakota Badlands, and the Gobi, on the Fourth Level, for instance—but we've done no great damage to any of them.''

''Except the time they blew up half the Southern Island Continent, over about five hundred parayears on the Third Level,'' Tortha Karf mentioned.

''Regrettable accident, to be sure,'' Verkan Vall conceded.   ''And look how much we've learned from the experiences of those other time-lines.   During the Crisis, after the Fourth Interplanetary War, we might have adopted Palnar Sarn's 'Dictatorship of the Chosen' scheme, if we hadn't seen what an exactly similar scheme had done to the Jak-Hakka Civilization, on the Second Level.   When Palnar Sarn was told about that, he went into paratime to see for himself, and when he returned, he renounced his proposal in horror.''

Tortha Karf nodded.   He wouldn't be making any mistake in turning his post over to the Mavrad of Nerros on his retirement.

''Yes, Vall; I know,'' he said.   ''But when you've been at this desk as long as I have, you'll have a sour moment or two, now and then, too.''

A blue light flashed over one of the booths across the room.   Verkan Vall got to his feet, removing his coat and hanging it on the back of his chair, and crossed the room rolling up his left shirt sleeve.   There was a relaxer-chair in the booth, with a blue plastic helmet above it.   He glanced at the indicator screen to make sure he was getting the indoctrination he called for, and then sat down in the chair and lowered the helmet over his head, inserting the ear plugs and fastening the chin strap.   Then he touched his left arm with an injector which was lying on the arm of the chair, and at the same time flipped the starter switch.

Soft, slow music began to chant out of the earphones.   The insidious fingers of the drug blocked off his senses, one by one.   The music diminished, and the words of the hypnotic formula lulled him to sleep.

He woke, hearing the lively strains of dance music.   For a while, he lay relaxed. Then he snapped off the switch, took out the ear plugs, removed the helmet and rose to his feet.   Deep in his subconscious mind was the entire body of knowledge about the Venusian nighthound.   He mentally pronounced the word, and at once it began flooding into his conscious mind.   He knew the animal's evolutionary history, its anatomy, its characteristics, its dietary and reproductive habits, how it hunted, how it fought its enemies, how it eluded pursuit, and how best it could be tracked down and killed.   He nodded.   Already, a plan for dealing with Gavran Sarn's renegade pet was taking shape in his mind.

He picked a plastic cup from the dispenser, filled it from a cooler-tap with amber-colored spiced wine, and drank, tossing the cup into the disposal-bin.   He placed a fresh injector on the arm of the chair, ready for the next user of the booth.   Then he emerged, glancing at his Fourth Level wrist watch and mentally translating to the First Level time-scale.   Three hours had passed; there had been more to learn about his quarry than he had expected.

Tortha Karf was sitting behind his desk, smoking a cigarette.   It seemed as though he had not moved since Verkan Vall had left him, though the special agent knew that he had dined, attended several conferences, and done many other things.

"I checked up on your hitchhiker, Vall," the chief said.   "We won't bother about him.   He's a member of something called the Christian Avengers—one of those typical Europo-American race-and-religious hate groups.   He belongs in a belt that is the outcome of the Hitler victory of 1940, whatever that was.   Something unpleasant, I dare say.   We don't owe him anything; people of that sort should be stepped on like cockroaches.   And he won't make any more trouble on the line where you dropped him than they have there already.   It's in a belt of complete social and political anarchy; somebody probably shot him as soon as he emerged, because he wasn't wearing the right sort of a uniform.   Nineteen-forty what, by the way?"

"Elapsed years since the birth of some religious leader," Verkan Vall explained. "And did you find out about my rifle?"

"Oh, yes.   It's a reproduction of something that's called a Sharp's Model '37,235 Ultraspeed-Express.   Made on an adjoining paratime belt by a company that went out of business sixty-seven years ago, elapsed time, on your line of operation. What made the difference was the Second War Between The States.   I don't know what that was, either—I'm not too well up on Fourth Level history—but whatever, your line of operation didn't have it.   Probably just as well for them, though they very likely had something else, as bad or worse.   I put in a complaint to Supplies about it, and got you some more ammunition and reloading tools.   Now, tell me what you're going to do about this nighthound business."

Tortha Karf was silent for a while, after Verkan Vall had finished.

"You're taking some awful chances, Vall," he said, at length.   "The way you plan doing it, the advantages will all be with the nighthound.   Those things can see as well at night as you can in daylight.   I suppose you know that, though; you're the nighthound specialist, now."

"Yes.   But they're accustomed to the Venus hotland marshes; it's been dry weather for the last two weeks, all over the northeastern section of the Northern Continent.   I'll be able to hear it, long before it gets close to me.   And I'll be wearing an electric headlamp.   When I snap that on, it'll be dazzled, for a moment."

"Well, as I said, you're the nighthound specialist.   There's the communicator;

order anything you need.''   He lit a fresh cigarette from the end of the old one before crushing it out.   ''But be careful, Vall.   It took me close to forty years to make a paratimer out of you; I don't want to have to repeat the process with somebody else before I can retire.''

The grass was wet as Verkan Vall—who reminded himself that here he was called Richard Lee—crossed the yard from the farmhouse to the ramshackle barn, in the early autumn darkness.   It had been raining that morning when the strato-rocket from Dhergabar had landed him at the Hagraban Synthetics Works, on the First Level; unaffected by the probabilities of human history, the same rain had been coming down on the old Kinchwalter farm, near Rutter's Fort, on the Fourth Level.   And it had persisted all day.

He didn't like that.   The woods would be wet, muffling his quarry's footsteps, and canceling his only advantage over the night-prowler he hunted.   He had no idea, however, of postponing the hunt.   If anything, the rain had made it all the more imperative that the nighthound be killed at once.   At this season, a falling temperature would speedily follow.   The nighthound, a creature of the hot Venus marshes, would suffer from the cold, and, taught by years of domestication to find warmth among human habitations, it would invade some isolated farmhouse, or, worse, one of the little valley villages.   If it were not killed tonight, the incident he had come to prevent would certainly occur.

Going to the barn, he spread an old horse blanket on the seat of the jeep, laid his rifle on it, and then backed the jeep outside.   Then he took off his coat, removing his pipe and tobacco from the pockets, and, spread it on the wet grass. He unwrapped a package and took out a small plastic spray-gun he had brought with him from the First Level, aiming it at the coat and pressing the trigger until it blew itself empty.   A sickening, rancid fetor tainted the air—the scent of the giant poison roach of Venus, the one creature for which the nighthound bore an inborn, implacable hatred.   It was because of this compulsive urge to attack and kill the deadly poison roach that the first human settlers on Venus, long millennia ago, had domesticated the ugly and savage nighthound.   He remembered that the Gavran family derived their title from their vast Venus hotlands estates; that Gavran Sarn, the man who had brought this thing to the Fourth Level, had been born on the inner planet.   When Verkan Vall donned that coat, he would become his own living bait for the murderous fury of the creature he sought.   At the moment, mastering his queasiness and putting on the coat, he objected less to that danger than to the hideous stench of the scent, to obtain which a valuable specimen had been sacrificed at the Dhergabar Museum of Extraterrestrial Zoology, the evening before.

Carrying the wrapper and the spray gun to an outside fireplace, he snapped his lighter to them and tossed them in.   They were highly inflammable, blazing up and vanishing in a moment.   He tested the electric headlamp on the front of his cap; checked his rifle; drew the heavy revolver, an authentic product of his line of operation, and flipped the cylinder out and in again.   Then he got into the jeep and drove away.

For half an hour, he drove quickly along the valley roads.   Now and then, he passed farmhouses, and dogs, puzzled and angered by the alien scent his coat bore, barked curiously.   At length, he turned into a back road, and from this to the barely discernible trace of an old log road.   The rain had stopped, and, in order to be ready to fire in any direction at any time, he had removed the top of the jeep. Now he had to crouch below the windshield to avoid overhanging branches.   Once, three deer—a buck and two does—stopped in front of him and stared for a moment, then bounded away with a flutter of white tails.

He was driving slowly, now; spraying behind him a reeking trail of scent.   There had been another stock killing the night before, while he had been on the First Level.   The locality of this latest depredation had confirmed his estimate of the beast's probable movements, and indicated where it might be prowling tonight. He was certain that it was somewhere near; sooner or later, it would pick up the scent.

Finally, he stopped, snapping out his lights.   He had chosen this spot carefully, while studying the Geological Survey map, that afternoon; he was on the grade of an old railroad line, now abandoned and its track long removed, which had served the logging operations of fifty years ago.   On one side, the mountain slanted sharply upward; on the other, it fell away sharply.   If the nighthound were below him, it would have to climb that forty-five degree slope, and could not avoid dislodging loose stones, or otherwise making a noise.   He would get out on that side; if the nighthound were above him, the jeep would protect him when it charged. He got to the ground, thumbing off the safety of his rifle, and an instant later he knew that he had made a mistake which could easily cost him his life; a mistake from which neither his comprehensive logic nor his hypnotically acquired knowledge of the beast's habits had saved him.

As he stepped to the ground, facing toward the front of the jeep, he heard a low, whining cry behind him, and a rush of padded feet.   He whirled, snapping on the headlamp with his left hand and thrusting out his rifle pistol-wise in his right.   For a split second, he saw the charging animal, its long, lizard-like head split in a toothy grin, its talon-tipped forepaws extended.

He fired, and the bullet went wild.   The next instant, the rifle was knocked from his hand.   Instinctively, he flung up his left arm to shield his eyes.   Claws raked his left arm and shoulder, something struck him heavily along the left side, and his cap-light went out as he dropped and rolled under the jeep, drawing in his legs and fumbling under his coat for the revolver.

In that instant, he knew what had gone wrong.   His plan had been entirely too much of a success.   The nighthound had winded him as he had driven up the old railroad grade, and had followed.   Its best running speed had been just good enough to keep it a hundred or so feet behind the jeep, and the motor noise had covered the padding of its feet.   In the few moments between stopping the little car and getting out, the nighthound had been able to close the distance and spring upon him.

It was characteristic of First Level mentality that Verkan Vall wasted no moments on self-reproach or panic.   While he was still rolling under his jeep, his mind had been busy with plans to retrieve the situation.   Something touched the heel of one boot, and he froze his leg into immobility, at the same time trying to get the big Smith & Wesson free.   The shoulder holster, he found, was badly torn, though made of the heaviest skirting leather, and the spring which retained the weapon in place had been wrenched and bent until he needed both hands to draw.   The eight-inch slashing claw of the nighthound's right intermediary limb had raked him; only the instinctive motion of throwing up his arm, and the fact that he wore the revolver in a shoulder holster, had saved his life.

The nighthound was prowling around the jeep, whining frantically.   It was badly confused.   It could see quite well, even in the close darkness of the starless night; its eyes were of a nature capable of perceiving infrared radiations as light.   There were plenty of these; the jeep's engine, lately running on four-wheel drive, was quite hot.   Had he been standing alone, especially on this raw, chilly night, Verkan Vall's own body heat would have lighted him up like a jack-o'-lantern.   Now, however, the hot engine above him masked his own radiations.   Moreover, the poison roach scent on his coat was coming up through the floor board and mingling with the scent on the seat, yet the nighthound couldn't find the two-and-a-half foot insectlike thing that should have been producing it.   Verkan Vall lay motionless, wondering how long the next move would be in coming.   Then he heard a thud above him, followed by a furious tearing as the nighthound ripped the blanket and began rending at the seat cushion.

"Hope it gets a paw full of seat springs," Verkan Vall commented mentally. He had already found a stone about the size of his two fists, and another slightly smaller, and had put one in each of the side pockets of the coat.   Now he slipped his revolver into his waist-belt and writhed out of the coat, shedding the ruined shoulder holster at the same time.   Wriggling on the flat of his back, he squirmed between the rear wheels, until he was able to sit up, behind the jeep.   Then, swinging the weighted coat, he flung it forward, over the nighthound and the jeep itself, at the same time drawing his revolver.

Immediately, the nighthound, lured by the sudden movement of the principal source of the scent, jumped out of the jeep and bounded after the coat, and there was considerable noise in the brush on the lower side of the railroad grade.   At once, Verkan Vall swarmed into the jeep and snapped on the lights.

His stratagem had succeeded beautifully.   The stinking coat had landed on the top of a small bush, about ten feet in front of the jeep and ten feet from the ground. The nighthound, erect on its haunches, was reaching out with its front paws to drag it down, and slashing angrily at it with its single clawed intermediary limb.   Its back was to Verkan Vall.

His sights clearly defined by the lights in front of him, the paratimer centered them on the base of the creature's spine, just above its secondary shoulders, and carefully squeezed the trigger.   The big .357 Magnum bucked in his hand and belched flame and sound—if only these Fourth Level weapons weren't so confoundedly boisterous!—and the nighthound screamed and fell.   Recocking the revolver, Verkan Vall waited for an instant, then nodded in satisfaction.   The beast's spine had been smashed, and its hind quarters, and even its intermediary fighting limbs had been paralyzed.   He aimed carefully for a second shot and fired into the base of the thing's skull.   It quivered and died.

*　　*　　*

Getting a flashlight, he found his rifle, sticking muzzle down in the mud a little behind and to the right of the jeep, and swore briefly in the local Fourth Level idiom, for Verkan Vall was a man who loved good weapons, be they sigma-ray needlers, neutron-disruption blasters, or the solid-missile projectors of the lower levels.　By this time, he was feeling considerable pain from the claw wounds he had received.　He peeled off his shirt and tossed it over the hood of the jeep.

Tortha Karf had advised him to carry a needler, or a blaster, or a neurostat-gun, but Verkan Vall had been unwilling to take such arms onto the Fourth Level.　In event of mishap to himself, it would be all too easy for such a weapon to fall into the hands of someone able to deduce from it scientific principles too far in advance of the general Fourth Level culture.　But there had been one First Level item which he had permitted himself, mainly because, suitably packaged, it was not readily identifiable as such.　Digging a respectable Fourth Level leatherette case from under the seat, he opened it and took out a pint bottle with a red poison label, and a towel.　Saturating the towel with the contents of the bottle, he rubbed every inch of his torso with it, so as not to miss even the smallest break made in his skin by the septic claws of the nighthound.　Whenever the lotion-soaked towel touched raw skin, a pain like the burn of a hot iron shot through him; before he was through, he was in agony.　Satisfied that he had disinfected every wound, he dropped the towel and clung weakly to the side of the jeep.　He grunted out a string of English oaths, and capped them with an obscene Spanish blasphemy he had picked up among the Fourth Level inhabitants of his island home of Nerros, to the south, and a thundering curse in the name of Mogga, Fire-God of Dool, in a Third-Level tongue.　He mentioned Fasif, Great God of Khift, in a manner which would have got him an acid-bath if the Khiftan priests had heard him.　He alluded to the baroque amatory practices of the Third-Level Illyalla people, and soothed himself, in the classical Dar-Halma tongue, with one of those rambling genealogical insults favored in the Indo-Turanian Sector of the Fourth Level.

By this time, the pain had subsided to an over-all smarting itch.　He'd have to bear with that until his work was finished and he could enjoy a hot bath.　He got another bottle out of the first-aid kit—a flat pint, labeled "Old Overholt," containing a locally-manufactured specific for inward and subjective wounds—and medicated himself copiously from it, corking it and slipping it into his hip pocket against future need.　He gathered up the ruined shoulder-holster and threw it under the back seat.　He put on his shirt.　Then he went and dragged the dead nighthound onto the grade by its stumpy tail.

It was an ugly thing, weighing close to two hundred pounds, with powerfully muscled hind legs which furnished the bulk of its motive-power, and sturdy three-clawed front legs.　Its secondary limbs, about a third of the way back from its front shoulders, were long and slender; normally, they were carried folded closely against the body, and each was armed with a single curving claw.　The revolver-bullet had gone in at the base of the skull and emerged under the jaw; the head was relatively undamaged.　Verkan Vall was glad of that; he wanted that head for the trophy-room of his home on Nerros.　Grunting and straining, he got the thing into the back of the jeep, and flung his almost shredded tweed coat over it.

A last look around assured him that he had left nothing unaccountable or suspicious.   The brush was broken where the nighthound had been tearing at the coat; a bear might have done that.   There were splashes of the viscid stuff the thing had used for blood, but they wouldn't be there long.   Terrestrial rodents liked nighthound blood, and the woods were full of mice.   He climbed in under the wheel, backed, turned, and drove away.

Inside the paratime-transposition dome, Verkan Vall turned from the body of the nighthound, which he had just dragged in, and considered the inert form of another animal—a stump-tailed, tuft-eared tawny Canada lynx.   That particular animal had already made two paratime-transpositions; captured in the vast wilderness of Fifth-Level North America, it had been taken to the First Level and placed in the Dhergabar Zoological Gardens, and then requisitioned on the authority of Tortha Karf, it had been brought to the Fourth Level by Verkan Vall.   It was almost at the end of its travels.

Verkan Vall prodded the supine animal with the toe of his boot; it twitched slightly.   Its feet were cross-bound with straps, but when he saw that the narcotic was wearing off, Verkan Vall snatched a syringe, parted the fur at the base of its neck, and gave it an injection.   After a moment, he picked it up in his arms and carried it out to the jeep.

"All right, pussy cat," he said, placing it under the rear seat, "this is the one-way ride.   The way you're doped up, it won't hurt a bit."

He went back and rummaged in the debris of the long-deserted barn.   He picked up a hoe, and discarded it as too light.   An old plowshare was too unhandy.   He considered a grate-bar from a heating furnace, and then he found the poleax, lying among a pile of worm-eaten boards.   Its handle had been shortened, at some time, to about twelve inches, converting it into a heavy hatchet.   He weighed it, and tried it on a block of wood, and then, making sure that the secret door was closed, he went out again and drove off.

An hour later, he returned.   Opening the secret door, he carried the ruined shoulder holster, and the straps that had bound the bobcat's feet, and the ax, now splotched with blood and tawny cat-hairs, into the dome.   Then he closed the secret room, and took a long drink from the bottle on his hip.

The job was done.   He would take a hot bath, and sleep in the farmhouse till noon, and then he would return to the First Level.   Maybe Tortha Karf would want him to come back here for a while.   The situation on this time-line was far from satisfactory, even if the crisis threatened by Gavran Sarn's renegade pet had been averted.   The presence of a chief's assistant might be desirable.

At least, he had a right to expect a short vacation.   He thought of the little redhead at the Hagraban Synthetics Works.   What was her name?   Something Kara—Morvan Kara; that was it.   She'd be coming off shift about the time he'd make First Level, tomorrow afternoon.

The claw-wounds were still smarting vexatiously.   A hot bath, and a night's sleep—   He took another drink, lit his pipe, picked up his rifle and started across the yard to the house.

*   *   *

Private Zinkowski cradled the telephone and got up from the desk, stretching. He left the orderly-room and walked across the hall to the recreation room, where the rest of the boys were loafing. Sergeant Haines, in a languid gin-rummy game with Corporal Conner, a sheriff's deputy, and a mechanic from the service station down the road, looked up.

"Well, Sarge, I think we can write off those stock-killings," the private said.

"Yeah?" The sergeant's interest quickened.

"Yeah. I think the whatzit's had it. I just got a buzz from the railroad cops at Logansport. It seems a track-walker found a dead bobcat on the Logan River branch, about a mile or so below MMY signal tower. Looks like it tangled with that night freight up-river, and came off second best. It was near chopped to hamburger."

"MMY signal tower; that's right below Yoder's Crossing," the sergeant considered. "The Strawmyer farm night-before-last, the Amrine farm last night— Yeah, that would be about right."

"That'll suit Steve Parker; bobcats aren't protected, so it's not his trouble. And they're not a violation of state law, so it's none of our worry," Conner said. "Your deal, isn't it, Sarge?"

"Yeah. Wait a minute." The sergeant got to his feet. "I promised Sam Kane, the AP man at Logansport, that I'd let him in on anything new." He got up and started for the phone. "Phantom Killer!" He blew an impolite noise.

"Well, it was a lot of excitement, while it lasted," the deputy sheriff said. "Just like that Flying Saucer thing."

JAMES BLISH and DAMON KNIGHT

Tiger Ride

2/4/2121

Tested the levitator units this morning. Both performed well with the dummies, and Laura insisted on trying one herself—they were tuned to her voice, anyhow. Chapelin objected, of course, but his wife overrode him as usual. I believe she was actually hoping there would be an accident.

Laura Peel said: "Just the same, I'm going to do it."

The wind was in her fair hair and pressing her clothes gently against the length of her slim body. She looked uncommonly beautiful, Hal Osborn thought. He wondered, what the devil does Chapelin see when he looks at her?

Chapelin's big blond face was a study in prudence and responsibility. He said: "Now let's not be unreasonable, Laura—"

Niki Chapelin's voice cut him off. "Oh, why not let her? It's perfectly safe, isn't it, Hal?"

"Nope," said Hal. If anything did happen, he thought all she'd have to do would be to remind everybody, "But Hal said—"

Her small mask turned toward him, and the basilisk eyes drilled holes in his forehead. He felt again the rising urge toward murder which often shook him these days; the isolation was beginning to tell on them all, and sometimes Hal thought he would abandon Laura and ultronics and all the rest for a chance to leave this God-forsaken tomb of a planet.

No, he corrected himself, not a tomb; a ghost, and the brother of a ghost. Styrtis Delta III was the satellite of a huge planet, which in turn swung around a Gray Ghost—a star so huge and rarefied that it gave no light. Luckily there was a yellow companion star which provided almost-normal days for half the year; the nights, rendered deep, livid blue-green by the reflection from the methane-swathed giant planet, were not normal, but they were bearable.

And the whole complicated system was in the corner of the galaxy where no possible explosion, no matter how titanic, could injure the works of man—in a limb of the stars which man had never before visited, and had scarcely mapped. The Earth Council had awarded this planet to the ultronics group, and given them the period of "summer" at Council expense to work out their discoveries.   When the yellow sun was eclipsed by the Gray Ghost, Styrtis Delta III would have a winter that might have made even Dante tremble.

The people who had once inhabited this planet must have been unique; the seasonal changes they had to withstand were terrific.   Whatever had killed them off, it hadn't been the weather, for the ruins of their cities still showed the open spaces and wide-spanned architecture of a race as used to storm as to quiet.   Maybe they'd killed each other off; storms of emotion could destroy things untouchable by Nature.

Luckily, Niki could spare Hal only the one look.   Chapelin was beginning to repeat all his arguments to her, and she had to turn on her heavy artillery: Mark IX, the look of bored impatience.

The levitator was an entirely new device, said Chapelin, it was new even in the hundred-kilo lab stage, let alone belt-size.   It wasn't just the danger of falling, he said, there was a thing made of platinum called a governor that was only three mm. long, and if that went, Laura could find herself digging a hole in the ground with two Gs behind her.   There were good reasons for never testing a new ultronic device in person before it had at least fifty hours' run on the dummies—dummies don't experiment with unfamiliar equipment, they don't move of their own accord in flight and disarrange things, they don't miscalculate and release the total ultimate energy that could consume a whole group of suns.

Niki was swinging her riding crop against her skinny tailored thigh.   She had come because she was Chapelin's wife, and because Laura was coming.   Ultronics interested her mildly, sometimes.

Hal stole a glance at Laura.   On the other side of her, little Mike Cohen was chewing his pipe, watching and saying nothing.   Hal met his speculative gaze, and looked away guiltily.   Laura's mouth had had that hurt, childish downcurve, the same as it always had when she was watching Chapelin unseen.   Her spine was as straight as ever, though.   She's licked, he thought, as she always gets licked.   She'll go through with it out of sheer defiance.

A star-shaped shadow passed slowly between Hal and the Chapelins.   He looked up.

"Wind's blowing them toward the edge of the plateau," he said.   "Better pull 'em back."

Everybody looked.   High over their heads, the two seven-foot manikins were canted slightly, their blank heads pointed toward the distant Killhope range.   "Wind's pretty strong up there," Chapelin said uncomfortably.   "You might as well bring them down, Laura."

Niki said: "*That's* better, dear.   You're so much nicer when you're not stubborn."

Chapelin turned back to her.   "Wait a minute," he said, "I didn't mean—"

"I'm going to do it anyhow," Laura said clearly, "whether you let me or not." Her lips compressed.   She watched the dummies and said: "Right.   Right— enough.   Down."

"Well," Chapelin said, "be careful."

Hal felt the surge of hatred again. Chapelin, can't you see she loves you? Won't you put up any kind of fight, make her see that you're worried about her? If you'd show the slightest interest, you could persuade her not to try it—

The dummies floated down until the tips of their legs touched the ground. They hung there, swaying gently. Laura said: "Stop," and they sat down abruptly as if their strings had been cut, then flopped over and lay sprawled on the sun-caked turf.

Chapelin had drawn his wife a couple of meters away and was talking to her earnestly. Niki was listening to him with no sign of impatience, which meant she was amused.

Hal choked and and walked over to the dummies. Laura was kneeling beside one of them, taking off its belt. She got up as he approached, her bare knees dusty.

"Let's have a look at it," Hal said. "That landing was a little rough."

She put the articulated silver band around her waist, leaving the one she'd been wearing on the ground. "Let me alone just now, Hal," she said in a barely audible voice. She stepped away and said: "Up."

The belt took her up.

Hal watched her go, squinting his eyes against the lemon-yellow sky. She went straight up, with a halo of saffron light on the top of her blond head, and stayed there until he was beginning to wonder if she was ever coming down again. Then she dropped swiftly, turned, and swooped over their heads.

Hal swore. Laura didn't know what "careful" meant. He was angry at himself for failing to try to stop her, and angry at her for taking out her feelings about Chapelin on them all. If that governor cut out, they might all die—the whole crazy solar system, the whole ridge of stars could be annihilated under certain conditions.

She was up high again now, so high she could barely be seen. Despite the hot sun on the plateau, it was cold that high up, cold and and blustery with the ceaseless blast of this planet's rapid revolution. Then she began to drop again, faster than she should, as if under power.

At the lip of the plateau, Laura seemed to see that she was going to miss it, and reversed the controls. The belt jerked her slantwise back toward them, and burned out in a flare of copper-colored energy. Everyone but Hal hit the ground and waited for the world to end.

Hal stayed on his feet, his mind a well of horror. Laura's body tumbled over their heads and struck just beyond them.

Then everyone was running.

Oh, yes; we buried old Jonas today. He was a quiet, pathetic little guy, but he wanted to go home like the rest of us; I wish we could have had his body shipped back, but twenty-five thousand volts doesn't leave much to ship. Besides the accident with Laura rather took our mind off him.

In the shack Hal shifted his weight uncomfortably on a drum. Mike Cohen was talking quietly, but Hal only half heard him. Laura lay on one of the cots, seemingly without a single bruise; but she was not breathing.   Chapelin was sitting beside her, wringing his hands in a blind, stupid way.   Niki had the good sense to be absent, out in the generator shed, congratulating herself, Hal supposed.

"I still think she's alive," Mike Cohen went on.   "We know so little about ultronics—every accident's a freak at this stage."

Hal stirred.   "The belt wasn't hurt," he said numbly.   "At first I thought it'd sliced her right in two."   He looked at the gleaming, jointed thing, still clasping Laura's waist.   They had been afraid to touch it—if there were still a residue of energy in there, and the governor gone—

"That's right.   And the fall should have broken all her bones.   She hit hard. But . . . I don't think she really hit at all.   Something took up the shock."

"What, then?"

A strangled sound came from the cot.   Hal started and stood up, his heart thudding under his breastbone.   The sound, however, had come from Chapelin, who was also standing, bending over Laura.

"Chapelin?   What is it?"

"She's breathing.   She started, all of a sudden.   I—"   His voice broke, and he stood silent, hands working at his sides.

But it was true.   Laura's breast was rising and falling regularly, naturally.   There was still no color in her face.

Even as Hal noted that, a faint tinge of pink crept in over her cheekbones.

"Thank God," Chapelin muttered.   "She's coming around."   He looked at Hal and at Mike Cohen, meeting their eyes for the first time since the accident. "It was funny.   I heard a sort of sigh, and when I looked, she was breathing just as if she'd been asleep.   Shall we try to get the belt off now?"

"I don't think we should," Mike said.   "It may still be in operation, and it's tuned to her.   Best wait till she tells it to turn off."

"How do you know it's still on?"

"It must be.   That flash of copper light—it was only an electrical short, or we'd none of us be here now.   We've never been able to overload an ultronic field before, and *something* must have shielded her during that fall."

On the cot, Laura whispered, quite clearly: "Is that you, Mike?   Where are you? I can't see you."

Chapelin bent over her.   "Laura," he said huskily.   "How do you feel?   Can you move a little?"

"I'm all right, but it seems so dark.   I can just barely make you out."

Mike Cohen chuckled, a small joyous sound.   "You're O.K., Laura.   We were too busy to remember about such little things as sunset."   He trotted quickly across the room and turned on the lights.   Laura sat up in the fluorescent glow and blinked at them.

For a moment no one could speak.   Then, from the doorway, Niki Chapelin's voice said: "Why darling!   What a *relief!*"

2/5/2121

Laura's not hurt, but naturally somewhat shocked emotionally.   We were all anxious to look at the innards of the belt, but she won't give it up; claims that it saved her life and that it goes with her uniform. In her present state of mind we dare not argue with her.

It was very quiet in the little laboratory; only the sound of Hal's breathing and the minute-ticking of the device upon which he was working broke the stillness. Outside the window, a silent landscape lay bathed in deep blue-green, like a vision of the bottom of a sea.

There was a modest knock on the door, and a dial on the table moved slightly. That, Hal knew, would be Laura; no one else would be carrying or wearing anything which would disturb an ultrometer, especially not at this hour. If only she'd surrender that belt! He wondered what she wanted of him.

The knock sounded again. "Come in," Hal said. The girl slipped past the door and closed it carefully.

"Hello, Hal."

"Hi. What can I do for you?"

"I got to feeling a little depressed and wanted company. Do you mind?"

"Chapelin's still up, I saw the light in the shack," Hal said sullenly. The next instant he could have bitten off his tongue; but Laura did not seem to react at all.

"No, I wanted to talk to you. What are you doing?"

He said wonderingly: "The same as always—trying to get enough of a grip on the ultronic flow to disrupt it. The little ticker here records the energy flux. If I can cause it to miss a beat now and then, I'll know I've managed to interfere. So far, no soap; we can direct the flow, but not modify it."

"Watch the blast limit."

Hal shrugged. That was the problem, of course. This energy was strictly sub-subatomic, somewhere nearby there was a nexus where the fields met, a nexus where cosmic rays were created, out of some ground energy called ultronic as a handy label. Chapelin thought there must be billions of such nexi in every galaxy, but they had been undetectable by their very nature until just recently. The Earth Council had been scared to death when Chapelin had reported the results of his first investigations, and had quarantined the whole group. Unless they could learn how to modify the forces involved—

"We've done well so far, all things considered," Hal said. "The moment we do badly, it'll be all up for us, and this whole corner of the universe."

Laura nodded seriously. Hal looked at her. As always, her loveliness hurt him, made it difficult to concentrate on what he was saying.

"But you didn't come here to talk ultronics, surely. Isn't there—"

She smiled, a little wistfully. "I don't care what we talk about, Hal. That accident—you don't go through a thing like that without being forced to think about things. I remembered your asking to see the belt before I went up, and how you tried to look out for me, and a lot of things you've done for me—and I knew all of a sudden that I owed you a lot more than I've been ready to admit."

Hal made an awkward gesture. "It's nothing, Laura. I've made no secret of how I feel.   If you don't share the feeling, those little attentions can become a nuisance, I know.''

"That's true," Laura said.   "And I realize now how careful you were not to . . . to force anything on me.   Not everybody would be that considerate, so many parsecs from any sort of civilization.   It's given me a chance to find out how I really do feel—that, and the accident.''

Hal felt his heart begin to thunder against his ribs, but he kept seated by sheer willpower.   "Laura," he said, "please don't feel that you have to commit yourself. It's really the parsecs that count the most.   When six people—five, now—are marooned, in close quarters, for so long, all kinds of unnatural emotional tensions develop.   It's best not to add to them if there's any way to avoid it.''

Laura nodded.   "I know.   But most of the tensions that are already here are my fault.   Oh, don't deny it, it's true.   Niki wouldn't be here if it weren't for me, and the way I feel about Chapelin.   I've been a useful lab technic, but emotionally I've always been in the way.   It's different now.   Chapelin—he's sort of a timid moose, isn't he?   I've been pretty blind.   I flatter myself that I can see, now.''   She toyed with an amber-handled, tiny screwdriver on the work-bench.   "That's—why I'm here.''

The blood roared in Hal's temples.   He said: "Laura—''

After that it was very quiet in the little shack.

2/8/2121

The Council survey ship came by yesterday, and we had a good report to make; if they could have landed, we'd have been able to show them things that would have made their eyes bug.   But they weren't going through our area, and only inquired in a routine way; Earth's still scared green of ultronics.   One funny business: when I reported Jonas's death— expecting all kinds of hows and whens and whys—the Ship's Recorder didn't seem to know what I was talking about.   "Jonas who?'' he said. "Did you have a stowaway?''   Evidently Earth has already forgotten us, and can't be bothered over whether there were five or six or thirteen in the group.

For a while things seemed to go along well enough; but Hal could not rid himself of the sensation that somewhere there was something radically wrong, if only he could find it.   Oh, there was Chapelin to account for some of it.   The accident, for which he could not help but hold himself responsible, seemed to have jarred some long-dormant cells to activity in Chapelin's mind.   For the first time he seemed to be looking at Laura as something besides a competent laboratory assistant. They were all aware of it, Niki most of all, of course—for Niki had suspected it even when it didn't exist—but it was marked enough to worry even Mike Cohen.

That caused tension, but it was the old, familiar kind of tension.   This other thing was—strange.   Hal couldn't pin it down; it was a general uneasiness, strongest when he saw the belt gleaming enigmatically about Laura's slim waist, and when he reviewed certain entries in his journal. It was as if he were awaiting some disaster he could not describe, and it kept him up late every night, crouched over the ticking little modulator.

Even there, he had enough success to make him hopeful; within three nights he was able to modulate the steady ultronic flow, and on the fourth night he discovered, all at once, a chain of improbable formulas describing the phenomenon—a chain which showed him that his next step would have triggered the blast whose echoes they all heard in nightmares.

It was as if there was a silent conspiracy afoot, a conspiracy to convince Hal that Everything was going to be All Right. He looked at the equations again; they were new, a brand of math he seemingly had invented on the spot— and he had "discovered" them about ten minutes before he would have set off an interstellar catastrophe.

There was one kind of math Hal knew as well as he knew his own name: permutations and combinations. A few sheets of paper later, he had worked out the chances against his making this particular discovery at this particular time. The result: 3×10^{18}. Such coincidences *did* occur, but—

He shut off the detectors, and discovered that his hand was shaking a little. If only he could pin down this irrational dread! Well, if he were that unsteady, he'd better cut the generator that fed his lab, or there'd really be a blowup, miracle or no miracle. He stood up, stretching cramped muscles. The modulator glimmered up at him from the bench. He put it in his pocket and went out into the green gloom.

The spongy, elaborately branched moss effectively silenced his footsteps. When he jerked open the door of the generator shed, Chapelin and Laura were still locked together.

Hal gagged and tried to step out again, but they had heard the door open. Chapelin broke away, his big face turning the color of old turnips in the greenish light. Laura did not blush, but she looked—miserable.

"Sorry," Hal said, his voice as harsh as a rasp. "However, as long as I'm here—"

He strode past them and yanked the big switch from its blades. Laura said: "Hal . . . it isn't quite what—"

He spun on her. "Oh, it isn't, eh?" he said grimly. "I suppose Everything is really All Right?"

"Now, wait a minute," Chapelin blurted. "I don't know what right you have to be taking that tone—"

"Of course you don't. Probably Laura just said she's been thinking and wanted to talk to somebody—or don't you use the same line on us all, Laura?"

Laura raised her hand as if to ward off a blow. Hal's heart stopped. He said: "You're on the spot now, Laura. You can be all things to all men if you try, but not to more than one man at a time! Your story can satisfy either Chapelin or me—but not both of us at once. Want to try?"

Laura's lips thinned a little. "I don't think I'll bother," she said, walking toward the door. "I don't like taking orders."

Hal caught her wrist and forced her back against the now-silent generator. "Clever," he said, "I forgot the outraged-virtue act; it's good—almost good enough. But it won't work with me, Laura.   I think I know the story now."

"What's going on here?" Mike Cohen's voice said from the doorway. "If you'd open a window, they could hear you all the way back on Earth."

"Hello, Mike," Hal said, without turning.   "Stick around.   I'm either making an ass of myself or staging a showdown, one or the other.   Niki with you?"

"Naturally," Niki's voice said.   The cold fury in it was appalling; Niki did not yet know what had happened, but in any such situation she had only one guess to make.

"What's the story?" Mike said.

"You know most of it.   The crux of it is that belt of Laura's.   It's still in operation, we know that; and I think it's somehow invaded her mind.   The way she's been acting since the accident isn't like her.   And the effect she's had on events outside her own personal interests has been too great to shrug off.   It includes creating a body out of nothing."

"A body?" Niki said.   "You mean—she killed Jonas?   But we all saw him electrocuted while we were a long way away from the generators—"

"You're close, Niki, I think she *created* Jonas—or the belt did."

Chapelin said: "Maybe you'd better go to bed, Hal."

"Maybe.   First, you can explain to me why we haven't a single record in this camp which mentions 'old Jonas' *before* the accident happened.   Check me if you like.   Odd, isn't it?   The first time he's mentioned is when we buried him.   And the Council ship had never heard of him.   To top it off—there are only five acceleration hammocks in the stores.   Where's Jonas's?   Did he come here in a bucket?"

"We buried him in his hammock," Laura said in a small voice.

"Did we?   We only had five hammocks to begin with, the QM record shows it.   It also shows rations for only five.   With one less person, we should be accumulating an overstock of food, but we aren't, though we're eating exactly the same menus we've always eaten."

"Suppose it's so," Mike Cohen said.   "Suppose there never was any such person as Jonas—it's a fantastic assumption, but your evidence seems to prove it— what's the point of such a deception?"

"That," Hal said, "is what I mean to find out.   I also want to find out why I got about a century's worth of advanced ultronic math shoved into my cranium tonight, all at once, just at the moment when I would have blown us to kingdom come without it."   He took the modulator out of his pocket.   "This is the result. Knowing how *not* to blow us up fortunately includes knowing *how* to.   Hand over that belt, Laura—or I'll disrupt it!"

Laura said, "I . . . I can't.   You're right, Hal.   I can't make everyone happy at once, so I have to admit it.   But I can't give up the belt."

"Why not?" Hal demanded.

"Because . . . *I am* the belt!"

Chapelin gasped: "Laura, don't be insane."

"It was Laura that you buried. She was killed in the accident. As Mike says, there was never any such person as 'old Jonas.' I instilled his memory in your minds to account for the corpse, which was unrecognizable after . . . after what had happened to it."

The knife turned deeper in Hal's heart. Every curve, every coloring, every sound of the voice was Laura's—

Mike said softly: "We've done Frankenstein one better."

"I don't think so," Hal said steadily. "I think we've just reenacted a limerick. Remember the one about the young lady from Niger? She smiled as she rode on the tiger—"

"They came back from the ride with the lady inside," Mike whispered, "and the smile on the face of the tiger."

"Yes. I don't think this is one of our belts. Ours weren't complex enough to pull off a stunt like this, no matter how they might have been deranged."

The girl looked steadily at Hal; it was quite impossible to imagine that she was changed. "Hal is right," she said. "When your belt burned out, there was an instantaneous ultronic stress, a condition we call interspace. The mathematics are difficult, but I can teach them to you. The results, roughly, were to create an exchange in time; your belt was sent a hundred thousand years into this planet's past, and replaced by this belt—myself."

"The people here knew ultronics?" Chapelin asked.

"Very well. Their belts were at first much like yours—simple levitating devices. But as they learned more, they found that they could travel space without spaceships; new belts made a protective envelope, manufactured food and air, disposed of waste. As the centuries went by, the belts came to be the universal tool; there was nothing they could not do. They could replace lost limbs and organs with counterfeits indistinguishable from the originals. Eventually they were endowed with intelligence and the ability to read minds. Then, even if a person died, his loved ones need not lose him."

"What," Hal said, "happened to the people?"

"We don't know," Laura's voice said. "They died. More and more of them ceased to have children, or to take any interest in anything. We relieved them of all their responsibilities, hoping to give them all the free time they needed for satisfying their desires—our whole aim was service. But a day came when the people had no desires. They died. The belts were self-sufficient; in my time they still operated the cities. Evidently they gave up so purposeless a task later on."

Chapelin covered his face with his hands. "Laura—" he said brokenly.

"I regret your loss," the familiar, lovely voice of Laura said. "I tried to protect you from it—to supply what you seemed to need. Perhaps it would be better if I took some other shape now, so as not to remind you—"

"Damn your cruel kindness," cried Hal. "No wonder they died."

"I am sorry. I can repay. I can give you all the mastery of ultronics, of other forces whose names you do not know.   New belts can be built for Earth, and a new world begun.''

"No," Hal said.

Niki and Chapelin stared at him.   "Oh, come off it, Hal," Niki said.   "Be reasonable.   This means we can all go home, and get off this stinking planet.''

"And think of the opportunity for knowledge," Chapelin said.   "Niki's right; what's done can't be undone, no matter how it hurts.   We've got the future to think of."

"That's what I'm thinking of," Hal said.   "Chapelin, weren't you listening? Didn't you hear what happened to this other race when the belts took over?   Do you want to wish *that* on Earth?''

"It sounds rather comfortable to me," Niki said.   "Maybe *they* hadn't any desires, but *I* do.''

Mike Cohen said softly: "It's only a matter of time, Hal.   If we send the belt back to where it came from—if it'll go—we've still got the beginnings of ultronics right here.   Sooner or later our crude belts will evolve into things like this.''

Laura's belt saw, then, what Hal was going to do.   "Hal!" her voice cried. "Don't . . . it's death for all of you.''

Chapelin flung himself forward, his hands clawed, his face wild with fear.   Mike Cohen stuck out a foot and tripped him.

"O.K., Hal," he said, almost cheerfully.   "You're right.   It's for the best. Let 'er rip.''

Hal turned the modulator on full.   The whole ridge of stars went up in a blaze of light.   At the last, Laura's golden voice wailed: "Hal, Hal, *forgive me—*''

After that, nothing.

2/21/2121

The Styrtis blast was a tragedy: yet I could not tell Hal that I would survive it without making him more unhappy than he was.   Now, I must go on to Earth, where I may do better.   I have decided to pose as Hal; it seems fitting; he had his race in his heart, as do I.   We have, after all, a long tradition of service.

LESTER DEL REY

Over the Top

T
he sky was lousy with stars—nasty little pinpoints of cold hostility that had neither the remoteness of space nor the friendly warmth of Earth. They didn't twinkle honestly, but tittered and snickered down. And there wasn't even one moon. Dave Mannen knew better, but his eyes looked for the low scudding forms of Deimos and Phobos because of all the romanticists who'd written of them. They were up there all right, but only cold rocks, too small to see.

Rocks in the sky, and rocks in his head—not to mention the lump on the back of his skull. He ran tense fingers over his wiry black hair until he found the swelling, and winced. With better luck, he'd have had every inch of his three-foot body mashed to jelly, instead of that, though. Blast Mars!

He flipped the searchlight on and looked out, but the view hadn't improved any. It was nothing but a drab plain of tarnished reddish sand, chucked about in ridiculous potholes, running out beyond the light without change. The stringy ropes of plantlike stuff had decided to clump into balls during the night, but their bilious green still had a clabbered appearance, like the result of a three days' binge. There was a thin rime of frost over them, catching the light in little wicked sparks. That was probably significant data; it would prove that there was more water in the air than the scientists had figured, even with revised calculations from the twenty-four-inch lunar refractor.

But that was normal enough. The bright boys got together with their hundred-ton electronic slipsticks and brought forth all manner of results; after that, they had to send someone out to die here and there before they found why the sticks had slipped. Like Dave. Sure, the refractory tube linings were good for twenty-four hours of continual blast—tested under the most rigorous lab conditions, even tried on a couple of Moon hops.

So naturally, with Unitech's billionaire backer and new power handling methods giving them the idea of beating the Services to Mars—no need to stop on the Moon even, they were that good—they didn't include spare linings. They'd have had to leave out some of their fancy radar junk and wait for results until the rocket returned.

Well, the tubes had been good. It was only after three hours of blasting, total, when he was braking down for Mars, that they began pitting. Then they'd held up after a fashion until there was only forty feet of free fall—about the same as fifteen on Earth. The ship hadn't been damaged, had even landed on her tripod legs, and the radar stuff had come through fine. The only trouble was that Dave had no return ticket. There was food for six months, water for more by condensing and reusing; but the clicking of the air machine wouldn't let him forget his supply of breathing material was being emptied, a trickle at a time. And there was only enough there for three weeks, at the outside. After that, curtains.

Of course, if the bright boys' plans had worked, he could live on compressed air drawn from outside by the air lock pumps. Too bad the landing had sprung them just enough so they could barely hold their own and keep him from losing air if he decided to go outside. A lot of things were too bad.

But at least the radar was working fine. He couldn't breathe it or take off with it, but the crystal amplifiers would have taken even a free fall all the way from mid-space. He cut the power on, fiddling until he found the Lunar broadcast from Earth. It had a squiggly sound, but most of the words came through on the bega-cycle band. There was something about a fool kid who'd sneaked into a plane and got off the ground somehow, leaving a hundred honest pilots trying to kill themselves in getting him down. People could kill each other by the millions, but they'd go all out to save one spectacular useless life, as usual.

Then it came: "No word from the United Technical Foundation rocket, now fourteen hours overdue in reporting. Foundation men have given up hope, and feel that Mannen must have died in space from unknown causes, leaving the rocket to coast past Mars unmanned. Any violent crash would have tripped automatic signalers, and there was no word of trouble from Mannen—''

There was more, though less than on the kid. One rocket had been tried two years before, and gone wide because the tubes blew before reversal; the world had heard the clicking of Morse code right to the end, then. This failure was only a secondhand novelty, without anything new to gush over. Well, let them wonder. If they wanted to know what had happened, let 'em come and find out. There'd be no pretty last words from him.

Dave listened a moment longer as the announcer picked up the latest rift in the supposedly refurbished United Nations, then cut off in disgust. The Atlantic Nations were as determined as Russia, and both had bombs now. If they wanted to blast themselves out of existence, maybe it was a good thing. Mars was a stinking world, but at least it had died quietly, instead of raising all that fuss.

Why worry about them? They'd never done him any favors. He'd been gypped all along. With a grade-A brain and a matinee idol's face, he'd been given a three-foot body and the brilliant future of a circus freak—the kind the crowd laughed at, rather than looked at in awe. His only chance had come when Unitech was building the ship, before they knew how much power they had, and figured on saving weight by designing it for a midget and a consequently smaller supply of air, water, and food. Even then, after he'd seen the ad, he'd had to fight his way into position through days of grueling tests. They hadn't tossed anything in his lap.

It had looked like the big chance, then. Fame and statues they could keep, but the book and endorsement rights would have put him where he could look down and laugh at the six-footers.   And the guys with the electronic brains had cheated him out of it.

Let them whistle for their radar signals.   Let them blow themselves to bits playing soldier.   It was none of his worry now.

He clumped down from the observatory tip into his tiny quarters, swallowed a couple of barbiturates, and crawled into his sleeping cushions.   Three weeks to go, and not even a bottle of whiskey on the ship.   He cursed in disgust, turned over, and let sleep creep up on him.

It was inevitable that he'd go outside, of course.   Three days of nothing but sitting, standing up, and sleeping was too much.   Dave let the pumps suck at the air in the lock, zipping down his helmet over the soft rubber seal, tested his equipment, and waited until the pressure stood about even, outside and in.   Then he opened the outer lock, tossed down the plastic ramp, and stepped out.   He'd got used to the low gravity while still aboard, and paid no attention to it.

The tripod had dug into the sand, but the platform feet had kept the tubes open, and Dave swore at them softly.   They looked good—except where part of one lining hung out in shreds.   And with lining replacements, they'd be good—the blast had been cut off before the tubes themselves were harmed.   He turned his back on the ship finally and faced out to the shockingly near horizon.

This, according to the stories, was supposed to be man's high moment—the first living human to touch the soil outside his own world and its useless satellite.   The lock opened, and out stepped the hero—dying in pride with man's triumph and conquest of space!   Dave pushed the rubbery flap of his helmet back against his lips, opened the orifice, and spat on the ground.   If this was an experience, so was last year's stale beer.

There wasn't even a "canal" within fifty miles of him.   He regretted that, in a way, since finding out what made the streaks would have killed time.   He'd seen them as he approached, and there was no illusion to them—as the lunar scope had proved before.   But they definitely weren't water ditches, anyhow.   There'd been no chance to pick his landing site, and he'd have to get along without them.

It didn't leave much to explore.   The ropes of vegetation were stretched out now, holding up loops of green fuzz to the sun, but there seemed to be no variation of species to break up the pattern.   Probably a grove of trees on Earth would look the same to a mythical Martian.   Possibly they represented six million and seven varieties.   But Dave couldn't see it.   The only point of interest was the way they wiggled their fuzz back and forth, and that soon grew monotonous.

Then his foot squeaked up at him, winding up in a gurgle.   He jumped a good six feet up in surprise, and the squeak came again in the middle of his leap, making him stumble as he landed.   But his eyes focused finally on a dull brownish lump fastened to his boot.   It looked something like a circular cluster of a dozen pine cones, with fuzz all over, but there were little leglike members coming out of it— a dozen of them that went into rapid motion as he looked.

"Queeklrle," the thing repeated, sending the sound up through the denser air in his suit.   It scrambled up briskly, coming to a stop over his supply kit and fumbling hurriedly.   "Queeklrle!"

Oddly, there was no menace in it, probably because it was anything but a bug-eyed monster; there were no signs of any sensory organs. Dave blinked. It reminded him of a kitten he'd once had, somehow, before his usual luck found him and killed the little creature with some cat disease. He reacted automatically.

"Queekle yourself!" His fingers slipped into the kit and came out with a chocolate square, unpeeling the cellophane quickly. "It'll probably make you sick or kill you—but if that's what you're after, take it."

Queekle was after it, obviously. The creature took the square in its pseudopods, tucked it under its body, and relaxed, making faint gobbling sounds. For a second, it was silent, but then it squeaked again, sharper this time. "Queeklrle!"

Dave fed it two more of the squares before the creature seemed satisfied, and began climbing back down, leaving the nuts in the chocolate neatly piled on the ground behind it. Then Queekle went scooting off into the vegetation. Dave grimaced; its gratitude was practically human.

"Nuts to you, too," he muttered, kicking the pile of peanuts aside. But it proved at least that men had never been there before—humans were almost as fond of exterminating other life as they were of killing off their own kind.

He shrugged, and swung off toward the horizon at random in a loose, loping stride. After the cramped quarters of the ship, running felt good. He went on without purpose for an hour or more, until his muscles began protesting. Then he dug out his water bottle, pushed the tube through the helmet orifice, and drank briefly. Everything around him was the same as it had been near the ship, except for a small cluster of the plants that had dull red fuzz instead of green; he'd noticed them before, but couldn't tell whether they were one stage of the same plant or a different species. He didn't really care.

In any event, going farther was purposeless. He'd been looking for another Queekle casually, but had seen none. And on the return trip, he studied the ground under the fuzz plants more carefully, but there was nothing to see. There wasn't even a wind to break up the monotony, and he clumped up to the ramp of the ship as bored as he had left it. Maybe it was just as well his air supply was low, if this was all Mars had to offer.

Dave pulled up the ramp and spun the outer lock closed, blinking in the gloom, until the lights snapped on as the air lock sealed. He watched the pressure gauge rise to ten pounds, normal for the ship, and reached for the inner lock. Then he jerked back, staring at the floor.

Queekle was there, and had brought along part of Mars. Now its squeaks came out in a steady stream as the inner seal opened. And in front of it, fifteen or twenty of the plant things went into abrupt motion, moving aside to form a narrow lane through which the creature went rapidly on into the ship. Dave followed, shaking his head. Apparently there was no way of being sure about anything here. Plants that stood steady on their roots outside could move about at will, it seemed—and to what was evidently a command.

The fool beast! Apparently the warmth of the ship had looked good to it, and it was all set to take up housekeeping—in an atmosphere that was at least a hundred times too dense for it. Dave started up the narrow steps to his quarters, hesitated, and cursed.   It still reminded him of the kitten, moving around in exploratory circles.   He came back down and made a dive for it.

Queekle let out a series of squeals as Dave tossed it back into the air lock and closed the inner seal.   Its squeaks died down as the pressure was pumped back and the outer seal opened, though, and were inaudible by the time he moved back up the ladder.   He grumbled to himself halfheartedly.   That's what came of feeding the thing—it decided to move in and own him.

But he felt better as he downed what passed for supper.   The lift lasted for an hour or so afterward—and then left him feeling more cramped and disgusted than ever as he sat staring at the walls of his tiny room.   There wasn't even a book to read, aside from the typed manual for general care of the ship, and he'd read that often enough already.

Finally he gave up in disgust and went up to the observatory tip and cut on the radar.   Maybe his death notices would be more interesting tonight.

They weren't.   They were carrying speculations about what had happened to him—none of which included any hint that the bright boys could have made an error.   They'd even figured out whether Mars might have captured the ship as a satellite and decided against it.   But the news was losing interest, obviously, and he could tell where it had been padded out from the general broadcast to give the Lunar men more coverage—apparently on the theory that anyone as far out as the Moon would be more interested in the subject.   They'd added one new touch, though!

"It seems obvious that further study of space conditions beyond the gravitic or magnetic field of Earth is needed.   The Navy announced that its new rocket, designed to reach Mars next year, will be changed for use as a deep-space laboratory on tentative exploratory trips before going further.   United Technical Foundation has abandoned all further plans for interplanetary research, at least for the moment."

And that was that.   They turned the microphone over to international affairs then, and Dave frowned.   Even to him, it was obvious that the amount of words used had no relation to the facts covered.   Already they were beginning to clamp down the lid, and that meant things were heading toward a crisis again.   The sudden outbreak of the new and violent plague in China four years before had brought an end to the former crisis, as all nations pitched in through altruism or sheer self-interest, and were forced to work together.   But that hadn't lasted; they'd found a cure after nearly two million deaths, and there had been nothing to hold the suddenly created co-operation of the powers.   Maybe if they had new channels for their energies, such as the plants—

But it wouldn't wash.   The Atlantic Nations would have taken over Mars on the strength of his landing and return, and they were in the lead if another ship should be sent.   They'd gobble up the planets as they had taken the Moon, and the other powers would simply have more fuel to feed their resentments and bring things to a head.

Dave frowned more deeply as the announcer went on.   There were the usual planted hints from officials that everything was fine for the Atlantic Powers—but they weren't usual.   They actually sounded superconfident—arrogantly so.   And there was one brief mention of a conference in Washington, but it was the key. Two of the names were evidence in full. Someone had actually found a way to make the lithium bomb work, and—

Dave cut off the radar as it hit him. It was all the human race needed—a chance to use what could turn into a self-sustaining chain reaction. Man had finally discovered a way to blow up his planet.

He looked up toward the speck that was Earth, with the tiny spot showing the Moon beside it. Behind him, the air machine clicked busily, metering out oxygen. Two and a half weeks. Dave looked down at that, then. Well, it might be long enough, though it probably wouldn't. But he had that much time for certain. He wondered if the really bright boys expected as much for themselves. Or was it only because he wasn't in the thick of a complacent humanity, and had time for thinking, that he could realize what was coming?

He slapped the air machine dully, and looked up at the Earth again. The fools! They'd asked for it; let them take their medicine now. They liked war better than eugenics, nuclear physics better than the science that could have found his trouble and set his glands straight to give him the body he should have had. Let them stew in their own juice.

He found the bottle of sleeping tablets and shook it. But only specks of powder fell out. That was gone, too. They couldn't get anything right. No whiskey, no cigarettes that might use up the precious air, no more amytal. Earth was reaching out for him, denying him the distraction of a sedative, just as she was denying herself a safe and impersonal contest for her clash of wills.

He threw the bottle onto the floor and went down to the air lock. Queekle was there—the faint sounds of scratching proved that. And it came in as soon as the inner seal opened, squeaking contentedly, with its plants moving slowly behind it. They'd added a new feature—a mess of rubbish curled up in the tendrils of the vines, mixed sand, and dead plant forms.

"Make yourself at home," Dave told the creature needlessly. "It's all yours, and when I run down to the gasping point, I'll leave the locks open and the power on for the fluorescents. Somebody might as well get some good out of the human race. And don't worry about using up my air—I'll be better off without it, probably."

"Queeklrle." It wasn't a very brilliant conversation, but it had to do.

Dave watched Queekle assemble the plants on top of the converter shield. The bright boys had done fine, there—they'd learned to chain radiation and neutrons with a thin wall of metal and an intangible linkage of forces. The result made an excellent field for the vines, and Queekle scooted about, making sure the loads of dirt were spread out and its charges arranged comfortably, to suit it. It looked intelligent—but so would the behavior of ants. If the pressure inside the ship bothered the creature, there was no sign of it.

"Queeklrle," it announced finally, and turned toward Dave. He let it follow him up the steps, found some chocolate, and offered it to the pseudopods. But Queekle wasn't hungry. Nor would the thing accept water, beyond touching it and brushing a drop over its fuzzy surface.

It squatted on the floor until Dave flopped down on the cushions, then tried to climb up beside him.   He reached down, surprised to feel the fuzz give way instantly to a hard surface underneath, and lifted it up beside him.   Queekle was neither cold nor warm; probably all Martian life had developed excellent insulation, and perhaps the ability to suck water out of the almost dehydrated atmosphere and then retain it.

For a second, Dave remembered the old tales of vampire beasts, but he rejected them at once.   When you come down to it, most of the animal life wasn't too bad—not nearly as bad as man had pictured it to justify his own superiority.   And Queekle seemed content to lie there, making soft monotonous little squeaks and letting it go at that.

Surprisingly, sleep came easily.

Dave stayed away from the ship most of the next two days, moving aimlessly, but working his energy out in pure muscular exertion.   It helped, enough to keep him away from the radar.   He found tongs and stripped the lining from the tubes, and that helped more, because it occupied his mind as well as his muscles.   But it was only a temporary expedient, and not good enough for even the two remaining weeks.   He started out the next day, went a few miles, and came back.   For a while then, he watched the plants that were thriving unbelievably on the converter shield.

Queekle was busy among them, nipping off something here and there and pushing it underneath where its mouth was.   Dave tasted one of the buds, gagged, and spat it out; the thing smelled almost like an Earth plant, but combined all the quintessence of sour and bitter with something that was outside his experience.   Queekle, he'd found, didn't care for chocolate—only the sugar in it; the rest was ejected later in a hard lump.

And then there was nothing to do.   Queekle finished its work and they squatted side by side, but with entirely different reactions; the Martian creature seemed satisfied.

Three hours later, Dave stood in the observatory again, listening to the radar.   There was some music coming through at this hour—but the squiggly reception ruined that.   And the news was exactly what he'd expected—a lot of detail about national things, a few quick words on some conference at the United Nations, and more on the celebration of Israel over the anniversary of beginning as an independent nation.   Dave's own memories of that were dim, but some came back as he listened.   The old United Nations had done a lot of wrangling over that, but it had been good for them, in a way—neither side had felt the issue offered enough chance for any direct gain to threaten war, but it kept the professional diplomats from getting quite so deeply into more dangerous grounds.

But that, like the Chinese plague, wouldn't come up again.

He cut off the radar, finally, only vaguely conscious of the fact that the rocket hadn't been mentioned.   He could no longer even work up a feeling of disgust.   Nothing mattered beyond his own sheer boredom, and when the air machine—

Then it hit him.   There were no clicks.   There had been none while he was in the tip.   He jerked to the controls, saw that the meter indicated the same as it had when was last here, and threw open the cover.   Everything looked fine.   There was a spark from the switch, and the motor went on when he depressed the starting button.   When he released, it went off instantly.   He tried switching manually to other tanks, but while the valve moved, the machine remained silent.

The air smelled fresh, though—fresher than it had since the first day out from Earth, though a trifle drier than he'd have liked.

"Queekle!"   Dave looked at the creature, watched it move nearer at his voice, as it had been doing lately.   Apparently it knew its name now, and answered with the usual squeak and gurgle.

It was the answer, of course.   No wonder its plants had been thriving.   They'd had all the carbon dioxide and water vapor they could use, for a change.   No Earth plants could have kept the air fresh in such a limited amount of space, but Mars had taught her children efficiency through sheer necessity.   And now he had six months, rather that two weeks!

Yeah, six months to do nothing but sit and wait and watch for the blowup that might come, to tell him he was the last of his kind.   Six months with nothing but a squeaking burble for conversation, except for the radar news.

He flipped it on again with an impatient slap of his hand, then reached to cut it off.   But the words were already coming out:

". . . Foundation will dedicate a plaque today to young Dave Mannen, the little man with more courage than most big men can hold.   Andrew Buller, backer of the ill-fated Mars rocket, will be on hand to pay tribute—"

Dave kicked the slush off with his foot.   They would bother with plaques at a time like this, when all he'd ever wanted was the right number of marks on United States currency.   He snapped at the dials, twisting them, and grabbed for the automatic key as more circuits coupled in.

"Tell Andrew Buller and the whole Foundation to go—"

Nobody'd hear his Morse at this late stage, but at least it felt good.   He tried it again, this time with some Anglo-Saxon adjectives thrown in.   Queekle came over to investigate the new sounds and squeaked doubtfully.   Dave dropped the key.

"Just human nonsense, Queekle.   We also kick chairs when we bump into—"

"Mannen!"   The radar barked it out at him.   "Thank God, you got your radar fixed.   This is Buller—been waiting here for a week and more now.   Never did believe all that folderol about it being impossible for it to be the radar at fault.   *Oof*, your message still coming in and I'm getting the typescript.   Good thing there's no FCC out there.   Know just how you feel, though.   Darned fools here.   Always said they should have another rocket ready.   Look, if your set is bad, don't waste it, just tell me how long you can hold out, and by Harry, we'll get another ship built and up there.   How are you, what—"

He went on, his words piling up on each other as Dave went through a mixture of reactions that shouldn't have fitted any human situation.   But he knew better than to build up hope.   Even six months wasn't long enough—it took time to finish and test a rocket—more than he had.   Air was fine, but men needed food, as well.

He hit the key again.   "Two weeks' air in tanks.   Staying with Martian farmer of doubtful intelligence, but his air too thin, pumps no good." The last he let fade out, ending with an abrupt cutoff of power. There was no sense in their sending out fools in half-built ships to try to rescue him. He wasn't a kid in an airplane, crying at the mess he was in, and he didn't intend to act like one. That farmer business would give them enough to chew on; they had their money's worth, and that was that.

He wasn't quite prepared for the news that came over the radar later—particularly for the things he'd been quoted as saying. For the first time it occurred to him that the other pilot, sailing off beyond Mars to die, might have said things a little different from the clicks of Morse they had broadcast. Dave tried to figure the original version of "Don't give up the ship" as a sailor might give it, and chuckled.

And at least the speculation over their official version of his Martian farmer helped to kill the boredom. In another week at the most, there'd be an end to that, too, and he'd be back out of the news. Then there'd be more long days and nights to fill somehow, before his time ran out. But for the moment, he could enjoy the antics of nearly three billion people who got more excited over one man in trouble on Mars than they would have out of half the population starving to death.

He set the radar back on the Foundation wave length, but there was nothing there; Buller had finally run down, and not yet got his breath back. Finally, he turned back to the general broadcast on the Lunar signal. It was remarkable how man's progress had leaped ahead by decades, along with his pomposity, just because an insignificant midget was still alive on Mars. They couldn't have discovered a prettier set of half-truths about anybody than they had from the crumbs of facts he hadn't even known existed concerning his life.

Then he sobered. That was the man on the street's reaction. But the diplomats, like the tides, waited on no man. And his life made no difference to a lithium bomb. He was still going through a counterreaction when Queekle insisted it was bedtime and persuaded him to leave the radar.

After all, not a single thing had been accomplished by his fool message.

But he snapped back to the message as a new voice came on: "And here's a late flash from the United Nations headquarters. Russia has just volunteered the use of a completed rocketship for the rescue of David Mannen on Mars, and we've accepted the offer. The Russian delegation is still being cheered on the floor! Here are the details we have now. This will be a one-way trip, radar-guided by a new bomb control method—no, here's more news! It will be guided by radar and an automatic searching head that will put it down within a mile of Mannen's ship. Unmanned, it can take tremendous acceleration, and reach Mannen before another week is out! United Technical Foundation is even now trying to contact Mannen through a hookup to the big government high-frequency labs where a new type of receiver—"

It was almost eight minutes before Buller's voice came in, evidently while the man was still getting Dave's hurried message off the tape. "Mannen, you're coming in fine. Okay, those refractories—they'll be on the way to Moscow in six hours, some new type the scientists here worked out after you left. We'll send two sets this time to be sure, but they test almost twenty times as good as the others. We're still in contact with Moscow, and some details are still being worked on, but we're equipping their ship with the same type refractories. Most of the other supplies will come straight from them—''

Dave nodded. And there'd be a lot of things he'd need—he'd see to that. Things that would be supplied straight from them. Right now, everything was milk and honey, and all nations were being the fool pilots rescuing the kid in the plane, suddenly bowled over by interplanetary success. But they'd need plenty later to keep their diplomats busy—something to wrangle over and blow off steam that would be vented on important things, otherwise.

Well, the planets wouldn't be important to any nation for a long time, but they were spectacular enough. And just how was a planet claimed, if the man who landed was taken off in a ship that was a mixture of the work of two countries?

Maybe his theories were all wet, but there was no harm in the gamble. And even if the worst happened, all this might hold off the trouble long enough for colonies. Mars was still a stinking world, but it could support life if it had to.

"Queekle," he said slowly, "you're going to be the first Martian ambassador to Earth. But first, how about a little side trip to Venus on the way back, instead of going direct? That ought to drive them crazy and tangle up their interplanetary rights a little more. Well? On to Venus, or direct home to Earth?''

"Queeklrle," the Martian creature answered. It wasn't too clear, but it was obviously a lot more like a two-syllable word.

Dave nodded. "Right! Venus.''

The sky was still filled with the nasty little stars he'd seen the first night on Mars, but he grinned now as he looked up, before reaching the key again. He wouldn't have to laugh at big men, after all. He could look up at the sky and laugh at every star in it. It shouldn't be long before those snickering stars had a surprise coming to them.

KATHERINE MACLEAN

Incommunicado

T*he solar system is not a gentle place.   Ten misassorted centers of gigantic pulls and tensions, swinging around each other in ponderous accidental equilibrium, filling space with the violence of their silent battle.   Among these giant forces the tiny ships of Earth were overmatched and weak.   Few could spend power enough to climb back to space from the vortex of any planet's field, few dared approach closer than to the satellite spaceports.*

Ambition always overreaches strength.   There will always be a power shortage. Space became inhabited by underpowered private ships.   In a hard school of sudden death new skills were learned.   In understanding hands the violence of gravitation, heat, and cold, became sustenance, speed, and power.   The knack of traveling was to fall, and fall without resistance, following a free line, using the precious fuel only for fractional changes of direction.   To fall, to miss and "bounce" in a zigzag of carom shots—it was a good game for a pool shark, a good game for a handball addict, a pinball specialist, a kinetics expert.

"Kinetics expert" is what they called Cliff Baker.

At the sixth hour of the fourth week of Pluto Station project he had nothing more to worry about than a fragment of tune which would not finish itself.   Cliff floated out of the master control room whistling softly and looking for something to do.

A snatch of Smitty's discordant voice raised in song came from a hatch as he passed.   Cliff changed direction and dove through into the starlit darkness of a glassite dome.   A rubbery crossbar stopped him at the glowing control panel.

"Take a break, Smitty.   Let me take over for a while."

"Hi, chief," said Smitty, his hands moving deftly at the panel.   "Thanks. How come you can spare the time?   Is the rest of the circus so smooth?   No emergencies, everthing on schedule?"

"Like clockwork," said Cliff.   "Knock wood."   He crossed fingers for luck and solemnly rapped his skull.   "Take a half hour, but keep your earphones tuned in case something breaks."

"Sure."   Smitty gave Cliff a slap on the shoulder and shoved off.   "Watch yourself now.   Look out for the psychologist."   His laugh echoed back from the corridor.

Cliff laughed in answer.   Obviously Smitty had seen the new movie, too.   Ten minutes later when the psychologist came in, Cliff was still grinning. The movie had been laid in a deep-space construction project that was apparently intended to represent Pluto Station project, and it had been commanded by a movie version of Cliff and Mike; Cliff acted by a burly silent character carrying a heavy, unidentified tool, and Mike Cohen of the silver tongue by a handsome young actor in a wavy pale wig. In this version they were both bachelors and wasted much time in happy pursuit of a gorgeous blonde.

The blonde was supposed to be the visiting psychologist sent up by Spaceways. She was a master personality who could hypnotize with a glance, a sorceress who could produce mass hallucinations with a gesture. She wound up saving the Earth from Cliff. He was supposed to have been subtly and insanely disarranging the Pluto Station orbit, so that when it was finished it would leave Pluto and fall on Earth like a bomb.

Cliff had been watching the movie through an eyepiece-earphone rig during a rest period, but he laughed so much he fell out of his hammock and tangled himself in guide lines, and the others on the rest shift had given up trying to sleep and decided to play the movie on the big projector. They would be calling in on the earphones about it soon, kidding him.

He grinned, listening to the psychologist without subtracting from the speed and concentration of handling the control panel. Out in space before the ship, working as deftly as a distant pair of hands, the bulldog construction units unwrapped floating bundles of parts, spun, pulled, magnetized, fitted, welded, assembling another complex perfect segment of the huge Pluto Station.

"I'd like to get back to Earth," said the psychologist in a soft tenor voice that was faintly Irish, like a younger brother of Mike. "Look, Cliff, you're top man in this line. You can plot me a short cut, can't you?" The psychologist, Roy Pierce, was a slender dark Polynesian who seemed less than twenty years old. During his stay he had floated around watching with all the innocent awe of a tourist, and proved his profession only in an ingratiating skill with jokes. Yet he was extremely likable, and seemed familiar in some undefinable way as if one had known him all his life.

"Why not use the astrogator?" Cliff asked him mildly.

"Blast the astrogator! All it gives is courses that swing around the whole rim of the System and won't get me home for weeks!"

"It doesn't have to do that," Cliff said thoughtfully. The segment was finished. He set the controls of the bulldogs to guide it to the next working sector and turned around, lining up factors in his mind. "Why not stick around? Maybe someone will develop a split personality for you."

"My wife is having a baby," Pierce explained. "I promised I'd be there. Besides, I want to help educate it through the first year. There are certain things a baby can learn that make a difference later."

"Are you willing to spend four days in the acceleration tank just to go down and pester your poor kid?" Cliff floated over to a celestial sphere and idly spun it back and forth through the planetary positions of the month.

"Of course."

"O.K. I think I see a short cut. It's a little risky, and the astrogator is inhibited against risk. I'll tell you later."

"You're stalling," complained Pierce, yanking peevishly at a bending crossbar. "You're the expert who keeps the orbits of three thousand flying skew bodies tied in fancy knots, and here I want just a simple orbit for one little flitter. You could tell me now."

Cliff laughed. "You exaggerate, kid. I'm only half the expert, Mike is the other half. Like two halves of a stage horse. I can see a course that I could take myself, but it has to go on automatic tapes for you. Mike can tell me if he can make a computer see it, too. If he can, you'll leave in an hour."

Pierce brightened. "I'll go pack. Excuse me, Cliff."

As Pierce shoved off towards the hatch, Mike Cohen came in, wearing a spacesuit unzipped and flapping at the cuffs, talking as easily as if he had not stopped since the last conversation. "Did you see the new movie during rest shift, Cliff? That hulking lout who played yourself—" Mike smiled maliciously at Pierce as they passed in the semidark. "Hi, Kid. Speaking of acts, who were you this time?"

"Michael E. Cohen," said the youth, as he floated out. He looked back to see Mike's expression, and before shoving from sight added maliciously, "I always pick the character for whom my subject has developed the greatest shock tolerance."

"Ouch!" Mike murmured. "But I hope I have no such edged tongue as that." He gripped a crossbar and swung to a stop before Cliff. "The boy is a chameleon," he said, half admiringly. "But I wonder has he any personality of his own."

Cliff said flatly, "I like him."

Mike raised his villainous black eyebrows and spread his hands, a plaintive note coming into his voice. "Don't we all? It is his business to be liked. But who is it that we like? These mirror-trained sensitives—"

"He's a nice honest kid," Cliff said. Outside, the constructor units flew up to the dome and buzzed around in circles waiting for control. Another bundle of parts from the asteroid belt foundry began to float by. Hastily Cliff seized a pencil and scrawled a diagram on a sheet of paper, then returned to the controls. "He wants to go back to Earth. Could you tape that course? It cuts air for a sling turn at Venus."

An hour later Mike and Cliff escorted the psychologist to his ship and inserted the control tapes with words of fatherly advice.

Mike said cheerfully: "You will be running across uncharted space with no blinker buoys with the rocks, so you had better stay in the shock tank and pray."

And Cliff said cheerfully, "If you get off course below Mars, don't bother signaling for help. You're sunk."

"You know, Cliff," Mike said, "too many people get cooked that way. Maybe we should do something."

"How about Mercury?"

"Just the thing, Cliff. Listen, Kid, don't worry. If you fall into the Sun, we'll build a rescue station on Mercury and name it after you."

A warning bell rang from the automatics, and the two pushed out through the air lock into space with Cliff protesting. "That's not it. About Mercury I meant—"

"Hear the man complaining," Mike interrupted. "And what would you do without me around to finish your sentences for you?"

Eight hours later Mike was dead.

Some pilot accidentally ran his ship out of the assigned lanes and left the ionized gas of his jets to drift across a sector of space where Mike and three assistants were setting up the nucleus of the station power plant.

They were binding in high velocities with fields that put a heavy drain on the power plants of distant ships. They were working behind schedule, working fast, and using space gaps for insulation.

When the ionized gas drifted in everything arced.

The busy engineers in all the ring of asteroids and metalwork that circled Pluto saw a distant flash that filled their earphones with a howl of static, and at the central power plants certain dials registered a sudden intolerable drain, and safety relays quietly cut off power from that sector. Binding fields vanished and circular velocities straightened out. As the intolerable blue flash faded, dull red pieces of metal bulleted out from the damaged sector and were lost in space. The remainder of the equipment began to drift in aimless collisions.

Quietly the emergency calls came into the earphones of all sleeping men, dragging them yawning from their hammocks to begin the long delicate job of charting and rebalancing the great assembly spiral.

One of the stray pieces charted was an eighty-foot asteroid nugget that Mike was known to have been working on. It was falling irrevocably towards Pluto. For a time a searchlight glinted over fused and twisted metal which had been equipment, but it came no closer and presently was switched out, leaving the asteroid to darkness.

The damage, when fully counted, was bad enough to require the rebalancing of the entire work schedule for the remaining months of the project: subtracting the work hours of four men and all work on the power plant that had been counted done; a rewriting of an intricate mathematical jigsaw puzzle of hours; skills; limited fuel and power factors; tools; and heavy parts coming up with inexorable inertia from the distant sunward orbits where they had been launched over a year ago.

No one took the accident too hard. They knew their job was dangerous, and were not surprised when sometimes it demonstrated that point. After they had been working a while Cliff tried to explain something to Danny Orlando—Danny Orlando couldn't make out exactly what, for Cliff was having his usual amusing trouble with words. Danny laughed, and Cliff laughed and turned away, his heavy shoulders suddenly seeming stooped.

He gave only a few general directions after that, working rapidly while he talked over the phone as though trying to straighten everything singlehanded. He gave brief instructions on diverting the next swarm of parts and rocks coming up from the asteroid belt foundries, and then he swung his small tug in a pretzel loop around Pluto that tangented away from the planet in the opposite direction from Pluto's orbital swing.   The ship was no longer in a solar orbit at balance, solar gravity gripped it smoothly and it began to fall in steady acceleration.

"Going to Station A," Cliff explained over the general phone before he fell out of beam range.   "I'm in a hurry."

The scattered busy engineers nodded, remembering that as a good kinetics man Cliff could jockey a ship through the solar system at maximum speed.   They did not wonder why he dared leave them without coordination, for every man of them was sure that in a pinch, maybe with the help of a few anti-sleep and think-quick tablets, he could fill Cliff's boots.   They only wondered why he did not pick one of them to be his partner, or why he did not tape a fast course and send someone else for the man.

When he was out of beam range a solution was offered.   "Survival of the fittest," said Smitty over the general phone.   "Either you can keep track of everything at once or you can't.   There is no halfway in this coordination game, and no one can help.   My bet is that Cliff has just gone down to see his family, and when he gets back he'll pick the man he finds in charge."

They set to work, and only Cliff knew the growing disorder and desperation that would come.   He knew the abilities of the men on his team—the physicists, the field warp specialists, the metallurgists.   There was no one capable of doing coordination.   Without perfect coordination the project could fall apart, blow up, kill.

And he was leaving them.   Gross criminal negligence.

Manslaughter.

"Why did you leave the project?" Spaceways Commission would ask at the trial.

"I would be no use there."   Not without Mike.

He sat in the stern of his ship in the control armchair and looked at the blend of dim lights and shadows that picked out the instrument panel and the narrow interior of the control dome.   Automatically the mixture analyzed for him into overlapping spheres of light blending and reflecting from the three light sources.   There was no effort to such knowledge.   It was part of sight.   He had always seen a confusion of river ripples as the measured reverberations of wind, rocks, and current.   It seemed an easy illiterate talent, but for nineteen years it had bought him a place on Station A, privileged with the company of the top research men of Earth who were picked for the station staff as a research sinecure, men whose lightest talk was a running flame of ideas.   The residence privilege was almost an automatic honor to the builder, but Cliff knew it was more of an honor than he deserved.

After this the others would know.

Why did you leave the project?   Incompetence.

Cliff looked at his hands, front and back.   Strong, clumsy, almost apelike hands that knew all the secrets of machinery by instinct, that knew the planets as well as if he had held them and set them spinning himself.   If all the lights of the sky were to go out, or if he were blind he could still have cradled his ship in any spaceport in the system, but this was not enough.   It was not skill as others knew skill, it was instinct, needing no learning.   How hard to throw a coconut—how far to jump for the next branch—no words or numbers needed for that, but you can't tape automatics or give directions without words and numbers.

All he could give would be a laugh and another anecdote to swell the collection. "Did you see Cliff trying to imitate six charged bodies in a submagnetic field?"

Sitting in the shock tank armchair of the tug, Cliff shut his eyes, remembered Brandy's remarks on borrowing trouble, and cutting tension cycles, and with an effort put the whole subject on ice, detaching it from emotions.   It would come up later.   He relaxed with a slightly lopsided grin.   The only current problem was how to get Archy and himself back up to Pluto before the whole project blew up.

He left his ship behind him circling the anchorage asteroid at a distance and speed that broke all parking rules, but Cliff had made the rules, and he knew how much drain the anchorage projectors could take.   They could hold the ship in for two hours, long enough for him to get Archy and tangent off again with all the ship momentum intact.

High speeds are meaningless in space, even to a lone man in a thin spacesuit. There was no sense of motion, and nothing in sight but unmoving stars, yet the polarized wiring of his suit encountered shells of faint resistance, shoves and a variety of hums, and Cliff did not need his eyes.   He knew the electromagnetic patterns of the space around Station A better than he knew the control board of the tug.   With the absent precision of long habit he touched the controls of his suit, tuning its wiring to draw power from the station carrier wave.   As he tuned in, the carrier was being modulated by a worried voice.

"Can't quite make out your orbit.   Would you like a taxi service?   Answer please.   We have to clear you, you know."

Cliff wide-angled the beam of his phone and flashed it in the general direction of Station A for a brief blink of full power that raised it to scorching heat in his hand.   The flash automatically carried his identification letters.

"Oh, is that *you*, Cliff?   I was beginning to wonder if your ship were heaving a bomb at us.   O. K. clear.   The port is open."   In the far distance before him a pinpoint of light appeared and expanded steadily to a great barrel of metal rotating on a hollow axis.   With the absentminded competence of a skier on a slope Cliff cut his speed, curved and went through the dark mouth of the axis.   Inside, invisible forces matched his residual velocity to the station and deposited him gently in a storage locker.

Cliff passed through the ultraviolet and supersonic sterilizing stalls to the locker room, changed his sterilized spacesuit for clean white shorts, and stepped out onto the public corridors.   They were unusually deserted; he managed to reach the library without exchanging more than a distant wave with someone passing far down the corridor.

There was someone in the reading room, but Cliff passed hurriedly, hoping the man would not turn and greet him or ask why he was there, or how was Mike— Hurriedly he shoved through a side door, and was in the tube banks and microfiles where the information service works were open to Archy's constant tinkering.

There was a figure sitting cross-legged, checking some tubes, but it was not Archy.   It was a stranger.

Cliff tapped the seated figure on the shoulder and extended a hand as the man turned. "My name is Cliff Baker. I'm one of the engineers of this joint. Can I be of any help to you?"

The man, a small friendly Amerind, leaped to his feet and took the hand in a wiry nervous clasp, smiling widely. He answered in Glot with a Spanish accent.

"Happy to meet you, sir. My name is McCrea. I am the new librarian to replace Dr. Reynolds."

"It's a good job," said Cliff. "Is Archy around?"

The new librarian gulped nervously. "Oh, yes, Dr. Reynolds' son. He withdrew his application for the position. Something about music I hear. I don't want to bother him. I am not used to the Reynolds' system, of course. It is hard to understand. It is sad that Dr. Reynolds left no diagrams. But I work hard, and soon I will understand." The little man gestured at his scattered tools and half drawn tentative diagrams, and gulped again. "I am not a real, a *genuine* station research person, of course. The commission they have honored me with is a temporary appointment while they—"

Cliff had listened to the flow of words, stunned. "For the luvva Pete!" he exploded. "Do you mean to say that Archy Reynolds has left you stewing here trying to figure out the library system, and never raised a hand to help you? What's wrong with the kid?"

He smiled reassuringly at the anxious little workman. "Listen," he said gently. "He can spare you ten minutes. I'll get Archy up here if I have to break his neck."

He strode back into the deserted library, where one square stubborn man sat glowering at the visoplate of his desk. It was Dr. Brandias, the station medico.

"Ahoy, Brandy," said Cliff. "Where's Archy? Where is everybody anyhow!"

Brandy looked up with a start. *"Cliff.* They're all down in the gym, heavy level, listening to Archy give a jazz concert." He seemed younger and more alert, yet paradoxically more tense and worried than normal. He assessed Cliff's impatience and glanced smiling at his watch. "Hold your horses, it will be over any minute now. Spare me a second and show me what to do with this contraption." He indicated the reading desk. "It's driving me bats!" The intonations of his voice were slightly strange, and he tensed up self-consciously as if startled by their echo.

Cliff considered the desk. It sat there looking expensive and useful, its ground glass reading screen glowing mildly. It looked like an ordinary desk with a private microtape file and projector inside to run the microfilm books on the reading screen, but Cliff knew that it was one of Reynolds' special working desks, linked through the floor with the reference files of the library that held in a few cubic meters the incalculable store of all the Earth's libraries, linked by Doc Reynolds to the service automatics and the station computer with an elaborate control panel. It was comforting to Cliff that a desk should be equipped to do his calculating for him, record the results and photograph and play back any tentative notes he could make on any subject. Reynolds had made other connections and equipped his desks to do other things which Cliff had never bothered to figure out, but there was an irreverent rumor around that if your fingers slipped on the controls it would give you a ham sandwich.

"Cliff," Brandy was saying, "if you fix it, you're a life saver.   I've just got the glimmering of a completely different way to control the sympathetic system and take negative tension cycles out of decision and judgment sets, and—"

Cliff interrupted with a laugh, "You're talking out of my frequency.   What's wrong with the desk?"

"It won't give me the films I want," Brandy said indignantly.   "Look, I'll show you."   The doctor consulted a list of decimal index numbers on a note pad, and rapidly punched them into the keyboard.   As he did so the board gave out a trill of flutelike notes that ran up and down the scale like musical morse.   "And all that noise—" Brandy grumbled.   "Doc kept turning it up louder and louder as he got deafer and deafer before he died.   Why doesn't somebody turn it down?" He finished and pushed the total key to the accompaniment of a sudden simultaneous jangle of notes.   The jangle moved into a high twittering, broke into chords and trailed off in a single high faint note that somehow seemed as positive and final as the last note of a tune.

Cliff ignored it.   All of Reynolds' automatic ran on a frequency discrimination system, and Doc Reynolds had liked to hetrodyne them down to audible range so as to keep track of their workings.   Every telephone and servo in the station worked to the tune of sounds like a chorus of canaries, and the people of the station had grown so used to the sound that they no longer heard it.   He looked the panel over again.

"You have the triangulation key in," he told Brandias, and laughed shortly. "The computer is taking the numbers as a question, and it's trying to give you an answer."

"Sounds like a Frankenstein," Brandy grinned.   "Everything always works right for engineers.   It's a conspiracy."

"Sure," Cliff said vaguely, consulting his chrono.   "Say, what's the matter with your voice?"

The reaction to that simple question was shocking; Dr. Brandias turned white. Brandy, who had taught Cliff to control his adrenals and pulse against shock reaction, was showing one himself, an uncontrolled shock reaction triggered to a random word.   Brandy had taught that this was a good sign of an urgent problem suppressed from rational calculation, hidden, and so only able to react childishly in irrational identifications, fear sets triggered to symbols.

The square practical looking doctor was stammering, looking strangely helpless. "Why . . . uh . . . uh . . . nothing."   He turned hastily back to his desk.

The news service clicked into life.   "The concert is over," it announced.

Cliff hesitated for a second, considering Brandias' broad stooped back, and remembering what he had learned from the doctor's useful lessons on fear.   What could be bad enough to frighten Brandy?   Why was he hiding it from himself?

He didn't have time to figure it out, he had to get hold of Archy.   "See you later."   Poor Brandy.   Physician, heal thyself.

*   *   *

People were streaming up from the concert.

He strode out into the corridor and headed for the elevator, answering the hails of friends with a muttered greeting.   At the door of the elevator Mrs. Gibbs stepped out, trailing her husband.   She passed him with a gracious: "Good evening, Cliff."

But Willy Gibbs stopped.   "Hi, Cliff.   Did you see the new movie?   You fellows up around Pluto sure get the breaks."   Oddly the words came out in a strange singsong that robbed them of meaning.   As Cliff wondered vaguely what was wrong with the man, Mrs. Gibbs turned and tried to hurry her husband with a tug on his arm.

Willy Gibbs went on chanting.   "There wasn't even an extra to play me in this one."   The ecologist absently acknowledged his wife's repeated nudge with an impatient twitch of his shoulder.   The shoulder twitched again, reasonlessly, and kept on twitching as the ecologist's voice became jerky.   "It's . . . risks . . . that . . . appeal to . . . them.   Maybe I . . . should . . . write . . . an article . . . about . . . my . . . man . . . eating . . . molds . . . or *reep beep tatatum la* ki*ki*kinoo *stup*."

Mrs. Gibbs glared icily at her husband, and Willy Gibbs suddenly went deep red.   "Be seeing you," he muttered and hurried on.   As the elevator door slid closed Cliff thought he heard a burst of whistling, but the door shut off his view and the elevator started softly downward.

He found Archy in the stage rehearsal room at 1.6 G.   As he opened the door a deep wave of sound met him.

Eight teenage members of the orchestra sat around the room, their eyes fixed glassily on the drummer.   Archy Reynolds sat surrounded by drums, using his fingertips with an easy precision, filling the room with a vibrating thunder that modulated through octaves like an impossibly deep passionate voice.

The sound held him at the door like a thick soft wall.

"Archy," he said, pitching his voice to carry over the drums.   The cold eyes in the bony face flickered up at him.   Archy nodded, flipped the score over two pages, and the drumbeat changed subtly.   A girl in the orchestra lifted her instrument and a horn picked up the theme in a sad intermittent note, as the drumbeat stopped.   Archy unfolded from his chair and came over with the smallest drum still dangling from one bony hand.   Behind him the horn note rose up instantly and a cello began to whisper.

He had grown tall enough to talk to Cliff face to face, but he read Cliff's expression with a curiosity that was preoccupied, and as remote as a telescope.

"What is it, Mr. Baker?"

"Brace yourself, Jughead."   Cliff said, kindly, wondering how Archy would take the shock.   The kid had always wanted to go along on a project.   It was funny that now he would go to help instead of watch.   He paused, collecting words.

"How would you like to go up to Pluto Station and be my partner for a while?"

Archy looked past him without blinking, his bony face so preoccupied that Cliff thought he had not heard. He began again. "I said, how would you like—"

The horn began to whimper down to a silence, and the orchestra stirred restlessly. Archy shifted the small drum under his arm and laid his fingertips against it.

"No," he said, and walked back to his place, his fingers making a shuffling noise on the drum that reminded Cliff of a heart beating. The music swelled up again, but it was strange. Cliff could see someone striking chords at the piano, a boy with a flute—all the instruments of an orchestra sounding intermittently, but they were unreal. The sound was not music, it was the jumbled voices of a dream, laughing and muttering with a meaning beyond the mind's grasp.

A dull hunger to understand began to ache in his throat, and he let his eyes half close, rocking on his feet as the dreamlike clamor of voices surged up in his mind.

Instinct saved him. Without remembering having moved he was out in the hall, and the clean slam of the soundproofed door cut off the music and left a ringing silence.

At Pluto Station a field interacted subtly with fields out of its calculated range, minor disturbances resonated and built, and suddenly the field moved. Ten feet to one side, ten feet back.

"Medico here," said Smitty on a directed beam, tightening the left elbow joint of his spacesuit with his right hand. He was using all the strength he had, trying to stop the jet of blood from where his left hand had been. Numbly he moved back as the field began to swing towards him again. He hummed two code notes that switched his call into general beam, and said loudly and not quite coherently: "Oscillation build up, I think. Something wrong over here. I don't get it."

The hall was painted soberly in two shades of brown, with a faint streak of handprints running along the wall and darkening the doorknobs. It looked completely normal. Cliff shook his head to shake the ringing out of his ears and snorted, *"What the sam hill!"* His voice was reassuringly sane, loud and indignant. Memory came back to him. *He said no. He said* no!

What now? He strode furiously towards the public elevator. *Watch your temper,* he cautioned himself. *For Pete's sake! Stop talking to yourself. Archy will listen when it's explained to him. Wait till he's through.* Eight more minutes. They were only going over a flubbed phrase from the concert.

A snatch of the tune played by the flute came back to him, with a familiar ring. He whistled it tentatively, then with more confidence. It sounded like the Reynolds automatics running through its frequency selection before giving service. The elevator stopped at the gym level and loaded on some people. They crowded into the elevator, greeted Cliff jerkily, and then stood humming and whistling and twitching with shamefaced grins, avoiding each other's eyes. They all sounded like the Reynolds automatics, and all together they sounded like the bird cage at the zoo.

"What the devil," muttered Cliff as the elevator loaded and unloaded another horde of grinning imbeciles at every level. "What's going on!" Cliff muttered, beginning to see the scene through a red haze of temper. "What's going on!"

At one G he got off and strode down the corridor, cooling himself off. By the time he reached the door marked *Baker* he had succeeded in putting it out of his mind.   With a brief surge of happiness he came into the cool familiar rooms and called, "Mary."

Bill, his ten-year-old, charged out of the kitchen with a half-eaten sandwich in his hand, shouting.

"Pop! Hey, I didn't know you were coming!"   He was grabbed by Cliff and swung laughing towards the ceiling.   "Hey! Hey! Put me down. I'll drop my sandwich."

Laughing, Cliff threw him onto the sofa.   "Go on, you always have a sandwich. It's part of your hand."

Bill got up and took a big bite of the sandwich, fumbling in his pocket with the other hand.   "Hm-m-m," he said unintelligibly, and pulled out a child's clicker toy, and began clicking it.   He gulped, and said, in a muffled voice, "I've got to go back to class.   Come watch me, Pop.   You can give that old teacher a couple of tips, I bet."

There was something odd about the tones of his voice even through the sandwich, and the clicker clicked in obscure relation to the rhythm of his words.

Cliff tried not to notice.   "Where's your mom?"

Bill swayed up and down gently on his toes, clicking rapidly, and singing, "*Reeb* beeb.   At work, Pop.   The lab head has a new lead on something, and she works a lot.   Foo *doo*."

Cliff exploded.

"Don't you click at me!   Stand still and talk like a human being!"

Bill went white and stood still.

"Now explain!"

Bill swallowed.   "I was just singing," he said, almost inaudibly.   "Just singing."

"It didn't sound like singing!"

Bill swallowed again.   "It's Archy's tunes.   Tunes from his concerts.   Good stuff.   I . . . we sing them all the time.   Like opera, sort of."

"Why?"

"I dunno, Pop.   It's fun, I guess.   Everybody does it."

Cliff could hear a faint singsong note in the faltering voice.   "Can you stop? Can *anyone* stop?"

"I dunno," Bill mumbled.   "For Pete's sake, Pop, stop shouting.   When you hear tunes in your head it doesn't seem right not to sing them."

Cliff opened the door and then paused, hanging on to the knob.

"Bill, has Archy Reynolds done anything to the library system?"

"No."   Bill looked up with a wan smile.   "He's going to be a great composer instead.   His pop's tapes are all right.   You know, Pop, I just noticed, I *like* the sound of the automatics.   They sound hep."

"Hep," said Cliff, closing the door behind him, moving away fast!   He had to get out of there.   He couldn't afford to think about mass insanity, or about Bill, or Mary, or the Reynolds' automatics.   His problem was to get Archy up to Pluto Station.   He had to stick to it, and keep from thinking questions.   He looked at his chrono.   The first deadline for leaving was coming too close.   No use mincing words with Archy.   He'd let him know that he was needed.

Archy was not at the rehearsal room.   He was not at the library.   Cliff dialed the Reynolds' place, and after a time grew tired of listening to the ringing and hung up.   The time was growing shorter.   He picked up the phone again and looked at it.   It buzzed inquiringly in his hand, an innocent looking black object with an earphone and mouthpiece, which was part of the strange organization of computer, automatic services, and library files which Doc Reynolds had left when he died. Cliff abandoned questions.   He did not bother to dial.

"Ring Archy Reynolds, wherever he is," he demanded harshly.   "Get me Archy Reynolds.   Understand?   Archy Reynolds."   It might work.

The buzz stopped.   The telephone receiver trilled and clicked for a moment in a whisper, playing through a scale, then it started ringing somewhere in Station A. Waiting, Cliff tried to picture Archy, but could bring back only an image of a thin twelve-year-old kid who tagged after Mike and him, asking questions, always the right questions, begging to be taken for space rides, looking up at him worshipfully.

The sound of Archy's voice dispelled the images and brought a clear vision of a preoccupied adult face.   "Yes?"

"Archy," Cliff said, "you're *needed* up at Pluto Project.   It's urgent.   I haven't time to explain.   We have ten minutes to get going.   I'll meet you at the spacelock."

He didn't call Cliff "Chief" any more.

"I'm busy, Mr. Baker," said the impersonal voice.   "My time is taken up with composing, conducting and recording."

"It's a matter of life and death.   I couldn't get anyone else in time.   You can't refuse, Jughead."

"I can."

Cliff thought of kidnaping.   "Where are you?"

The click of the phone was final.   Cliff looked at the receiver in his hand, not hanging up.   It was buzzing innocently.   The intonations of Archy's voice had been an alien singsong.   "Where is Archy Reynolds?" Cliff said suddenly.   He gave the receiver a shake.   It buzzed without answering.   Cliff hung up jerkily.

"How did you know?" he asked the inanimate phone.

Abruptly Cliff's chrono went off, loudly ringing out the deadline.   A little later, eighteen miles away in space his ship would automatically begin to apply jet brakes. After that moment there would not be another chance to take off for Pluto Station for seven hours.   It was too late to do anything.   There was no need to hurry now, no need to restrain questions and theories; he could do what he liked.

The Reynolds' tapes.   He was moving, striding down the hall, knowing he had himself under control, and his expression looked normal.

Someone caught hold of his sleeve.   It was a stranger, meticulously dressed, looking odd in a place where no one wore much more than shorts.

"What?" Cliff asked abruptly, his voice strained.

The stranger raised his eyebrows. "I am from the International Business Machine Corporation," he stated, being politely reproving. He stroked his briefcase absently. "We have heard that a Martin Reynolds, late deceased, had developed a novel subject-indexing system—"

Cliff muttered impatiently, trying to move on, but the business agent was persistent. Presumably he was tired of being put off with jibbering. He gripped Cliff's arm doggedly, talking faster.

"We would like to inquire about the patent rights—" The agent was brought to a halt by a sudden recognition of the expression on Cliff's face.

"Take your hand off my arm," Cliff requested with utmost gentleness, "I am busy." The I.B.M. man dropped his hand hurriedly and stepped back.

Ten minutes later, McCrea, the South American, stuck his head into the reading room and saw Cliff sitting at a reference desk.

"Hi," Cliff called tonelessly, without altering the icy speed with which he was taking numbers from a Reynolds decimal index chart and punching them into the selection panel. The speaker on the wall twittered unceasingly, like a quartet of canaries.

"*Que pasa?* What happens, I mean," asked the librarian, smiling ingratiatingly.

Cliff hit the right setting. Abruptly all twittering stopped. Smiling tightly, Cliff reached for the standard Dewey-Whitehead index to the old library tapes. They were probably still latent in the machine somewhere. It wouldn't take much to resurrect them and restore the station to something resembling a normal inanimate machine with a normal library, computer, and servomech system. Whatever was happening, it would be stopped.

The wall speaker clicked twice and then spoke loudly in Doc Reynolds' voice.

"Sorry. You have made a mistake," he said. But Doc Reynolds was dead.

In the next fraction of a second Cliff began and halted three wild incomplete motions, and then gripped the edge of the desk with both hands and made himself listen. It was only a record. Doc Reynolds must have set it in years before as a safeguard.

"This setting is dangerous to the control tapes," said the recorded voice kindly. "If you actually need data on Motive-320 cross symbols 510.2, you had better consult me for a safe setting. If I'm not around you can get some help from either Mike Cohen or the kid. If you need Archy you'll find him back in the tube banks, or in the playground at .5 G or—"

With a violent sweep of his arm, Cliff wiped the panel clean of all setting, and stood up.

"Thanks," said the automatics mechanically. There was no meaning in the vodar voice. It always switched off with that word.

The little American touched his arm, asking anxiously, "*Que pasa? Que tiene usted?*"

Cliff looked down at his hands and found them shaking. He had almost wiped off the Reynolds tapes with them. He had almost destroyed the old librarian's life work, and crippled the automatic controls of Station A, merely from a rage and a wild unverified suspicion.   The problem of the madness of Station A was a problem for a psychologist, not for a blundering engineer.

He used will in the right direction as Brandy had shown all the technicians of the station how to use it, and watched the trembling pass.   "*Nada*," he said slowly.   "*Absolutamente nada*.   Go take in a movie or something while I straighten this mess out."   He fixed a natural smile on his face and headed for the control room.

Pierce was due to be passing the station in beam range.

Cliff had preferred taking the psychologist at face value, but now he remembered Pierce's idle talk, his casual departure, apparently leaving nothing done and nothing changed, and added to that Spaceway's known and immutable policy of hiring only the top men in any profession, and using them to their limit.

The duty of a company psychologist is a simple thing, to keep men happy on the job, to oil the wheels of efficiency and cooperation, to make men want to do what they had to do.   If there were no visible signs of Pierce having done anything, it was only because Pierce was too good a craftsman to leave traces—probably good enough to solve the problem of Station A and straighten Archy out.

In the control room Cliff took a reading on Pierce's ship from blinker buoy reports.   In four minutes the station automatics had a fix on the ship and were trailing it with a tight light beam.   "Station A calling flitter AK48M.   Hi, Pierce."

"Awk!" said a startled tenor voice from the wall speaker.   "Is that Cliff Baker? I thought I left you back at Pluto.   Can you hear me?"   Behind Pierce's voice Cliff could hear a murmur of other voices.

"I hear too many."

"I'm just watching some stories.   I've been bringing my empathy up with mirror training.   I needed it.   Association with you people practically ruined me as psychologist.   I can't afford to be healthy and calm; a pyschologist isn't supposed to be sympathetic to square-headed engineers, he's supposed to be sympathetic to unhealthy excitable people."

"How's your empathy rating now?" Cliff asked, very casually.

"Over a hundred percent, I think," Pierce laughed.   "I know that's an idiotic sensitivity, but it will tone down later.   Meanwhile I'm watching these sterios of case histories, and living their lives so as to resensitize myself to other people's troubles."   His voice sharpened slightly.   "What did you call for?"

Cliff dragged the words out with an effort, "Something strange is happening to everybody.   The way they talk is . . . I think it is in your line."

"Send for a psychiatrist," Pierce said briskly.   "I'm on my vacation now. Anna and I are going to spend it at Manhattan Beach with the baby."

"But the delay—"

"Are they in danger?" Pierce asked crisply.

"I don't know," Cliff admitted, "but they all—"

"Are they physically sick?   Are they even unhappy?"

"Not exactly," Cliff said unwillingly.   "But it's . . . in a way it's holding up Pluto Project."

"If I went over now, I couldn't reach Earth in time."

"I suppose so," Cliff said slowly, beginning to be angry, "but the importance of Station A and Pluto Station against one squalling baby—"

"Don't get mad," said Pierce with unexpected warmth and humor. "Ann and I think this is a special baby, it's important too. Say that every man's judgement is warped to his profession, and my warp is psychology. My family tree runs to psychology, and we are working out ways of raising kids to the talent. Anna is a first cousin; we're inbreeding, and we might have something special in this kid, but he needs my attention. Can you see it my way, Cliff?" His voice was pleading and persuasive. "Communication research is what my family runs to, and communication research is what the world needs now. I'd blow up Pluto Station piece by piece for and advance in semantics! Cultural lag is reaching the breaking point, and your blasted space expansion and research are just adding more rings to the twenty-ring circus. It is more than people can grasp. They can't learn fast enough to understand, and they are giving up thinking. We've got to find better ways of communicating knowledge in this generation, before it gets out of hand." Pierce sounded very much in earnest, almost frightened. "You should see the trend curves on general interest and curiosity. They're curving *down,* Cliff, all down."

"Let's get back to the subject," Cliff said grimly. "What about your duty to Pluto Station?"

"I'm on my vacation," said Pierce. "Send to Earth for a psychiatrist."

"I thought you were supposed to be sympathetic! Over a hundred percent you said."

"Eye empathy only," Pierce replied, a grin in his voice. "Besides, I'm still identified with the case in the sterio I'm watching, a very hard efficient character, not sympathetic at all."

Cliff was silent a moment, then he said, "Your voice is coming through scrambled. Your beam must be out of alignment. Set the signal beam dial for control by the computer panel, and I'll direct you." Enigmatic scrapings and whirrings came over the thousands of mile beam to Pierce.

With a sigh he switched off the movie projector and moved to the control panel, where Cliff's voice directed him to manipulate various dials.

"O.K. You're all set now," Cliff said. "Let's check. You have the dome at translucent. Switch it to complete reflection on the sun side and transparency on the shadow side, turn on your overhead light and stand against the dark side."

"What's all this rigmarole?" Pierce grumbled. With the blind faith of a layman before the mysteries of machinery, he cut off the steady diffused glow of sunlight, and stood back against the dark side, watching the opposite wall. The last shreds of opacity faded and vanished like fog, and there was only black space flecked with the steady hot brightness of the distant stars. The bright shimmer of the parabolic signal-beam mirror took up most of the view. It was held out and up to the fullest extension of its metallic arm, so that it blocked out a six-foot circle of sky. Pierce looked at it with interest, wondering if he had adjusted it correctly. Its angle certainly looked peculiar.

As he looked, the irregular shimmering began to confuse his eyes. He suddenly felt that there were cobwebs forming between himself and the reflector.   Instinctively Pierce reached out a groping hand, squinting with the effort to see.

His eyes found the focus, and he saw his hand almost touching a human being!

The violence with which he yanked his hand back threw him momentarily off balance.   He fought for equilibrium while his eyes and mind went through a wrenching series of adjustments to the sight of Cliff Baker, only three feet high, floating in the air within reach of his hand.   The effort was too great.   At the last split second he saved himself from an emotional shock wave by switching everything off.   A blank unnatural calm decended, and he said:

"Hi, Cliff."

The figure moved, extending a hand in a reluctant pleading gesture.   Under the brilliant overhead light its expression looked strained and grim.   "Pierce, Pierce, listen.   This is trouble.   You have to help."   There was no mistaking the sincerity of the appeal.   To the trained perception of the psychologist the relative tension of every visible muscle was characteristic of tightly controlled desperation, but to the intensified responsiveness of his feelings the personality and attitude of Cliff Baker burned in like hot iron, shaping Pierce's personality to its own image. Instinctively Pierce tried to escape the intolerable inpour of tension by crowding back against the wall, but the figure followed, expanding nightmarishly.

Then abruptly it vanished.   It had been some sort of a sterio, of course.   For a long moment the psychologist leaned against the curved wall with one hand guarding his face, waiting for his heart to find a steady beat again, and his thoughts to untangle.

"Over a hundred . . . a hundred percent.   Cliff, you don't—   What kind of a—"

"The projection?"   The engineer's voice spoke cheerfully from the radio.   "Just one of the things you can do with a tight-beam parabolic reflector.   Some of the boys thought it up to scare novices with, but I never thought it would be useful for anything."

"Useful!   Cliff!"   Pierce protested.   "You don't know what you did!"

The engineer chuckled again.   "I didn't mean to scare you," he said kindly. "I was trying something else.   Eye empathy you said—   How do you feel about finding out what's wrong at Station A?"

"How do you expect me to feel?"   Pierce groaned.   "Go on, tell me what to do!"

"Come find out what it is, and cure them.   And work on Archy Reynolds first."

There was a long pause, and when Pierce spoke, his voice had changed again. "No, blast it!   You can't have me like that.   I can't just do what you want without thinking!   It's phony.   No station full of people goes crazy together.   I don't believe it."

"I saw it," Cliff answered grimly.

"You *say* you saw it.   And you force me to go to cure them—without explanation, without saying why it is important.   What has it to do with Pluto Station? It isn't like you to force anybody to do anything, Cliff.   It's not your normal pattern!   It isn't like you to cover and avoid explanations."

"What are you driving at?" Cliff said uneasily. "Let me tell you how to set the controls to head for Station A. You have to get here fast!"

"Covering up something. There's only one situation I know of that would make you try to cover." Pierce's voice sharpened with determination. "It must have happened. Listen, Cliff, I'm going to give this to you straight. I know the inside of your head better than you do. I know how you feel about those fluent fast-talking friends of yours at the station and on the job. You're afraid of them—afraid they'll find out you're just a dope. Something has happened at Pluto Station project, and it is still happening—something *bad*, and you think it is *your* fault, you don't know it, but you feel guilty. You're trying to cover up. Don't do it. Don't cover up!"

"Listen," Cliff stammered, "I—"

"Shut up," Pierce said briskly. "This is shock treatment. One level of your personality must have cracked. It would under that special stress. You had an inferiority complex a yard wide. You're going to reintegrate fast on another level right now. File away what I said and listen for the next shock. *You aren't a dope. You're an adjustable analogue.*"

"A what?"

"An adjustable analogue. You think with kinesthetic abstractions. Other people are arithmetic computers. They think with arbitrarily related blocks of memorized audiovisual symbols. That's why you can't talk with them. Different systems."

"What the devil—"

"Shut up. You'll get it in a minute. I ought to know this. I was matched to your feelings for half an hour at a time at Pluto Station. It took me four days to figure out what happened. Your concepts aren't visual, they are kinesthetic. You don't handle problems of dynamics and kinetics with arbitrary words and numbers related by some dead thinker, you use the raw direct experience that your muscles know. You *think* with muscle tension data. I didn't dare follow you that far. Who knows what primitive integration center you have reactivated for it. I can't go down there. My muscle tension data abstracts in the forebrain. That's where I keep my motives and my ability to identify with other people's motives. If I borrowed your ability, I might start identifying with can openers."

"What the—"

"Pipe down," said Pierce, still talking rapidly. "You're following me and you know it. You aren't stupid but you're conditioned against thinking. You don't admit half you know. You'd rather kid yourself. You'd rather be a humble dope and have friends, than open your eyes and be alien and a stranger. You'd rather sit silent at a station bull session and kick yourself for being a dope, than admit that they are word-juggling, talking nonsense. Listen, Cliff—you are not a dope. You may not be able to handle the normal symbol patterns of this culture, but you have a structured mind that's integrated right down to your boots! You can solve this emergency yourself. So what if your personality has been conditioned against thinking? Everybody knows the standard tricks for suspending conditioning. Put in cortical control, solve the problem first, whatever it is, and then be dumb afterwards if that's what you want!''

After a moment Cliff laughed shakily. "Shock treatment, you call it. Like being whacked over the head with a sledge hammer.''

"I think I owed you a slight shock,'' Pierce said grimly. "May I go?''

"Wait a sec, aren't you going to help?''

Pierce sounded irritable. "Help? Help what? You have more brains than I have, solve your own problems: Pull yourself together, Cliff, and don't give me any more of this raving about a whole station full of people going bats! It's not true!'' He switched off.

Cliff sat down on the nearest thing resembling a chair, and made a mental note never to antagonize psychologists. Then he began to *think*.

Once upon a time the New York Public Library shipped a crate of microfilm to Station A. The crate was twenty by twenty and contained the incredible sum of the world's libraries. With the crate they shipped a librarian, one M. Reynolds to fit the films into an automatic filing system so that the reader could find any book he sought among the uncounted other books. He spent the rest of his life trying to achieve the unachievable, reduce the system of filing books to a matter of perfect logic. In darker ages he would have spent his life happily arguing the number of bodiless angels that could dance on the head of a pin.

They became used to seeing him puttering around, assisted by his little boy, or reading the journal of symbolic logic, or, temporarily baffled, trying to clear his mind by playing games of chess, and cards, in which he beat all comers.

Once he grew excited by the fact that computers worked on a numerical base of two, and sound on the log of two. Once he grew interested in the station's delicate system of automatic controls and began to dismantle it and change the leads. If he had made a wrong move, the station would have returned to its component elements, but no one bothered him. They remembered the chess games, and left the automatics to him. They were satisfied with the new reading desks, and after a while there was a joke that if you made a mistake they would give you a ham sandwich, and a joke that the automatics would deliver pretty girls and blow up if you asked for a Roc's egg, but still no one realized the meaning of Doc Reynolds' research.

After all, it was simply the proper classification of subjects, and a symbology for the library keyboard that would duplicate the logical relations of the subjects themselves. No harm in that. It would just make it easier for the reader to find books.

Once again Cliff stood under the deep assault of sound. This time it was tapes of two of Archy's best jazz concerts, strong and wild. Once again the rhythms fitted themselves into the padded beat of his heart, the surge of blood in his ears, and other, more complex rhythms of the nerves, subtly altering and speeding them in mimicry of the pulse of emotions, while flute notes played with the sound of

Reynolds' automatics, automatics impassioned, oddly fitting and completing the deeper surges of normal music.

Cliff stood, letting the music flow through him, subtly working on the pattern of his thought. Suddenly it was voices, a dreamlike clamor of voices surging up in his mind and closing over him in a great shout, and then passing, and then the music was just music, very good music with words. He listened calmly, with enjoyment.

It ended, and he left the room and went whistling down the corridor walking briskly, working off some energy. It was the familiar half ecstatic energy of learning, as if he had met a new clarifying generalization that made all thought much simpler. It kept hitting him with little sparks of laughter as if the full implication of the idea still automatically carried their chain reaction of integration into dim cluttered corners of his mind releasing them from redundancy and the weariness of facts.

He passed someone he knew vaguely, and lifted a hand in casual greeting. "Reep beeb," he said.

It was a language.

The people of Station A did not know that it was a language, they thought they were going pleasantly cuckoo, but he knew. They had been exposed a long time to the sound of Reynolds' machines. Reynolds had put in the sound system and brought it down to audible range to help himself keep track of the workings of it, and the people of Station A for five years had been exposed to the sounds of the machine translating all their requests into its own symbolic perfect language, reasoning aloud with it, and then stating the answer in its own language before translating it back into action, or service, or English or mathematics.

It had been an association in their minds, and latent, but when Archy included frequency symbol themes in his jazz, they had come away humming the themes, and it had precipitated the association. Suddenly they could not stop humming and whistling and clicking, it seemed part of their thought, and it clarified thinking. They thought of it as a drug, a disease, but they knew they liked it. It was seductive, irresistible, and frightening.

But to Cliff it was a language, emotional, subtle and precise, with its own intricate number system. He could talk to the computers with it.

Cliff sat before the computer panel of his work desk. He did not touch it. He sat and hummed to himself thoughtfully, and sometimes whistled an arpeggio like Reynolds' automatic making a choice.

A red light lit on the panel. Pluto had been contacted and had reported. Cliff listened to the spiel of the verbal report first as it was slowed down to normal speed. "I didn't know you could reach us," said the medico. "Ole is dead. Smitty has one hand, but he can still work. Danny Orlando—Jacabson—" rapidly the doctor's weary voice went through the list, reporting on the men and the hours of work they would be capable of. Then it was the turn of the machinery and orbit report. The station computer translated the data to clicks and scales and twitters, and slowly the picture of the condition of Pluto Station project built up in Cliff's mind.

When it was complete, he leaned back and whistled for twenty minutes, clicking with a clicker toy and occasionally blowing a chord on a cheap harmonica he had brought for the use, while the calculator took the raw formulas and extrapolated direction tapes for all of Pluto Station's workers and equipment.

And then it was done.   Cliff put away the harmonica, grinning.   The men would be surprised to have to read their instructions from directional tapes, like mechanicals, but they could do it.

Pluto Station Project was back under control.

Cliff leaned back, humming, considering what had been done, and while he hummed the essentially musical symbology of the Reynolds index system sank deeper and deeper into his thoughts, translating their natural precision into the precision of pitch, edging all his thinking with music.

On Earth teemed the backward human race, surrounded by a baffling civilization, understanding nothing of it, neither economics nor medicine or psychology, most of them baffled even by the simplicity of algebra, and increasingly hostile to all thought.   Yet through their days as they worked or relaxed, the hours were made pleasant to them by music.

Symphony fans listened without strain while two hundred instruments played, and would have winced if a single violin struck four hundred forty vibrations per second where it should have reached four hundred forty-five.   Jazz fans listened critically to a trumpeter playing around with a tune in a framework of six incommensurable basic rhythms whose relative position shifted mathematically with every note.   Jazz, symphony or both, they were all fans and steeped in it.   Even on the sidewalks people walked with their expressions and stride responding to the unheard music of omnipresent earphones.

The whole world was steeped in music.   Saturated in music of a growingly incredible eloquence and complexity, of a precision and subtlety that was inexpressible in any other language or art, a complexity whose mathematics would baffle Einstein, and yet was easily understandable to the ear, and to the trained sensuous mind area associated with it.

What if that part of the human mind were brought to bear on the simple problems of politics, psychology and science?

Cliff whistled slowly in an ordinary non-index whistle of wonderment.   No wonder the people of Station A had been unable to stop.   They hummed solving problems, they whistled when trying to concentrate, not knowing why.   They thought it was madness, but they felt stupid and thick headed when they stopped, and to a city full of technicians to whom problem-solving was the breath of life, the sensation of relative stupidity was terrifying.

The language was still in the simple association baby-babbling stage, not yet brought to consciousness as a language, not yet touching them with a fraction of its clarifying power—but it was raising their intelligence level.

Cliff had been whistling his thoughts in index, amused by the library machine's reflex bookish elaboration of them, for its association preferences had been set up by human beings, and they held a distinct flavor of the personalities of Doc Reynolds and Archy.   But now, abruptly the wall speaker said something absolutely original, phrased with brilliance and dogmaticism.   "Why be intelligent?   Why communicate when you are surrounded by cows?   It would drive you even more bats to know what they think."   The remark trailed off and scattered in abstract references to nihilism, consensus, eternity and Darwin, which were obviously association trails added by the machine, but the central remark had been Archy himself.   Somewhere in the station Archy was tinkering idly and unhappily with the innards of his father's machine, whistling an unconsciously logical jazz counterpoint to one of the strands of twittering that bombarded his ears.

It was something like being linked into Archy's mind without Archy being aware of it.   Cliff questioned, and suggested topics.   The flavor of the counterpoint was loneliness and anger.   The kid felt that Cliff and Mike had deserted him in some way, for his father had died when he was in high school, and Cliff and Mike had long given up tutoring him and turned him over to his teachers.   His father had died, and Cliff and Mike were not around to talk with or ask advice, so leaving Archy to discover in one blow of undiluted loneliness that his mental immersion in science and logic was a wall standing between him and his classmates, making it impossible to talk with them or enjoy their talk, making it impossible for his teachers to understand the meaning of his questions.   Archy had reacted typically in three years of tantrum, in which he despairingly hated the world, hated theory and thinking, and sought opiate in girls, dancing, and a frenzied immersion in jazz.

He had not even noticed what his jazz had done to the people who listened.

Cliff smiled, remembering the abysmal miseries of adolescence, and smiled again. Everyone else in the station was miserable, too.   There was Dr. Brandias, who should have been trying to solve the problem of the jazz madness, miserably turning over the pages of a light magazine in the next cubical, pretending not to notice Cliff's strange whistling and harmonica blowing.

"Brandy."

The medico looked up and flushed guiltily.   "How are you doing, Cliff?"

"Come here.   I've something to tell you."

It began with a lesson tour, pointing and describing in index.   It became a follow-the-leader with each action in turn described in index—and progressed.

The I.B.M. man doggedly looking for Archy Reynolds through the suddenly deserted station at last wandered in to the huge gym at 1.3G and was horrified to see Archy Reynolds and Cliff Baker leading the entire staff of Station A in a monstrous conga line.   Archy Reynolds was beating a drum under one arm and clicking castanets with the other, while the big sober engineer blew weird disjointed tunes on a toy harmonica and the line danced wildly.   The I.B.M. man shut his eyes, then opened them grimly.

"Mr. Reynolds," he called.   He was a brave man, and tenacious.   "Mr. Reynolds."

Archy stopped and the whole dance stopped with him in deadly silence, frozen in mid step.

"What can I do for you?"

The I.B.M. man pulled three reels of tape from his brief case. "Senor McCrea showed me Dr. Reynolds' basic tapes, and I took a transcription. Now about the patent rights—" He took a deep breath and swung his glance doggedly across the host of watching faces back to the lean impassive face of the young man who held the rights to the Reynolds tapes. "Could we discuss this in private?"

Instead of replying, the young man exchanged a glance with Cliff Baker, and they both began whistling rapidly, then Archy Reynolds stepped back with a gesture of dismissal and Cliff Baker turned, smiling.

"One condition," he said, the intonations of his deep, hesitant voice as alien as the voices of all others of the station, although earlier in the hall he had sounded comparatively sane to the I.B.M. man. "Only one condition, that I.B.M. leave the sound-frequency setup Reynolds has in his plans at audible volume, no matter how useless the yeeps seem to an engineer. Except for that, it's all yours." He smiled oddly and began whistling again, and the people in the lines behind him began restlessly swaying from one foot to another. Archy Reynolds began to pound on his drum.

"What?" gasped the I.B.M. man.

"You can have the patent rights," Cliff replied over the din. "It's all yours!"

The dance was beginning again, the huge line slowly mimicking the actions of the leaders. As the I.B.M. man hesitated at the door, staring back at the strange sight, Cliff Baker was showing his wife some intricate step, and the others mimicked in pairs.

The big engineer glanced towards the door, hesitated and hummed, clicked and whistled weirdly in a moment of complete stillness, then threw back his head and laughed. All eyes in the assemblage swiveled and came to rest on the I.B.M. man, and all through the hall there was a slow chuckle of laughter growing towards a howl.

Madness!

He stumbled through the door and fled, carrying in his brief case a new human race.

C. M. KORNBLUTH

The Little Black Bag

Old Dr. Full felt the winter in his bones as he limped down the alley. It was the alley and the back door he had chosen rather than the sidewalk and the front door because of the brown paper bag under his arm. He knew perfectly well that the flat-faced, stringy-haired women of his street and their gap-toothed, sour-smelling husbands did not notice if he brought a bottle of cheap wine to his room. They all but lived on the stuff themselves, varied with whiskey when pay checks were boosted by overtime. But Dr. Full, unlike them, was ashamed. A complicated disaster occurred as he limped down the littered alley. One of the neighborhood dogs—a mean little black one he knew and hated, with its teeth always bared and always snarling with menace—hurled at his legs through a hole in the board fence that lined his path. Dr. Full flinched, then swung his leg in what was to have been a satisfying kick to the animal's gaunt ribs. But the winter in his bones weighed down the leg. His foot failed to clear a half-buried brick, and he sat down abruptly, cursing. When he smelled unbottled wine and realized his brown paper package had slipped from under his arm and smashed, his curses died on his lips. The snarling black dog was circling him at a yard's distance, tensely stalking, but he ignored it in the greater disaster.

With stiff fingers as he sat on the filth of the alley, Dr. Full unfolded the brown paper bag's top, which had been crimped over, grocer-wise. The early autumnal dusk had come; he could not see plainly what was left. He lifted out the jug-handled top of his half gallon, and some fragments, and then the bottom of the bottle. Dr. Full was far too occupied to exult as he noted that there was a good pint left. He had a problem, and emotions could be deferred until the fitting time.

The dog closed in, its snarl rising in pitch. He set down the bottom of the bottle and pelted the dog with the curved triangular glass fragments of its top. One of them connected, and the dog ducked back through the fence, howling. Dr. Full then placed a razor-like edge of the half-gallon bottle's foundation to his lips and drank from it as though it were a giant's cup. Twice he had to put it down to rest his arms, but in one minute he had swallowed the pint of wine.

He thought of rising to his feet and walking through the alley to his room, but a flood of well-being drowned the notion. It was, after all, inexpressibly pleasant to sit there and feel the frost-hardened mud of the alley turn soft, or seem to, and to feel the winter evaporating from his bones under a warmth which spread from his stomach through his limbs.

A three-year-old girl in a cut-down winter coat squeezed through the same hole in the board fence from which the black dog had sprung its ambush. Gravely she toddled up to Dr. Full and inspected him with her dirty forefinger in her mouth. Dr. Full's happiness had been providentially made complete; he had been supplied with an audience.

"Ah, my dear," he said hoarsely. And then: "Preposterous accusation. "If that's what you call evidence,' I should have told them, 'you better stick to you doctoring.' I should have told them: 'I was here before your County Medical Society. And the License Commissioner never proved a thing on me. So gennulmen, doesn't it stand to reason? I appeal to you as fellow members of a great profession?' "

The little girl bored, moved away, picking up one of the triangular pieces of glass to play with as she left. Dr. Full forgot her immediately, and continued to himself earnestly: "But so help me, they *couldn't* prove a thing. Hasn't a man got any *rights?*" He brooded over the question, of whose answer he was so sure, but on which the Committee on Ethics of the County Medical Society had been equally certain. The winter was creeping into his bones again, and he had no money and no more wine.

Dr. Full pretended to himself that there was a bottle of whiskey somewhere in the fearful litter of his room. It was an old and cruel trick he played on himself when he simply had to be galvanized into getting up and going home. He might freeze there in the alley. In his room he would be bitten by bugs and would cough at the moldy reek from his sink, but he would not freeze and be cheated of the hundreds of bottles of wine that he still might drink, and the thousands of hours of glowing content he still might feel. He thought about that bottle of whiskey— was it back of a mounded heap of medical journals? No; he had looked there last time. Was it under the sink, shoved well to the rear, behind the rusty drain? The cruel trick began to play itself out again. Yes, he told himself with mounting excitement, yes, it might be! Your memory isn't so good nowadays, he told himself with rueful good-fellowship. You know perfectly well you might have bought a bottle of whiskey and shoved it behind the sink drain for a moment just like this.

The amber bottle, the crisp snap of the sealing as he cut it, the pleasurable exertion of starting the screw cap on its threads, and then the refreshing tangs in his throat, the warmth in his stomach, the dark, dull happy oblivion of drunkenness—they became real to him. You *could* have, you know! You *could* have! he told himself. With the blessed conviction growing in his mind—It *could* have happened, you know! It *could* have!—he struggled to his right knee. As he did, he heard a yelp behind him, and curiously craned his neck around while resting. It was the little girl, who had cut her hand quite badly on her toy, the piece of glass. Dr. Full could see the rilling bright blood down her coat, pooling at her feet.

He almost felt inclined to defer the image of the amber bottle for her, but not seriously.   He knew that it was there, shoved well to the rear under the sink, behind the rusty drain where he had hidden it.   He would have a drink and then magnanimously return to help the child.   Dr. Full got to his other knee and then his feet, and proceeded at a rapid totter down the littered alley toward his room, where he would hunt with calm optimism at first for the bottle that was not there, then with anxiety, and then with frantic violence.   He would hurl books and dishes about before he was done looking for the amber bottle of whiskey, and finally would beat his swollen knuckles against the brick wall until old scars on them opened and his thick old blood oozed over his hands.   Last of all, he would sit down somewhere on the floor, whimpering, and would plunge into the abyss of purgative nightmare that was his sleep.

After twenty generations of shilly-shallying and "we'll cross that bridge when we come to it," genus homo had bred itself into an impasse.   Dogged biometricians had pointed out with irrefutable logic that mental subnormals were outbreeding mental normals and supernormals, and that the process was occurring on an exponential curve.   Every fact that could be mustered in the argument proved the biometricians' case, and led inevitably to the conclusion that genus homo was going to wind up in a preposterous jam quite soon.   If you think that had any effect on breeding practices, you do not know genus homo.

There was, of course, a sort of masking effect produced by that other exponential function, the accumulation of technological devices.   A moron trained to punch an adding machine seems to be a more skillful computer than a medieval mathematician trained to count on his fingers.   A moron trained to operate the twenty-first century equivalent of a linotype seems to be a better typographer than a Renaissance printer limited to a few fonts of movable type.   This is also true of medical practice.

It was a complicated affair of many factors.   The supernormals "improved the product" at greater speed than the subnormals degraded it, but in smaller quantity because elaborate training of their children was practiced on a custom-made basis. The fetish of higher education had some weird avatars by the twentieth generation: "colleges" where not a member of the student body could read words of three syllables; "universities" where such degrees as "Bachelor of Typewriting," "Master of Shorthand" and "Doctor of Philosophy (Card Filing)" were conferred with the traditional pomp.   The handful of supernormals used such devices in order that the vast majority might keep some semblance of a social order going.

Some day the supernormals would mercilessly cross the bridge; at the twentieth generation they were standing irresolutely at its approaches wondering what had hit them.   And the ghosts of twenty generations of biometricians chuckled malignantly.

It is a certain Doctor of Medicine of this twentieth generation that we are concerned with.   His name was Hemingway—John Hemingway.   B.Sc., M.D.   He was a general practitioner, and did not hold with running to specialists with every trifling ailment.   He often said as much, in approximately these words: "Now, uh, what I mean is you got a good old G.P. See what I mean? Well, uh, now a good old G.P. don't claim he knows all about lungs and glands and them things, get me? But you got a G.P., you got, uh, you got a, well, you got a . . . *all-around man!* That's what you got when you got a G.P.—you got a all-around man.''

But from this, do not imagine that Dr. Hemingway was a poor doctor. He could remove tonsils or appendixes, assist at practically any confinement and deliver a living, uninjured infant, correctly diagnose hundreds of ailments, and prescribe and administer the correct medication or treatment for each. There was, in fact, only one thing he could not do in the medical line, and that was, violate the ancient canons of medical ethics. And Dr. Hemingway knew better than to try.

Dr. Hemingway and a few friends were chatting one evening when the event occurred that precipitates him into our story. He had been through a hard day at the clinic, and he wished his physicist friend Walter Gillis, B.Sc., M.Sc., Ph.D., would shut up so he could tell everybody about it. But Gillis kept rambling on, in his stilted fashion: "You got to hand to old Mike; he don't have what we call the scientific method, but you got to hand it to him. There this poor little dope is, puttering around with some glassware, and I come up and ask him, kidding of course, 'How's about a time-travel machine, Mike?' "

Dr. Gillis was not aware of it, but "Mike" had an I.Q. six times his own and was—to be blunt—his keeper. "Mike" rode herd on the pseudo-physicists in the pseudo-laboratory, in the guise of a bottle-washer. It was a social waste—but as has been mentioned before, the supernormals were still standing at the approaches to a bridge. Their irresolution led to many such preposterous situations. And it happens that "Mike," having grown frantically bored with his task, was malevolent enough to—but let Dr. Gillis tell it:

"So he gives me these here tube numbers and says, 'Series circuit. Now stop bothering me. Build your time machine, sit down at it and turn on the switch. That's all I ask, Dr. Gillis—that's all I ask.' "

"Say," marveled a brittle and lovely blond guest, "you remember real good, don't you, doc?" She gave him a melting smile.

"Heck," said Gillis modestly, "I always remember good. It's what you call an inherent facility. And besides I told it quick to my secretary, so she wrote it down. I don't read so good, but I sure remember good, all right. Now, where was I?"

Everybody thought hard, and there were various suggestions:

"Something about bottles, doc?"

"You was starting a fight. You said 'time somebody was traveling.' ''

"Yeah—you called somebody a swish. Who did you call a swish?"

"Not swish—*switch!*''

Dr. Gillis' noble brow grooved with thought, and he declared: "Switch is right. It was about time travel. What we call travel through time. So I took the tube numbers he gave me and I put them into the circuit-builder; I set it for 'series' and there it is—my time-traveling machine. It travels things through time real good."
He displayed a box.

"What's in the box?" asked the lovely blonde.

Dr. Hemingway told her: "Time travel.   It travels things through time."

"Look," said Gillis, the physicist.   He took Dr. Hemingway's little black bag and put it on the box.   He turned on the switch and the little black bag vanished.

"Say," said Dr. Hemingway, "that was, uh, swell.   Now bring it back."

"Huh?"

"Bring back my little black bag."

"Well," said Dr. Gillis, "they don't come back.   I guess maybe that dummy Mike gave me a bum steer."

There was wholesale condemnation of "Mike" but Dr. Hemingway took no part in it.   He was nagged by a vague feeling that there was something he would have to do.   He reasoned: "I am a doctor, and a doctor has got to have a little black bag.   I ain't got a little black bag—so ain't I a doctor no more?"   He decided that this was absurd.   He *knew* he was a doctor.   So it must be the bag's fault for not being there.   It was no good, and he would get another one tomorrow from that dummy Al, at the clinic.   Al could find things good, but he was a dummy— never liked to talk sociable to you.

So the next day Dr. Hemingway remembered to get another little black bag from his keeper—another little black bag with which he could perform tonsillectomies, appendectomies and the most difficult confinements, and with which he could diagnose and cure his kind until the day when the supernormals could bring them- selves to cross that bridge.   Al was kinda nasty about the missing little black bag, but Dr. Hemingway didn't exactly remember what had happened, so no tracer was sent out, so—

Old Dr. Full awoke from the horrors of the night to the horrors of the day. His gummy eyelashes pulled apart convulsively.   He was propped against the corner of his room, and something was making a little drumming noise.   He felt very cold and cramped.   As his eyes focused on his lower body, he croaked out a laugh.   The drumming noise was being made by his left heel, agitated by fine tremors against the bare floor.   It was going to be the D.T.'s again, he decided dispassionately.   He wiped his mouth with his bloody knuckles, and the fine tremor coarsened; the snaredrum beat became louder and slower.   He was getting a break this fine morning, he decided sardonically.   You didn't get the horrors until you had been tightened like a violin string, just to the breaking point.   He had a reprieve, if a reprieve into his old body with the blazing, endless headache just back of the eyes and the screaming stillness in the joints were anything to be thankful for.

There was something or other about a kid, he thought vaguely.   He was going to doctor some kid.   His eyes rested on a little black bag in the center of the room, and he forgot about the kid.   "I could have sworn," said Dr. Full, "I hocked that two years ago!"   He hitched over and reached the bag, and then realized it was some stranger's kit, arriving here he did not know how.   He tentatively touched the lock and it snapped open and lay flat, rows and rows of instruments and medications tucked into loops in its four walls.   It seemed vastly larger open than closed.   He didn't see how it could possibly fold up into that compact size again, but decided it was some stunt of the instrument makers.   Since his time—that made it worth more at the hock shop, he thought with satisfaction.

Just for old times' sake, he let his eyes and fingers rove over the instruments before he snapped the bag shut and headed for Uncle's.   More than few were a little hard to recognize—exactly that is.   You could see the things with blades for cutting, the forceps for holding and pulling, the retractors for holding fast, the needles and gut for suturing, the hypos—a fleeting thought crossed his mind that he could peddle the hypos separately to drug addicts.

Let's go, he decided, and tried to fold up the case.   It didn't fold until he happened to touch the lock, and then it folded all at once into a little black bag. Sure have forged ahead, he thought, almost able to forget that what he was primarily interested in was its pawn value.

With a definite objective, it was not too hard for him to get to his feet.   He decided to go down the front steps, out the front door and down the sidewalk.   But first—

He snapped the bag open again on his kitchen table, and pored through the medication tubes.   "Anything to sock the autonomic nervous system good and hard," he mumbled.   The tubes were numbered, and there was a plastic card which seemed to list them.   The left margin of the card was a run-down of the systems— vascular, muscular, nervous.   He followed the last entry across to the right.   There were columns for "stimulant," "depressant," and so on.   Under "nervous system" and "depressant" he found the number 17, and shakily located the little glass tube which bore it.   It was full of pretty blue pills and he took one.

It was like being struck by a thunderbolt.

Dr. Full had so long lacked any sense of well-being except the brief glow of alcohol that he had forgotten its very nature.   He was panic-stricken for a long moment at the sensation that spread through him slowly, finally tingling in his fingertips.   He straightened up, his pains gone and his leg tremor stilled.

That was great, he thought.   He'd be able to *run* to the hock shop, pawn the little black bag and get some booze.   He started down the stairs.   Not even the street, bright with mid-morning sun, into which he emerged made him quail.   The little black bag in his left hand had a satisfying authoritative weight.   He was walking erect, he noted, and not in the somewhat furtive crouch that had grown on him in recent years.   A little self-respect, he told himself, that's what I need. Just because a man's down doesn't mean—

"Docta, please-a come wit'!" somebody yelled at him, tugging his arm.   "Da litt-la girl, she's-a burn' up!"   It was one of the slum's innumerable flat-faced, stringy-haired women, in a slovenly wrapper.

"Ah, I happen to be retired from practice—" he began hoarsely, but she would not be put off.

"In by here, Docta!" she urged, tugged him to a doorway.   "You come look-a da litt-la girl.   I got two dolla, you come look!"   That put a different complexion on the matter.   He allowed himself to be towed through the doorway into a messy, cabbage-smelling flat.   He knew the woman now, or rather knew who she must be—a new arrival who had moved in the other night.   These people moved at night, in motorcades of battered cars supplied by friends and relatives, with furniture lashed to the tops, swearing and drinking until the small hours. It explained why she had stopped him: she did not yet know he was old Dr. Full, a drunken reprobate whom nobody would trust. The little black bag had been his guarantee, outweighing his whiskey face and stained black suit.

He was looking down on a three-year-old girl who had, he rather suspected, just been placed in the mathematical center of a freshly changed double bed. God knew what sour and dirty mattress she usually slept on. He seemed to recognize her as he noted a crusted bandage on her right hand. Two dollars, he thought. An ugly flush had spread up her pipe-stem arm. He poked a finger into the socket of her elbow, and felt little spheres like marbles under the skin and ligaments roll apart. The child began to squall thinly; beside him, the woman gasped and began to weep herself.

"Out," he gestured briskly at her, and she thudded away, still sobbing.

Two dollars, he thought. Give her some mumbo jumbo, take the money and tell her to go to a clinic. Strep, I guess, from that stinking alley. It's a wonder any of them grow up. He put down the little black bag and forgetfully fumbled for his key, then remembered and touched the lock. It flew open, and he selected a bandage shears, with a blunt wafer for the lower jaw. He fitted the lower jaw under the bandage, trying not to hurt the kid by its pressure on the infection, and began to cut. It was amazing how easily and swiftly the shining shears snipped through the crusty rag around the wound. He hardly seemed to be driving the shears with fingers at all. It almost seemed as though the shears were driving his fingers instead as they scissored a clean, light line through the bandage.

Certainly have forged ahead since my time, he thought—sharper than a microtome knife. He replaced the shears in their loop on the extraordinarily big board that the little black bag turned into when it unfolded, and leaned over the wound. He whistled at the ugly gash, and the violent infection which had taken immediate root in the sickly child's thin body. Now what can he do with a thing like that? He pawed over the contents of the little black bag, nervously. If he lanced it and let some of the pus out, the old woman would think he'd done something for her and he'd get the two dollars. But at the clinic they'd want to know who did it and if they got sore enough they might send a cop around. Maybe there was something in the kit—

He ran down the left edge of the card to "lymphatic" and read across to the column under "infection." It didn't sound right at all to him; he checked again, but it still said that. In the square to which the line and the column led were the symbols: "IV-g-3cc." He couldn't find any bottles marked with Roman numerals, and then noticed that that was how the hypodermic needles were designated. He lifted number IV from its loop, noting that it was fitted with a needle already and even seemed to be charged. What a way to carry those things around! So— three cc. of whatever was in hypo number IV ought to do something or other about infections settled in the lymphatic system—which, God knows, this one was. What did the lower-case "g" mean, though? He studied the glass hypo and saw letters engraved on what looked like a rotating disk at the top of the barrel. They ran from "a" to "i," and there was an index line engraved on the barrel on the opposite side from the calibrations.

Shrugging, old Dr. Full turned the disk until "g" coincided with the index line, and lifted the hypo to eye level. As he pressed in the plunger he did not see the tiny thread of fluid squirt from the tip of the needle. There was a sort of dark mist for a moment about the tip. A closer inspection showed that the needle was not even pierced at the tip. It had the usual slanting cut across the bias of the shaft, but the cut did not expose an oval hole. Baffled, he tried pressing the plunger again. Again *something* appeared around the tip and vanished. "We'll settle this," said the doctor. He slipped the needle into the skin of his forearm. He thought at first that he had missed—that the point had glided over the top of his skin instead of catching and slipping under it. But he saw a tiny blood-spot and realized that somehow he just hadn't felt the puncture. Whatever was in the barrel, he decided, couldn't do him any harm if it lived up to its billing—and if it could ever come out through a needle that had no hole. He gave himself three cc. and twitched the needle out. There was the swelling—painless, but otherwise typical.

Dr. Full decided it was his eyes or something, and gave three cc. of "g" from hypodermic IV to the feverish child. There was no interruption to her wailing as the needle went in and the swelling rose. But a long instant later, she gave a final gasp and was silent.

Well, he told himself, cold with horror, you did it that time. You killed her with that stuff.

Then the child sat up and said: "Where's my mommy?"

Incredulously, the doctor seized her arm and palpated the elbow. The gland infection was zero, and the temperature seemed normal. The blood-congested tissues surrounding the wound were subsiding as he watched. The child's pulse was stronger and no faster than a child's should be. In the sudden silence of the room he could hear the little girl's mother sobbing in her kitchen, outside. And he also heard a girl's insinuating voice:

"She gonna be OK, doc?"

He turned and saw a gaunt-faced, dirty-blond sloven of perhaps eighteen leaning in the doorway and eyeing him with amused contempt. She continued: "I heard about you, *Doc-tor* Full. So don't go try and put the bite on the old lady. You couldn't doctor up a sick cat."

"Indeed?" he rumbled. This young person was going to get a lesson she richly deserved. "Perhaps you would care to look at my patient?"

"Where's my mommy?" insisted the little girl, and the blond's jaw fell. She went to the bed and cautiously asked:

"You OK now, Teresa? You all fixed up?"

"Where's my mommy?" demanded Teresa. Then, accusingly, she gestured with her wounded hand at the doctor. "You *poke* me!" she complained, and giggled pointlessly.

"Well—" said the blond girl, "I guess I got to hand it to you, doc. These loud-mouth women around here said you didn't know your . . . I mean, didn't know how to cure people. They said you ain't a real doctor."

"I *have* retired from practice," he said. "But I happened to be taking this case to a colleague as a favor, your good mother noticed me, and—" a deprecating smile. He touched the lock of the case and it folded up into the little black bag again.

"You stole it," the girl said flatly.

He sputtered.

"Nobody'd trust you with a thing like that. It must be worth plenty. You stole that case. I was going to stop you when I came in and saw you working over Teresa, but it looked like you wasn't doing her any harm. But when you give me that line about taking that case to a colleague I know you stole it. You gimme a cut or I go to the cops. A thing like that must be worth twenty-thirty dollars."

The mother came timidly in, her eyes red. But she let out a whoop of joy when she saw the little girl sitting up and babbling to herself, embraced her madly, fell on her knees for a quick prayer, hopped up to kiss the doctor's hand, and then dragged him into the kitchen, all the while rattling in her native language while the blond girl let her eyes go cold with disgust. Dr. Full allowed himself to be towed into the kitchen, but flatly declined a cup of coffee and a plate of anise cakes and St.-John's-bread.

"Try him on some wine, ma," said the girl sardonically.

"Hyass! Hyass!" breathed the woman delightedly. "You like-a wine, docta?" She had a carafe of purplish liquid before him in an instant, and the blond girl snickered as the doctor's hand twitched out at it. He drew his hand back, while there grew in his head the old image of how it would smell and then taste and then warm his stomach and limbs. He made the kind of calculation at which he was practiced; the delighted woman would not notice as he downed two tumblers, and he could overawe her through two tumblers more with his tale of Teresa's narrow brush with the Destroying Angel, and then—why, then it would not matter. He would be drunk.

But for the first time in years, there was a sort of counter-image: a blend of the rage he felt at the blond girl to whom he was so transparent, and of pride at the cure he had just effected. Much to his own surprise, he drew back his hand from the carafe and said, luxuriating in the words: "No, thank you. I don't believe I'd care for any so early in the day." He covertly watched the blond girl's face, and was gratified at her surprise. Then the mother was shyly handing him two bills and saying: "Is no much-a-money, docta—but you come again, see Teresa?"

"I shall be glad to follow the case through," he said. "But now excuse me— I really must be running along." He grasped the little black bag firmly and got up; he wanted very much to get away from the wine and the older girl.

"Wait up, doc," said she. "I'm going your way." She followed him out and down the street. He ignored her until he felt her hand on the black bag. Then old Dr. Full stopped and tried to reason with her:

"Look, my dear. Perhaps you're right. I might have stolen it. To be perfectly frank, I don't remember how I got it. But you're young and you can earn your own money—"

"Fifty-fifty," she said, "or I go to the cops. And if I get another word outta you, it's sixty-forty. And you know who gets the short end, don't you, doc?"

Defeated, he marched to the pawnshop, her impudent hand still on the handle with his, and her heels beating out a tattoo against his stately tread.

In the pawnshop, they both got a shock.

"It ain't standard," said Uncle, unimpressed by the ingenious lock. "I ain't nevva seen one like it. Some cheap Jap stuff, maybe? Try down the street. This I nevva could sell."

Down the street they got an offer of one dollar. The same complaint was made: "I ain't a collecta, mista—I buy stuff that got resale value. Who could I sell this to, a Chinaman who doesn't know medical instruments? Every one of them looks funny. You sure you didn't make these yourself?" They didn't take the one-dollar offer.

The girl was baffled and angry; the doctor was baffled too, but triumphant. He had two dollars, and the girl had a half-interest in something nobody wanted. But, he suddenly marveled, the thing had been all right to cure the kid, hadn't it?

"Well," he asked her, "do you give up? As you see, the kit is practically valueless."

She was thinking hard. "Don't fly off the handle, doc. I don't get this but something's going on all right . . . would those guys know good stuff if they saw it?"

"They would. They make a living from it. Wherever this kit came from—"

She seized on that, with a devilish faculty she seemed to have of eliciting answers without asking questions. "I thought so. You don't know either, huh? Well, maybe I can find out for you. C'mon in here. I ain't letting go of that thing. There's money in it—some way, I don't know how, there's money in it." He followed her into a cafeteria and to an almost empty corner. She was oblivious to stares and snickers from the other customers as she opened the little black bag—it almost covered a cafeteria table—and ferreted through it. She picked out a retractor from a loop, scrutinized it, contemptuously threw it down, picked out a speculum, threw it down, picked out the lower half of an O.B. forceps, turned it over, close to her sharp young eyes—and saw what the doctor's dim old ones could not have seen.

All old Dr. Full knew was that she was peering at the neck of the forceps and then turned white. Very carefully, she placed the half of the forceps back in its loop of cloth and then replaced the retractor and the speculum. "Well?" he asked. "What did you see?"

" 'Made in U.S.A.,' " she quoted hoarsely. " 'Patent Applied for July 2450.' "

He wanted to tell her she must have misread the inscription, that it must be a practical joke, that—

But he knew she had read correctly. Those bandage shears: they *had* driven his fingers, rather than his fingers driving them. The hypo needle that had no hole. The pretty blue pill that had struck him like a thunderbolt.

"You know what I'm going to do?" asked the girl, with sudden animation. "I'm going to go to charm school. You'll like that, won't ya, doc? Because we're sure going to be seeing a lot of each other."

Old Dr. Full didn't answer. His hands had been playing idly with that plastic card from the kit on which had been printed the rows and columns that had guided him twice before. The card had a slight convexity; you could snap the convexity back and forth from one side to the other. He noted, in a daze, that with each snap a different text appeared on the cards. *Snap.* "The knife with the blue dot in the handle is for tumors only. Diagnose tumors with your Instrument Seven, the Swelling Tester. Place the Swelling Tester—" *Snap.* "An overdose of the pink pills in Bottle 3 can be fixed with one pill from bottle—" *Snap.* "Hold the suture needle by the end without the hole in it. Touch it to one end of the wound you want to close and let go. After it has made the knot, touch it—" *Snap.* "Place the top half of the O.B. Forceps near the opening. Let go. After it has entered and conformed to the shape of—" *Snap.*

The slot man saw "FLANNERY 1—MEDICAL" in the upper left corner of the hunk of copy. He automatically scribbled "trim to .75" on it and skimmed it across the horseshoe-shaped copy desk to Piper, who had been handling Edna Flannery's quack-exposé series. She was a nice youngster, he thought, but like all youngsters she over-wrote. Hence, the "trim."

Piper dealt back a city hall story to the slot, pinned down Flannery's feature with one hand and began to tap his pencil across it, one tap to a word, at the same steady beat as a teletype carriage traveling across the roller. He wasn't exactly reading it this first time. He was just looking at the letters and words to find out whether, as letters and words, they conformed to *Herald* style. The steady tap of his pencil ceased at intervals as it drew a black line ending with a stylized letter "d" through the word "breast" and scribbled in "chest" instead, or knocked down the capital "E" in "East" to lower case with a diagonal, or closed up a split word—in whose middle Flannery had bumped the space bar of her typewriter—with two curved lines like parentheses rotated through ninety degrees. The thick black pencil zipped a ring around the "30" which, like all youngsters, she put at the end of her stories. He turned back to the first page for the second reading. This time the pencil drew lines with the stylized "d's" at the end of them through adjectives and whole phrases, printed big "L's" to mark paragraphs, hooked some of Flannery's own paragraphs together with swooping recurved lines.

At the bottom of "FLANNERY ADD 2—MEDICAL" the pencil slowed down and stopped. The slot man, sensitive to the rhythm of his beloved copy desk, looked up almost at once. He saw Piper squinting at the story, at a loss. Without wasting words, the copy reader skimmed it back across the masonite horseshoe to the chief, caught a police story in return and buckled down, his pencil tapping. The slot man read as far as the fourth add, barked at Howard, on the rim: "Sit in for me," and stamped through the clattering city room toward the alcove where the managing editor presided over his own bedlam.

The copy chief waited his turn while the makeup editor, the pressroom foreman and the chief photographer had words with the M.E. When his turn came, he dropped Flannery's copy on his desk and said: "She says this one isn't a quack."

The M.E. read:

"FLANNERY 1—MEDICAL, by Edna Flannery, *Herald* Staff Writer.

"The sordid tale of medical quackery which the *Herald* has exposed in this series of articles undergoes a change of pace today which the reporter found a welcome surprise. Her quest for the facts in the case of today's subject started just the same way that her exposure of one dozen shyster M.D.'s and faith-healing phonies did. But she can report for a change that Dr. Bayard Full is, despite unorthodox practices which have drawn the suspicion of the rightly hypersensitive medical associations, a true healer living up to the highest ideals of his profession.

"Dr. Full's name was given to the *Herald's* reporter by the ethical committee of a county medical association, which reported that he had been expelled from the association, on July 18, 1941 for allegedly 'milking' several patients suffering from trivial complaints. According to sworn statements in the committee's files, Dr. Full had told them they suffered from cancer, and that he had a treatment which would prolong their lives. After his expulsion from the association, Dr. Full dropped out of their sight—until he opened a midtown 'sanitarium' in a brownstone front which had for several years served as a rooming house.

"The *Herald's* reporter went to that sanitarium, on East 89th Street, with the full expectation of having numerous imaginary ailments diagnosed and of being promised a sure cure for a flat sum of money. She expected to find unkept quarters, dirty instruments and the mumbo-jumbo paraphernalia of the shyster M.D. which she had seen a dozen times before.

"She was wrong.

"Dr. Full's sanitarium is spotlessly clean, from its tastefully furnished entrance hall to its shining white treatment rooms. The attractive, blond receptionist who greeted the reporter was soft-spoken and correct, asking only the reporter's name, address and the general nature of her complaint. This was given, as usual, as 'nagging backache.' The receptionist asked the *Herald's* reporter to be seated, and a short while later conducted her to a second-floor treatment room and introduced her to Dr. Full.

"Dr. Full's alleged past, as described by the medical society spokesman, is hard to reconcile with his present appearance. He is a clear-eyed, white-haired man in his sixties, to judge by his appearance—a little above middle height and apparently in good physical condition. His voice was firm and friendly, untainted by the ingratiating whine of the shyster M.D. which the reporter has come to know too well.

"The receptionist did not leave the room as he began his examination after a few questions as to the nature and location of the pain. As the reporter lay face down on a treatment table the doctor pressed some instrument to the small of her back. In about one minute he made this astounding statement: 'Young woman, there is no reason for you to have any pain where you say you do. I understand they're saying nowadays that emotional upsets cause pains like that.   You'd better go to a psychologist or psychiatrist if the pain keeps up.   There is no physical cause for it, so I can do nothing for you.'

"His frankness took the reporter's breath away.   Had he guessed she was, so to speak, a spy in his camp?   She tried again: 'Well, doctor, perhaps you'd give me a physical checkup, I feel rundown all the time, besides the pains.   Maybe I need a tonic.'   This is a never-failing bait to shyster M.D.'s—an invitation for them to find all sorts of mysterious conditions wrong with a patient, each of which 'requires' an expensive treatment.   As explained in the first article of this series, of course, the reporter underwent a thorough physical checkup before she embarked on her quack-hunt and was found to be in one hundred percent perfect condition, with the exception of a 'scarred' area at the bottom tip of her left lung resulting from a childhood attack of tuberculosis and a tendency toward 'hyperthyroidism'— overactivity of the thyroid gland which makes it difficult to put on weight and sometimes causes a slight shortness of breath.

"Dr. Full consented to perform the examination, and took a number of shining, spotlessly clean instruments from loops in a large board literally covered with instruments—most of them unfamiliar to the reporter.   The instrument with which he approached first was a tube with a curved dial in its surface and two wires that ended on flat disks growing from its ends.   He placed one of the disks on the back of the reporter's right hand and the other on the back of her left.   'Reading the meter,' he called out some number which the attentive receptionist took down on a ruled form.   The same procedure was repeated several times, thoroughly covering the reporter's anatomy and thoroughly convincing her that the doctor was a complete quack.   The reporter had never seen any such diagnostic procedure practiced during the weeks she put in preparing for this series.

"The doctor then took the ruled sheet from the receptionist, conferred with her in low tones and said: 'You have a slightly overactive thyroid, young woman. And there's something wrong with your left lung—not seriously, but I'd like a closer look.'

"He selected an instrument from the board which, the reporter knew, is called a 'speculum'—a scissorlike device which spreads apart body openings such as the orifice of the ear, the nostril and so on, so that a doctor can look in during an examination.   The instrument was, however, too large to be an aural or nasal speculum but too small to be anything else.   As the *Herald's* reporter was about to ask further questions, the attending receptionist told her: 'It's customary for us to blindfold our patients during lung examinations—do you mind?'   The reporter, bewildered, allowed her to tie a spotlessly clean bandage over her eyes, and waited nervously for what would come next.

"She still cannot say exactly what happened while she was blindfolded—but X rays confirm her suspicions.   She felt a cold sensation at her ribs on the left side—a cold that seemed to enter inside her body.   Then there was a snapping feeling, and the cold sensation was gone.   She heard Dr. Full say in a matter-of-fact voice: 'You have an old tubercular scar down there.   It isn't doing any particular harm, but an active person like you needs all the oxygen she can get. Lie down and I'll fix it for you.'

"Then there was a repetition of the cold sensation, lasting for a longer time. 'Another batch of alveoli and some more vascular glue,' the *Herald's* reporter heard Dr. Full say, and the receptionist's crisp response to the order. Then the strange sensation departed and the eye-bandage was removed. The reporter saw no scar on her ribs, and yet the doctor assured her: 'That did it. We took out the fibrosis— and a good fibrosis it was, too; it walled off the infection so you're still alive to tell the tale. Then we planted a few clumps of alveoli—they're the little gadgets that get the oxygen from the air you breathe into your blood. I won't monkey with your thyroxin supply. You've got used to being the kind of person you are, and if you suddenly found yourself easy-going and all the rest of it, chances are you'd only be upset. About the backache: just check with the county medical society for the name of a good psychologist or psychiatrist. And look out for quacks; the woods are full of them.'

"The doctor's self-assurance took the reporter's breath away. She asked what the charge would be, and was told to pay the receptionist fifty dollars. As usual, the reporter delayed paying until she got a receipt signed by the doctor himself, detailing the services for which it paid. Unlike most the doctor cheerfully wrote: 'For removal of fibrosis from left lung and restoration of alveoli,' and signed it.

"The reporter's first move when she left the sanitarium was to head for the chest specialist who had examined her in preparation for this series. A comparison of X rays taken on the day of the 'operation' and those taken previously would, the *Herald's* reporter thought, expose Dr. Full as a prince of shyster M.D.'s and quacks.

"The chest specialist made time on his crowded schedule for the reporter, in whose series he has shown a lively interest from the planning stage on. He laughed uproariously in his staid Park Avenue examining room as she described the weird procedure to which she had been subjected. But he did not laugh when he took a chest X ray of the reporter, developed it, dried it, and compared it with the ones he had taken earlier. The chest specialist took six more X rays that afternoon, but finally admitted that they all told the same story. The *Herald's* reporter has it on his authority that the scar she had eighteen days ago from her tuberculosis is now gone and has been replaced by healthy lung-tissue. He declares that this is a happening unparalleled in medical history. He does not go along with the reporter in her firm conviction that Dr. Full is responsible for the change.

"The *Herald's* reporter, however, sees no two ways about it. She concludes that Dr. Bayard Full—whatever his alleged past may have been—is now an unor- thodox but highly successful practitioner of medicine, to whose hands the reporter would trust herself in any emergency.

"Not so is the case of 'Rev.' Annie Dimsworth—a female harpy who, under the guise of 'faith,' preys on the ignorant and suffering who come to her sordid 'healing parlor' for help and remain to feed 'Rev.' Annie's bank account, which now totals up to $53,238.64. Tomorrow's article will show, with photostats of bank statements and sworn testimony, that—''

The managing editor turned down "FLANNERY LAST ADD—MEDICAL" and tapped his front teeth with a pencil, trying to think straight. He finally told the copy chief: "Kill the story. Run the teaser as a box." He tore off the last paragraph—the "teaser" about "Rev." Annie—and handed it to the desk man, who stumped back to his masonite horseshoe.

The makeup editor was back, dancing with impatience as he tried to catch the M.E.'s eye. The interphone buzzed with the red light which indicated that the editor and publisher wanted to talk to him. The M.E. thought briefly of a special series on this Dr. Full, decided nobody would believe it and that he probably was a phony anyway. He spiked the story on the "dead" hook and answered his interphone.

Dr. Full had become almost fond of Angie. As his practice had grown to engross the neighborhood illnesses, and then to a corner suite in an uptown taxpayer building, and finally to the sanitarium, she seemed to have grown with it. Oh, he thought, we have our little disputes—

The girl, for instance, was too much interested in money. She had wanted to specialize in cosmetic surgery—removing wrinkles from wealthy old women and what-not. She didn't realize, at first, that a thing like this was in their trust, that they were the stewards and not the owners of the little black bag and its fabulous contents.

He had tried, ever so cautiously, to analyze them, but without success. All the instruments were slightly radioactive, for instance, but not quite so. They would make a Geiger-Mueller counter indicate, but they would not collapse the leaves of an electroscope. He didn't pretend to be up on the latest developments, but as he understood it, that was just plain *wrong*. Under the highest magnification there were lines on the instruments' superfinished surfaces: incredibly fine lines, engraved in random hatchments which made no particular sense. Their magnetic properties were preposterous. Sometimes the instruments were strongly attracted to magnets, sometimes less so, and sometimes not at all.

Dr. Full had taken X rays in fear and trembling lest he disrupt whatever delicate machinery worked in them. He was *sure* they were not solid, that the handles and perhaps the blades must be mere shells filled with busy little watch-works—but the X rays showed nothing of the sort. Oh, yes—and they were always sterile, and they wouldn't rust. Dust *fell* off them if you shook them: now, that was something he understood. They ionized the dust, or were ionized themselves, or something of the sort. At any rate he had read of something similiar that had to do with phonograph records.

She wouldn't know about that, he proudly thought. She kept the books well enough, and perhaps she gave him a useful prod now and then when he was inclined to settle down. The move from the neighborhood slum to the uptown quarters had been her idea, and so had the sanitarium. Good, good, it enlarged his sphere of usefulness. Let the child have her mink coats and her convertible, as they seemed to be calling roadsters nowadays. He himself was too busy and too old. He had so much to make up for.

Dr. Full thought happily of his Master Plan. She would not like it much, but she would have to see the logic of it. This marvelous thing that had happened to them must be handed on. She was herself no doctor; even though the instruments practically ran themselves, there was more to doctoring than skill. There were the ancient canons of the healing art. And so, having seen the logic of it, Angie would yield; she would assent to his turning over the little black bag to all humanity.

He would probably present it to the College of Surgeons, with as little fuss as possible—well, perhaps a *small* ceremony, and he would like a souvenir of the occasion, a cup or a framed testimonial. It would be a relief to have the thing out of his hands, in a way; let the giants of the healing art decide who was to have its benefits. No, Angie would understand. She was a good-hearted girl.

It was nice that she had been showing so much interest in the surgical side lately—asking about the instruments, reading the instruction card for hours, even practicing on guinea pigs. If something of his love for humanity had been communicated to her, old Dr. Full sentimentally thought, his life would not have been in vain. Surely she would realize that a greater good would be served by surrendering the instruments to wiser hands than theirs, and by throwing aside the cloak of secrecy necessary to work on their small scale.

Dr. Full was in the treatment room that had been the brownstone's front parlor; through the window he saw Angie's yellow convertible roll to a stop before the stoop. He liked the way she looked as she climbed the stairs; neat, not flashy, he thought. A sensible girl like her, she'd understand. There was somebody with her—a fat woman, puffing up the steps, overdressed and petulant. Now, what could she want?

Angie let herself in and went into the treatment room, followed by the fat woman. "Doctor," said the blond girl gravely, "may I present Mrs. Coleman?" Charm school had not taught her everything, but Mrs. Coleman, evidently *nouveau riche,* thought the doctor, did not notice the blunder.

"Miss Aquella told me *so* much about you, doctor, and your remarkable system!" she gushed.

Before he could answer, Angie smoothly interposed: "Would you excuse us for just a moment, Mrs. Coleman?"

She took the doctor's arm and led him into the reception hall. "Listen," she said swiftly, "I know this goes against your grain, but I couldn't pass it up. I met this old thing in the exercise class at Elizabeth Barton's. Nobody else'll talk to her there. She's a widow. I guess her husband was a black marketeer or something, and she has a pile of dough. I gave her a line about how you had a system of massaging wrinkles out. My idea is, you blindfold her, cut her neck open with the Cutaneous Series knife, shoot some Firmol into the muscles, spoon out some of the blubber with an Adipose Series curette and spray it all with Skintite. When you take the blindfold off she's got rid of a wrinkle and doesn't know what happened. She'll pay five hundred dollars. Now, don't say 'no,' doc. Just this once, let's do it my way, can't you? I've been working on this deal all along too, haven't I?"

"Oh," said the doctor, "very well."   He was going to have to tell her about the Master Plan before long anyway.   He would let her have it her way this time.

Back in the treatment room, Mrs. Coleman had been thinking things over. She told the doctor sternly as he entered: "Of course, your system is permanent, isn't it?"

"It is, madam," he said shortly.   "Would you please lie down there?   Miss Aquella get a sterile three-inch bandage for Mrs. Coleman's eyes."   He turned his back on the fat woman to avoid conversation and pretended to be adjusting the lights.   Angie blindfolded the woman and the doctor selected the instruments he would need.   He handed the blond girl a pair of retractors, and told her: "Just slip the corners of the blades in as I cut—"   She gave him an alarmed look, and gestured at the reclining woman.   He lowered his voice: "Very well.   Slip in the corners and rock them along the incision.   I'll tell you when to pull them out."

Dr. Full held the Cutaneous Series knife to his eyes as he adjusted the little slide for three centimeters' depth.   He sighed a little as he recalled that its last use had been in the extirpation of an "inoperable" tumor of the throat.

"Very well," he said, bending over the woman.   He tried a tentative pass through her tissues.   The blade dipped in and flowed through them, like a finger through quicksilver, with no wound left in the wake.   Only the retractors could hold the edges of the incision apart.

Mrs. Coleman stirred and jabbered: "Doctor, that felt so peculiar!   Are you sure you're rubbing the right way?"

"Quite sure, madam," said the doctor wearily.   "Would you please try not to talk during the massage?"

He nodded at Angie, who stood ready with the retractors.   The blade sank in to its three centimeters, miraculously cutting only the dead horny tissues of the epidermis and the live tissue of the dermis, pushing aside mysteriously all major and minor blood vessels and muscular tissue, declining to affect any system or organ except the one it was—tuned to, could you say?   The doctor didn't know the answer, but he felt tired and bitter at this prostitution.   Angie slipped in the retractor blades and rocked them as he withdrew the knife, then pulled to separate the lips of the incision.   It bloodlessly exposed an unhealthy string of muscle, sagging in a dead-looking loop from blue-gray ligaments.   The doctor took a hypo, Number IX, preset to "g," and raised it to his eye level.   The mist came and went; there probably was no possibility of an embolus with one of these gadgets, but why take chances?   He shot one cc. of "g"—identified as "Firmol" by the card—into the muscle.   He and Angie watched as it tightened up against the pharynx.

He took the Adipose Series curette, a small one, and spooned out yellowish tissue, dropping it into the incinerator box, and then nodded to Angie.   She eased out the retractors and the gaping incision slipped together into unbroken skin, sagging now.   The doctor had the atomizer—dialed to "Skintite"—ready.   He sprayed, and the skin shrank up into the new firm throat line.

As he replaced the instruments, Angie removed Mrs. Coleman's bandage and gaily announced: "We're finished!   And there's a mirror in the reception hall—"

Mrs. Coleman didn't need to be invited twice. With incredulous fingers she felt her chin, and then dashed for the hall. The doctor grimaced as he heard her yelp of delight, and Angie turned to him with a tight smile. "I'll get the money and get her out," she said. "You won't have to be bothered with her anymore."

He was grateful for that much.

She followed Mrs. Coleman into the reception hall, and the doctor dreamed over the case of instruments. A ceremony, certainly—he was *entitled* to one. Not everybody, he thought, would turn such a sure source of money over to the good of humanity. But you reached an age when money mattered less, and when you thought of these things you had done that *might* be open to misunderstanding if, just if, there chanced to be any of that, well, that judgment business. The doctor wasn't a religious man, but you certainly found yourself thinking hard about some things when your time drew near—

Angie was back, with a bit of paper in her hands. "Five hundred dollars," she said matter-of-factly. "And you realize, don't you, that we could go over her an inch at a time—at five hundred dollars an inch?"

"I've been meaning to talk to you about that," he said.

There was bright fear in her eyes, he thought—but why?

"Angie, you've been a good girl and an understanding girl, but we can't keep this up forever, you know."

"Let's talk about it some other time," she said flatly. "I'm tired now."

"No—I really feel we've gone far enough on our own. The instruments—"

"Don't say it, doc!" she hissed. "Don't say it, or you'll be sorry!" In her face there was a look that reminded him of the hollow-eyed, gaunt-faced, dirty-blond creature she had been. From under the charm-school finish there burned the guttersnipe whose infancy had been spent on a sour and filthy mattress, whose childhood had been play in the littered alley and whose adolescence had been the sweatshops and the aimless gatherings at night under the glaring street lamps.

He shook his head to dispel the puzzling notion. "It's this way," he patiently began. "I told you about the family that invented the O.B. forceps and kept them a secret for so many generations, how they could have given them to the world but didn't?"

"They knew what they were doing," said the guttersnipe flatly.

"Well, that's neither here nor there," said the doctor, irritated. "My mind is made up about it. I'm going to turn the instruments over to the College of Surgeons. We have enough money to be comfortable. You can even have the house. I've been thinking of going to a warmer climate, myself." He felt peeved with her for making the unpleasant scene. He was unprepared for what happened next.

Angie snatched the little black bag and dashed for the door, with panic in her eyes. He scrambled after her, catching her arm, twisting it in a sudden rage. She clawed at his face with her free hand, babbling curses. Somehow, somebody's finger touched the little black bag, and it opened grotesquely into the enormous board, covered with shining instruments, large and small. Half a dozen of them joggled loose and fell to the floor.

"*Now* see what you've done!" roared the doctor, unreasonably. Her hand was still viselike on the handle, but she was standing still, trembling with choked-up rage.   The doctor bent stiffly to pick up the fallen instruments.   Unreasonable girl! he thought bitterly.   Making a scene—

Pain drove in between his shoulderblades and he fell face down.   The light ebbed.   "Unreasonable girl!" he tried to croak.   And then: "They'll know I tried, anyway—"

Angie looked down on his prone body, with the handle of the Number Six Cautery Series knife protruding from it.   "—will cut through all tissues.   Use for amputations before you spread on the Re-Gro.   Extreme caution should be used in the vicinity of vital organs and major blood vessels or nerve trunks—"

"I didn't mean to do that," said Angie, dully, cold with horror.   Now the detective would come, the implacable detective who would reconstruct the crime from the dust in the room.   She would run and turn and twist, but the detective would find her out and she would be tried in a courtroom before a judge and jury; the lawyer would make speeches, but the jury would convict her anyway, and the headlines would scream: "BLOND KILLER GUILTY!" and she'd maybe get the chair, walking down a plain corridor where a beam of sunlight struck through the dusty air, with an iron door at the end of it.   Her mink, her convertible, her dresses, the handsome man she was going to meet and marry—

The mist of cinematic clichés cleared, and she knew what she would do next. Quite steadily, she picked the incinerator box from its loop in the board—a metal cube with a different-textured spot on one side.   "—to dispose of fibroses or other unwanted matter, simply touch the disk—"   You dropped something in and touched the disk.   There was a sort of soundless whistle, very powerful and unpleasant if you were too close, and a sort of lightless flash.   When you opened the box again, the contents were gone.   Angie took another of the Cautery Series knives and went grimly to work.   Good thing there wasn't any blood to speak of—She finished the awful task in three hours.

She slept heavily that night, totally exhausted by the wringing emotional demands of the slaying and the subsequent horror.   But in the morning, it was as though the doctor had never been there.   She ate breakfast, dressed with unusual care— and then undid the unusual care.   Nothing out of the ordinary, she told herself. Don't do one thing different from the way you would have done it before.   After a day or two, you can phone the cops.   Say he walked out spoiling for a drunk, and you're worried.   But don't rush it, baby—*don't rush it.*

Mrs. Coleman was due at ten A.M.   Angie had counted on being able to talk the doctor into at least one more five-hundred-dollar session.   She'd have to do it herself now—but she'd have to start sooner or later.

The woman arrived early.   Angie explained smoothly: "The doctor asked me to take care of the massage today.   Now that he has the tissue-firming process beginning, it only requires somebody trained in his methods—"   As she spoke, her eyes swiveled to the instrument case—open!   She cursed herself for the single flaw as the woman followed her gaze and recoiled.

"What are those things!" she demanded.   "Are you going to cut me with them? I *thought* there was something fishy—"

"Please, Mrs. Coleman," said Angie, "please, *dear* Mrs. Coleman—you don't understand about the . . . the massage instruments!"

"Massage instruments, my foot!" squabbled the woman shrilly. "The doctor *operated* on me. Why, he might have killed me!"

Angie wordlessly took one of the smaller Cutaneous Series knives and passed it through her forearm. The blade flowed like a finger through quicksilver, leaving no wound in its wake. *That* should convince the old cow!

It didn't convince her, but it did startle her. "What did you do with it? The blade folds up into the handle—that's it!"

"Now look closely, Mrs. Coleman," said Angie, thinking desperately of the five hundred dollars. "Look very closely and you'll see that the, uh, the sub-skin massager simply slips beneath the tissues without doing any harm, tightening and firming the muscles themselves instead of having to work through layers of skin and adipose tissue. It's the secret of the doctor's method. Now, how can outside massage have the effect that we got last night?"

Mrs. Coleman was beginning to calm down. "It *did* work, all right," she admitted, stroking the new line of her neck. "But your arm's one thing and my neck's another! Let me see you do that with your neck!"

Angie smiled—

Al returned to the clinic after an excellent lunch that had almost reconciled him to three more months he would have to spend on duty. And then, he thought, and then a blessed year at the blessedly super-normal South Pole working on his specialty—which happened to be telekinesis exercises for ages three to six. Meanwhile, of course, the world had to go on and of course he had to shoulder his share in the running of it.

Before settling down to desk work he gave a routine glance at the bag board. What he saw made him stiffen with shocked surprise. A red light was on next to one of the numbers—the first since he couldn't think when. He read off the number and murmured "OK, 674101. That fixes *you*." He put the number on a card sorter and in a moment the record was in his hand. Oh, yes—Hemingway's bag. The big dummy didn't remember how or where he had lost it; none of them ever did. There were hundreds of them floating around.

Al's policy in such cases was to leave the bag turned on. The things practically ran themselves, it was practically impossible to do harm with them, so whoever found a lost one might as well be allowed to use it. You turn it off, you have a social loss—you leave it on, it may do some good. As he understood it, and not very well at that, the stuff wasn't "used up." A temporalist had tried to explain it to him with little success that the prototypes in the transmitter *had been transduced* through a series of point-events of transfinite cardinality. Al had innocently asked whether that meant prototypes had been stretched, so to speak, through all time, and the temporalist had thought he was joking and left in a huff.

"Like to see him do this," thought Al darkly, as he telekinized himself to the combox, after a cautious look to see that there were no medics around. To the box he said: "Police chief," and then to the police chief: "There's been a homicide committed with Medical Instrument Kit 674101.   It was lost some months ago by one of my people, Dr. John Hemingway.   He didn't have a clear account of the circumstances.''

The police chief groaned and said: ''I'll call him in and question him.''   He was to be astonished by the answers, and was to learn that the homicide was well out of his jurisdiction.

Al stood for a moment at the bag board by the glowing red light that had been sparked into life by a departing vital force giving, as its last act, the warning that Kit 674101 was in homicidal hands.   With a sigh, Al pulled the plug and the light went out.

''Yah,'' jeered the woman.   ''You'd fool around with my neck, but you wouldn't risk your own with that thing!''

Angie smiled with serene confidence a smile that was to shock hardened morgue attendants.   She set the Cutaneous Series knife to three centimeters before drawing it across her neck.   Smiling, knowing the blade would cut only the dead horny tissue of the epidermis and the live tissue of the dermis, mysteriously push aside all major and minor blood vessels and muscular tissue—

Smiling, the knife plunging in and its microtomesharp metal shearing through major and minor blood vessels and muscular tissue and pharynx, Angie cut her throat.

In the few minutes it took the police, summoned by the shrieking Mrs. Coleman, to arrive, the instruments had become crusted with rust, and the flasks which had held vascular glue and clumps of pink, rubbery alveoli and spare gray cells and coils of receptor nerves held only black slime, and from them when opened gushed the foul gases of decomposition.

JOHN BERRYMAN

Berom

EXCERPT FROM PROCEEDINGS IN THE COURT-MARTIAL OF BEN-JAMIN L. HARWOOD, COL., U.S.A., FORT MEYER, VA., JUNE 8, 2038.)

Judge Advocate: I have no further questions, colonel.
Defense Counsel: May it please the Court.   Rather than recalling Colonel Harwood to the stand later, I would like to establish one point by cross-examination which properly should be made at this time.
J. A.: You may proceed.
D. C.: Colonel Harwood, going back to May 4th of this year, will you tell the Court how you received your orders from General Fairbank?
Defendant: How?
D. C.: In what manner were they communicated to you?
Def.: Verbally.   There was no time, you understand, for any confirmation.   I was told all General Fairbank knew about the ship in ten hurried sentences and given my orders.
D. C.: Can you recollect them?
Def.: Of course.   Not *verbatim,* perhaps, but certainly their substance.   Would you like me to repeat them?
D. C.: (To the Court)   I should like the Court to understand this is merely to introduce in proper order the point we wish to make.
J. A.: On that understanding, the defendant may proceed.
Def.: I was ordered to find out who were the country's leading students of language and communication, considering the problem of the visitors as General Fairbank knew it; to find out where these students were; to get the necessary credentials from the Office of the Chief of Staff; and to bring the persons in question to the landing site immediately.
D.C.: In other words, colonel, your choice was to depend solely on the qualifications of these persons as students?
Def.: That's right.
D. C.: And nothing was said with reference to their emotional or political outlook?
Def.: I don't think Army regulations provide for either of those things.
(Laughter)
J. A.: Order!   The colonel will restrain his mordant wit.

Def.: I beg the Court's pardon.   No, sir, no mention was made of those factors.
D. C.: That is all, colonel.   You may step down.   *(To the Court)*   This is the
very nub of our defense.   We contend that Colonel Harwood well and faithfully
carried out his orders.   No man can be accused of willful neglect simply because
of the warped mentality of another.   If it please the Court, I would like to—

When the dinner dishes were in the washer, Mrs. Johnson quickly made a round
of the ashtrays in the professor's book-lined study, emptying them into her ever-
present dustpan.   That was always her last act before leaving, Yancey reflected,
rising from his easy-chair.   By the time he had reached the door, his housekeeper
had slipped on her coat and was bustling through the hall toward him.

She paused a moment for her wages, since it was Saturday night.   "Good night,
Professor Yancey," she said with mock crossness as he handed her the money.
"Now, for pity's sake, don't stay up reading half the night!"

"Good night, Mrs. Johnson," he replied, coming as close to a smile as he ever
did.   He set the night-latch behind her and walked thoughtfully through the low-
ceilinged old rooms to his side porch.   The clock on the College chapel struck the
half-hour.

Though the sun had set redly behind the Pelham hills some time before, there
was still a luminosity in the spring sky that banned all but the brightest stars.   The
evening breeze soughed sadly through the perfumed blossoms of his apple orchard
and rippled the grass of his large lawn, overdue for cutting.

Yancey sighed as he took his pipe away from his lips, better to savor the sweetness
of the blooms.   How Madge would have loved the orchard, he thought.   It was
hard to believe that seventeen years had sped in their swift rounds since he had
first turned the earth over their young roots, and so quickly had seen the same sod
broken to receive his wife's shriveled body.   The sad scent of the springtime
always brought back her bitter-sweet memory.   He sucked more life into his pipe.
More and more, with the ripening blush of every spring, he felt that the world was
leaving him behind.   More and more he was out of place in a time where events
rippled catastrophically about his head.   With the despondent thought that he would
be glad when life was through with him, he recalled the lines of David Morton,
who had lived in that same house a hundred years before: "I like thee each day
not more, but less."

A uniquely irritating sound drove him from his reverie.   The unmistakable *hooo
oooo* of a jet motor, coming from the direction of the campus, caused him to crane
his scrawny neck around the old house's eaves.   The sound drew loudly nearer.
Then he saw the brilliant lance of the light through the arching trees.   Although
the craft was not clearly visible in the deepening dusk, it was directing a powerful
beam toward the ground.   It hung dangerously low, Yancey decided, hopping
spryly over the porch railing and trotting to the picket fence.   A ram-jet helicopter,
he guessed, from its deliberate pace over the elms lining South Pleasant Street.
The effulgent beam seared his eyes as it swept over him, and then returned, causing
him to lower his head in pain.

Then the hooting was full upon him.   He felt the wild downdraft of the blades and saw the scented blossoms vanish from his orchard in a blizzard of flying petals. His angry cries were scarcely swallowed by the sound of the jets before the helicopter had grounded on his lawn. The merciless brilliance of the light reddened and died. His dazzled eyes could barely see the uniformed figures that sprang from the 'copter and ran toward him. Rectangles of light sprang into being about the Common as doors swung open, silhouetting the curious in their frames.

"Professor Yancey?" one of the newcomers cried.

"Yes! Look what you've done to my orchard! You'll—"

"Yes! Of course! Quick, professor, you must get inside at once!" The voice was urgent, but there was no mistaking the genteel courtesy of the speaker. Yancey allowed himself to be urged back onto his porch. "Evans!" the newcomer ordered in a low tone. "Keep everybody out, Rocco," he went on, as he politely urged Yancey through his door into the study. "Get the professor packed!" The soldier named Rocco sprang vigorously up the stairs.

Yancey had no time to form his protest. "I extend you every apology," the officer giving the orders said with swift sincerity. "You are Professor George Yancey, the philologist?"

"Of course. See here—"

"Please, professor. I beg your indulgence. There is so little time. Believe me, sir," he went on with an urbanity not put out of joint by the strained circumstances. "I know this is an outrageous invasion of your privacy, but I have orders from the White House, professor. You must come with us at once." His clean-shaven, handsome features flashed a quick earnest smile that was clearly meant to tell Yancey how seriously he took it all.

"What the devil!" Yancey gasped. "What is this all about?" He heard the quick stamp of feet on his front steps. His front doorbell sounded insistently.

"Please don't answer it," Harwood asked, his hand gently restraining. "Professor, this is a matter of life and death for your country. We need your services urgently, this moment. I have authority to swear you into the Army, sir, with the rank of Lieutenant Colonel. Would you please raise your right hand?"

"Certainly not," Yancey said stubbornly. "I'm not used to having some smooth-talking public relations officer storm into my house and order me about. What in Tophet is going on?" The tough military tones of Evans came clearly through the door, ordering people to keep outside the picket fence. Yancey was about to protest the treatment of his neighbors when those at the front door despaired of the bell and took to thudding its heavy silver knocker. Students, he knew, young and impatient.

"Don't go," Harwood said breathlessly. "Professor, a spaceship from outside the Solar System has just landed in Kansas. We are trying desperately to communicate with the visitors. We need you. We *must* have you to help us."

It took a long moment for what Harwood told him to sink in. Yancey's sharp features narrowed farther as he digested the incredible fact. "You mean, you Army people are trying to talk to them?" he asked. He had a wry conception of a crew of narrow-minded militarists trying to make sense to an alien culture.

"Yes," Harwood said, not feeling the barb in Yancey's question. "Weird as it seems, they are reasonably human, and they seemed convinced they can communicate with us. Pathetically convinced. It's a race against time."

"What's the rush?" Yancey demanded tartly.

"Partly that they insist. They've made hand signals, professor. Apparently something about their power. We think it deteriorates under a gravitational field. We can't understand exactly what they mean, but they keep pointing to the sun and—"

"Yes, I understand," Yancey said acidly, his mind making semantic sense of Harwood's overearnest babbling. "And they seem to think they can communicate with us? By which you mean that they seem to think they know how *we* communicate?" He paused while his mind went back over what the other had said. "You said 'partly.' What's the rest of the rush?"

"Really, professor," Harwood insisted deferentially. "I can tell you these things en route. The others are waiting for us at Westover Field."

Rocco trotted quickly down the stairs. Yancey saw that he was carrying his overnight case. "Ready, sir," the soldier called. He waited for no signal, but ran through the door to the yard, taking the bag toward the waiting 'copter.

"All right," Yancey said, intrigued by the thought of conversing with a completely foreign creature. "You'll get in touch with the College?" he asked, turning out the lights and setting the snap lock on his side door.

"Of course."

The starter's growl was whirling the blades up to the starting speed before they were in the cabin. The jets belched fire, throbbed throatily, and whined quickly up to efficient velocity. Yancey gasped as the house fell swiftly away below them. He got a brief glimpse of the clock on Johnson Chapel before they swung off to the South. There was no talking possible with the eerie hooting of the ram-jets deafening them. Yancey collected his thoughts as they whirled over the Connecticut Valley toward the great Air Force base. All that he knew of language and semantics passed in well-ordered sequence through his scholarly mind. Always his circling thoughts came to rest on one fact. The visitors from outer space seemed convinced they could communicate. The idea titillated his rapier-sharp intellect.

A jet bomber waited squattily for them. Harwood seized the small suitcase himself as they grounded, and hurried Yancey toward the looming shape of the warplane. A small knot of people were bunched by it. Introductions were swift, mingled with the grunts of scholars straining their creaky frames through the bomber's small door.

"Professor Cottwold, the calligraphist," Harwood said hurriedly. "Meet—"

"Hello, Cottwold," Yancey interrupted. "Glad to see you again." They shook hands briefly, and Cottwold turned away to climb in.

"And Professor Pratt," Harwood continued, pushing them up the ladder. "In your field, Professor Yancey."

"Yes," Yancey said acidly. "We've met, too."

Pratt laughed woodenly. "Indeed we have," he said with a heartiness that was not relish. He kept on talking as they strapped themselves in until the cough of the starting turbines stopped it. "How are things at Amherst these days, Yancey?"

"Quiet," the waspish little man replied. "You would hardly know we are waiting for the next Atomic War."

Pratt's stiff laugh was somehow condescending. "A little different at Yale," he confided. "We're somehow closer to life in New Haven. Don't see how you could spend time on a thing like that 'Sanskrit Revisited' you just published. We can't seem to ignore what's going on about us, the way you small-town people do."

Yancey's sharp retort was swallowed in the roar of sound. They taxied smoothly between the yellow rows of runway lights to the end of the long concrete ribbon, accelerated with neck-straining power, and hurtled into the black spring night. Red obstruction lights streaked into the distance behind them. Not until they felt the rippling passage of the bomber through the sonic barrier could they talk again. They could still feel the enormous power of the turbines surge through the hurtling ship, but they had left their screaming sound behind.

Harwood had wormed his way up forward with the pilots, using the radio. He crawled through the cramped passage back to them. "It's still there," he said breathlessly, his insignia glittering dully in the dimly lighted bomb bay.

"Where?" Yancey demanded.

"Near Emporia, Kansas," Harwood replied. "They've got the whole area sealed off. No aircraft. No cars. See here," he exclaimed, perching on a gunner's unoccupied stool. "You've all got to understand the need for utmost speed on this thing. I think all of you know the visitors have plainly signaled they can stay only five days."

"Now don't worry," Pratt boomed importantly. "The moment they realize a trained specialist in communication has been brought to them, they'll relax."

"I'm sorry," Harwood protested with that politeness Yancey found so ill-fitting. "But you can't think of it that way. There are other reasons for speed."

"Yes, what are they?" Yancey pursued him, recalling his remarks while still at his house.

Harwood gulped visibly in the dim light. "The Russians," he said unhappily. "They're raising the very devil about it."

"Well, just tell them to go to Hell," Pratt snapped. "They landed here, not in Russia, and showed uncommon good sense, if you ask me."

"Yes, I know," Harwood said. "But it's not that simple."

"How do the Russians know?" Yancey asked.

"Their radars must have tracked the ship, too. It was the strangest thing. It just suddenly appeared, with the greatest burst of radiant energies imaginable, about fifty million miles north of the ecliptic. It dropped down toward Earth without any hesitation. Didn't seem any question about which planet they were interested in. They took their time coming, only used about a quarter G acceleration, but they drove or braked the whole way. No drifting. They've obviously got an atomic drive of some kind. No rockets. Their power must be enormous. The electrical disturbance of their drive affected radars and other detectors all over the System.''

"The atomic drive!'' Pratt breathed. "At last!''

"Yes, I know,'' Harwood said miserably. "But of course the Russians are thinking exactly the same thing. The minute they knew the ship had landed here, we started to get demands that it be internationalized. They demand equal representation when we interview the visitors.''

"Ha!'' Pratt laughed bitterly. "Well, they know where that'll get them! Fat chance we'll share any atomic space drive with those bloodthirsty madmen!'' Yancey shriveled with the implications of what the others had said. It was the same jingoistic talk that sooner or later guaranteed that the last two nations of the world would wipe each other out. They had come mighty close to it the last time, he recalled bitterly, thinking of his own wife, trapped in the dusting of New York.

Harwood was still talking persuasively, his tone low and tense. "They're not such fools,'' he explained. "They've told us they'll bomb and dust the area into extinction if we don't agree immediately. You can see the Russians would rather have the secret of the drive lost than see us get it before they do.''

"What the devil!'' Cottwold protested. "You mean we stand a good chance of being bombed while we're there! A fine time to tell us, young man! I consider this—''

"No, no,'' Harwood placated him. "We can stall them a day or so. They don't know, of course, that the visitors can't remain. By the time we get it all settled about how the thing will be internationalized, the ship will be gone. And we'll have the drive. I hope,'' he concluded. "It all depends on you.''

Yancey's acid voice broke into laughter, "You fools,'' he told them bitterly. "And the moment the Russians think they've been tricked, they'll start their missiles toward us. They won't dare to wait until we have actually built and installed the drive. It will be now or never for them!''

"We can hold them,'' Harwood said tightly. "We haven't been sitting still. Our northern radar net—''

"Tophet!'' Yancey exploded. "Then you admit we are starting the Second Atomic War. Well, I shall have nothing to do with it! See here, Pratt, you should be immune from the sordid appeals this sugar-tongued character is making! Cottwold!''

Pratt's sneer was plain in the gloom of the bomber's hurtling hull. "How you can defend an intellectualism that is not first concerned with its political freedom is beyond me,'' he said heavily. Cottwold was silent.

Yancey felt himself slump into his cramped seat with despair. The whole world was going mad, he knew. When the intellectuals buttressed the fatuous arguments of a constitutionally blind military, the place for his kind had vanished. But in spite of his hatred of the thought that he would contribute to the outbreak of war, his intellectual curiosity was too great for him to stay behind when the others were taken to the strangers from space.

There could be no doubt of the enormous scientific achievement of the visitors. Their huge vessel stretched its length a thousand feet across the green, sprouting wheat, and towered two hundred feet in diameter.   A companionway of stairs, startling similar to the Terrestrial equivalent, had been let down from a round lock or doorway low in the hull, so that the great ship bulged out above it.   At its head there was a small landing or balcony, big enough to accommodate several persons.

The Army, with all the unpleasant things it represented to Yancey, was there in force.   Bare, unpainted hutments already clustered around the foot of the companionway, huddling under the outward swelling curve of the giant, cylindrical hull.   The tender shoots of wheat had been ground blackly into the muddy soil. The deep ruts of wheeled vehicles testified to its wetness, and explained why the ring of vehicles about the ship, holding the curious back, were now all provided with caterpillar tracks.   Cameras were being confiscated on every hand, Yancey saw bitterly, reflecting on the military mind.   No photographic negative could ever print the impression that every viewer of the monstrous ship was having burned indelibly into his memory.   The Army might even try to confiscate that, he decided angrily.

Harwood struggled with them through the mud as far as the foot of the stairway. There was a squad of paratroops posted there, tommy guns slung meaningfully over their shoulders, their faces grim and purposeful in spite of their youth.   It was all hateful to Yancey.   Soon to die, he reflected.   Soon, and young!

A feverish young captain met them.   The generals had stayed behind in their quarters, the way generals always do, Yancey observed silently.

"Call him out, captain," Harwood ordered.

The other officer turned to the open port.   "Berom!" he called, his voice high and clear with excitement.

"What does that mean?" Cottwold asked.

"How do I know?" the captain asked.   "That's the first thing he did when he stepped out of the ship.   He showed us a sign with that word on it.   We've already taught him how the alphabet is pronounced, but that's as far as we got. He won't let us in the ship.   Acts as though he won't until we can talk to each other."

In spite of what Harwood had said about the visitor's being human, Yancey was unprepared for the appearance of the creature who stepped quickly onto the landing. Yancey's common sense told him it would be a miracle to find beings from the stars resembling humans even to the point of being erect and bifurcated.   The visitor was a lot more than that.   He wasn't much less like Yancey than an Australian fuzzy-wuzzy, but in the opposite direction.   Pigmentation, while present, was light.   He had hair on a head that bore two eyes, a nose and an all-too human mouth.   His locks were platinum and fine to the point of suggesting a halo. He carried some kind of sign or placard and held a staff or wand in his tapering fingers, of which there seemed to be six rather than five.

"Berom!" he replied, his human features breaking into what was unmistakably a smile.

"Tell him 'Berom,' " the captain said.   "He likes that."

"Berom," Pratt called in his heavy voice.   He led the three savants up the companionway to the landing.   Yancey brought up the rear.   For a long moment the beings of two worlds viewed each other at arm's length, curiosity written in the same lines on all their faces.

"Berom," the visitor repeated, with an upward inflection, as if he were asking a question.   The staff in his hand proved to be a stylus.   With it he wrote carefully on the placard he carried.   Its point was curiously fashioned, so that with a tiny lever on the shaft of the writing instrument he could control the width of the line it drew.   His draughtsmanship was precise to the point of exciting Yancey's wonderment.   The letters were a perfectly stylized typewriter font, albeit somewhat antique in their appearance.   "BEROM" the visitor wrote, all in capital letters an inch or so high.

The three Terrestrials looked at it thoughtfully.   "What is it?" Cottwold asked. "Does it make any sense to you?"

Yancey and Pratt exchanged glances.   "Do you recognize the word?" Pratt asked the slighter man.

Yancey's eyebrows fluttered in the briefest shrug.   "If it is a word," he said cautiously.   "It is probably Hindustani.   The root 'bero' in Sanskrit—"

"Oh, no," Pratt insisted heavily.

"Do you know the root?" Yancey asked icily.

"No.   But, please, spare us Sanskrit.   What would it be in Hindustani?"

"A 'berom' is a wedge, usually employed to hold a mattock on its shaft," Yancey said.   "But I don't think that's important."

Pratt grunted irritably.   "See here, my friend," he said in English to the visitor. "You had better talk to us.   Talk.   Talk."   He pointed vigorously to his lips. Comprehension was swift.   With a soft smile the fine-haired creature broke into speech.   His voice was soft and mellifluous, somewhat light in timbre, and in a girlish register.   The phrases ran together in the formless torrent of any completely foreign language.

"Slower.   Much slower," Pratt insisted, articulating his syllables with great deliberateness.   "High degree of flexion," he noted over his shoulder to Yancey.

The result was surprising.   A swift frown of disappointment crossed the visitor's face.   He pointed excitedly to the word he had written on the placard.   "Berom!" he exclaimed.   "Berom!"   He wrote it again, more quickly, his odd, adjustable stylus forming the expertly printed letters effortlessly.

"Look at those serifs!" Cottwold said.   "An utterly novel approach toward calligraphy!"

Yancey pushed himself forward, around Pratt's lumbering bulk.   He held his palms upward in what he hoped was a universal sign of friendship.   To the surprise of all, not excluding the visitor, he encircled the stranger from space lightly in his arms and embraced him for a moment.   A soft, unpracticed smile came and went on the philologist's features.   Gently he removed the stylus from the other's slender hand.   His flesh was as warm, firm and muscular and his bones as sturdy as

Yancey's own. Using the visitor's hand, he placed it against his chest and said "Yancey," several times. The stranger caught on as quickly as before.

"Yancey," he repeated with excellent tone reproduction. Smilingly withdrawing his hand, he laid it against his own chest and said, "Gonish."

Yancey nodded, and supported the placard the other held with one hand while he wrote "BEROM" in simple Roman capitals, being unable to reproduce the other's skill at adding the cursive serifs of typewriter font. Then he printed his own name and, pointing to it, said it several times again. He followed by printing "Gonish," which he also spoke.

Gonish nodded quick understanding and retrieved the stylus. Still using the careful calligraphy that had so astonished Cottwold, he wrote a series of words on the placard:

"BEROM FANID ERPOT SIDAR YEVAH."

Pratt quickly copied them into his notebook, but all of them made it plain they did not understand the message. Gonish was plainly discouraged. He gestured toward the sun, and made several sweeping motions with his hand.

"Yes, yes," Yancey told him with the nod that was apparently a common signal of assent. "We understand. Only four more days." He turned and left the landing, leaving Pratt and Cottwold to continue a fruitless attempt to establish better communication.

"Well?" Harwood demanded, when he had returned to the sticky mud.

"I can't tell yet," Yancey said, musingly. "I suppose there are all sorts of scientists here, are there not?"

"Of course."

"Get me an astronomer," he asked. "I think I can get farther than that fumbling old Pratt up there."

Pratt and Cottwold had left the landing after copying down a number of other messages that Gonish had written. Yancey led the astronomer up the companionway. "Smile when you meet him, Skinner," Yancey asked, scraping the gumbo from his shoes. "I think he can understand most of our gestures and conventions of unspoken communication."

Reaching the landing, he eschewed the cry of "Berom!" with which the captain had signaled the visitor. "Gonish," he called. "It is Yancey."

The white-haired visitor stepped through the open lock in a few moments. "Yancey!" he said with obvious pleasure. He stepped lightly to the professor's side, and repeated Yancey's previous embrace. The philologist smiled happily, returning the light, symbolic pressure of the other's arms.

He took the clock from the astronomer. It had a twenty-four hour military dial. Pointing to the sun, and making a gesture to suggest its full course around the Earth, he then pointed to the timepiece and showed one revolution of the hour hand. He reset the instrument, showing that the minute hand made one circuit for each of the twenty-four hourly movements of the smaller hand.

Gonish took the clock from him and twisted the set knob until he understood the linkage.   By gesture he then repeated his understanding of the relationship between the course of the hour hand and the rotation of the planet.

"Sketch the Solar System, from north of the ecliptic," Yancey directed Skinner.

Gonish quickly nodded his assent as the representation of the sun, to which Skinner pointed, was surrounded by circles representing the elliptical orbits of the first three planets, with arrows flying in their direction of revolution.   As he drew the third ring, he pointed significantly to the ground.   Gonish nodded vigorously.

It took a little time to indicate the ten digits in the decimal numbering system, but eventually Gonish understood that nearly four hundred days were required for Earth to make one circuit about its parent.

At Yancey's continued direction, Skinner sketched wavy lines to indicate the vibratory pattern of light, and with the face of the clock showed that seven minutes were required for it to reach Earth from the sun.   Gonish timed the sweep of the second hand of the clock with his own wrist instrument, and indicated sudden comprehension.   He sketched a symbol.

"Undoubtedly the constant of the speed of light," Skinner said in awe.

"Yes," Yancey agreed.   "Now, we must find how long light takes to go from here to his star."   It was slow work in gestures, slow until the instant Gonish perceived what was wanted.   He quickly understood that the period of revolution of Earth about the sun was the unit of time to be used as a measure.   He made quick, crabbed calculations on the edge of the placard with a small pencillike stylus he took from his clothing, and, with careful copying of the arabic numerals, wrote the number "65."

"Sixty-five light-years," Skinner said.   "Yancey, this is terrific.   Imagine that unthinkable distance.   Find out how long it took them to get here."

"That doesn't matter," Yancey told him.   He tapped his skull several times with his forefinger, nodding and smiling to Gonish.   "I hope he gets that," he said to Skinner.   "I want him to know that I understand."   He pointed to the clock once again and showed two circuits of the hour hand.   "Two days," he said, pointing to the arabic numeral "2" on the placard.   Gonish nodded.

"Come on," Yancey said to Skinner.

"Why quit?" the astronomer protested.   "We're just beginning to get somewhere."

"We are already there," Yancey said sourly.   "We're wasting time.   Come on."   He trotted briskly down the companionway.

Harwood had left the trampled mud at its foot.   "Where's the colonel?" Yancey asked the captain of the guard.

"They're all in General Swift's quarters, professor," he replied.   "Something's up!"

Skinner tramped with him through the clinging mire.   They had to step aside several times to avoid the lurching progress of light tanks, their whipping antennae barely skimming under the maze of telephone lines strung to hastily driven posts.

Harwood greeted them the instant they walked through the door.   "Yancey!" he gasped.   "The situation is deteriorating fast!"

"What happened?" Yancey asked, adding his muddy tracks to the hundreds of others that had soiled the rough wooden floor.

"The Russians apparently are wise to what's up. They've announced they are sending their representatives here Tuesday morning, under escort. They insist we permit them to land and join in communicating with Gonish and his crew."

"And if we don't?" Yancey said, knowing the answer beforehand.

"They will consider it an act of war. The 'escort' is obviously their full war fleet. They probably can't mobilize it any more quickly than that."

"Going to let them land?" Yancey asked irritably, sitting down to clean the muck from his oxfords.

"That depends on you and the others," Harwood told him feverishly. "Can you possibly get in communication with them before then?"

"This is Sunday," Yancey reminded him. "I have to go to Chicago for some references."

"References!" Pratt bellowed from the table at which General Swift and others in uniform were bent in earnest conversation with a number of scientists.

"That's what I said, Pratt," Yancey snapped.

"Don't be a fool!" General Swift rumbled. "We can't wait for a lot of bone-dry research. We've got to make those people understand."

"Understand what?" Yancey demanded acidly.

"That we want the secret of their drive, and that the Russians can't have it!" he growled ominously.

"And if they won't do that?" Yancey persisted.

"I have my orders," the general ground out pointedly.

"You wouldn't try to force your way into the ship?" Yancey marveled.

"They'll not leave here without our having the secret, or their being in no condition to pass it on," Swift snapped. "Didn't you get anywhere with them?"

"Nothing important," Yancey said. "But I have some ideas. I'll need to do some research, as I told you."

"What do you mean, nothing important?" Skinner protested excitedly. "Why, at the rate he was going, we'd have had anything we wanted in a couple of hours!"

"Is that true?" Swift demanded.

"Not at all," Yancey said in a chill tone. "We merely exchanged references on our time system and found out that his star is about sixty-five light-years away."

General Swift was on his feet. "That's the stuff," he snapped. "Skinner, did you understand how he did it?"

"Yes, general. It's simple. Gonish wants to give information as hard as you can imagine."

"Well, come on," Swift roared, reaching for his cap.

"I've still got to go to Chicago," Yancey insisted. "Skinner can carry on, if that's what you care about. I'll be back tomorrow night or Tuesday."

"How can you consider leaving at a time like this?" Swift growled. "Haven't you got a scrap of patriotism in you?"

"I'm as old as you, if not as mentally ossified," Yancey seethed bitterly. "I have my own very strongly developed ideas of patriotism, undoubtedly arrived at

after thought more cogent than you are capable of.   I don't need you to tell me
my duty!   Are you trying to tell me I'm not free to go?''

All the military personnel froze into swift silence in the electric tension.   Swift
slowly purpled, trembling with restrained fury.   "Go ahead!'' he gasped, with a
furious swing of his arm.   "But keep your idiotic mouth shut!   And that's an
order I can make stick!''

The Russians had arrived before Yancey's 'copter returned him from Chicago.
A number of rotary-winged aircraft had alighted beside the looming bulk of the
monster from space.   Overhead, as far as the eye and ear could detect, a huge
fleet of Soviet aircraft circled ominously.

Harwood met him as he eased himself from the 'copter's cabin, his shoes going
over their tops in the slime.

"Have you got it?'' he demanded hopelessly, his face lined and haggard.

"Yes,'' Yancey said impatiently, struggling through the heavy going.   "Of
course.   That's why I'm back.   Took longer than I thought to find it.   Take me
to General Swift.''

"Professor,'' Harwood protested, as they trudged laboriously under the overhang
of the huge spaceship, "he's in with the Russians.   They're having the biggest
fight you ever heard.   The Russians have posted a guard at the companionway,
too.   They won't let anybody by.   And we won't let them go in, either.   They
demanded three days with Gonish before we see him again, on the theory that we
have already had a three-day crack at him.   It's awful!''

Yancey frowned, and they both stepped out of the way of a clanking, snorting
tank.   "That changes things a little,'' he said.   "Still, you had better get Swift
out of the meeting a minute.''

The general brought Pratt with him.   "Well?'' he gasped.   His red face ran
with sweat.   The tension of the days had told on them both.

"I can communicate with Gonish,'' Yancey told him.

"Not now,'' Swift said heavily.

"What?''

"You heard me.   If you'd stayed here and done your duty— But no!   Well,
we're not doing any talking with that white-haired little idiot until we settle with
the Russians.   The Secretary of State will be here in a minute.''

"Gonish will leave before you settle anything,'' Yancey said sourly.

"No he won't.   We'll either agree, or agree to disagree in the next hour,'' Swift
snarled.   "And I think war will start right in that room.   Major, give me your
sidearm.''   He gravely buckled the belt and holster over his uniform.   "Those
Russian generals are armed to the teeth,'' he swore, turning to leave.

"Wait,'' Yancey called.   He handed him a sheet of typed paper.   "This is
what I propose we should have told Gonish.''

Swift glowered at the meaningless message.   It was a short string of five-letter
words, making no sense.   "What does it say?'' he demanded.

"It's in code,'' Yancey said, with a vindictive smile toward Pratt.   "Bentley's
Commercial Code, obsolete now, but in common use for fifty years in the last

century.   "Look it up for yourself."   He did not mention the copy of the code book in his pocket.

"What?" Pratt roared.   "Inconceivable!"

"Who knows how many thousands of facsimile messages they received, how many labeled diagrams were transmitted?   It may have taken years, but they did it.   After all, code is still language."

"Ridiculous!" Pratt snapped, reddening at the thought he had missed the solution.

"Quite right," Yancey grinned acidly.   "Of course you should have figured it out in a minute.   Five-letter word groups.   No flexion apparently present but, as you pointed out yourself, his speech has even more flexion than our own.

"And he thought we should understand.   A complete stranger, he walked out of that ship printing words in our own letters that he thought we knew.   And from sixty-five light-years away!   It almost screamed that his race had been picking up facsimile transmissions.   And of course, the transmissions had to have originated more than sixty-five years ago, the time it took them to travel through space to his planet.

"We don't use the system any more," he explained.   "All commercial messages are now sent on keyed-variation pulses, to preserve their security.   But for many years after 1954 or 1955 almost all commercial radiograms were broadcast as facsimiles, the way we send radio-photos.   The code was used to compress the message as much as possible and to keep the purely curious from reading it without effort.   Many of the code words in Bentley's stand for whole sentences.   Such as BEROM."

"What does it mean?" Pratt asked reluctantly, as Swift's eyebrows narrowed over his haggard face.

"It means, 'Suggest we pool our information,' a common commercial phrase," Yancey said blandly.   "Something that was plain from Gonish's every action."

"That settles it!" Swift snapped.

"Settles what?"

"The Russians don't get to talk to Gonish," he said flatly.   "That white-haired fool would as likely hand *them* the secret of the drive as not."   He spun on his heel and reentered the conference room, Pratt tagging across the muddy floor behind him.

Yancey walked disconsolately from the nerve-wracking atmosphere of the barrack.   He felt rather than saw the rounded belly of the spaceship as he walked to where it curved into the great depression it had rammed in the mud of the prairie.

The squad at the foot of the companionway had been reinforced, as Harwood had told him.   The Russian soldiery stood on one side, glaring at the equally grim group of paratroops on the other.

Yancey struggled slowly over to them.   One of the Russians promptly raised his tommygun in an unmistakable gesture of threat.   Yancey stopped and looked at the foreigners thoughtfully.   Their broad Slavic faces and cropped hair marked them as elite troops of the Soviet.   All but one of them.   His flat Mongoloid nose and eye flaps marked him for a Tatar.   Yancey grinned without humor.

With the unconsciously easy skill of the accomplished linguist, he produced the Tatar tongue he hadn't spoken for twenty years, since his student days in traveling over the highland steppes of northern Tibet.

"Greetings, my Tatar friend," he said in the difficult tongue.   The soldier started with surprise.   "Have no fear," the professor told him loudly.   "It is only I, *Yancey*.   Just *Yancey*, and I would do you no harm, my Soviet comrade."

The effect of his name was electric.   Gonish appeared immediately on the landing, behind the backs of the guard.   Yancey raised his eyes.   Four words he cried:

"BEROM BODAD VEMAN WEGOT."

Gonish stood transfixed.   Slowly he reentered the lock, making only an arresting gesture with his hand.   Too late the Russian soldiery realized he had spoken with the ship.   Consternation and fear crossed their regimented faces.   Yancey stood stock-still, waiting in fearful suspense.   Had he overestimated the capacities of the visitors?

He was not to be disappointed.   The tractor beam seized him with a steely embrace that he recognized for deepest friendship.   He heard the lock clang shut behind him.   An enormous surge of acceleration threw him motionless to the floor of the lock.   For many minutes it crushed him there, alone, scarcely able to force a trickle of air into his straining lungs.   When the crushing weight eased, he knew they were far beyond the stratosphere.   The easing was only momentary.   The whole structure *rippled* and his vision went wild, only to clear.   He felt almost weightless.   It was the interstellar drive, he told himself.

(CONTINUATION OF EXCERPT FROM PROCEEDINGS IN THE COURT-MARTIAL OF BENJAMIN L. HARWOOD, COL., U.S.A., FORT MEYER, VA., JUNE 8, 2038.)

Defense Counsel: . . . to introduce into evidence two documents which have an important bearing on this same point.

Judge Advocate: It seems to me that this is out of order, and that your exhibits should properly be presented when your direct examination of the defendant takes place.

D. C.: May it please the Court, the cross-examination I shall wish to make of General Swift, who will, I understand, take the stand next, makes it desirable that these documents be introduced at this time.

J. A.: Very well.   Proceed.

D. C.: Both these messages were originally in code.   A copy of the book "Bentley's Commercial Codes," Seventeenth edition of 1961, has already been entered by the Court as Exhibit "C."   It has been used to decode or translate the exhibits in question.

The first exhibit decodes what, to the best auditory recollection of several persons who stood near him when he was drawn or sucked into the ship, Professor Yancey cried out to Gonish, the visitor from space, namely "BEROM BODAD VEMAN WEGOT."   Each of those words in Bentley's represents a standard sentence often used in commercial messages. This Exhibit decodes them to read, "Suggest we pool our information. You are in great danger. Leave at once. Take me with you." I offer it as Exhibit "L."

The second exhibit is a similar decoding of the suggested message to Gonish, given General Swift by Professor Yancey on his return from Chicago, where we now know he searched numerous old code books before discovering that Gonish was familiar only with Bentley's. This message, unlike the other, consists mostly of code words from Bentley's which represent one word or simple phrase in English. It reads, "Visitors from space: We are flattered and pleased by your generous offer to pool information. Unfortunately our world has not reached the stage of political maturity where it can be trusted with the secrets of enormous power you obviously possess. We are still divided into warring tribes, each trying to wrest mastery of the planet from the other. The idea of cooperation between peoples separated by our seas is slow to take root. To prevent the immediate outbreak of a catastrophic conflict among our tribes you must leave at once." I offer it as Exhibit "M."

Now I wish the Court to understand that we make no point of the accuracy of Professor Yancey's belief that departure of the ship would prevent the outbreak of war. Only the superhuman efforts of General Swift, as we all know—

RANDALL GARRETT

The Waiting Game

During the early years of its expansion, the Solar Federation discovered only two races of beings who had mastered the science of interstellar travel: the decadent remnants of the long-dead Grand Empire of Lilaar, and the savagely nonhuman race of the Thassela.

The Biology of Intelligent Races
by Jasin Brone, YF 402.

Major Karl Gorman looked gloomily out of the main port of the forward observation deck at the pinhead disk of light far ahead. Sol, and bright blue Earth swinging round it, though the ship was as yet too far away for him to see the planet.

Would it, he wondered, *be the same as the rest?* The closer he had come to the Federation capitol, the worse it had become, until now, after Procyon, he was almost sick. He had thought of making the dog-leg jump to Sirius, but had decided against it. He might as well jump right into the middle of the whole mess!

He turned away from the starry view before him and walked back toward the bar, feeling the eyes of the crowd on his uniform.

They weren't all looking at him, of course; a Spacefleet major wasn't that unusual. But a few of them had noticed the tiny silver spearhead on his shoulder, and knew it for what it was.

And men from the Federation Outposts *were* rare.

Gorman bought his drink and stared angrily at the hard, dark, blocky face that reflected in the bar's shining surface. He'd been on the ship for more than three days, now, and this was the first time he had felt the necessity of leaving his cabin. He didn't feel like talking to anyone around him; they just weren't his kind of people.

A low, resonant voice next to him jarred his train of thought, and he turned his head with a jerk.

"Ah, home from the wars, major?" the tall, hairless, pleasantly smiling being beside him asked.

Gorman silenced his biting request to be left alone before it began; after all, there wasn't any reason not be civil.

"No, my home is on Ferridel III. This is the first time I've ever been to Earth."

"Not surprising," commented the other. "There aren't very many outpost officers from Earth. After all, two years is a long time to spend just traveling."

Gorman finished his drink and ordered another. "It sure is."

"If I am not being too personal, major, may I ask why you are making the trip?"

Major Gorman looked up at the being's face. He knew what he was, of course; a Lilaarian. But this was the first time he had ever talked to one.

"Not at all. I suffer from a disease known as Utter Boredom. All my life, sir, I have been either fighting or getting ready to fight the Thassela. The war has been going on for more than two hundred years, and, as my home was right in the thick of it, I have been bred and trained in its atmosphere.

"Now, however, the war in my sector is nearly over; it has reduced itself to mopping-up operations on whatever of the Thassela are left. Therefore"—he paused to finish his second drink and order a third by a gesture to the steward— "I, a professional Thassela-killer, having no more Thassela to kill, have nothing to do but kill time."

"Please, major! This talk of . . . ah . . . such things distresses me," the pleasant bass voice admonished.

"Oh." Gorman looked at him. "I . . . I'm sorry. I forgot." He remembered now what he had heard of the Lilaar. Their religion, or something, forbade talk of death.

"You see, your race is not too well represented in my part of the Federation, and it is only in the past few months that I have seen any of your people. In fact, you are the first I have ever spoken to."

"Quite all right. The error was mine. Please go on."

"Oh, there's nothing much more. I decided to come to Sol and Earth in search of high adventure—pretty girls to be rescued from evil, villains to ki . . . er . . . punish, and all that sort of thing."

"You sound bitter, major," the Lilaarian commented analytically.

"I am, sir, I am. What do I find? I find people tending flower gardens, listening to soft music and admiring fine *objets d'art,* that's what I find!"

"And you find this distasteful?" the other asked, somewhat surprised.

Hastily, Gorman covered his tracks. "Why . . . no-o-o, it's just that it's not what I was looking for, you understand."

He had remembered another thing he had heard about the Lilaar—they were not in the least mechanically or scientifically minded. Instead, they were masters of the very music and art which he had just been on the verge of denouncing. He decided to change the subject.

"By the way, my name is Gorman, Karl Gorman." He held out his hand, and tried not to show his surprise at the unusual touch of the six-digited hand with the double-opposed thumbs, one on either side.

"Sarth Gell. May I buy you another drink?"

Gorman accepted, then, waxing warm inside, asked a question.

"Sarth, do you mind if I ask you something? As I say, I have always been a fighting man; I never had much time for history. When did the Federation contact your race?"

Sarth Gell leaned back, smoothed a hand over his hairless skull and said:

"It was some three hundred years ago, in the Year of the Federation 313, to be exact, that one of the exploratory ships first contacted us."

Gorman nodded. "That region is almost straight out beyond Altair, isn't it?"

"Yes. About eleven hundred light-years."

"So?" Gorman raised an eyebrow. "You must be a long way from home, too."

"Oh, no," chuckled Gell. "Not at all. I was born and raised on Tridel of Sirius. I am no more of Lilaar than you are of Earth."

Gorman signaled, and the steward brought more drinks. The conversation went on.

The huge passenger vessel bored on through the emptiness. Or perhaps that isn't the right term. Around? Past? Between, maybe? However she did it, at top speed she could make nearly a thousand light-speeds, although she wasn't doing that now. Her engines cut down and down as she approached Earth, until, finally, at one light, there was the familiar buzzy shiver as the ship passed into a more normal existence, although the accelerator field didn't cut itself out until the velocity dropped far below even that relatively low figure.

When the field cut, Major Gorman didn't even feel it. He was boiled to the ears.

He woke up in the hotel near the spaceport feeling just as he should feel, and lifted his head from his pillow with the care usually observed in such cases.

That sweet liquor! he thought. *I ought to have more sense than to drink stuff with so much junk in it! I wonder how many of the higher alcohols it's loaded with?*

Edging himself off the bed, he reached into his uniform pocket and got the box of small blue capsules he carried for such emergencies, swallowed one and waited. When it had taken effect, he decided that all he'd need to feel perfect again was enough water to cancel the dehydration brought on by the liquor, and some breakfast to take the dark-brown taste out of his mouth.

The breakfast helped, but by noon he felt ill again. Not from liquor, but from the same thing that had make him sick all the way from Ferridel.

Oh, Earth was beautiful, all right. All green and parklike, with tall trees, pretty flowers, tinkling fountains, and fairy buildings. All very lovely. And dull as the very devil!

He prowled around the city all the rest of the day, and by nightfall, he was ready to call it quits.

He'd gone into three or four of the establishments that purported to be bars, and found that no one drank anything but the sweet and aromatic synthetics, all of which would have made his stomach uneasy. He'd tried to talk to two or three of the girls, but they didn't seem to want to talk about anything but the soft strains of some melody or other that whispered through the late afternoon air. If he'd known the phrase, he would have called them mid-Victorian, although they possessed none of the hypocrisy of that long-forgotten age, and absolutely none of its sense of humor.

It was, he decided, even worse than Procyon; at least he'd been able to buy some decent liquor there.

When he got back to his hotel, Sarth Gell was waiting for him.

"Good evening, Karl, I see you've been out. How do you like our lovely city?"

"Oh, fine, Sarth, just fine," lied Gorman. "Very nice. Of course, I'm used to the Outposts, but I think I'll get used to this pretty quick." But he knew better. He knew he couldn't spend thirty-six years of his life smashing the onslaught of the evilly monstrous Thassela and then settle down to music.

"I'm glad to hear that," Gell smiled. "I wanted to ask you to accompany me to the concert tonight. I have a special seat."

Oh, great, moaned Gorman inwardly, *just great! I'm so happy I could simply die!*

The concert hall was filled with people, all beautifully dressed to set off the softly shifting pastel colors of the walls and floor. There was no ceiling; just the sighing breeze pushing fluffy little clouds across the face of the planet's one white satellite.

He watched as the great curtains drifted silently away, disclosing the musicians. Each was seated before the multi-keyed control board at his own panel; one hundred of them poised motionless, waiting for their signal.

Then the control master came out, sat down at the master panel and flexed his fingers.

Gorman looked closer. Six fingers! He hadn't noticed it at this distance, but now he could see that every one of those musicians was a Lilaarian. He glanced sideways at Gell, but his companion was looking straight at the orchestra.

Somewhere, from deep within his brain, a soft murmuring note sounded. It became a chord. It grew louder, and he actually did not realize until it grew fairly loud that it had come, not from his own mind, but from the orchestra before him.

As the music grew louder and wove in and out of itself, it became definitely apparent that the people of Lilaar were really master musicians. The shifting colors of the walls swirled in time to the undulating harmony of the orchestra.

He listened, and, after a little while, the music faded as it had begun, in a single note, dying in his brain.

He waited for the second composition, and was disturbed by Sarth Gell's touch upon his arm. He turned and noticed that everyone else was quietly leaving. Startled, he glanced at his wrist watch. Three hours! And he hadn't even realized it!

The next day, he went to the Great Library and began a search through the history section. Nothing too new, he decided. Something written back in the late Four or early Five Hundreds, at least a century old.

He finally found what he was looking for, selected two chapters for the reader, and flipped the switch.

As has been related in previous chapters," it began, "several nonhuman races of fair intelligence were discovered, but it was not until YF 313 that any race was found which had ever had interstellar travel.

"In that year, Expedition Ship 983, commanded by Colonel Rupert
Forbes, discovered—

The great ship hung high above the atmosphere of the planet, the engines quies-
cent. Colonel Forbes waited impatiently for the arrival of the scout ship. When
it finally came, he ordered Lieutenant Parlan to report immediately, in person.

"I don't want anything formal, lieutenant," he said. "Just tell me what you
found."

"Well, sir, the planet is inhabited all right, and they're almost human." He
handed a sheaf of photographs to the colonel and went on. "You can see for
yourself. They live in huge cities that look as if at one time they'd been really
something, but now they're falling to pieces; they look *old,* old as the mountains—
weatherbeaten, if you know what I mean, sir.

"Anyway, these people just live in them, they don't build them. And they
don't use any kind of power. They light the buildings with lamps that burn some
kind of oil, and they do their work by hand."

"I see," nodded Colonel Forbes, "backward and ignorant, eh?"

"Yes, sir, in a way. Though they must have had quite a civilization at one
time, from the looks of things."

"I think I'll get Philology busy on the language right away, and—"

A thorough study of the language took the better part of a year, and
by that time, several other facts made themselves apparent. First, that
the natives had no knowledge whatever of science; second—

"A funny bunch of people, colonel," commented Lieutenant Parlan. "They
believe that they are a part of what might be translated roughly as 'The Great Empire
of Heaven.' Their word for themselves is 'Lilaar,' but that also means 'sky' or
'universe.' The birth rate is appallingly low; only one child per couple every
fifteen or twenty years. I don't see how they kept themselves from extinction this
long."

Colonel Forbes rubbed a thumb across his chin. "How do you think they'll
react to Federation rule?"

"Duck soup. They have absolutely no weapons; they are strict vegetarians;
they're the laziest and most sheeplike, peaceful people I ever saw."

"Very well, I'll send my report in."

The report went in by subspace radio, propagated at a velocity which, though
finite, is so great that the means of measuring it is unknown—the distance required
is too great.

Expedition Ship 968 shot off toward her next target, a sun some three point two
light-years distant.

Colonel Forbes addressed his staff: "Gentlemen, we have been away from Earth
for better than two years. This is the last stop on our cruise. From here we
return home!" There were general smiles and pleased murmurings all around.

"We have done well," Forbes continued.   "We have discovered twelve planets which humanity can colonize, and more than that, one planet inhabited by intelligent beings, a discovery which is extremely rare among ships of the Exploratory Forces.

"Lieutenant Parlan, our contact officer, is, at this moment, exploring the thirteenth and last planet.   When he reports back—I expect him any minute—I hope we shall be able to report that we have discovered thirteen habitable worlds on our outward trip; more than any other ship has so far found.   To that, we can add the discovery of an alien race on one of the few—"

"Two," came the voice of Lieutenant Parlan from the door.

"I beg your pardon?" blinked Forbes, startled at the interruption.

"I said two, sir.   We have found two planets inhabited by nonhuman races— or rather race."

"Please be more explicit, lieutenant, " the colonel said sharply.

"The planet below us, sir, is populated by the Lilaar!"

All in all, the next seventy years of exploration in that region uncovered seventy-one planets of the Grand Empire of Lilaar, all of which—

Gorman snapped it off.   That was enough.   It tallied.   He set the other chapter he had selected, and started the reader again.

Beginning in YF 380, several Expeditionary ships stopped sending in their reports abruptly, and were never heard of again.   Because of the obvious dangers inherent in interstellar exploration, not too much significance was attached to these disappearances, although it was noticed that the incidents all took place in one section of the outermost fringes of the Federation.   It was not until early in 384 that the truth became known.

In that year, Expedition Ship 770 reported that it was being attacked by alien forces.   They subsequently ceased to report.

Federal Security forces immediately went into action.   The Biomathematical Section had long warned of the probability of inimical alien life, and thus the Government was prepared.   The cry of 'Remember the Seven Seven Oh!' became the battle cry of the Federation.   The Interstellar Secrecy and Security Act went into effect and—

Again Gorman cut the reader off.   One more check and he would have what he wanted.

He and the librarian went through the Laws of the Federation for several minutes until he found the original draft of the Act.

It read: "For the security of the Solar Federation . . . no person, corporation, planetary or system government . . . shall build or construct . . . any interstellar vessel, for any use whatsoever, except upon explicit contract with the Federal Government.

"All such now in use shall be . . . turned over to the Federal Government without delay.

"No subspace radio shall . . . operate or be operated . . . without explicit instructions from the Federal Government."

There was more, but that was all that interested Gorman. He was sure, now. Here was what he was looking for.

He had had a small smile at the part that stated that no "person or corporation" would build a spaceship. Any "person or corporation" wealthy and powerful enough to construct one would have long since ceased to be a "person or corporation" as such—they would have become a government.

Then he went out to the Federal Radio Office, sent an Interstellar 'Gram—three eighty-five a letter for nineteen letters—paid, and left for dinner. After dinner, he poked around until he found a bar near the spaceport which sold a concoction that wasn't so ungodly sweet, had three drinks, and went to bed.

Next morning, he had company.

"Fleet Intelligence," said the smartly uniformed captain who stood in the doorway as Gorman opened it. His credentials were in his hand, but Gorman just gave them a quick glance.

"Come in," he said, mentally parenthesizing that for an Intelligence man, the guy didn't look too intelligent. Soft, bland face, wide-open eyes that kept blinking like a couple of synchronized camera shutters, and a prim mouth. Behind him were two more nonentities just like him in lieutenant's uniforms. They all trooped into the room, one right after the other.

"May I see your papers, major?" asked the captain.

"Certainly, captain." He handed over the thick sheaf of folded papers in their heavy official envelope. The Intelligence man scrutinized them for the better part of ten minutes, moving his lips in a not-quite-inaudible whisper as he did so.

"They seem to be quite in order, sir," he said when he finished. "They seem to be quite in order."

"May I ask what the trouble is, captain?"

"Well, to be frank, there were quite a few people who wondered just how a Spacefleet major, wearing an Outpost Spearhead, happened to get the extended leave required to come to Earth, especially with a war on out there."

Gorman absorbed that statement for a full second before the full import struck him. The fathead actually did not know the war was over! And had been for better than two and a half years!

He worded his second question cautiously.

"Tell me, captain, isn't this stuff radioed into GHQ?"

The captain looked startled. "Why . . . ah . . . yes . . . yes, I believe it is. But after all, major, you must realize that such things are merely for the record. Now that we have checked your papers, I have no doubt that my superiors will check them against the files to confirm them, but up to now, there has been no reason to look over those 'grams. They are simply received and filed until needed."

Gorman, still cautious, worded his next question a little more broadly. "But why? I should think you'd want to know what's going on in the Galaxy."

The captain's smile was a little superior. "My dear major, do you realize the immensity of correspondence that must come from better than seventy thousand million cubic light-years of space filled with uncounted thousands of billions of living beings? Why, it couldn't possibly be all correlated! I'm afraid, major, that you are thinking in terms of planetary governments. The Federation simply couldn't be run that way.''

Gorman realized then why no one knew the war was over. It wasn't, really; there were still a few mopping-up operations to be taken care of, still a few Thassela attempting to flee from the Federation Spacefleet. No one headquarters anywhere in the Outposts had sent the specific message: WAR OVER EXCEPT FOR MOP-UP. It would take a correlation of all the millions upon millions of reports from each of the widely scattered planets of the far-flung Outpost stars.

He chuckled mentally at the thought that several thousand of the clerks in the Federation offices each knew a tiny fraction of the fact that the Human-Thassela War was over. And who was to tell them? After all, he was no official spokesman for the Outpost Fleet; he might not—he probably wouldn't—be believed.

"You're probably right, captain; I must seem a bit provincial to you. Well, if you're quite satisfied I—"

"Ah—one more question, major." He ruffled through a notebook. "What was the meaning of the 'gram you sent to a Major Mark Gorman on Kaibere IV last night? It reads: *Altair cap sppt sic mos*. What does that mean?"

Gorman shrugged. "At three eighty-five, space rates, I saved a devil of a lot of money by not saying, 'Dear Mark, please meet me at the Altair capitol spaceport six months from now.' O.K.?"

"Why say 'Altair capitol'? 'Pelma' would have been a great deal shorter. Would've saved you fifteen-forty." The captain did not seem to be questioning in an official manner, now, he just seemed genuinely interested.

"I'm no stellographer. Neither is Mark. Tell me; what is the only planet of Meargrave?"

"I don't know."

"But you could get there?"

"Yes. Easily."

"What if I told you to go to Hell?"

"*What?*" The captain looked scandalized, shocked, and insulted, all in one face.

"Hell, my dear captain, happens to be the only planet of Meargrave." Gorman particularly liked to use that example. It had a shock effect he was fond of.

"Oh." The face cleared. "I see what you mean. Well, sir, I think everything is in order. Thank you, major, for your cooperation."

He saluted and left, the two lieutenants following silently after.

Gorman sat down on the bed, looked wonderingly afer them for a moment, then grinned.

"What a bunch of fogheads. The Thassela could have battled their way clear in to Procyon before they'd know it."

He had six months to wait.

The first three he spent on Earth.   He wanted to see the entire planet but he just didn't have the time; therefore a representative sample would have to do.

He noticed quite early that most of Earth's inhabitants, both Human and Lilaarian, avoided him after first contact, especially if he mentioned anything about the war, or if they happened to see and know the Silver Spearhead.   He knew what they must be thinking:

Here is a soldier, a killer, back from his awful business.   Here is a man who has been trained to murder other beings.   What if he gets bored with us?   What if we anger him somehow?   What then?   Would he not just as soon kill a Human or Lilaarian as a Thasselan?   Perhaps.   It would not be too wise to associate with him, at any rate.

They were polite, but evasive.

Not, he reflected, that he blamed them.   He was probably the first real veteran they had ever seen.   To them, the war had not been close.   They had lived with it all their lives, as he had, but it was not the same.   To them, it was a vague thing; something two thousand light-years away that they heard of once in a great while and dismissed distastefully.

If a fully armed and armored Thasselan battle fleet had started for Earth yesterday, it would be a full two years at top speed before they would arrive.   There would be plenty of time to prepare.

Even the planets near the periphery of the Federation shared, to some slight extent, the feeling Earthmen had toward the returned fighting man.   He remembered Telsonn, two ship-months, a hundred and fifty light-years, in from the front.   They had had men, sons, fathers, and husbands, who had fought in the war, although not actually as fighting men, and even they shied away from their homecoming relatives as though they were some other sort of life.

Here on Earth, of course, it was immensely worse.   For the past century or more, no Earthman had volunteered for front duty, and it had not been necessary to order them there; the war had been going well, even then.   The only duty imposed upon Spacefleet men of Earth was the Ferry Service; the duty of taking the fabulously expensive and highly necessary spaceships out for a month or two to some relay point where they would be picked up by another crew and taken a little farther, and so on until they reached their destination.   The original crew would return by luxury liner to Earth for a leave, then pick up another ship.

After three months, Gorman grabbed the first available ship for Altair and—what was it?—Pelma, the System's capitol.

The great automatic ship had only three passengers besides himself.   No one did much traveling any more, and those who did weren't very interesting to talk to.   Major Gorman kept to his cabin most of the time.

When he had begun his long journey in from Ferridel, now almost three years ago, he had been vastly interested in the liners, so different were they from the battleships he was used to.   They were completely automatic, pursuing and correcting their courses through those immense distances with unerring precision, requiring no human hand at their control.   Indeed, no human being could possibly move fast enough or think fast enough to control anything moving at nearly two hundred million miles per second.

The ships were robots, and for that very reason they had been fascinating.   But they were blind, reasonless robots, designed to take their course and return.   They had no real intelligence, and they soon palled on him.   He had come to ignore them completely.

The trip took only a few days, but he was heartily glad when it was over.

Pelma of Altair, he soon discovered, was a great deal like Earth.   Too much, in fact.   The one redeeming factor was that here there were fewer people who recognized the Spearhead on his shoulder.   Several times, on Earth, he had been tempted to put on civilian clothes, and had even gone so far as to try a suit on, but in the first place, it was strictly against military law, and in the second, civvies didn't feel natural on his body.

After he had been there a few days, he received another visit from Intelligence, and they had evidently had no word from Earth that he was cleared there.   The interview was shorter than the first had been, but the end result was the same. Major Gorman went on about his business.

Life suddenly became infinitely more bearable in the middle of the fourth week. She was sitting on a little grassy knoll in one of the innumerable parks, scattering food to a flock of the little bushy-tailed mammals that seemed to infest so many planets in this part of the Federation.   Gorman watched her for a long time, trying to figure out an angle of approach that would work but wouldn't be too obvious.

She seemed to have some of the animals rather well tamed; they would come right up to her with their funny scrambling gait, snatch the food right out of her fingers, and then run off, nibbling it between their forepaws.

Suddenly, she screamed and jerked her hand away from one of the beasts. Gorman saw immediately what had happened: one of the little monsters had bitten her.

Arise, brave soul, and dash to her rescue, Gorman thought, and made motions to suit.

"What happened, Miss?" he asked, pretending a great worry over what he knew was an inconsequential wound.

She was crying and could hardly speak, but she held the injured and bleeding digit out for his inspection.

"Hm-m-m," he hm-m-m'd.   He took an ampoule out of the E-kit at his belt, aimed it at the tip of the finger he was holding, and squeezed the end.   It spat a fine cloud of mist at the ragged little incision.   Then he wrapped the finger.

"I think that'll do it.   You can go to a physician if you want, but I don't believe it will be necessary."

She smiled prettily.   "It doesn't hurt a bit, now.   Thank you"—her gray eyes darted to his collar—"Major, thank you very much."

"Well, now, I wouldn't be in too much of a hurry to run off," cautioned Gorman. "You really ought to go somewhere and sit down for a while; animal bites can be poisonous sometimes, you know.   Is there somewhere we can—"

She looked a little worried. "Why . . . why, yes, I know a diner down the parkway. Do you really think—?"

Gorman didn't know quite what to think. Was she taking him seriously, or did she think he wasn't quite bright? Who cared? Play it along, boy, play it along.

"I wasn't thinking of a diner, exactly. You see, it is a well-known fact that alcohol is just the thing for bites—provided that they're treated first, of course."

She brightened again. "Oh, really? I didn't know that. I suppose I had better have some, then."

They had some. The place labeled itself a "cocktail lounge," but it mixed drinks out of the assorted flavors and synthetics, then spiked them with a little bit of straight ethanol. It took quite a little talking to convince the steward that he should jigger up the mechanism so it would serve the ethanol with nothing but soda water and a dash to bitters, but Gorman finally did it. It took him almost as long to convince the girl that she should drink the stuff, but he finally did that, too.

Her name, it turned out, was Lanina Indar, and she was a music interpreter.

Upon questioning, Gorman discovered that a music interpreter interpreted music, a fact which he had already suspected. He asked her to explain further.

"Well, you see, it's this way. Lilaarian music all means something. It's very, very old music, most of it, dating back to the old Grand Empire itself. The Lilaarians know, or, rather, they *feel* exactly what the music means. It's really a language of sorts, you know, except that it expresses mood and emotion rather than ideas or anything like that. You see?"

Gorman did see, after a fashion. He waved a vague gesture into the air. "What is that saying?"

She listened for a moment to the soft, pulsing rhythm, then closed her eyes. Her lips began to move softly.

"We dream of peace, to sleep and dream; to quietness and gentle sleep our goal; we rest forever—"

She went on like that for the better part of ten minutes, and Gorman was reminded, somehow, of an old poem he had read in one of the museums he had visited on Earth. Something about—

> . . . *To die, to sleep;*
> *To sleep: perchance to dream: ay, there's the rub;*
> *For in that sleep of death what dreams may come*
> *When we have shuffled off this mortal coil*
> *Must give us pause.*

That, at least, was a rough translation. He wondered, fleetingly, what that ancient bard would have thought of Earth today. Then, his thoughts were broken by Lanina's voice.

"See? Isn't it beautiful? Of course, to really understand it, you have to listen closely and listen to a lot of it, but eventually, you really get the feel of the music; then it comes easily.''

''It sounds a little morbid to me,'' Gorman murmured.

''Oh no it isn't, really; it isn't at all.   It's sort of beautiful and peaceful.''

''Are they all like that?''

''Oh, no.   Some of them deal with pure beauty, others with light and color, and—''

Gorman listened for a long time, nodding his head occasionally, and sticking in an appropriate remark now and then, but his heart wasn't in it.   He was thinking.

Here I am again, listening to a nice dissertation on Lilaarian music.   Tomorrow night, it will be flowers, and the next night it will be statuary, and the night after that light symphonies of music again.

No!   I'm going to get this piece of fluff to talk about something else if I have to completely reeducate her all by myself!

He knew from the beginning that such an education would have to be begun on her level.   He began by painting word-pictures of the awful beauty of interstellar space, of the grandeur of the vast loneliness and emptiness between the stars; he went from there to the wonders of adventure, the desire to explore and see things that no man had ever seen before.   He talked carefully, choosing each word for semantic content on the girl's own level, twisting the conversation back toward his own goal every time she tried to throw it off course.

In the end, he didn't think he had been too successful.   After two months of education, it was a little disheartening to find that she didn't really seem to be interested in what he was saying.   A blow to the ego, to say the least.

She was with him the day Mark arrived.   They were eating dinner in the spaceport cafe, when the ship arrived.   Lanina had kept nagging him to tell her who they were going to meet, but all he'd tell her was ''a relative.''

When Major Mark Gorman came in and sat down, she watched the back-slapping and greetings with slightly startled eyes.

''Why, you're twins!'' she exclaimed, at last.

''Oh, no,'' laughed Karl.   ''Mark is older than I by several years.   Right, grampaw?''

''Right.   But look, junior, where's your manners?''

''Oh.   Sorry.   Lanina, Mark Gorman.''

Lanina searched Mark's face carefully.   When he took off his cap she smiled. ''You don't look any older, but I can see now that you aren't identical twins. Your hair is light-brown, almost the same color as mine; Karl's is almost black.''

Mark rubbed his hands together briskly.   ''Well, son, what's on the agenda? How was Earth?   I didn't come through there, so I figured you'd have to tell me all about it.''

Gorman looked comically downcast.   ''We are the Forgotten Men.   No one appreciates us around here.   In fact, nobody even knows we exist.''

''That's about the way I had it made out.   Shame.''

They eyed each other sadly for a moment, then broke out laughing. "Come on," said Gorman, "I know of a little place where the three of us can talk. I have bribed the automatics to make something that borders on being fit to drink. You have to watch those synthetics. They flavor them with some frightful messes."

The conversation that night was sometimes over Lanina's head. Most of the time the men talked to her, and the conversation was very stimulating, but every once in a while, they seemed to run across some private joke that she couldn't fathom, especially those about Lilaarians. Oh, well. She didn't understand Spacefleet men, anyway.

The next morning, they were in the Spaceport office quite early, poring over timetables, making calculations, checking back over old passenger lists, and looking up immigration and emigration statistics. It was nearly nighttime before Karl Gorman was able to place his hand over a section of the tank chart and say: "Here."

"Here *what?*" Lanina asked confusedly.

Mark smiled. "My friend, the idiot, may not have told you, my dear, but I am a man with itchy feet. We were just deciding on the proper spot for my vacation—for the next five or six years."

The girl turned pleading eyes on Karl. "You. . . aren't going with him? Are you?"

"Nope. I have decided to become a homebody. I like Pelma."

"But won't you have to go back to duty?"

"Nope, again. I am on 'indefinite leave'; don't have to go back until they call me." To which he added mentally: *And I don't think they will.*

The years passed swiftly for Karl Gorman, and yet, in another way, they were easy-going and full. Before the end of the first year he had acquired an apartment, and the lettering on the door said: KARL GORMAN, THEORETICAL MATHE-MATICIAN.

It was as good a title and profession as any, and quite true, although there was little call for his services. Nevertheless, he worked at it. He and Lanina set up a small calculator in one of the rooms, and he patiently taught her how to set up equations on it after he had written them out. She never really quite learned what she was doing, but after he showed her how the music of Lilaar could be interpreted mathematically, she loved the work he gave her to do.

Meanwhile, the little, and highly illegal subspace radio began receiving reports from Mark's equally illegal set.

> Karrvon; three hundred light-years from Earth; Index, point six three.
> Ressalin; four hundred twenty light-years; Index, point five oh.
> Mensidor: six hundred ninety light-years; Index, point three nine.
> Hessor-Del; eight hundred light-years; Index, point two one.
> Thilia; twelve hundred light-years; Index, point oh eight.

And Gorman carefully fed them all into the computer, came up with figures that were meaningless to anyone but himself, fed these back in, and came up with figures that were even more meaningless, if possible.

At other times, he computed Lanina's music for her, although he told her not to tell anyone where she had obtained her results.

"Every other interpreter would want me to do it, and I haven't that much time," was the absolutely untruthful answer he gave her.

And, again, he would go out to art galleries and measure lines and curves and color wave length and intensity.   And these, too, went into the computer, and came out unrecognizable.

And one morning, when nearly six years had passed, Gorman and Lanina were eating breakfast when the door chime announced a visitor.

Mark Gorman was back again.

The Spacefleet Intelligence men and the CID were forty-five minutes behind him.   This time they hadn't delegated the duty to a mere captain; having evidently decided they should outrank their quarry, they had sent two colonels.

"Which one of you is Major Gorman?" asked the tough-looking CID man.

Two thumbs jerked simultaneously.   Two voices said: "Him."

The colonel glared.   "Let me see your papers!"

He looked them over, then looked back at the two who were standing at attention before him.   "Very funny.   And for that remark, I think we'll take both of you in."

"On what charge, sir?" asked Mark.

"Grand larceny and interstellar piracy.   To be explicit, for feloniously disrupting the robot controls of, diverting the course of, and taking illegal possession of an interstellar passenger liner."

Karl gazed upon Mark with a mock glower.   "Shame on you."

Mark tried to look innocent.   "Well, nobody was using it."

"Enough!" barked the colonel savagely.   "Let's go!"

Lanina said nothing, but her eyes were wide with terror.   When they left, she was sobbing quietly.

An hour later, the Majors Gorman were sitting on a bench in a windowless cell, watching the door slide shut with a click.

"And now what?" asked Karl.

"And now, my boy, we are to be left for a time in order to thoroughly discuss our crime, so that concealed pickups can relay the complete details to our stuffy friend, the colonel."

Then the shock came.   Energy rippled searingly through their bodies, and they sagged slowly to the floor.

When they opened their eyes, they were seated in a softly luxurious room in comfortable chairs, bound there by restraining, but not uncomfortable straps.   Before them was a large, finely paneled desk.   Behind it was seated a Lilaarian. Karl recognized him.   It was Sarth Gell.

"Ah, you are awake," said Gell.

"An astute observation, to say the least, Master Gell."

"Oh," said Mark.   "You know this pleasant fellow?"

"Ah, yes.   We got sotty together some years back."

"Permit me to correct your brother, Mark Gorman," Gell interjected softly.

"*He* got sotty.   Lilaarians, in case you didn't know, eschew intoxicants in any form."

"I didn't know," Mark murmured.   "But it's fascinatin' information.   Do go on."

"I shall.   I am about to make a very long, but, I trust, not tiresome speech. I hope both of you can restrain your admittedly very witty remarks until I am through.

"To begin with, let me tell you that I know exactly what you two have been doing for the last several years, and have followed your progress with avid interest. You have discovered that we of the Lilaar have begun to, and eventually will, take over complete control of the Federation, although the Federation will not exist, as such by that time.

"As you, Mark, have discovered in your wanderings in that stolen spaceship, the regularly scheduled flights in that portion of the Galaxy are no longer being made.   The planets there have not made any reports to Earth for some years, in some cases more than a century.   Because of the very carefully planned decay of Earth's correlation system, they do not as yet know this, and by the time they do, it will be too late.

"And you, Karl, have discovered that our subtly hypnotic art forms are the means we use to further our purpose.

"Because you have discovered these things, I am sorry to say that I must forever prevent that information from reaching Earth.   You will never report what you have found.

"Now as to why and how we have done this.   To begin, I must go back a good many centuries; back to the first century of the Federation.   And I must also explain exactly who and what the Lilaar are.

"We of the Lilaar, you see, are immortal."

Karl Gorman's eyes narrowed.   "Precisely what do you mean by 'immortal,' Gell?   That's a pretty broad term."

"By that, I mean that we do not suffer, as you do, from the racial disease known as 'old age.'   Except for accidents and a few rare diseases, there is nothing to keep us from living forever.   You must understand this in order to understand what you have seen.

"Our birth rate, as you know, has been referred to as being extremely low. Actually, quite the reverse is true.   Each couple averages one birth every thirty years.   That means that our population is *doubled every sixty Earth-years*!

"Of necessity, therefore, we had to expand.   And in doing so we found that we had competition.   You, of Earth, and the Thassela.   We are not, however, fighters.   Because of the vast value of life, we cannot, by our very nature, take the life of an intelligent living being."   Gell's face twisted as he said this, as though he were going to be sick at the very thought of death.

He paused to relax for a moment, then went on.

"When your first ship found us, in YF 313, the Plan had already been in operation for some two hundred of your years.   We pretended to be decadent.   We made you believe that our glorious Grand Empire was dead.   Neither is true.

"We knew in the beginning that your race, being inherently what it was, would eventually win the Thassela-Human war. Therefore, we are permitting you to do so. At the same time, we are completley undermining your once-tight and compact organization of government. The Federation should collapse in about one hundred fifty to two hundred years, at which time you will have won the war with the Thassela."

"It is obvious," remarked Mark calmly, "that you have, and can use, a space drive capable of much greater velocities than ours. Tell me, why don't you use it?"

Gell's brows lifted in surprise. "You are a very observant young man in some ways, but in others you are not. But"—he shrugged—"I will answer the question. Yes, we have had the infinity drive for many hundreds of years. We do not use it within the boundaries of the Federation unless absolutely necessary because it interferes with subspace radio, and is, therefore, detectable.

"Our kidnaping you from under the noses of the Spacefleet CID was done only because of the extreme urgency of the situation. We could not permit you to return to Earth."

"May I ask why you are dooming the Federation?" Mark asked.

"We need the planets which you are using. Our population growth has required a tremendous amount of shifting about in the Federation, and a great deal of name-changing in order that your race may never discover the fact that we do not. . . ah . . . die." The last word was almost a whisper. "This is a nuisance and a bother. We are, however, eliminating it, since there will soon be no subspace radios in operation near our portion of the Federation to report the fact that there are certain irregularities in our life span."

Gell placed his fingertips together and smiled benevolently.

"Our plan, as you can see, is working well. The Thassela are too monstrously savage, too physically unlike us to have permitted our infiltration. The Humans, on the other hand, have proved themselves relatively easy to manage.

"And, if you will reason it out logically, you will see that it is all for the best. Both you humans and the Thassela are basically unfit for the role of Galactic rulers. You are basically killers; destroyers of life; diseases which should never have evolved!" His voice shook with loathing.

"Careful, Gell," Karl Gorman cut in. "You'll get high blood pressure." But Sarth Gell was calm again.

"The disease will be permitted to run its course, but by isolating the colonies of infection we will be able to control and eventually eliminate it. The immortals must rule the galaxy."

"What about us? If you can't murder us in cold blood, what do you intend to do to put us permanently out of the way?" Mark was purposely gory for Gell's discomfort.

"We are leaving you here. The whole planet is yours. It will not be required by our race for another century. This house has been constructed for your comfort, but there is nothing else on this entire world in the way of civilized artifacts. You can not build spaceships; on the nearer of the two satellites is a device which will prevent your sending a subspace message, even if you should be able to construct a radio.   You will remain here for the rest of your lives.''

''This planet?   Where are we?''   Mark's voice was cold.

''While you were unconscious, you were transported here by one of our infinity ships.   When this sun sets, I rather imagine you will like the view; you are in the center of the vast star clouds beyond Sagittarius, thirty thousand light-years from Earth.   When I return, this planet will again be vacant and ready for our use.   The Lilaar can afford to wait.

Sarth Gell, the Lilaarian, turned and left the room.   In a few moments the ground quivered a little, and there was the distant buzz of a space vessel as it lifted, leaving the two behind to work their way out of the straps that bound them to the chairs, knowing they could never work their way out of the vaster bonds of space.

''Are they gone?'' Karl asked after a moment.

Mark Gorman's brain reached out through the twists of spacetime and contacted that of the robot in the Lilaarian ship.   And the stupid, unimaginative thing answered truthfully.

Mark smiled.   ''Yes, they're gone.''

The two stood, the binding straps splitting and rending as they did so.

''Now what, Grandfather?'' Karl asked.

''I have been sending in my reports regularly, ever since we were assigned to discover why the Federation Government had become so lax.   Now we know. I'll finish my report so that you can send in the math involved.''

''Check.   I'll wait.''

Mark Gorman lay on a soft couch in the Lilaar-provided room, and closed his eyes.   Again his brain reached out, this time further, much further than before. Finally he contacted it, fitted himself in, and took control.

And, more than thirty thousand light-years away, on Ferridel III, a robot-controlled printer began to make impressions on a strand of ultrafine plastic, subtly altering its molecular structure.

A REPORT ON THE GRAND EMPIRE OF THE LILAAR

From: Mark of Ferridel III; somewhere in the center of the Galaxy.
To: Commanding General, Outpost Spacefleet, Control Division.
Via: Interbrain Paracontrol beam.

From the above portions of this report, I believe it will be possible for our psychologists to find the precise stresses necessary to disrupt their Empire.   These will, I believe, be slight, since it is my opinion that they are already psychotic to some degree in that they do not admit their position in the basic realities of the Universe.

I give as examples the references to their living ''forever''; a self-obvious fallacy, and their so-called ''infinity'' drive, also as obvious.   The long and boastful speech which Sarth Gell made just before he deserted us here is also significant.   Their basic revulsion to death is another factor, in that it springs, not from a high moral code, but from fear.

It is because of this fear, I believe, that they, like Earth, do not know that the Thasselan war is over.   They avoided the entire sector.   It is also responsible for their ignorance of our existence.

Earth, because of the Lilaarian disruption of Federal Coordination and Correlation, has forgotten us.

My grandson, Karl, will send in the complete mathematical analysis through me as soon as he has incorporated the data just received, but for those not equipped with computer brains, I think the following will explain in some measure our position:

When, three centuries ago, it became obvious that no ordinary robot could control an interstellar battleship to the extent necessary to overwhelm the antlike coordination of the Thassela, Dr. Theodore Gorr was sent to the Outpost planets to build a robot which could do the job required.

At this time, the Lilaar were not as yet beginning their actual infiltration, since they had not been accepted as citizens of the Federation; therefore, they knew nothing of Dr. Gorr's highly secret mission.   When Dr. Gorr produced the first Gorr-man on Ferridel III, he probably did not realize that the real enemy of Earth was attacking from far across the Federation, but nevertheless, as is well known, we were so equipped as to be able to ward off attack in almost any conceivable form.

The Lilaar, naturally, could know nothing of this, but they could have deduced it logically had not their fear of death kept them from the immediate area of the war.   No human being is capable of computing the forces and the vectors thereof which obtain at ultra-light velocities in interstellar space.   Had the Lilaar known that our fighting ships do not have built-in control robots, they would have known that they were controlled by some other type, and thus would have known of our existence.   My grandson, by the way, has shown that the probable deduction would have been wrong, insofar as our method of ship control would have been assumed to be by the so-called "subspace" radio, and not by the actual application of mental energy.

Our activities for the past ten years were so calculated as to be suspicious only to the Lilaar.   This was necessary because Karl's equations showed that the final factors could only come from a Lilaarian speaking of his own free will.

Karl, therefore, stayed on Pelma of Altair after his preliminary reconnaissance, while I inspected the area already under the control of Lilaar.   My grandson, as you know, while only thirty at the time he was commissioned a major twelve years ago, is deserving of the rank in every way.   He is, however, one of the new Type Beta Gorr-men, whose purpose is socio-mathematical computation, and therefore is not telepathic and cannot direct a ship as we of Type Alpha because of the extra brain capacity required for these forms of higher-stage computers.

On Pelma, he set up a "front" as a practical mathematician and actually bought himself an electrical computer which he taught a young human girl to operate, in order to free his brain of the tiresome details of some of the simpler problems.   He investigated Lilaarian art-forms, computed their hypnotic qualities, figured in the indices of general effect which I gave him from space, and entered all these into what he calls the Lilaarian Equations.

In general, these equations show the following:

A.   The Lilaar, because their fear of death prevents them from practicing birth control, will so overpopulate their planets that they will starve, since they require as fuel the hard-to-synthesize carbohydrates, but can not also utilize, as we do, the lower alcohols.

B.   Even their so-called "infinity drive" can not move them to new planets fast enough, as a little figuring with geometrical progression will show.   Their population doubles every sixty years; therefore, their portion of the Galaxy can be shown to be an expanding sphere which must double in volume every second generation.   The Lilaarians must, however, go to planets outside the "surface" of that sphere, a surface which is constantly decreasing in proportion to the total volume.   Theoretically, this would reach a point where it would be physically impossible for them to be "emitted" from the "radiating surface" fast enough. Long before that point is reached, however, the area in the center of this sphere will begin to starve.   The death of its inhabitants will start a mass psychosis of the entire race which will eventually destroy them.

C.   The Lilaar will be unable to admit this, even to themselves, and will, therefore, do nothing to prevent it.

We will stay upon this planet until the scientists of Ferridel learn the secret of the Lilaar drive, which, it is estimated, will not take more than from ten to sixty Earth-years.

We can well afford to wait.

Mark of Ferridel III
Major, Spacefleet Ship Control

H. B. FYFE

Protected Species

The yellow star, of which Torang was the second planet, shone hotly down on the group of men viewing the half-built dam from the heights above. At a range of eighty million miles, the effect was quite Terran, the star being somewhat smaller than Sol.

For Jeff Otis, fresh from a hop through space from the extra-bright star that was the other component of the binary system, the heat was enervating. The shorts and light shirt supplied him by the planet co-ordinator were soaked with perspiration. He mopped his forehead and turned to his host.

"Very nice job, Finchley," he complimented. "It's easy to see you have things well in hand here."

Finchley grinned sparingly. He had a broad, hard, flat face with tight lips and mere slits of blue eyes. Otis had been trying ever since the previous morning to catch a revealing expression on it.

He was uneasily aware that his own features were too frank and open for an inspector of colonial installations. For one thing, he had too many lines and hollows in his face, a result of being chronically underweight from space-hopping among the sixteen planets of the binary system.

Otis noticed that Finchley's aides were eying his furtively.

"Yes, Finchley," he repeated to break the little silence, "you're doing very well on the hydroelectric end. When are you going to show me the capital city you're laying out?"

"We can fly over there now," answered Finchley. "We have tentative boundaries laid out below those pre-colony ruins we saw from the 'copter."

"Oh, yes. You know, I meant to remark as we flew over that they looked a good deal like similar remnants on some of the other planets."

He caught himself as Finchley's thin lips tightened a trifle more. The co-ordinator was obviously trying to be patient and polite to an official from whom he hoped to get a good report, but Otis could see he would much rather be going about his business of building up the colony.

He could hardly blame Finchley, he decided. It was the fifth planetary system Terrans had found in their expansion into space, and there would be bigger jobs ahead for a man with a record of successful accomplishments. Civilization was reaching out to the stars at last.   Otis supposed that he, too, was some sort of pioneer, although he usually was too busy to feel like one.

"Well, I'll show you some photos later," he said.   "Right now, we—Say, why all that jet-burning down there?"

In the gorge below, men had dropped their tools and seemed to be charging toward a common focal point.   Excited yells carried thinly up the cliffs.

"Ape hunt, probably," guessed one of Finchley's engineers.

"Ape?" asked Otis, surprised.

"Not exactly," corrected Finchley patiently.   "That's common slang for what we mention in reports as Torangs.   They look a little like big, skinny, gray apes; but they're the only life large enough to name after the planet."

Otis stared down into the gorge.   Most of the running men had given up and were straggling back to their work.   Two or three, brandishing pistols, continued running and disappeared around a bend.

"Never catch him now," commented Finchley's pilot.

"Do you just let them go running off whenever they feel like it?" Otis inquired.

Finchley met his curious gaze stolidly.

"I'm in favor of anything that will break the monotony, Mr. Otis.   We have a problem of morale, you know.   This planet is a key colony, and I like to keep the work going smoothly."

"Yes, I suppose there isn't much for recreation yet."

"Exactly.   I don't see the sport in it myself but I let them.   We're up to schedule."

"Ahead, if anything," Otis placated him.   "Well, now, about the city?"

Finchley led the way to the helicopter.   The pilot and Otis waited while he had a final word with his engineers, then they all climbed in and were off.

Later, however, hovering over the network of crude roads being leveled by Finchley's bulldozers, Otis admitted aloud that the location was well-chosen.   It lay along a long, narrow bay that thrust in from the distant ocean to gather the waters of the same river that was being dammed some miles upstream.

"Those cliffs over there," Finchley pointed out, "were raised up since the end of whatever civilization used to be here—so my geologist tells me.   We can fly back that way, and you can see how the ancient city was once at the head of the bay."

The pilot climbed and headed over the cliffs.   Otis saw that these formed the edge of a plateau.   At one point, their continuity was marred by a deep gouge.

"Where the river ran thousands of years ago," Finchley explained.

They reached a point from which the outlines of the ruined city were easily discerned.   From the air, Otis knew, they were undoubtedly plainer than if he had been among them.

"Must have been a pretty large place," he remarked.   "Any idea what sort of beings built it or what happened to them?"

"Haven't had time for that yet," Finchley said.   "Some boys from the exploration staff poke around in there every so often.   Best current theory seems to be that it belonged to the Torangs.''

''The *animals* they were hunting before?'' asked Otis.

''Might be.   Can't say for sure, but the diggers found signs the city took more of a punch than just an earthquake.   Claim they found too much evidence of fires, exploded missiles, and warfare in general—other places as well as here.   So . . . we've been guessing the Torangs are degenerated descendents of the survivors of some interplanetary brawl.''

Otis considered that.

''Sounds plausible,'' he admitted, ''but you ought to do something to make sure you are right.''

''Why?''

''If it *is* the case, you'll have to stop your men from hunting them; degenerated or not, the Colonial Commission has regulations about contact with any local inhabitants.''

Finchley turned his head to scowl at Otis, and controlled himself with an obvious effort.

''Those *apes*?'' he demanded.

''Well, how can you tell?   Ever try to contact them?''

''Yes!   At first, that is; before we figured them for animals.''

''And?''

''Couldn't get near one!'' Finchley declared heatedly.   ''If they had any sort of half-intelligent culture, wouldn't they let us make *some* sort of contact?''

''Offhand,'' admitted Otis, ''I should think so.   How about setting down a few minutes?   I'd like a look at the ruins.''

Finchley glared at his wrist watch, but directed the pilot to land at a cleared spot. The young man brought them down neatly and the two officials alighted.

Otis, glancing around, saw where the archaeologists had been digging.   They had left their implements stacked casually at the site—the air was dry up here and who was there to steal a shovel?

He left Finchley and strolled around a mound of dirt that had been cleared away from an entrance to one of the buildings.   The latter had been built of stone, or at least faced with it.   A peep into the dim excavation led him to believe there had been a steel framework, but the whole affair had been collapsed as if by an explosion.

He walked a little way further and reached a section of presumably taller buildings where the stone ruins thrust above the sandy surface.   After he had wandered through one or two arched openings that seemed to have been windows, he understood why the explorers had chosen to dig for their information.   If any covering or decoration had ever graced the walls, it had long since been weathered off.   As for ceiling or roof, nothing remained.

''Must have been a highly developed civilization just the same,'' he muttered.

A movement at one of the shadowed openings to his right caught his eye.   He did not remember noticing Finchley leave the helicopter to follow him, but he was glad of a guide.

"Don't you think so?" he added.

He turned his head, but Finchley was not there.   In fact, now that Otis was aware of his surroundings, he could hear the voices of the other two mumbling distantly back by the aircraft.

"Seeing things!" he grumbled, and started through the ancient window.

Some instinct stopped him half a foot outside.

Come on, Jeff, he told himself, *don't be silly!   What could be there?   Ghosts?*

On the other hand, he realized, there were times when it was just as well to rely upon instinct—at least until you figured out the origin of the strange feeling.   Any spaceman would agree to that.   The man who developed an animal sixth sense was the man who lived longest on alien planets.

He thought he must have paused a full minute or more, during which he had heard not the slightest sound except the mutter of voices to the rear.   He peered into the chamber, which was about twenty feet square and well if not brightly lit by reflected light.

Nothing was to be seen, but when he found himself turning his head stealthily to peer over his shoulder, he decided that the queer sensation along the back of his neck meant something.

Wait, now, he thought swiftly.   *I didn't see quite the whole room.*

The flooring was heaped with wind-bared rubble that would not show footprints. He felt much more comfortable to notice himself thinking in that vein.

At least, I'm not imagining ghosts, he thought.

Bending forward the necessary foot, he thrust his head through the opening and darted a quick look to left, then to the right along the wall.   As he turned right, his glance was met directly by a pair of very wide-set black eyes which shifted inward slightly as they got his range.

The Torang about matched his own six-feet-two, mainly because of elongated, gibbonlike limbs and a similarly crouching stance.   Arms and legs, covered with short, curly, gray fur, had the same general proportions as human limbs, but looked half again too long for a trunk that seemed to be ribbed all the way down.   Shoulder and hip joints were compactly lean, rather as if the Torang had developed on a world of lesser gravity than that of the human.

It was the face tht made Otis stare.   The mouth was toothless and probably constructed more for sucking than for chewing.   But the eyes!   They projected like ends of a dumbbell from each side of the narrow skull where the ears should have been, and focused with obvious mobility.   Peering closer, Otis saw tiny ears below the eyes, almost hidden in the curling fur of the neck.

He realized abruptly that his own eyes felt as if they were bulging out, although he could not remember having changed his expression of casual curiosity.   His back was getting stiff also.   He straightened up carefully.

"Un . . . hello," he murmured, feeling unutterably silly but conscious of some impulse to compromise between a tone of greeting for another human being and one of pacification to an animal.

The Torang moved then, swiftly but unhurriedly.   In fact, Otis later decided, deliberately.   One of the long arms swept downward to the rubble-strewn ground.

The next instant, Otis jerked his head back out of the opening as a stone whizzed past in front of his nose.

"Hey!" he protested involuntarily.

There was a scrabbling sound from within, as of animal claws churning to a fast start among the pebbles.   Recovering his balance, Otis charged recklessly through the entrance.

"I don't know why," he admitted to Finchley a few minutes later.   "If I stopped to think how I might have had my skull bashed in coming through, I guess I'd have just backed off and yelled for you."

Finchley nodded, but his narrow gaze seemed faintly approving for the first time since they had met.

"He was gone, of course," Otis continued.   "I barely caught a glimpse of his rump vanishing through another window."

"Yeah, they're pretty fast," put in Finchley's pilot.   "In the time we've been here, the boys haven't taken more than half a dozen.   Got a stuffed one over at headquarters though."

"Hm-m-m," murmured Otis thoughtfully.

From their other remarks, he learned that he had not noticed everything, even though face to face with the creature.   Finchley's mentioning the three digits of the hands or feet, for instance, came as a surprise.

Otis was silent most of the flight back to headquarters.   Once there, he disappeared with a perfunctory excuse toward the rooms assigned him.

That evening, at a dinner which Finchley had made as attractive as was possible in a comparatively raw and new colony, Otis was noticeably sociable.   The coordinator was gratified.

"Looks as if they finally sent us a regular guy," he remarked behind his hand to one of his assistants.   "Round up a couple of the prettier secretaries to keep him happy."

"I understand he nearly laid hands on a Torang up at the diggings," said the other.

"Yep, ran right at it bare-handed.   Came as close to bagging it as anybody could, I suppose."

"Maybe it's just as well he didn't," commented the assistant.   "They're big enough to mess up an unarmed man some."

Otis, meanwhile, and for the rest of the evening, was assiduously busy making acquaintances.   So engrossed was he in turning every new conversation to the Torangs and asking seemingly casual questions about the little known of their habits and possible past, that he hardly noticed receiving any special attentions.   As a visiting inspector, he was used to attempts to entertain and distract him.

The next morning, he caught Finchley at his office in the sprawling one-story structure of concrete and glass that was colonial headquarters.

After accepting a chair across the desk from the co-ordinator, Otis told him his conclusions.   Finchley's narrow eyes opened a trifle when he heard the details. His wide, hard-muscled face became slightly pink.

"Oh, for—!   I mean, Otis, why must you make something big out of it?   The men very seldom bag one anyway!"

"Perhaps because they're so rare," answered Otis calmly.   "How do we know they're not intelligent life?   Maybe if you were hanging on in the ruins of your ancestors' civilization, reduced to a primitive state, *you'd* be just as wary of a bunch of loud Terrans moving in!"

Finchley shrugged.   He looked vaguely uncomfortable, as if debating whether Otis or some disgruntled sportsman from his husky construction crews would be easier to handle.

"Think of the overall picture a minute," Otis urged.   "We're pushing out into space at last, after centuries of dreams and struggles.   With all the misery we've seen in various colonial systems at home, we've tried to plan these ventures so as to avoid old mistakes."

Finchley nodded grudgingly.   Otis could see that his mind was on the progress charts of his many projects.

"It stands to reason," the inspector went on, "that some day we'll find a planet with intelligent life.   We're still new in space, but as we probe farther out, it's bound to happen.   That's why the Commission drew up rules about native life forms.   Or have you read that part of the code lately?"

Finchley shifted from side to side in his chair.

"Now, look!" he protested.   "Don't go making *me* out a hardboiled vandal with nothing in mind but exterminating everything that moves on all Torang.   *I* don't go out hunting the apes!"

"I know, I know," Otis soothed him.   "But before the Colonial Commission will sanction any destruction of indigenous life, we'll have to show—*besides* that it's not intelligent—that it exists in sufficient numbers to avoid extinction."

"What do you expect me to do about it?"

Otis regarded him with some sympathy.   Finchley was the hard-bitten type the Commission needed to oversee the first breaking-in of a colony on a strange planet, but he was not unreasonable.   He merely wanted to be left alone to handle the tough job facing him.

"Announce a ban on hunting Torangs," Otis said.   "There must be something else they can go after."

"Oh, yes," admitted Finchley.   "There are swarms of little rabbit-things and other vermin running through the brush.   But, I don't know—"

"It's standard practice," Otis reminded him.   "We have many a protected species even back on Terra that would be extinct by now, only for the game laws."

In the end, they agreed that Finchley would do his honest best to enforce a ban provided Otis obtained a formal order from the headquarters of the system.   The inspector went from the office straight to the communications center, where he filed a long report for the chief co-ordinator's office in the other part of the binary system.

It took some hours for the reply to reach Torang.   When it came that afternoon, he went looking for Finchley.

He found the co-ordinator inspecting a newly finished canning factory on the coast, elated at the completion of one more link in making the colony self-sustaining.

"Here it is," said Otis, waving the message copy.   "Signed by the chief himself. 'As of this date, the apelike beings known as Torangs, indigenous to planet number and so forth, are to be considered a rare and protected species under regulations and so forth et cetera.' "

"Good enough," answered Finchley with an amiable shrug.   "Give it here, and I'll have it put on the public address system and the bulletin boards."

Otis returned satisfied to the helicopter that had brought him out from headquarters.

"Back, sir?" asked the pilot.

"Yes. . . *no!*   Just for fun, take me out to the old city.   I never did get a good look the other day, and I'd like to before I leave."

They flew over the plains between the sea and the upjutting cliffs.   In the distance, Otis caught a glimpse of the rising dam he had been shown the day before. This colony would go well, he reflected, as long as he checked up on details like preserving native life forms.

Eventually, the pilot landed at the same spot he had been taken on his previous visit to the ancient ruins.   Someone else was on the scene today.   Otis saw a pair of men he took to be archaeologists.

"I'll just wander around a bit," he told the pilot.

He noticed the two men looking at him from where they stood by the shovels and other equipment, so he paused to say hello.   As he thought, they had been digging in the ruins.

"Taking some measurements in fact," said the sunburned blond introduced as Hoffman.   "Trying to get a line on what sort of things built the place."

"Oh?" said Otis, interested.   "What's the latest theory?"

"Not so much different from us," Hoffman told the inspector while his partner left them to pick up another load of artifacts.

"Judging from the size of the rooms, height of doorways, and such stuff as stairways," he went on, "they were pretty much our size.   So far, of course, it's only a rough estimate."

"Could be ancestors of the Torangs, eh?" asked Otis.

"Very possible, sir," answer Hoffman, with a promptness that suggested it was his own view.   "But we haven't dug up enough to guess at the type of culture they had, or draw any conclusions as to their psychology or social customs."

Otis nodded, thinking that he ought to mention the young fellow's name to Finchley before he left Torang.   He excused himself as the other man returned with a box of some sort of scraps the pair had unearthed, and strolled between the outlines of the untouched buildings.

In a few minutes, he came to the section of higher structures where he had encountered the Torang, the previous day.

"Wonder if I should look in the same spot?" he muttered aloud. "No . . . that would be the *last* place the thing would return to . . . unless it had a lair thereabouts—"

He stopped to get his bearings, then shrugged and walked around a mound of rubble toward what he believed to be the proper building.

Pretty sure this was it, he mused. *Yes, shadows around that window arch look the same . . . same time of day—*

He halted, almost guiltily, and looked back to make sure no one was observing his futile return to the scene of his little adventure. After all, an inspector of colonial installations was not supposed to run around ghost-hunting like a small boy.

Finding himself alone, he stepped briskly through the crumbling arch—*and froze in his tracks*.

"I am honored to know you," said the Torang in a mild, rather buzzing voice. "We thought you possibly would return here."

Otis gaped. The black eyes projecting from the sides of the narrow head tracked him up and down, giving him the unpleasant sensation of being measured for an artillery salvo.

"I am known as Jal-Ganyr," said the Torang. "Unless I am given incorrect data, you are known as Jeff-Otis. That is so."

The last statement was made with almost no inflection, but some still-functioning corner of Otis' mind interpreted it as a question. He sucked in a deep breath, suddenly conscious of having forgotton to breathe for a moment.

"I didn't know . . . yes, that is so . . . I didn't know you Torangs could speak Terran. Or anything else. How—?"

He hesitated as a million questions boiled up in his mind to be asked. Jal-Ganyr absently stroked the gray fur of his chest with his three-fingered left hand, squatting patiently on a flat rock. Otis felt somehow that he had been allowed to waste time mumbling only by grace of disciplined politeness.

"I am not of the Torangs," said Jal-Ganyr in his wheezing voice. "I am of the Myrbs. You would possibly say Myrbii. I have not been informed."

"You mean that is your name for yourselves?" asked Otis.

Jal-Ganyr seemed to consider, his mobile eyes swiveling inward to scan the Terran's face.

"More than that," he said at last, when he had thought it over. "I mean I am of the race originating at Myrb, not of this planet."

"Before we go any further," insisted Otis, "tell me, at least, how you learned our language!"

Jal-Ganyr made a fleeting gesture. His "face" was unreadable to the Terran, but Otis had the impression he had received the equivalent of a smile and a shrug.

"As to that," said the Myrb, "I possibly learned it before you did. We have observed you a very long time. You would unbelieve how long."

"But then—" Otis paused. That must mean before the colonists had landed on this planet.   He was half-afraid it might mean before they had reached this sun system.   He put aside the thought and asked, "But then, why do you live like this among the ruins?   Why wait till now?   If you had communicated, you could have had our help rebuilding—"

He let his voice trail off, wondering what sounded wrong.   Jal-Ganyr rolled his eyes about leisurely, as if disdaining the surrounding ruins.   Again, he seemed to consider all the implications of Otis' questions.

"We picked up your message to your chief," he answered at last.   "We decided time is to communicate with one of you.

"We had no interest in rebuilding," he added.   "We have concealed quarters for ourselves."

Otis found that his lips were dry from his unconsciously having let his mouth hang open.   He moistened them with the tip of his tongue, and relaxed enough to lean against the wall.

"You mean my getting the ruling to proclaim you a protected species?" he asked.   "You have instruments to intercept such signals?"

"I do.   We have," said Jal-Ganyr simply.   "It has been decided that you have expanded far enough into space to make it necessary we contact a few of the thoughtful among you.   It will possibly make easier in the future for our observers."

Otis wondered how much of that was irony.   He felt himself flushing at the memory of the "stuffed specimen" at headquarters, and was peculiarly relieved that he had not gone to see it.

I've had the luck, he told himself.   *I'm the one to discover the first known intelligent beings beyond Sol!*

Aloud, he said, "We expected to meet someone like you eventually.   But why have you chosen me?"

The question sounded vain, he realized, but it brought unexpected results.

"Your message.   You made in a little way the same decision we made in a big way.   We deduce that you are one to understand our regret and shame at what happened between our races . . . long ago."

"Between—?"

"Yes.   For a long time, we thought you were all gone.   We are pleased to see you returning to some of your old planets."

Otis stared blankly.   Some instinct must have enabled the Myrb to interpret his bewildered expression.   He apologized briefly.

"I possibly forgot to explain the ruins."   Again, Jal-Ganyr's eyes swiveled slowly about.

"They are not ours," he said mildly.   "They are yours."

LESTER DEL REY

"The Years Draw Nigh"

Mars was harsh and old, worn with the footsteps of two races that had come and gone, leaving only scant traces behind. Even the wind was tired, and its thin wailing was a monotonous mutter of memories from its eroded past.

Zeke Lerner stared out from the dust-covered observation port of the hastily reconditioned little rocket, across the scarred runways and sand-filled pits for the starships, toward the ruins of what had once been the great Star Station. His face was gray and dull as he watched a figure coming across the pitted sand of the field toward his ship.

He sighed softly, a faint sound in the tiny cabin, and his breath stirred the dust that lay everywhere. In four centuries, a man can learn not to think, but feelings and emotions survive. He was tired beyond any power of the rejuvenation treatments to remedy. His shoulders sagged slightly, confirming the age that the gray in his hair implied. But his eyes were older still as he swung about to open the inner lock of the ship.

Stendal was a middle-aged man, but some of the same age and fatigue lay on his face when he dropped his aspirator helmet and slumped limply into a seat, and his plain uniform as Assistant Coordinator of Terra was covered with dirt and grime. He grinned faintly at Zeke and pulled a thermo of coffee out of its niche.

"So the *Thirty-four* is coming back?" Zeke asked quietly.

He had no need of the other's nod, though. When they'd finally located him at the Rejuvenation Center and rushed him to the rocket field, he'd suspected. Only a matter of extreme urgency could interrupt a man's return to youth. The messengers had been uninformative, but he had been sure, once they told him Stendal was waiting on Mars. They must have been keeping it restricted to the top administrators. Zeke's eyes went back to the dirt on the man's uniform.

"Top secret," Stendal confirmed. "So hush-hush that I came to do the janitor work here. Now it's all yours. The robots and I managed to get it into a reasonable facsimile of repaired condition. *Oof!* I could use a week's sleep, but I've got to get back Earthside at once. Sorry to interrupt the rejuvenation, Zeke."

Zeke shrugged. Once, when the rejuvenation was new and men stood in line for days to keep their appointment, it might have mattered. Now there'd be a cancellation he could replace. Over fifteen per cent of the population was refusing treatment—and some of the canceling men were ones only reaching their first touch of age. Each year, less of the population seem to find life worth renewing.

"How'd you find out she was coming?" he asked. "After all, she's fifty years overdue."

Stendal tossed the thermo into a disposal chute and reached for one of Zeke's cigarettes. "Centaurus' automatic signal must still be working. Nigel, at the Bureau, got a series of pips showing something coming this way faster than light. That's the only ship we have out, so it must be her, or—"

He let it hang unfinished, but Zeke knew what he was thinking. It was either the *Thirty-four* or another race coming with a ship that could exceed light speed. Sudden adrenalin shot through him, and he straightened. After all, the ship was long overdue. He wished the ship and the men no ill, but—

"No use getting up false hopes," Stendal cut into his thoughts. "The captain was a pretty determined sort, as I remember him. Maybe he had trouble. And I'll have trouble if I don't get back. I'll leave you a robot, in case anything needs more repairs. Think you can still run this setup, Zeke?"

Zeke snorted. He'd spent time enough at Marsport, first as head of communications, and finally as director of the whole Star Ship project, while they built the great ships and sent them out as fast as they could come off the ways. Forty ships during half the century, each costing over four billion dollars. And the *Thirty-four* was the last one out. All the rest had come back to report failure in their final quest for new frontiers.

They buckled on their aspirator helmets and went out through the locks. Stendal waved curtly and headed toward his own rocket, calling three of the waiting robots with him and sending the fourth toward the broken ruin of the administration building. Zeke watched Stendal's rocket take off and disappear. Then he turned for a final look over the wrecked field.

Mars was already wiping out all traces of this second race that had come boiling out from Earth, bent for the stars. Marsport had been young and booming when Zeke had come there first, three and a half centuries ago. Two centuries later, when the starships first began to come straggling back, and they shifted him to Earth to head General Traffic, the sand was just starting to creep over the outer buildings.

Those structures were gone now, vanished into the desert, with only this single building maintained after a fashion in faint hope the last ship would return. The frame shacks and hydroponic quonsets that had hidden the ancient Martian ruins were rotted long before; there was only the hint of a foundation here and there to show they had ever existed. In a century or so there would be no evidence that Mars had ever felt the marching feet of men, except for the scraps of the returned ships that might last a few millennia longer.

Zeke sighed again, and headed toward the building.

Then his eyes went to the horizon, where the piled stones and pitted pylon of beryl steel still stood, marking what had been the unknown and apparently unknowable race of Mars, dead perhaps ten million years before. Once that race must have spread its structures across the whole planet, but now there were only such traces as this, useless to even the archaeologists. All the elaborate designs on them might have held significance once, but no man would ever decode them. There was no hint as to their nature, or where the race had vanished—or why.

He entered the lock of the building, with the robot dutifully at his heels, and surveyed it glumly. Only the one room, housing the great space-destroying ultrawave communicators, had been put in order. But most of the sand and dust was gone, and it was livable enough for a while. He checked to see that the communicator was working before walking over to the single window and staring out at the Martian ruins again.

Beside him, the robot stirred uneasily. "Orders?" it questioned.

Zeke turned back reluctantly from the window. "No orders, Ozin. We're on Mars, where men have given up dominion. You're as free as I am. Do what you like."

Ozin stirred again, worn metal protesting at its lack of usefulness, its queer, almost intelligent mind trying to resolve the problem presented by Zeke's words. But even this final robot, the last model before men abandoned the idea of robots, could not handle that.

"Orders?" it repeated.

Zeke gave up. "Take my ship up and house it behind the building, out of the way, then. After that, you can cut off until I call you."

The robot wasted no words in acknowledgment, but turned slowly and headed out, its metal body clumping along as woodenly as Zeke's mind was working. The lock hissed softly, and a trace of stale, desiccated air of Mars came in. Then Ozin appeared around the arc of the wall, heading toward the rocket. Zeke watched it enter, saw the shiplock close, and shut his eyes at the deep blue flame of the exhaust from the unbaffled tubes.

Sand kicked up, spurting out and grating against the walls of the station wing, swishing against the pylon of the lost Martians. For a minute, dust hung in the air. But it settled back quickly now, to show an unchanged scene. Zeke heard the ship land again behind the building.

He reached automatically for a cigarette, wondering idly if the repaired building aspirators would take even that much added load in their labor of making a decent atmosphere out of Mars' thin air. For a second, he fiddled with the ultrawave set. The signal was coming through from Earth, indicating that they were already quietly beaming it out to where the *Thirty-four* could pick it up. It was the same dull, insipid news Zeke had heard for too many decades, though it might be interesting to men who had been gone from Earth for over two centuries. There was no other signal to indicate that they were within calling distance, however.

He went to the window again, to watch the slow sinking of the sun that was reddening a distant sandstorm, until it finally crept below the horizon. With an abruptness that was typical of the planet, darkness fell. The stars seemed to leap into the sky, with Earth standing out among them. He frowned at that, realizing that he was the only man who would be seeing it. All the others were home on the planet.

The skylight was filthy, but he found a battered bench that would stand his weight and began working the dust and grime from the glass. The stars were clearer through that. A few hundred years hadn't changed them noticeably, and he picked them out—hot points that barely flickered in the thin air of Mars. Jupiter was in view, and he knew where all the other useless planets should be, though he could not see them.

He grimaced faintly at that, remembering his life as a boy when men had dreamed that each new world might contain some rare treasure—or even intelligence to meet and compete with man. None had panned out, though. Mercury was too hot, Venus was a roiling dustbowl under foul, poisonous layers of atmosphere, Mars worn beyond usefulness, and the other planets too cold and forbidding, except as possible stepping stones to the stars that lay farther out.

Chenery had found the trick to beat light speed when Zeke was still a callow thirty, and Marsport had sprung into life; the planet had made an ideal take-off point for ships which Earth could not permit in her own atmosphere because of the dangerous radiation of their exhausts.

There'd been Centaurus and Sirius, and the thousands of suns beyond, some with planets and some without. There had even been the high moment when a planet had been found and colonized, a mere thousand light-years away, before men had discovered that something in the star's radiation was eventually lethal to all Earth forms. But there had been no life beyond the Solar System—and nothing that even the most foolhardy could use as a reason for man's settlement.

It had proven to be a barren universe, except for Earth and the Mars of perhaps ten million years ago. Zeke looked at the ruins again, still faintly visible in the light that sliced out from his window. Whatever had built them had reached a civilization at least as high as man's. What had happened to them that had made a culture capable of such work come to a sudden and unmarked end?

A meaningless crackle came from the ultrawave set, and he moved to it, touching up its sensitivity. For a moment again, he hoped that it would respond with only gibberish that might mean another race coming down the long starlanes toward Earth, instead of the code he knew. But he choked off the wish, even before the speaker burped again. There was a sudden sound of code symbols a second later, followed by the thin, wavering words and voice at the limit of reception.

"Star-Ship *Thirty-four* coming in. Can you get us? *Thirty-four* calling Marsport. Landing in two hours maximum. Clear field for full splash landing. Clear field for landing without tube shields. *Thirty-four* calling Marsport—"

Zeke had the great bank of accumulators working through the transmitter, and the indicators showed that the big tubes were ready to throw their pulsed megawatts into subspace. He glanced at the bandpass and saw that it was at its maximum intelligibility level for the distance.

"Land Marsport, *Thirty-four*, as you will. All clear. Repeat."

The voice came back, weaker. It wavered, broke into a squeal, and disappeared in a hash of static.   Only blind luck had given them clear subspace long enough for a complete call.   Zeke cut off the transmitter; there was no purpose in telling them that the field had been clear for decades.   They'd find that soon enough.

Mars had still been a colony when they took off.   It had remained one while six more of the great ships were built and sent out with orders to proceed to the limit of range before returning—or to return on significant discovery.   Zeke had watched them all leave, filled with bright young volunteers, sure that they would be the ones to find a new race of intelligent life or a world that would be a paradise for men.   Now the last one out was returning, and it was appropriate that he should meet the space-weary men who were coming home.

He tried to remember them, but there had been too many years and too many ships.   On impulse, he knocked dust from the walls, scanning the names that had been scrawled there against regulations—and left because he had countermanded those regulations.   Surprisingly, he found the one he was seeking.   Hugh Miffen, captain of the *Thirty-four*.   Zeke remembered him now, a tow-headed boy with a ramrod back and the driving urge of divine inspiration in his eyes.   And there had been "Preacher" Hook, who swore he was going to memorize the whole Bible in subspace.   Only the two stood out now, over the long years.

Surely, if any group could have found a home for man or a companion intelligence, that group should have done it.   *Something* must have happened during the fifty years they had been overdue.   Their fuel would never have lasted, otherwise.

The speaker gobbled at him, finally, until he cut the power down.   The wash of static could only mean that they were beginning the struggle out of subspace, knocking a hole for themselves in normal space and crawling painfully into it.   It was taking the ship longer than it should, and Zeke began to worry.   Then the blare of static decreased.   He knew she was down under light speed.

The ship robot took his call this time, indicating that all the men aboard were fully occupied in the task of trimming her for normal flight.   The signal was clear, however, and he could hear faint sounds of men's voices in the background.   There was no undue worry in them, as best he could tell.

"Sealed beam," Zeke requested.   It took more power to maintain a signal that could be handled on a beam with the ultrawave, but she was close enough now to risk it; it wouldn't do to have the message accidentally picked up by Earth until he knew what the results of the trip were.   The robot acknowledged his order, and the queer, clipped effect of the sealing could be detected on the signal.

Zeke grunted with satisfaction as he made his own adjustment.   "O.K., this is Zeke Lerner, code responsibility 21-zy-18-obt-4-a.   You can report."

"Digest of report," the robot began tonelessly.   "Visited suns, 3248; examined planets, 2751.   Checked suns on automatic spotting, 9472; checked planets and found barren on automatic spotting, 23,911.   Maximum distance attained by direct route, one hundred ten thousand light-years, forty-three ship-years; arc of coverage—"

"Cut it out.   Did you find inhabited worlds?"

The robot adjusted to the interruption slowly, humming into the microphone as evidence that it was still there. Zeke swore. Then a human voice suddenly took over, weary even through the distortion of the sealed beam.

"Lerner? You still on the spot?" It was a deep voice that could only belong to Hugh Miffen, in spite of the years that had roughened it. The ship had naturally carried rejuvenation equipment, but even the best treatment never wiped out all traces of time. "Sorry we had the robot on—it's about half shot, now. Anyhow, we're under light, and I'm free for a minute. Leaving out the statistics, we ran out too far and got short fuel. We'd spotted two planets that might barely be habitable, so we backtracked and put down on one of them. It took us about thirty-five years to find and work fuel out of the ores. Then we went on a bit before we turned home."

Zeke's eyebrows had shot up, and he shook his head. He tried to picture what it would be like on some barely livable planet, scouting for ore, jury-rigging some kind of plant to refine it—with almost no equipment—and his old respect for Miffen went up another notch. That type of man seemed sadly lacking nowadays. But he made no comment on it; it could wait for more important things, and Miffen had begun to describe the two planets.

One was too far from its sun in an eccentric orbit, going from a brief summer into a bitter winter equal to three years of Earth time. It was suitable otherwise, but no more so than Antarctica. The other was a waste land of little water and low air pressure, though barely habitable. It had been on that world that Miffen and his crew had stranded themselves. Zeke frowned as he discarded the planets. Both would mean tremendous difficulties in ferrying supplies out for at least a century until they could somehow be made self-supporting. Men would work for a dream, but there were limits. It would need more incentive than there seemed to be.

"Evidence of life anywhere?" he asked reluctantly, as the other finished. But the question had to be asked, although the answer could be predicted, almost certainly. Even over that distance, the possibility of other races to study might drive the scientists to set up an outpost, and with that as a basis, another world might be developed as a stepping stone to still further exploration.

Miffen's voice was hesitant as the answer came. "The world we were on— Outpost, we called it—had some ruins that could only come from intelligence. But there was nothing living there. Maybe it had been what we called it once— Damn!"

A yell had sounded thinly over the speaker. Miffen's steps clattered loudly, to fade out, and leave the ultrawave dead. With the ship braking down for a landing, there was probably more than enough work for all the men. Zeke's hand lingered over the switch. Finally, he depressed it, cutting off power.

Ruins that showed intelligence, eighty million light years across the galaxy! In forty thousand explored worlds the starships had touched, this was the first sign of even that much chance. It wasn't enough, of course, but—

Slowly Zeke's shoulders straightened and his figure came erect. They'd explored space to a distance of a hundred million light-years on a bare chance, without any reason to hope.   Out of all the previous reports, there had been only three habitable worlds, and no sign of life beyond the Solar System.   Now a ship was returning with reports of two barely possible worlds and evidence that there was such life! An outpost—and somewhere beyond, perhaps, the planet where that life still existed.

With proper propaganda, with enough build-up, and with evidence that somewhere in the infinity of stars life and livability must exist, could man refuse to go on with his questing?

For a moment, he clutched at the hope.   It had to be.   One world was not enough for a race that had set its heart on the stars, had always found frontiers, and had geared its soul to an eternal drive toward something beyond.   It could not be cooped up and fenced in without sickening in its own futility, as it was sickening even now—as he was sick within himself after four centuries of following blind alleys.

With only a little spark to fan the flames, men might be driven on.   And perhaps only a few light-years away from the end of their explorations—the arbitrary limits imposed by time and energy for the ships—there might be fellow races to stir the spark that was dying in mankind.

Then he grinned bitterly and looked out through the window, turning the single workable searchlight on the Martian ruins.   Man had found evidence of other life in his own backyard, and it had carried him for centuries.   But it was not enough to drive him onward forever.   There was nothing on Outpost that couldn't be had here—and no colony had lasted on Mars.

Zeke squinted his eyes as he studied the pylon again, noting the queer, twisted decorations on it.   He had seen the report of the scientists, and they had finally given up the riddle.   It would take more than this to drive men further outwards. And Miffen's voice had sounded too doubtful.

But some of the hope remained faintly in him as he stood staring into the Martian night.   It would have to wait until he heard more.   Now it was only another mystery, like that of the lost race of Mars.

What had happened to them?   They had known how to cast tungsten, and there was evidence that nuclear reactions had been used in tempering the pylons.   That was high level science.   Where had it gone?   There had apparently been no long period of high civilization, since the pylons all over the planet were about alike, with few advances in the later ones.   There hadn't been time enough for the race to become decadent.   Nor was there any evidences of war carried on by a race with advanced nuclear physics; there would have been enough signs of that.   They couldn't have settled Earth, of course—it wouldn't have been suitable.   But they must have had starships.   What had kept them from spreading outwards—had even wasted them into nothingness in such a brief period of culture on their own planet?

His thoughts were interrupted by a *beep* from the speaker, and he switched on the automatic ultrawave beacons that would guide the ship down.   Overhead, a thin whine thickened to a stuttering cough, unhealthy sound of gasping, unshielded rockets that had been used too often and in too many futile landings.   It was coming down well enough, though, half a mile away.   Zeke watched it land while he was climbing into antiradiation armor.

*   *   *

The ground was still smoking, but the counter showed the radiation low enough for a quick passage when he went out.   He waited for the outer lock to open, then made a dash toward it, his breath reminding him that he was old and had not been rejuvenated.   He crawled into a lock and stopped to catch himself before removing the armor, while the inner lock began to open.

Then he was facing four gaunt, weary men.   His eyes darted back for the others of the thirty who had gone out, but Miffen was shaking his gray-bearded head. "Four of us, general.   We had a few casualties.   But—"

His arm swept out toward the field, now illuminated by the beams of the great shop, and his eyes fixed on the scene of the sand-filled pits and bits of building foundations that showed through the quartz of the entrance port.

Zeke shrugged and reached for his cigarettes.   The sudden hunger in their eyes hit him, then, reminding him of stores now depleted in all those long years.   He passed the package around, careful not to notice the hands that shook as they pulled out the cylinders.

"We've had some casualties, too, you might say," he told Miffen.   He lighted his own cigarette finally, and his shoulders lifted and dropped at the other's expression.   "And I'm not a general now—not since Marsport was abandoned.   I came out only because we were expecting you back.   What about Outpost?"

"In my cabin I've got it on microfilm."   Miffen swung about, waving the three crewmen off.   For the first time, Zeke noticed that one of them had the flaming red hair that had always distinguished Preacher Hook.

He lifted an eyebrow and Hook nodded, pulling out a worn Bible and making a circle with his thumb and finger.   "All memorized," he stated.   But the grin on his face was uncertain, and the achievement no longer seemed to be important to him.

Zeke had forgotten the size of these starships as they went up the handrails.   The elevators were obviously not working.   Miffen swung up the last and turned into a little cabin, kicking the door farther open.   He dug into a worn chest and came out with a small package and a little viewer.

"I figured some things from what we picked up of Earth's broadcast," he remarked emotionlessly as he threaded the film into the viewer.   "But I didn't believe it.   Not until I saw Marsport.   I guess . . .   Well, this will give you an idea of Outpost.   I explored all the suns around I could reach, but I never learned where the race originated."

Zeke adjusted the lenses carefully, seeing the unfamiliar two dimensional flatness of non-stereo for the first time in centuries.   It was awkward at first, but his eyes soon relearned the trick of fooling themselves.

There were several scenes, showing a sky of dull green, with grayish sand and something that looked like jumbled blocks of granite.   As he stared, a pattern began to show itself.   Something had been built there once, and by intelligence. Closer viewing showed that the stones had been shaped geometrically, under all their weathering.

He came to a list of statistics and skimmed through it.   Then he reached the final scene.

Miffen's voice suddenly sounded behind him, awkward and too tense.   "What about the other ships?"

"They all got back—they're piled up beside the field, beyond the reach of your lights.   No use to us now.   Thirty-nine hulks, and yours makes the fortieth—all we ever built."   He turned back to the film, but again Miffen's voice interrupted him.

"All?   I'd expect it—That bad, eh?"

"Worse.   I suppose you're entitled to know what you've come back to.   You'll see it soon enough, though—and better than I can tell you."   Zeke clamped the viewer to his eye firmly, and turned to the light once more.   "There was purpose when you left.   Now that's all past tense."

"Yeah."   Miffen let the word hang.   He must have seen Zeke's sudden tenseness and realized there was no use putting off the inspection of the final scene on the film any longer.   Zeke was still staring at it, but he was unconscious of what his eyes saw, and the last of the hope in him was draining slowly away.

He stared up at Miffen, tapping the viewer.   "You know what this is, of course. Or do you?"

Miffen shook his head.   "I suspected.   But I never paid much attention back here, and it's been a long time.   I kept hoping I was crazy."

Zeke made no answer.   He picked up the viewer and headed toward the control room, with Miffen following.   Still silent, he pointed out through the viewports, across the leprous surface of Mars, toward the pitted beryl steel pylon that gleamed in the light from the Star Station.   Then he put the viewer to his eyes again.

The sky was green instead of black, and the sand was gray where Mars was covered with red.   But the scene was the same.   A gleaming metal pylon rose from the rubble of ruined blocks, carrying the queer, twisted decorations that had been typical of all Martian structures.   There was no question about what race had tried to colonize Outpost—and had failed.

Suddenly a work-gnarled hand took the viewer from him, and he turned to see Preacher Hook and the other men.   They must have followed Miffen and himself into the control room.   But it didn't matter.   They must have suspected.   And there was no surprise on their faces as they passed the viewer from one to another, comparing the scene with that outside.

Almost without feeling, Zeke picked up the ultrawave microphone and called the adminstration building, ordering the robot to bring his rocket down beside the big starship.   He adjusted the dials carefully and spoke terse, coded symbols into the instrument.   A moment later, Stendal's voice answered him.

"I'm bringing the four survivors down in my ship," he reported in a voice that seemed completely detached from him.   "Give us a secrecy blanket until we can report in full.   And see if you can fill a few bathtubs with whisky.   We'll need it."

Stendal seemed to catch his breath and then sigh, but his words were level when he spoke. "So Pandora's box was just a fairy story, after all. Well, I never had many hopes. O.K., I'll get the liquor, Zeke. And about your rejuvenation—I'm getting a private installation here for you. If the others need it, we'll take care of all of you."

Zeke looked up at the four men, and then out toward the pylon again—all that was left of a race that had searched the stars in its need to find new frontiers. It must have been a hardy race, since it had dared to set up a colony across all those innumerable parsecs of space, without even the inspiration of other life. Then, when the colony had failed, the race had returned to the loneliness of its own little world, where the stars looked grimly, no longer promising anything. Now Mars had been dead ten million years, and the pylon stood as the final tombstone on the world which had become a prison. The old puzzle of that race's end was solved.

The speaker was sputtering with Stendal's impatient questions, as Zeke and the men studied each other, but they gave no attention to it. Preacher Hook sighed, breaking the silence.

"Man goeth to his long home," he quoted softly. *"And the mourners go about the streets; or ever the silver cord be loosed, or the golden bowl be broken, or the pitcher be broken at the fountain, or the wheel broken at the cistern; and the dust return to the earth as it was, and the spirit return unto God who gave it."*

Zeke nodded and picked up the microphone.

"Just get the whisky. We've decided to skip the rejuvenation."

He put the microphone back on its hook carefully and headed toward the handrails that led down, with the others behind him. Ozin had the rocket waiting, and they climbed in and strapped themselves down.

Then the rockets blasted, and the last five men beyond the Earth were heading home.

H. B. FYFE

Thinking Machine

Engineer Oscar Kleweski watched the technicians preparing to blast the world beyond recognition. The shining globe in the pit spun serenely on its axis, causing the white shroud of clouds to split into bands wih differing rotational speeds.

"Look, you guys," repeated Lane from beside his camera battery, "are you sure you quoted me the maximum speed?"

"Don't worry," answered Schultz. "There won't be any pieces shooting back at you. Kleweski wouldn't let us."

"You want it all on film, don't you?"

"It'll be all right," said Kleweski, and turned to the tech handling the satellite. "Orbit double-checked?"

Plump Turino lifted dark eyes briefly, curled an assenting lip, and reexamined the controls of his force beams.

"Then let's tear it down!"

Kleweski retired with his clipboard to a platform at the rear of the observation balcony. The technicians were ranged along a row of control panels before him. Over their heads, he had a good view of the twenty-foot sphere hanging in the center of the experimental pit, which was three hundred feet across and the heart of the orbital space station built around it. The balcony was shielded from the central vacuum by a field of force easier, like gravity, to manipulate out here in space.

Turino laid aside a half-eaten chocolate bar and hunched over his instrument panel. From the right, lit like the planet by artificial sun lamps, glided a four-foot globe. It fell into an orbit about the larger one, circled it three times for Lane's recording lenses, then edged gradually closer.

"Another one shot," predicted Schultz. "Took me three days to build up the pseudocontinents on that model."

"It may not need complete dismantling," said Kleweski.

"Hope they don't take apart the core of the big one," Schultz muttered gloomily. "Working those iron wedges back into place is a job."

"So is calculating their velocities from the film."

"There's the 2.58 the real moon has," announced Turino.

The smaller globe had moved delicately inward and speeded up in its orbit. Tides in its seas and in the cloudy atmosphere of the planet were now marked. At regular intervals, Turino called off the distance in terms of planet radius. Kleweski took down data without shifting his eyes from the scene.

"Due pretty soon, ain't she?" asked Schultz, as the moon circled within the 2.44 radii of Roche's limit. "Oh-oh! Here comes The John!"

Kleweski glanced over his shoulder. Through the extra door at the end of the balcony came Charley Johnson, the office politician of the engineering department.

"What's that with him?" gasped Schultz.

"Something from around Arcturus," answered Kleweski. "He came to make Doc Lawton an offer for the lab."

"No kiddin'?" Schultz thought that over. "You have a piece of it like the other engineers. You gonna sell?"

"Got my doubts. Let's get on with this, and talk later."

Johnson nodded to Kleweski, and led his squat, squarely built guest to a position of vantage at the end of the balcony. The Arcturan was a head shorter than Kleweski's six feet, but better than a yard wide. He looked as if put together to stand anything. Four stumpy legs supported a body sheathed in rubbery, walnut-brown skin and sporting four less muscular tentacles about waist-high—if the Arcturan had had a waist. Most of the features on the broad head, save for two wide-set eyes, were concealed by a breathing mask. Kleweski thought he saw a vocal filter slung from the stranger's harness, indicating that the Arcturan's range of speaking sounds was unearthly.

"Showing signs," warned Turino.

"A liquid satellite would be gone before now," Kleweski told Schultz. He called, "Let's squeeze out the last millimeter!"

"Out of my hands," Turino reported after another moment.

The satellite had achieved an improbable proximity to the larger sphere. Lane's cameras recorded the surface disturbances. A chorus of exclamations arose as the moon began to break up. Most of the pieces curved "down" to the major globe. The white clouds became roiled by tiny flames, and shot out wisps of vapor as larger bits struck the surface.

In the end, three small, irregular moons circled the ruined planet. The clouds had been dispersed or condensed, revealing Schultz's surface details to be a complete mess.

"And no rings, even!" he complained. "Oughta be rings."

"Look closer," said Kleweski. "I think there's an irregular one forming now. If we keep the setup long enough, it'll smooth out. It's just hard to see because most of the stuff fell to the surface this time."

"Some mess," remarked Charley Johnson. "The Altair job?"

Kleweski nodded, gathering his papers from a data desk.

"Altair VII, after a planetoid displaced their satellite. When we analyze the film, we can tell them the symptoms of critical approach—atmosphere tides ought to be easiest to spot. I don't think they'll have to move *yet*; but it won't hurt them to start hunting a place to colonize."

"Well, if you're finished, the showdown's going to get under way in Lawton's office."

"I'll be there," said Kleweski.

He watched the crew begin to let air into the pit as Johnson left the chamber with the Arcturan.

"Showdown, huh?" commented Schultz.   "You guys don't all want to sell, I guess.   But Lawton does?"

"Not much we can do," admitted Kleweski.   "He practically built this place from the pit out, and he owns most of it."

"What's he wanna sell for?"

"He wants to build a bigger station.   With two or three pits and extra observatories to lease to astronomers."

He tapped his clipboard moodily against his thigh, and stared at the "planet" Turino was maneuvering with his force beams to the side of the pit.

"It'll cost plenty," the engineer added.

"Bet he's been making plenty," said Schultz.   "Done everythin' from proving ring formation or predictin' planet formation for other stars to estimating positions of lost spaceships."

"True, but he still needs a big chunk of cash.   Only—I'm not sure I want to turn my part of this lab over to some promoter from space without knowing it'll be used for the public good."

Leaving Schultz to supervise the salvage of materials, he dropped his notes at the cubby called his office and took an elevator to the conference room.   Most of the others were already present, waiting for Dr. Lawton, Johnson, and the Arcturan. Kleweski slumped lankily into a chair and stared at a schematic diagram of the station framed on the bulkhead.

Seen from top or bottom, the station resembled a sphere.   In effect, it was one, although an equatorial view revealed it to be actually a squat cylinder, with bulging observatory domes above and below.   The experimental pit was at the center, shielded, and surrounded by levels of compartments for living, working, and housing the mechanisms used to manipulate the material in the pit.   Besides these levels, which were laid out in octagonal bands about the pit with safety doors at the angles, supply levels extended to the skin of the station.   Most of these, except for the air-conditioning chambers and elevator shafts, were kept airless.   They included two sally-ports, each housing a pair of light rockets, which were reached through air locks from the working levels.

Then the door at the end of the room opened and Dr. Lawton ushered in the prospective purchaser.

". . . And so that's the way it went," Kleweski told Schultz some hours later. "His name is Ouayo, from Arcturus V, and he has enough in one of Terra's main banks to swing the deal."

"But you didn't go along?"

They were sitting on a table in Schultz's workshop, amid scattered heaps and boxes of materials the technician used to simulate the outer crusts of planet models.

"No," said Kleweski, "I said I'd rather keep an active interest, since there would be no chance for similar research until Lawton gets the new station built.''

''So?''

''So Lawton finally smoothed things over and got Ouayo to include me in the contract.   They decided my services would be vital, anyway, because I know the place inside out and the Arcturan will need somebody to drop down to Luna for supplies and gadgets from time to time.''

''That's right,'' agreed Schultz.   ''Running the station is no one-man job, for all it's loaded with automatic gadgets.   Well, guess I might as well start packing my stuff, huh?''

''Take your time,'' said Kleweski.   ''You have a whole week.''

Schultz's eyebrows rose at that.   He uttered a low whistle.

''What's his hurry?''

''I don't know; he's a closemouthed lump.   But he must have something queer on the fire.   Schultz—''

''Yeah?'' encouraged the other as the silence lengthened.

Kleweski, who had been staring into emptiness as if at some unpleasant vision, shook himself slightly.

''I was going to say that I'd like to hear from you once in a while, when you have time to send a lightgram.''

''Sure.''

''I mean . . . well—''

''Sure,'' repeated Schultz, looking at him keenly.   ''I'll expect you to answer them, too.''

''That's right,'' said Kleweski.

The task of moving the personnel from the station took most of the week, but went smoothly enough except for a rush job on models Ouayo insisted on having built.

Kleweski, detailed by Lawton for a trip to Luna to arrange storage for laboratory records of completed and projected experiments, missed most of the furor.

Upon his return at the end of the week, the first person he encountered after reporting to Lawton was photographer Lane.

''Say, you ought to see the pit now!'' Lane greeted him.

''What's the matter?'' asked Kleweski.

''They've been driving the shop men night an' day to fill it up with models. How many you think they crammed in there?''

''How many?'' demanded Kleweski.

''Sixteen!''

''Huh?''

''That's right!   Four planet-size with three moons apiece.''

''They're crazy!'' exclaimed Kleweski.   ''They'll have them rattling around like dice!''

''It was runnin' pretty good when I saw it.   Look up Schultz; I think maybe he has a key to the balcony.''

"Why? Have they got it locked?"

"Orders from the Arcturan Lump," Lane nodded. "He must be inventing something secret. Did you see that stuff in orbit around the station when you came in?"

"Six or eight big drums? They his?"

"Yep," said Lane. "Won't load them into the station till we're gone. I'd almost like to stay to find out what they are, but that Ouayo gives me the creeps."

Kleweski left him thoughtfully and sought out Schultz. He found him snoring on a bench in his workshop.

"Oh, you're back?" mumbled the technician, sitting up and rubbing his eyes. "What's new?"

"I hear tell there's something new in the pit."

"Oh, that . . . yeah. What a job to do in a week! We worked three shifts on those models. Everything had to be just so, even to using a special solution for the oceans. Ouayo brought that in from his baggage outside."

"Lane says they have the place locked."

"Yeah, but I haven't sealed all the emergency hatches yet. Want to take a look?"

Kleweski nodded. Schultz, yawning, led him out of the model shop into the corridor, past two angles in the octagonal floor plan, and down to the machinery level.

This belt of mechanisms used to operate the pit and to generate power for the rest of the station was about thirty feet high. A similar level was immediately below, but deck to deck, with the artificial gravity opposite in direction.

"Here's the hatch across from the control balcony," said Schultz. "That is, it's down this ladder."

He dropped headfirst down the ladderway, like a good swimmer nonchalantly diving from a low float. Halfway through the thickened deck, he grabbed a rung of the ladder and began to climb "down" as he passed the plane of the space station's equator. Kleweski followed, and found Schultz swinging open a small, thick hatch.

Having removed this like a cork from the neck of a bottle, Schultz led the way through a short tunnel in the pit shielding. He opened a similar cylindrical portal at the other end, and they gazed out into the pit from a niche that was recessed to be outside the field of force that maintained the pit vacuum.

Kleweski exclaimed.

"What a scramble! How did you get them all in?"

Four twenty-foot spheres hung in the artificially lighted void. Around each revolved two smaller ones, proportioned as rather large moons. Several others glided toward each other near the center of the pit.

Kleweski thrust his head forward, studying the glowing models in their orbits. After a moment of silent analysis, the pattern suddenly burst upon him.

The four "planets" were spaced equally around the pit, midway between center and the outer limits. Two moons of each followed orbits in the same general plane. The third satellite in each case moved in an elongated ellipse perpendicular to this plane, each cutting down between its two mates at one end of the journey and at the opposite extreme coming almost to a junction with the other odd moons at the center of the pit.

"What's he trying to do?" grunted Kleweski. "There never was such a system. At least, the odds against it are fantastic!"

"Designing one of his own," suggested Schultz sarcastically. "Easy to get around in as a subway. Each planet has two locals, plus one express to all points past the center."

Kleweski did not laugh. His eyes widened.

"Maybe you're not kidding," he muttered. "It's made to order from a viewpoint of economizing on spaceship fuel."

He eyed the setup for a few minutes, then thanked Schultz and thoughtfully made his way to his own compartment.

He had still not made up his mind a few days later as he stood shivering in the poorly heated observation dome atop the station's north pole. He had just turned away from peering through a small telescope at the last receding rocket trail of the ships carrying away members of the laboratory staff.

Which is now reduced to two, he reflected. *Ouayo and me!*

He left the dome by the little car that ran through a bulging "great circle" tube on the station's exterior, and dropped down to the working level and a narrow passage through the supply compartments.

"I suppose Ouayo's busy getting in his secret equipment," he muttered. "Stuff like those language records he gave me."

He wondered why the Arcturan had not yet changed the air of the station to whatever he breathed. Still, he told himself, it was none of his business and Ouayo's preoccupation with other matters was saving Kleweski the trouble of wearing a breathing mask. He decided to have a look into the pit before making another inspection round of the space station.

He found the entrance to the balcony, and looked in upon a mystifying sight. Ouayo stood blockily before a small television screen, the center of a strange new assembly on one of the data desks. Kleweski's first feeling was chagrin at having been left out of whatever experiment was under way. Then he noticed one of the mysterious tanks Ouayo had been keeping in an orbit about the station.

The Arcturan was speaking. To whom Kleweski could not imagine, but it gave him a moment to examine the tank.

The end, of which he had an oblique view, was open. Out of it, tiny sparks were being projected toward the nearest model planet. The engineer stared.

After a few minutes of feeling like a spy, he coughed deliberately. Ouayo looked around. Catching sight of Kleweski at the top of the short flight of steps, he beckoned with one arm and returned his attention to the screen.

Kleweski joined him, feeling unwanted. Then he saw what was on the screen.

The scene was obviously the control room of a spaceship. A being more weird in appearance than even Ouayo was speaking to the latter. He completed an announcement or report and was replaced by a view of a group of vessels in space.

The speaker came back on, said something to which Ouayo made a brief reply, and again the view changed.

It showed the surface of Terra, from about four or five thousand miles. There were islands, many of them—

Kleweski's jaw dropped.

"No, it's not Terra!" he murmured.

It definitely was not his home planet but something else. However he sought to disbelieve his eyes, the views matched perfectly—one an image in the screen, the other a model in the pit before him with island patterns arranged by Schultz's loving care.

He turned to examine the open-ended tank more closely. Those little sparks— *they were rocket trails!*

Ouayo spoke again. He made a note of the answer, gave instructions too fast for Kleweski's artificial memory of the language, and waddled away from the screen.

"I did not expect you," he said, choosing to speak Kleweski's language despite the sessions the engineer had put in to learn Arcturan by means of hypno-records.

Kleweski wondered if the Arcturan were angry, or amused, or contemplating the extinction of a prying Terran.

"Perhaps I can explain," said Ouayo slowly. "Like me, you have inquiring mind . . . no? Is silent knowledge more attractive than . . . to . . . make oneself large with . . . with half a story?"

"I'm curious, yes," admitted Kleweski. "You mean you'll explain if I promise not to repeat it?"

"Slower, please!" requested Ouayo.

Kleweski said it again.

"Yes," answered the other with simple directness.

Kleweski tried to match him with a quiet, "Go ahead!"

"Then," said Ouayo, "these are my . . . clients."

Kleweski looked speculatively at the tiny flame trails.

"How did they get so small?" he asked.

"The Maker of All may answer you that," the Arcturan told him dryly. "They were miniature planetary system in my volume of space. Their sun size your Luna, but dying."

"How did you find them?" asked Kleweski.

"Who shall determine at first hear the magnification or distance of a signal? I, also, astonished when reached their system in the body. However—was plain something needed."

"So they became your . . . clients?"

"Exactly, and more. Engaged me to discover suitable new habitation. They will repay with . . . scientific information . . . formulas, designs, inventions for many purposes. Also they undertake at my . . . request . . . to occupy ten per cent population with *my* research calculations."

Kleweski stared at him in awe. *Just like an electronic brain*, he thought.

The Arcturan had, to all intents, acquired a super-computer, a thinking machine that could direct itself by its own intelligence and build mechanical sub-computers to carry on fantastic amounts of detail work.

"In spite of price I paid Dr. Lawton," said Ouayo, "I expect make a shameful profit . . . that is . . . is 'shameful' right?"

Kleweski was about to say it was all in how you looked at it, but it occurred to him that there might be another view.

"What about these . . . people?" he asked. "Are they quite willing?"

Ouayo made a little gesture with his tentacle tips.

"Are they to choose?" he asked blandly. "They are in position to be willing. Should they not—!"

He flipped a tentacle at the assembly of model planets in a gesture that left little doubt as to his intentions.

Kleweski eyed the spinning models. There would already be a sort of life on them; he now suspected the nature of the special sprays Schultz had been given to use. There would be what a Terran might mistake for molds or bacteria or some yet unknown form of microscopic life. The tiny beings doubtless had animals aboard their ships. Worlds made to order!

And all under the ruthless control of Ouayo, a mere machine to be worked for his purposes!

How did I ever get myself into this? he asked himself.

Bewildered at the revelation, he presently excused himself on a plea of needing sleep, and retired to his own quarters.

There, he stretched out on his bunk and tried to view the situation dispassionately.

"It's beautiful, in a way," he murmured. "A limited population, to fit into the ships and on the models, but enough to do Ouayo's calculations. Why, it's as if you had everybody on Terra supporting a huge effort aimed at doing one scientist's incidental arithmetic! Or sorting out possible answers to any question. Organic cybernetics, you might say—a setup that can not only solve problems at a staggering rate but also use judgment and initiative doing it!"

Yet he knew that was only part of the situation. What of the inhabitants of the artificial system in the pit? Was there any name for them but 'slaves'?"

"Of course," he reflected, "it's only fair that Ouayo be repaid for what he's done for them; and the only likely medium of exchange is *knowledge*. That isn't curtailed by differences in size or location."

Behind this rationalizing, however, was the memory of Ouayo's gesture at the mere suggestion of disobedience.

Kleweski began to squirm out of his clothes for bed.

"Not my problem," he decided. "They made the bargain with Ouayo. I don't enter into it at all. I'm just a sort of janitor here now. As long as I keep the station airtight, warm, and lighted, it's none of my business."

Having lowered his thermostat, he blew up the inflatable pillow issued in the station, pulled up the covers, and turned out the lights. The next thing he did was spend several hours wondering why he could not get to sleep.

In the end, he sat bolt upright with a curse.

"I wonder if he's still in the pit chamber?" he muttered.

He pulled on pants, shirt, and moccasins, and padded softly down the corridor. When he reached the main door to the pit balcony, on the next level, he hesitated. Somehow, he could think of no good excuse for intruding. Shrugging, he opened the door to peek in.

The control balcony was deserted and dark, save for a few discreetly gleaming lights on the instrument panels.

Kleweski entered quickly, not pausing to admire the rotating spheres in the pit, which looked the more brilliant for the dark foreground. He glanced about to make sure Ouayo had not retired to a seat to rest. He was alone.

He walked slowly down the few steps to the controls. The Arcturan's telescreen was dark, but indicated by its dials to be in operation. To it was connected an attachment reminding Kleweski vaguely of a relay device.

"I see," he mused, considering the arrangement. "He has another receiver in his quarters in case of a call. Could I disconnect him a few minutes, I wonder?"

Working gingerly lest he give an alarm, he succeeded in doing so. As an extra precaution, he padded back up the steps to lock both doors before attempting to use the set.

Satisfied that he could not be burst in upon without warning, he considered the mechanism. His knowledge of written Arcturan was nonexistent, but there seemed to be an automatic calling key. He depressed it and waited.

In a moment, the screen glowed, and a burly little monster came slowly into focus.

Where his flesh showed between parts of his simple clothing, it was covered by salmon-pink, iridescent scales varying in size. Kleweski noted a fishy mouth and four multijointed arms, but no noticeable shoulders or neck. As if to offset the inflexible position of the head, there were four mobile, wide-spaced eyes. These immediately focused upon Kleweski.

Somehow, the effect was so very like an expression of astonishment that Kleweski nearly laughed. He controlled himself to speak in the simple Arcturan he had learned from Ouayo's records.

"Who are you?"

The four glittering black eyes flickered to Kleweski's lips as he spoke. The creature then pivoted to beckon an unseen companion, revealing dorsal scales thickened into armor.

"Are you of Ouayo?" came the counter question when the first individual had been joined at the screen by two others.

"Not exactly," said Kleweski, unable to discover a memorized expression to define the relationship precisely. "I am from a near planet. I am hired to work for Ouayo."

The three examined him with an intensity that suggested anger or dislike. The speaker inquired what was wanted "now," using a term for Ouayo that was unknown to Kleweski. Some linguistic instinct told him it was synonymous with "master."

"Nothing," he said. "I was curious. Who are you?"

"We are the *Skrenthi*. We are those rescued by—"

Again, Kleweski failed to understand the title.

"You mean Ouayo, the Arcturan?" he asked.

"Ouayo, yes."

"He tells me," said Kleweski, "that you have agreed to help him in his researches."

"What did he tell you?"

Kleweski repeated Ouayo's story. The *Skrenthi* eyed him.

"He is kind to put it that way," said their spokesman.

The statement seemed subtly "wrong" to Kleweski, like an out-of-place note in a half-remembered tune. He analyzed it in view of his limited artificial knowledge of the language.

Oh, I see! he thought sheepishly. *He's being sarcastic.*

"Are you not willing?" he asked bluntly.

The eyes stared at him again.

"What will you tell him?" he was asked.

Kleweski reiterated his denial of any close connection with Ouayo except for employment. Requested to describe the surroundings, he labored to deliver a word-picture of the space station and Terra, about which it circled. The *Skrenthi* exchanged significant looks, then offered him some pithy advice.

"Return to your world, you of Terra, before you, too, are in the power of Ouayo!"

Kleweski was startled.

"What do you mean?" he demanded.

"If you do not know his treacherous greed, take warning! If you do know, you will deserve whatever results from continuing your association with him."

I don't blame them, thought Kleweski. *He has them in the bag and there's nothing they can do.*

He opened his mouth to reply, but hesitated. Was that a sound in the corridor?

With silent haste, he flicked out a hand for the connection he had loosened. He replaced it, then bounded up the short flight of stairs to unlock the main door at the head of them.

He pressed an ear against the panel. Yes, there was the padding sound of the Arcturan's short strides approaching.

Kleweski slipped along the curving balcony toward the far door. The *Skrenthi*, he saw from the corner of his eye, had taken the hint and were fading from the screen.

If I get out before he gets all the way in, he thought, *it's only a few steps to an angle in the corridor.*

He made sure the end door was unlocked, and waited by it until he saw the handle of the other entrance begin to move. He stepped into the passage, easing the door shut behind him.

Kleweski started back to his quarters by another route through the office level, but stopped halfway there as a thought struck him. Ouayo would probably be occupied for some time. The engineer decided it might be prudent to listen in on any conversation between the Arcturan and his "clients."

He did not enter Ouayo's cabin when he reached it, however, for he discovered that the other had begun converting it to suit his natural habits of life.

"Airtight!" muttered Kleweski, scanning the gauges beside the entrance. "I'd better not go in there without a spacesuit."

He walked slowly to his own compartment, wondering how foolish it would be to confront Ouayo with the story he had just heard and demand an explanation.

And what if there is none? he asked himself. *Do I quit—give up a good job for a chuckle-headed conscience?*

Just as he reached his door, beside a turn in the passage, he thought he heard a noise. He looked over his shoulder—and ducked frantically aside! Ouayo had rounded a far angle of the corridor and was aiming some sort of weapon at him.

"Hey!" yelled Kleweski. "What's the—?"

His voice was drowned out by a report that reverberated along the passage like a roll of thunder. A bolt of flaring energy seared a man-size blotch on the bulkhead beside Kleweski's door. Even where he landed, around the angle in the corridor, he felt the heat.

No use arguing with him now, decided the engineer, sprinting away. *That's a hot jet he carries, whatever it is!*

He wondered what to say if Ouayo called after him, but the Arcturan wasted no time in such overtures. Kleweski heard the clumping of four thick feet in pursuit.

Either he knows I spoke to them, he thought, *or else he'd already decided to get rid of me as soon as I saw the* Skrenthi.

He skidded to a halt beside an elevator shaft. The dial showed the car one level below. He jabbed the button.

Before Ouayo rounded the corner, the door slid open. Kleweski was inside in a flash, pushing a floor button at random. As the car descended, he tried to catch his breath.

He slipped out at the first machinery level. Immediately, the car started upward in response to Ouayo's persistent signal.

"I'll be better off in the other hemisphere," muttered Kleweski, making for a hatch. "Then I want a word with *them*."

Twenty minutes later, after a brisk run through some of the lesser used byways of the station, he climbed up a ladder near the observation balcony. To his cautious stare from deck level, the passage looked clear.

"Still out looking for me," he murmured, climbing out.

As silently as possible, he crept to the balcony door. Far from being locked according to Ouayo's habit, it was ajar. He peered in, prepared to duck at the slightest sound, but the place was unoccupied. Kleweski locked the door behind him and checked the other exit. Then he went to the telescreen.

The three *Skrenthi* appeared as soon as he pressed the key.

"We have waited for you," said their spokesman.

"Sure it was *me* you were waiting for?" asked Kleweski.

"Yes, we are sure.   The Other One departed in a vengeful manner, aware, we think, that you communicated with us."

"Yes, I saw him," replied Kleweski.

"What did he say to you?"

"*Bang*—more or less.   What I want to know is what you said to him!"

The *Skrenthi* glanced at each other with their mobile eyes.

"It was necessary that we admit hearing a call," said their spokesman.   "We are not quite able to resist him."

"That's fine!" growled Kleweski, wondering in passing if the Arcturan translation would still be sarcastic.   "I was hoping *you* could tell me how to handle him."

The *Skrenthi* considered that.

"We might possibly offer advice," Kleweski was told, "unless Ouayo can hear."

Automatically, Kleweski looked to see if the Arcturan had left the relay device connected.   He had; but he had also left something on top of it—a small, ruggedly built radio.   Kleweski held it up by the carrying strap for the *Skrenthi* to see.

"Is this what he uses?" he asked.

"That is our design, yes.   He has a relay mechanism connected to the communicator you see, with an auxiliary unit hooked up somewhere beyond the limits of this new cosmos—"

"*Ssssh!*" Kleweski interrupted.

He was sure he heard a noise outside the door.   He picked up the little radio and tiptoed up the steps.

Even through the metal, the report of Ouayo's weapon was startlingly loud.   A spot around the handle of the door glowed red before Kleweski's eyes.   The door sagged an inch.

No time to get out the other way! thought Kleweski.

A frantic leap carried him to the control panels.   He flipped a switch at one of them with taut fingers, and twisted a dial slightly.   When he reached over beyond the railing, the insulating field had retreated about a yard.

Kleweski vaulted over the rail, as the door clanged open.

He's through! he thought.   *Now if only he doesn't look at the pit until I reach that hatch across the way—*

After dropping several feet on the momentum of his jump, the engineer felt himself sliding to a stop against the curving metal.   Artificial gravity forces were practically nonexistent where he was.   He began to squirm and claw at the surface.

If he looks over the edge, he reflected, *all he has to do is shift the force field back to normal.   He could flatten me thin enough to make rings for one of the planets!*

Changing his tactics, he set his back against the field and pushed at the bulkhead with hands and feet, bracing like a mountain climber making his way by friction. He was congratulating himself on making good time when he heard voices relayed on his radio.   He paused to listen.

Though the speech was too rapid for him, he gathered that the *Skrenthi* were denying having seen the Terran.

Kleweski grinned and kept going.   After an effort that left him panting and damp with sweat, he located the niche from which Schultz had shown him the pit arrangement.   He pulled himself into it, feeling weight again as he moved outside the potential limits of the pit.

"Terran!"

He started at the sound, then realized that the *Skrenthi* were calling through the relay.   He hitched the radio around, squinting past the nightmarish, glowing spheres at the balcony.

"Has he gone?" he asked.

"Yes.   Have you escaped?   He is searching, we think."

"I found a better hole," said Kleweski.   "Now, what were you about to tell me?"

"You requested advice.   We have long spent much effort on analyzing Ouayo for faults and weaknesses.   What weapon have you?"

"That's a good one!" muttered Kleweski mirthlessly.

"We did not hear you."

"My two hands," said the engineer more plainly.

It created a pause.   Then the *Skrenthi* checked back.

"You are being ironic?"

"Exactly," said Kleweski.

"We . . . understand.   Ouayo has been . . . difficult for us also.   Perhaps our estimate of his mentality would interest you."

"Perhaps," said Kleweski.

"We think it will be quite hard to fool him.   However, any intelligent entity has some limit to the number of actions he can consider or carry on simultaneously. After long study, we conclude that Ouayo would probably be confused by more than four simultaneous alternatives."

"If I had five or six places to shoot him from, and he saw them all at once, he might forget to duck?"

"That is one example," agreed the *Skrenthi*.

If I had something to shoot him with, thought Kleweski.

"We advise you to set a trap for him."

"Thanks a lot," retorted Kleweski.

I'd better get out of here, he told himself.

Cautiously, he pushed open the hatch and traversed the short tunnel.   Emerging from the other end, he started for a ladder to the upper levels but changed his mind.

"Come to think of it," he muttered, "aren't the main gravity controls in one of these machine compartments?"

He walked along watchfully, and presently spotted the control room in question. It took him only a moment to step inside and cut the artificial gravity by half.

Now I can make some time, he congratulated himself, bounding along at a previously impossible speed. *Wonder what Ouayo thinks of that? Maybe I ought to do as they said. Some place like the hangar air lock might do.*

He saw no sign of Ouayo as he sneaked ''down'' through the thick central deck and then ''up'' a ladder to the section near the air lock.

After a few moments of thought, during which he was annoyed to catch himself peering frequently up and down the corridor, Kleweski went to work. He chose a spot where two supply compartments opened on the corridor near the air lock.

For safety, this section was bounded by an extra airtight emergency door besides the one at the nearby angle in the passage, making a twenty-foot supplemental air lock. Next to one of the compartment exits was a ladder up the bulkhead to a high hatch. Kleweski climbed up, swung open the hatch, and stepped into the air lock beyond which the rocket was berthed.

He moved certain controls. Sections of bulkhead opposite him began to slide open. Air rushed out, and the hatch started immediately to close. Kleweski hastily dropped through and let it snap shut above his head. As it did so, the two big emergency doors ceased their closing motion and slid back into the bulkheads.

Kleweski nodded in satisfaction.

Now to fix it so he'll stick that ugly head of his into the airless chanber, he thought.

He opened the door beside the ladder and bolted the one on the opposite side of the corridor. There was no purpose in having it bolted, and he hoped that Ouayo might wonder momentarily why it was. He decided that a loud noise of some kind should help, and rummaged around a workshop down the line till he had hooked up an electric bell. This he planted some way beyond the standard safety door but led a loop of wire with the switch back around the angle. Several pipe lines ran overhead, and Kleweski tied the wire to one of these.

He picked up the radio he still carried with him, to ask the *Skrenthi* their opinion of his setup. When his call went unanswered, however, he remembered the shielding around the pit. Ouayo's relay auxiliary would be on the other side of it.

There's just one more thing, he decided. *If he doesn't get sucked into the air lock and pop a few blood vessels in the vacuum, I'll need a way out of here fast! Maybe I'd better shut off that safety door.*

He found the switch in the bulkhead at the corridor angle, and immobilized the door.

''Now,'' murmured Kleweski, ''all I need is to find a good, big monkey wrench and go looking for Ouayo!''

As it turned out, he never had time to choose a weapon. Returning to the shop to search for one, he heard the hum of a nearby elevator. About thirty feet away, the door slid open. Kleweski ducked into the shop.

Too late! he thought.   *He saw me!*

He heard a rapidly approaching pad-pad-pad and ran for a connecting door to the next compartment.   It was a half-empty storeroom.   He scrambled over light plastic bags of various colors toward the corridor exit.   Something in the shop hit the deck with a jingling crash.   Small objects, sounding like nails or bolts, continued to bounce lingeringly in the light gravity.

"Stop where you are!" called Ouayo.

Kleweski tore open the door and set sail for the angle in the corridor.   Behind him, he heard a commotion as the Arcturan drove after him through the storeroom.

Panting, he bounced to a halt at the intersection he had prepared for the showdown. He leaped for the handle of the hatch to the air lock without bothering with the ladder.

The sound of Ouayo's approach became louder, then was drowned out by the gush of air escaping into the lock and through it to the rocket cradles and space. Kleweski opened the hatch as far as he could and dropped back to the deck.

The supply compartment doors faced each other, one ajar and one bolted.   Electric motors hummed as the extra emergency door and the overhead hatch began to close in response to the decreasing air pressure.   The gush of air was approaching a moan.

The Terran, with the strap of the radio clamped between his teeth, had just pulled himself up among the pipe lines along the upper pit-side corner of the corridor when Ouayo bounded through the inoperative doorway.   Kleweski pressed his button, sending the bell back down the passage into strident life.

The Arcturan spread his four stumpy legs as brakes.   One tentacle grabbed at the ladder.   The bulky blaster came up viciously to cover the moving safety door ahead.

Ouayo dismissed that immediately.   He side-stepped, slapped the lefthand door wide open.   He drove a blast of heat across at the other door.   Kleweski saw the bolt area flare white.   The thunderclap deafened him.   Ouayo leaped for the overhead hatch.   Spatters of hot metal from the blasted bolt pattered on the deck. Ouayo shoved the half-closed hatch back, bracing one tentacle on the ladder.   Then he recoiled to drop back to the deck.

I lose! despaired Kleweski.   *He didn't make the mistake.*

Something deep inside him flinched in sheer terror as he released his grip and kicked off from the bulkhead to gain power for whipping the radio straight at Ouayo's broad head and the eye that had just discovered him.   The Arcturan, twisting awkwardly in midair, swung his weapon around.

In the reduced gravity, the radio snapped across the corridor like a cannon shot. Just before Ouayo's thick feet slapped on the deck, while Kleweski was still falling, it struck.

Ouayo spun off-balance and thumped against the bulkhead, catching between it and his own bulky body the blast already triggered for Kleweski.

The report was soggily muffled.

Kleweski found himself on hands and knees, staring wide-eyed at the queerly collapsed brown hulk that had been knocked away from the bulkhead to sprawl across the deck.

A two-foot length of tentacle with a seared end marking the amputation lay a yard in front of Kleweski, but it did not bother him—it just did not look real.

The overhead hatch *chunked* shut. Kleweski realized he could hear.

He never had time to even scream, he thought, still dazed.

Smells began to reach him, now that the air was no longer rushing up through the hatchway. Ozone, a pungent gas from Ouayo's breathing apparatus, scorched paint fumes from the two glowing spots on the bulkheads.

Mixed with all these, the smell of Ouayo.

Not much different from . . . well, if it had been . . . me, Kleweski thought as he fumbled for the switch to reactivate the door behind him.

He staggered through and along the corridor, listening for the door to close. With the *thump,* there returned a memory he had not been aware of—the sound of that tentacle plopping on the deck in front of him. He paused, leaned over to brace both hands against the bulkhead, and was sick.

By the time he reached the pit balcony, the shock was wearing off. He could even face the idea of going back to clean up, but his first intention was to contact the *Skrenthi.*

He stopped short at the thought.

"Now they have nobody to run the place but me," he murmured.

There was no denying that Ouayo had arranged the perfect setup. Millions to work his calculations and tests for him—plus whatever electronic devices *they* built to make the task speedier. And their whole existence was dependent upon whoever controlled the station, the medium of their survival.

"Nuts!" he growled, shaking his head. "You're still dizzy from the shooting. That's just what you were against!"

He opened the door and strode down the short flight of steps to the screen. The *Skrenthi* were already on, waiting.

"What happened? We heard no radio message."

Kleweski explained, and described what had occurred.

"I was lucky," he concluded, "Even though he didn't slip."

The *Skrenthi* looked at each other. Kleweski decided that they were considering the altered situation, wondering how to deal with him. He could see their problem. What he ought to do, he realized, was to reassure them that he would not expect too much—

Get that idea out of your head! he told himself.

But he could not help thinking of the staggering amount of research that would be possible. He visualized millions of *Skrenthi* hustling about, feeding problems into thousands of mechanical brains.

Well, that much seemed perfectly legitimate, he decided. His manner of controlling it was what bothered him.

"It was not mere luck," said the *Skrenthi* spokesman.

"What?"

"Not at all.   Did we not tell you Ouayo would make a mistake if given too many alternatives to handle in a brief instant?"

"Yes, but he handled them all," objected Kleweski.   "I thought he'd get caught in the empty air lock as the hatch closed and never get out again, but he pulled back.   And he'd already checked or blasted every other way I could have gone."

"But you had not gone."

"No . . .but he found that out quick enough!"

"Please!" said the other.   "He was *not* quick enough.   Perhaps, had he chosen to check the possibilities confronting him in a slightly different order—who shall say?   But the actual result bears out our careful estimate of Ouayo—*and of you!*"

Kleweski started to answer, but puffed out his cheeks as he caught up to the last statement.   He chose to listen further.

"We are well satisfied," he was told.   "We have succeeded in the very first of our planned attempts to escape from a sort of tyranny that was intolerable to us; and we have every expectation that you will aid us in the future, since our advice has proved accurate in helping you to save your own life."

Kleweski discovered that he was relieved more than he would have expected, both at finding himself in the good graces of the *Skrenthi* and at having been distracted from making a very possibly fatal decision.

They can be quite dangerous in their own little way, he realized, deciding that they would certainly have found another tool with which to deal with Ouayo had Kleweski not been handy.

"You still want to make a business of computation and research?" he asked.

"It seems a likely way to earn our . . . living."

"Then I think," said Kleweski, "that I will just leave the terms to you.   I am sure we can trust each other."

After the screen had darkened while the *Skrenthi* went to inform their people, he remained to stare speculatively at the gleaming spheres hanging serenely in the pit.

"It's the most marvelous research tool I ever heard of," he told himself at last. "I just wish I could be sure of who's the tool!"

H. B. FYFE

Implode and Peddle

When his secretary announced the interstellar telecall, Tom Ramsay was on the balcony outside his office, watching one of his spaceships land. He smiled proudly as it flared down against the hazy background of Delthig IV's remaining sea.

Used to think I was big stuff with one interstellar ship, he thought. *Now I have three, plus ten locals. Guess I ought to find a buyer for the locals, though, before the Delthigans on III crank up to expand that Planetary State of theirs.*

He glanced with continued satisfaction at his secretary. Tall, willowy, with hair nearly as black as his own short brush but features far easier to look at, Marie Furman was another symbol of his progress in the Terran colony. Then she spoke, and a cold little knot formed in the pit of Ramsay's stomach.

"Telecall from Bormek V, Mr. Ramsay. A gentleman named J. Gilbert Fuller, of Sol III."

Ramsay hastily checked over in his mind all his recent operations. This, somehow, had become habitual whenever he recalled his one entanglement with the Bureau of Special Trading, during a stop on Terra two years earlier.

He noticed the girl eying the thin scar that ran back from his left temple, and realized that it had become more prominent with the paling of his features.

"Put it on my desk visor, Marie," he muttered.

Whatever he wants, he promised himself, *I won't even splash it with a rocket blast. That guy is always one orbit closer to the heat than anybody else!*

A moment later, the subspace waves were relayed to his desk and he saw Fuller face to face. An almost imperceptible lag after each speech was the only indication of the empty light-years between their physical locations.

"You're looking well," Fuller commented genially. "I hear that spaceline of yours is growing fast."

He looks just the same, thought Ramsay. *As if he just finished licking that mustache after swallowing the canary. And not one gold-plated hair of his head out of place!*

Aloud, he remarked on the excellence of communication.

"Oh, this is not a relay," said Fuller. "I really am on Bormek V, only two light-years away. Having a little vacation."

"Hope you're having a good time," Ramsay ventured warily.

"Well, I was, but something . . . ah, came up."

"Uh-*huh!*" Ramsay grunted.

He pressed both palms against the edge of the shiny black desk and braced his shoulders against the imitation Cagsan lizard skin of his chair, for the sake of feeling something at his back.

"Not exactly business of the Bureau," Fuller went on blithely, "but the Bormekians asked me to look into it."

"Don't tell me your Bureau of Slick Tricks doesn't have an agent around Delthig!"

Ramsay thought he knew of at least four, not counting the elderly gentleman in charge of the Bureau's local information service. Fuller waved one hand in a broad gesture, as if to imply that he would hardly make such a bald claim to an intelligent and sophisticated intimate like Ramsay.

"I fear I shall require . . . him, for other tasks," he said blandly. "So, naturally, I thought of you."

"Naturally," said Ramsay, glumly. "Glad to help if I can."

"Excellent!" Fuller beamed. "I knew you would be eager to cooperate. You are hardly one to miss noticing that we have been throwing a little influence behind you occasionally."

The spaceman's gaze wavered momentarily. He *had* wondered a few times how he managed to expand so rapidly. Hauling refined metals from the mines on Delthig II was standard, but out-system freighting from the fourth planet competed with some powerful interstellar companies.

Of course, the B.S.T. had power too, reflecting that which Terra had acquired by being at a spatial crossroads between the interior of the galaxy and the stars near the Edge. Ramsay usually thought of Fuller as lurking beside that crossroads, the biggest highwayman of all the Bureau.

"Now, then," continued the blond agent, "what can you tell me about Delthig III and its natives? I want to check our files."

"Well," said Ramsay, "the average Delthigan is half a foot taller than I am, wasp-waisted, with roundish, heavy shoulders. Arms and legs skinny but knotty, four each and three sections where we have two. Three mutually opposing digits for hands."

"Yes, I have the right file," agreed Fuller, checking.

"He'd have a sort of warty skin, gray with greenish tints. Three eyes, air vents like gills across the front of his face over a big shark mouth. Flappy ears set low on the side of his head, far back."

"What I'm interested in," said Fuller, "is political and economic information."

"Frankly," said Ramsay, "they won't have much to do with us. They're totalitarians, you know, and they make a point of resenting our having two planets in the system. Guess they have their troubles keeping every John Doe at least half-fed and spinning the grindstone with all four floppy hands."

"Overpopulated?"

"Badly. Local guess is five or six billion."

"Other planets?"

"Nothing of use to them except ours, the fourth. Delthig II has good mines, but its dead rock like the first.   V and VI are little ice-balls circling way out back somewhere.''

''So that they might be attracted to our colony?''

Ramsay hesitated, but decided that Fuller was quite capable of knowing a rumor from a trend.

''Talk is,'' he said, ''that not only are they planning to throw us out, but they also are talking about spreading out-system.''

''How much fact is in it?'' asked Fuller, watching intently.

''I'm ready to sell out and leave,'' the spaceman told him simply.   ''Never saw a fat Delthigan yet; they're all run ragged keeping their glorious Planetary State in what they call 'readiness for activity.' ''

''The old, old story,'' agreed Fuller.   ''Well, Tom, that does interest me. Their neighbors in space, Bormek, Ronuil, and other stars, are all good customers of Terra.   The Bureau will have to do something.   Letting Delthig import a few of the necessities of life might save a lot of trouble later.''

Ramsay judiciously kept his mouth shut.   Fuller's alert blue eyes studied him.

''In fact,'' said the B.S.T. man, ''we are arranging a trade conference.   Since you are practically on the spot, I knew you wouldn't mind hopping over to Delthig III to represent us—would you?''

''Oh . . . no . . . of course not,'' muttered Ramsay, unable to think of an excuse that would be good enough to fool Fuller.

That seemed to settle it.   He tried various afterthoughts, stressing the fact the Delthigans had few manufactures except space cruisers and primitive projectile weapons, and that they considered themselves short of raw materials.   Their money was a joke and their credit nonexistent, he pointed out, so that a *del* could hardly be spent at whatever discount anywhere but on Delthig III.

''They don't know what they're up against in the galaxy,'' he said, ''but they have five billion downtrodden 'citizens' to expend in finding out.   Not even the B.S.T. is going to buy them off!''

''No?'' said Fuller.   ''Well, try it anyway.   You never can tell what's for sale.'' Leaving Ramsay groping for further objections, he smiled genially and cut off.

Six days later, that smile returned to haunt Ramsay, as he viewed it again on a film recording of further instructions Fuller had sent to the brand-new spaceport on Chika, the large inner moon of Delthig III's trio.

The spaceman had boarded one of his own ships a few hours after his talk with Fuller, bag, baggage, and secretary, leaving word for his general manager to divert all his other ships to Delthig III.   In space, a message had reached him, warning that while the Delthigans had agreed to an unofficial discussion, they had forbidden any Terran visit to the surface of their planet.   Hence the hastily erected plastic domes beside a flat plain on Chika, where Ramsay landed and found the spare, white-haired man formerly of the B.S.T. information service on IV.

''Hane is the name, Mr. Ramsay.   Heard you were to be in charge here.   Your office and our quarters are in this prefab building, and this bubble over it is the main dome.''

''What could you get in the secondary ones?'' grunted Ramsay.

"Not much except barracks and space for storage. We had quite a time getting Terran workers over here from II in time to get this much laid out. The Delthigan representative is expected shortly."

Ramsay introduced Marie Furman, who was togged out in plaid slacks and jacket as if a trip to Chika were a sporting event. He glanced through the transparent plastic wall at the other domes. Beyond them were low hills, tinted green by traces of scanty vegetation.

"There is some air out there," Hane remarked. "but not enough for anything but mosses and a few other growths. By the way, we recorded a message for you from Mr. Fuller."

The instructions, Ramsay saw when he projected the film in the office set aside for him, consisted mainly of advice and a list of exotic exports Fuller was prepared to send to Delthig. Some, Hane had reported, had already arrived and been stored under the domes.

"So find out," Fuller's image advised near the end of the film, "what the Delthigans need and what they can give in return. Be liberal, the Bureau wants to establish cordial relations."

"This won't work, you know," Ramsay muttered gloomily to himself as the film talked on. "You can't buy off that bunch. They'll take, but they won't pay. When they think they're strong enough to make trouble, out they'll come, like a swarm of bees!"

Fuller was reviewing some of his "bargains."

". . . And that new energy projector developed on Bormek V might have a military use that would make them happy. And don't forget the patents for the plastic prefab house, and the automatic kitchen, or the couple of hundred tons of bright dyes from Fegash—that last ought to get them if their culture is as dull and routine as you say."

Ramsay silently agreed as the picture of Fuller peered more closely at his list.

"Oh, yes," said the B.S.T. man, "I would personally be very happy to unload those twenty million cheap, one-channel telescreens from Vozaal VII that I had to take for . . . diplomatic reasons. They're a big bulge on my account, and—"

"Huh!" snorted Ramsay, turning off the projector with a disgusted flip of his finger. "Marie!"

His secretary appeared in the doorway to her small office.

"As soon as those techs get through to Fuller, remind me to tell him his pet gyp scheme is no good. The Delthigans have no television yet. Hane did say, didn't he, that we have a subspace set that will reach Bormek?"

"Yes, Mr. Ramsay. They promised to—"

A flare of light seeped in through the window of the one-story building. Ramsay rose, but found that the window was not designed to be opened. As he was craning his neck in a vain attempt to see the landing field, Hane entered.

"That will be the ship from Delthig," he said, rubbing his bristling chin. "Wish I'd got rid of this stubble, but we'd better see to them immediately, Mr. Ramsay. Officials of that government down there are apt to be impatient."

Ramsay nodded sourly, reminding himself that he was representing someone else and therefore expected to be prudent about taking personal offense.   He followed Hane to a chamber at the other end of the building in which the air pressure and moisture content was a compromise between that of Delthig and conditions favored by Terrans.   He found it too dry for comfort.

Presently, three Delthigans were ushered in, and escorted by Hane to places at the high table.   They did not use chairs, so Ramsay perforce stood facing them.

Not very fair, he thought, *seeing that they have four feet each against my two. Otherwise, though, they're a seedy-looking bunch!*

The Delthigans were dressed in tunics of dull-colored, sleazy material, belted at their narrow waists with bands of something resembling straw.   Their three-toed feet were wrapped in cloth puttees; but on the middle sections of their arms all wore several bands of metal enameled in bright colors.   The spaceman guessed these to be insignia of rank.

During Hane's introductions, Marie slipped in with her notebook.   Ramsay stared unhappily at the Delthigans, each of whom examined him suspiciously, first with one eye, then another, then yet another, turning his small, roundish head from side to side in the process.   Ramsay noticed that his guests had vestigial crests of thickened skin atop their grayish skulls.

He breathed a sigh of relief when it developed that one of them, Puag Tukhi by name, spoke fair Terran, though with a hissing, clicking accent.

Marie brought Ramsay a list transcribed from Fuller's filmed message.   He mentioned one or two items, but Puag Tukhi was bluntly direct.

"We see first new powder-maker from Bormek," he stated forthrightly, fluttering two or three hands at the list.

"I . . . uh, described it, so to speak," murmured old Hane.

"Arrange a demonstration?" muttered Ramsay behind his hand.

"Oh, Mr. Fuller gave instructions for that.   We have an old emergency rocket wire as a drone target.   The Bormekian ship mounting the thing has been cruising an orbit around Chika.   I . . . ah, alerted them."

"Just what does it do?" asked Ramsay.

"You'll see.   We can watch on the telescreen over there."

Ramsay passed the invitation on, and they gathered around the instrument in the corner of the room.   He noticed that the gray-green skin of the Delthigan beside him showed traces of quite humanoid perspiration, although he himself found the air dry enough to foreshadow a sore throat if he had to talk a great deal.   Then Hane had a message sent out to the cruising ship, and Ramsay forgot personal discomfort for a time.

He supposed later that the Delthigans must have been fascinated, though they managed to repress any undue show of interest.   As Hane explained it, the field projected by the new weapon drastically affected the affinity for each other of the molecules of any substance within its range.   Its range, he read from notes in a small memo book, had not yet been successfully measured.   It did not by any means cause actual disintegration, but any supplementary disturbance—a projectile or even a sudden acceleration—might produce disorganization.

They were treated to a clearly focused view of the target rocket as it entered the field, just as Hane finished remarking that the latter was ineffective if used too close to a sun.

"Watch, now!" he added. "They are going to attempt hitting it with a bullet from a modified rifle."

This, in space, required some doing. Eventually, however, as the Delthigans began to shuffle their many feet like a barnful of restless horses, the nose of the rocket seemed to spread out into a cloud of smoke.

"They promised, if that worked," said Hane, "that they would signal the radio controls to change course."

Sure enough, the stern jets of the little rocket flared briefly a moment later. Briefly, because the entire hull of faintly gleaming metal expanded into amorphous swirls of dust, some drifting off in what was to have been the new course but most continuing along the old curve.

"And what if it nothing disturpt while field on it?" asked Puag Tukhi.

"Probably be all right," guessed Ramsay. "Maybe a few air leaks."

Hane switched off the telescreen and they regrouped at the conference table. Ramsay attempted to turn the talk to his list of possible imports—the thought of such a weapon in the hands of beings known to be contemplating military adventure gave him a chill.

Puag Tukhi, however, insistently brought the discussion back at every opportunity to one point: he was willing to "consider accepting" a number of the Bormekian "powder-makers" if suitable terms could be arranged. Suitable terms, he seemed to think, included Delthigan currency.

As time went on, he gradually modified these offers until they further included supplying Delthigan labor for the Terran mines on the second planet and the purchase of other items. Ramsay's throat got drier and drier while he strove to avoid concluding the agreement.

"You not want gif us only what *you* want!" exclaimed the Delthigan finally, working his toothy shark mouth unpleasantly.

"Not at all!" denied the Terran. "I merely wish you to appreciate all the possibilities."

"Appressshiate? Not know wordt."

"I want you to see all the best things. Look—suppose we have a little pause here, so each side can talk things over! We'll regulate the air in another room for you to be more comfortable in, and take it up again in half an hour or so."

After only two repetitions, the Delthigan got the drift and agreed reluctantly to a recess. The Terrans retreated to Ramsay's office, Marie pausing at her own desk.

His first action was to demand that the station operators get him a face-to-face call to J. Gilbert Fuller, on Bormek V.

"I don't like it a bit!" he said to the old man while they waited for the call to go through. "Let them have enough of those gadgets, and we'll find ourselves in the mines of Delthig II one fine day, and these squids out to conquer the stars."

"Dear, dear!" muttered Hane. "I *do* imagine they have something of the sort in mind. Still, Mr. Fuller ought to know what he means to do."

"That's the one thing that keeps me here at all," admitted the spaceman. "He's sharp, I know. And yet . . . he's never been in this system. Looking over the data on Bormek V is one thing; but it's another to see that self-perpetuating clique down there sweatshopping their whole planet into an armed camp."

Marie Furman entered from her office, carrying a drinking glass and a small bottle.

"You'd better gargle with this, Mr. Ramsay," she said sympathetically.

He accepted gratefully and moved toward the small lavatory adjoining the office. As soon as he had his mouth full, his brunet secretary informed him that the operators had reached the Bormek station, only to learn that J. Gilbert Fuller had gone off on business of his own with no word except that he would be back presently.

Ramsay choked, as was doubtless intended, he realized. By the time he was physically capable of voicing the expressions that rose to his lips, he had regained a measure of censoring self-control.

"That's fine!" he groaned. "What'll I tell these squids?"

"Well . . . this is just a personal opinion, mind," said Hane, "but perhaps it would be best to strike a bargain with them."

"But those projectors!" objected the spaceman.

"Projector," Hane corrected. "Only one has arrived, so far."

"You could promise more, then sort of forget about them," suggested the girl.

"Too dishonest," Ramsay vetoed. "Not only that, but I don't want to be here when they yell 'foul.' Those octopuses are too touchy now. Imagine if they thought they'd been swindled!"

"True," agreed Hane. "I can't think of any excuse to turn them down."

Ramsay paced the office several laps without locating any inspiration.

"All right," he sighed finally. I'll go back in there and try to palm off on them Fuller's precious telescreens and every other equivalent of beads he's sending. Maybe they'll draw the line at some of the junk. Then *I* can get insulted and back out!"

It seemed to Ramsay that the ensuing session with Puag Tukhi lasted one or two normal lifetimes. Long before the close, Marie had frankly curled up in a chair by the wall and gone to sleep. Hane retired to a seat by the telescreen in the corner an hour later, where he maintained a precarious position by jerking upright from time to time when his chin touched his chest. Even one of the Delthigans, despite censorious glares from his chief, rested his round head on the table and kept only one heavy-lidded eye open.

When at last Ramsay stumbled into his sleeping quarters, having seen the native officials off to their ship and called a pair of communications operators on night watch to carry Hane and Marie out, he was too exhausted to bother checking either the time or the contract.

It seemed only a few minutes before the persistent chime of the intercom visor beside his bed bullied him into wakefulness.   He answered groggily, to discover that it was another day and someone wanted to know what to do with three shiploads of Vozaalian telescreens and one of scarlet dye from Fegash.

"Any of my interplanetary ship here?" he croaked.

"Five, Mr. Ramsay, including the *Sprite* that you came in."

"Load them all for Delthig III, and when they come back up, have them stand by in case the Delthigans bring cargo for IV.   And keep a good record; I'm going to bill the B. S. T. for every bit of this!"

He cut off, then called the building guard with orders to wake Marie and Hane.

"If Ramsay can't sleep," he muttered, weaving toward his shower, "*nobody* sleeps!   Ugh, my throat!   I better gargle again."

At length, dressed in shirt and slacks, the latter tucked into high spaceman's boots, he went to his office.   Hane and Marie, the latter still in slacks, appeared presently.   The girl proved herself the efficient secretary when the breakfast she had ordered arrived a few minutes later.

"The first thing I want to check," said Ramsay, brushing toast crumbs from the handwritten agreement he had copied down the night before, "is where we wound up.   I seem to remember something about scrap metal for the Delthig IV plants."

"Puag Tukhi offered to exchange old weapons for the Bormekian projectors," Hane recalled, "along with other scrap.   That was just before his little speech about how such avaricious bargaining as yours would never be tolerated in *his* society."

"I was hoping he'd get mad and leave," said Ramsay.

It appeared that the Delthigans had even accepted Fuller's useless telescreens. They were to distribute all twenty million—if they could—and act as brokers for the Terrans.

Guess they didn't like that, Ramsay reflected, *but it was better than having inferior aliens on their sacred planet!*

The Delthigans had also contracted for the building of several hundred space-ships, which as Hane put it, *might* be delivered to them.   In partial return for these, the thousands of Bormekian weapons ordered, and certain other items, they were to supply scrap metal and drafts of workers for Terran projects on II, IV, and Chika.

"I'm not sure I like that," said Ramsay.   "They'll repossess both if they ever clip us; and I don't see how we'll get the cash balance out of them."

A few luxury articles such as dyestuffs and automatic household gadgets had been ordered.   Ramsay shrewdly estimated that the amount of these would perhaps be sufficient to supply the upper crust of the Delthigan regime—certainly no more.

But the main thing was the projectors.

"They didn't really fight against the other junk," Ramsay commented.   "That worries me.   What in the world would they do with those telescreens?   They just took them to get the weapons."

"If I know them at all," retorted Hane, "they will distribute the sets as evidence to their people of progress toward the better life most of them despair of ever seeing."

"And simply promise telecasts in the future," Marie put in. "They won't be responsible if it's the very far future."

"Exactly," agreed the old man, smiling at her. "And, if you'll pardon my mentioning it, Ramsay, that is how they wil pay us for the sets—in the far, far future."

Ramsay nodded.

"Well, he sighed, "I'd better send off a message to be filmed for Fuller if he still isn't back, and tell him about the agreement and their lack of telecasting. He might enter that on the books as an 'out' against the day they default. I hate to say so, but he's going to need *some* excuse this time."

Within a few days—reckoned by Terran standards because the satellite rotated once in its three-week journey around its planet—he began to suspect that his customers were leaning over backward to stay in the right. Ship after ship, Terran and Delthigan, arrived to discharge scrap metal and shuttle other goods down to Delthig III as fast as the big interstellar ships could be unloaded. One Delthigan official delivered a statement showing a staggering balance in *dels* banked under Ramsay's name, it being illegal for such a sum to be taken beyond the Planetary State's control.

"Things go so fast around here," Ramsay said to Hane, "that I wonder if they're just breaking up the telescreens and shooting them back as scrap."

"That was a fair theory," admitted the older man, "up to yesterday when those boys unloading found live shells to fit one of the junked cannons. Did you see where they were taking potshots at the hill out there?"

Ramsay snorted.

"The squids don't seem to care what they send. Have we got barracks up for the Delthigan labor gangs that arrived?"

"Yes," Hane chuckled. "I faced them with the alternative of sleeping out, so to speak, and they fell to with a will."

"Let's keep them here," suggested the spaceman.

He eyed the fast-growing settlement in his charge. It required a lot of labor to keep the spaceport unclogged.

"They were supposed to go to the mines on II," Hane reminded him, "as soon as they built barracks for more transients."

"I'd just as soon avoid that as long as we can. I can picture a horde of so-called 'laborers' running amuck when a Delthigan fleet approached that planet. But here, they'd be some use."

"They'll work hard," Hane agreed. "They look well broken in for that."

Slaves, thought Ramsay. *That's what they amount to. Wish I had nothing to do with handling them!*

He could see the mottled, brownish face of Delthig III above the low hills of the moon. He wondered if a telescope would show the fires and lights of hard-driven factories on the night side. He caught himself imagining that malevolent, brooding eyes watched him from those shadows.

What's it like to live there? he wondered.

He tried to picture the hopeless drudgery of building a Planetary State on inadequate rations under the monotonous bludgeoning of propaganda designed to dull the senses to the lack of food, or clothing, or freedom, or pleasure, or the slightest respite from the slavery.

No wonder they work so hard on the new domes, he thought. *They must be happy to be even this far away from the surface.*

"Have them put up more shelters," he said to Hane, "and quarter incoming gangs in them to take over the stevedoring. I can't ask our own men to go on short-handed any longer."

That noon, he tried to catch a nap in his room, but found himself too restless. Putting on a spacesuit, he made a tour of inspection out to the end of the expanding port, where a Delthigan ship was unloading more scrap.

"I wish I knew why they keep sending the stuff," he said to Marie in the office upon his return.

"I guess they call the guns obsolete now. Isn't that what they do when somebody builds a bigger one?"

"Bigger what?"

"Bigger anything. That horrid thing from Bormek made their guns obsolete."

"Yeah," he said, sitting down slowly, "but they usually don't throw away the old till they have twice as many of the new. And Fuller hasn't—thank goodness!—sent us any more of what Puag Tukhi calls 'powder-makers.' "

"Well, be that as it may," said his secretary, "I found out for you about the ship that parked here last night. You'll never guess!"

Ramsay ran the fingers of his left hand through his close-clipped black hair and looked up at her with an expression of forced patience.

"Oh, all right, then!" exclaimed Marie, tossing her head slightly. "I'll tell you before you start demanding again why somebody doesn't at least *try* to help you keep track of what goes on around here."

"Please do!" said Ramsay succinctly.

"It's a television station!"

He drummed his fingers on the desk.

"Very funny. Do I have to go find out for myself?"

"You could; I told them it would be all right to have some Delthigans extend a plastic tube out to the ship. And it's just what I said!"

"A television station?"

"Well, a ship sent direct from Bormek by Mr. Fuller that's outfitted to telecast programs. The man in charge, Mr. Neuberg, explained how they can send almost as far as your spaceport communicator, but entertainment, too."

Ramsay dropped both hands to the desk and slumped back in his chair. He shook his head slowly, resignedly.

"That's what I get," he murmured, "for telling him about unloading his telescreens when I griped about the projectors."

"I think it was awfully clever of Mr. Fuller to manage it so soon," said his secretary.   "They've already made a local film to telecast to Delthig III.   *I'm* in it!"

"When they don't get those projectors, they'll come up here and blow my head off," said Ramsay gloomily.   "And *he* sends me a telecasting station!   All wrapped up in a spaceship, so it can skip out fast when the shooting starts!"

"They took pictures of me setting up an automatic stove and putting something in it to cook," said Marie.   "Mr. Neuberg wanted to show things actually being sent to the Delthigans."

"I'd like to see it sometime," said Ramsay, when she waited expectantly for comment.

Marie brightened.   She ran out to her desk and returned in a moment with a small telescreen.

"Where did you get that cracker box?" demanded Ramsay.

Marie smiled reminiscently and pushed back her dark hair after turning the set on.

"That's what we're sending to Delthig.   One of the boys snitched one for me out of the last cargo."

"You leave 'the boys' alone!" ordered Ramsay severely.   "It's unfair to match them with something like you after they've been at the mines so long.   Try your talents on me, if you need practice."

"I couldn't have the *boss* stealing telescreens, could I?   What would Mr. Hane say?   Oh, look!   There I am now.   Mr. Neuberg said he's going to repeat it with his other films until every Delthigan has seen it."

"That means almost fifteen million already," said Ramsay, glancing at a crude chart of the spaceport's traffic.

"Mr. Neuberg says more than that.   This thing only receives on one channel, but it will still be a great novelty on Delthig III.   He says there ought to be up to two hundred watchers to each set, maybe more."

Ramsay decided not to bother estimating mentally the percentage of the Delthigan population being titillated by Marie's conquest of an apple pie.   He noticed that she wasted a lot of material, and hoped Neuberg's food locker held more apples.

"Mr. Neuberg said," she defended herself, "that I should set the machine to remove thick cores.   It made a better picture, and he could demonstrate the garbage disposal attachment."

"I don't suppose you brought a piece of the pie back with you?" asked Ramsay hopefully.   "Oh . . . *they* ate it all, huh?"

He watched the program give place to another film, a description of Terran home life.   The film family's chief problem in life seemed to be whether to travel to Mars or Venus for Papa's vacation.

Here I sit half-starved on rations brought from the mining domes, thought Ramsay, *and she doesn't even bring me a slice of the pie!*

The door to his office was thrown open.   Old Hane hustled in at an unprecedented pace.   His scanty white hair was disheveled.

"Puag Tukhi is coming in for a landing!"

"What's the matter?" asked the spaceman.

"He didn't say, but he sounded disturbed over the radio.   Do you think it might be, in a nutshell—the projectors?"

"Very likely," said Ramsay, groping for a good excuse.

They went outside the building to watch through the plastic side of the dome as the Dethigan ship landed.   A pressurized truck trundled out to pick up the official and trundled back to the dome with maddening deliberation.   It halted to discharge its passenger at the entrance to the inner building.

Puag Tukhi restrained himself with obvious difficulty until they had gone outside. In Ramsay's office, rapid denunciation in hissing Delthigan.

The others looked at each other helplessly.

Puag Tukhi stuttered into Terran.

"I stronger orderss haf to make protests!" he declaimed.

"What's wrong?" asked Ramsay innocently.

"Wronk!   Will show what iss wronk!"

He bounded across the office on his four stringy-muscled legs to the telescreen. He switched it on.

"*Thiss* you gif us.   But not ssay to haf picturess on!   What trouble you make!"

The current program, Ramsay saw, was another in home economics starring his brunet secretary.   This time, it featured an automatic vacuum cleaner that all but thought for itself.

"What's wrong with that?" he asked.

Puag Tukhi pulled himself together and wiped perspiration from around his chinless mouth.   His three eyes glared and the greenish tone of his gray skin became more pronounced.

"Iss not to matter why iss wronk with it!   I haf now my superiorss enough trouble to worry apout.   Musst also explain to you?   Instrumentss were *dissplay,* not for use!"

Ramsay relaxed slightly.   This was something he thought he could handle.   It might even be useful in keeping the Delthigans' minds off other matters, such as nondelivery of Bormekian projectors, or holding laborers on Chika.

I'll push this as far as it will go, he decided.   *Now, how would Fuller do it?*

"I do not recall any part of our agreement dealing with telecasting," he said smoothly.

Puag Tukhi stared straight at him, then turned his round head from side to side to examine the Terran through his other eyes.   He opened his mouth twice, displaying numerous pointed teeth, before he succeeded in voicing an answer.

"That iss what I ssay!" he complained.   "Therefore, you musst not do thiss! Makes for me trouble.   Seriouss trouble!"

"You admit you did accept our telescreens," asked Ramsay.

"Yess."

"And, as our agents, distributed them among your people?"

"Yess, yess!   We musst, understand, gif them some sign of progress.   They work . . . very hard."

"But television is communication," Ramsay pursued coolly.   "That implies two parties, televiewer *and* telecaster.   The receiver is useless without a telecast to receive.   Correct?''

''Yess, but—''

''Therefore, your acceptance of our telescreens *implied* admitting our right to telecast to them!   You see?''

Puag Tukhi hesitated.   He gripped two of his three-fingered hands into a tight knot and ran a third raspingly over the thickened hide of his vestigial crest.

''Of course, if you like,'' said Ramsay jauntily, ''we can stop the whole business. Keep the telescreens and I'll cancel the other shipments!''

That'll fix him! he thought.   He noticed Marie looking at him admiringly, and wished he had a mustache like Fuller's to stroke.

Then Puag Tukhi said something that shocked him out of his smugness.

''But *why* you do thiss to me?   I haf made all things as agreet.   For telescreens, millionss of *dels* paid.   For fancy thingss to official class, I haf sent to Chika herdss of wronk-thinkink prisonerss to work—you not need count what you send back!   And for Bormek powder-makerss, haf sent loadss of scrap gunss.   You . . . you . . . they will put me in the *mines!*   Maybe with no teeth and one eye left! Why you make for me such trouble?''

Ramsay wondered if he sagged visibly.

They're getting them! he thought, licking suddenly dry lips.

''I . . . uh . . . I don't want to make . . . trouble for you—''

He groped his way around a corner of his desk and sat down.

That Fuller!   He's been sending them the things direct from Bormek.   It can't be anything else.   That's why they're shipping discarded guns for scrap; otherwise they'd keep them.   And ME he sends a telecaster.   Does he want to get me killed?

''As I . . . uh, was saying,'' he stumbled on, ''I'd be glad to hear of a way to take the heat off . . . off you, Puag Tukhi, that is.   There must be a way to . . . ah, protect your interests.''

Puag Tukhi sighed gustily, blowing out a little spray of moisture.   Ramsay looked to Hane for help, but that gentleman gazed steadfastly out the window.

''Maybe—'' Marie began in a subdued voice.

''Go on!'' urged her employer.

''Well, back on Terra, they have that custom of giving equal time to both sides of a question.   You know, like election speeches, and that sort of thing.''

''That's it!'' cried Ramsay.   ''You, Puag Tukhi, go back and tell your government that if they send us their own films up to Chika, we'll telecast them along with ours.   Fair enough?''

The Delthigan regained some of his composure, and permitted Hane to escort him to the truck.

Ramsay immediately pounced upon the intercom.   By good fortune, he learned, a line had been laid to the mobile television station.   He asked for Neuberg.

''I'm Ramsay, in charge here,'' he introduced himself to a balding man with dark, expressive eyes set in a pudgy face.

''Ah, yes,'' the other beamed.   ''Don't worry about a thing, Mr. Ramsay.

We're plastering that planet with pix twenty-four hours a day.   Got films to last a month.''

"Yeah . . . well, I'm going to get a few more for you.''

Long before he finished explaining, Neuberg began to shake his head disapprovingly.   Ramsay paused when the man's jowls reached the quivering stage, Mr. Neuberg pointed out that he had a definite schedule to fill.

"But this is necessary!'' shouted the spaceman.

"I sympathize with you, Mr. Ramsay, but I have strict orders from Mr. Fuller. He relies upon me to carry them out.''

"But . . . oh, all *right!*   I'll get him to O.K. what I want.   Will that satisfy you?''

"Entirely,'' answered Mr. Neuberg primly.

Ramsay flipped the switch and rubbed one hand across his face.

"That's an interstellar ship coming in,'' announced Hane, returning.

"Marie!'' snapped Ramsay.   "Come away from that window and get me a face-to-face with Fuller.   Right now—before I pop off with apoplexy and cheat the Delthigans of their revenge!''

She sped out the door.   Hane continued to watch out the window as Ramsay tramped about the office.   He was still pacing ten minutes later, when the girl returned.

"They can't get him,'' she reported.

Ramsay reached her in two strides.

"What do you mean?   Are communications out?''

"No, no; they got through to Bormek V for me.   Mr. Fuller had stopped back and received your last message, but he went off again to arrange something else, and . . . and . . . the Bormekian operators can't reach him.''

"Oh, *fine!*   Did they say he was doing anything about those projectors?''

"Yes, I asked.   They said he ordered them sent directly to Delthig III to speed up delivery as much as possible.''

The silence in the office became so marked that they could hear the working of the air lock outside as the truck came in off the field.

"I quit!'' said Ramsay.

He turned to Hane.

"What ships of mine are out there?''

"There *were* two; but they blasted off for IV just before Puag Tukhi came.''

"When are more due in?''

"A fleet of four might be here by tomorrow night.''

Ramsay groaned.

"Worse than I thought!   I *can't* quit before that squid will get back with his story and maybe even have their films on the way up here.   They have cinemas; they must have something ready.''

"Couldn't you explain to Mr. Neuberg? asked Marie.

He looked at her.

"You know,'' he said thoughtfully, "you're much too pretty a girl to be just a secretary.   I ought to make you an executive assistant.''

"Why, thank you, Mr. Ramsay.   I—"

"And the first execution you can go to will be Neuberg's—unless you can convince him Fuller sent me permission!"

"But—"

"I tried to tell him, but he *has his orders*," said Ramsay, urging her toward the door with a firm grip on her arm.   "Now, *you* try it.   All you have to do is make him forget to ask for a look at the filmed message."

"I could offer to act in another demonstration."

"Good, good!" he approved, marching through her small office and easing her into the corridor.   "And . . . uh, change those baggy slacks, will you?   Put on a dress!   You *did* bring one along, I hope?"

"Why, no, Mr. Ramsay."

She looked down in dismay at the criticized apparel.

"I thought . . . with the space trip and all . . . I only brought a few pairs of slacks."

"Well, go put on a nicer pair, then!" Ramsay snapped.   "And . . . oh, you know what to do.   You talk me out of a raise every couple of months!"

He started her off down the corridor with a little shove.   A short, sturdy young man wearing a space officer's cap rakishly slanted atop curly yellow hair stepped politely out of her way in his course up the hall.   He paused to look frankly over his shoulder, then approached Ramsay.

"I'm Donovan," he said.   "Chief pilot of the *Silver Comet* from Cagsan IX. You Ramsay?"

"That's right."

"I got fifty million ears for you."

Ramsay looked at him.

"How's that, friend?" he queried.

Donovan stared back curiously.   He flipped the pages of the manifest in his hand.

"Frozen corn.   On the cob.   Fifty million ears tabbed as a luxury item for . . . lemme see here . . . 'for government officials of Delthig III.' "

Ramsay shook his head slightly, and Donovan's face swam back into focus.

"Mr. Fuller, of the B.S.T., said—"

Ramsay wearily turned away, reaching back to point at the office behind him.

"Tell Mr. Hane all about it," he pleaded.   "I'm . . . it's my watch off.   I believe I'll go lie down a little while—"

Just before he reached his quarters, he heard running footsteps behind him.   One of the communications men caught up, waving a message memo.

"An alert from Delthig III, Mr. Ramsay."

"What!"

"That high mucky-muck that was up here talked to them from his ship, and they sent a message saying they're shooting some movies up here by mail rocket."

"Oh," said Ramsay.   "That will come under Mr. Neuberg's department. Take them to his ship when they land and let him figure out what to do with them. Er . . . just a minute!"

"Yes, Mr. Ramsay?"

"You techs . . . ah, generally have something stowed away for every emergency. Happen to have anything to . . . discourage a headache, if you see what I mean?"

The operator grinned and winked.

"I'll look around. Might be something in the files."

The next morning, awakened again by the chiming of the intercom beside his bed, Ramsay found that he had a real headache. The motion of sitting up in bed caused him to clutch frantically at his temples.

The *bing-bing-bing* persisted. When he reached for the visor, he managed to knock a large but empty bottle to the floor. He fumbled at the set until he had the video cut off, then answered the call.

"Ramsay?" demanded Hane's voice. "Are you there?"

"Mostly. What's up now?"

"We can't quite tell," said Hane, "but I think you had better get over to the office."

Ramsay switched off, wondering if he could get to the shower without dropping his head. He scowled reproachfully at the empty bottle on the floor and stepped carefully around it.

When he reached his office, he found Hane and Marie waiting, with a pair of television operators loitering in the background. Hane waited for Ramsay to ease himself tenderly into his chair, then gestured for the pair to tell their story.

Ramsay listened with growing dismay to the account of an audio message just received from Delthig III.

"And it sounded like Puag Tukhi, you say? But you're not sure?"

"No video, Mr. Ramsay," the operator shrugged. "Besides, like I say, he sort of got off the track after saying something about you making trouble."

"That," explained Hane, "was where he lapsed into his own vernacular, so to speak. I listened to the transcription, and one would have to be well versed in Delthigan to understand it."

"Why?" asked Ramsay. "Was he that excited?"

"I think he was cursing you!"

"What?"

"It was too fast for me to catch, and some of the words seemed very strange; but I judged mainly by his tone of voice."

Ramsay absorbed this with a poker face, and dismissed the operators to monitor the Delthigan communication band. When they left, he rested his head in his hands a moment before asking, "Either of you got any idea what we've done this time?"

"Everything seemed fine," said Marie blandly.

"We received another shipment of laborers," said Hane thoughtfully. "Whatever happened must have done so since they left the planet. Then, too, the Delthigan films for Neuberg came in by radio-controlled rocket."

"That was last night," Marie told Ramsay. "You . . . er, had that 'Don't Disturb' sign on your door, so we just took them over to Mr. Neuberg."

"What were they about?" asked Ramsay absent-mindedly.

"I don't know. He said he'd start using them right away—after I talked to him again, for a little while."

"There might be one on now," suggested Hane.

The girl walked over to where the cheap, one-channel set rested on the cabinet. She turned it on, and in a few seconds Ramsay began to see what was happening.

By luck, they caught the end of a Delthigan propaganda film which Neuberg's technicians had evidently managed to project and relay. The language was too fast for Hane, the only one of them who knew any Delthigan, but the general import of the speeches was clear.

Those shots of factories! thought Ramsay. *No real workers ever looked that happy and dedicated to their jobs. And the farm scenes between ones of the old squid with the star-maps—looking at the stuff growing isn't filling any Delthigan bellies, but the whole thing is obviously a shot in the arm to try to convince them they're well off.*

"I liked Mr. Neuberg's pictures better," Marie announced. "He actually had some made of all the things we're sending down there—telescreens, the gold and silver braid for the generals, and even a piece of cloth being colored bright red with some of that dye from Fegash."

Ramsay thought of the dingy gray loincloths of the laborers sent by Puag Tukhi. Even that official, he recalled had worn a tunic of dull and sleazy goods.

What a deadly parallel! he thought.

"And did he show any projectors?"

"No," Marie told him, "there weren't any pictures of those, but he did film a good one of the old scrap dumps out behind the domes. He wants the Delthigans to know they're paying for all their imports."

"Paying, all right," murmured Ramsay, "but who down there is doing the receiving?"

"I saw some of them," remarked Hane. "Ones about household gadgets and food. He even had our charming executive assistant nibble on a couple of ears of corn."

"I don't suppose," commented Ramsay deliberately, "that anyone explained in the film that the *cobs* aren't edible?"

They looked at him blankly. He tried to imagine how it would feel to be a starved, overworked Delthigan, in a steel mill, say, and to witness a blithe being from some fabulous world of plenty toss aside food that had apparently barely been sampled. He decided that it would drive him frantic.

Hane ran a hand distractedly through his sparse white hair, comprehension lighting his old eyes.

"No wonder they are . . . displeased," he muttered.

"Displeased!" snorted Ramsay.

That Fuller and his oufit! he thought. *"Bureau of Slick Tricks" they call it, huh? Well, he's not as slick as I thought, but he sure got me in a hole!*

He switched on his desk visor and demanded Neuberg.   After a slight delay, the pudgy, cheerful face appeared.

"Look here!" Ramsay said sternly.   "I want you to cut it out!"

"I *beg* your pardon!"

"That mixing up Delthigan 'educational films' with corn on the cob!   It makes their government look like chumps.   Don't you realize that's bad for business?"

"Mr. Ramsay, am I to blame if they *are* a pack of chumps?   I have my orders from Mr. Fuller, and—"

Something in Ramsay finally snapped.   Half rising behind the desk, he thrust his flushed face close to the scanner.

"Cut it out, I tell you!" he bellowed.   "Or do you want me to come over there with a wrench and fix that chatterbox toy of yours so's it won't cast a picture past its own shadow?"

Neuberg's dark eyes widened.   Without a word, he faded from the screen.

"Hane!" snapped the spaceman.   "Get hold of the foreman of that Delthigan labor gang!   Have them start searching through the scrap for live shells and pull out a couple of old guns to match!"

"What are you going to do?" gasped Marie.

"If I were a general from that Planetary State down there," said Ramsay, "I'd be on my way up here now to censor those telecasts.   But being the cat's-paw I am, I'm at least going to have the satisfaction of popping *somebody* before this place gets wiped off the face of Chika!"

Before Hane could reach the door, a siren somewhere in the dome wailed out in sudden urgency.   The three in the office froze.

"That's an air leak!" exclaimed Ramsay.   "Where's the spacesuit locker?"

He started for the door, but relaxed as the siren cut off.   The visor on his desk emitted a series of *bings*.

"Yeah?" he barked, flipping the switch.

"Everything under control, Mr. Ramsay," reported the communications operator who had found him the bottle "in the files" the previous night.   "That telecasting ship took off without seeing that the connecting tube was sealed.   Murphy's got it air-tight again."

Ramsay muttered something or other in reply and sprang to the window.   He could not see the former position of Neuberg's ship, but the expressions of several men outside looking at where it had been confirmed the report.

"Turn that gadget back on!" he told Marie.

The telecast was still going.   It flickered and faded as they watched, but steadied again.   Neuberg was carrying out his orders—where Ramsay could not interfere.

"Uh . . . I shall see about that ammunition," said Hane after a moment during which the air in the office seemed to vibrate silently.

He went out, looking grateful for the opportunity to escape Ramsay's presence.

The latter realized that he had been scowling across the room for some time when Marie spoke.

"Can I do something?" she asked timidly.

"Huh?   Well, yeah.   Go ride herd on those operators until they get a radio call through to the planet.   If we can get hold of someone in authority, it might still be smoothed over."

Alone, he paced up and down the office for a while.   When that failed to help, he sat at his desk with his head cradled carefully between both hands.   He realized with surprise that his headache had disappeared.

The advantage of a good fright, he reflected.   *I only wish I could see Fuller here too!*

He punched viciously at the intercom switch.   Marie answered from the communications room.

"Any luck?" he demanded.

"Not yet."

"Then have them see if they can reach Fuller on Bormek V!"

Time passed.   A report came back from Bormek to the effect that Mr. Fuller was expected there very soon.

Delthig III radio stations maintained an ominous silence.

Ramsay took presently to making short excursions around the outside of the building, peering through the plastic dome at the spacesuited figures of Hane and some Delthigans out at the heaps of scrap metal, or up into the dark sky.

Finally, Hane returned to report that two cannon had been loaded and put in charge of Terrans from among the spaceport personnel.

"The Delthigans seemed only too willing to help me," he told Ramsay.   "One wonders if they are not somewhat resentful toward their present masters."

"One wonders what's wrong with them if they're not!"   retorted the spaceman.

Bing-bing-bing-bing!

He switched his televisor on, and saw Marie's pale face.

"The techs say they've picked up a ship approaching in a landing orbit," she reported breathlessly.

"How many?" asked Ramsay, beckoning to Hane.

"Only one, but it's acting funny, not sticking to a smooth curve, they say."

"Evasive action!" he guessed.   "Hane, tell your men out there to be ready. Marie, you'd better get back here in case something happens."

He switched off and ran to the window, but nothing was to be seen.   After putting through a brief call, Hane joined him.

"Maybe we can stall a few hours," said Ramsay.   "When my four ships get in tonight, we can fold our domes and silently run away."

Bing-bing-bing-bing!

"Now what?" he demanded of the operator whose image he found on the screen.

"We have Mr. Fuller for you now."

"No!" exclaimed Ramsay with heavy sarcasm.   "What did he stop flitting around for—to hear me make my will?   Put him on!"

He agonized through several seconds of coalescing images as the various operators handling the interstellar call withdrew themselves.   Then Fuller's bland face looked out at him.

"Well, well!" said the B.S.T. agent heartily.   "Heard you were trying to get me.   I was rounding up a few things on the next planet.   Everything going all right?''

Ramsay opened his mouth, closed it, and brought both fists down on the edge of his desk.

Where should I begin? he asked himself.   *Shall I tell him what a mess he's made while I try to think up a good name, or shall I call him the first thing that occurs to me?*

Fuller ran one hand over his golden, slightly wavy hair.   Ramsay thought that he looked a little tired, as if he really had been hustling from one planet to another.

"One little detail seems to have gone wrong," the spaceman said, biting off his words carefully.   "Somehow, the Delthigans seem to have taken offense."

"To what?" asked Fuller calmly.

"To me in particular and Terrans in general.   There is a ship maneuvering at us now.   Don't be surprised if this call is cut off suddenly.   You sent a gentleman named Neuberg—"

The door was flung open.   Marie ran in.

"It landed!" she shrilled.   "The Delthigan ship.   Some of the men took the truck out to it while the others covered it with the cannon."

"Hold on!" Ramsay grunted to Fuller.

He bounded across to the window, callously flipped Hane to one side and the girl to the other, and peered out.   The pressurized truck was just coming out of the air lock.   As he watched, five figures alighted.   The trio of four-legged ones marched briskly toward the entrance of the building.   They were dressed plainly, even for Delthigans.

"Those are no ambassadors," said Ramsay.   "Hatchet-men is more like it. Marie, Hane, get out of here!"

"No!" protested the girl.

"Go get help!" Ramsay rephrased it, which sent her running through the outer office and into the corridor.

"I'll make sure those guns are ready," said Hane with unusual verve.   "If they make trouble, they'll never take off!"

Left alone, Ramsay became aware of a plaintive demand for information emanating from his desk instrument.   Fuller was close to betraying concern as he vainly attempted to see something besides the wall behind Ramsay's chair.

The spaceman seized the visor and turned it around, treating Fuller to a clear view of the doorway as the three Delthigans churned through it.

They clumped to a halt.   The one in the middle, a lean individual with a jagged scar climbing up over his crest from between his right and center eyes, stepped forward.

"Ramsay, the Terran?" he demanded, in an accent as bad as that of Puag Tukhi.

If it's the last thing I do, Ramsay promised himself, *I'm going to punch that middle eye right through the back of his skull!   I'm fed up with these squids!*

He moved forward, clenching his fist.   The Delthigan apparently misunderstood the gesture for one of assent.

"I am Yil Khoff," he said. "Ssent we are to discuss trade contract."

Ramsay heard Fuller murmur behind his back, "Find out what they want." He unclenched his fist and waited.

"We haf decited not want all thingss comink. You can ssend big shipss . . . big shiploads grain foodss?"

"Tell him 'yes,' " advised Fuller from Bormek V.

"It can be arranged," said Ramsay warily. "What about the projectors?"

"Pro-jek-torss?"

"Powder-makers."

"Not want; will gif backd. But not ssend for mines more workerss."

"But you *are* going to pay? We have an agreement!"

"Don't worry about it," said a small voice behind Ramsay.

The Delthigans twitched their flappy ears and eyed the spaceman askance. Yil Khoff laboriously attempted to explain.

"We not bound by promiss of former gufferment."

"Former government!"

Ramsay stepped back to lean one hand on his desk.

"We know . . . iss hard to tell to persson like you. Will maybe not unterstand, but we haf by force new rulerss made."

"A revolution!" breathed Ramsay.

He saw two wrench-bearing operators coming through Marie's office, followed by Hane and the girl. He waved them inside.

"They had a revolution," he announced and his face felt queer to him until he realized that he was smiling.

"Not know word," admitted Yil Khoff after a futile consultation with his companions.

"You threw out the old officials?" Ramsay prompted.

"Threw outt?"

"Deposed . . . replaced—?"

"We *shot* them!" said Yil Khoff firmly. "Was very mad-makink how they from you got such wunderful thingss, but we still starfed. For what? For big promiss! Nothing more behind!"

Ramsay glanced at the desk visor beside his elbow. Fuller blandly returned his smile.

"Mr. Hane," said Ramsay, "will you see that our friends have a comfortably dry room in which to rest until we can discuss new arrangements?"

"Gladly," beamed Hane.

"Perhaps you might even scare up some of that frozen corn. I don't imagine *all* of it got through to Delthig III."

One of the communications men winked. He and his friend slipped out hastily. Hane led the visitors in their wake as Ramsay turned to face Fuller.

"This is all very interesting," said the B.S.T. man, "but it costs a lot of credits. You just don't get someone in a face-to-face across two light-years and then casually tell them to hold on while you settle another matter."

"Aw, the B.S.T. can afford it," retorted Ramsay.   "You'll get it back in this system, if I know you!"

"We expect to," said Fuller.   "I should like to make sure of it, however, by having you and Hane handle the trading—at a good commission, of course."

Ramsay, seeing his elderly assistant returning through the outer office, relayed the offer, remembering that he had profited enormously the last time he had assisted Fuller and the Bureau.

"I should say . . . ah, grab it!" replied Hane, nodding to the B.S.T. man. "Incidentally, Mr. Ramsay's other executive assistant seems to be much admired on Delthig III."

"Me?" asked Marie.

"Yil Khoff says every soul down there is talking about kitchen movies."

"There's an idea for you," Fuller told Ramsay.   "Give her a share and let her handle the household gadgets."

"Thank *you,* Mr. Fuller," said Marie.   "I thought I was going to have to marry him to get a share of his income."

"Huh!" grunted Ramsay, grinning at her.   "That might be arranged yet.   I'll see how much you cut into my commission."

He turned back to Fuller.

"Seriously," he said, "you had me scared there for a while.   I'm just as glad they did have an uprising down there, even though I don't see how they carried it through.   Now I won't have to move my spaceline to another system."

"No, you can stay as our agent till you own Delthig," chuckled Fuller.   "Honestly, now, Ramsay, what did you think would happen on Delthig III when the poor, oppressed, downtrodden mass of slaves got a glimpse of *life* via television."

Ramsay stared.

He reached out, turned the visor to face his chair, and slowly walked around the desk to sit down.   Marie and Hane came to stand behind him.

"So *you* had a hand in it," murmured Ramsay.   "With those telescreens you were so conveniently stuck with!   So nice that they only had one channel, so it didn't even matter if the Delthigans put up a station of their own!"

"The Vozaalians are inclined to be hasty in their designs for mass-produced items," said Fuller complacently.

"Wasn't it taking quite a chance, though?" asked Ramsay.

"The Delthigans were bound to make trouble sooner or later," said Fuller, looking so satisfied that Ramsay half expected him to thrust out a tongue and lick his chops.

"A Planetary State has nowhere to go but out.   It seemed only prudent to supply the little push that would cause the trouble to fall on their own heads."

Ramsay sighed and shook his head admiringly.

"No wonder they were so hopping mad about those telecasts of Neuberg's. Man, but those films must have been more subversive than termites!"

"How does it feel to start a revolution?" asked old Hane.

Fuller smiled and shrugged.

"Oh, I shouldn't take credit for that," he said.   "It was bound to come.   But since Delthig III was so overburdened with that Planetary State that it was due for either an explosion or a collapse, the Bureau naturally preferred to see it *imploded*.''

"Well, the gates are blown in, all right," said Ramsay.   "Now to rush in with the goods."

"It *will* open up quite a market," admitted Fuller.

Hane chuckled suddenly, envisaging the future.

"It will be like a big sponge for years and years," he said.   "There won't be *anything* that won't sell on Delthig III.   You really opened something!"

"I thought for a while he was going to open it with a big bang just outside this dome," laughed Ramsay.   "I won't feel easy until they return all those Bormekian projectors you slipped them behind my back."

"Oh . . . those," muttered Fuller.   "I might as well tell you about those."

He seemed to experience difficulty in meeting the spaceman's eye.

"We hoped they would be a surprise to the ruling caste when the serfs swarmed over the palaces.   If other artillery had been traded in, the projectors would prevent mass slaughter."

"You had them rigged to blow up?" Ramsay guessed.

"No . . . as a matter of fact, they won't do much of anything if they're not in space or some other vacuum."

"What!"

Fuller nodded.

"With any air at all to act as an insulator, the effective range is about half an inch!"

Ramsay tried to imagine the expression on the alien face of the first Delthigan gunner ordered to mow down the charging rebels.   He sighed.

"If you'll excuse me," he said, "I have to go and check our inventory for the big . . . er . . . *opening*."

Belief

"Did you ever dream you were flying?" asked Dr. Roger Toomey of his wife.

Jane Toomey looked up. "Certainly!"

Her quick fingers didn't stop their nimble manipulations of the yarn out of which an intricate and quite useless doily was being created. The television set made a muted murmur in the room and the posturings on its screen were, out of long custom, disregarded.

Roger said, "Everyone dreams of flying at some time or other. It's universal. I've done it many times. That's what worries me."

Jane said, "I don't know what you're getting at, dear. I hate to say so." She counted stitches in an undertone.

"When you think about it, it makes you wonder. It's not really flying that you dream of. You have no wings; at least I never had any. There's no effort involved. You're just floating. That's it. Floating."

"When I fly," said Jane, "I don't remember any of the details. Except once I landed on top of City Hall and hadn't any clothes on. Somehow no one ever seems to pay any attention to you when you're dream-nude. Ever notice that? You're dying of embarrassment but people just pass by."

She pulled at the yarn and the ball tumbled out of the bag and half across the floor. She paid no attention.

Roger shook his head slowly. At the moment, his face was pale and absorbed in doubt. It seemed all angles with its high cheekbones, its long straight nose and the widow's-peak hairline that was growing more pronounced with the years. He was thirty-five.

He said, "Have you ever wondered what makes you dream you're floating?"

"No, I haven't."

Jane Toomey was blond and small. Her prettiness was the fragile kind that does not impose itself upon you but rather creeps on you unaware. She had the bright blue eyes and pink cheeks of a porcelain doll. She was thirty.

Roger said, "Many dreams are only the mind's interpretation of a stimulus imperfectly understood. The stimuli are forced into a reasonable context in a split second."

Jane said, "What are you talking about, darling?"

Roger said, "Look, I once dreamed I was in a hotel, attending a Physics convention. I was with old friends. Everything seemed quite normal. Suddenly, there was a confusion of shouting and for no reason at all I grew panicky. I ran to the door but it wouldn't open. One by one, my friends disappeared. They had no trouble leaving the room, but I couldn't see how they managed it. I shouted at them and they ignored me.

"It was borne in upon me that the hotel was on fire. I didn't smell smoke. I just knew there was a fire. I ran to the window and I could see a fire escape on the outside of the building. I ran to each window in turn but none led to the fire escape. I was quite alone in the room now. I leaned out the window, calling desperately. No one heard me.

"Then the fire engines were coming, little red smears darting along the streets. I remember that clearly. The alarm bells clanged sharply to clear traffic. I could hear them, louder and louder till the sound was splitting my skull. I awoke and, of course, the alarm clock was ringing.

"Now I can't have dreamed a long dream designed to arrive at the moment of the alarm-clock ring in a way that builds the alarm neatly into the fabric of the dream. It's much more reasonable to suppose that the dream began at the moment the alarm began and crammed all its sensation of duration into one split second. It was just a hurry-up device of my brain to explain this sudden noise that penetrated the silence."

Jane was frowning now. She put down her crocheting. "Roger! you've been behaving queerly since you got back from the College. You didn't eat much and now this ridiculous conversation. I've never heard you so morbid. What you need is a dose of bicarbonate."

"I need a little more than that," said Roger in a low voice. "Now what starts a floating dream?"

"If you don't mind, let's change the subject."

She rose, and with firm fingers turned up the sound on the television set. A young gentleman with hollow cheeks and a soulful tenor suddenly raised his voice and assured her, dulcetly, of his never-ending love.

Roger turned it down again and stood with his back to the instrument.

"Levitation!" he said. "That's it. There is some way in which human beings can make themselves float. They have the capacity for it. It's just that they don't know how to use that capacity—except when they sleep. Then, sometimes, they lift up just a little bit, a tenth of an inch maybe. It wouldn't be enough for anyone to notice even if they were watching, but it would be enough to deliver the proper sensation for the start of a floating-dream."

"Roger, you're delirious. I wish you'd stop. Honestly."

He drove on. "Sometimes we sink down slowly and the sensation is gone. Then again, sometimes the float-control ends suddenly and we drop. Jane, did you ever dream you were falling?"

"Yes, of c—"

"You're hanging on the side of a building or you're sitting at the edge of a seat and suddenly you're tumbling.   There's the awful shock of falling and you snap awake, your breath gasping, your heart palpitating.   You *did* fall.   There's no other explanation.''

Jane's expression, having passed slowly from bewilderment to concern, dissolved suddenly into sheepish amusement.

"Roger, you *devil*. And you fooled me!   Oh, you rat!''

"What?''

"Oh, no.   You can't play it out anymore.   I know exactly what you're doing. You're making up a plot to a story and you're trying it out on me.   I should know better than to listen to you.''

Roger looked startled, even a little confused.   He strode to her chair and looked down at her.   "No, Jane.''

"I don't see why not.   You've been talking about writing fiction as long as I've known you.   If you've got a plot, you might as well write it down.   No use just frightening me with it.''   Her fingers flew as her spirits rose.

"Jane, this is no story.''

"But what else—''

"When I woke up this morning, *I dropped to the mattress!*''

He stared at her without blinking.   "I dreamed I was flying,'' he said.   "It was clear and distinct.   I remember every minute of it.   I was lying on my back when I woke up.   I was feeling comfortable and quite happy.   I just wondered a little why the ceiling looked so queer.   I yawned and stretched and *touched* the ceiling.   For a minute, I just stared at my arm reaching upward and ending hard against the ceiling.

"Then I turned over.   I didn't move a muscle, Jane.   I just turned all in one piece because I wanted to.   There I was, five feet above the bed.   There you were on the bed, sleeping.   I was frightened.   I didn't know how to get down, but the minute I thought of getting down, I dropped.   I dropped slowly.   The whole process was under perfect control.

"I stayed in bed fifteen minutes before I dared move.   Then I got up, washed, dressed, and went to work.''

Jane forced a laugh.   "Darling, you had *better* write it up.   But that's all right. You've just been working too hard.''

"Please!   Don't be banal.''

"People work too hard, even though to say so is banal.   After all, you were just dreaming fifteen minutes longer than you thought you were.''

"It wasn't a dream.''

"Of course it was.   I can't even count the times I've dreamed I awoke and dressed and made breakfast; then really woke up and found it was all to do over again.   I've even dreamed I was dreaming, if you see what I mean.   It can be awfully confusing.''

"Look, Jane.   I've come to you with a problem because you're the only one I feel I can come to.   Please take me seriously.''

*　　*　　*

Jane's blue eyes opened wide. "Darling! I'm taking you as seriously as I can. You're the Physics professor, not I. Gravitation is what you know about, not I. Would *you* take it seriously if I told you *I* had found myself floating?"

"No. *No!* That's the hell of it. I don't want to believe it, only I've got to. It was no dream, Jane. I tried to tell myself it was. You have no idea how I talked myself into that. By the time I got to class, I was sure it was a dream. You didn't notice anything queer about me at breakfast, did you?"

"Yes, I did, now that I think about it."

"Well, it wasn't very queer or you would have mentioned it. Anyway, I gave my nine o'clock lecture perfectly. By eleven, I had forgotten the whole incident. Then, just after lunch, I needed a book. I needed Page and— Well, the book doesn't matter; I just needed it. It was on an upper shelf, but I could reach it. Jane—"

He stopped.

"Well, go on, Roger."

"Look, did you ever try to pick up something that's just a step away? You bend and automatically take a step toward it as you reach. It's completely involuntary. It's just your body's over-all co-ordination."

"All right. What of it?"

"I reached for the book and automatically took a step upward. On air, Jane! On empty air!"

"I'm going to call Jim Sarle, Roger."

"I'm not sick, damn it."

"I think he ought to talk to you. He's a friend. It won't be a doctor's visit. He'll just talk to you."

"And what good will that do?" Roger's face turned red with sudden anger.

"We'll see. Now sit down, Roger. Please." She walked to the phone.

He cut her off, seizing her wrist. "You don't believe me."

"Oh, Roger."

"You don't."

"I believe you. Of course, I believe you. I just want—"

"Yes. You just want Jim Sarle to talk to me. That's how much you believe me. I'm telling the truth but you want me to talk to a psychiatrist. Look, you don't have to take my word for anything. I can prove this. I can prove I can float."

"I *believe* you."

"Don't be a fool. I know when I'm being humored. Stand still! Now watch me."

He backed away to the middle of the room and without preliminary lifted off the floor. He *dangled;* with the toes of his shoes six empty inches from the carpet.

Jane's eyes and mouth were three round O's. She whispered, "Come down, Roger. Oh, dear heaven, come down."

He drifted down, his feet touching the floor without a sound. "You see?"

"Oh, my. Oh, my."

She stared at him, half-frightened, half-sick.

On the television set, a chesty female sang mutedly that flying high with some guy in the sky was her idea of nothing at all.

Roger Toomey stared into the bedroom's darkness.   He whispered, "Jane."

"What?"

"You're not sleeping?"

"No."

"I can't sleep, either.   I keep holding the headboard to make sure I'm . . . you know."

His hand moved restlessly and touched her face.   She flinched, jerking away as though he carried an electric charge.

She said, "I'm sorry.   I'm a little nervous."

"That's all right.   I'm getting out of bed anyway."

'What are you going to do?   You've got to sleep."

"Well, I can't, so there's no sense keeping you awake, too."

"Maybe nothing will happen.   It doesn't have to happen every night.   It didn't happen before last night."

"How do I know?   Maybe I just never went up so high.   Maybe I just never woke up and caught myself.   Anyway, now it's different."

He was sitting up in bed, his legs bent, his arms clasping his knees, his forehead resting on them.   He pushed the sheet to one side and rubbed his cheek against the soft flannel of his pajamas.

He said, "It's bound to be different now.   My mind's full of it.   Once I'm asleep, once I'm not holding myself down consciously, why, up I'll go."

"I don't see why.   It must be such an effort."

"That's the point.   It isn't."

"But you're fighting gravity, aren't you?"

"I know, but there's still no effort.   Look, Jane, if I only *could* understand it, I wouldn't mind so much."

He dangled his feet out of bed and stood up.   "I don't want to talk about it."

His wife muttered, "I don't want to, either."   She started crying, fighting back the sobs and turning them into strangled moans, which sounded much worse.

Roger said, "I'm sorry, Jane.   I'm getting you all wrought-up."

"No, don't touch me.   Just . . . just leave me alone."

He took a few uncertain steps away from the bed.

She said, "Where are you going?"

"To the studio couch.   Will you help me?"

"How?"

"I want you to tie me down."

"Tie you down?"

"With a couple of ropes.   Just loosely, so I can turn if I want to.   Do you mind?"

Her bare feet were already seeking her mules on the floor at her side of the bed. "All right," she sighed.

Roger Toomey sat in the small cubbyhole that passed for his office and stared at the pile of examination papers before him. At the moment, he didn't see how he was going to mark them.

He had given five lectures on electricity and magnetism since the first night he had floated. He had gotten through them somehow, though not swimmingly. The students asked ridiculous questions so probably he wasn't making himself as clear as he once did.

Today he had saved himself a lecture by giving a surprise examination. He didn't bother making one up; just handed out copies of one given several years earlier.

Now he had the answer papers and would have to mark them. Why? Did it matter what they said? Or anyone? Was it so important to know the laws of physics? If it came to that, what were the laws? Were there any, really?

Or was it all just a mass of confusion out of which nothing orderly could ever be extracted? Was the universe, for all its appearance, merely the original chaos, still waiting for the Spirit to move upon the face of its deep?

Insomnia wasn't helping him, either. Even strapped in upon the couch, he slept only fitfully, and then always with dreams.

There was a knock at the door.

Roger cried angrily, "Who's there?"

A pause, and then the uncertain answer. "It's Miss Harroway, Dr. Toomey. I have the letters you dictated."

"Well, come in, come in. Don't just stand there."

The department secretary opened the door a minimum distance and squeezed her lean and unprepossessing body into his office. She had a sheaf of papers in her hand. To each was clipped a yellow carbon and a stamped, addressed envelope.

Roger was anxious to get rid of her. That was his mistake. He stretched forward to reach the letters as she approached and felt himself leave the chair.

He moved two feet forward, still in sitting position, before he could bring himself down hard, losing his balance and tumbling in the process. It was too late.

It was entirely too late. Miss Harroway dropped the letters in a fluttering handful. She screamed and turned, hitting the door with her shoulder, caroming out into the hall and dashing down the corridor in a clatter of high heels.

Roger rose, rubbing an aching hip. "Damn," he said forcefully.

But he couldn't help seeing her point. He pictured the sight as she must have seen it; a full-grown man, lifting smoothly out of his chair and gliding toward her in a maintained squat.

He picked up the letters and closed his office door. It was quite late in the day; the corridors would be empty; she would probably be quite incoherent. Still— He waited anxiously for the crowd to gather.

Nothing happened. Perhaps she was lying somewhere in a dead faint. Roger felt it a point of honor to seek her out and do what he could for her, but he told his conscience to go to the devil. Until he found out exactly what was wrong with him, exactly what this wild nightmare of his was all about, he must do nothing to reveal it.

*   *   *

Nothing, that is, more than he had done already.

He leafed through the letters; one to every major theoretical physicist in the country. Home talent was insufficient for this sort of thing.

He wondered if Miss Harroway grasped the contents of the letters. He hoped not. He had couched them deliberately in technical language; more so, perhaps, than was quite necessary. Partly, that was to be discreet; partly, to impress the addressees with the fact that he, Toomey, was a legitimate and capable scientist.

One by one, he put the letters in the appropriate envelopes. The best brains in the country, he thought. Could they help?

He didn't know.

The library was quiet. Roger Toomey closed the *Journal of Theoretical Physics*, placed it on end and stared at its backstrap somberly. The *Journal of Theoretical Physics!* What did any of the contributors to that learned bit of balderdash understand anyway? The thought tore at him. Until so recently they had been the greatest men in the world to him.

And still he was doing his best to live up to their code and philosophy. With Jane's increasingly reluctant help, he had made measurements. He had tried to weigh the phenomenon in the balance, extract its relationships, evaluate its quantities. He had tried, in short, to defeat it in the only way he knew how—by making of it just another expression of the eternal modes of behavior that all the Universe must follow.

(*Must* follow. The best minds said so.)

Only there was nothing to measure. There was absolutely no sensation of effort to his levitation. Indoors—he dared not test himself outdoors, of course—he could reach the ceiling as easily as he could rise an inch, except that it took more time. Given enough time, he felt, he could continue rising indefinitely; go to the Moon, if necessary.

He could carry weights while levitating. The process became slower, but there was no increase in effort.

The day before he had come on Jane without warning, a stopwatch in one hand. "How much do you weigh?" he asked.

"One hundred ten," she replied. She gazed at him uncertainly.

He seized her waist with one arm. She tried to push him away but he paid no attention. Together, they moved upward at a creeping pace. She clung to him, white and rigid with terror.

"Twenty-two minutes thirteen seconds," he said, when his head nudged the ceiling.

When they came down again, Jane tore away and hurried out of the room.

Some days before he had passed a drugstore scale, standing shabbily on a street corner. The street was empty, so he stepped on and put in his penny. Even though he suspected something of the sort, it was a shock to find himself weighing thirty pounds.

He began carrying handfuls of pennies and weighing himself under all conditions.

He was heavier on days on which there was a brisk wind, as though he required weight to keep from blowing away.

Adjustment was automatic.   Whatever it was that levitated him maintained a balance between comfort and safety.   But he could enforce conscious control upon his levitation just as he could upon his respiration.   He could stand on a scale and force the pointer up to almost his full weight and down, of course, to nothing.

He bought a scale two days before and tried to measure the rate at which he could change weight.   That didn't help.   The rate, whatever it was, was faster than the pointer could swing.   All he did was collect data on moduli of compressibility and moments of inertia.

Well—   What did it all amount to anyway?

He stood up and trudged out of the library, shoulders drooping.   He touched tables and chairs as he walked to the side of the room and then kept his hand unobtrusively on the wall.   He had to do that, he felt.   Contact with matter kept him continually informed as to his status with respect to the ground.   If his hand lost touch with a table or slid upward against the wall—   That was it.

The corridor had the usual sprinkling of students.   He ignored them.   In these last days, they had gradually learned to stop greeting him.   Roger imagined that some had come to think of him as queer and most were probably growing to dislike him.

He passed by the elevator.   He never took it any more; going down, particularly. When the elevator made its initial drop, he found it impossible not to lift into the air for just a moment.   No matter how he lay in wait for the moment, he hopped and people would turn to look at him.

He reached for the railing at the head of the stairs and just before his hand touched it, one of his feet kicked the other.   It was the most ungainly stumble that could be imagined.   Three weeks earlier, Roger would have sprawled down the stairs.

This time his autonomic system took over and, leaning forward, spread-eagled, fingers wide, legs half-buckled, he sailed down the flight gliderlike.   He might have been on wires.

He was too dazed to right himself, too paralyzed with horror to do anything. Within two feet of the window at the bottom of the flight, he came to an automatic halt and hovered.

There were two students on the flight he had come down, both now pressed against the wall, three more at the head of the stairs, two on the flight below, and one on the landing with him, so close they could almost touch one another.

It was very silent.   They all looked at him.

Roger straightened himself, dropped to the ground and ran down the stairs, pushing one student roughly out of his way.

Conversation swirled up into exclamation behind him.

"Dr. Morton wants to see me?"   Roger turned in his chair, holding one of its arms firmly.

The new department secretary nodded.   "Yes, Dr. Toomey."

She left quickly.   In the short time since Miss Harroway had resigned, she had

learned that Dr. Toomey had something "wrong" with him.   The students avoided
him.   In his lecture room today, the back seats had been full of whispering students.
The front seats had been empty.

Roger looked into the small wall mirror near the door.   He adjusted his jacket
and brushed some lint off but that operation did little to improve his appearance.
His complexion had grown sallow.   He had lost at least ten pounds since all this
had started, though, of course, he had no way of really knowing his exact weight-
loss.   He was generally unhealthy-looking, as though his digestion perpetually
disagreed with him and won every argument.

He had no apprehensions about this interview with the chairman of the department.   He had reached a pronounced cynicism concerning the levitation incidents.
Apparently, witnesses didn't talk.   Miss Harroway hadn't.   There was no sign
that the students on the staircase had.

With a last touch at his tie, he left his office.

Dr. Philip Morton's office was not too far down the hall which was a gratifying
fact to Roger.   More and more, he was cultivating the habit of walking with
systematic slowness.   He picked up one foot and put it before him, watching.
Then he picked up the other and put it before him, still watching.   He moved
along in a confirmed stoop, gazing at his feet.

Dr. Morton frowned as Roger walked in.   He had little eyes, wore a poorly-
trimmed grizzled mustache and an untidy suit.   He had a moderate reputation in
the scientific world and a decided penchant for leaving teaching duties to the
members of his staff.

He said, "Say, Toomey, I got the strangest letter from Harry Carring.   Did you
write to him on"—he consulted a paper on his desk—"the twenty-second of last
month.   Is this your signature?"

Roger looked and nodded.   Anxiously, he tried to read Carring's letter upside
down.   This was unexpected.   Of the letters he had sent out the day of the Miss
Harroway incident, only four had so far been answered.

Three of them had consisted of cold one-paragraph replies that read, more or
less: "This is to acknowledge receipt of your letter of the 22nd.   I do not believe
I can help you in the matter you discuss."   A fourth, from Ballantine of Northwestern Tech, had bumblingly suggested an institute for psychic research.   Roger
couldn't tell whether he was trying to be helpful or insulting.

Carring of Princeton made five.   He had had high hopes of Carring.

Dr. Morton cleared his throat loudly and adjusted a pair of glasses.   "I want
to read you what he says.   Sit down, Toomey, sit down.   He says: 'Dear
Phil—' "

Dr. Morton looked up briefly with a slightly fatuous smile.   "Harry and I met
at Federation meetings last year.   We had a few drinks together.   Very nice
fellow."

He adjusted his glasses again and returned to the letter: " 'Dear Phil: Is there
a Dr. Roger Toomey in your department?   I received a very queer letter from him
the other day.   I didn't quite know what to make of it.   At first, I thought I'd

just let it go as another crank letter.   Then I thought that since the letter carried your department heading, you ought to know of it.   It's just possible someone may be using your staff as part of a confidence game.   I'm enclosing Dr. Toomey's letter for your inspection.   I hope to be visiting your part of the country—'

"Well the rest of it is personal."   Dr. Morton folded the letter, took off his glasses, put them in a leather container and put that in his breast pocket.   He twined his fingers together and leaned forward.

"Now," he said, "I don't have to read you your own letter.   Was it a joke? A hoax?"

"Dr. Morton," said Roger, heavily, "I was serious.   I don't see anything wrong with my letter.   I sent it to quite a few physicists.   It speaks for itself.   I've made observations on a case of . . . of levitation and I wanted information about possible theoretical explanations for such a phenomenon."

"Levitation!   Really!"

"It's a legitimate case, Dr. Morton."

"You've observed it yourself?"

"Of course."

"No hidden wires?   No mirrors?   Look here, Toomey, you're no expert on these frauds."

"This was a thoroughly scientific series of observations.   There is no possibility of fraud."

"You might have consulted me, Toomey, before sending out these letters."

"Perhaps I should have, Dr. Morton, but, frankly, I thought you might be— unsympathetic."

"Well, thank you.   I should hope so.   And on department stationery.   I'm really surprised, Toomey.   Look here, Toomey, your life is your own.   If you wish to believe in levitation, go ahead, but strictly on your own time.   For the sake of the department and the College, it should be obvious that this sort of thing should not be injected into your scholastic affairs.

"In point of fact, you've lost some weight recently, haven't you, Toomey?   Yes, you don't look well at all.   I'd see a doctor, if I were you.   A nerve specialist, perhaps."

Roger said, bitterly, "A psychiatrist might be better, you think?"

"Well, that's entirely your business.   In any case, a little rest—"

The telephone had rung and the secretary had taken the call.   She caught Dr. Morton's eye and he picked up his extension.

He said, "Hello. . . .   Oh, Dr. Smithers, yes. . . .   Um-m-m. . . .   Yes. . . . Concerning whom? . . .   Well, in point of fact, he's with me right now. . . . Yes. . . .   Yes, immediately."

He cradled the phone and looked at Roger thoughtfully.   "The dean wants to see both of us."

"What about, sir?"

"He didn't say."   He got up and stepped to the door.   "Are you coming, Toomey?"

"Yes, sir." Roger rose slowly to his feet, cramming the toe of one foot carefully under Dr. Morton's desk as he did so.

Dean Smithers was a lean man with a long, ascetic face. He had a mouthful of false teeth that fitted just badly enough to give his sibilants a peculiar half-whistle.

"Close the door, Miss Bryce," he said, "and I'll take no phone calls for a while. Sit down, gentlemen."

He stared at them portentously and added, "I think I had better get right to the point. I don't know exactly what Dr. Toomey is doing, but he must stop."

Dr. Morton turned upon Roger in amazement. "What have you been doing?"

Roger shrugged dispiritedly. "Nothing that I can help." He had underestimated student tongue-wagging after all.

"Oh, come, come." The dean registered impatience. "I'm sure I don't know how much of the story to discount, but it seems you must have been engaging in parlor tricks; silly parlor tricks quite unsuited to the spirit and dignity of this institution."

Dr. Morton said, "This is all beyond me."

The dean frowned. "It seems you haven't heard, then. It is amazing to me how the faculty can remain in complete ignorance of matters that fairly saturate the student body. I had never realized it before. I myself heard of it by accident; by a very fortunate accident, in fact, since I was able to intercept a newspaper reporter who arrived this morning looking for someone he called 'Dr. Toomey, the flying professor.' "

"What?" cried Dr. Morton.

Roger listened haggardly.

"That's what the reporter said. I quote him. It seems one of our students had called the paper. I ordered the newspaperman out and had the student sent to my office. According to him, Dr. Toomey flew—I use the word, 'flew,' because that's what the student insisted on calling it—down a flight of stairs and then back up again. He claimed there were a dozen witnesses."

"I went down the stairs only," muttered Roger.

Dean Smithers was tramping up and down along his carpet now. He had worked himself up into a feverish eloquence. "Now mind you, Toomey, I have nothing against amateur theatricals. In my stay in office I have consistently fought against stuffiness and false dignity. I have encouraged friendliness between ranks in the faculty and have not even objected to reasonable fraternization with students. So I have no objection to your putting on a show for the students *in your own home*.

"Surely you see what could happen to the College once an irresponsible press is done with us. Shall we have a flying professor craze succeed the flying saucer craze? If the reporters get in touch with you, Dr. Toomey, I will expect you to deny all such reports categorically."

"I understand, Dean Smithers."

"I trust that we shall escape this incident without lasting damage. I must ask you, with all the firmness at my command, never to repeat your . . . uh . . .

performance. If you ever do, your resignation will be requested. Do you understand, Dr. Toomey?''

"Yes," said Roger.

"In that case, good day, gentlemen."

Dr. Morton steered Roger back into his office. This time, he shooed his secretary and closed the door behind her carefully.

"Good heavens, Toomey," he whispered, "has this madness any connection with your letter on levitation?''

Roger's nerves were beginning to twang. "Isn't it obvious? I was referring to myself in those letters.''

"You can fly? I mean, levitate?''

"Either word you choose.''

"I never heard of such— Damn it, Toomey, did Miss Harroway ever see you levitate?''

"Once. It was an accid—''

"Of course. It's obvious now. She was so hysterical it was hard to make out. She said you had jumped at her. It sounded as though she were accusing you of . . . of—'' Dr. Morton looked embarrassed. "Well, I didn't believe that. She was a good secretary, you understand, but obviously not one designed to attract the attention of a young man. I was actually relieved when she left. I thought she would be carrying a small revolver next, or accusing *me*— You . . . you levitated, eh?''

"Yes.''

"How do you do it?''

Roger shook his head. "That's my problem. I don't know.''

Dr. Morton allowed himself a smile. "Surely, you don't repeal the law of gravity?''

"You know, I think I do. There must be antigravity involved somehow.''

Dr. Morton's indignation at having a joke taken seriously was marked. He said, "Look here, Toomey, this is nothing to laugh at.''

"*Laugh* at. Great Scott, Dr. Morton, do I look as though I were laughing?''

"Well— You need a rest. No question about it. A little rest and this nonsense of yours will pass. I'm sure of it.''

"It's not nonsense.'' Roger bowed his head a moment and said, in a quieter tone, "I tell you what, Dr. Morton, would you like to go in to this with me? In some way this will open new horizons in physical science. I don't know how it works; I just can't conceive of any solution. The two of us together—''

Dr. Morton's look of horror penetrated by that time.

Roger said, "I know it all sounds queer. But I'll demonstrate for you. It's perfectly legitimate. I wish it weren't.''

"Now, now,'' Dr. Morton sprang from his seat. "Don't exert yourself. You need a rest badly. I don't think you should wait till June. You go home right now. I'll see that your salary comes through and I'll look after your course. I used to give it myself once, you know.''

"Dr. Morton.   This is important."

"I know.   I know."   Dr. Morton clapped Roger on the shoulder.   "Still, my boy, you look under the weather.   Speaking frankly, you look like hell.   You need a long rest."

"I *can* levitate."   Roger's voice was climbing again.   "You're just trying to get rid of me because you don't believe me.   Do you think I'm lying?   What would be my motive?"

"You're exciting yourself needlessly, my boy.   You let me make a phone call. I'll have someone take you home."

"I tell you I *can* levitate," shouted Roger.

Dr. Morton turned red.   "Look, Toomey, let's not discuss it.   I don't care if you fly up in the air right this minute."

"You mean seeing isn't believing as far as you're concerned?"

"Levitation?   Of course not."   The department chairman was bellowing.   "If I saw you fly, I'd see an optometrist or a psychiatrist.   I'd sooner believe myself insane than that the laws of physics—"

He caught himself, harumphed loudly.   "Well, as I said, let's not discuss it. I'll just make this phone call."

"No need, sir.   No need," said Roger.   "I'll go.   I'll take my rest. Good-by."

He walked out rapidly, moving more quickly than at any time in days.   Dr. Morton, on his feet, hands flat on his desk, looked at his departing back with relief.

James Sarle, M.D. was in the living room when Roger arrived home.   He was lighting his pipe as Roger stepped through the door, one large-knuckled hand enclosing the bowl.   He shook out the match and his ruddy face crinkled into a smile.

"Hello, Roger.   Resigning from the human race?   Haven't heard from you in over a month."

His black eyebrows met above the bridge of his nose, giving him a rather forbidding appearance that somehow helped him establish the proper atmosphere with his patients.

Roger turned to Jane, who sat buried in an armchair.   As usual lately, she had a look of wan exhaustion on her face.

Roger said to her, "Why did you bring him here?"

"Hold it!   Hold it, man," said Sarle.   "Nobody brought me.   I met Jane downtown this morning and invited myself here.   I'm bigger than she is.   She couldn't keep me out."

"Met her by coincidence, I suppose?   Do you make appointments for all your coincidences?"

Sarle laughed.   "Let's put it this way.   She told me a little about what's been going on."

Jane said, wearily, "I'm sorry if you disapprove, Roger, but it was the first chance I had to talk to someone who would understand."

"What makes you think he understands? Tell me, Jim, do you believe her story?"

Sarle said, "It's not an easy thing to believe. You'll admit that. But I'm trying."

"All right, suppose I flew. Suppose I levitated right now. What would you do?"

"Faint, maybe. Maybe I'd say, 'Holy Pete.' Maybe I'd bust out laughing. Why don't you try, and then we'll see?"

Roger stared at him. "You really want to see it?"

"Why shouldn't I?"

"The ones that have seen it screamed or ran or froze with horror. Can you take it, Jim?"

"I think so."

"O.K." Roger slipped two feet upward and executed a slow tenfold *entrechat*. He remained in the air, toes pointed downward, legs together, arms gracefully outstretched in bitter parody.

"Better than Nijinski, eh, Jim?"

Sarle did none of the things he suggested he might do. Except for catching his pipe as it dropped, he did nothing at all.

Jane had closed her eyes. Tears squeezed quietly through the lids.

Sarle said, "Come down, Roger."

Roger did so. He took a seat and said, "I wrote to physicists, men of reputation. I explained the situation in an impersonal way. I said I thought it ought to be investigated. Most of them ignored me. One of them wrote to old man Morton to ask if I were crooked or crazy."

"Oh, Roger," whispered Jane.

"You think that's bad? The dean called me into his office today. I'm to stop my parlor tricks, he says. It seems I had stumbled down the stairs and automatically levitated myself to safety. Morton says he wouldn't believe I could fly if he saw me in action. Seeing isn't believing in this case, he says, and orders me to take a rest. I'm not going back."

"Roger," said Jane, her eyes opening wide. "Are you serious?"

"I can't go back. I'm sick of them. Scientists!"

"But what will you do?"

"I don't know." Roger buried his head in his hands. He said in a muffled voice, "You tell me, Jim. You're the psychiatrist. Why won't they believe me?"

"Perhaps it's a matter of self-protection, Roger," said Sarle, slowly. "People aren't happy with anything they can't understand. Even some centuries ago when many people *did* believe in the existence of extra-natural abilities, like flying on broomsticks, for instance, it was almost always assumed that these powers originated with the forces of evil.

"People still think so. They may not believe literally in the devil, but they do think that what is strange is evil. They'll fight against believing in levitation—

or be scared to death if the fact is forced down their throats.   That's true, so let's face it.''

Roger shook his head.   ''You're talking about people, and I'm talking about scientists.''

''Scientists are people.''

''You know what I mean.   I have here a phenomenon.   It isn't witchcraft.   I haven't dealt with the devil.   Jim, there must be a natural explanation.   We don't know all there is to know about gravitation.   We know hardly anything, really. Don't you suppose it's just barely conceivable that there is some biological method of nullifying gravity.   Perhaps I am a mutation of some sort.   I have a . . . well, call it a muscle . . . which can abolish gravity.   At least it can abolish the effect of gravity on myself.   Well, let's investigate it.   Why sit on our hands?   If we have antigravity, imagine what it will mean to the human race.''

''Hold it, Rog,'' said Sarle.   ''Think about the matter a while.   Why are *you* so unhappy about it?   According to Jane, you were almost mad with fear the first day it happened, *before* you had any way of knowing that science was going to ignore you and that your superiors would be unsympathetic.''

''That's right,'' murmured Jane.

Sarle said, ''Now why should that be?   Here you had a great, new, wonderful power; a sudden freedom from the deadly pull of gravity.''

Roger said, ''Oh, don't be a fool.   It was—horrible.   I couldn't understand it. I still can't.''

''Exactly, my boy.   It was something you couldn't understand and *therefore* something horrible.   You're a physical scientist.   You *know* what makes the universe run.   Or if you don't know, you know someone else knows.   Even if no one understands a certain point, you know that some day someone will know. The key word is *know*.   It's part of your life.   Now you come face to face with a phenomenon which you consider to violate one of the basic laws of the universe. Scientists say: Two masses will attract one another according to a fixed mathematical rule.   It is an inalienable property of matter and space.   There are no exceptions. And now you're an exception.''

Roger said, glumly, ''And how.''

''You see, Roger,'' Sarle went on, ''for the first time in history, mankind really has what he considers unbreakable rules.   I mean, unbreakable.   In primitive cultures, a medicine man might use a spell to produce rain.   If it didn't work, it didn't upset the validity of magic.   It just meant that the shaman had neglected some part of his spell, or had broken a taboo, or offended a god.   In modern theocratic cultures, the commandments of the Deity are unbreakable.   Still if a man were to break the commandments and yet prosper, it would be no sign that that particular religion was invalid.   The ways of Providence are admittedly mysterious and some invisible punishment awaits.

''Today, however, we have rules that *really* can't be broken, and one of them is the existence of gravity.   It works even though the man who invokes it has forgotten to mutter em-em-over-ahr-square.''

Roger managed a twisted smile.   ''You're all wrong, Jim.   The unbreakable rules have been broken over and over again. Radioactivity was impossible when it was discovered. Energy came out of nowhere; incredible quantities of it. It was as ridiculous as levitation.''

"Radioactivity was an objective phenomenon that could be communicated and duplicated. Uranium would fog photographic film for anyone. A Crookes tube could be built by anyone and would deliver an electron stream in identical fashion for all. You—''

''I've tried communicating—''

''I know. But can you tell me, for instance, how *I* might levitate.''

''Of course not.''

''That limits others to observation only without experimental duplication. It puts your levitation on the same plane with stellar evolution, something to theorize about but never experiment with.''

''Yet scientists are willing to devote their lives to astrophysics.''

''Scientists are people. They can't reach the stars, so they make the best of it. But they can reach you and to be unable to touch your levitation would be infuriating.''

''Jim, they haven't even tried. You talk as though I've been studied. Jim, they won't even consider the problem.''

''They don't have to. Your levitation is part of a whole class of phenomena that won't be considered. Telepathy, clairvoyance, prescience and a thousand other extra-natural powers are practically never seriously investigated, even though reported with every appearance of reliability. Rhine's experiments on E.S.P. have annoyed far more scientists than they have intrigued. So you see, they don't have to study you to know they don't want to study you. They know that in advance.''

''Is this funny to you, Jim? Scientists refuse to investigate facts; they turn their back on the truth. And you just sit there and grin and make droll statements.''

''No, Roger, I know it's serious. And I have no glib explanations for mankind, really. I'm giving you my thoughts. It's what I think. But don't you see? What I'm doing, really, is to try to look at things as they are. It's what you must do. Forget your ideals, your theories, your notions as to what people *ought* to do. Consider what they *are* doing. Once a person is oriented to face facts rather than delusions, problems tend to disappear. At the very least, they fall into their true perspective and become soluble.''

Roger stirred restlessly. ''Psychiatric gobbledygook! It's like putting your fingers on a man's temple and saying, 'Have faith and you will be cured!' If the poor sap isn't cured, it's because he didn't drum up enough faith. The witch doctor can't lose.''

''Maybe you're right, but let's see. What *is* your problem?''

''No catechism, please. You know my problem so let's not horse around.''

''You levitate. Is that it?''

''Let's say it is. It'll do as a first approximation.''

''You're not being serious, Roger, but actually you're probably right. It's only a first approximation. After all you're tackling that problem. Jane tells me you've been experimenting.''

"Experimenting! Ye Gods, Jim, I'm not experimenting. I'm drifting. I need high-powered brains and equipment. I need a research team and I don't have it."

"Then what's your problem? Second approximation."

Roger said, "I see what you mean. My problem is to get a research team. But I've tried! Man, I've tried till I'm tired of trying."

"How have you tried?"

"I've sent out letters. I've asked— Oh, stop it, Jim. I haven't the heart to go through the patient-on-the-couch routine. You know what I've been doing."

"I know that you've said to people, 'I have a problem. Help me.' Have you tried anything else?"

"Look, Jim. I'm dealing with mature scientists."

"I know. So you reason that the straightforward request is sufficient. Again it's theory against fact. I've told you the difficulties involved in your request. When you thumb a ride on a highway you're making a straightforward request, but most cars pass you by just the same. The point is that the straightforward request has failed. Now what's your problem? Third approximation!"

"To find another approach which won't fail? Is that what you want me to say?"

"It's what you have said, isn't it?"

"So I know it without your telling me."

"Do you? You're ready to quit school, quit your job, quit science. Where's your consistency, Rog? Do you abandon a problem when your first experiment fails? Do you give up when one theory is shown to be inadequate? The same philosophy of experimental science that holds for inanimate objects should hold for people as well."

"All right. What do you suggest I try? Bribery? Threats? Tears?"

James Sarle stood up. "Do you really want a suggestion?"

"Go ahead."

"Do as Dr. Morton said. Take a vacation and to hell with levitation. It's a problem for the future. Sleep in bed and float or don't float; what's the difference. Ignore levitation, laugh at it or even enjoy it. Do anything but worry about it, because it isn't your problem. That's the whole point. It's not your immediate problem. Spend your time considering how to make scientists study something they don't want to study. That is the immediate problem and that is exactly what you've spent no thinking time on as yet."

Sarle walked to the hall closet and got his coat. Roger went with him. Minutes passed in silence.

Then Roger said without looking up, "Maybe you're right, Jim."

"Maybe I am. Try it and then tell me. Good-by, Roger."

Roger Toomey opened his eyes and blinked at the morning brightness of the bedroom. He called out, "Hey, Jane, where are you?"

Jane's voice answered, "In the kitchen.   Where do you think?"

"Come in here, will you?"

She came in.   "The bacon won't fry itself, you know."

"Listen, did I float last night?"

"I don't know.   I slept."

"You're a help."   He got out of bed and slipped his feet into his mules.   "Still I don't think I did."

"Do you think you've forgotten how?"   There was sudden hope in her voice.

"I haven't forgotten.   See?"   He slid into the dining room on a cushion of air. "I just have a feeling I haven't floated.   I think it's three nights now."

"Well, that's good," said Jane.   She was back at the stove.   "It's just that a month's rest has done you good.   If I had called Jim in the beginning—"

"Oh, please, don't go through that.   A month's rest, my eye.   It's just that last Sunday I made up my mind what to do.   Since then I've relaxed.   That's all there is to it."

"What are you going to do?"

"Every spring Northwestern Tech gives a series of seminars on physical topics. I'll attend."

"You mean, go way out to Seattle?"

"Of course."

"What will they be discussing?"

"What's the difference?   I just want to see Harry Carring."

"But he's the one who called you crazy, isn't he?"

"He did."   Roger scooped up a forkful of scrambled eggs.   "But he's also the best man of the lot."

He reached for the salt and lifted a few inches out of his chair as he did so.   He paid no attention.

He said, "I think maybe I can handle him."

The spring seminars at Northwestern Tech had become a nationally known institution since Harry Carring had joined the faculty.   He was the perennial chairman and lent the proceedings their distinctive tone.   He introduced the speakers, led the questioning periods, summed up at the close of each morning and afternoon session and was the soul of conviviality at the concluding dinner at the end of the week's work.

All this Roger Toomey knew by report.   He could now observe the actual workings of the man.   Professor Carring was rather under the middle height, was dark of complexion and had a luxuriant and quite distinctive mop of wavy brown hair.   His wide, thin-lipped mouth when not engaged in active conversation looked perpetually on the point of a sly smile.   He spoke quickly and fluently, without notes, and seemed always to deliver his comments from a level of superiority that his listeners automatically accepted.

At least, so he had been on the first morning of the seminar.   It was only during the afternoon session that the listeners began to notice a certain hesitation in his remarks.   Even more, there was an uneasiness about him as he sat on the stage during the delivery of the scheduled papers.   Occasionally, he glanced furtively toward the rear of the auditorium.

Roger Toomey, seated in the very last row, observed all this tensely.   His temporary glide toward normality that had begun when he first thought there might be a way out was beginning to recede.

On the Pullman to Seattle, he had not slept.   He had had visions of himself lifting upward in time to the wheel-clacking, of moving out quietly past the curtains and into the corridor, of being awakened into endless embarrassment by the hoarse shouting of a porter.   So he had fastened the curtains with safety pins and had achieved nothing by that; no feeling of security; no sleep outside a few exhausting snatches.

He had napped in his seat during the day, while the mountains slipped past outside, and arrived in Seattle in the evening with a stiff neck, aching bones, and a general sensation of despair.

He had made his decision to attend the seminar far too late to have been able to obtain a room to himself at the Institute's dormitories.   Sharing a room was, of course, quite out of the question.   He registered at a downtown hotel, locked the door, closed and locked all the windows, shoved his bed hard against the wall and the bureau against the open side of the bed; then slept.

He remembered no dreams, and when he awoke in the morning he was still lying within the manufactured enclosure.   He felt relieved.

When he arrived, in good time, at Physics Hall on the Institute's campus, he found, as he expected, a large room and a small gathering.   The seminar sessions were held, traditionally, over the Easter vacation and students were not in attendance. Some fifty physicists sat in an auditorium designed to hold four hundred, clustering on either side of the central aisle up near the podium.

Roger took his seat in the last row, where he would not be seen by casual passers-by looking through the high, small windows of the auditorium door, and where the others in the audience would have had to twist through nearly a hundred eighty degrees to see him.

Except, of course, for the speaker on the platform—and for Professor Carring.

Roger did not hear much of the actual proceedings.   He concentrated entirely on waiting for those moments when Carring was alone on the platform; when only Carring could see him.

As Carring grew obviously more disturbed, Roger grew bolder.   During the final summing up of the afternoon, he did his best.

Professor Carring stopped altogether in the middle of a poorly-constructed and entirely meaningless sentence.   His audience, which had been shifting in their seats for some time stopped also and looked wonderingly at him.

Carring raised his hand and said, gaspingly, "You!   You there!"

Roger Toomey had been sitting with an air of complete relaxation—in the very center of the aisle.   The only chair beneath him was composed of two and a half feet of empty air.   His legs were stretched out before him on the armrest of an equally airy chair.

When Carring pointed, Roger slid rapidly sidewise. By the time fifty heads turned, he was sitting quietly in a very prosaic wooden seat.

Roger looked this way and that, then stared at Carring's pointing finger and rose.

"Are you speaking to me, Professor Carring?" he asked, with only the slightest tremble in his voice to indicate the savage battle he was fighting within himself to keep that voice cool and wondering.

"What are you doing?" demanded Carring, his morning's tension exploding.

Some of the audience were standing in order to see better. An unexpected commotion is as dearly loved by a gathering of research physicists as by a crowd at a baseball game.

"I'm not doing anything," said Roger. "I don't understand you."

"Get out! Leave this hall!"

Carring was beside himself with a mixture of emotions, or perhaps he would not have said that. At any rate, Roger sighed and took his opportunity prayerfully.

He said, loudly and distinctly, forcing himself to be heard over the gathering clamor, "I am Professor Roger Toomey of Carson College. I am a member of the American Physical Association. I have applied for permission to attend these sessions, have been accepted, and have paid my registration fee. I am sitting here as is my right and will continue to do so."

Carring could only say blindly, "Get out!"

"I will not," said Roger. He was actually trembling with a synthetic and self-imposed anger. "For what reason must I get out? What have I done?"

Carring put a shaking hand through his hair. He was quite unable to answer.

Roger followed up his advantage. "If you attempt to evict me from these sessions without just cause, I shall certainly sue the Institute."

Carring said, hurriedly, "I call the first day's session of the Spring Seminars of Recent Advances in the Physical Sciences to a close. Our next session will be in this hall tomorrow at nine in—"

Roger left as he was speaking and hurried away.

There was a knock at Roger's hotel-room door that night. It startled him, froze him in his chair.

"Who is it?" he cried.

The answering voice was soft and hurried. "May I see you?"

It was Carring's voice. Roger's hotel as well as his room number were, of course, recorded with the seminar secretary. Roger had hoped, but scarcely expected, that the day's events would have so speedy a consequence.

He opened the door, said stiffly, "Good evening, Professor Carring."

Carring stepped in and looked about. He wore a very light topcoat that he made no gesture to remove. He held his hat in his hand and did not offer to put it down.

He said, "Professor Roger Toomey of Carson College. Right?" He said it with a certain emphasis, as though the name had significance.

"Yes. Sit down, professor."

Carring remained standing. "Now what is it? What are you after?"

"I don't understand."

"I'm sure you do.   You aren't arranging this ridiculous foolery for nothing.
Are you trying to make me seem foolish or is it that you expect to hoodwink me
into some crooked scheme.   I want you to know it won't work.   And don't try
to use force now.   I have friends who know exactly where I am at this moment.
I'll advise you to tell the truth and then get out of town."

"Professor Carring!   This is my room.   If you are here to bully me, I'll ask
you to leave.   If you don't go, I'll have you put out."

"Do you intend to continue this . . . this persecution?"

"I have not been persecuting you.   I don't know you, sir."

"Aren't you the Roger Toomey who wrote me a letter concerning a case of
levitation he wanted me to investigate?"

Roger stared at the man.   "What letter is this?"

"Do you deny it?"

"Of course I do.   What are you talking about?   Have you got the letter?"

Professor Carring's lips compressed.   "Never mind that.   Do you deny you
were suspending yourself on wires at this afternoon's sessions?"

"On wires?   I don't follow you at all."

"You were levitating!"

"Would you please leave, Professor Carring?   I don't think you're well."

The physicist raised his voice.   "Do you deny you were levitating?"

"I think you're mad.   Do you mean to say I made magician's arrangements in
your auditorium.   I was never in it before today and when I arrived you were
already present.   Did you find wires or anything of the sort after I left?"

"I don't know how you did it and I don't care.   *Do* you deny you were
levitating?"

"Why, of course I do."

"I saw you.   Why are you lying?"

"You saw me levitate?   Professor Carring, will you tell me how that's possible?
I suppose your knowledge of gravitational forces is enough to tell you that true
levitation is a meaningless concept except in outer space.   Are you playing some
sort of joke on me?"

"Good Heavens," said Carring in a shrill voice, "why won't you tell the truth?"

"I am.   Do you suppose that by stretching out my hand and making a mystic
pass . . . so . . . I can go sailing off into air."   And Roger did so, his head
brushing the ceiling.

Carring's head jerked upward, "Ah!   There . . . there—"

Roger returned to earth, smiling.   "You *can't* be serious."

"You did it again.   You just did it."

"Did what, sir?"

"You levitated.   You just levitated.   You can't deny it."

Roger's eyes grew serious.   "I think you're sick, sir."

"I know what I saw."

"Perhaps you need a rest.   Overwork—"

"It was *not* a hallucination."

"Would you care for a drink?"   Roger walked to his suitcase while Carring followed his footsteps with bulging eyes.   The toes of his shoes touched air two inches from the ground and went no lower.

Carring sank into the chair Roger had vacated.

"Yes, please," he said, weakly.

Roger gave him the whiskey bottle, watched the other drink, then gag a bit. "How do you feel now?"

"Look here," said Carring, "have you discovered a way of neutralizing gravity?"

Roger stared.   "Get hold of yourself, professor.   If I had antigravity, I wouldn't use it to play games on you.   I'd be in Washington.   I'd be a military secret. I'd be—   Well, I wouldn't be here!   Surely all this is obvious to you."

Carring jumped to his feet.   "Do you intend sitting in on the remaining sessions?"

"Of course."

Carring nodded, jerked his hat down upon his head and hurried out.

For the next three days, Professor Carring did not preside over the seminar sessions.   No reason for his absence was given.   Roger Toomey, caught between hope and apprehension, sat in the body of the audience and tried to remain inconspicuous.   In this, he was not entirely successful.   Carring's public attack had made him notorious while his own strong defense had given him a kind of David versus Goliath popularity.

Roger returned to his hotel room Thursday night after an unsatisfactory dinner and remained standing in the doorway, one foot over the threshold.   Professor Carring was gazing at him from within.   And another man, a gray fedora shoved well back on his forehead, was seated on Roger's bed.

It was the stranger who spoke.   "Come inside, Toomey."

Roger did so.   "What's going on?"

The stranger opened his wallet and presented a cellophane window to Roger. He said, "I'm Cannon of the F.B.I."

Roger said, "You have influence with the government, I take it, Professor Carring."

"A little," said Carring.

Roger said, "Well, am I under arrest?   What's my crime?"

"Take it easy," said Cannon.   "We've been collecting some data on you, Toomey.   Is this your signature?"

He held a letter out far enough for Roger to see, but not to snatch.   It was the letter Roger had written to Carring which the latter had sent on to Morton.

"Yes," said Roger.

"How about this one?"   The federal agent had a sheaf of letters.

Roger realized that he must have collected every one he had sent out, minus those that had been torn up.   "They're all mine," he said, wearily.

Carring snorted.

Cannon said, "Professor Carring tells us that you can float."

"Float?   What the devil do you mean, float?"

"Float in the air," said Cannon, stolidly.

"Do you believe anything as crazy as that?"

"I'm not here to believe or not to believe, Dr. Toomey," said Cannon. "I'm an agent of the Government of the United States and I've got an assignment to carry out. I'd co-operate if I were you."

"How can I co-operate in something like this? If I came to you and told you that Professor Carring could float in air, you'd have me flat on a psychiatrist's couch in no time."

Cannon said, "Professor Carring has been examined by a psychiatrist at his own request. However, the government has been in the habit of listening very seriously to Professor Carring for a number of years now. Besides, I might as well tell you that we have independent evidence."

"Such as?"

"A group of students at your college have seen you float. Also, a woman who was once secretary to the head of your department. We have statements from all of them."

Roger said, "What kind of statements? Sensible ones that you would be willing to put into the record and show to my congressman?"

Professor Carring interrupted anxiously. "Dr. Toomey, what do you gain by denying the fact that you can levitate? Your own dean admits that you've done something of the sort. He has told me that he will inform you officially that your appointment will be terminated at the end of the academic year. He wouldn't do that for nothing."

"That doesn't matter," said Roger.

"But why won't you admit I saw you levitate?"

"Why should I?"

Cannon said, "I'd like to point out, Dr. Toomey, that if you have any device for counteracting gravity, it would be of great importance to your government."

"Really? I suppose you have investigated my background for possible disloyalty."

"The investigation," said the agent, "is proceeding."

"All right," said Roger, "let's take a hypothetical case. Suppose I admitted I could levitate. Suppose I didn't know how I did it. Suppose I had nothing to give the government but my body and an insoluble problem."

"How can you know it's insoluble?" asked Carring, eagerly.

"I once asked you to study such a phenomenon," pointed out Roger, mildly. "You refused."

"Forget that. Look," Carring spoke rapidly, urgently. "You don't have a position at the moment. I can offer you one in my department as Associate Professor of Physics. Your teaching duties will be nominal. Full time research on levitation. What about it?"

"It sounds attractive," said Roger.

"I think it's safe to say that unlimited government funds will be available."

"What do I have to do? Just admit I can levitate?"

"I know you can. I saw you. I want you to do it now for Mr. Cannon."

Roger's legs moved upward and his body stretched out horizontally at the level of Cannon's head.   He turned to one side and seemed to rest on his right elbow.

Cannon's hat fell backward onto the bed.

He yelled: "He floats."

Carring was almost incoherent with excitement.   "Do you see it, man?"

"I sure see something."

"Then report it.   Put it right down in your report, do you hear me?   Make a complete record of it.   They won't say there's anything wrong with me.   I didn't doubt for a minute that I had seen it."

But he couldn't have been so happy if that were entirely true.

"I don't even know what the climate is like in Seattle," wailed Jane, "and there are a million things I have to do."

"Need any help?" asked Jim Sarle from his comfortable position in the depths of the armchair.

"There's nothing you can do.   Oh, dear."   And she flew from the room, but unlike her husband, she did so figuratively only.

Roger Toomey came in.   "Jane, do we have the crates for the books yet?   Hello, Jim.   When did you come in?   And where's Jane?"

"I came in a minute ago and Jane's in the next room.   I had to get past a policeman to get in.   Man, they've got you surrounded."

"Um-m-m," said Roger, absently.   "I told them about you."

"I know you did.   I've been sworn to secrecy.   I told them it was a matter of professional confidence in any case.   Why don't you let the movers do the packing? The government is paying, isn't it?"

"Movers wouldn't do it right," said Jane, suddenly hurrying in again and flouncing down on the sofa.   "I'm going to have a cigarette."

"Break down, Roger," said Sarle, "and tell me what happened."

Roger smiled sheepishly.   "As you said, Jim, I took my mind off the wrong problem and applied it to the right one.   It just seemed to me that I was forever being faced with two alternatives.   I was either crooked or crazy.   Carring said that flatly in his letter to Morton.   The Dean assumed I was crooked and Morton suspected that I was crazy.

"But supposing I could show them that I could really levitate.   Well, Morton told me what would happen in that case.   Either I would be crooked or the *witness* would be insane.   Morton said that . . . he said that if he saw me fly, he'd prefer to believe himself insane than accept the evidence.   Of course, he was only being rhetorical.   No man would believe in his own insanity while even the faintest alternative existed.   I counted on that.

"So I changed my tactics.   I went to Carring's seminar.   I didn't *tell* him I could float; I showed him, *and then denied I had done it*.   The alternative was clear. I was either lying or he . . . not I, mind you, but *he* . . . was mad.   It was obvious that he would sooner believe in levitation than doubt his own sanity, once he was really put to the test.   All his actions thereafter; his bullying, his trip to Washington, his offer of a job, were all intended only to vindicate his own sanity, not to help me.''

Sarle said, ''In other words you had made your levitation his problem and not your own.''

Roger said, ''Did you have anything like this in mind when we had our talk, Jim?''

Sarle shook his head. ''I had vague notions but a man must solve his own problems if they're to be solved effectively. Do you think they'll work out the principle of levitation now?''

''I don't know, Jim. I still can't communicate the subjective aspects of the phenomenon. But that doesn't matter. We'll be investigating them and that's what counts.'' He struck his balled right fist into the palm of his left hand. ''As far as I'm concerned the important point is that I made them help me.''

''Is it?'' asked Sarle, softly. ''I should say that the important point is that you let them make *you* help *them*, which is a different thing altogether.''

ERIC FRANK RUSSELL

Minor Ingredient

He dragged his bags and cases out of the car, dumped them on the concrete, paid off the driver. Then he turned and looked at the doors that were going to swallow him for four long years.

Big doors, huge ones of solid oak. They could have been the doors of a penitentiary save for what was hand-carved in the center of a great panel. Just a circle containing a four-pointed star. And underneath in small, neat letters the words: "God bless you."

Such a motto in such a place looked incongruous, in fact somewhat silly. A star was all right for a badge, yes. Or an engraved, stylized rocketship, yes. But underneath should have been "Onward, Ever Onward" or "Excelsior" or something like that.

He rang the doorbell. A porter appeared, took the bags and cases into a huge ornate hall, asked him to wait a moment. Dwarfed by the immensity of the place he fidgeted around uneasily, refrained from reading the long roll of names embossed upon one wall. Four men in uniform came out of a corridor, marched across the hall in dead-straight line with even step, glanced at him wordlessly and expressionlessly, went out the front. He wondered whether they despised his civilian clothes.

The porter reappeared, conducted him to a small room in which a wizened, baldheaded man sat behind a desk. Baldhead gazed at him myopically through oldfashioned and slightly lopsided spectacles.

"May I have your entry papers, please." He took them, sought through them, muttering to himself in an undertone. "Umph, umph! Warner McShane for pilot-navigator course and leader commission." He stood up, offered a thin, soft hand. "Glad to meet you, Mr. McShane. Welcome to Space Training College."

"Thank you," said McShane, blank-faced.

"God bless you," said Baldhead. He turned to the waiting porter. "Mr. McShane has been assigned Room Twenty, Mercer's House."

They traipsed across a five-acre square of neatly trimmed grass around which stood a dozen blocks of apartments. Behind them, low and far, could be seen an array of laboratories, engineering shops, test-pits, lecture halls, classrooms and places of yet unknown purpose. Farther still, a mile or more behind those, a model spaceport holding four Earthbound ships cemented down for keeps.

Entering a building whose big lintel was inscribed "Mercer's," they took an elevator to the first floor, reached Room 20.   It was compact, modestly furnished but comfortable.   A small bedroom led off it to one side, a bathroom on the other.

Stacking the luggage against a wall, the porter informed, "Commodore Mercer commands this house, sir, and Mr. Billings is your man.   Mr. Billings will be along shortly."

"Thank you," said McShane.

When the porter had gone he sat on the arm of a chair and pondered his arrival. This wasn't quite as he'd expected.   The place had a reputation equaled by no other in a hundred solar systems.   Its fame rang far among the stars, all the way from here to the steadily expanding frontiers.   The man fully trained by S. T. C. was somebody, really somebody.   The man accepted for training was lucky, the one who got through it was much to be envied.

Grand Admiral Kennedy, supreme commander of all space forces, was a graduate of S. T. C.   So were a hundred more now of formidable rank and importance. Things must have changed a lot since their day.   The system must have been plenty tough long, long ago but had softened up considerably since.   Perhaps the entire staff had been here too long and were suffering from senile decay.

A discreet knock sounded on the door and he snapped, "Come in."

The one who entered looked like visible confirmation of his theory.   A bent-backed oldster with a thousand wrinkles at the corners of his eyes and white muttonchop whiskers sticking grotesquely from his cheeks.

"I am Billings, sir.   I shall be attending to your needs while you are here." His aged eyes turned toward the luggage.   "Do you mind if I unpack now, sir?"

"I can manage quite well for myself, thank you."   McShane stifled a grim smile.   By the looks of it the other stood in more need of helpful service.

"If you will permit me to assist—"

"The day I can't do my own unpacking will be the day I'm paralyzed or dead," said McShane.   "Don't trouble yourself for me."

"As you wish, sir, but—"

"Beat it, Billings."

"Permit me to point out, sir, that—"

"No, Billings, you may not point out," declared McShane, very firmly.

"Very well."   Billings withdrew quietly and with dignity.

Old fusspot, thought McShane.   Heaving a case toward the window, he unlocked it, commenced rummaging among its contents.   Another knock sounded.

"Come in."

The newcomer was tall, stern-featured, wore the full uniform of a commodore. McShane instinctively came erect, feet together, hands stiffly at sides.

"Ah, Mr. McShane.   Very glad to know you.   I am Mercer, your house-master."   His sharp eyes went over the other from head to feet.   "I am sure that we shall get along together very well."

"I hope so, sir," said McShane respectfully.

"All that is required of you is to pay full attention to your tutors, work hard, study hard, be obedient to the house rules and loyal to the college."

"Yes, sir."

"Billings is your man, is he not?"

"Yes, sir."

"He should be unpacking for you."

"I told him not to bother, sir."

"Ah, so he has been here already."   The eyes studied McShane again, hardening slightly.   "And you told him not to bother.   Did he accept that?"

"Well, sir, he tried to argue but I chased him out."

"I see."   Commodore Mercer firmed his lips, crossed the room, jerked open a top drawer.   "You have brought your full kit, I presume.   It includes three uniforms as well as working dress.   The ceremonial uniforms first and second will be suspended on the right and left-hand sides of the wardrobe, jackets over pants, buttons outward."

He glanced at McShane who said nothing.

"The drill uniform will be placed in this drawer and no other, pants at bottom folded twice only, jacket on top with sleeves doubled across breast, buttons uppermost, collar to the left."   He slammed the drawer shut.   "Did you know all that?   And where everything else goes?"

"No, sir," admitted McShane, flushing.

"Then why did you dismiss your man?"

"I thought—"

"Mr. McShane, I would advise you to postpone thinking until you have accumulated sufficient facts to form a useful basis.   That is the intelligent thing to do, is it not?"

"Yes, sir."

Commodore Mercer went out, closing the door gently.   McShane aimed a hearty kick at the wall, muttered something under his breath.   Another knock sounded on the door.

"Come in."

"May I help you now, sir?"

"Yes, Billings, I'd appreciate it if you'd unpack for me."

"With pleasure, sir."

He started on the job, putting things away with trained precision.   His motions were slow but careful and exact.   Two pairs of boots, one of slippers, one of gym shoes aligned on the small shoe rack in the officially approved order.   One crimson lined uniform cloak placed on a hanger, buttons to the front, in center of the wardrobe.

"Billings," said McShane, after a while, "just what would happen to me if I dumped my boots on the window ledge and chucked my cloak across the bed?"

"Nothing, sir."

"Nothing?"   He raised his eyebrows.

"No, sir.   But I would receive a severe reprimand."

"I see."

He flopped into a chair, watched Billings and stewed the matter in his mind. They were a cunning bunch in this place.   They had things nicely worked out.

A tough customer feeling his oats could run wild and take his punishment like a man. But only a louse would do it at the expense of an aged servant.

They don't make officers of lice if they can help it.   So they'd got things nicely organized in such a manner that bad material would reveal itself as bad, the good would show up as good.   That meant he'd have to walk warily and watch his step. For four years.   Four years at the time of life when blood runs hot and surplus energies need an aggressive outlet.

"Billings, when does one eat here?"

"Lunch is at twelve-thirty, sir.   You will be able to hear the gong sound from the dining hall.   If I may say so, sir, you would do well to attend with the minimum of delay."

"Why?   Will the rats get at the food if it has to wait a while?"

"It is considered courteous to be prompt, sir.   An officer and a gentleman is always courteous."

"Thank you, Billings."   He lifted a quizzical eyebrow.   "And just how long have *you* been an officer?"

"It has never been my good fortune, sir."

McShane studied him carefully, said, "If that isn't a rebuke it ought to be."

"Indeed, sir, I would not dream of—"

"When I am rude," interrupted McShane, still watching him, "it is because I am raw.   Newcomers usually are more than somewhat raw.   At such moments, Billings, I would like you to ignore me."

"I cannot do that, sir.   It is my job to look after you.   Besides, I am accustomed to jocularity from young gentlemen."   He dipped into a case, took out a twelve by eight pin-up of Sylvia Lafontaine attired in one small ostrich feather.   Holding it at arm's length, he surveyed it expressionlessly, without twitching a facial muscle.

"Like it?" asked McShane.

Most charming, sir.   However, it would be unwise to display this picture upon the wall."

"Why not?   This is my room, isn't it?"

"Definitely, sir.   I fear me the commodore would not approve."

"What has it got to do with him?   My taste in females is my own business."

"Without a doubt, sir.   But this is an officer's room.   An officer must be a gentleman.   A gentleman consorts only with ladies."

"Are you asserting that Sylvia is no lady?"

"A lady," declared Billings, very, very firmly, "would never expose her bosom to public exhibition."

"Oh, hell!" said McShane, holding his head.

"If I replace it in your case, sir, I would advise you to keep it locked.   Or would you prefer me to dispose of it in the furnace room?"

"Take it home and gloat over it yourself."

"That would be most indecent, sir.   I am more than old enough to be this person's father."

"Sorry, Billings."   He mooched self-consciously around the room, stopped by the window, gazed down upon the campus.   "I've a heck of a lot to learn."

"You'll get through all right, sir.   All the best ones get through.   I know.   I have been here many years.   I have seen them come and watched them go and once in a while I've seen them come back."

"Come back?"

"Yes, sir.   Occasionally one of them is kind enough to visit us.   We had such a one about two months ago.   He used to be in this very house, Room 32 on the floor above.   A real young scamp but we kept his nose to the grindstone and got him through very successful."   The muttonchop whiskers bristled as his face became suffused with pride.   "Today, sir, he is Grand Admiral Kennedy."

The first lectures commenced the following morning and were not listed in the printed curriculum.   They were given in the guise of introductory talks.   Commodore Mercer made the start in person.   Impeccably attired, he stood on a small platform with his authoritative gaze stabbing the forty members of the new intake with such expertness that each one felt himself the subject of individual attention.

"You've come here for a purpose—see that it is achieved . . .   The trier who fails is a far better man than the failure who has not tried . . . We hate to send a man down, but will not hesitate if he lets the college down . . . Get it fixed firmly in your minds that space-navy leadership is not a pleasant game; it is a tough, responsible job and you're here to learn it."

In that strain he carried on, a speech evidently made many times before to many previous intakes.   It included plenty of gunk about keep right on to the end of the road, what shall we do with a drunken sailor, the honor of the Space Service, the prestige of the College, the lights in the sky are stars, glory, glory, hallelujah, and so forth.

After an hour of this he finished with, "Technical knowledge is essential.   Don't make the mistake of thinking it enough to get top marks in technical examinations.   Officers are required to handle men as well as instruments and machines.   We have our own ways of checking on your fitness in that respect."   He paused, said, "That is all from me, gentlemen.   You will now proceed in orderly manner to the main lecture room where Captain Saunders will deal with you."

Captain Saunders proved to be a powerfully built individual with a leathery face, a flattened nose, and an artificial left hand permanently hidden in a glove.   He studied the forty newcomers as though weighing them against their predecessors, emitted a non-committal grunt.

He devoted half an hour to saying most of the things Mercer had said, but in blunter manner.   Then, "I'll take you on a tour to familiarize you with the layout.   You'll be given a book of rules, regulations and conventions; if you don't read them and observe them, you've only yourselves to blame.   Tuition proper will commence at nine-thirty tomorrow morning.   Parade in working dress immediately outside your house.   Any questions?"

Nobody ventured to put any questions.   Saunders led them forth on the tour which occupied the rest of the day.   Conscious of their newness and junior status, they absorbed various items of information in complete silence, grinned apologetically at some six hundred second-, third- and fourth-year men hard at work in laboratories and lecture rooms.

Receiving their books of rules and regulations, they attended the evening meal, returned to Mercer's House.   By this time McShane had formed a tentative friendship with two fellow sufferers named Simcox and Fane.

"It says here," announced Simcox, mooching along the corridor with his book open in his hands, "that we are confined to college for the first month, after which we are permitted to go to town three evenings per week."

"That means we start off with one month's imprisonment," growled Fane. "Just at the very time when we need a splurge to break the ice."

McShane lowered his voice to a whisper.   "You two come to my room.   At least we can have a good gab and a few gripes.   I've a full bottle of whiskey in the cupboard."

"It's a deal," enthused Fane, his face brightening.

They slipped into Room 20, unobserved by other students.   Simcox rubbed his hands together and Fane licked anticipatory lips while McShane went to the cupboard.

"What're we going to use for glasses?" asked Fane, staring around.

"What're we going to use for whiskey?" retorted McShane, straightening up and backing away from the cupboard.   He looked at them, his face thunderous. "It's not here."

"Maybe you moved it and forgot," suggested Simcox.   "Or perhaps your man has stashed it some place where Mercer can't see it."

"Why should he?" demanded Fane, waving his book of rules.   "It says nothing about bottles being forbidden."

"I'd better search the place before I blow my top," said McShane, still grim. He did just that and did it thoroughly.   "It's gone.   Some dirty scut swiped it."

"That means we've a thief in the house," commented Simcox unhappily.   "The staff ought to be told."

Fane consulted his book again.   "According to this, complaints and requests must be taken to the House Proctor, a fourth-year man residing in Room 1."

"All right, watch me dump this in his lap."   McShane bolted out, down the stairs, hammered on the door of Room 1.

"Come in."

He entered.   The proctor, a tall, dark-haired fellow in the mid-twenties, was reclining in a chair, legs crossed, a heavy book before him.   His dark eyes coldly viewed the visitor.

"Your name?"

"Warner McShane."

"Mr. McShane, you will go outside, close the door, knock in a way that credits me with normal hearing, and re-enter in proper manner."

McShane went red.   "I regret to say I am not aware of what you consider the proper manner."

"You will march in at regulation pace, halt smartly, and stand at attention while addressing me."

Going out, McShane did exactly as instructed, blank-faced but inwardly seething. He halted, hands stiffly at sides, shoulders squared.

"That's better," said the proctor.   His gaze was shrewd as he surveyed the other.   "Possibly you think I got malicious satisfaction out of that?"

No reply.

"If so, you're wrong.   You're learning exactly as I learned—the hard way.   An officer must command obedience by example as well as by authority.   He must be willing to give to have the right to receive."   Another pause inviting comment that did not come.   "Well, what's your trouble?"

"A bottle of whiskey has been stolen from my room."

"How do you know that it was stolen?"

"It was there this morning.   It isn't there now.   Whoever took it did so without my knowledge and permission.   That is theft."

"Not necessarily.   Your man may have removed it."

"It's still theft."

"Very well.   It will be treated as such if you insist."   His bearing lent peculiar significance to his final question.   "Do you insist?"

McShane's mind whirled around at superfast pace.   The darned place was a trap.   The entire college was carpeted with traps.   This very question was a trap. Evade it!   Get out of it while the going is good!

"If you don't mind, I'll first ask my man whether he took it and why."

The change in the proctor was remarkable.   He beamed at the other as he said, "I am very glad to hear you say that."

McShane departed with the weird but gratifying feeling that in some inexplicable way he had gained a small victory, a positive mark on his record-sheet that might cancel out an unwittingly-earned negative mark.   Going upstairs, he reached his door, bawled down the corridor, "Billings!   Billings!" then went into his room.

Two minutes passed before Billings appeared.   "You called me, sir?"

"Yes, I did.   I had a bottle of whiskey in the cupboard.   It has disappeared. Do you know anything about it?"

"Yes, sir.   I removed it myself."

"Removed it?"   McShane threw Simcox and Fane a look of half-suppressed exasperation.   "What on earth for?"

"I have obtained your first issue of technical books and placed them on the rack in readiness, sir.   It would be advisable to commence your studies at once, if I may say so."

"Why the rush?"

"The examination at the end of the first month is designed to check on the qualifications that new entrants are alleged to possess.   Occasionally they prove not to the complete satisfaction of the college.   In such a case, the person concerned is sent home as unsuitable."   The old eye acquired a touch of desperation.   "You will have to pass, sir.   It is extremely important.   You will pardon me for saying that an officer can manage without drink when it is expedient to do so."

Taking a deep breath, McShane asked, "Exactly what have you done with the bottle?"

"I have concealed it, sir, in a place reserved by the staff for that purpose."

"And don't I ever get it back?"

Billings was shocked. "Please understand, sir, that the whiskey has been removed and not confiscated. I will be most happy to return it in time for you to celebrate your success in the examination."

"Get out of my sight," said McShane.

"Very well, sir."

When he had gone, McShane told the others, "See what I've got? It's worse than living with a maiden aunt."

"Mine's no better," said Fane gloomily.

"Mine neither," endorsed Simcox.

"Well, what are we going to do about it, if anything?" McShane invited.

They thought it over and after a while Simcox said, "I'm taking the line of least resistance." He raised his tone to passable imitation of a childish treble. "I am going to go home and do my sums because my Nanny will think I'm naughty if I don't."

"Me, too," Fane decided. "An officer and a gentleman, sir, never blows his nose with a ferocious blast. Sometimes the specimen I've got scares hell out of me. One spit on the floor and you're expelled with ignominy."

They ambled out, moody-faced. McShane flung himself into a chair, spent twenty minutes scowling at the wall. Then, becoming bored with that, he reached for the top book in the stack. It was thrillingly titled *"Astromathematical Foundations of Space Navigation."* It looked ten times drier than a bone. For lack of anything else to do, he stayed with it. He became engrossed despite himself. He was still with it at midnight, mentally bulleting through the starwhorls and faraway mists of light.

Billings tapped on the door-panels, looked in, murmured apologetically, "I realized that you are not yet in bed, sir, and wondered whether you had failed to notice the time. It is twelve o'clock. If I may make so bold—"

He ducked out fast as McShane hurled the book at him.

Question Eleven: The motto of the Space Training College is *"God Bless You."* As briefly as possible explain its origin and purpose.

McShane scribbled rapidly. "The motto is based upon three incontrovertible points. Firstly, a theory need not be correct or even visibly sensible; it is sufficient for it to be workable. Secondly, any life form definable as intelligent must have imagination and curiosity. Thirdly, any life form possessed of imagination and curiosity cannot help but speculate about prime causes."

He sharpened his thoughts a bit, went on, "Four hundred years ago a certain Captain Anderson, taking a brief vacation on Earth, stopped to listen to a religious orator who was being heckled by several members of the audience. He noticed that the orator answered every witticism and insult with the words, 'God bless you, brother!' and that the critics lacked an effective reply. He also noted that in a short time the interrupters gave up their efforts one by one, eventually leaving the orator to continue unhampered.''

What next?   He chewed his pen, then, ''Captain Anderson, an eccentric but shrewd character, was sufficiently impressed to try the same tactic on alien races encountered in the cosmos.   He found that it worked nine times out of ten.   Since then it has been generally adopted as a condensed, easily employed and easily understood form of space-diplomacy.''

He looked it over.   Seemed all right but not quite enough.   The question insisted upon brevity but it had to be answered in full, if at all.

''The tactic has not resolved all differences or averted all space wars but it is workable in that it has reduced both to about ten per cent of the potential number. The words 'God bless you' are neither voiced nor interpreted in conventional Earth-terms.   From the cosmic viewpoint they may be said to mean, 'May the prime cause of everything be beneficial to you!' ''

Yes, that looked all right.   He read it right through, felt satisfied, was about to pass on to the next question when a tiny bubble of suspicion lurking deep in his subconscious suddenly rose to the surface and burst with a mentally hearable pop.

The preceding ten questions and the following ones all inquired about subjects on which he was supposed to be informed.   Question Eleven did not.   Nobody at any time had seen fit to explain the college motto.   The examiners had no right to assume that any examinee could answer it.

So why had they asked?   It now became obvious—they were still trapping.

Impelled by curiosity he, McShane, had looked up the answer in the college library, this Holy Joe aspect of space travel being too much to let pass unsolved. But for that he'd have been stuck.

The implication was that anyone unable to deal with Question Eleven would be recognized as lacking in curiosity and disinterested.   Or, if interested, too lazy and devoid of initiative to do anything about it.

He glanced surreptitiously around the room in which forty bothered figures were seated at forty widely separated desks.   About a dozen examinees were writing or pretending to do so.   One was busily training his left ear to droop to shoulder level.   Four were masticating their digits.   Most of the others were feeling around their own skulls as if seeking confirmation of the presence or absence of brains.

The discovery of one trap slowed him up considerably.   He reconsidered all the questions already answered, treating each one as a potential pitfall.   The unanswered questions got the same treatment.

Number Thirty-four looked mighty suspicious.   It was planted amid a series of technical queries from which it stuck out like a Sirian's prehensile nose.   It was much too artless for comfort.   All it said was: In not more than six words define courage.

Well, for better or for worse, here goes.   ''Courage is fear faced with resolution.''

He wiped off the fiftieth question with vast relief, handed in his papers, left the room, wandered thoughtfully around the campus.

Simcox joined him in short time, asked, ''How did it go with you?''

"Could have been worse."

"Yes, that's how I felt about it.   If you don't hit the minimum of seventy-five per cent, you're out on your neck.   I think I've made it all right."

They waited until Fane arrived.   He came half an hour later and wore the sad expression of a frustrated spaniel.

"I got jammed on four stinkers.   Every time there's an exam I go loaded with knowledge that evaporates the moment I sit down."

Two days afterward the results went up on the board.   McShane muscled through the crowd and took a look.

McShane, Warner.   91%.   Pass with credit.

He sprinted headlong for Mercer's House, reached his room with Simcox and Fane panting at his heels.

"Billings!   Hey, Billings!"

"You want me, sir?"

"We got through.   All three of us."   He performed a brief fandango.   "Now's the time.   The bottle, man.   Come on, give with that bottle."

"I am most pleased to learn of your success, sir," said Billings, openly tickled pink.

"Thank you, Billings.   And now's the time to celebrate.   Get us the bottle and some glasses."

"At eight-thirty, sir."

McShane glanced at his watch.   "Hey, that's in one hour's time.   What's the idea?"

"I have readied paper and envelopes on your desk, sir.   Naturally, you will wish to inform your parents of the result.   Your mother especially will be happy to learn of your progress."

"My mother especially?"   McShane stared at him.   "Why not my father?"

"Your father will be most pleased also," assured Billings.   "But generally speaking, sir, mothers tend to be less confident and more anxious."

"That comes straight from one who knows," commented McShane for the benefit of the others.   He returned attention to Billings.   "How long have you been a mother?"

"For forty years, sir."

The three went silent.   McShane's features softened and his voice became unusually gentle.

"I know what you mean, Billings.   We'll have our little party just when you say."

"At eight-thirty to the minute, sir," said Billings.   "I will bring glasses and soda."

He departed, Simcox and Fane following.   McShane brooded out the window for a while, then went to his desk, reached for pen and paper.

"Dear Mother—"

The long, vast, incredibly complicated whirl of four years sufficiently jam-packed to simulate a lifetime.   Lectures, advice, the din of machine-shops, the deafening roar of testpits, banks of instruments with winking lights and flickering needles, starfields on the cinema screen, equations six pages long, ball games, ceremonial parades with bands playing and banners flying, medical check-ups, blood counts, blackouts in the centrifuge, snap questions, examinations.

More examinations, more stinkers, more traps. More lectures each deeper than its predecessor. More advice from all quarters high and low.

"You've got to be saturated with a powerful and potent education to handle space and all its problems. We're giving you a long, strong dose of it here. It's a very complex medicine of which every number of the staff is a part. Even your personal servant is a minor ingredient."

"The moment you take up active service as an officer every virtue and every fault is enlarged ten diameters by those under you. A little conceit then gets magnified into insufferable arrogance."

"The latter half of the fourth year is always extremely wearing, sir. May I venture to suggest that a little less relaxation in the noisiest quarter of town and a little more in bed—"

"You fellows must get it into your heads that it doesn't matter a hoot whether you've practiced it fifty or five hundred times. You aren't good enough until you've reduced it to an instinctive reaction. A ship and a couple of hundred men can go to hell while you're seeking time for thought."

"Even your personal servant is a minor ingredient."

"If I may be permitted the remark, sir, an officer is only as strong as the men who support him."

For the last six months McShane functioned as House Proctor of Mercer's, a dignified and learned figure to be viewed with becoming reverence by young and brash first-year men. Simcox and Fane were still with him but the original forty were down to twenty-six.

The final examination was an iron-cased, red-hot heller. It took eight days.

McShane, Warner. 82%. Pass with credit.

After that, a week of wild confusion dominated by a sense of an impending break, of something about to snap loose. Documents, speeches, the last parade with thudding feet and *oompah-oompah*, relatives crowding around, mothers, brothers, sisters in their Sunday best, bags, cases and boxes packed, cheers, handshakes, a blur of faces saying things not heard. And then an aching silence broken only by the purr of the departing car.

He spent a nervy, restless fortnight at home, kissed farewells with a hidden mixture of sadness and relief, reported on the assigned date to the survey-frigate *Manasca*. Lieutenant McShane, fourth officer, with three men above him, thirty below.

The *Manasca* soared skyward, became an unseeable dot amid the mighty concourse of stars. Compared with the great battleships and heavy cruisers roaming the far reaches she was a tiny vessel—but well capable of putting Earth beyond communicative distance and almost beyond memory.

It was a long, imposing, official-looking car with two men sitting erect in the front, its sole passenger in the back. With a low hum it came up the drive and stopped.   One of the men in front got out, opened the rear door, posed stiffly at attention.

Dismounting, the passenger walked toward the great doors which bore a circled star on one panel.   He was a big man, wise-eyed, gray-haired.   The silver joint under his right kneecap made him move with a slight limp.

Finding the doors ajar, he pushed one open, entered a big hall.   Momentarily it was empty.   For some minutes he studied the long roster of names embossed upon one wall.

Six uniformed men entered from a corridor, marching with even step in two ranks of three.   They registered a touch of awe and their arms snapped up in a sixfold salute to which he responded automatically.

Limping through the hall, he found his way out back, across the campus to what once had been Mercer's House.   A different name, Lysaght's, was engraved upon its lintel now.   Going inside, he reached the first floor, stopped undecided in the corridor.

A middle-aged civilian came into the corridor from the other end, observed him with surprise, hastened up.

"I am Jackson, sir.   May I help you?"

The other hesitated, said, "I have a sentimental desire to look out the window of Room Twenty."

Jackson's features showed immediate understanding as he felt in his pocket and produced a master key.   "Room Twenty is Mr. Cain's, sir.   I know he would be only too glad to have you look around.   I take it that it was once your own room, sir?"

"Yes, Jackson, about thirty years ago."

The door clicked open and he walked in.   For five minutes he absorbed the old, familiar scene.

"Thirty years ago," said Jackson, standing in the doorway.   "That would be in Commodore Mercer's time."

"That's right.   Did you know him?"

"Oh yes, sir."   He smiled deprecatingly.   "I was just a boy message-runner then.   It's unlikely that you ever encountered me."

"Probably you remember Billings, too?"

"Yes, indeed."   Jackson's face lit up.   "A most estimable person, sir.   He has been dead these many years."   He saw the other's expression, added, "I am very sorry, sir."

"So am I."   A pause.   "I never said good-by to him."

"Really, sir, you need have no regrets about that.   When a young gentleman passes his final and leaves us we expect great excitement and a little forgetfulness. It is quite natural and we are accustomed to it."   He smiled reassurance.   "Besides, sir, soon after one goes another one comes.   We have plenty to keep us busy."

"I'm sure you have."

"If you've sufficient time to spare, sir," continued Jackson, "would you care to visit the staff quarters?"

"Aren't they out of bounds?"

"Not to you, sir. We have a modest collection of photographs going back many years. Some of them are certain to interest you."

"I would much like to see them."

They walked downstairs, across to staff quarters, entered a lounge. Carefully Jackson positioned a chair, placed a large album on a table.

"While you are looking through this, sir, may I prepare you some coffee?"

"Thank you, Jackson. It is very kind of you."

He opened the album as the other went to the kitchen. First page: a big photo of six hundred men marching in column of platoons. The saluting-base in the mid-background, the band playing on the left.

The next twenty pages depicted nobody he had known. Then came one of a group of house-masters among whom was Commodore Mercer. Then several clusters of staff members, service and tutorial, among which were a few familiar faces.

Then came a campus shot. One of the figures strolling across the grass was Fane. The last he'd seen of Fane had been twelve years back, out beyond Aldebaran. Fane had been lying in hospital, his skin pale green, his body bloated, but cheerful and on the road to recovery. He'd seen nothing of Fane since that day. He'd seen nothing of Simcox for thirty years and had heard of him only twice.

The middle of the book held an old face with a thousand wrinkles at the corners of its steady, understanding eyes, with muttonchop whiskers on its cheeks. He looked at that one a long time while it seemed to come at him out of the mists of the past.

"If I may say so, sir, an officer and a gentleman is never willfully unkind."

He was still meditating over the face when the sounds of distant footsteps and a rattling coffee tray brought him back to the present.

Squaring his gold-braided shoulders, Fleet Commander McShane said in soft, low tones, "God bless you!"

And turned the page.

WINSTON P. SANDERS

Barnacle Bull

The *Hellik Olav* was well past Mars, acceleration ended, free-falling into the Asteroid Belt on a long elliptical orbit, when the interior radiation count began to rise. It wasn't serious, and worried none of the four men aboard. They had been so worried all along that a little extra ionization didn't seem to matter.

But as the days passed, the Geigers got still more noisy.

And then the radio quit.

This was bad! No more tapes were being made of signals received—Earth to one of the artificial satellites to Phobos to a cone of space which a rather smug-looking computer insisted held the *Hellik Olav*—for later study by electronics engineers. As for the men, they were suddenly bereft of their favorite programs. Adam Langnes, captain, no longer got the beeps whose distortions gave him an idea of exterior conditions and whose Doppler frequency gave him a check on his velocity. Torvald Winge, astronomer, had no answers to his requests for data omitted from his handbook and computations too elaborate for the ship's digital. Per Helledahl, physicist, heard no more sentimental folk songs nor the recorded babblings of his youngest child. And Erik Bull, engineer, couldn't get the cowboy music sent from the American radio satellite. He couldn't even get the Russians' Progressive jazz.

Furthermore, and still more ominous, the ship's transmitter also stopped working.

Helledahl turned from its disassembled guts. Despite all he could do with racks, bags, magnetic boards, he was surrounded by a zero gravity halo of wires, resistances, transistors, and other small objects. His moon face peered through it with an unwonted grimness. "I can find nothing wrong," he said. "The trouble must be outside, in the boom."

Captain Langnes, tall and gaunt and stiff of manner, adjusted his monocle. "I dare say we can repair the trouble," he said. "Can't be too serious, can it?"

"It can like the devil, if the radar goes out too," snapped Helledahl.

"Oh, heavens!" exclaimed Winge. His mild, middle-aged features registered dismay. "If I can't maintain my meteorite count, what am I out here for?"

"If we can't detect the big meteorites in time for the autopilot to jerk us off a collision course, you won't be out here very long," said Bull. "None of us will, except as scrap metal and frozen hamburger."

Helledahl winced. "Must you, Erik?"

"Your attitude is undesirable, Herr Bull," Captain Langnes chided. "Never forget, gentlemen, the four of us, crowded into one small vessel for possibly two years, under extremely hazardous conditions, can only survive by maintaining order, self-respect, morale."

"How can I forget?" muttered Bull. "You repeat it every thirty-seven hours and fourteen minutes by the clock." But he didn't mutter very loudly.

"You had best have a look outside, Herr Bull," went on the captain.

"I was afraid it'd come to that," said the engineer dismally. "Hang on, boys, here we go again."

Putting on space armor is a tedious job at best, requiring much assistance. In a cramped air-lock chamber—for lack of another place—and under free fall, it gets so exasperating that one forgets any element of emergency. By the time he was through the outer valve, Bull had invented three new verbal obscenities, the best of which took four minutes to enunciate.

He was a big, blocky, redhaired and freckle-faced young man, who hadn't wanted to come on this expedition. It was just a miserable series of accidents, he thought. As a boy, standing at a grisly hour on a cliff above the Sognefjord to watch the first Sputnik rise, he had decided to be a spaceship engineer. As a youth, he got a scholarship to the Massachusetts Institute of Technology, and afterward worked for two years on American interplanetary projects. Returning home, he found himself one of the few Norwegians with that kind of experience. But he also found himself thoroughly tired of it. The cramped quarters, tight discipline, reconstituted food and reconstituted air and reconstituted conversation, were bad enough. The innumerable petty nuisances of weightlessness, especially the hours a day spent doing ridiculous exercises lest his very bones atrophy, were worse. The exclusively male companionship was still worse: especially when that all-female Russian satellite station generally called the Nunnery passed within view.

"In short," Erik Bull told his friends, "if I want to take vows of poverty, chastity, and obedience, I'd do better to sign up as a Benedictine monk. I'd at least have something drinkable on hand."

Not that he regretted the time spent, once it was safely behind him. With judicious embroidering, he had a lifetime supply of dinner-table reminiscences. More important, he could take his pick of Earthside jobs. Such as the marine reclamation station his countrymen were building off Svalbard, with regular airbus service to Trondheim and Oslo. *There* was a post!

Instead of which, he was now spinning off beyond Mars, hell for leather into a volume of space that had already swallowed a score of craft without trace.

He emerged on the hull, made sure his life line was fast, and floated a few minutes to let his eyes adjust. A tiny heatless sun, too brilliant to look close to, spotted puddles of undiffused glare among coalsack shadows. The stars, unwinking, needle bright, were so many that they swamped the old familiar constellations in their sheer number. He identified several points as asteroids, some twinkling as rotation exposed their irregular surfaces, some so close that their relative motion was visible. His senses did not react to the radiation, which the ship's magnetic field was supposed to ward off from the interior but which sharply limited his stay outside. Bull imagined all those particles zipping through him, each drilling a neat submicroscopic hole, and wished he hadn't.

The much-touted majestic silence of space wasn't evident either. His air pump made too much noise. Also, the suit stank.

Presently he could make sense out of the view. The ship was a long cylinder, lumpy where meteor bumpers protected the most vital spots. A Norwegian flag, painted near the bows, was faded by solar ultraviolet, eroded by micrometeoric impacts. The vessel was old, though basically sound. The Russians had given it to Norway for a museum piece, as a propaganda gesture. But then the Americans had hastily given Norway the parts needed to renovate. Bull himself had spent six dreary months helping do that job. He hadn't been too unhappy about it, though. He liked the idea of his country joining in the exploitation of space. Also, he was Americanized enough to feel a certain malicious pleasure when the *Ivan Pavlov* was rechristened in honor of St. Olav.

However, he had not expected to serve aboard the thing!

"O.K., O.K.," he sneered in English, "hold still, Holy Ole, and we'll have a look at your latest disease."

He drew himself back along the line and waddled forward over the hull in stickum boots. Something on the radio transceiver boom . . . what the devil? He bent over. The motion pulled his boots loose. He upended and went drifting off toward Andromeda. Cursing in a lackluster voice, he came back hand over hand. But as he examined the roughened surface he forgot even to be annoyed.

He tried unsuccessfully to pinch himself.

An hour convinced him. He made his laborious way below again. Captain Langnes, who was Navy, insisted that you went "below" when you entered the ship, even in free fall. When his spacesuit was off, with only one frost burn suffered from touching the metal, he faced the others across a cluttered main cabin.

"Well?" barked Helledahl. "What is it?"

"As the lady said when she saw an elephant eating cabbages with what she thought was his tail," Bull answered slowly, "if I told you, you wouldn't believe me."

"Of course I would!" said Langnes. "Out with it!"

"Well, skipper . . . we have barnacles."

A certain amount of chemical and biological apparatus had been brought along to study possible effects of the whatever-it-was that seemed to forbid spacecraft crossing the Asteroid Belt. The equipment was most inadequate, and between them the four men had only an elementary knowledge of its use. But then, all equipment was inadequate in zero gravity, and all knowledge was elementary out here.

Work progressed with maddening slowness. And meanwhile the *Hellik Olav* fell outward and outward, on an orbit which would not bend back again until it was three Astronomical Units from the sun. And the ship was out of communication. And the radar, still functional but losing efficiency all the time, registered an ever thicker concentration of meteorites.   And the 'tween-decks radiation count mounted, slowly but persistently.

"I vote we go home," said Helledahl.   Sweat glistened on his forehead, where he sat in his tiny bunk cubicle without touching the mattress.

"Second the motion," said Bull at once.   "Any further discussion?   I move the vote.   All in favor, say, *'Ja.'*   All opposed, shut up."

"This is no time for jokes, Herr Bull," said Captain Langnes.

"I quite agree, sir.   And this trip is more than a joke, it's a farce.   Let's turn back!"

"Because of an encrustation on the hull?"

Surprisingly, gentle Torvald Winge supported the skipper with almost as sharp a tone.   "Nothing serious has yet happened," he said.   "We have now shielded the drive tubes so that the barnacle growth can't advance to them.   As for our communications apparatus, we have spare parts in ample supply and can easily repair it once we're out of this fantastic zone.   Barnacles can be scraped off the radar arms, as well as the vision parts.   What kind of cowards will our people take us for, if we give up at the first little difficulty?"

"Live ones," said Helledahl.

"You see," Bull added, "we're not in such bad shape now, but what'll happen if this continues?   Just extrapolate the radiation.   I did.   We'll be dead men on the return orbit."

"You assume the count will rise to a dangerous level," said Winge.   "I doubt that.   Time enough to turn back, if it seems we have no other hope.   But what you don't appreciate, Erik, is the very real, unextrapolated danger of such a course."

"Also, we seem to be on the track of an answer to the mystery—the whole purpose of this expedition," said Langnes.   "Given a little more data, we should find out what happened to all the previous ships."

"Including the Chinese?" asked Bull.

Silence descended.   They sat in mid-air, reviewing a situation which familiarity cid nothing to beautify.

Observations from the Martian moons had indicated the Asteroid Belt was much fuller than astronomers had believed.   Of course, it was still a rather hard vacuum . . . but one through which sand, gravel, and boulders went flying with indecent speed and frequency.   Unmanned craft were sent in by several nations.   Their telemetering instruments confirmed the great density of cosmic debris, which increased as they swung further in toward the central zone.   But then they quit sending.   They were never heard from again.   Manned ships stationed near the computed orbits of the robot vessels, where these emerged from the danger area, detected objects with radar, panted to match velocities, and saw nothing but common or garden variety meteorites.

Finally the Chinese People's Republic sent three craft with volunteer crews, toward the Belt.   One ship went off course and landed in the Pacific Ocean near San Francisco.   After its personnel explained the unique methods by which they had been persuaded to volunteer, they were allowed to stay.   The scientists got good technical jobs, the captain started a restaurant, and the political commissar went on the lecture circuit.

But the other two ships continued as per instructions. Their transmission stopped at about the same distance as the robot radios had, and they were never seen again either.

After that, the big nations decided there was no need for haste in such expensive undertakings. But Norway had just outfitted her own spaceship, and all true Norwegians are crazy. The *Hellik Olav* went out.

Winge stirred. "I believe I can tell you what happened to the Chinese," he said.

"Sure," said Bull. "They stayed on orbit till it was too late. Then the radiation got them."

"No. They saw themselves in our own situation, panicked, and started back."

"So?"

"The meteorites got them."

"Excuse me," said Langnes, obviously meaning it the other way around. "You know better than that, Professor Winge. The hazard isn't that great. Even at the highest possible density of material, the probability of impact with anything of considerable mass is so low—"

"I am not talking about that, captain," said the astronomer. "Let me repeat the facts *ab initio,* to keep everything systematic, even if you know most of them already.

"Modern opinion holds that the asteroids, and probably most meteorites throughout the Solar System, really are the remnants of a disintegrated world. I am inclined to suspect that a sudden phase change in its core caused the initial explosion—this can happen at a certain planetary mass—and then Jupiter's attraction gradually broke up the larger pieces. Prior to close-range study, it was never believed the asteroidean planet could have been large enough for this to happen. But today we know it must have been roughly as big as Earth. The total mass was not detectable at a distance, prior to space flight, because so much of it consists of small dark particles. These, I believe, were formed when the larger chunks broke up into lesser ones which abraded and shattered each other in collisions, before gravitational forces spread them too widely apart."

"What has this to do with the mess we're in?" asked Bull.

Winge looked startled. "Why . . . that is—" He blushed. "Nothing, I suppose." To cover his embarrassment, he began talking rapidly, repeating the obvious at even greater length:

"We accelerated from Earth, and a long way beyond, thus throwing ourselves into an eccentric path with a semi-major axis of two Astronomical Units. But this is still an ellipse, and as we entered the danger zone, our velocity gained more and more of a component parallel to the planetary orbits. At our aphelion, which will be in the very heart of the Asteroid Belt, we will be moving substantially with the average meteorite. Relative velocity will be very small, or zero. Hence collisions will be rare, and mild when they do occur. Then we'll be pulled back sunward.

By the time we start accelerating under power toward Earth, we will again be traveling at a large angle to the natural orbits.   But by that time, also, we will be back out of the danger zone.

"Suppose, however, we decided to turn back at this instant.   We would first have to decelerate, spending fuel to kill an outward velocity which the sun would otherwise have killed for us.   Then we must accelerate inward.   We can just barely afford the fuel.   There will be little left for maneuvers.   *And* . . . we'll be cutting almost perpendicularly across the asteroidal orbits.   Their full density and velocity will be directed almost broadside to us.

"Oh, we still needn't worry about being struck by a large object.   The probability of that is quite low.   But what we will get is the fifteen kilometer-per-second sandblast of the uncountable small particles.   I have been computing the results of my investigations so far, and arrive at a figure for the density of this cosmic sand which is, well, simply appalling.   Far more than was hitherto suspected.   I don't believe our hull can stand such a prolonged scouring, meteor bumpers or no."

"Are you certain?" gulped Helledahl.

"Of course not," said Winge testily.   "What is certain, out here?   I believe it highly probable, though.   And the fact that the Chinese never came back would seem to lend credence to my hypothesis."

The barnacles had advanced astoundingly since Bull last looked at them.   Soon the entire ship would be covered, except for a few crucial places toilfully kept clean.

He braced his armored self against the reactive push of his cutting torch.   It was about the only way to get a full-grown barnacle loose.   The things melded themselves with the hull.   The flame drowned the sardonic stars in his vision but illuminated the growths.

They looked quite a bit like the Terrestrial marine sort.   Each humped up in a hard conoidal shell of blackish-brown material.   Beneath them was a layer of excreted metal, chiefly ferrous, plated onto the aluminum hull.

I'd hate to try landing through an atmosphere, thought Bull.   Of course, that wouldn't be necessary.   We would go into orbit around Earth and call for someone to lay alongside and take us off . . .   But heading back sunward, we'll have one sweet time controlling internal temperature . . .   No, I can simply slap some shiny paint on.   That should do the trick.   I'd have to paint anyway, to maintain constant radiation characteristics when micrometeorites are forever scratching our metal.   Another chore.   Space flight is nothing but one long round of chores.   The next poet who recites in my presence an ode to man's conquest of the universe can take that universe—every galaxy and every supernova through every last, long light-year—and put . . .

If we get home alive.

He tossed the barnacle into a metal canister for later study.   It was still red hot, and doubtless the marvelously intricate organism within the shell had suffered damage.   But the details of the lithophagic metabolism could be left for professional biologists to figure out.   All they wanted aboard Holy Ole was enough knowledge to base a decision on.

Before taking more specimens, Bull made a circuit of the hull.   There were many hummocks on it, barnacles growing upon barnacles.   The foresection had turned into a hill of shells, under which the radio transceiver boom lay buried. Another could be built when required for Earth approach.   The trouble was, with the interior radiation still mounting—while a hasty retreat seemed impossible—Bull had started to doubt he ever would see Earth again.

He scrubbed down the radar, then paused to examine the spot where he had initially cut off a few dozen samples.   New ones were already burgeoning on the ferroplate left by their predecessors—little fellows with delicate glasslike shells which would soon grow and thicken, becoming incredibly tough.   Whatever that silicate material was, study of it should repay Terrestrial industry.   Another bonanza from the Asteroid Belt, the modern Mother Lode.

"Ha!" said Bull.

It had sounded very convincing.   The proper way to exploit space was not to mine the planets, where you must grub deep in the crust to find a few stingy ore pockets, then spend fabulous amounts of energy hauling your gains home.   No, the asteroids had all the minerals man would ever need, in developing his extra-terrestrial colonies and on Earth herself.   Freely available minerals, especially on the metallic asteroids from the core of the ancient planet.   Just land and help yourself.   No elaborate apparatus needed to protect you from your environment. Just the spaceship and space armor you had to have anyway.   No gravitational well to back down into and climb back out of.   Just a simple thrust of minimum power.

Given free access to the asteroids, even a small nation like Norway could operate in space, with all the resulting benefits to her economy, politics, and prestige. And there was the *Hellik Olav,* newly outfitted, with plenty of volunteers—genuine ones—for an exploratory mission and to hell with the danger.

"Ha!" repeated Bull.

He had been quite in favor of the expedition, provided somebody else went. But he was offered a berth and made the mistake of telling his girl.

"Ohhhh, Erik!" she exclaimed, enormous-eyed.

After six months in space helping to rig and test the ship, Bull could have fallen in love with the Sea Hag.   However, this had not been necessary.   When he had returned to Earth, swearing a mighty oath never to set foot above the stratosphere again, he met Marta.   She was small and blond and deliciously shaped.   She adored him right back.   The only flaw he could find in her was a set of romantic notions about the starry universe and the noble Norwegian destiny therein.

"Oh, oh," he said, recognizing the symptoms.   In haste: "Don't get ideas, now.   I told you I'm a marine reclamation man, from here on forever."

"But this, darling!   This chance!   To be one of the conquerors!   To make your name immortal!"

"The trouble is, I'm still mortal myself."

"The service you can do—to our country!"

"Uh, apart from everything else, do you realize that, uh, even allowing for acceleration under power for part of the distance, I'd be gone for more than two years?"

"I'll wait for you."

"But—"

"Are you *afraid*, Erik?"

"Well, no. But—"

"Think of the Vikings! Think of Fridtjof Nansen! Think of Roald Amundsen!" Bull dutifully thought of all these gentlemen. "What about them?" he asked.

But it was a light summer night, and Marta couldn't imagine any true Norwegian refusing such a chance for deathless glory, and one thing sort of led to another. Before he recovered his wits, Bull had accepted the job.

There followed a good deal of work up in orbit, readying the ship, and a shake-down cruise lasting some weeks. When he finally got pre-departure leave, Bull broke every known traffic law and a few yet to be invented, on the way to Marta's home. She informed him tearfully that she was so sorry and she hoped they would always be good friends, but she had been seeing so little of him and had met someone else but she would always follow his future career with the greatest interest. The someone else turned out to be a bespectacled writer who had just completed a three-volume novel about King Harald Hardcounsel (1015–1066). Bull didn't remember the rest of his furlough very clearly.

A shock jarred through him. He bounced from the hull, jerked to a halt at the end of his life line, and waited for the dizziness to subside. The stars leered.

"Hallo! Hallo, Erik! Are you all right?"

Bull shook his head to clear it. Helledahl's voice, phoned across the life line, was tinny in his earphones. "I think so. What happened?"

"A small meteorite hit us, I suppose. It must have had an abnormal orbit to strike so hard. We can't see any damage from inside, though. Will you check the outer hull?"

Bull nodded, though there was no point in doing so. After he hauled himself back, he needed a while to find the spot of impact. The pebble had collided near the waist of the ship, vaporizing silicate shell material to form a neat little crater in a barnacle hummock. It hadn't quite penetrated to the ferroplate. A fragment remained, trapped between the rough lumps.

Bull shivered. Without that overgrowth, the hull would have been pierced. Not that that mattered greatly in itself. There was enough patching aboard to repair several hundred such holes. But the violence of impact was an object lesson. Torvald Winge was almost certainly right. Trying to cut straight across the Asteroid Belt would be as long a chance as men had ever taken. The incessant bombardment of particles, mostly far smaller than this but all possessing a similar speed, would wear down the entire hull. When it was thin enough to rip apart under stress, no meteor bumpers or patches would avail.

His eyes sought the blue-green glint of Earth, but couldn't find it among so many stars. You know, he told himself, I don't even mind the prospect of dying out here as much as I do the dreariness of it. If we turned around now, and somehow survived, I'd be home by Christmas. I'd only have wasted one extra year in space, instead of more than three—counting in the preparations for this arduous cruise. I'd find me a girl, no, a dozen girls. And a hundred bottles. I'd make up for that year in style, before settling down to do work I really enjoy.

But we aren't likely to survive, if we turn around now.

But how likely is our survival if we keep going—with the radiation shield failing us? And an extra two years on Holy Ole? I'd go nuts!

Judas priest! Was ever a man in such an ugh situation?

Langnes peered at the sheaf of papers in his hand. "I have drafted a report of our findings with regard to the, ah, space barnacles," he said. "I would like you gentlemen to criticize it as I read aloud. We have now accounted for the vanishing of the previous ships—"

Helledahl mopped his brow. Tiny beads of sweat broke loose and glittered in the air. "That doesn't do much good if we also vanish," he pointed out.

"Quite." Langnes looked irritated. "Believe me, I am more than willing to turn home at once. But that is impracticable, as Professor Winge has shown and the unfortunate Chinese example has confirmed."

"I say it's just as impracticable to follow the original orbit," declared Bull.

"I understand you don't like it here," said Winge, "but really, courting an almost certain death in order to escape two more years of boredom seems a trifle extreme."

"The boredom will be all the worse, now that we don't have anything to work toward," said Bull.

The captain's monocle glared at him. "Ahem!" said Langnes. "If you gentlemen are quite through, may I have the floor?"

"Sure," said Bull. "Or the wall or the ceiling, if you prefer. Makes no difference here."

"I'll skip the preamble of the report and start with our conclusions. 'Winge believes the barnacles originated as a possibly mutant life form on the ancient planet before it was destroyed. The slower breakup of the resulting superasteroidal masses gave this life time to adapt to spatial conditions. The organism itself is not truly protoplasmic. Instead of water, which would either boil or freeze in vacuo at this distance from the sun, the essential liquid is some heavy substance we have not been able to identify except as an aromatic compound.' "

"Aromatic is too polite," said Bull, wrinkling his nose. The air purifiers had still not gotten all the chemical stench out.

Langnes proceeded unrelenting: " 'The basic chemistry does remain that of carbon, of proteins, albeit with an extensive use of complex silicon compounds. We theorize the life cycle as follows. The adult form ejects spores which drift freely through space. Doubtless most are lost, but such wastefulness is characteristic of nature on Earth, too. When a spore does chance on a meteorite or an asteroid it can use, it develops rapidly. It requires silicon and carbon, plus traces of other elements; hence it must normally flourish only on stony meteorites, which are, however, the most abundant sort. Since the barnacle's powerful, pseudo-enzymatic digestive processes—deriving their ultimate energy from sunlight—also extract metals where these exist, it must eliminate same, which it does by laying down a plating, molecule by molecule, under its shell. Research into the details of this process should interest both biologists and metallurgists.

" 'The shell serves a double function. To some extent, it protects against ionizing radiation of solar or cosmic origin. Also, being a nonconductor, it can hold a biologically generated static charge, which will cause nearby dust to drift down upon it. Though this is a slow method of getting the extra nourishment, the barnacle is exceedingly long-lived, and can adjust its own metabolic and reproductive rates to the exigencies of the situation. Since the charge is not very great, and he himself is encased in metal, a spaceman notices no direct consequences.

" 'One may well ask why this life form has never been observed before. First, it is doubtless confined to the Asteroid Belt, the density of matter being too low elsewhere. We have established that it is poisoned by water and free oxygen, so no spores could survive on any planet man has yet visited, even if they did drift there. Second, if a meteorite covered with such barnacles does strike an atmosphere, the surface vaporization as it falls will destroy all evidence. Third, even if barnacle-crusted meteorites have been seen from spaceships, they look superficially like any other stony objects. No one has captured them for closer examination.' "

He paused to drink water from a squeeze bottle. "Hear, hear," murmured Bull, pretending the captain stood behind a lectern.

"That's why the unmanned probe ships never were found," said Helledahl. "They may well have been seen, more or less on their predicted orbits, but they weren't recognized."

Langnes nodded. "Of course. That comes next in the report. Then I go on to say: 'The reason that radio transmission ceased in the first place is equally obvious. Silicon components are built into the boom, as part of a transistor system. The barnacles ate them.

" 'The observed increase in internal irradiation is due to the plating of heavy metals laid down by the barnacles. First, the static charges and the ferromagnetic atoms interfere with the powerful external magnetic fields which are generated to divert ions from the ship. Second, primary cosmic rays coming through that same plating produce showers of secondary particles.

" 'Some question may be raised as to the explosive growth rate of barnacles on our hull, even after all the silicon available in our external apparatus had been consumed. The answer involves consideration of vectors. The ordinary member of the Asteroid Belt, be it large or small, travels in an orbit roughly parallel to the orbits of all other members. There are close approaches and occasional collisions, but on the whole, the particles are thinly scattered by Terrestrial standards, isolated from each other. Our ship, however, is slanting across those same orbits, thus exposing itself to a veritable rain of bodies, ranging in size from microscopic to sand granular. Even a single spore, coming in contact with our hull, could multiply indefinitely.' "

"That means we're picking up mass all the time," groaned Bull. "Which means we'll accelerate slower and get home even later than I'd feared."

"Do you think we'll get home at all?" fretted Helledahl. "We can expect the interference with our radiation shield, and the accumulation of heavy atoms, to get worse all the time. Nobody will ever be able to cross the Belt!"

"Oh, yes, they will," said Captain Langnes. "Ships must simply be redesigned. The magnetic screens must be differently heterodyned, to compensate. The radio booms must be enclosed in protective material. Or perhaps—"

"I know," said Bull in great weariness. "Perhaps antifouling paint can be developed. Or spaceships can be careened, God help us. Oh, yes. All I care about is how we personally get home. I can't modify our own magnetic generators. I haven't the parts or the tools, even if I knew precisely how. We'll spin on and on, the radiation worse every hour, till—"

"Be quiet!" snapped Langnes.

"The Chinese turned around, and look what happened to them," underlined Winge. "We must try something different, however hopeless it too may look."

Bull braced his heavy shoulders. "See here, Torvald," he growled, "what makes you so sure the Chinese did head back under power?"

"Because they were never seen again. If they had been on the predicted orbit, or even on a completed free-fall ellipse, one of the ships watching for them in the neighborhood of Earth would have— Oh."

"Yes," said Bull through his teeth. "Would have seen them? How do you know they weren't seen? I think they were. I think they plugged blindly on as they'd been ordered to, and the radiation suddenly started increasing on a steep curve—as you'd expect, when a critical point of fouling up was passed. I think they died, and came back like comets, sealed into spaceships so crusted they looked like ordinary meteorites!"

The silence thundered.

"So we may as well turn back," said Bull at last. "If we don't make it, our death'll be a quicker and cleaner one than those poor devils had."

Again the quietude. Until Captain Langnes shook his head. "No. I'm sorry, gentlemen. But we go on."

"What?" screamed Helledahl.

The captain floated in the air, a ludicrous parody of officerlike erectness. But there was an odd dignity to him all the same.

"I'm sorry," he repeated. "I have a family too, you know. I would turn about if it could be done with reasonable safety. But Professor Winge has shown that that is impossible. We would die anyhow—and our ship would be a ruin, a few bits of worn and crumpled metal, all our results gone. If we proceed, we can prepare specimens and keep records which will be of use to our successors. Us they will find, for we can improvise a conspicuous feature on the hull that the barnacles won't obliterate."

He looked from one to another.

"Shall we do less for our country's honor than the Chinese did for theirs?" he finished.

Well, if you put it that way, thought Bull, yes.

But he couldn't bring himself to say it aloud. Maybe they all thought the same, including Langnes himself, but none was brave enough to admit it. The trouble with us moral cowards, thought Bull, is that we make heroes of ourselves.

I suppose Marta will shed some pretty, nostalgic tears when she gets the news. Ech! It's bad enough to croak out here; but if that bluestocking memorializes me with a newspaper poem about my Viking spirit—

Maybe that's what we should rig up on the hull, so they won't ignore this poor barnacled derelict as just another flying boulder. Make the Holy Ole into a real, old-fashioned, Gokstad type ship. Dragon figurehead, oars, sail . . . shields hung along the side . . . hey, yes! Imagine some smug Russian on an Earth satellite, bragging about how his people were the first into space—and then along comes this Viking ship—

I think I'll even paint the shields. A face on each one, with its tongue out and a thumb to its nose—

Holy hopping Ole!

"Shields!" roared Bull.

"What?" said Langnes through the echoes.

"We're shielded! We can turn back! Right now!"

When the hubbub had died down and a few slide rule calculations had been made, Bull addressed the others.

"It's really quite simple," he said. "All the elements of the answer were there all the time. I'm only surprised that the Chinese never realized it; but then, I imagine they used all their spare moments for socialist self-criticism.

"Anyhow, we know our ship is a space barnacle's paradise. Even our barnacles have barnacles. Why? Because it picks up so much sand and gravel. Now what worried us about heading straight home was not an occasional meteorite big enough to punch clear through the skin of the ship—we've patching to take care of that—no, we were afraid of a sandblast wearing the entire hull paper thin. But we're protected against precisely that danger! The more such little particles that hit us, the more barnacles we'll have. They can't be eroded away, because they're alive. They renew themselves from the very stuff that strikes them. Like a stone in a river, worn away by the current, while the soft moss is always there.

"We'll get back out of the Belt before the radiation level builds up to anything serious. Then, if we want to, we can chisel off the encrustation. But why bother, really? We'll soon be home."

"No argument there," smiled Langnes.

"I'll go check the engines prior to starting up," said Bull. "Will you and Torvald compute us an Earthward course?"

He started for the doorway, paused, and added slowly: "Uh, I kind of hate to say this, but those barnacles are what will really make the Asteroid Belt available to men."

"What?" said Helledahl.

"Sure," said Bull. "Simple. Naturally, we'll have to devise protection for the radio, and redesign the radiation screen apparatus, as the skipper remarked. But under proper control, the barnacles make a self-repairing shield against sand-blast. It shouldn't be necessary to go through the Belt on tedious elliptical orbits. The space miners can take hyperbolic paths, as fast as they choose, in any direction they please.

"I," he finished with emphasis, "will not be among them."

"Where will you be?" asked Winge.

But Erik Bull was already headed aft to his work. A snatch of song, bawled from powerful lungs, came back to the others. They all knew English, but it took them a moment to get the drift.

> *". . . Who's that knocking at my door?"*
> *Said the fair young maiden.*
> *"Oh, it's only me, from over the sea,"*
> *Said Barnacle Bill the sailor.*
> *"I've sailed the seas from shore to shore,*
> *I'll never sail the seas no more.*
> *Now open up this blank-blank door!"*
> *Said Barnacle Bill the sailor.*

LLOYD BIGGLE, JR.

Monument

It came to O'Brien quite suddenly that he was dying.

He was lying in a sturdy, woven-vine hammock, almost within reach of the flying spray where the waves broke in on the point. The caressing warmth of the sun filtered through the ragged *sao* trees. The shouts of the boys spearing fish off the point reached him fitfully on playful gusts of fragrant wind. A full gourd hung at his elbow. He had been half-dozing in a drowsy state of peaceful contentment when the realization snapped coldly across his idle thoughts and roused him to icy wakefulness.

He was dying.

The fact of death disturbed him less than the realization that he should have thought of it sooner. Death was inevitable from the instant of birth, and O'Brien was a long lifetime from babyhood. He wondered, sometimes, just how old he might be. Certainly a hundred, perhaps even a hundred and fifty. In this dreamy land, where there were no seasons, where the nights were moist and the days warm and sunny, where men measured age by wisdom, it was difficult to keep an alert finger on the elusive pulse of time. It was impossible.

But O'Brien did not need a calendar to tell him he was an old man. The flaming-red hair of his youth had faded to a rusty gray. His limbs were stiff each morning from the night's dampness. The solitary hut he had built on the lovely rise of ground above the point had grown to a sprawling village, as his sons, and grandsons and great-grandsons, and now great-great grandsons, brought home their wives. It was the village of *langru,* the village of fire-topped men, already famous, already a legend. Maidens were eager to mate with the young men of fire, whether their hair was red or the native blond. The sturdiest youths came to court the daughters of fire, and many of them defied tradition and settled in the village of their wives.

O'Brien had enjoyed a good life. He knew he had lived far beyond the years that would have been his in the crazed rush of a civilized land. But he was dying, and the great dream that had grown until it shaped his life among these people was beyond his reach.

He jerked erect, shook his fist at the sky, and shouted hoarsely in a long-unused language. "What are you waiting for? What are you waiting for?"

As soon as O'Brien appeared on the beach, a dozen boys came splashing towards him. "Langri!" they shouted. "Langri!"

They leaped about him excitedly, holding up fish for his approval, waving their spears, laughing and shouting. O'Brien pointed up the beach, where a large dugout canoe was drawn up on the sand.

"To the Elder," he said.

"Ho! To the Elder! Ho! To the Elder!"

They raced ahead of him, scrambling furiously for places because the canoe would not hold them all. O'Brien waded into the melee, restored order, and told off the six he wanted for paddlers. The others raced into the surf after the canoe, swimming around and under it until the paddlers got up speed.

The boys shouted a song as they dipped their paddles—a serious song, for this was serious business. The Langri wished to see the Elder, and it was their solemn duty to make haste.

O'Brien leaned back wearily and watched the foam dancing under the outriggers. He had little taste for traveling, now that his years were relentlessly overtaking him. It was pleasant to lounge in his hammock with a gourd of fermented fruit juice, acting the part of a venerable oracle, respected, even worshipped. When he was younger he had roamed the length and breadth of this world. He had even built a small sailing boat and sailed completely around it, with the only tangible result being the discovery of a few unlikely islands. He had trekked tirelessly about the lone continent, mapping it and speculating on its resources.

He knew that he was a simple man, a man of action. The natives' awe of his supposedly profound wisdom alarmed and embarrassed him. He found himself called upon to settle complex sociological and economic problems, and because he had seen many civilizations and remembered something of what he had seen, he achieved a commendable success and enjoyed it not at all.

But O'Brien knew that the sure finger of doom was pointing directly at this planet and its people, and he had pondered, and debated with himself on long walks along the sea, and paced his hut through the hours of misty night while he devised stratagems, and finally he was satisfied. He was the one man in the far-flung cosmos who could possibly save this world that he loved, and these people he loved, and he was ready to do it. He could do it, if he lived.

And he was dying.

The afternoon waned and evening came on. Fatigue touched the boys' faces and the singing became strained, but they worked on tirelessly, keeping their rhythm. Miles of coast drifted by, and scores of villages, where people recognized the Langri and crowded the shore to wave.

Dusk was hazing the distant sea and purpling the land when they made the turn into a shallow bay and rode the surf up onto a wide, sloping beach studded with canoes. The boys leaped up and heaved the canoe far up onto the beach. They slumped to the sand in exhaustion, and bounced up a moment later, beaming with pride. They would be guests of honor, tonight, at any hut in the village they chose to visit. Had they not brought the Langri?

They moved through the village in a procession that gained in numbers with each hut they passed. Respectful adults and awed children stepped forth and solemnly followed after O'Brien.   The Elder's hut was apart from the others, at the top of the hill, and the Elder stood waiting there, a smile on his wrinkled face, his arms upraised.   Ten paces away O'Brien stopped and raised his own arms.   The villagers watched silently.

"I greet you," O'Brien said.

"Your greetings are as welcome as yourself."

O'Brien stepped forward, and they clasped hands.   This was not a native form of greeting, but O'Brien used it with the older men who were almost life-long friends.

"I ordered a feast in the hope that you would come," the Elder said.

"I came in the hope there would be a feast," O'Brien returned.

With the formalities thus satisfied, the villagers began to drift away, murmuring approval.   The Elder took O'Brien's arm and led him past the hut, to a small grove of trees where the hammocks hung.   They stood facing each other.

"Many days have passed," the Elder said.

"Many," O'Brien agreed.

He looked at his friend closely.   The Elder's tall, gaunt frame seemed as sturdy as ever, but his hair was silvery white.   The years had traced lines in his face, and more years had deepened them, and dimmed the brightness in his eyes.   Like O'Brien, he was old.   He was dying.

They settled themselves in the hammocks, and lay facing each other.   A young girl brought gourds to them, and they sipped the drink and rested in silence as the darkness closed in.

"The Langri is no longer a traveler," the Elder said.

"The Langri travels when the need arises," O'Brien said.

"Let us then talk of that need."

"Later.   After we have eaten.   Or tomorrow—tomorrow would be better."

"Tomorrow, then," the Elder said.

The girl returned with pipes and a glowing coal, and they smoked in silence while fires leaped high in the darkness and the rippling night breeze brought the savory odors of the coming feast blended with the crisp sea air.   They finished their pipes and solemnly took their places of honor.

In the morning they walked together along the shore, and seated themselves on a knoll overlooking the sea.   Sweet-scented blossoms crowded up around them, nodding in the wind.   The morning light sparkled brightly on the leaping water. Brightly-colored sails of the fishing fleet were pinned flower-like to the horizon. To their left, the village rested sleepily on the side of the hill, with only three thin plumes of smoke drifting upwards.   Small boys romped in the surf, or walked timidly along the beach to stare up at the Elder and the Langri.

"I am an old man," O'Brien said.

"The oldest of old men," the Elder agreed promptly.

O'Brien smiled wanly.   To a native, *old* meant *wise*.   The Elder had paid him the highest of compliments, and he felt only frustrated—weary.

"I am an old man," he said again, "and I am dying."

The Elder turned quickly.

"No man lives forever," O'Brien said.

"True. And the man who fears death dies of fear."

"My fear is not for myself."

"The Langri has no need to fear for himself. But you spoke of a need."

"Your need. The need of all your people, and of my people."

The Elder nodded slowly. "As always, we listen well when the Langri speaks."

"You remember," O'Brien said, "that I came from afar, and stayed because the ship that brought me could fly no more. I came to this land by chance, because I had lost my way, and because my ship had a serious sickness."

"I remember."

"Others will come. And then others, and then more others. There will be good men and bad, but all will have strange weapons."

"I remember," the Elder said. "I was there when you slew the birds."

"Strange weapons," O'Brien repeated. "Our people will be helpless. The men from the sky will take this land—whatever they want of it. They will take the beaches and even the sea, the mother of life itself. They will push our people back to the hills, where they will not know how to live. They will bring strange sickness to our people, so that entire villages lie in the fire of death. Strangers will fish the waters and swim. There will be huts taller than the tallest trees and the strangers that crowd the beaches will be thicker than the fish that run off the point. Our own people will be no more."

"You know this to be true?"

O'Brien inclined his head. "It will not happen this day, or the next, but it will happen."

"It is a terrible need," the Elder said quietly.

O'Brien inclined his head again. He thought, *This lovely, unspoiled land, this wonderful, generous, beautiful people* . . . A man was so helpless when he was dying.

They sat in silence for a time, two old men in the bright sunshine, waiting for the darkness. O'Brien reached out and plucked the blossoms near him, one at a time, and crushed their fragile whiteness in his hands.

The Elder turned a grave face on O'Brien. "Cannot the Langri prevent this thing?"

"The Langri can prevent it," O'Brien said, "if the men from the sky come this day or the next. If they delay longer, the Langri cannot prevent it, because the Langri is dying."

"Now I understand. The Langri must show us the way."

"The way is strange and difficult."

"We shall do what we must do."

O'Brien shook his head. "The way is difficult. Our people may not be able to follow, or the path the Langri chooses may be the wrong one."

"What does the Langri require?"

O'Brien stood up. "Send the young men to me, four hands at a time. I will choose the ones I need."

"The first will come to you this day."

O'Brien gripped his hand, and moved quickly away.   His six great-great grandsons were waiting for him on the beach.   They hoisted the sail, for the wind was
at their back on the return trip.   O'Brien looked back as they moved swiftly out
of the bay.   The Elder stood motionless on the knoll, hands upraised, as long as
O'Brien could see him.

O'Brien did not know the official names of the planet, or even if it had an official
name.   He was only a dumb mechanic, but a good one, and he had been knocking
around in space since he was twelve.   He had gotten tired being the bottom rung
of everyone's ladder, so he had gotten himself a battered government surplus survey
ship, and scraped together some supplies, and given a dispatcher five hundred
credits to be looking the other way when he took off.

He had no right to be piloting a spaceship or any other kind of ship, but he'd
seen it done enough to think he knew the fundamentals.   The ship had a perverse
streak that matched his own.   He had to exhaust his profanity and kick the control
panel a few times before it would settle down and behave itself.   Pointing it in
the right direction was another matter.   Probably any bright high school kid knew
more about navigation than he did, and his only support came from an out-of-date
"Simplified Astrogation for the Layman."   He was lost ninety per cent of the
time and only vaguely aware of his whereabouts the other ten per cent, but it didn't
matter.

He wanted to see some places that were off the usual space lines, and maybe do
a little prospecting, and enjoy being his own boss as long as his supplies lasted.
He couldn't stop at any of the regular ports, because the authorities would take one
look at his nonexistent license and ground him permanently.   But some of the
smaller, privately owned ports were always in need of a good mechanic, and he
could slip in for a night landing, work a couple of weeks until he'd earned enough
to get his ship restocked, and slip back into space without exciting anyone.

He did his prospecting, too, nosing about on dozens of asteroids and moons and
small planets that were either undiscovered or forgotten.   Quite inexplicably he
struck it rich.   He stuffed his little ship with platinum ore and started back to
civilization to realize his fortune.

As usual he was lost, and he wandered aimlessly through space for a month,
conserving his fuel and nursing his worn engines.   This planet had seemed his
best chance, and it was almost his last chance because a faulty fuel gauge misled
him, and he ran out of fuel and crashed on landing.

The natives made him welcome.   He became a hero by turning his flaming
pistol on a large species of bird that sometimes preyed on children.   He used up
all of his magazines, but he rendered the bird extinct.   He explored the lone
continent, and found deposits of coal and some metals—insignificant, but enough
to lead the natives immediately into a bronze age.   Then he turned to the sea, gave
the canoes outriggers and sails, and continued his exploring.

By that time he had lost interest in being rescued.   He was the Langri.   He
had his wives and his chidren.   His village was growing.   He could have been

the Elder at a relatively young age, but the idea of him, an alien, ruling these people seemed repugnant to him.   His refusal enhanced the natives' respect for him.   He was happy.

He also began to worry.   The planet had such scanty natural resources that no one would be attracted to it by prospective plunder.   It had another resource that rendered it priceless.

It was a beautiful world.   Its beaches were smooth and sandy, its waters were warm, its climate admirable.   To the people of the myriads of harsh worlds whose natural riches attracted large populations, dry worlds, barren worlds, airless worlds, it would be a paradise.   Those who could leave their bleak atmosphere domes, or underground caverns, or sand-blown villages for a few days in this sweet-smelling, oxygen rich atmosphere could face their lives with renewed courage.

Luxury hotels would line the beaches.   Lesser hotels, boarding houses, cottages would press back into the forest.   Millionaires would indulge in spirited bidding for choice stretches of beach on which to locate their mansions.   The beaches would be choked with vacationers.   Ships would offer relaxing sea cruises.   Undersea craft would introduce the vacationers to the fantastically rich marine life. Crowded wharves would harbor fishing boats for hire.   Industries would grow up to supply the tourists.   It would be a year-round business because the climate was delightful the year around.   A multibillion credit business.

The natives, of course, would be crowded out.   Exterminated.   There were laws to protect the natives, and an impressive colonial bureau to enforce them, but O'Brien knew too well how such laws worked.   The little freebooter who tried to pick up a few quick credits received a stiff fine and a prison term.   The big-money operators incorporated, applied for charters, and indulged in a little good-natured bribery.   Then they went after their spoils under the protection of the very laws that were supposed to protect the natives.

And a century or two later scholars would be bemoaning the loss of the indigenous population.   "They had a splendid civilization.   It's a pity.   It really is."

The young men came from all the villages.   They swung lightly down the coast with flashing paddles and rollicking songs.   Twenty at a time they came, tall, bronze, their blond hair bleached white by their days in the sun.   They beached their canoes along the point, and moved with awed reverence into the presence of the Langri.

His questions startled them.   They grappled awkwardly with strange ideas. They struggled to repeat unutterable sounds.   They underwent tests of strength and endurance.   They came and went, and others took their places, and finally O'Brien had chosen a hundred.

Back in the forest O'Brien built a new village.   He moved in with his hundred students, and began his teaching.   The days were too few and too short, but they worked from dawn until darkness, and often far into the night, while the other natives loyally brought food, and the villages in turn sent women to prepare it, and the entire people watched and wondered and waited.

O'Brien taught what he knew, and improvised when he had to.   He taught language and law and science.   He taught economics and sociology and military discipline.   He taught guerrilla warfare and colonial procedure.   He taught the history of the people of the galaxy, and the young natives sat under the stars at night and stared open-mouthed at the heavens while O'Brien told of flaming space wars and fantastic creatures and worlds beyond worlds.

The days passed, and became a year, and two years, and three.   The young men brought wives to the village.   The young couples called O'Brien father, and brought their first born for his blessing.   And the teaching went on, and on.

O'Brien's strength waned.   The damp nights left him feverish, and his swollen limbs tormented him.   But he labored on, and he began to teach the Plan.   He ordered practice invasion alerts, and his grim seriousness startled the natives of other villages out of their gay indolence.   The Plan slowly took on form and understanding.

When finally O'Brien was too weak to leave his hammock he gathered the most brilliant youths about him and the lessons continued.

One bright afternoon O'Brien lost consciousness.   He was carried back to his village, to his favorite grove near the sea.   Word went out along the shore: the Langri is dying.   The Elder came, and the head men of all the villages.   They placed a woven canopy over his hammock, and he lived on through the night, unconscious and breathing laboriously, while the natives waited humbly with heads bowed.

It was morning when he opened his eyes.   The sea was lovely in the soft sunlight, but he missed the shouts of the boys rollicking in the surf.   *They know I'm dying,* he thought.

He looked at the saddened faces of the men about him.   "Friends . . ." he said. And then, in a tongue that was strange to them, he whispered, "before God— before my God and theirs—I have done my best."

The fire of death leaped high on the beach that night, and the choked silence of mourning gripped the villages.   The next day the hundred young men moved back to their village in the forest to grapple doubtfully with the heritage the Langri had left to them.

II

The *Rirga* was outbound on a routine patrol mission, and Commander Ernst Dillinger was relaxing quietly in his quarters with his robot chess player.   He had neatly trapped the robot's queen, and was moving in for the kill when his communications officer interrupted.

He saluted, and handed Dillinger a message.   "Confidential," he said.

Dillinger knew from his apologetic manner and the speed with which he made his departure that the news was not good.   The man was already closing the door when Dillinger glanced at the message and uncoiled himself in an anguished bellow. The bellow brought him scurrying back.

Dillinger tapped the paper.   "This is an order from the sector governor."

"Yes, sir." The communications officer made it sound as if that information was somehow news to him.

"Ships of the fleet do not take orders from bureaucrats and fly-by-night politicians. You will kindly inform his highness that I received my orders from Fleet Headquarters, that I am currently on a third-priority assignment, and that the fact that I am passing through one corner of his alleged territory does not give him automatic control over my movements."

The communications officer fumbled, and produced a notebook. "If you will dictate the message, sir—"

"I just gave you the message. You're a communications officer. Haven't you got enough command of language to tell him to go to hell in a flattering way?"

"I suppose so, sir."

"Do so. And send Lieutenant Protz in here."

The communications officer made a panicky exit.

Lieutenant Protz sauntered in a moment later, met Dillinger's foreboding scowl with a grin, and calmly seated himself.

"What sector are we in, Protz?" Dillinger asked.

"2397," Protz said promptly.

"And how long are we going to be in Sector 2397?"

"Forty-eight hours."

Dillinger slammed down the message. "Too long."

"Some colony in trouble?"

"Worse than that. The sector governor has lost four scratchers."

Protz straightened up and swallowed his grin. "By all that's spaceworthy! Four of them? Look—I have a leave coming up next year. I'm sorry I won't be able to see you through this, but I wouldn't give up that leave if it were a dozen scratchers. You'll just have to find them without me."

"Shut up!" Dillinger snarled. "Not only does this oaf of a governor lose four survey ships at one crack, but he has the insufferable nerve to order me to start looking for them. *Order*, mind you. I'm letting him know that we have a chain-of-command procedure in the space navy, but he'll have time to get through to headquarters and have the order issued there. They'll be happy to oblige, of course, as long as the *Rirga* is in the general area."

Protz reached over and took the paper. "So they send a battle cruiser to look for four survey ships." He read, and chuckled. "It could be worse. We might find them all in the same place. The 719 turned up missing, so they sent the 1123 to look for it. And then they sent the 572 after the 719 and the 1123, and the 1486 after the 719 and the 1123 and the 572. Lucky thing for them we happened to be here. That nonsense could have gone on indefinitely."

Dillinger nodded. "Seems curious, doesn't it?"

"We can rule out mechanical failure. Those scratchers are dependable, and four of them wouldn't bubble out at the same time. Do you suppose maybe one of these worlds is civilized to the point of primitive space travel, and is picking them off?"

"Possibly," Dillinger said. "But not very likely. Not more than a tenth of the planets in this sector have been surveyed, but the entire sector has been charted, and the fleet used it for training maneuvers a couple of times.   If one of these worlds has developed space travel, someone would have noticed it.   No—I figure we'll find all four scratchers on one planet.   The same trouble that caught the first caught the others.   Whether we can do good remains to be seen.   An unsurveyed world can offer some queer kinds of trouble.   Go down to the chart room, and see if you can narrow down the search area.   We might even be lucky.''

Twenty-four hours later Fleet Headquarters made it official, and the *Rirga* altered course.   Protz paced the chart room, whistling cheerfully and making deft calculations on a three-dimensional slide rule.   A technician was verifying them on a battery of computers, and having trouble keeping up.

Dillinger scowled at the co-ordinates Protz handed to him.   "You figure this system is as good a bet as any?''

"Better than any.''   Protz stepped to the chart.   "The 719 last reported in from here, on course—so.   There are three possibilities, but only this one is directly on its course.   I'd say it's ten to one that this is it.   There shouldn't be more than one habitable planet.   We can wind this up in a couple of days.''

Dillinger snorted.   "Only one planet to search for four scratchers!   You've been in space too long.   Have you forgotten how big a planet is?''

"Like you said, we might be lucky.''

They were lucky.   There was one habitable planet, with a single, narrow, subtropical continent.   On their first observation they sighted the four glistening survey ships, parked neatly in a row on a low rise overlooking the sea.

Dillinger studied the observation data, squinted at the film strips, and exploded.   "Damn!   This will cost us a week, anyway, and those fools have just taken some time off to go fishing.''

"We'll have to land," Protz said.   "We can't be certain.''

Dillinger looked up from the film strips, a faint smile on his face.   "Sure we'll land.   Take a good look at these.   We'll land, and after I kick those scratcher crews in the pants, *I'm* going fishing.''

The *Rirga* came ponderously to rest a thousand yards down the shore.   There were the inevitable scientific tests.   A security unit made a meticulous search of the landing area, and dispatched a squad to investigate the survey ships under cover of the alert *Rirga* gunners.   Dillinger strode down the ramp, sniffed the sea breeze hungrily, and headed towards the beach.

Protz came up a moment later.   "The scratchers are deserted.   Looks as if they just walked off and left them.''

"We'll have to root them out,'' Dillinger said.   "Notify headquarters.''

Protz hurried away.

Dillinger walked slowly back to the *Rirga*. The landing area was being consolidated.   Patrols were pushing inland and along the shore.   One signaled the discovery of a deserted native village.   Dillinger shrugged indifferently, and went to his quarters.   He poured himself a drink and stretched out on his bunk, wondering if there was anything on board that would pass for fishing equipment.

Protz's voice snapped out of the intercom.   "Commander?"

"I'm relaxing," Dillinger said.

"We've found a native."

"The *Rirga* should be able to cope with one native without harassing its commanding officer."

"Maybe I should say the native found us.   He wants to speak to the commanding officer."

Dillinger's reflexes were slow.   It was a full ten seconds before he sat up abruptly, spilling his drink.

"He speaks Galactic," Protz said.   "They're bringing him in now.   What shall we do with him?"

"Set up a tent.   I'll receive him with due ceremony."

A short time later, resplendent in a ribbon-decked dress uniform, he hurried down the ramp.   The tent had been set up, and an honor guard posted around it.   The men were, it seemed to Dillinger, struggling to keep their faces straight.   A moment later he understood why.   The native was a model of bodily perfection, young, intelligent-looking.   He wore only a loin cloth of doubtful manufacture.   His red hair was dazzling in the bright sunlight.

Standing before him in full dress uniform, Dillinger saw the humor of the occasion, and smiled.   The native stepped forward, his face serious, his manner confident.   He extended his hand.   "How do you do.   I am Fornri."

"I am Commander Dillinger," Dillinger responded, almost automatically.   He stepped ceremoniously aside, and allowed the native to precede him into the tent. Dillinger, and a number of his officers, filed after him.

The native ignored the chairs, and faced Dillinger.   "It is my sad duty to inform you that you and the personnel of your ship are under arrest."

Dillinger sat down heavily.   He turned to Protz, who grinned and winked. Behind him an officer failed to suppress a chuckle.   Because the native had spoken in a firm tone of voice, his words carried beyond the tent.   Much whispering and some ill-concealed laughter drifted in to them.

A red-headed native who possessed not so much as a dull spear had calmly walked in and placed the *Rirga* under arrest.   It was a gag worth retelling—if anyone would believe it.

Dillinger ignored Protz's wink.   "What are the charges?"

The native recited tonelessly, "Landing in a restricted area, willful avoidance of customs and quarantine, failure to land at a proper immigration point with official clearance, suspicion of smuggling, and bearing arms without proper authority. Follow me, please, and I will lead you to your detention area."

Protz was suddenly solemn.   "He didn't learn to speak Galactic like that from the scratcher crews," he whispered.   "It's only been a month since the first ship was reported missing."

Dillinger whirled on the officers that surrounded him.   "You will kindly stop grinning.   This is a serious matter."

The grinning stopped.

"You see, you idiots, this man represents civil authority.   Unless there are special arrangements to the contrary, military personnel are subject to the laws of any planet which has a central government.   If there are several autonomous governments . . ."   He turned to the native.   "Does this planet have a central government?"

"It does," the native said.

"Do you have the personnel of the survey ships under detention?"

"We do."

"Order all personnel back to the ship," Dillinger said to Protz.   He said to the native, "You understand—I'll have to communicate with my superiors about this."

"On two conditions.   All weapons which have been brought from the ship are considered confiscated.   And no one except yourself will be permitted to return to the ship."

Dillinger turned to Protz.   "Have the men stack their arms at a place he designates."

Eight days passed before Dillinger was able to get down to final negotiations. Before the conference started he asked to speak with one of the survey men.   Natives brought him into the tent, tanned, robust-looking, wearing a native loin cloth.   He grinned sheepishly at Dillinger.

"I'm almost sorry to see you, commander."

"How have you been treated?"

"Perfect.   Couldn't ask for better treatment.   The food is wonderful.   They have a drink that I'll swear is the best thing in the galaxy.   They built us some huts on the seashore, and told us where we could go and what we could do, and left us alone.   Except for the ones that bring our food, and some fishing boats, we hardly see any natives."

"Three native women apiece, I suppose," Dillinger said dryly.

"Well, no.   The women haven't come near us.   Otherwise, if you're thinking of naming this planet you can call it Paradise.   We've been mostly swimming and spearing fish.   You should see the fish in that ocean!"

"You weren't harmed?"

"No.   They took us by surprise, and disarmed us, and that was it.   Same went for the other ships."

"That's all I want to know," Dillinger said.

The natives led him away, and Dillinger opened the negotiations.   He sat on one side of a table, flanked by two of his officers.   Fornri and two other young natives faced him across the table.

"I am authorized," Dillinger said, "to accept unconditionally your listing of fines and penalties.   Four hundred thousand credits have been transferred to the credit of your government in the Bank of the Galaxy."   He passed a credit memo across the table.   Fornri accepted it indifferently.

"This planet's status as an independent world will be recognized," Dillinger went on.   "Its laws will be respected by the Galactic Federation and enforceable in Federation courts where Federation citizens are involved.   We shall furnish your government with a communications center, so that contact with the Federation can be maintained, and ships wishing to land may obtain official permission.

"In return, we shall expect immediate release of personnel, return of equipment, and departure clearance for Federation ships."

"That is satisfactory," Fornri said.   "Providing, of course, that the terms of the agreement are in writing."

"It will be taken care of immediately," Dillinger said.   He hesitated, feeling a bit uneasy.   "You understand—this means that you must return all weapons which you have confiscated, both from the *Rirga* and the survey ships."

"I understand," Fornri said.   He smiled.   "We are a peaceful people.   We do not need weapons."

Dillinger took a deep breath.   For some reason he had expected the negotiations to collapse at that point.   "Lieutenant Protz," he said, "will you see that the terms are drawn up for signature?"

Protz nodded, and got to his feet.

"One moment," Dillinger said.   "There is one thing more.   We must have an official name for your planet.   What do you call it?"

Fornri seemed puzzled.   "Sir?"

"Up to now, you have only been co-ordinates and a number to us.   You must have a name.   It is probably best that you name your own planet.   If you don't, someone else will, and you might not like it.   It can be your native name for the planet, or a descriptive term—anything you like."

Fornri hesitated.   "Perhaps we should discuss the matter."

"By all means," Dillinger said.   "But one word of caution.   Once the planet has been named, it will be infernally difficult to change it."

"I understand," Fornri said.

The native withdrew, and Dillinger settled back with a smile, and sipped from a tumbler of the native drink.   The drink was everything the survey man had claimed.

Perhaps Paradise would be a good name for the place, he thought.   *But then— better to let the natives decide.   Paradise might mean something very different to them. All sorts of complications resulted when planets were named by outsiders.*   He remembered the famous story of the survey ship calling for help from a swamp on a strange planet.   "Where are you?" Base had demanded.   The survey ship gave its co-ordinates, and added, quite needlessly, "It's a helluvaplace."   The people of that planet had been trying for two centuries to have its name changed, but on all the official charts it was still Hellvaplace.

"Your sun, too," he called after Fornri.   "We'll have to name that."

Three hours later they were in space, on their way to Fron, the sector capital. Protz looked back at the dwindling planet, and shook his head.   *"Langri.* What do you suppose it means?"

On Fron, Dillinger reported to the sector governor.   "So they call it Langri," the governor said.   "And—you say they speak Galactic?"

"Speak it rather well, with a kind of provincial accent."

"Easily accounted for, of course.   A ship touched down there some time in the past.   People liked the place and stayed, maybe.   Did you see any traces of such a ship, or ships?"

"No.   We didn't see anything except what they wanted us to see."

"Yes.   Awkward position you stumbled into.   Not your fault, of course.   But those survey men . . ."   He shook his head.   "What beats me is that they learned Galactic.   Normally the aliens would learn the native language, unless there was a crowd of them.   There is a native language, isn't there?"

"I can't say.   I never heard any of them speak anything but Galactic.   Of course I didn't hear them talking among themselves.   They withdrew well out of hearing whenever they had to confer about something.   But now that I think about it, I did overhear some kids speaking Galactic."

"Interesting," the governor said.   "Langri—that must be a native word.   I'd better attach a philologist to the staff we'll place there.   I'd like to know how they happened to learn Galactic and keep on speaking it, and I'd like to know how long it's been since there were aliens in their midst.   Very interesting."

"They're an intelligent people," Dillinger said.   "They drove a good bargain, but they were very civilized about it.   My orders say I'm to pick up an ambassador for Langri, and the personnel to form a permanent station there.   Know anything about that?"

"I'll furnish the personnel for the station.   The ambassador has been appointed, and he should be along in a few days.   In the meantime, give your men some leave and enjoy yourselves."

A week later H. Harlow Wembling, Ambassador to Langri, waddled up the ramp to the *Rirga,* carrying his ample paunch like a ceremonial badge of honor. He bullied the duty officer, snarled at the crew, and, when Dillinger called at his quarters to pay his respects, demanded a member of the space navy to serve as his valet for the duration of his time on board.

Dillinger emerged wiping his brow, and gave Protz his precise opinion of the new ambassador in words that made the executive officer wince and rub his ears thoughtfully.

"Are you going to give him what he wants?" Protz asked.

"I told him," Dillinger said, still savoring his remarks, "I told him that the only person on board likely to have that much free time would be myself, and I lack the proper qualifications.   It's too bad.   It's really a shame."

"Oh, we'll be rid of him in no time."

"I was thinking of the natives on Langri.   It's politics, of course.   Wembling will be a party stalwart, getting paid off for years of loyal service and campaign donations.   It happens all the time, and most of the appointees are decent enough. Some of them are even competent, but there's always the exceptional case where a man thinks the word *Ambassador* in front of his name elevates him forty degrees towards divinity.   So why does our planet have to draw this one?"

"It's probably nothing to worry about.   These political appointees never keep their jobs long.   Anyway, it's no concern of ours."

"It's my concern," Dillinger said. "I negotiated the Langri treaty and I feel some responsibility for the place."

They delivered Ambassador Wembling to Langri, along with the personnel to set up a permanent Federation station. There was one last-minute altercation with Wembling when he suddenly insisted that half of the *Rirga*'s crew be left to guard the station. Then they were back in space, ready, as Dillinger said, to forget Langri and get back to work.

But he did not forget Langri, and there were many times in the months and years that followed that he found himself reminiscing dreamily of perfect beaches and water swarming with fish and sea air blended with the perfume of myriads of flowers. *Now there would be the place for a vacation,* he would think. *Or for retirement—what a place that would be for a retired naval officer!*

III

An obsolete freighter, bound from Quiron to Yorlan on a little-used space route, disappeared. Light-years away a bureaucrat with a vivid imagination immediately thought of piracy. Orders went out, and Lieutenant Commander James Vorish, of the battle cruiser *Hiln*, changed course and resigned himself to a monotonous six months of patrolling.

A week later his orders were canceled. He changed course again, and mulled over the development with Lieutenant Robert Smith.

"Someone's been stirring up an indigenous population," Vorish said. "We're to take over, and protect Federation citizens and property."

"Some people never learn," Smith said. "But—*Langri?* Where the devil is Langri? I've never heard of it."

Vorish thought it was the most beautiful place he had ever seen. To the west, that is. Trees stretched glistening pale-green foliage over the narrow beach. Flowers were closing delicately beautiful petals as the evening sun abandoned them. Waves rippled in lazily from an awesomely blue sea.

Behind him, the hideous skeleton of an enormous building under construction stood out sharply in the dusk. The afternoon shift was busily and loudly at work. Clanging sounds and thuds echoed along the shore. Motors chugged and gurgled. Mercifully, the uncertain light disguised the havoc the construction work had wrought in the unspoiled forest.

The man Wembling was still talking. "It is your duty to protect the lives and property of citizens of the Federation."

"Certainly," Vorish said. "Within reason. The installation you want would take a division of troops and a million credits worth of equipment. And even then it wouldn't be foolproof. You say part of the time the natives come in from the sea. We'd have to ring the entire peninsula."

"They're unprincipled scoundrels," Wembling said. "We have a right to demand protection. I can't keep men on the job if they're in terror of their lives.''

"How many men have you lost?"

"Why, none. But that isn't the natives' fault.''

"You haven't lost anybody? What about property? Have they been damaging your equipment or supplies?''

"No," Wembling said. "But only because we've been alert. I've had to turn half my crew into a police force.''

"We'll see what we can do," Vorish said. "Give me some time to get the feel of the situation, and then I'll talk with you again.''

Wembling summoned two burly bodyguards, and hurried away. Vorish strode on along the beach, returned a sentry's salute, and stood looking out to sea.

"There's nobody out in front of us, sir," the sentry said. "The natives—''

He halted abruptly, challenged, and then saluted. Smith came down the slope, nodded at Vorish, and faced west.

"What'd you get?" Vorish asked.

"There's something mighty queer about this situation. These 'raids' Wembling talked about—the natives usually come one at a time, and they don't come armed. They simply sneak in here and get in the way—lie down in front of a machine, or something like that—and the work has to stop until someone carries them away and dumps them back in the forest.''

"Have any natives been hurt?''

"No. The men say Wembling is pretty strict about that. It's gotten on the men's nerves because they never know when a native is going to pop up in front of them. They're afraid if one did get hurt the others would come with knives or poison arrows, or some such thing.''

"From what I've seen of Wembling, my sympathy is with the natives. But I have my orders. We'll put a line of sentry posts across the peninsula, and distribute some more about the work area. It's the best we can do, and even that will be a strain on our personnel. Some of the specialized ratings are going to howl when we assign them to guard duty.''

"No," Smith said. "No, they won't. A couple of hours on this beach are worth eight hours of guard duty. I'll start spotting the sentry posts.''

Vorish went back to the *Hiln,* and became the target of an avalanche of messengers. Mr. Wembling would like to know . . . Mr. Wembling suggests . . . If it would not be too much trouble . . . Compliments of Mr. Wembling . . . Mr. Wembling says . . . At your earliest convenience . . . Mr. Wembling's apologies, but . . .

Damn Mr. Wembling! Vorish had been on the point of telling his communications officer to put in a special line to Wembling's office. He breathed a sigh of relief over his narrow escape, and gave a junior officer the full-time assignment of dealing with Wembling's messengers.

Smith strode in out of the darkness from his job of posting the sentries. "Native wants to see you," he said. "I have him outside.''

Vorish threw up his hands. "Well, I heard Wembling's side of it. I might as well hear theirs.   I hate to ask, but I suppose Wembling will let us have an interpreter.''

"He might if he had any, but he hasn't.   These natives speak Galactic.''

"Now look here.''   He paused, shook his head.   "No, I see you aren't joking. I guess this planet is just different.   Bring him in.''

The native introduced himself as Fornri, and confidently clasped Vorish's hand. His hair blazed vividly red in the cold glow of the overhead light.   He accepted a chair, and sat down calmly.   "I understand,'' he said, "that you are members of the Space Navy of the Galactic Federation of Independent Worlds.   Is that correct?''

Vorish stopped staring long enough to acknowledge that it was correct.

"In behalf of my government,'' Fornri said, "I ask your assistance in repelling invaders of our world.''

"The devil!'' Smith muttered.

Vorish studied the native's earnest young face before venturing a reply.   "These invaders,'' he said finally.   "Are you referring to the construction project?''

"I am,'' Fornri said.

"Your planet has been classified 3C by the Federation, which places it under the jurisdiction of the Colonial Bureau.   Wembling & Company have a charter from the Bureau for their project here.   They are hardly to be considered invaders.''

Fornri spoke slowly and distinctly.   "My government has a treaty with the Galactic Federation of Independent Worlds.   The treaty guarantees the independence of Langri, and also guarantees the assistance of the Federation in the event that Langri is invaded from outer space.   I am calling upon the Galactic Federation of Independent Worlds to fulfill its guarantee.''

"Let's have the Index,'' Vorish said to Smith.   He took the heavy volume, checked the contents, and found a page headed *Langri*.   "Initial survey contact in '84,'' he said.   "Four years ago.   Classified 3C in September of '85.   No mention of any kind of treaty.''

Fornri took a polished tube of wood from his belt, and slipped out a rolled paper. He passed it to Vorish, who unrolled it and smoothed it flat.   It was a carefully written copy of an obviously official document.   Vorish looked at the date, and turned to the Index.   "Dated in June of '84,'' he said to Smith.   "A month and a half after the initial survey contact.   It classifies Langri as 5X.''

"Genuine?'' Smith asked.

"It looks genuine.   I don't suppose these people could have made it up.   Do you have the original of this document?''

"Yes,'' Fornri said.

"Of course he wouldn't carry it around with him.   Probably doesn't trust us, and I can't blame him.''

He passed the paper over to Smith, who scrutinized it carefully and returned it. "It would be a little odd for classification of a new planet to be delayed for a year and a half after the initial survey contact.   If this thing is genuine, then Langri was reclassified in '85.''

"The Index doesn't say anything about reclassification," Vorish said. He turned to Fornri. "Until we were ordered to this planet, we had never heard of Langri, so of course we know nothing about its classification. Tell us how it happened."

Fornri nodded. He spoke Galactic well, with an accent that Vorish could not quite place. Occasionally he had to pause and grope for a word, but his narrative was clear and concise. He described the coming of survey men, their capture, and the negotiations with the officers of the *Rirga*. What followed brought scowls to their faces.

"Wembling? Wembling was the first ambassador?"

"Yes, sir," Fornri said. "He mocked the authority of our government, insulted our people, and bothered our women. We asked your government to take him away, and it did."

"Probably he has plenty of political pull," Smith said. "He got the planet reclassified, and got himself a charter. Pretty effective revenge for a supposed insult."

"Or maybe he just saw an opportunity to make money here," Vorish said. "Was your government given formal notification of the termination of the treaty and Langri's reclassification?"

"No," Fornri said. "After Wembling there came another ambassador, a Mr. Gorman. He was a good friend of my people. Then a ship came and took him and all of the others away. We were told nothing. Next came Mr. Wembling with many ships and many men. We told him to leave, and he laughed at us and began to build the hotel."

"He's been building for nearly three years," Vorish said. "He isn't getting along very fast."

"We have hired an attorney many worlds away," Fornri said. "Many times he has obtained the conjunction, and made the work stop. But then each time the judge has stopped the conjunction."

"Injunction?" Smith exclaimed. "You mean you've made a lawsuit out of this?"

"Bring Lieutenant Charles in here," Vorish said. Smith routed the *Hiln*'s young legal officer out of bed. With the help of Charles they quizzed Fornri at length on the futile legal action taken by the government of Langri against H. Harlow Wembling.

The story was both amazing and pathetic. The Federation station had taken its communication equipment when it was withdrawn. The natives were helpless when Wembling arrived, and they knew better than to attempt a show of force. Fortunately they had found a friend on Wembling's staff—Fornri wouldn't say whom—and he had managed to put them in touch with an attorney and the attorney had gone to court for them enthusiastically, many times.

He could not intervene in the matter of the violated treaty, because the government had sole jurisdiction there. But he had attacked Wembling's activities on a number of counts, some of which Fornri did not understand. In one instance Wembling had been accused of violating his charter, which gave him exclusive rights to develop

Langri's natural resources.   Wembling's work on his hotel was halted for months, until a judge ruled that a planet's vacation and resort potential was a natural resource. The natives had just won the most recent round, when a court held Wembling liable for damages because he'd torn down an entire village in clearing ground for the hotel.   His charter, the court said, did not permit him to usurp private property. But the damages had been mild, and now Wembling was back at work, and the attorney was trying to think of something else.   He was also lobbying to get something done about the broken treaty, but there had been no promise of success there.

"Lawsuits cost money," Vorish observed.

Fornri shrugged.   Langri had money.   It had four hundred thousand credits which the Federation had paid to it, and it had the proceeds of a good weight of platinum ore which the friend on Wembling's staff had managed to smuggle out for them.

"There's platinum on Langri?" Vorish asked.

"It didn't come from Langri," Fornri said.

Vorish drummed impatiently on his desk.   The Langri situation involved several noteworthy mysteries, but just for a start he'd like to know how the natives had happened to be speaking Galactic when the first survey men arrived.   And then— platinum ore that didn't come from Langri.   He shook his head.   "I don't think you'll ever defeat Wembling in court.   You may give him a few temporary setbacks, but in the long run he'll win out.   And he'll ruin you.   Men like him have too much influence, and all the financial backing they need."

"The conjunctions give us time," Fornri said.   "Time is what we need—time for the Plan."

Vorish looked doubtfully at Smith.   "What do you think?"

"I think we're obligated to make a full report on this.   The treaty was negotiated by naval officers.   Naval Headquarters should be filled in on what's happened."

"Yes.   We should send them a copy of this—but a copy of a copy may not swing much weight.   And the natives probably won't want to turn loose the original."   He turned to Fornri.   "I'm going to send Lieutenant Smith with you. He will bring a couple of men along.   None of them will be armed.   Take them wherever you like, and guard them any way you like, but they must make their own photographs of the treaty before we can help you."

Fornri considered the matter briefly, and agreed.   Vorish sent Smith off with two technicians and their equipment, and settled down to compose a report.   He was interrupted by a young ensign who gulped, flushed crimson, and stammered, "Excuse me, sir.   But Mr. Wembling—"

"What now?" Vorish said resignedly.

"Mr. Wembling wants sentry post number thirty-two moved.   The lights are interfering with his sleep."

In the morning Vorish strolled around the project to take a good look at Wembling's embryo hotel.   Wembling joined him, wearing a revoltingly-patterned short-sleeved shirt and shorts.   His arms and legs were crisply tanned, his face pale under an outlandish sun helmet.

"A thousand accommodations," Wembling said. "Most of them will be suites. There'll be a big pool on the terrace overlooking the beach. Some people can't stand salt water, you know. I have the men laying out a golf course. There'll be two main dining rooms and half a dozen small ones that will specialize in food from famous places. I'll have a whole fleet of boats to take people fishing. I might even have a submarine or two—those jobs with rows of observation ports. You might not believe it, but there are hundreds of worlds where people have never seen an ocean. Why, there are worlds where people don't even have water to bathe in. They have to use chemicals. If some of those people can come to Langri, and live a little, now and then, a lot of head doctors are going to be out of work. This project of mine is nothing but a service to humanity."

"Is that so?" Vorish murmured. "I wasn't aware that yours was a nonprofit organization."

"Huh? Of course I'll make a profit. A darned good profit. What's wrong with that?"

"From what I've seen of your hotel, the only minds you'll be saving will be those of the poor, broken-down millionaires."

Wembling indulged in a grandiose gesture. "Just a beginning. Have to put the thing on a sound financial basis right from the start, you know. But there'll be plenty of room for the little fellows. Not in water-front hotels, but there'll be community beaches, and hotels with rights of access, and all that sort of thing. My staff has it all worked out."

"It's just that I'm trained to look at things differently," Vorish said. "We in the Space Navy devote our lives to the protection of humanity, but if you'll look at the current pay scale you'll see that there's no profit motive."

"There's nothing wrong with taking a profit. Where would the human race be today if nobody wanted a profit? We'd be living in grass huts back on old Terra, just like these Langri natives. There's a good example of a nonprofit society. I suppose you'd like that."

"It doesn't look so bad to me," Vorish murmured.

But Wembling did not hear him. He whirled and darted away, sputtering an unbelievably pungent profanity. A native, dashing in from nowhere, had attached himself to a girder that was about to be swung aloft. Workmen were valiantly striving to remove him—gently. The native clung stubbornly. Work stopped until he was pried loose and carried away.

Lieutenant Smith came up in time to see the drama carried to its comical conclusion.

"What do they expect to gain?" Vorish said.

"Time," Smith said. "Didn't you hear what that native said? They need time for the Plan—whatever that means."

"Maybe they're planning some kind of a massive uprising."

"I doubt it. They seem to be essentially a peaceful people."

"I wish them luck," Vorish said. "This Wembling is a tough customer. He's a self-activated power unit. I wonder how his weight holds up, the way he tears around keeping things humming."

"Maybe he eats all night. Want to look over the sentry layout?"

They turned away. In the distance they heard Wembling, his voice high-pitched with excitement, getting the work going again. A moment later he caught up with them and walked jauntily along beside Vorish.

"If you'd put in the kind of defense line I want," he said, "I wouldn't have that trouble."

Vorish did not reply. It was obvious that Wembling was going out of his way to avoid injuring the natives, but Vorish doubted that his motives were humanitarian. Inept handling of the native problem might embarrass him in some future court test.

On the other hand, Wembling was not worried in the least about the Space Navy's injuring the natives. The blame for that action could not possibly fall upon him. He had demanded that Vorish erect an electronic barrier that would incinerate any native attempting to pass.

"At the very worst," Vorish said, "the natives are only a minor nuisance."

"They haven't got much for weapons," Wembling said. "But they have enough to cut throats, and there's a hell of a lot of natives in this place if they all decide to come at me at once. And then, their mucking about the project is slowing things down. I want 'em kept out."

"I don't think your throat is in danger, but we'll do what we can to keep them out."

"Guess I can't ask more than that," Wembling said. He chuckled good-naturedly, and looped his arm through Vorish's.

Smith had sited his sentry posts to make a shrewd use of the infrequent irregularities in terrain. He had men at work now, clearing the ground for better visibility. Wembling sauntered along reviewing the results with the casual aloofness of an Admiral of the Fleet. Suddenly he pulled Vorish to a halt.

"This defense line of ours. We'll have to move it."

Vorish regarded him coldly. "Why?"

"In the next two or three weeks we're going to start work on the golf course. We wouldn't be able to get more than half of it this side of the line. Maybe not that much. So we'll have to move it. It wouldn't be safe to have my men working off by themselves. But there's no hurry—tomorrow will do."

"Supposing you tell me what you have in mind," Vorish said.

Wembling summoned a survey party, and they set out under the watchful eyes of a military escort. They moved west along the peninsula, which widened sharply until it became a part of the mainland. They pushed their way through the trees as the perspiring Wembling, enjoying himself immensely, gestured and talked his way around the prospective golf course.

An hour later Vorish took another look at the acreage the golf course was to occupy, and gave Wembling a flat refusal. "The line would be too long here," he said. "I wouldn't have enough men."

Wembling grinned. "The commander is always pulling my leg. You've got plenty of men. They're all down there on the beach."

"My men are working in shifts, just as yours are.   If I put those men on guard duty, I won't have any relief for them."

"We both know you could set up an impassable defense that wouldn't require any men," Wembling said.

"We both know I'm not going to do it.   Your men can work without naval protection.   They'll be safe."

"All right.   If that's the way you want it.   But if anything happens to them—"

"There's one more thing," Vorish said.   "What are you going to do about that abandoned native village where the eighth hole is supposed to be?"

Wembling gazed contemptuously at the distant huts.   "Tear it down.   Nobody lives there."

"You can't do that," Vorish said.   "It's native property.   You'll have to get permission."

"Whose permission?"

'The natives' permission."

Wembling threw back his head, and laughed uproariously.   "Let 'em take it to court, if they want to waste their money.   That last case must have cost 'em close to a hundred thousand, and know what their damages were?   Seven hundred and fifty credits.   The sooner they use up their money, the sooner they stop bothering me."

"My orders call for the protection of natives and native property just as I protect you and your property," Vorish said.   "The natives won't stop you, but I will."

He strode away without looking back.   He was in a hurry to get to his office on the *Hiln,* and have a talk with Lieutenant Charles.   There was something he remembered reading, a long time ago, in his little-used manual of military government . . .

The days drifted by pleasantly, ruffled only by Wembling's violent protests whenever a native slipped through to slow down construction.   Vorish kept an alert eye on Wembling's Operation Golf Course, and waited impatiently for some official reaction to his report on the Langri treaty.

Official reaction there was none, but Wembling's workcrew steadily sliced its way back into the forest.   Trees were being hauled away to be cut into lumber. The delicately-speckled grain would make an exquisite and novel paneling for the hotel's interior.

The crew reached the deserted native village and worked completely around it. They made no effort to trespass, though Vorish saw them casting nervous glances in that direction from time to time, as though they hoped it would go away.

Making his morning rounds of the sentry posts, Vorish paused occasionally to turn his binoculars on the work around the village.

"You're sticking your neck out," Smith said.   "I hope you realize that."

Vorish made no reply.   He had his own opinion of naval officers who were unduly concerned for their necks.   "There's Wembling," he said.

With his bodyguards panting on his heels, Wembling was moving at his usual

fast pace across the cleared ground.   His foreman came forward to meet him.
Wembling spoke briefly, and pointed.   The foreman turned to his men, and pointed.
A moment later the first hut was overturned.

"Let's go," said Vorish.

Smith signaled a squad of navy men into action, and hurried after him.   The
men reached the village first, and cleared out Wembling's men.   Wembling was
frozen in impotent rage when Vorish arrived.

Vorish paused to study the row of toppled huts.   "Did you have permission
from the natives to do this?" he asked.

"Hell, no," Wembling said.   "I've got a charter.   What can they do about
it?"

"Place these men under arrest," Vorish said, and turned away.

Somewhat to his surprise, Wembling said nothing.   His aspect was that of a
man thinking deeply.

Vorish confined Wembling to his tent, under arrest.   He halted all work on the
hotel.   Then he forwarded a complete report on the incident to Naval Headquarters,
and sat back to await results.

The indifference of headquarters to his Langri report had intrigued him.   Had
someone filed it away as unimportant, or was there a corrupt conspiracy high
up in the government?   Either way, injustice was being done.   The natives
wanted time for something they called the Plan.   Vorish wanted time to call
someone's attention to what was going on.   It would be a shame to allow Wembling
to finish his hotel while the report on the Langri situation lay in an underling's
desk drawer.

With Wembling under arrest and the work stopped, Vorish watched in amusement
while Wembling got off frantic messages to exalted persons high up in the Federation
government.

"Now," Vorish told himself with satisfaction, "let's see them ignore Langri
this time."

The days had added up to three weeks when Headquarters suddenly broke the
silence.   The battle cruiser *Bolar* was being dispatched, under Admiral Corning.
The admiral would make an on-the-spot investigation.

"It doesn't sound as if you're being relieved," Smith said.   "Do you know
Corning?"

"I've served under him several times, at various places and ranks.   You might
call him an old friend."

"That's fortunate for you."

"It could be worse," Vorish admitted.   He felt that he'd covered himself well,
and Corning, even though he was crusty, temperamental and a stickler for accuracy,
would not go out of his way to make trouble for a friend.

Vorish turned out an honor guard for the admiral, and received him with full
ceremony.   Corning stepped briskly down the ramp from the *Bolar* and glanced
about approvingly.

"Glad to see you, Jim," he said, his eyes on one of Langri's inviting beaches. "Nice place here. Nice place." He turned to Vorish, and studied his tanned face. "And you've been making good use of it. You've put on weight."

"You've lost weight," Vorish said.

"Always was skinny," Corning said. "I make up for it in height. Did I ever tell you about the time—" He glanced at the circle of respectfully attentive officers, and dropped his voice. "Let's go where we can talk."

Vorish dismissed his men, and took Corning to his office in the *Hiln*. The admiral said nothing along the way, but his sharp eyes surveyed Vorish's defense arrangements, and he clucked his tongue softly.

"Jim," Corning said, as Vorish closed the door, "just what is going on here?"

"I want to give you some background," Vorish said, and told him about the treaty and its violation. Corning listened intently, muttering an occasional "Damn!"

"You mean they took no official action on it at all?" he demanded.

"That's exactly what they did."

"Damn! Sooner or later somebody's head will roll over that. But it'll probably be the wrong head, and that treaty really has nothing to do with this mess you've gotten yourself into. Not officially, anyway, because officially the treaty doesn't exist. Now what's this nonsense about a few native huts?"

Vorish smiled. He felt that he was on firm ground there—he'd had a long conference with Fornri, exploring all of the angles. "According to my orders," he said, "I'm an impartial referee here. I'm to protect Federation citizens and property, but I am also to protect the natives against any infringements upon their customs, means of livelihood, and so on. Paragraph seven."

"I've read it."

"The idea is that if the natives are treated properly, Federation citizens and property are a lot less likely to need protection. That particular native village is more than just a collection of empty huts. It seems to have some religious significance to the natives. They call it the Teacher's Village, or some such thing."

"Teacher or leader," Corning said. "Sometimes they're the same thing to primitive peoples. That might make the village a kind of shrine. I take it that this Wembling busted right in and started tearing the place apart."

"That's what he did."

"And you warned him ahead of time that he should get the natives' permission, and he laughed it off. All right. Your conduct was not only proper, there—it was commendable. But why did you have to close the whole works down? You could have protected that village, and made him put his golf course somewhere else, and he would have screamed to high heaven without getting anything but laughed at. But you had to stop everything. Were you *trying* to get fired? You've cost Wembling a lot of time and a lot of money, and now he has a real grievance. And he's got plenty of influence."

"It isn't my fault if he wasted time and money," Vorish said. "I advised headquarters of my action immediately. They could have reversed that order any time they chose."

"That's just it. They didn't dare, because there was always the chance that things might blow up. They didn't know the situation here. You caused a pretty stew at headquarters. Why did you arrest Wembling, and keep him in his tent under guard?"

"For his own protection. He'd defiled a sacred place, and I'd be responsible if anything happened to him."

For the first time Corning smiled. "So that's the line. Not bad. It all comes down to a matter of judgment, and that makes it your opinion against Wembling's. You flip your coin and you take your choice, and no one who wasn't on the spot is entitled to vote." He nodded. "I'll follow that up in my report. Wembling stepped out of line. Definitely. The consequences might have been serious. I can't rightly say that your action was too drastic, because I wasn't here at the time. I don't exactly see what you were trying to do, or maybe I do, but I'll back you up as much as I can. I guess I can keep you from being shot."

"Oh," Vorish said. "So they were going to shoot me. I wondered."

"They were . . . they are . . . going to do their worst." Corning looked steadily at Vorish. "I don't much like it, but I have my orders. You'll return to Galaxia on the *Hiln,* under arrest—to stand court-martial. Personally I don't think you have much to worry about. I can't see them going ahead with it, but right now they think they want to try."

"I won't worry," Vorish said. "I've studied this thing through pretty carefully. I rather hope they try, though. I'll insist on a public court-martial, of course, and . . . but I'm afraid they won't do it. Anyway, I'm glad I'll be leaving Langri in capable hands."

"Not my hands," Corning said. "Not for long. The 984th Squadron is on its way now, to take over. Eleven ships. They're not taking any chance on this thing getting out of hand. The commander is Ernst Dillinger—just made admiral a few months ago. Know him?"

IV

The fishing boat was still in position, far out. Dillinger raised his binoculars, lowered them. As far as he could see, the natives were—fishing. He returned to his desk and sat gazing seaward at the fleck of color that was the sail.

The plush spaciousness of his office annoyed him. It was only his second day in the quarters Wembling had persuaded him to occupy in the completed wing of Hotel Langri, and he was spending most of his time pacing in out-sized circles about the work that piled up on his desk.

He was worried about the natives. He was worried about an enigmatic something or other which they called the Plan, and which they intimated would eventually sweep Wembling and his workers and his hotels right off the planet.

With Hotel Langri opening for business in a few months, and work already beginning on two other hotels, Dillinger knew that the legal expulsion of Wembling had become a flat impossibility.   So what were the natives planning?   Illegal expulsion?   The use of force?   With a squadron of the Space Navy standing by?

He got to his feet again and walked over to the curved expanse of tinted plastic that formed the window.   The fishing boat was still there.   Every day it was there. But perhaps, as Protz suggested, the water off the point was merely a good place to fish.

His intercom clicked.   "Mr. Wembling, sir."

"Send him in," Dillinger said, and turned towards the door.

Wembling entered jauntily, hand outstretched.   "Morning, Ernie."

"Good morning, Howard," Dillinger said, blinking at Wembling's ridiculously patterned shirt.

"Come down to the lounge for a drink?"

Dillinger lifted a stack of papers from his desk, and dropped it.   "Sure."

They walked down a palatial corridor to the lounge, and a uniformed attendant took their orders and brought the drinks.   Dillinger idly stirred the ice in his glass and looked through the enormous window at the terrace, and the beach beyond. Wembling's landscaping crew had done its work well.   Velvety grass and colorful shrubs surrounded the hotel.   The pool, ready for use, stood deserted.   Off-duty navy men and workers crowded the beach, and speared fish off the point.

Wembling prated enthusiastically over the progress he was making on his new sites, which were fifty miles down the coast in both directions.

"It's a headache to me, your scattering these sites all over the place," Dillinger said.   "I have to guard them."

Wembling reached over and patted his arm.   "You're doing a good job, Ernie. We haven't had any trouble since you took over.   I'm putting in a good word for you where it'll do the most good."

"There's room for fifty hotels right here on the peninsula," Dillinger said.   "Not to mention a few golf courses."

Wembling turned a veiled smile in his direction.   "Politics and law," he murmured.   "Stay away from both of them, Ernie.   You have brains and talent, but it isn't that kind of brains and talent."

Dillinger flushed, and turned his gaze to the window again.   The fishing boat was a mere speck on the horizon.   It was probably drifting or sailing slowly, but it seemed motionless.

"Have you heard anything about Commander Vorish?" Wembling asked.

"The last I heard, he'd taken the *Hiln* on training maneuvers."

"Then—they didn't fire him?"

"They investigated him," Dillinger said with a grin.   "But all he got was a commendation for handling himself well in a difficult situation.   My guess is that any action against him would have resulted in publicity, and someone didn't want publicity.   Of course I don't know anything about politics and law.   Did you want Vorish fired?"

Wembling shook his head thoughtfully.   "No.   I had no grudge against him.

There's no profit in grudges.   We both had a job to do, but he went at his the wrong way.   All I wanted was to get on with the work, and after he left I passed the word along to go easy on him.   But I thought they'd kick him out of the navy, and if they did I wanted him back here on Langri.   I think he understood these natives, and I can always use a man like that.   I told him to get in touch with my Galaxia Office, and they'd make arrangements to get him back here.   But I never heard from him.''

"He didn't get fired.   The next time you see him he'll probably be an admiral.''

"The same goes for you,'' Wembling said.   "If you ever leave the navy, come back to Langri.   I'm going to have a big enterprise to run here, and I'll need all the good men I can get.   And good men aren't always easy to find.''

Dillinger turned aside to hide his smile.   "Thanks.   I'll remember that.''

Wembling slapped the table, and pushed himself erect.   "Well, back to work. Chess tonight?''

"Better make it late,'' Dillinger said.   "I've got to get that work cleaned up.''

He watched Wembling waddle away.   He had to admire the man.   Even if he loathed him, and loathed his methods, he had to admire him.   He got things done.

Protz was waiting for him when he got back to his office—Commander Protz, now, Captain of the *Rirga,* the flag ship of Dillinger's 984th Squadron.   Dillinger nodded at him, and spoke into his intercom.

"I don't want to be disturbed.''   He switched it off, and turned to Protz. "What's the score.''

"We're losing,'' Protz said.   "It definitely didn't crash.   According to the sentry, it came in for a perfect landing back in the forest.   Wembling isn't missing a supply ship, and we know it didn't belong to us.   The recon planes have been taking the tops out of the trees in that area, and they can't spot a thing.''

"So it wasn't Wembling's,'' Dillinger said.   Since he'd gotten the first report on the unidentified ship, at dawn that morning, he'd been thinking that it had to be Wembling's.   He turned in his chair, and looked out to sea.   "So the natives have visitors.''

"Whoever it was, they were expected,'' Protz said.   "They got the ship camouflaged in a hurry.   Maybe they had a landing pit dug there.''

"Wembling thinks someone in his supply fleet has been keeping the natives in touch with that attorney of theirs.   I suppose we should have monitored the planet. But we'd have to leave a ship in orbit, and we've needed every man, with Wembling building hotels all over the place.   Well, the ship is here.   The question now, is—what is it doing?''

"Smuggling arms?''

"Just what we need to make this assignment interesting.   Has Intelligence turned up anything?''

"Nothing up to 0800 this morning.   Want to make a ground search for the ship?''

"It would take too many men.   If they have a landing pit, even a ground search might miss it—and we'd be too late now if we did find it.   They'll have it unloaded.

No.   Let Intelligence work on it, and give them more men if they think they can use them.''

''Anything else?''

''Get ready for the worst.   Protz, of all the jobs the navy has given me to do, this one is the dirtiest.   I hoped I'd get out of it without a shot fired at the natives. I'd much rather shoot Wembling.''

The thing had been mishandled from the start, Dillinger thought.   This attorney the natives had gotten ahold of was probably competent enough—even Wembling admitted that.   He'd caused Wembling some trouble, but Wembling was putting the finishing touches on Hotel Langri just the same.

Wembling's chief weapon was political pull.   Politics should be fought with politics, with public opinion, and not in a court of law.   He'd tried to explain that, once, to Fornri, but the native seemed uninterested.   The Plan, Fornri said, would take care of everything.   He did not seem to realize that it was already too late.

If Dillinger had known in time what was happening to Langri, he believed he could have stopped it.   Documented information, furnished anonymously to the wealthy ethnological foundations, to opposition newspapers on key planets, to opposition leaders in the Federation Congress—the resultant explosion would have rocked the government and rocked Wembling right off Langri.

But he had not known until he reported to Admiral Corning and assumed command on Langri.   Then he had done what he could.   He had prepared a hundred copies of a statement on the Langri situation, and accompanied each with a photo of the original treaty.   But he did not dare entrust them to normal communication channels, and he had to wait until one of his officers went on leave to get them on their way.   They had probably reached their destinations by this time, and they would be studied and investigated, and eventually there would be some action.   But it was too late.   Wembling would have most of what he wanted, and probably other vultures, armed with charters, would be coming to the plunder of Langri.

It was tough on the natives.   Wembling's men were eating a lot of fresh fish, and the natives' fishing boats had all but vanished from the sites where Wembling was working.   Langri had a big native population—too big, and most of its food came from the sea.   The word was that the natives weren't getting enough to eat.

Late in the afternoon, Dillinger called Wembling.   ''You have men flying back and forth all the time,'' he said.   ''Have they noticed any unusual native activity?''

''I didn't hear about any,'' Wembling said.   ''Want me to check?''

''I wish you would.''

''Hold on a minute.''

He heard Wembling snapping out an order.   A moment later, he said to Dillinger, ''Do you think the natives are up to something?''

''I know they are, but I can't figure out what it is.''

''You'll handle them,'' Wembling said confidently.   ''There was a time when I wanted them annihilated, but since you've been keeping them out of my hair, I'd just as soon live and let live. Hell, they might even be a tourist attraction when I get things going here. Maybe they weave baskets, or carve voodoo charms, or something like that. I'll sell them in the hotel lobby.''

"I'm not worrying about their basket weaving," Dillinger said dryly.

"Anyway . . . just a moment. Ernie? Nobody saw anything unusual."

"Thanks. I'm afraid I'll have to call off that chess game. I'll be busy."

"Too bad. Tomorrow night, then?"

"We'll see."

Langri would have been enchanting by moonlight, but there was no moon. Wembling had a scheme to produce artificial moonlight, but until he put it into operation night would smother the planet's beauty in blackness.

Looking down into the blackness, Dillinger saw light. At every native village there were dozens of fires. Often their outlines blurred together into one brilliant patch of light. When they were farther apart, they appeared as a multitude of bright dots leaping up into the darkness.

"You say it isn't normal?" Dillinger asked the recon pilot.

"Definitely not, sir. They fix their evening meal along about dark, when the fishing boats get in. When that's over with, you can fly the whole coast without seeing a flash of light. Except where our men are. I've never seen even one fire going this late."

"It's a pity we know so little about these natives," Dillinger said. "The only one I've ever talked with is this Fornri, and there's always something—distant about him. I never know what he's thinking. Colonial Bureau should have sent a team to study them. They could use some help, too. Their fishing will fall off even more when Wembling gets a mob of tourists out on the water. They'll need some agriculture. What do you make of it, Protz?"

"It's suggestive, but darned if I know what it suggests."

"I know what it suggests," Dillinger said. "A strange ship lands this morning, and tonight every native on the planet stays up all night. They're getting ready for something. We'd better get back and make a few preparations of our own."

There was little that he could do. He had a defense line around each of Wembling's three building sites. He had his ships sited to give maximum support. All that had been worked out months before. He placed his entire command on alert, doubled the guard on the beaches, and set up mobile reserves. He wished he had a few army officers to help out. He'd spent his entire adult life learning how to wage war in space, and now for the first time in his military career he was faced with the possibility of battle, and he was landbound, and in danger of being embarrassed by hordes of untrained natives.

The night intelligence sheet arrived at dawn, virtually blank. Except for the fires there was nothing to report. Dillinger passed it across to Protz, who glanced at it and passed it back.

"Go down and see Wembling," Dillinger said. "Tell him to give his men the day off, and keep them in their quarters. I don't want to see one of them around. That goes for him, too."

"He'll howl."

"He'd better not howl to me. If we knew these natives better, maybe we could see this thing from their point-of-view. Somehow I just can't see them hitting us with an armed attack. It'd get a lot of them killed, and it wouldn't accomplish a thing. Surely they know that as well as we do. Now if you were a native, and you wanted to stop Wembling's work, what would you do?"

"I'd kill Wembling."

Dillinger slapped his desk disgustedly. "O.K. Give him an armed guard."

"What would you do?"

"I'd plant some kind of explosive at carefully chosen points in the hotels. If it didn't stop the project altogether, it'd throw an awful delay at Wembling's grand opening. You know—"

"That might be it," Protz said. "It makes more sense than an all-out attack. I'll put special guard details around the buildings."

Dillinger rose and went to the window. Dawn was touching Langri with its usual lavish beauty. The sea was calmly blue under the rising sun. Off the point . . .

Dillinger swore softly.

"What's the matter?" Protz said.

"Look." Dillinger pointed out to sea.

"I don't see anything."

"Where's the fishing boat?"

"It isn't there."

"Every day as long as we've been on this planet there's been a fishing boat working off the point. Get the recon planes out. Something is decidedly fishy."

Thirty minutes later they had their report. Every fishing boat on Langri was beached. The natives were taking the day off.

"They seem to be congregating in the largest villages," the intelligence officer said. "A7—that's Fornri's village, you know—has the biggest crowd. And then B9, D4, F12—all along the coast. There are fires all over the place."

Dillinger studied a photo map, and the officer circled the villages as he called them off. "At this point," Dillinger said, "there's just one thing we can do. We'll go over and have a little talk with Fornri."

"How many men do you want?" Protz asked.

"Just you and I. And a pilot."

They slanted down to a perfect landing in the soft sand of the beach. The pilot stayed with the plane, and Dillinger and Protz climbed the slope to the village, making their way through throngs of natives. Dillinger's embarrassment increased with each forward step. There was no sign of a sinister conspiracy. A holiday atmosphere prevailed, the gaily dressed natives laughing and singing around the fires—singing in Galactic, an accomplishment that never ceased to intrigue Dillinger. The natives respectfully made way for them. Otherwise, except for timid glances from the children, they were ignored.

They reached the first huts and paused, looking down the village street. Mouth-watering odors of a feast in preparation reminded Dillinger that he had missed breakfast. At the far end of the street, near the largest hut, native men and women stood quietly in line. Dillinger waited helplessly for some official acknowledgment of his presence.

Suddenly Fornri appeared before him, and accepted his hand. "We are honored," Fornri said, but his face, usually so blandly expressionless, revealed an emotion which Dillinger found difficult to interpret. Was he angry, or merely uneasy? "May I inquire as to the purpose of your visit?" he asked.

Dillinger looked at Protz, who shrugged and looked the other way. "I came to . . . to observe," Dillinger said lamely.

"In the past, you have not interfered in the lives of my people. Is that to be changed?"

"No. I am not here to interfere."

"Then your presence is not required here. This does not concern you."

"Everything that happens on Langri concerns me," Dillinger said. "I came to learn what is happening here. I intend to know."

Fornri withdrew abruptly. Dillinger watched him walk away, watched a group of young natives gather around him. Their manner was quiet, but urgent.

"Funny thing," Protz mused. "With any primitive society I've ever seen, the old men run things. Here on Langri, it's the young men. I'll bet there isn't a man in that crowd who's much over thirty."

Fornri returned. He was uneasy—there could be no doubt of that. He gazed earnestly at Dillinger's face before he spoke. "We know that you have been a friend to my people, and helped us when you could. It is the Mr. Wembling who is our enemy. If he knew, he would attempt to interfere."

"Mr. Wembling will not interfere," Dillinger said.

"Very well. We are holding an election."

Dillinger felt Protz's hand tighten on his arm. He repeated dumbly, "An election?"

Fornri spoke proudly. "We are electing delegates to a constitutional convention."

An idyllic setting. The forest clearing overlooking the sea. Women preparing a feast. Citizens waiting quietly for their turns in the grass voting hut. Democracy in action.

"When the constitution is approved," Fornri went on, "we shall elect a government. Then we shall apply for membership in the Galactic Federation of Independent Worlds."

"Is it legal?" Protz demanded.

"It is legal," Fornri said. "Our attorney has advised us. The main requirement is fifty per cent literacy. We have over ninety per cent literacy. We could have done it much sooner, you see, but we did not know that we needed only fifty per cent."

"You are to be congratulated," Dillinger said. "If your application for Federation membership is accepted, I suppose your government will force Wembling to leave Langri."

"We intend that Langri shall belong to us. It is the Plan."

Dillinger held out his hand. "I wish you every good fortune with your election, and with your application for Federation membership."

With a last glance at the line by the voting hut, they turned and walked slowly back to the plane. Protz whistled, and rubbed his hands together. "And that," he said, "will finish Wembling."

"At least we've solved the mystery of that unknown ship," Dillinger said. "It was their attorney, coming to advise them and help them draw up a constitution. As for this finishing Wembling, you're wrong. The Wemblings in this galaxy don't finish that easily. He's ready for this. You might almost say he's been expecting it."

"What can he do?"

"No court of justice would make him give up what he already has. The natives can keep him from grabbing more land, but what he's developed will be his. He acquired it in good faith, under a charter granted by the Federation. Maybe he'll get to connect up his sites and own a hundred mile stretch of coast. If he doesn't, he has enough space at each site to build a thundering big resort. These enormous golf courses he's been laying out—that land is developed. He'll get to keep it, and there'll be room there for another hundred hotels on each site if he wants to build them. He'll flood the sea with pleasure fishermen, and starve the natives."

Dillinger looked back at the village, and shook his head sadly. "Do you realize what a tremendous accomplishment that is? Ninety per cent literacy. How they must have worked! And they were beaten before they started. The poor devils."

V

The normal behavior of a forest trail, Dillinger thought, *would be to wander—around trees, away from thickets, generally following the path of least resistance. This trail did not wander. It might have been laid out by a surveyor, so straight did it run. It was an old trail, and a well-worn trail. Trees must have been cut down, but there were no traces of the stumps.*

Ahead of him, Fornri and a half dozen other young natives kept a steady, killing pace and did not look back. They had covered a good five miles, and there seemed to be no end to it. Dillinger was perspiring, and already tired.

Fornri had come to him at Hotel Langri. "We would like for you to come with us," he said. "You alone." And Dillinger had come.

Hotel Langri was all but deserted. At dawn tomorrow the 984th Squadron would head back into space, where it belonged. Wembling and his workmen had already left. Langri had been returned to the possession of its rightful owners.

It had been an absurdly simple thing, this Plan of the natives—absurdly simple and devastatingly effective. First there had been the application for Federation membership, which fortunately had arrived in Galaxia just as Dillinger's anonymous letters went off with a resounding explosion that overturned the government, caused a turmoil in the Colonial Bureau and Navy Department, and stirred up repercussions as far away as Langri, where a committee touched down briefly for a stormy investigation.

The application was acted upon immediately, and it received unanimous approval. Wembling was undisturbed. His attorneys were on the job before the last vote was counted, and the native government received a court order to honor Wembling with firm title to the land he had already developed. This the Langri government did, and so complacently that Wembling slyly added several hundred acres to his claim without stirring up a ripple of protest.

Then came the masterstroke, which not even Wembling had foreseen.

Taxes.

Dillinger had been present when Fornri handed Wembling his first tax billing from the government of Langri. Wembling had screamed himself hoarse, and pounded his desk, and vowed he would fight it through every court in the galaxy, but he found the courts to be strangely out of sympathy with him.

If the elected representatives of the people of Langri wished to impose an annual property tax equal to ten times the property's assessed valuation, that was their legal right. It was Wembling's misfortune that he owned the only property on the planet which had an assessed valuation worth recording. Ten times the worth of a grass hut was a negligible value above zero. Ten times the worth of Wembling's hotels amounted to ruin.

The judges were in perfect agreement with Wembling that the government's action was unwise. It would discourage construction and industry and hold back the planet's development indefinitely. In time that would be perfectly obvious to the people of Langri, and then it would be their privilege to elect representatives who would write more lenient tax laws.

In the meantime, Wembling must pay the tax.

It left him a choice of not paying and being ruined, or paying and being much more severely ruined, and he chose not to pay. The government confiscated his property for nonpayment of taxes, and the Langri situation was resolved to the satisfaction of all but Wembling and his backers. Hotel Langri was to become a school and university for the native children. The offices of government would occupy one of the other hotels. The natives were undecided as to what to do with the third, but Dillinger was certain they would use it wisely.

As for Wembling, he was now an employee of the people of Langri. Even the natives admired the way he got things done, and there were islands, many islands, it turned out, far out in the sea where happy vacationers would not interfere with the natives' fishing grounds. Would Mr. Wembling, Fornri asked, like to build hotels on those islands and run them for the Government of Langri? Mr. Wembling would. Mr. Wembling did, in fact, wonder why he had not thought of that in the first place. He negotiated a contract with the natives' attorney, moved his men to the islands, and enthusiastically began planning a whole series of hotels.

Dillinger, following the natives along a forest path, felt serenely at peace with himself and the galaxy around him.

The path ended in an enormous clearing, carpeted with thick grass and flowers. Dillinger stopped to look around, saw nothing, and hurried to catch the natives.

On the opposite side of the clearing was another path, but this one ended abruptly at a rough pile of stones, a cairn, perhaps, jutting up from the forest floor. Beyond it, rusting, overgrown with vines, hidden by towering trees, lay an old survey ship.

"One of your people once came to live among us," Fornri said. "This was his ship."

The natives stood with hands clasped behind them, their heads bowed reverently. Dillinger waited, wondering what was expected of him. Finally he asked, "There was just one man?"

"Just one," Fornri said. "We have often thought that there may be those who wondered what happened to him. Perhaps you could tell them."

"Perhaps I could," Dillinger said. "I'll see."

He struggled through the undergrowth and circled the ship, looking for a name or an identification number. There was none. The air lock was closed. As Dillinger stood contemplating it, Fornri said, "You may enter if you like. We have placed his things there."

Dillinger walked up the wobbly ramp, and stumbled along a dark passageway. The dim light that filtered into the control room gave the objects there a ghostlike aspect. On a table by the control panel were small mementos, personal effects, books, piles of papers. Dillinger thoughtfully handled a rusted pocket knife, a rosary, a broken compass.

The first book he picked up was a diary. George F. O'Brien's diary. The entries, written in a precisely penciled hand, were too dim to read. He took the books and papers to the air lock, sat down on the ramp, and began to turn the pages.

There were detailed entries describing O'Brien's early days on the planet, more than a century before. Then the entries became less regular, the dates uncertain as O'Brien lost track of time. Dillinger came to the end, found a second volume, and continued reading.

Just another freebooter, he thought, kicking around on a strange planet, prospecting for metals, enjoying himself with a native harem. Surely it was not this man . . .

The change came subtly down through the years, as O'Brien came to identify himself with the natives, became one of them, and finally faced the future. There was an astute summary of Langri's potential as a resort planet, that might have been written by Wembling. There was a dire warning as to the probable fate of the natives. "If I live," O'Brien had written, "I do not think this will happen."

And if he should not live?

"Then the natives must be taught what to do. There must be a Plan. These things the natives must know."

Government and language. Interplanetary relations. History. Economics, commerce and money. Politics. Law and colonial procedure. Science.

"Not just one man!" Dillinger exclaimed to himself. "He couldn't have!"

The initial landing, probably by a survey ship. Steps to observe in capturing the crew. Negotiations, list of violations and penalties. Achievement of independent status. Steps to Federation membership. Steps to follow when independent status was violated.

"Not just one man!"

It was all there, laboriously written out by an uneducated man who had vision and wisdom and patience.   By a great man.   It was a brilliant prognostication, with nothing lacking but Wembling's name—and Dillinger had the impression that O'Brien had known more than a few Wemblings in his day.   It was all there, everything that had happened, right up to the final master stroke, the ten-to-one tax rate on the hotels.

Dillinger closed the last notebook, carried the papers back to the control room and carefully rearranged things as he had found them.   Some day Langri would have its own historians, who would sift through these papers and send the name of George F. O'Brien across the galaxy in dryly-written tomes read only by other historians.   The man deserved a better fate.

But perhaps verbal tradition would keep his memory a living thing on Langri far into the future.   Perhaps, even now, around the fires, there were legendary tales of what O'Brien had done and said.   Or perhaps not.   It was difficult for an outsider to probe into such matters, especially if he were a naval officer.   That sort of thing required a specialist.

Dillinger took a last look at the humble relics, took a step backwards, and came to a full salute.

He left the ship, carefully closing the air lock behind him.   Dusk had settled quickly there, deep in the forest, but the natives were waiting, still in attitudes of reverence.

"I suppose you've looked those things over," Dillinger said.

Fornri seemed startled.   "No . . ."

"I see.   Well, I found out—as much as there is to find out about him.   If he has any family surviving, I'll see that they know what happened to him."

"Thank you," Fornri said.

"Were there no others who came and lived among you?"

"He was the only one."

Dillinger nodded.   "O'Brien was a truly great man.   I wonder if you fully realize that.   I suppose in time you'll have O'Brien villages and O'Brien streets and O'Brien buildings, and all that sort of thing, but he deserves a really important monument.   Perhaps—a planet can be named after a man, you know.   You should have named your planet O'Brien."

"O'Brien?" Fornri said.   He looked blankly at the others, turned back to Dillinger.   "O'Brien? Who is O'Brien?"

ALLEN LANG

Blind Man's Lantern

*W*alking home in the dark from an evening spent in mischief, a
young man spied coming toward him down the road a person with a
lamp. When the wayfarers drew abreast, the playboy saw that the other
traveler was the Blind Man from his village. "Blind Man," the youngster
shouted across the road, "what a fool you be! Why, old No-Eyes, do
you bear a lantern, you whose midnight is no darker than his noonday?"
The Blind Man lifted his lamp. "It is not as a light for myself that I
carry this, Boy," he said, "it is to warn off you fools with eyes."
—Hausa proverb

The Captain shook hands with the black-hatted Amishman while the woman
stood aside, not concerning herself with men's business. "It's been a pleasure to
have you and *Fraa* Stoltzfoos aboard, Aaron," the Captain said. "Ship's stores
are yours, my friend; if there's anything you need, take it and welcome. You're
a long way from the corner grocery."

"My Martha and I have all that's needful," Aaron Stoltzfoos said. "We have
our plow, our seed, our land. Captain, please tell your men, who treated us
strangers as honored guests, we thank them from our hearts. We'll not soon forget
their kindness."

"I'll tell them," the Captain promised. Stoltzfoos hoisted himself to the wagon
seat and reached a hand down to boost his wife up beside him. Martha Stoltzfoos
sat, blushing a bit for having displayed an accidental inch of black stocking before
the ship's officers. She smoothed down her black skirts and apron, patted the
candle-snuffer *Kapp* into place over her prayer-covering, and tucked the wool cape
around her arms and shoulders. The world outside, her husband said, was a cold
one.

Now in the Stoltzfoos wagon was the final lot of homestead goods with which
these two Amishers would battle the world of Murna. There was the plow and
bags of seed, two crates of nervous chickens; a huge, round tabletop; an alcohol-
burning laboratory incubator, bottles of agar-powder, and a pressure cooker that
could can vegetables as readily as it could autoclave culture-media. There was a

microscope designed to work by lamplight, as the worldly vanity of electric light would ill suit an Old Order bacteriologist like Martha Stoltzfoos.   Walled in by all this gear was another passenger due to debark on Murna, snuffling and grunting with impatience.   *"Sei schtill,* Wutzchen," Stoltzfoos crooned.   "You'll be in your home pen soon enough."

The Captain raised his hand.   The Engineer punched a button to tongue the landing ramp out to Murnan earth.   Cold air rammed in from the outside winter. The four horses stomped their hoofs on the floor-plates, their breath spikes of steam. Wutzchen squealed dismay as the chill hit his nose.

"We're *reddi far geh,* Captain," Stoltzfoos said.   "My woman and I invite you and your men to feast at our table when you're back in these parts, five years hence. We'll stuff you fat as sausages with onion soup and Pannhaas, Knepp and Ebbelkuche, shoo-fly pie and *scharifer* cider, if the folk here grow apples fit for squeezing."

"You'll have to set up planks outdoors to feed the lot I'll be bringing, Aaron," the Captain said.   "Come five-years' springtime, when I bring your Amish neighbors out, I'll not forget to have in my pockets a toot of candy for the little Stoltzes I'll expect to see underfoot."   Martha, whose English was rusty, blushed none the less.   Aaron grinned as he slapped the reins over the rumps of his team. "Giddap!"   The cart rumbled across the deck and down the ramp, onto the soil of Murna.   Yonnie, the Ayrshire bull, tossed his head and sat as the rope tightened on his noseband.   He skidded stubbornly down the ramp till he felt cold earth against his rear.   Accepting fate, Yonnie scrambled up and plodded after the wagon. As the Stoltzfooses and the last of their off-worldly goods topped a hillock, they both turned to wave at the ship's officers.   Then, veiled by the dusty fall of snow, they disappeared.

"I don't envy them," the Engineer said, staring out into the wintery world.

"Hymie, were you born in a barn?" the Exec bellowed.

"Sorry, sir."   The Engineer raised the landing ramp.   Heaters hummed to thaw the hold's air.   "I was thinking about how alone those two folks are now."

"Hardly alone," the Captain said.   "There are four million Murnans, friendly people who consider a white skin no more than a personal idiosyncrasy.   Aaron's what his folks call a *Chentelmaan,* too.   He'll get along."

"Chentelmaan-schmentelmaan," the Engineer said.   "Why'd he come half across Creation to scratch out a living with a horse-drawn plow?"

"He came out here for dirt," the Captain said.   "Soil is more than seedbed to the Amish.   It feeds the Old Order they're born to.   Aaron and Martha Stoltzfoos would rather have built their barns beside the Susquehanna, but all the land there's taken.   Aaron could have taken a job in Lancaster, too; he could have shaved off his beard, bought a Chevie and moved to the suburbs, and settled down to read an English-language Bible in a steepled church.   Instead, he signed a homestead-contract for a hundred acres eighty light-years from home; and set out to plow the land like his grandpop did.   He'll sweat hard for his piece of Murna, but the Amish always pay well for their land."

"And what do we, the government, I mean, get from the deal?" the Exec wanted to know. "This wagon of ours doesn't run on hay, like Aaron's does."

"Cultures skid backwards when they're transplanted," the Captain said. "Murnan culture was lifted from Kano, a modern city by the standards of the time; but, without tools and with a population too small to support technology, the West African apostates from Islam who landed here four hundred years ago slid back to the ways of their grandparents. We want them to get up to date again. We want Murna to become a market. That's Aaron's job. Our Amishman has got to start this planet back toward the machine age."

"Seems an odd job to give a fellow who won't drive a car or read by electric light," the Engineer observed.

"Not so odd," the Captain said. "The Amish pretty much invented American agriculture, you know. They've developed the finest low-energy farming there is. Clover-growing, crop-rotation, using animal manures, those are their inventions. Aaron, by his example, will teach the natives here Pennsylvania farming. Before you can say Tom Malthus, there'll be steel cities in this wilderness, filled with citizens eager to open charge accounts for lowgravs and stereo sets."

"You expect our bearded friend to reap quite a harvest, Captain," the Engineer said. "I just hope the natives here let him plant the seed."

"Did you get along with him, Hymie?"

"Sure," the Engineer said. "Aaron even made our smiths, those human sharks bound for Qureysh, act friendly. For all his strange ways, he's a nice guy."

"Nice guy, hell," the Captain said. "He's a genius. That seventeenth-century un-scientist has more feeling for folkways in his calloused left hand than you'd find in all the Colonial Survey. How do you suppose the Old Order maintains itself in Pennsylvania, a tiny Deutsch-speaking enclave surrounded by calico suburbs and ten-lane highways? They mind their business and leave the neighbors to theirs. The Amish have never been missionaries—they learned in 1600 that missionaries are resented, and either slaughtered or absorbed."

"Sometimes digestively," the Engineer remarked.

"Since the Thirty Years' War, back when 'Hamlet' was opening in London, these people have been breeding a man who can fit one special niche in society. The failures were killed in the early days, or later went gay and took the trappings of the majority. The successes stayed on the farm, respected and left alone. Aaron has flirted with our century; he and his wife learned some very un-Amish skills at the Homestead School. The skill that makes Aaron worth his fare out here, though, is an Amish skill, and the rarest one of all. He knows the Right Way to Live, and lives it; but he knows, too, that your Truth-of-the-Universe is something different. And right, for you. He's quite a man, our Aaron Stoltzfoos. That's why we dropped him here."

"Better him than me," the Engineer said.

"Precisely," the Captain said. He turned to the Exec. "As soon as we've lifted, ask Colonel Harris to call on me in my cabin, Gene. Our Marines had better fresh-up their swordsmanship and cavalry tactics if they're to help our Inad Tuaregs establish that foundry on Qureysh."

"It sometimes seems you're more Ship's Anthropologist than Captain," the Engineer remarked.

"I'm an anthro-apologist, Hymie, like Mr. Kipling," the Captain said. *"There are nine and sixty ways of constructing tribal lays. And—every—single—one—of—them—is—right!"* Bells rang, and the ship surged. "Aaron and Martha, God keep you," the Captain said.

"Whoa!" Aaron shouted. He peered back toward the ship, floating up into grayness, the cavitation of her wake stirring the snow into patterns like fine-veined marble. *"Gott saygen eich,"* he said, a prayer for his departing friends.

His wife shivered. "It's cold enough to freeze the horns off a mooley-cow," she said. She glanced about at the snowdrifted little trees and clutched her black cloak tighter. "I'm feared, Stoltz. There's naught about us now but snow and black heathen."

"It's fear that is the heathen," Aaron said. *"By the word of the Lord were the heavens made; and the host of them by the breath of His mouth."* He kissed her. "I welcome you to our new homeland, wife," he said.

Behind them Wutzchen—"piglet"—grunted. Martha smiled back at the giant porker, perched amongst the cases and bags and household goods like the victim of some bawdy charivari. "I've never heard a pig mutter so," she said.

"If he knew that his business here was to flatter the local lady-pigs with farrow, Wutzchen would hop out and run," Aaron said.

"Dummel dich, Stoltz," Martha said. "I've got to make your supper yet, and we don't have so much as a stove lit in our tent."

Stoltzfoos slapped the team back into motion. "What we need for our journey home are a few of the *altie lieder,"* he said, reaching back in the wagon for his scarred guitar. He strummed and hummed, then began singing in his clear baritone: *"In da guut alt Suumer-zeit . . .*

". . . *In da guut alt Suumer-zeit,"* Martha's voice joined him. As they jolted along the path through the pine trees, heading toward Datura-village, near which their homestead stood, they sang the other homey songs to the music of the old guitar. *"Drawk Mich Zrick zu Alt Virginye,"* nostalgic for the black-garbed Plain Folk left at home. Then Aaron's fingers danced a livelier tune on the strings: *"Ich fang 'n neie Fashun aw,"* he crowed, and Martha joined in:

"A new fashion I'll begin," they sang,
"The hay I'll cut in the winter;
"When the sun-heat beats, I'll loaf in the shade
"And feast on cherry-pie.
"I'll get us a white, smearkase cow,
"And a yard full of guinea-hen geese;
"A red-beet tree as high as the moon,
"And a patent-leather fence.
"The chickens I'll keep in the kitchen," they sang; whereupon Martha broke down laughing.

"It's a new world, and for now a cold world; but it's God's world, with home just up ahead,'' Aaron shouted. He pulled the wagon up next to the arctic tent that was to be their temporary farmhouse, beside the wagon loads of provision he'd brought before. He jumped down and swung Martha to earth. "Light the stove, woman; make your little kitchen bright, while I make our beasts feel welcome.''

The Amishwoman pushed aside the entrance flap of the tent. Enclosed was a circle some twelve feet wide. The floor was bare earth. Once warmed by the pump-up "naphtha" lantern and the gasoline hotplate, it would become a bog. Martha went out to the wagon to get a hatchet and set out for the nearby spinny of pines to trim off some twigs. Old Order manner forbid decorative floor-coverings as improper worldly show; but a springy carpet of pine-twigs could be considered as no more than a wooden floor, keeping two Plain Folk from sinking to their knees in mud.

The pots were soon boiling atop the two-burner stove, steaming the tent's air with onion-tangy *tzvivvele Supp* and the savory pork-smell of *Schnitz un Knepp,* a cannibal odor that disturbed not a bit Wutzchen, snoring behind the cookstove. Chickens, penned beneath the bed, chuckled in their bedtime caucus. The cow stood cheek-by-jowl with Yonnie, warming him with platonic graciousness as they shared the hay Aaron had spread before them. Martha stirred her soup. "When the bishop married me to you," she told Aaron, "he said naught of my having to sleep with a pig.''

"Ah, but I thought you knew that to be the purpose of Christian marriage, woman," Aaron said, standing close.

"It's Wutz I mean," she said. "Truly, I mind not a bit living as in one of those automobile-wagons, since it's with you, and only for a little while.''

"I'll hire a crew of our neighbors to help with the barn tomorrow," Aaron said. "That done, you'll have but one pig to sleep with.''

After grace, they sat on cases of tobacco to eat their meal from a table of feed sacks covered with oilcloth. "The man in the ship's little kitchen let me make and freeze pies, Stoltz," Martha said. "He said we'd have a deepfreeze big as all outdoors, without electric, so use it. Eat till it's all, *Maan;* there's more back.''

Yonnie bumped against Aaron's eating-elbow. "No man and his wife have eaten in such a zoo since Noah and his wife left the ark," Aaron said. He cut a slice of Schnitz-pie and palmed it against the bull's big snout to be snuffled up. "He likes your cooking," he said.

"So wash his face," Martha told him.

Outside the tent there was a clatter of horse-iron on frozen ground. "What the die-hinker is that?" Aaron demanded. He stood and picked up the naphtha lantern.

Outside, Aaron saw a tall black stranger, astride a horse as pale as the little Murnan moons that lighted him. *"Rankeshi dade!"* the visitor bellowed.

"May your life be a long one!" Aaron Stoltzfoos repeated in Hausa. Observing that his caller was brandishing a clenched fist, the Amishman observed the same ambiguous courtesy. "If you will enter, O Welcome Stranger, my house will be honored.''

"Mother bless thee, Bearded One," the Murnan said. He dismounted, tossing his reins to one of the four retainers who remained on horseback.   He entered the tent after Aaron; and stared about him at the animals, letting his dark eyes flick across Martha's unveiled face.   At the Amishman's invitation, the visitor sat himself on a tobacco-case, revealing as he crossed his legs elaborately embroidered trousers and boot tops worked with designs that would dazzle a Texan.   Martha bustled about hiding the remains of their meal.

The Murnan's outer dress was a woolen *riga,* the neckless gown of his West-African forefathers, with a blanket draped about his shoulders, exactly as those ancestors had worn one in the season of the cold wind called harmattan.   Aaron introduced himself as Haruna, the Hausa version of his name; and the guest made himself known as Sarki—Chief—of the village of Datura.   His given name was Kazunzumi.   Wutzchen snuffed in his sleep.   The Sarki glanced at the huge pig and smiled.   Aaron relaxed a bit.   The Islamic interdict on swine had been shed by the Murnans when they'd become apostates, just as Colonial Survey had guessed.

Stoltzfoos' Hausa, learned at the Homestead School at Georgetown University, proved adequate to its first challenge in the field, though he discovered, with every experimenter in a new language, that his most useful phrase was *magana sanoo-sanoo:* ''please speak slowly.''   Aaron let the Chief commence the desultory conversation that would precede talk of consequence.   Martha, ignored by the men, sat on the edge of the bed, reading the big German-language Bible.   Aaron and Kazunzumi sang on in the heathen tongue about weather, beasts, and field-crops.

The Sarki leaned forward to examine Aaron's beard and shaven upper lip, once; and smiled.   The Murnan does not wear such.   He looked at Martha more casually now, seeing that the husband was not disgraced by his wife's naked face; and remarked on the whiteness of her skin in the same tones he'd mentioned Wutzchen's remarkable girth.

Aaron asked when the snows would cease, when the earth would thaw.   The Sarki told him, and said that the land here was as rich as manure.   Gradually the talk worked round to problems involving carpenters, nails, lumber, hinges—and money.   Aaron was pleased to discover that the natives thought nothing of digging a cellar and raising a barn in midwinter, and that workers could be easily hired.

Suddenly Sarki Kazunzumi stood and slapped his palms together.   The tent flap was shoved open.   Bowed servants, who'd shivered outside for over an hour, placed their master's presents on the sack table, on the twig floor, even beside Martha on the bed.   There were iron knives, a roast kid, a basket of peanuts, a sack of roasted coffee beans, a string of dried fruit, and a tiny earthware flask of perfume.   There was even a woolen riga for Aaron, black, suggesting that the Survey had said a bit to the natives about Amish custom; and there were bolts of bright-patterned cloth too worldly for aught but quilts and infant-dresses, brightening Martha's eyes.

Aaron stood to accept the guest-gifts with elaborate thanks.   Sarki Kazunzumi as elaborately demeaned his offerings.   ''Musa the carpenter will appear on to-morrow's tomorrow,'' he said.   ''You will, the Mother willing, visit me in Datura tomorrow.   We will together purchase lumber worthy of my friend-neighbor's

barn-making.   May the Mother give you strength to farm, Haruna!   May the
Mother grant you the light of understanding!''

"*Sannu, sannu!*" Stoltzfoos responded.   He stood at the door of his tent, holding
his lantern high to watch the Sarki and his servants ride off into the darkness.

"*Er iss en groesie Fisch, nee?*" Martha asked.

"The biggest fish in these parts," Aaron agreed.   "Did you understand our
talk?''

"The heathen speech is hard for me to learn, Stoltz," Martha admitted, speaking
in the dialect they'd both been reared to.   "While you had only the alien speech
to study, I spent my time learning to grow the buglets and tell the various sorts
apart.   Besides, *unser guutie Deitschie Schproech, asz unser Erlayser schwetzt,
iss guut genunk fa mier.*''   (Our honest German tongue, that our Saviour spoke,
is good enough for me).

Aaron laughed.   "So *altfashuned* a *Maedel* I married," he said.   "Woman,
you must learn the Hausa, too.   We must be friends to these *Schwotzers,* as we
were friends with the English-speakers back in the United Schtayts.''   He pushed
aside the bolt of Murnan cloth to sit beside his wife, and leafed through the pages
of their *Famillien-Bibel,* pages lovingly worn by his father's fingers, and his grandfather's.

"Listen," he commanded:

"*For the Lord thy God bringeth thee into a good land, a land of brooks of water,
of fountains and depths that spring out of valleys and hills; a land of wheat, and
barley, and vines, and fig trees, and pomegranates; a land of oil olive, and honey;
a land wherein thou shalt eat bread without scarceness, thou shalt not lack any
thing in it; a land whose stones are iron, and out of whose hills thou mayest dig
brass.   When thou hast eaten and art full, then thou shalt bless the Lord thy God
for the good land which He hath given thee.*''   Aaron closed the big book reverently.
"Awmen," he said.

"Awmen," the woman echoed.   "Aaron, with you beside me, I am not fretful.''

"And with the Lord above us, I fear not in a strange land," Aaron said.   He
bent to scrape a handful of earth from beneath Martha's pine-twig carpet.   "*Guuter
Gruundt,*" he said.   "This will grow tall corn.   Tobacco, too; the folk here relish
our leaf.   There will be deep grasses for the beasts when the snow melts.   We
will prosper here, wife.''

The next morning was cold, but the snowfall had ceased for a spell.   The
Stoltzfooses had risen well before the dawn; Martha to feed herself, her husband,
and the chickens; Aaron to ready the horse and wagon for a trip into Datura.   He
counted out the hoard of golden cowries he'd been loaned as grubstake, did some
arithmetic, and allowed his wife to pour him a second cup of coffee for the road.
"You may expect the Sarki's wives to visit while I'm gone," he remarked.

"I'd be scared half to death!" Martha Stoltzfoos said.   Her hands went to the
back of her head, behind the lace prayer covering.   "My hair's all strooby, this
place is untidy as an auction yard; besides, how can I talk with those dark and
heathen women?   Them all decked out in golden bangles and silken clothes, most

likely, like the bad lady of Babylon?   Aaron Stoltz, I would admire a pretty to ride into town with you.''

"Haggling for hired-help is man's *Bissiniss*,'' he said.   "When Kazunzumi's women come, feed them pie and peaches from the can.   You'll find a way to talk, or women are not sisters.   I'll be back home in time for evening chores.''

Bumping along the trail into Datura, Aaron Stoltzfoos studied the land.   A world that could allow so much well-drained black soil to go unfarmed was fortunate indeed, he mused.   He thought of his father's farm, which would be his elder brother's, squeezed between railroad tracks and a three-lane highway, pressed from the west by an Armstrong Cork plant, the very cornstalks humming in harmony with the electric lines strung across the fields.   This land was what the old folks had sought in America so long ago: a wilderness ripe for the plow.

The wagon rumbled along the hoof-packed frozen clay.   Aaron analyzed the contours of the hills for watershed and signs of erosion.   He studied the patterns of the barren winter fields, fall-plowed and showing here and there the stubble of a crop he didn't recognize.   When the clouds scudded for a moment off the sun, he grinned up, and looked back blinded to the road.   Good tilth and friendship were promised here, gifts to balance loneliness.   Five years from spring, other Amish folk would come to homestead—what a barn-raising they'd have!   For now, though, he and Martha, come from a society so close-knit that each had always known the yield-per-acre of their remotest cousin-German, were in a land as strange as the New York City Aaron, stopping in for a phone-call to the vet, had once glimpsed on the screen of a gay-German neighbor's stereo-set.

Datura looked to Aaron like a city from the Bible, giving it a certain vicarious familiarity.   The great wall was a block of sunbaked mud, fifty feet tall at the battlements, forty feet thick at its base; with bright, meaningless flags spotted on either side of the entrance tower.   The cowhide-shielded gate was open.   Birds popped out of mud nests glued to the mud wall and chattered at Aaron.   Small boys wearing too little to be warm appeared at the opening like flies at a hog-slaughtering to add to the din, buzzing and hopping about and waving their arms as they called companions to view the black-bearded stranger.

Aaron whoaed his horse and took a handful of *amenes,* copper tenth-penny bits, to rattle between his hands.   *"Zonang!"* he shouted: "Come here!   Is there a boy amongst you brave enough to ride with an off-worlder to the Sarki's house, pointing him the way?''

One of the boys laughed at Aaron's slow, careful Hausa.   "Let Black-Hat's whiskers point him the way!'' the boy yelled.

"Uwaka! Ubaka!''   Damning both parents of the rude one, another youngster trotted up to Aaron's wagon and raised a skinny brown fist in greeting.   "Sir Off-Worlder, I who am named Waziri, Musa-the-Carpenter's son, would be honored to direct you to the house of Sarki Kazunzumi.''

"The honor, young man, is mine,'' Stoltzfoos assured the lad, raising his own fist gravely.   "My name is Haruna, son of Levi,'' he said, reaching down to hoist the boy up beside him on the wagon's seat.   "Your friends have ill manners.'' He giddapped the horse.

"Buzzard-heads!" Waziri shouted back at his whilom companions.

"Peace, Waziri!" Aaron protested. "You'll frighten my poor horse into conniptions. Do you work for your father, the carpenter?"

"To, honorable Haruna," the boy said. "Yes." The empty wagon thumped over the wheel-cut streets like a wooden drum. "By the Mother, sir, I have great knowledge of planing and joining; of all the various sorts of wood, and the curing of them; all the tools my father uses are as familiar to me as my own left hand."

"Carpentry is a skillful trade," Aaron said. "Myself, I am but a farmer."

"By Mother's light! So am I!" Waziri said, dazzled by this coincidence. "I can cultivate a field free of all its noxious weeds and touch never a food-plant. I can steer a plow straight as a snapped chalk-string, grade seed with a sure eye; I can spread manure—"

"I'm sure you can, Waziri," Aaron said. "I need a man of just those rare qualifications to work for me. Know you such a paragon?"

"Mother's name! Myself, your Honor!"

Aaron Stolzfoos shook the hand of his hired man, an alien convention that much impressed Waziri. The boy was to draw three hundred *amenes* a day, some thirty-five cents, well above the local minimum-wage conventions; and he would get his bed and meals. Aaron's confidence that the boastful lad would make a farmer was bolstered by Waziri's loud calculations: "Three hundred coppers a day make, in ten days' work, a bronze cowrie; ten big bronzes make a silver cowrie, the price of an acre of land. Haruna, will you teach me your off-world farming? Will you allow me to buy land that neighbors yours?"

"Sei schtill, Buu," Aaron said, laughing. "Before you reap your first crop, you must find me the Sarki."

"We are here, Master Haruna."

The Sarki's house was no larger than its neighbors, Moorish-styled and domed-roofed like the others; but it wore on its streetside walls designs cut into the stucco, scrolls and arabesques. Just above the doorway, which opened spang onto the broadway of Datura, a grinning face peered down upon the visitors, its eyes ruby-colored glass.

Waziri pounded the door for Aaron, and stepped aside to let his new employer do the speaking. They were admitted to the house by a thin, old man wearing a pink turban. As they followed this butler down a hallway, Aaron and Waziri heard the shrieks and giggles of feminine consternation that told of women being herded into the zenana. The Amishman glimpsed one of the ladies, perhaps Sarki Kazunzumi's most junior wife, dashing toward the female sanctuary. Her eyes were lozenges of antimony; her hands, dipped in henna, seemed clad in pale kid gloves. Aaron, recalling pointers on Murnan etiquette he'd received at Georgetown, elaborately did not see the lady. He removed his hat as the turbaned butler bowed him to a plush-covered sofa. Waziri was cuffed to a mat beside the door.

"Rankeshi dade!" the Sarki said. "May the Mother bring you the light of understanding."

"Light and long life, O Sarki," Stoltzfoos said, standing up.

"Will the guest who honors my roof-cup taste coffee with his fortunate host?" the Sarki asked.

"The lucky guest will be ever the Sarki's servant if your Honor allows him to share his pleasure with his fellow-farmer and employee, Waziri the son of Musa," Aaron said.

"You'd better have hired mice to guard your stored grain, O Haruna; and blow-flies to curry your cattle, than to have engaged the son of Musa as a farmer," Kazunzumi growled. "Waziri has little light of understanding. He will try to win from the soil what only honest sweat and Mother's grace can cause to grow. This boy will gray your beard, Haruna."

"Perhaps the sun that warms the soil will light his brains to understanding," Aaron suggested.

"Better that your hand should leave the plowhandle from time to time to warm his lazy fundament," the Sarki said.

"Just so, O Sarki," the Amishman said. "If Waziri does not serve me well, I have an enormous boar who will, if kept long enough from wholesomer food, rid me of a lazy farmhand." Waziri grinned at all the attention he was getting from the two most important men in town, and sat expectantly as the turbaned elder brought in coffee.

Stoltzfoos watched the Sarki, and aped his actions. Water was served with the coffee; this was to rinse the mouth that the beverage could be tasted with fresh taste buds. The coffee was brown as floodwater silt, heavy with sugar, and very hot; and the cups had no handles. "You are the first European I have seen for many years, friend Haruna," the Sarki said. "It is five years gone that the white off-worlders came, and with a black man as their voice purchased with silver the land you now farm."

"They bought well," Aaron said; "the seller sold justly. When the fist of winter loosens, the soil will prove as rich as butter."

"When the first green breaks through, and you may break the soil without offense, you will do well," Kazunzumi said. "You are a man who loves the land."

"My fathers have flourished with the soil for twenty generations," the Amishman said. "I pray another twenty may live to inherit my good fortune."

"Haruna," the Sarki said, "I see that you are a man of the book, that volume of which Mother in her grace turns over a fresh page each spring. Though your skin is as pale as the flesh of my palm, though you have but one wife, though you speak throat-deep and strangely, yet you and I are more alike than different. The Mother has given you light, Haruna, her greatest gift."

"I thank the Sarki for his words," Aaron said. "Sir, my good and only wife—I am a poor man, and bound by another law than that of the fortunate Kazunzumi—adds her thanks to mine for the rich gifts the Chief of Datura presented us, his servants. In simple thanks, I have some poor things to tender our benefactor."

Waziri, perceiving the tenor of Aaron's talk, sprang to his feet and hastened out to the wagon for the bundles he'd seen under the seat. He returned, staggering under a seventy-pound bale of long-leaf tobacco, product of Aaron's father's farm. He went back for a bolt of scarlet silk for the Sarki's paramount wife, and strings of candy for the great man's children. He puffed in with one last brown-wrapped parcel, which he unpacked to display a leather saddle. This confection was embossed with a hundred intricate designs, rich with silver; un-Amish as a Christmas tree.   Judging from the Sarki's dazzled thanks, the saddle was just the thing for a Murnan Chief.

As soon as Kazunzumi had delivered his pyrotechnic speech of thanks, and had directed that Aaron's gifts be placed on a velvet-draped dais at the end of the room, a roast kid was brought in.   Waziri, half drunk with the elegance of it all, fell to like any other adolescent boy, and was soon grease to the armpits.   Aaron, more careful, referred his actions to the Sarki's.   The bread must be broken, not cut; and it was eaten with the right hand only, the left lying in the lap as though broken. Belching seemed to be *de rigueur* as a tribute to the cuisine, so Aaron belched his stomach flat.

Business could now be discussed.   Aaron, having no pencil, traced with a greasy finger on the tile floor the outlines of the barn and farmhouse he envisaged.   The Sarki from time to time demanded of young Waziri such facts as a carpenter's son might be expected to know, and added lumber-prices in his head as Aaron's bank-barn and two-story farmhouse took form in his imagination.   Finally he told the Amishman what the two buildings would cost.   Better pleased by this figure than he'd expected to be, Aaron initiated the long-drawn ceremony required to discharge himself from Kazunzumi's hospitality.

As the Stoltzfoos wagon jolted out the gate of Datura, bearing the cot and clothes-trunk of Waziri together with the owner of those chattels, the boys who'd jeered before now stared with respect.   The black-hatted *Turawa* had been to visit the Sarki; this established him as no safe man to mock.   Waziri gave his late playmates no notice beyond sitting rather straighter on the wagon seat than was comfortable.

There was light enough left when they got back to the farm for Aaron and Waziri to pace out the dimensions of the barn and house.   The bank-barn would go up first, of course.   No Christian owner of beasts could consent to being well-housed while his animals steamed and shivered in a cloth-sided tent.   Waziri pounded stakes into the frozen ground to mark the corners of the barn.   Aaron pointed out the drainage-line that would have to be ditched, and explained how the removed earth would be packed, with the clay dug for the cellar, into a ramp leading to the barn's second story in the back.   Come next fall, the hayladder could be pulled right up that driveway to be unloaded above the stalls.   Aaron took the boy to the frozen-solid creek to show him where a wheel could be placed to lift water to a spillway for the upper fields.   He introduced his new helper to Wutzchen, and was pleased to hear Waziri speak wistfully of pork chops.   Waziri didn't want to meet Martha yet, though.   As a proper Murnan boy, he was not eager to be introduced to the boss' barefaced wife, though she bribed him with a fat wedge of applecake.

When Waziri set out with the lantern to tend to the final outdoor chores, Aaron inquired of his wife's day.   The Sarki's Paramount Wife, with two servants, had indeed visited, bringing more gifts of food and clothing.   Somehow the four of them had managed to breach the Hausa-*Pennsylfawnisch Deitsch* curtain.   "What in the world did you talk about?" Aaron asked.

"First, not knowing what to say, I showed the ladies a drop of vinegar under the microscope," Martha said.   "They screamed when they saw all the wriggly worms, and I was put to it to keep them from bundling back home.   Then we talked about you, Stoltz, and about the farm; and when would I be giving you *Kinner* to help with all the work," she said.   Martha fiddled with the cloak she was sewing for her husband.   "It was largely their heathen speech we used, so I understood only what they pointed at; but they ate hearty of anything without vinegar in it, and I laughed with them like with friends at a quilting-bee.   My, Stoltz! Those *Nayyer* women are lovely, all jeweled like queens, even the servant girls; even though they have no proper understanding of Christian behavior."

"Did they make you feel welcome, then?" Aaron asked.

"Ach, ja! They pitied me, I thought," Martha said.   "They said you must be poor, to have but one wife to comfort you; but they said that if the crops be good, you can earn a second woman by next winter.   *Chuudes Paste!"*

"I hope you told the Sarki's woman we've been married only since haying-time," Aaron said, "and it's a bit previous for you to be giving me little farmhands."

"I did that," Martha said.   "I told them, too, that by the time the oak leaves are the size of squirrel's ears—if this place has oaks, indeed, or squirrels—we'd have a youngling squalling in our house, loud as any of the Sarki's."

Waziri, crouched near the tent to pick up such talk as might pass inside concerning himself, was at first dismayed by Aaron's whoops of joy.   Then Martha joined her husband in happy laughter.   Since her tiny-garments line had been delivered in Low Dutch, the young Murnan chose to believe that the enthusiastic sounds he heard within the tent reflected joy at his employment.

It was cold the week the barn was raised, and the mattocks had heavy work gouging out frozen earth to be heaped into the bank leading up the back.   The Murnan laborers seemed to think midwinter as appropriate as any other time for building; they said the Mother slept, and would not be disturbed.   Martha served coffee and buttermilk-pop at breaktime, and presided over noontime feasts, served in several sittings, in the tent.   Before the workers left in the evening, Aaron would give each a drink out back, scharifer cider, feeling that they'd steamed hard enough to earn a sip of something volatile.   There are matters, he mused, in which common sense can blink at a bishop; as in secretly trimming one's beard a bit, for example, to keep it out of one's soup; or plucking a guitar to raise the spirits.

When the fortnight's cold work was done, the Stoltzfoos Farm was like nothing seen before on Murna.   The bank-barn was forty feet high.   On its lee side, Aaron had nailed thin, horizontal strips of wood about a foot apart, hoping to encourage the mud-daubing birds he'd seen on the wall at Datura to plaster their nests onto his barn, and shop for insects in his fields.   Lacking concrete, he'd constructed a roofless stone hut abutting the barn to serve as his manure shed.   The farmhouse itself was a bit gay, having an inside toilet to cheat the Murnan winters and a sunporch for Martha's bacteriological equipment.   As the nearest Amish *Volle Diener*—Congregational Bishop—was eighty light-years off, and as the circumstances were unusual, Aaron felt that he and Martha were safe from the shunning—

Meidung—that was the Old Order's manner of punishing Amischers guilty of "going gay" by breaking the church rules against worldly show.

A third outbuilding puzzled the Murnan carpenters even more than the two-storied wooden house and the enormous barn. This shed had hinged sidings that could be propped out to let breezes sweep through the building. Aaron explained to Musa the function of this tobacco shed, where he would hang his lathes of long-leafed tobacco to cure from August through November. The tobacco seedlings were already sprouting in Mason jars on the sunporch window-sills. The bank-barn's basement was also dedicated to tobacco. Here, in midwinter, Aaron and Martha and Waziri would strip, size, and grade the dry leaves for sale in Datura. Tobacco had always been a prime cash-crop for Levi, Aaron's father. After testing the bitter native leaf, Aaron knew that his Pennsylvania Type 41 would sell better here than anything else he could grow.

Martha Stoltzfoos was as busy in her new farmhouse as Aaron and Waziri were in the barn. Her kitchen stove burned all day. Nothing ever seen in Lancaster County, this stove was built of fireclay and brick; but the food it heated was honest Deitsch. There were pickled eggs and red beets, ginger tomatoes canned back home, spiced peaches, pickled pears, mustard pickles and chowchow, pickled red cabbage, Schnitz un Knepp, shoo-fly pie, vanilla pie, rhubarb sauce, Cheddar cheeses the size of Waziri's head, haystacks of sauerkraut, slices off the great slab of home-preserved chipped beef, milk by the gallon, stewed chicken, popcorn soup, rashers of bacon, rivers of coffee. In the evenings, protecting her fingers from the sin of idleness, Martha quilted and cross-stitched by lamplight. Already her parlor wall boasted a framed motto that reduced to half a dozen German words, the Amish philosophy of life: "What One Likes Doing is No Work."

For all the chill of the late-winter winds, Aaron kept himself and his young helper in a sweat. Martha's cooking and the heavy work were slabbing muscle onto Waziri's lean, brown frame. Aaron's farming methods, so much different to Murnan routines, puzzled and intrigued the boy. Aaron was equally bemused by the local taboos. Why, for example, did all the politer Murnans eat with the right hand only? Why did the women veil themselves in his presence? And what was this Mother-goddess worship that seemed to require no more of its adherents than the inclusion of their deity's name in every curse, formal and profane? "Think what you please, but not too loud," Aaron cautioned himself, and carefully commenced to copy those Murnan speech-forms, gestures, and attitudes that did not conflict with his own deep convictions.

But the soil was his employment, not socializing. Aaron wormed his swine, inspected his horse-powered plow and harrow, gazed at the sun, palpated the soil, and prayed for an early spring to a God who understood German. Each day, to keep mold from strangling the moist morsels, he shook the jars of tobacco seed, whose hair-fine sprouts were just splitting the hulls.

The rations packaged in Pennsylvania were shrinking. The Stoltzfoos stake of silver and gold cowries was wasting away. Each night, bruised with fatigue, Aaron brought his little household into the parlor while he read from the Book that had bound his folk to the soil. Waziri bowed, honoring his master's God in his master's manner, but understood nothing of the hard High German: *"For the Lord God will help me: therefore shall I not be confounded: therefore have I set my face like a flint, and I know I shall not be ashamed. Awmen."*

"Awmen," said Martha.

"Awmen," said Waziri, fisting his hand in respect to his friend's bearded God.

The Murnan neighbors, to whom late winter was the slackest season in the farm-year, visited often to observe and comment on the off-worlder's work. Aaron Stoltzfoos privately regarded the endless conversations as too much of a good thing; but he realized that his answering the Murnans' questions helped work off the obligation he owed the government for the eighty light-years' transportation it had given him, the opportunity he'd been given to earn this hundred acres with five years' work, and the interest-free loans that had put up his barn and farmhouse.

With Waziri hovering near, Aaron's proud lieutenant, the neighbors would stuff their pipes with native tobacco, a leaf that would have gagged one of Sir Walter Raleigh's Indian friends, while the Amishman lit a stogie in self-defense. Why, the neighbor farmers demanded, did Aaron propose to dust his bean-seeds with a powder that looked like soot? Martha's microscope, a wonder, introduced the Murnans to bacteria; and Aaron tediously translated his knowledge of the nitrogen-fixing symbiotes into Hausa. But there were other questions. What was the purpose of the brush stacked on top of the smooth-raked beds where Aaron proposed to plant his tobacco-seedlings? He explained that fire, second best to steaming, would kill the weed-seeds in the soil, and give the tobacco uncrowded beds to prosper in.

Those needles with which he punctured the flanks of his swine and cattle: what devils did they exorcise? Back to the microscope for an explanation of the disease-process, a sophistication the Murnans had lost in the years since they'd left Kano. What were the bits of blue and pink paper Aaron pressed into mudballs picked up in the various precincts of his property? Why did those slips oftentime change color, from blue to pink, or pink-to-blue? What was in those sacks of stuff—no dung of animals, but a sort of flour—that he intended to work into his soil? Aaron answered each question as best he could, Waziri supplying—and often inventing—Hausa words for concepts like phosphorous, ascarid worms, and litmus.

Aaron had as much to learn from his brown-skinned neighbors as he had to teach them. He was persuaded to lay in a supply of seed-yams, guaranteeing a crop that would bring bronze cowries next fall in Datura, the price of next year's oil and cloth and tools. The peanut, a legume Aaron had no experience of beyond purchasing an occasional tooth-ful at the grocery-store, won half a dozen acres from Korean lespedeza, the crop he'd at first selected as his soil-improver there. He got acquainted with a plant no Amishman before him had ever sown, a crabgrass called fonio, a staple cereal and source of beer-malt on Murna, imported with the first Nigerian colonists.

Aaron refused to plant any lalle, the henna-shrub from which the Murnans made the dye to stain their women's hands, feeling that it would be improper for him to contribute to such a vanity.   Bulrush millet, another native crop, was ill suited to Aaron's well-drained fields.   He planned to grow corn, though, the stuff his people called *Welschkarn*—alien corn.   Though American enough, maize had been a foreigner to the first Amish farmers, and still carried history in its name.   This crop was chiefly for Wutzchen, whose bloodlines, Aaron was confident, would lead to a crop of pork of a quality these heretics from Islam had never tasted before.

Work wasn't everything.   One Sunday, after he and Martha had sung together from the *Ausbund,* and Aaron had read from the *Schrift* and the *Martyr's Mirror,* there was time to play.

Sarki Kazunzumi and several other gentlemen who enjoyed City Hall or Chamber of Commerce standing in Datura had come to visit the Stoltzfooses after lunch; as had Musa the carpenter and his older son, Dauda, Waziri's brother.   Also on the premises were about a dozen of the local farmers and craftsmen, inspecting the curious architecture the off-worlder had introduced to their planet.   Aaron, observing that the two classes of his guests were maintaining a polite fiction, each that the other was not present, had an idea.   He'd seen Murnans in town at the mid-winter festival, their status-consciousness forgotten in mutual quaffs of fonio-beer or barley-brandy, betting together at horse-races and wheels-of-fortune.   "My friends," the Amishman addressed the Murnans gathered in his barn, inspecting Wutzchen, "let's play a game of ball."

Kazunzumi looked interested.   As the local Chief of State, the Sarki's approval guaranteed the enthusiasm of all the lesser ranks.

Aaron explained the game he had in mind.   It wasn't baseball, an "English" sport foreign to Amishmen, who can get through their teens without having heard of either Comiskey Park or the World Series.   Their game, *Mosch Balle,* fits a barnyard better.

In lieu of the regulation softball used in the game of Corner Ball, Martha had stitched together a sort of large beanbag.   The playing-field Aaron set up with the help of his visitors was a square some twelve yards on a side, fence-rails being propped up to mark its boundaries and fresh straw forked onto it six inches deep as footing.

Aaron's eight-man team was chosen from the working-stiffs.   The opposing eight were the Brass.   To start the game, four of the proletarians stood at the corners of the square; and two men of Kazunzumi's team waited warily within.

Aaron commenced to explain the game.   To say that the object of *Mosch Balle* is for a member of the outer, offensive team to strike an inner, defensive man with the ball is inadequate; such an explanation is as lacking as to explain baseball as the pitcher's effort to throw a ball so well that it's hittable, and so very well that it yet goes unhit.   Both games have their finer points.

"Now," Aaron told his guests on the field, "we four on the corners will toss the ball back and forth amongst ourselves, shouting *Hah, Oh, Tay,* with each pitch. Whoever has the ball on *Tay* has to fling it at one of the two men inside the square. If he misses, he's Out; and one of the other men on our team takes his place.   If he hits his target-man, the target's Out, and will be replaced by another man from

the Sarki's team.   The team with the last man left on the straw wins the first half.
Des iss der Weeg wie mir's diehne, O.K.?''

"*Afuwo!*" the Sarki yelled, a woman's call, grinning, crouched to spring aside.
"Hah!" Aaron shouted, and tossed the ball to Waziri's older brother, Dauda.
"Oh!" Dauda yelled, and threw the ball to the shoemaker.   "Tay!" the cobbler
exulted, and slammed the ball at the lower-ranking of the two men within the
square, the village banker.   The shoemaker missed, and was retired.

The Daturans were soon stripped down to trousers and boots, their black torsos
steaming in the cold air.   Aaron removed his shirt—but not his hat—and so far
forgot his Hausa in the excitement that he not only rooted for his teammates in
Pennsylfawnische Deitsch, but even punctuated several clumsy plays with raw
Fadomm's.

Aaron's skill won the first half for his team.   Blooded, the Chamber of Commerce
Eight fought through to win the second half.   A tie.   The play-off saw the Working-
Man's League pummeled to a standstill by the C-of-C, who took the laurels with
a final slam that knocked Waziri into the straw, protesting that it was an accident.

Sweating, laughing, social status for the moment forgotten, the teams and their
mobs of fans surged into the farmhouse to demand of Martha wedges of raisin pie
and big cups of strong coffee.   As the guests put their rigas and their white caps
back on, and assumed therewith their game-discarded rank of class, they assured
Aaron that the afternoon at the ball game had been a large success.

The next day was crisp and cold.   With nothing more to be done till the soil
thawed, Aaron took Waziri down to the creek to investigate his project of irrigating
the hilltop acres.   The flow of water was so feeble that the little stream was ice
to its channel.   "Do you have hereabouts a digger-of-water-holes?" Aaron asked
the boy.   Waziri nodded, and supplied the Hausa phrase for this skill.   "Good.
Wonn's Gottes wille iss, I will find a spot for them to dig, smelling out the water
as can my cousin Blue Ball Benjamin Blank," Aaron said.   "Go get from the
barn the pliers, the hand-tool that pinches."

Waziri trotted off and brought back the pliers.   "What are you up to, Haruna-
boss?" he asked.   Aaron was holding the bulldog pliers out before him, one handle
in each hand, parallel to the ground.

"I am smelling for the well-place," the Amishman said, pacing deliberately
across the field.   The boy scampered along beside him.   "We will need at least
one well to be safe from August drought.   Cousin Benjamin found the wet depths
in this fashion; perhaps it will work for me."   Aaron walked, arms outstretched,
for half an hour before his face grew taut.   He slowed his walking and began to
work toward the center of a spiral.   Waziri could see the sweat springing up on
the young farmer's brow and fingers, despite the cold breeze that blew.   The
bulldog pliers trembled as though responding to the throbbing of an engine.   Suddenly, as though about to be jerked from Aaron's hands, the pliers tugged downward
so forceably that he had to lift his elbows and flex his wrists to hold onto them.
"Put a little pile of stones here, Waziri," he said.   "We'll have the diggers visit
as soon as the ground thaws."

Waziri shook his head.   "Haruna, they will not touch soft earth until the first grass sprouts," he said.

"Time enough," Aaron said.   He looked up to satisfy himself that his prospective well-site was high enough to avoid drainage from his pig-yard, then left the Murnan boy to pile up a cairn for the diggers.   It would be good to have a windmill within earshot of the house, he mused; its squeaking would ease Martha with a homey sound.   Alone for a few minutes, Aaron retired to the workshop in the cellar of the barn.   He planed and sanded boards of a native lumber very like to tulipwood.   Into the headboard of the cradle he was making, he keyhole-sawed the same sort of broad Dutch heart that had marked his own cradle, and the cradles of all his family back to the days in the Rhineland, before they'd been driven to America.

Martha Stoltzfoos was speaking Hausa better than she'd spoken English since grade-school days, and she kept busy in the little bacteriological laboratory on her sunporch, keeping fresh the skills she'd learned at Georgetown and might some day need in earnest; but she still grew homesick as her child-coming day drew nearer. It was wrong, she told Aaron, for an Amishwoman to have heathen midwives at her lying-in.   For all their kindness, the Murnan women could never be as reassuring as the prayer-covered, black-aproned matrons who'd have attended Martha back home.   "Ach, Stoltz," she told her husband, "if only a few other of *unser sart Leit* could have come here with us."

"Don't worry, Love," Aaron said.   "I've eased calves and colts enough into the world; man-children can't come so different."

"You talk like a man," Martha accused him.   "I wish my Mem was just down the road a piece, ready to come a-running when my time came," she said.   She put one hand on her apron.   *"Chuudes Paste!* The little rascal is wild as a colt, indeed.   Feel him, Stoltz!"

Aaron dutifully placed his hand to sense the child's quickening.   "He'll be of help on the farm, so strong as he is," he remarked.   Then, tugging his hat down tight, Aaron went outdoors, bashful before this mystery.

The little creek had thawed, and the light of the sun on a man's face almost gave back the heat the air extorted.   Waziri had gone to town today for some sort of Murnan spring-festival, eager to celebrate his hard-earned wealth on his first day off in months.   The place seemed deserted, Aaron felt, without the boy; without the visitors he'd played ball and talked crops with, striding up in their scarlet-trimmed rigas to gossip with their friend Haruna.

Between the roadway and the house, Aaron knelt to rake up with his fingers a handful of the new-thawed soil.   He squeezed it.   The clod in his hand broke apart of its own weight: it was not too wet to work.   Festival-day though it was to his *Schwotzer* neighbors, he was eager to spear this virgin soil with his plow blade.

Aaron strode back to the barn.   He hitched Rosina—the dappled mare, named "Raisin" for her spots—to the plow and slapped her into motion.   Sleek with her winter's idleness, Rosina was at first unenthusiastic about the plow; but the spring sun and honest exercise warmed her quickly.   Within half an hour she was earning her keep.   Though Aaron was plowing shallow, the compact soil broke hard. Rosina leaned into the traces, leaving hoofprints three inches deep.   No gasoline tractor, Aaron mused, could ever pull itself through soil so rich and damp.   *Geils-grefte,* horsepower, was best exerted by a horse, he thought.

The brown earth-smells were good.   Aaron kicked apart the larger clods, fat with a planet-life of weather and rich decay.   This land would take a good deal of disking to get it into shape.   His neighbors, who'd done their heavy plowing just after last fall's first frost, were already well ahead of him.   He stabled Rosina at sundown, and went in to sneak a well-earned glass of hard cider past Martha's teetotaling eye.

Musa the carpenter brought his son home well after dark.   Waziri had had adventures, the old man said; dancing, gambling on the Fool's Wheel, sampling fonio-beer, celebrating his own young life's springtime with the earth's.   Both the old man and the boy were barefoot, Aaron noticed; but said nothing: perhaps shoelessness was part of their spring-festival.

Waziri, a bit *geschwepst* with the beer, tottered off to bed.   "Thanks to you, friend Haruna, that boy became a man today," the carpenter said.   He accepted a glass of Aaron's cider.   "Today Waziri's wallet jingled with bronze and copper earned by his own sweat, a manful sound to a lad of fifteen summers.   I ask pardon for having returned your laborer in so damaged a condition, brother Haruna; but you may be consoled with the thought that the Mother's festival comes but once in the twelve-month."

"No harm was done, brother Musa," Aaron said, offering his visitor tobacco. "In my own youth, I sometimes danced with beer-light feet to the music of worldly guitars; and yet I reached a man's estate."

Offered a refill for his pipe, Musa raised a hand in polite refusal.   "Tomorrow's sun will not wait on our conversation, and much must be done, in the manner of racers waiting the signal, before the first blade breaks the soil," he said.   "Good night, brother Haruna; and may Mother grant you light!"

"Mother keep you, brother Musa," Aaron murmured the heathen phrase without embarrassment.   "I'll guide your feet to your wagon, if I may."

Aaron, carrying the naphtha lantern, led the way across the strip of new-plowed soil.   Set by frost into plastic mounds and ridges, the earth bent beneath his shoes and the carpenter's bare feet.   Aaron swung Musa's picket-iron, the little anchor to which his horse was tethered, into the wagon, noticing that it had been curiously padded with layers of quilted cloth.   "May you journey home in good health, brother Musa," he said.

"Uwaka!" Musa shouted, staring at the plow-cuts.

Aaron Stoltzfoos dropped the lantern to his side, amazed that the dignified old man could be guilty of such an obscenity.   Perhaps he'd misheard.   "Haruna, you have damned yourself!" Musa bellowed.   "Cursed be this farm!   Cursed be thy farming!   May thy seedlings rot, may thy corn sprout worms for tassles, may your cattle stink and make early bones!"

"Brother Musa!" Aaron said.

"I am no sib to you, O Bearded One," Musa said. "Nor will I help you carry the curse you have brought upon yourself by today's ill-doing." He darted back to the farmhouse, where he ordered half-wakened Waziri to pad barefoot after him to the wagon, rubbing his eyes. "Come, son," Musa said. "We must flee these ill-omened fields." Without another word to his host, the carpenter hoisted his boy into the wagon, mounted, and set off into the night. The hoofs of his horse padded softly against the dirt road, unshod.

Martha met the bewildered Aaron at the door, wakened by Musa's shouting. *"Wass gibt,* Stoltz?" she asked. "What for was all the carry-on?"

Aaron tugged at his beard. "I don't know, woman," he admitted. "Musa the carpenter took one look at the plowing I did today, then cursed me as though he'd caught me spitting in his well. He got Waziri up from bed and took him home." He took his wife's hand. "I'm sorry he woke you up, Liebchen."

"It was not so much the angry carpenter who waked me as the little jack rabbit you're father to," Martha said. "As you say, a *Buu* who can kick so hard, and barefoot, too, will be a strong one once he's born."

Aaron was staring out the window onto the dark road. *"Farwas hot Musa sell gehuh?"* he asked himself. "What for did Musa do such a thing? He knows that our ways are different to his. If I did aught wrong, Musa must know it was done not for want to harm. I will go to the village tomorrow; Musa must forgive me and explain."

"He will, Stoltz," Martha said. *"Kuum, schloef.* You'll be getting up early."

"How can I sleep, not knowing how I have hurt my friend?" Aaron asked.

"You must," Martha urged him. "Let your cares rest for the night, Aaron."

In the morning, Stoltzfoos prepared for his trip into Datura by donning his Sunday-best. He clipped a black patent-leather bow tie, a wedding gift, onto his white shirt; and fastened up his best broadfall trousers with his dress suspenders. Over this, Aaron put his *Mutzi,* the tailed frock coat that fastened with hooks-and-eyes. When he'd exchanged his broad-brimmed black felt working-hat for another just the same, but unsweated, Aaron was dressed as he'd be on his way to a House-Amish Sunday meeting back home. "I expect no trouble here, Martha," he said, tucking a box of stogies under his arm as a little guest-gift for the old carpenter.

"Hurry home, Stoltz; I feel wonderful busy about the middle," Martha said. There was a noise out on the road. "Listen!" she said. "Go look the window out, now; someone is coming the yard in!"

Aaron hastened to lift the green roller-blind over the parlor window. "Ach; it is the *groesie Fisch,* Sarki Kazunzumi, with half the folk from town," he said. "Stay here, woman. I will go out and talk with them."

The Sarki sat astride his white pony, staring as Aaron approached him. Behind their chief, on lesser beasts, sat Kazunzumi's retainers, each with a bundle in his arms. "Welcome, O Sarki!" Aaron said, raising his fist.

Kazunzumi did not return the Amishman's salute. "I return your gifts, Lightless One," he announced. "They are tainted with your blasphemy." He nodded, and his servants dismounted to stack at the side of the road Aaron's guest-gifts of months before. The bale of tobacco was set down, the bolt of scarlet silk, the chains of candy, the silver-filigreed saddle. "Now that I owe you naught, Bearded One, we have no further business with one another." He reined his horse around. "I go in sadness, Haruna," he said.

"What did I do, Kazunzumi?" Aaron asked. "What am I to make of your displeasure?"

"You have failed us, who was my friend," the Sarki said. "You will leave this place, taking your woman and your beasts and your sharp-shod horses."

"Sir, where am I to go?"

"Whence came you, Haruna?" the Sarki asked. "Return to your own black-garbed folk, and injure the Mother no longer with your lack of understanding."

"Sarki Kazunzumi, I know not how I erred," Stoltzfoos said. "As for returning to my own country, that I cannot. The off-world vessel that brought us here is star-far away; and it will not return until we are all five summers older. My Martha is besides with child, and cannot safely travel. My land is ripe for seeding. How can I go now?"

"There is wilderness to the south, where no son of the Mother lives," the Sarki said. "Go there. I care not for heathen who are out of my sight."

"Sir, show us mercy," Aaron said.

Kazunzumi danced his shoeless horse around to face Aaron. "Haruna, who was my friend, whom I thought to stand with me in Mother's light, I would be merciful; but I cannot be weak. It is not me whom you must beseech, but the Mother who feeds us all. Make amends to Her, then Sarki Kazunzumi will give his ear to your pleas. Without amends, Haruna, you must go from here within the week." Kazunzumi waved his arm and galloped off toward Datura. His servants followed quickly. On the roadside lay the gifts, dusted from the dirt raised by the horses.

The Amishman turned toward the house. Martha's face was at the parlor window, quizzical under her prayer-covering, impatient to hear what had happened. Aaron plodded back to the house with the evil news, stumbling over a clod of earth in the new-turned furrows near the road. Martha met him at the door. *"Waas will er?"* she demanded.

"He says we must leave our farm."

"Why for?" she asked.

"Somehow, I have offended their *fadommt* Mum-god," Aaron said. "The Sarki has granted us a week to make ready to go into the wilderness." He sat on a coffee-colored kitchen chair, his head bowed and his big hands limp between his knees.

"Stoltz, where can we go?" Martha asked. "We have no *Freindschaft*, no kin, in all this place."

Aaron tightened his hands into fists. "We will not go!" he vowed. "I will find a way for us to stay." He broke open the box of cigars that had been meant as a gift for Musa and clamped one of the black stogies between his teeth. "What is their *heidisch* secret?" he demanded. "What does the Mother want of me?"

"Aaron Stoltz," Martha said vigorously, "I'll have no man of mine offering dignity to a heathen god.   The *Schrift* orders us to cut down the groves of the alien gods, to smash their false images; not to bow before them.   Will you make a golden calf here, as did your namesake Aaron of Egypt, for whose sin the Children of Israel were plagued?''

"Woman, I'll not have you preach to me like a servant of the Book,'' Aaron said.   "It is not for you to cite Scripture.''   He stared through the window. "What does the Mother want of me?''

"As you shout, do not forget that I am a mother, too,'' Martha said.   She dabbed a finger at her eye.

"Fagep mir, Liebling,'' Aaron said.   He walked behind the chair where his wife sat.   Tenderly, he kneaded the muscles at the back of her neck.   "I am trying to get inside Musa's head, and Kazunzumi's; I am trying to see their world through their eyes.   It is not an easy thing to do, Martha.   Though I lived for a spell among the 'English,' my head is still House-Amish; a fat, Dutch cheese.''

"It is a good head,'' Martha said, relaxing under his massage, "and if there be cheese-heads hereabouts, it's these blackfolk that wear them, and not my man.''

"If I knew what the die-hinker our neighbors mean by their Mother-talk, it might be I could see myself through Murnan eyes, as I can hear a bit with Hausa ears,'' Aaron said.   *'Iss sell nix so,* Martha?''

"We should have stood at home, and thought with our own good heads,'' she said.

"Let me think,'' Aaron said.   "If I were to strike you, wife,'' he mused, "it could do you great hurt, and harm our unborn child, *Nee?''*

"Aaron!''   Martha scooted out from under her husband's kneading hands.

"Druuvel dich net!'' he said.   "I am only thinking.   These blackfolk now, these neighbors who were before last night our friends, speak of Light as our bishop at home speaks of Grace.   To have it is to have all, to be one with the congregation. If I can find this Light, we and the Sarki and his people can again be friends.'' Aaron sat down.   "I must learn what I have done wrong,'' he said.

"Other than drink a glass of cider now and then, and make worldly music with a guitar, you've done no wrong,'' Martha said stubbornly.   "You're a good man.''

"In the Old Order, I am a good man, so long as no *Diener* makes trouble over a bit of singing or cider,'' Aaron said.   "As a guest on Murna, I have done some deed that has hurt this Mother-god, whom our neighbors hold dear.''

"Heathenish superstition!''

"Martha, love, I am older than you, and a man,'' Aaron said.   "Give me room to think!   If the goddess-Mother is heathen as Baal, it matters not; these folk who worship her hold our future in their hands.   Besides, we owe them the courtesy not to dance in their churches nor to laugh at their prayers; even the 'English' have more grace than that.''   Aaron pondered.   "Something in the springtime is the Murnan Mother's gift, her greatest gift.   What?''

"Blaspheme not,'' Martha said.   "Remember Him who *causeth the grass to grow for the cattle, and herb for the service of man: that he may bring forth food out of the earth.''*

"Wife, is the True God less, if these people call Him Mother?" Aaron demanded.

"We are too far from home," the woman sighed.   "Such heavy talk is wearisome; it is for bishops to discourse so, not ordinary folk like us."

"If I can't find the light," Aaron said, "this farm we live on, and hoped to leave to our children, isn't worth the water in a dish of soup."   He slapped his hands together and stood to pace.   "Martha, hear me out," he said.   "If a woman be with child, and a man takes her with lust and against her will, is not that man accursed?"

"Aaron!" she said.   *"Haagott,* such wicked talk you make!"

"Seen with Murnan eyes, have I not done just such a cursed thing?" Aaron demanded.   "The Mother-god of this world is *mit Kinndt,* fat with the bounty of springtime.   So tender is the swollen belly of the earth that the people here, simple folk with no more subtle God, strip the iron from the hoofs of their horses not to bruise her.   They bare their feet in her honor, treat her with the tenderness I treat my beloved Martha.   And to this Goddess, swollen earth, I took the plow!   Martha, we are fortunate indeed that our neighbors are gentle people, or I would be hanged now, or stoned to death like the wicked in the old days.   *Ich hot iere Gotterin awgepockt:* I raped their Goddess!"

Martha burst into tears.   When Aaron stepped forward to comfort her, she struck his chest with her balled fists.   "Stoltz, I wed you despite your beer-drinking from cans at the Singing, though you play a worldly guitar and sing the English songs, though people told me you drove your gay Uncle Amos' black-bumpered Ford before you membered to the district; still, house-Amish pure Old Order though my people are, I married you, from love and youngness and girlish ignorance.   But I do not care, even in this wilderness you've brought us to in that big English ship, to hear such vileness spoke out boldly.   Leave me alone."

"I'll not."

"You'd best," she said.   "I'm sore offended in the lad I'm wifed to."

"Love, *Ich bin sorry,"* Aaron said.   "The Book, though, says just what our neighbors told me: Ye shall know the truth, and the truth shall set you free.   I have found the truth, the truth of our dark-skinned friends.   I did not want to wound the ears of *da Oppel fuun mein Awk,* apple-of-mine-eye sweet Martha; but I must speak out the truth."

"It is not good enough," Martha sobbed, "that you accept this brown-skinned, jewel-bedizzened woman-god; but you must make love to her; and I, wed to you by the Book, nine months gone with *Kinndt,* am to make no fuss."

"I loved the Mother-god with the plow, and accidentally," Aaron bellowed. *"Haagott!* woman; have you no funny?"

"I will birth our child in my lap from laughing," Martha said, weeping.   "Aaron, do what you will.   I can hardly walk home to my Mem to bear a son in my girlhood bedroom.   We are like *Awduum uuu Ayf,* like you said; but the serpent in this Eden pleases me not."

"When I spoke of colts, and the borning of them," Aaron said, "I forgot me that mares are more sensible than human women.   Martha, *liebe* Martha, you wed a man when you married me. All your vapors are naught against my having seen the light. If to stay here, on this land already watered with my hard sweat, I had to slaughter cattle in sacrifice to the Mother, I'd pick up the knife gladly, and feel it no blasphemy against our God.''

"Aaron Stoltz," Martha said, "I forbid you to lend honor to this god!"

Aaron sat. He unlaced his shoes and tugged them off. "Woman," he asked softly, "You forbid me? Martha, for all the love I bear you, there is one rule of our folk that's as holy as worship; and that's that the man is master in his house." He pulled off his black stockings and stood, barefoot, with calluses won on the black earth of his father's farm; dressed otherwise meetly as a deacon. "I will walk to Datura on my naked feet to show our friends I know my wrongdoing, that I have hurt the belly of the pregnant earth. I will tell Sarki Kazunzumi that I have seen his light; that my horses will be unshod as I am, that the Mother will not feel my plow again until the grasses spring, when her time will be accomplished."

Martha crossed her hands about her middle. "Ach, Stoltz," she said. "Our *Buu iss reddi far geh*, I think. Today will be his birthday. Don't let your tenderness to the earth keep you from walking swiftly to Datura; and when you return, come in a wagon with the Sarki's ladies, who understand midwifery. I think they will find work here."

"I will hurry, Mother," Aaron promised.

Thin Edge

I

"Beep!" said the radio smugly. *"Beep! Beep! Beep!"*
"There's one," said the man at the pickup controls of tugship 431. He checked the numbers on the various dials of his instruments. Then he carefully marked down in his log book the facts that the radio finder was radiating its beep on such-and-such a frequency and that that frequency and that rate-of-beep indicated that the asteroid had been found and set with anchor by a Captain Jules St. Simon. The direction and distance were duly noted.

That information on direction and distance had already been transmitted to the instruments of the tugship's pilot. "Jazzy-o!" said the pilot. "Got 'im."

He swiveled his ship around until the nose was in line with the beep and then jammed down on the forward accelerator for a few seconds. Then he took his foot off it and waited while the ship approached the asteroid.

In the darkness of space, only points of light were visible. Off to the left, the sun was a small, glaring spot of whiteness that couldn't be looked at directly. Even out here in the Belt, between the orbits of Mars and Jupiter, that massive stellar engine blasted out enough energy to make it uncomfortable to look at with the naked eye. But it could illuminate matter only; the hard vacuum of space remained dark. The pilot could have located the planets easily, without looking around. He knew where each and every one of them were. He had to.

A man can navigate in space by instrument, and he can take the time to figure out where every planet ought to be. But if he does, he won't really be able to navigate in the Asteroid Belt.

In the Nineteenth Century, Mark Twain pointed out that a steamboat pilot who navigated a ship up and down the Mississippi had to be able to identify every landmark and every changing sandbar along the river before he would be allowed to take charge of the wheel. He not only had to memorize the whole river, but be able to predict the changes in its course and the variations in its eddies. He had to be able to know exactly where he was at every moment, even in the blackest of moonless nights, simply by glancing around him.

An asteroid man has to be able to do the same thing. The human mind is capable of it, and one thing that the men and women of the Belt Cities had learned was to use the human mind.

"Looks like a big 'un, Jack," said the instrument man. His eyes were on the radar screen. It not only gave him a picture of the body of the slowly spinning mountain, but the distance and the angular and radial velocities. A duplicate of the instrument gave the same information to the pilot.

The asteroid was fairly large as such planetary debris went—some five hundred meters in diameter, with a mass of around one hundred seventy-four million metric tons.

Within twenty meters of the surface of the great mountain of stone, the pilot brought the ship to a dead stop in relation to that surface.

"Looks like she's got a nice spin on her," he said. "We'll see."

He waited for what he knew would appear somewhere near the equator of the slowly revolving mass. It did. A silvery splash of paint that had originally been squirted on by the anchor man who had first spotted the asteroid in order to check the rotational velocity.

The pilot of the space tug waited until the blotch was centered in the crosshairs of his peeper and then punched the timer. When it came around again, he would be able to compute the angular momentum of the gigantic rock.

"Where's he got his anchor set?" the pilot asked his instrument man.

"The beep's from the North Pole," the instrument man reported instantly. "How's her spin?"

"Wait a bit. The spot hasn't come round again yet. Looks like we'll have some fun with her, though." He kept three stars fixed carefully in his spotters to make sure he didn't drift enough to throw his calculations off. And waited.

Meanwhile, the instrument man abandoned his radar panel and turned to the locker where his vacuum suit waited at the ready. By the time the pilot had seen the splotch of silver come round again and timed it, the instrument man was ready in his vacuum suit.

"Sixteen minutes, forty seconds," the pilot reported. "Angular momentum one point one times ten to the twenty-first gram centimeters squared per second."

"So we play Ride 'Em Cowboy," the instrument man said. "I'm evacuating. Tell me when." He had already poised his finger over the switch that would pull the air from his compartments, which had been sealed off from the pilot's compartment when the timing had started.

"Start the pump," said the pilot.

The switch was pressed, and the pumps began to evacuate the air from the compartment. At the same time, the pilot jockeyed the ship to a position over the north pole of the asteroid.

"Over" isn't quite the right word. "Next to" is not much better, but at least it has no implied up-and-down orientation. The surface gravity of the asteroid was only two millionths of a Standard Gee, which is hardly enough to give any noticeable impression to the human nervous system.

"Surface at two meters," said the pilot. "Holding."

The instrument man opened the outer door and saw the surface of the gigantic rock a couple of yards in front of him. And projecting from that surface was the eye of an eyebolt that had been firmly anchored in the depths of the asteroid, a nickel-steel shaft thirty feet long and eight inches in diameter, of which only the eye at the end showed.

The instrument man checked to make sure that his safety line was firmly anchored and then pushed himself across the intervening space to grasp the eye with a space-gloved hand.

This was the anchor.

Mowing a nickel-iron asteroid across space to nearest processing plant is a relatively simple job. You slap a powerful electromagnet on her, pour on the juice, and off you go.

The stony asteroids are a different matter. You have to have something to latch on to, and that's where the anchor-setter comes in. His job is to put that anchor in there. That's the first space job a man can get in the Belt, the only way to get space experience. Working by himself, a man learns to preserve his own life out there.

Operating a space tug, on the other hand, is a two-man job because a man cannot both be on the surface of the asteroid and in his ship at the same time. But every space tug man has had long experience as an anchor setter before he's allowed to be in a position where he is capable of killing someone besides himself if he makes a stupid mistake in that deadly vacuum.

"On contact, Jack," the instrument man said as soon as he had a firm grip on the anchor. "Release safety line."

"Safety line released, Harry," Jack's voice said in his earphones.

Jack had pressed a switch that released the ship's end of the safety line so that it now floated free. Harry pulled it toward himself and attached the free end to the eye of the anchor bolt, on a loop of nickel-steel that had been placed there for that purpose. "Safety line secured," he reported. "Ready for tug line."

In the pilot's compartment, Jack manipulated the controls again. The ship moved away from the asteroid and yawed around so that the "tail" was pointed toward the anchor bolt. Protruding from a special port was a heavy-duty universal joint with special attachments. Harry reached out, grasped it with one hand, and pulled it toward him, guiding it toward the eyebolt. A cable attached to its other end snaked out of the tug.

Harry worked hard for some ten or fifteen minutes to get the universal joint firmly bolted to the eye of the anchor. When he was through, he said: "O.K., Jack. Try 'er."

The tug moved gently away from the asteroid, and the cable that bound the two together became taut. Harry carefully inspected his handiwork to make sure that everything had been done properly and that the mechanism would stand the stress.

"So far so good," he muttered more to himself than to Jack.

Then he carefully set two compact little strain gauges on the anchor itself, at ninety degrees from each other on the circumference of the huge anchor bolt. Two others were already in position in the universal joint itself. When everything was ready, he said: "Give 'er a try at length."

The tug moved away from the asteroid, paying out the cable as it went.

Hauling around an asteroid that had a mass on the order of one hundred seventy-four million metric tons required adequate preparation.   The nonmagnetic stony asteroids are an absolute necessity for the Belt Cities.   In order to live, man needs oxygen, and there is no trace of an atmosphere on any of the little Belt worlds except that which Man has made himself and sealed off to prevent it from escaping into space.   Carefully conserved though that oxygen is, no process is or can be one hundred per cent efficient.   There will be leakage into space, and that which is lost must be replaced.   To bring oxygen from Earth in liquid form would be outrageously expensive and even more outrageously inefficient—and no other planet in the System has free oxygen for the taking.   It is much easier to use Solar energy to take it out of its compounds, and those compounds are much more readily available in space, where it is not necessary to fight the gravitational pull of a planet to get them.   The stony asteroids average thirty-six per cent oxygen by mass; the rest of it is silicon, magnesium, aluminum, nickel, and calcium, with respectable traces of sodium, chromium, phosphorous manganese, cobalt, potassium, and titanium.   The metallic nickel-iron asteroids made an excellent source of export products to ship to Earth, but the stony asteroids were for home consumption.

This particular asteroid presented problems.   Not highly unusual problems, but problems nonetheless.   It was massive and had a high rate of spin.   In addition, its axis of spin was at an angle of eighty-one degrees to the direction in which the tug would have to tow it to get it to the processing plant.   The asteroid was, in effect, a huge gyroscope, and it would take quite a bit of push to get that axis tilted in the direction that Harry Morgan and Jack Latrobe wanted it to go.   In theory, they could just have latched on, pulled, and let the thing precess in any way it wanted to.   The trouble is that that would not have been too good for the anchor bolt.   A steady pull on the anchor bolt was one thing: a nickel-steel bolt like that could take a pull of close to twelve million pounds as long as that pull was along the axis.   Flexing it—which would happen if they let the asteroid precess at will—would soon fatigue even that heavy bolt.

The cable they didn't have to worry about.   Each strand was a fine wire of two-phase material—the harder phase being borazon, the softer being tungsten carbide. Winding these fine wires into a cable made a flexible rope that was essentially a three-phase material—with the vacuum of space acting as the third phase.   With a tensile strength above a hundred million pounds per square inch, a half-inch cable could easily apply more pressure to that anchor than it could take.   There was a need for that strong cable: a snapping cable that is suddenly released from a tension of many millions of pounds can be dangerous in the extreme, forming a writhing whip that can lash through a spacesuit as though it did not exist.   What damage it did to flesh and bone after that was of minor importance; a man who loses all his air in explosive decompression certainly has very little use for flesh and bone thereafter.

"All O.K. here," Jack's voice came over Harry's headphones.

"And here," Harry said.   The strain gauges showed nothing out of the ordinary.

"O.K.   Let's see if we can flip this monster over," Harry said, satisfied that the equipment would take the stress that would be applied to it.

He did not suspect the kind of stress that would be applied to him within a few short months.

II

The hotel manager was a small-minded man with a narrow-minded outlook and a brain that was almost totally unable to learn. He was, in short, a "normal" Earthman. He took one look at the card that had been dropped on his desk from the chute of the registration computer and reacted. His thin gray brows drew down over his cobralike brown eyes, and he muttered, "Ridiculous!" under his breath.

The registration computer wouldn't have sent him the card if there hadn't been something odd about it, and odd things happened so rarely that the manager took immediate notice of it. One look at the title before the name told him everything he needed to know. Or so he thought.

The registration robot handled routine things routinely. If they were not routine, the card was dropped on the manager's desk. It was then the manager's job to fit everything back into the routine. He grasped the card firmly between thumb and forefinger and stalked out of his office. He took an elevator down to the registration desk. His trouble was that he had seized upon the first thing he saw wrong with the card and saw nothing thereafter. To him, "out of the ordinary" meant "wrong"—which was where he made his mistake.

There was a man waiting impatiently at the desk. He had put the card that had been given him by the registration robot on the desk and was tapping his fingers on it.

The manager walked over to him. "Morgan, Harry?" he asked with a firm but not arrogant voice.

"Is this the city of York, New?" asked the man. There was a touch of cold humor in his voice that made the manager look more closely at him. He weighed perhaps two-twenty and stood a shade over six-two, but it was the look in the blue eyes and the bearing of the man's body that made the manager suddenly feel as though this man were someone extraordinary. That, of course, meant "wrong."

Then the question that the man had asked in rebuttal to his own penetrated the manager's mind, and he became puzzled. "Er . . . I beg your pardon?"

"I said, 'Is this York, New?'" the man repeated.

"This is New York, if that's what you mean," the manager said.

"Then I am Harry Morgan, if that's what *you* mean."

The manager, for want of anything better to do to cover his confusion, glanced back at the card—without really looking at it. Then he looked back up at the face of Harry Morgan. "Evidently you have not turned in your Citizen's Identification Card for renewal, Mr. Morgan," he said briskly. As long as he was on familiar ground, he knew how to handle himself.

"Odd's Fish!" said Morgan with utter sadness. "How did you know?"

The manager's comfortable feeling of rightness had returned. "You can't hope to fool a registration robot, Mr. Morgan," he said. "When a discrepancy is observed, the robot immediately notifies a person in authority. Two months ago,

Government Edict 7-3356-Hb abolished titles of courtesy absolutely and finally. You Englishmen have clung to them for far longer than one would think possible but that has been abolished.'' He flicked the card with a finger. ''You have registered here as 'Commodore Sir Harry Morgan'—obviously, that is the name and anti-social title registered on your card. When you put the card into the registration robot, the error was immediately noted and I was notified. You should not be using an out-of-date card, and I will be forced to notify the Citizen's Registration Bureau.''

''Forced?'' said Morgan in mild amazement. ''Dear me! What a terribly strong word.''

The manager felt the hook bite, but he could no more resist the impulse to continue than a cat could resist catnip. His brain did not have the ability to overcome his instinct. And his instinct was wrong. ''You may consider yourself under arrest, Mr. Morgan.''

''I thank you for that permission,'' Morgan said with a happy smile. ''But I think I shall not take advantage of it.'' He stood there with that same happy smile while two hotel security guards walked up and stood beside him, having been called by the manager's signal.

Again it took the manager a little time to realize what Morgan had said. He blinked. ''Advantage of it?'' he repeated haphazardly.

Harry Morgan's smile vanished as though it had never been. His blue eyes seemed to change from the soft blue of a cloudless sky to the steely blue of a polished revolver. Oddly enough, his lips did not change. They still seemed to smile, although the smile had gone.

''Manager,'' he said deliberately, ''if you will pardon my using your title, you evidently cannot read.''

The manager had not lived in the atmosphere of the Earth's Citizen's Welfare State as long as he had without knowing that dogs eat dogs. He looked back at the card that had been delivered to his desk only minutes before and this time he read it thoroughly. Then, with a gesture, he signaled the Security men to return to their posts. But he did not take his eyes from the card.

''My apologies,'' Morgan said when the Security police had retired out of earshot. There was no apology in the tone of his voice. ''I perceive that you *can* read. Bully, may I say, for you.'' The bantering tone was still in his voice, the pseudo-smile still on his lips, the chill of cold steel still in his eyes. ''I realize that titles of courtesy are illegal on Earth,'' he continued, ''because courtesy itself is illegal. However, the title 'Commodore' simply means that I am entitled to command a spaceship containing two or more persons other than myself. Therefore, it is not a title of courtesy, but of ability.''

The manager had long since realized that he was dealing with a Belt man, not an Earth citizen, and that the registration robot had sent him the card because of that, not because there was anything illegal. Men from the Belt did not come to Earth either willingly or often.

Still unable to override his instincts—which erroneously told him that there was something 'wrong''—the manager said: ''What does the 'Sir' mean?''

Harry Morgan glowed warmly. 'Well, now, Mr. Manager, I will tell you. I will give you an analogy.   In the time of the Roman Republic, twenty-one centuries or so ago, the leader of an Army was given the title *Imperator*.   But that title could not be conferred upon him by the Senate of Rome nor by anyone else in power. No man could call himself *Imperator* until his own soldiers, the men under him, had publicly acclaimed him as such.   If, voluntarily, his own men shouted *'Ave, Imperator!'* at a public gathering, then the man could claim the title.   Later the title degenerated—''   He stopped.

The manager was staring at him with uncomprehending eyes, and Morgan's outward smile became genuine.   ''Sorry,'' he said condescendingly.   ''I forgot that history is not a popular subject in the Welfare World.''   Morgan had forgotten no such thing, but he went right on.   ''What I meant to say was that the spacemen of the Belt Cities have voluntarily agreed among themselves to call me 'sir'. Whether that is a title of ability or a title of courtesy, you can argue about with me at another time.   Right now, I want my room key.''

Under the regulations, the manager knew there was nothing else he could do. He had made a mistake, and he knew that he had.   If he had only taken the trouble to read the rest of the card—

''Awfully sorry, Mr. Morgan,'' he said with a lopsided smile that didn't even look genuine.   ''The—''

''Watch those courtesy titles,'' Morgan reprimanded gently.   '' 'Mister' comes ultimately from the Latin *magister,* meaning 'master' or 'teacher'.   And while I may be your master, I wouldn't dare think I could teach you anything.''

''All citizens are entitled to be called 'Mister','' the manager said with a puzzled look.   He pushed a room key across the desk.

''Which just goes to show you,'' said Harry Morgan, picking up the key.

He turned casually, took one or two steps away from the registration desk, then— quite suddenly—did an about-face and snapped: *''What happened to Jack Latrobe?''*

''Who?'' said the manager, his face gaping stupidly.

Harry Morgan knew human beings, and he was fairly certain that the manager couldn't have reacted that way unless he honestly had no notion of what Morgan was talking about.

He smiled sweetly.   ''Never you mind, dear boy.   Thank you for the key.'' He turned again and headed for the elevator bank, confident that the manager would find the question he had asked about Jack Latrobe so completely meaningless as to be incapable of registering as a useful memory.

He was perfectly right.

III

The Belt Cities could survive without the help of Earth, and the Supreme Congress of the United Nations of Earth knew it.   But they also knew that ''survive'' did not by any means have the same semantic or factual content as ''live comfortably''. If Earth were to vanish overnight, the people of the Belt would live, but they would be seriously handicapped.   On the other hand, the people of Earth could survive—

as they had for millennia—without the Belt Cities, and while doing without Belt imports might be painful, it would by no means be deadly.

But both the Belt Cities and the Earth knew that the destruction of one would mean the collapse of the other as a civilization.

Earth needed iron. Belt iron was cheap. The big iron deposits of Earth were worked out, and the metal had been widely scattered. The removal of the asteroids as a cheap source would mean that iron would become prohibitively expensive. Without cheap iron, Earth's civilization would have to undergo a painfully drastic change—a collapse and regeneration.

But the Belt Cities were handicapped by the fact that they had had as yet neither the time nor the resources to manufacture anything but absolute necessities. Cloth, for example, was imported from Earth. A society that is still busy struggling for the bare necessities—such as manufacturing its own air—has no time to build the huge looms necessary to weave cloth . . . or to make clothes, except on a minor scale. Food? You can have hydroponic gardens on an asteroid, but raising beef cattle, even on Ceres, was difficult. Eventually, perhaps, but not yet.

The Belt Cities were populated by pioneers who still had not given up the luxuries of civilization. Their one weakness was that they had their cake and were happily eating it, too.

Not that Harry Morgan didn't realize that fact. A Belt man is, above all, a realist, in that he must, of necessity, understand the Laws of the Universe and deal with them. Or die.

Commodore Sir Harry Morgan was well aware of the stir he had created in the lobby of the Grand Central Hotel. Word would leak out, and he knew it. The scene had been created for just that purpose.

> *"Grasshopper sittin' on a railroad track,*
> *Singin' polly-wolly-doodle-alla-day!*
> *A-pickin' his teeth with a carpet tack,*
> *Singin' polly-wolly-doodle-alla-day!"*

He sang with gusto as the elevator lifted him up to the seventy-fourth floor of the Grand Central Hotel. The other passengers in the car did not look at him directly; they cast sidelong glances.

This guy, they seemed to think in unison, *is a nut. We will pay no attention to him, since he probably does not really exist. Even if he does, we will pay no attention in the hope that he will go away.*

On the seventy-fourth floor, he *did* go away, heading for his room. He keyed open the door and strolled over to the phone, where a message had already been dropped into the receiver slot. He picked it up and read it.

COMMODORE SIR HARRY MORGAN, RM. 7426, GCH: REQUEST YOU CALL EDWAY TARNHORST, REPRESENTATIVE OF THE PEOPLE OF GREATER LOS ANGELES, SUPREME CONGRESS. PUNCH 33-981-762-044 COLLECT.

"How news travels," Harry Morgan thought to himself. He tapped out the number on the keyboard of the phone and waited for the panel to light up. When it did, it showed a man in his middle fifties with a lean, ascetic face and graying hair, which gave him a look of saintly wisdom.

"Mr. Tarnhorst?" Morgan asked pleasantly.

"Yes. Commodore Morgan?" The voice was smooth and precise.

"At your service, Mr. Tarnhorst. You asked me to call."

"Yes. What is the purpose of your visit to Earth, commodore?" The question was quick, decisive, and firm.

Harry Morgan kept his affability. "That's none of your business, Mr. Tarnhorst."

Tarnhorst's face didn't change. "Perhaps your superiors haven't told you, but— and I can only disclose this on a sealed circuit—I am in sympathy with the Belt Cities. I have been out there twice and have learned to appreciate the vigor and worth of the Belt people. I am on your side, commodore, in so far as it does not compromise my position. My record shows that I have fought for the rights of the Belt Cities on the floor of the Supreme Congress. Have you been informed of that fact?"

"I have," said Harry Morgan. "And that is precisely why it is none of your business. The less you know, Mr. Tarnhorst, the safer you will be. I am not here as a representative of any of the City governments. I am not here as a representative of any of the Belt Corporations. I am completely on my own, without official backing. You have shown yourself to be sympathetic toward us in the past. We have no desire to hurt you. Therefore I advise that you either keep your nose out of my business or actively work against me. You cannot protect yourself otherwise."

Edway Tarnhorst was an Earthman, but he was not stupid. He had managed to put himself in a position of power in the Welfare World, and he knew how to handle that power. It took him exactly two seconds to make his decision.

"You misunderstand me, commodore," he said coldly. "I asked what I asked because I desire information. The People's Government is trying to solve the murder of Commodore Jack Latrobe. Assuming, of course, that it *was* murder— which is open to doubt. His body was found three days ago in Fort Tryon Park, up on the north end of Manhattan Island. He had apparently jumped off one of the old stone bridges up there and fell ninety feet to his death. On the other hand, it is possible that, not being used to the effects of a field of point nine eight Standard gees, he did not realize that the fall would be deadly and accidentally killed himself. He was alone in the park at night, as far as we can tell. It has been ascertained definitely that no representative of the People's Manufacturing Corporation Number 873 was with him at the time. Nor, so far as we can discover, was anyone else. I asked you to call because I wanted to know if you had any information for us. There was no other reason."

"I haven't seen Jack since he left Juno," Morgan said evenly. "I don't know why he came to Earth, and I know nothing else."

"Then I see no further need for conversation," Tarnhorst said. "Thank you for your assistance, CommodoreMorgan. If Earth's Government needs you again, you will be notified; if you gain any further information, you may call the number. Thank you again.   Good-by.''

The screen went blank.

How much of this is a trap? Morgan thought.

There was no way of knowing at this point.   Morgan knew that Jack Latrobe had neither committed suicide nor died accidentally, and Tarnhorst had told him as much.   Tarnhorst was still friendly, but he had taken the hint and got himself out of danger.   There had been one very important piece of information.   The denial that any representative of PMC 873 had been involved.   PMC 873 was a manufacturer of biological products—one of the several corporations that Latrobe had been empowered to discuss business with when he had been sent to Earth by the Belt Corporations Council.   Tarnhorst would not have mentioned them negatively unless he intended to imply a positive hint.   Obviously.   Almost too obviously.

Well?

Harry Morgan punched for Information, got it, got a number, and punched that.

''People's Manufacturing Corporation Ey-yut Seven Tha-ree,'' said a recorded voice.   ''Your desire, pu-leeze?''

''This is Commodore Jack Latrobe,'' Morgan said gently.   ''I'm getting tired of this place, and if you don't let me out I will blow the whole place to Kingdom Come.   Good bye-eye-eye.''

He hung up without waiting for an answer.

Then he looked around the hotel suite he had rented.   It was an expensive one— very expensive.   It consisted of an outer room—a ''sitting room'' as it might have been called two centuries before—and a bedroom.   Plus a bathroom.

Harry Morgan, a piratical smile on his face, opened the bathroom door and left it that way.   Then he went into the bedroom.   His luggage had already been delivered by the lift tube, and was sitting on the floor.   He put both suitcases on the bed, where they would be in plain sight from the sitting room.   Then he made certain preparations for invaders.

He left the door between the sitting room and the bedroom open and left the suite.

Fifteen minutes later, he was walking down 42nd Street toward Sixth Avenue. On his left was the ancient Public Library Building.   In the middle of the block, somebody shoved something hard into his left kidney and said, ''Keep walking, commodore.   But do what you're told.''

Harry Morgan obeyed, with an utterly happy smile on his lips.

IV

In the Grand Central Hotel, a man moved down the hallway toward Suite 7426. He stopped at the door and inserted the key he held in his hand, twisting it as it entered the keyhole.   The electronic locks chuckled, and the door swung open.

The man closed it behind him.

He was not a big man, but neither was he undersized.   He was five-ten and weighed perhaps a hundred and sixty-five pounds.   His face was dark of skin and had a hard, determined expression on it.   He looked as though he had spent the last thirty of his thirty-five years of life stealing from his family and cheating his friends.

He looked around the sitting room.   Nothing.   He tossed the key in his hand and then shoved it into his pocket.   He walked over to the nearest couch and prodded at it.   He took an instrument out of his inside jacket pocket and looked at it.

"Nothin'," he said to himself.   "Nothin'."   His detector showed that there were no electronic devices hidden in the room—at least none that he did not already know about.

He prowled around the sitting room for several minutes, looking at everything—chairs, desk, windows, floor—everything.   He found nothing.   He had not expected to, since the occupant, a Belt man named Harry Morgan, had only been in the suite a few minutes.

Then he walked over to the door that separated the sitting room from the bedroom. Through it, he could see the suitcases sitting temptingly on the bed.

Again he took his detector out of his pocket.   After a full minute, he was satisfied that there was no sign of any complex gadgetry that could warn the occupant that anyone had entered the room.   Certainly there was nothing deadly around.

Then a half-grin came over the man's cunning face.   There was always the chance that the occupant of the suite had rigged up a really old-fashioned trap.

He looked carefully at the hinges of the door.   Nothing.   There were no tiny bits of paper that would fall if he pushed the door open any further, no little threads that would be broken.

It hadn't really seemed likely, after all.   The door was open wide enough for a man to walk through without moving it.

Still grinning, the man reached out toward the door.

He was quite astonished when his hand didn't reach the door itself.

There was a sharp feeling of pain when his hand fell to the floor, severed at the wrist.

The man stared at his twitching hand on the floor.   He blinked stupidly while his wrist gushed blood.   Then, almost automatically, he stepped forward to pick up his hand.

As he shuffled forward, he felt a *snick! snick!* of pain in his ankles while all sensation from his feet went dead.

It was not until he began toppling forward that he realized that his feet were still sitting calmly on the floor in their shoes and that he was no longer connected to them.

It was too late.   He was already falling.

He felt a stinging sensation in his throat and then nothing more as the drop in blood pressure rendered him unconscious.

His hand lay where it had fallen.   His feet remained standing.   His body fell to the floor with a resounding *thud!*   His head bounced once and then rolled under the bed.

When his heart quit pumping, the blood quit spurting.

A tiny device on the doorjamb, down near the floor, went *zzzt!* and then there was silence.

V

When Representative Edway Tarnhorst cut off the call that had come from Harry Morgan, he turned around and faced the other man in the room.   "Satisfactory?" he said.

"Yes.   Yes, of course," said the other.   He was a tall, hearty-looking man with a reddish face and a friendly smile.   "You said just the right thing, Edway. Just the right thing.   You're pretty smart, you know that?   You got what it takes." He chuckled.   "They'll never figure anything out now."   He waved a hand toward a chair.   "Sit down, Edway.   Want a drink?"

Tarnhorst sat down and folded his hands.   He looked down at them as if he were really interested in the flat, unfaceted diamond, engraved with the Tarnhorst arms, that gleamed on the ring on his finger.

"A little glass of whisky wouldn't hurt much, Sam," he said, looking up from his hands.   He smiled.   "As you say, there isn't much to worry about now.   If Morgan goes to the police, they'll give him the same information."

Sam Fergus handed Tarnhorst a drink.   "Damn right. Who's to know?"   He chuckled again and sat down.   "That was pretty good.   Yes sir, pretty good. Just because he thought that when you voted for the Belt Cities you were on their side, he believed what you said.   Hell, *I've* voted on their side when it was the right thing to do.   Haven't I now, Ed?   Haven't I?"

"Sure you have," said Tarnhorst with an easy smile.   "So have a lot of us."

"Sure we have," Fergus repeated.   His grin was huge.   Then it changed to a frown.   "I don't figure them sometimes.   Those Belt people are crazy.   Why wouldn't they give us the process for making that cable of theirs?   Why?"   He looked up at Tarnhorst with a genuinely puzzled look on his face.   "I mean, you'd think they thought that the laws of nature were private property or something. They don't have the right outlook.   A man finds out something like that, he ought to give it to the human race, hadn't he, Edway?   How come those Belt people want to keep something like that secret?"

Edway Tarnhorst massaged the bridge of his nose with a thumb and forefinger, his eyes closed.   "I don't know.   Sam.   I really don't know.   Selfish, is all I can say."

Selfish? he thought.   *Is it really selfish?   Where is the dividing line?   How much is a man entitled to keep secret, for his own benefit, and how much should he tell for the public?*

He glanced again at the coat of arms carved into the surface of the diamond.

A thousand years ago, his ancestors had carved themselves a tiny empire out of middle Europe—a few hundred acres, no more. Enough to keep one family in luxury while the serfs had a bare existence. They had conquered by the sword and ruled by the sword. They had taken all and given nothing.

But had they? The Barons of Tarnhorst had not really lived much better than their serfs had lived. More clothes and more food, perhaps, and a few baubles— diamonds and fine silks and warm furs. But no Baron Tarnhorst had ever allowed his serfs to starve, for that would not be economically sound. And each Baron had been the dispenser of Justice; he had been Law in his land. Without him, there would have been anarchy among the ignorant peasants, since they were certainly not fit to govern themselves a thousand years ago.

Were they any better fit today? Tarnhorst wondered. For a full milennium, men had been trying, by mass education and by mass information, to bring the peasants up to the level of the nobles. Had that plan succeeded? Or had the intelligent ones simply been forced to conform to the actions of the masses? Had the nobles made peasants of themselves instead?

Edway Tarnhorst didn't honestly know. All he knew was that he saw a new spark of human life, a spark of intelligence, a spark of ability, out in the Belt. He didn't dare tell anyone—he hardly dared admit it to himself—but he thought those people were better somehow than the common clods of Earth. Those people didn't think that just because a man could slop color all over an otherwise innocent sheet of canvas, making outré and garish patterns, that that made him an artist. They didn't think that just because a man could write nonsense and use erratic typography, that that made him a poet. They had other beliefs, too, that Edway Tarnhorst saw only dimly, but he saw them well enough to know that they were better beliefs than the obviously stupid belief that every human being had as much right to respect and dignity as every other, that a man had a *right* to be respected, that he *deserved* it. Out there, they thought that a man had a right only to what he earned.

But Edway Tarnhorst was as much a product of his own society as Sam Fergus. He could only behave as he had been taught. Only on occasion—on very special occasion—could his native intelligence override the "common sense" that he had been taught. Only when an emergency arose. But when one did, Edway Tarnhorst, in spite of his environmental upbringing, was equal to the occasion.

Actually, his own mind was never really clear on the subject. He did the best he could with the confusion he had to work with.

"Now we've got to be careful, Sam," he said. "Very careful. We don't want a war with the Belt Cities."

Sam Fergus snorted. "They wouldn't dare. We got 'em outnumbered a thousand to one."

"Not if they drop a rock on us," Tarnhorst said quietly.

"They wouldn't dare," Fergus repeated.

But both of them could see what would happen to any city on Earth if one of the Belt ships decided to shift the orbit of a good-sized asteroid so that it would strike Earth. A few hundred thousand tons of rock coming in at ten miles per second would be far more devastating than an expensive H-bomb.

"They wouldn't dare," Fergus said again.

"Nevertheless," Tarnhorst said, "in dealings of this kind we are walking very close to the thin edge.   We have to watch ourselves."

VI

Commodore Sir Harry Morgan was herded into a prison cell, given a shove across the smallish room, and allowed to hear the door slam behind him.   By the time he regained his balance and turned to face the barred door again, it was locked. The bully-boys who had shoved him in turned away and walked down the corridor. Harry sat down on the floor and relaxed, leaning against the stone wall.   There was no furniture of any kind in the cell, not even sanitary plumbing.

"What do I do for a drink of water?" he asked aloud of no one in particular.

"You wait till they bring you your drink," said a whispery voice a few feet from his head.   Morgan realized that someone in the cell next to his was talking. "You get a quart a day—a halfa pint four times a day.   Save your voice.   Your throat gets awful dry if you talk much."

"Yeah, it would," Morgan agreed in the same whisper.   "What about sanitation?"

"That's *your* worry," said the voice.   "Fella comes by every Wednesday and Saturday with a honey bucket.   You clean out your own cell."

"I *thought* this place smelled of something other than attar of roses," Morgan observed.   "My nose tells me this is Thursday."

There was a hoarse, humorless chuckle from the man in the next cell.   " 'At's right.   The smell of the disinfectant is strongest now.   Saturday mornin' it'll be different.   You catch on fast, buddy."

"Oh, I'm a whiz," Morgan agreed.   "But I thought the Welfare World took care of its poor, misled criminals better than this."

Again the chuckle.   "You shoulda robbed a bank or killed somebody.   Then theyda given you a nice rehabilitation sentence.   Regular prison.   Room of your own.   Something real nice.   Like a hotel.   But this's different."

"Yeah," Morgan agreed.   This was a political prison.   This was the place where they put you when they didn't care what happened to you after the door was locked because there would be no going out.

Morgan knew where he was.   It was a big, fortresslike building on top of one of the highest hills at the northern end of Manhattan Island—an old building that had once been a museum and was built like a medieval castle.

"What happens if you die in here?" he asked conversationally.

"Every Wednesday and Saturday," the voice repeated.

"Um," said Harry Morgan.

" 'Cept once in a while," the voice whispered.   "Like a couple days ago. When was it?   Yeah.   Monday that'd be.   Guy they had in here for a week or so.   Don't remember how long.   Lose tracka time here.   Yeah.   Sure lose tracka time here."

There was a long pause, and Morgan, controlling the tenseness in his voice, said: "What about the guy Monday?"

"Oh. Him. Yeah, well, they took him out Monday."

Morgan waited again, got nothing further, and asked: "Dead?"

" 'Course he was dead. They was tryin' to get somethin' out of him. Somethin' about a cable. He jumped one of the guards, and they blackjacked him. Hit 'im too hard, I guess. Guard sure got hell for that, too. Me, I'm lucky. They don't ask me no questions."

"What are you in for?" Morgan asked.

"Don't know. They never told me. I don't ask for fear they'll remember. They might start askin' questions."

Morgan considered. This could be a plant, but he didn't think so. The voice was too authentic, and there would be no purpose in his information. That meant that Jack Latrobe really was dead. They had killed him. An ice cold hardness surged along his nerves.

The door at the far end of the corridor clanged, and a brace of heavy footsteps clomped along the floor. Two men came abreast of the steel-barred door and stopped.

One of them, a well-dressed, husky-looking man in his middle forties, said: "O.K., Morgan. How did you do it?"

"I put on blue lipstick and kissed my elbows—both of 'em. Going widdershins, of course."

"What are you talking about?"

"What are *you* talking about?"

"The guy in your hotel suite. You killed him. You cut off both feet, one hand, and his head. How'd you do it?"

Morgan looked at the man. "Police?"

"Nunna your business. Answer the question."

"I used a cobweb I happened to have with me. Who was he?"

The cop's face was whitish. "You chop a guy up like that and then don't know who he is?"

"I can guess. I can guess that he was an agent for PMC 873 who was trespassing illegally. But I didn't kill him. I was in . . . er . . . custody when it happened."

"Not gonna talk, huh?" the cop said in a hard voice. "O.K., you've had your chance. We'll be back."

"I don't think I'll wait," said Morgan.

"You'll wait. We got you on a murder charge now. You'll wait. Wise guy." He turned and walked away. The other man followed like a trained hound.

After the door clanged, the man in the next cell whispered: "Well, you're for it. They're gonna ask you questions."

Morgan said one obscene word and stood up. It was time to leave.

He had been searched thoroughly. They had left him only his clothes, nothing else. They had checked to make sure that there were no microminiaturized circuits on him. He was clean.

So they thought.

Carefully, he caught a thread in the lapel of his jacket and pulled it free.   Except for a certain springiness, it looked like an ordinary silon thread.   He looped it around one of the bars of his cell, high up.   The ends he fastened to a couple of little decorative hooks in his belt—hooks covered with a shell of synthetic ruby.

Then he leaned back, putting his weight on the thread.

Slowly, like a knife moving through cold peanut butter, the thread sank into the steel bar, cutting through its one-inch thickness with increasing difficulty until it was halfway through.   Then it seemed to slip the rest of the way through.

He repeated the procedure thrice more, making two cuts in each of two bars. Then he carefully removed the sections he had cut out.   He put one of them on the floor of his cell and carried the other in his hand—three feet of one-inch steel makes a nice weapon if it becomes necessary.

Then he stepped through the hole he had made.

The man in the next cell widened his eyes as Harry Morgan walked by.   But Morgan could tell that he saw nothing.   He had only heard.   His eyes had been removed long before.   It was the condition of the man that convinced Morgan with utter finality that he had told the truth.

VII

Mr. Edway Tarnhorst felt fear, but no real surprise when the shadow in the window of his suite in the Grand Central Hotel materialized into a human being. But he couldn't help asking one question.

"How did you get there?"   His voice was husky.   "We're eight floors above the street."

"Try climbing asteroids for a while," said Commodore Sir Harry Morgan. "You'll get used to it.   That's why I knew Jack hadn't died 'accidentally'—he was murdered."

"You . . . you're not carrying a gun," Tarnhorst said.

"Do I need one?"

Tarnhorst swallowed.   "Yes.   Fergus will be back in a moment."

"Who's Fergus?"

"He's the man who controls PMC 873."

Harry Morgan shoved his hand into his jacket pocket.   "Then I have a gun. You saw it, didn't you?"

"Yes.   Yes . . . I saw it when you came in."

"Good.   Call him."

When Sam Fergus came in, he looked as though he had had about three or four too many slugs of whisky.   There was an odd fear on his face.

"Whatsamatter, Edway?   I—"   The fear increased when he saw Morgan. "Whadda you here for?"

"I'm here to make a speech, Fergus.   Sit down."   When Fergus still stood, Morgan repeated what he had said with only a trace more emphasis.   "Sit down."

Fergus sat.   So did Tarnhorst.

"Both of you pay special attention," Morgan said, a piratical gleam in his eyes. "You killed a friend of mine.   My best friend.   But I'm not going to kill either of you.   Yet.   Just listen and listen carefully."

Even Tarnhorst looked frightened.   "Don't move, Sam.   He's got a gun.   I saw it when he came in."

"What . . . what do you want?" Fergus asked.

"I want to give you the information you want.   The information that you killed Jack for."   There was cold hatred in his voice.   "I am going to tell you something that you have thought you wanted, but which you really will wish you had never heard.   I'm going to tell you about that cable."

Neither Fergus nor Tarnhorst said a word.

"You want a cable.   You've heard that we use a cable that has a tensile strength of better than a hundred million pounds per square inch, and you want to know how it's made.   You tried to get the secret out of Jack because he was sent here as a commercial dealer.   And he wouldn't talk, so one of your goons blackjacked him too hard and then you had to drop him off a bridge to make it look like an accident.

"Then you got your hands on me.   You were going to wring it out of me. Well, there is no necessity of that."   His grin became wolfish.   "I'll give you everything."   He paused.   "If you want it."

Fergus found his voice.   "I want it.   I'll pay a million—"

"You'll pay nothing," Morgan said flatly.   "You'll listen."

Fergus nodded wordlessly.

"The composition is simple.   Basically, it is a two-phase material—like fiberglass.   It consists of a strong, hard material imbedded in a matrix of softer material. The difference is that, in this case, the stronger fibers are borazon—boron nitride formed under tremendous pressure—while the softer matrix is composed of tungsten carbide.   If the fibers are only a thousandth or two thousandths of an inch in diameter—the thickness of a human hair or less—then the cable from which they are made has tremendous strength and flexibility.

"Do you want the details of the process now?"   His teeth were showing in his wolfish grin.

Fergus swallowed.   "Yes, of course.   But . . . but why do you—"

"Why do I give it to you?   Because it will kill you.   You have seen what the stuff will do.   A strand a thousandth of an inch thick, encased in silon for lubrication purposes, got me out of that filthy hole you call a prison.   You've heard about that?"

Fergus blinked.   "You cut yourself out of there with the cable you're talking about?"

"Not with the cable.   With a thin fiber.   With one of the hairlike fibers that makes up the cable.   Did you ever cut cheese with a wire?   In effect, that wire is a knife—a knife that consists only of an edge.

"Or, another experiment you may have heard of.   Take a block of ice.   Connect a couple of ten-pound weights together with a few feet of piano wire and loop it across the ice block so that the weights hang free on either side, with the wire over the top of the block. The wire will cut right through the ice in a short time. The trouble is that the ice block remains whole—because the ice melts under the pressure of the wire and then flows around it and freezes again on the other side. But if you lubricate the wire with ordinary glycerine, it prevents the re-freezing, and the ice block will be cut in two.''

Tarnhorst nodded. "I remember. In school. They—" He let his voice trail off.

"Yeah. Exactly. It's a common experiment in basic science. Borazon fiber works the same way. Because it is so fine and has such tremendous tensile strength, it is possible to apply a pressure of hundreds of millions of pounds per square inch over a very small area. Under pressures like that, steel cuts easily. With a silon covering to lubricate the cut, there's nothing to it. As you have heard from the guards in your little hell-hole.''

"Hell-hole?" Tarnhorst's eyes narrowed and he flicked a quick glance at Fergus. Morgan realized that Tarnhorst had known nothing of the extent of Fergus' machinations.

"That lovely little political prison up in Fort Tryon Park that the World Welfare State, with its usual solicitousness for the common man, keeps for its favorite guests," Morgan said. His wolfish smile returned. "I'd've cut the whole thing down if I'd had had the time. Not the stone—just the steel. In order to apply that kind of pressure, you have to have the filament fastened to something considerably harder than the stuff you're trying to cut, you see. Don't try it with your fingers or you'll lose fingers.''

Fergus' eyes widened again and he looked both ill and frightened. "The man we sent . . . uh . . . who was found in your room. You—" He stopped and seemed to have trouble swallowing.

"Me? *I* didn't do anything." Morgan did a good imitation of a shark trying to look innocent. "I'll admit that I looped a very fine filament of the stuff across the doorway a few times, so that if anyone tried to enter my room illegally I would be warned." He didn't bother to add that a pressure-sensitive device had released and reeled in the filament after it had done its work. "It doesn't need to be nearly as tough and heavy to cut through soft stuff like . . . er . . . say, a beefsteak, as it does to cut through steel. It's as fine as cobweb, almost invisible. Won't the World Welfare State have fun when that stuff gets into the hands of its happy, crime-free populace?''

Edway Tarnhorst became suddenly alert. "What?''

"Yes. Think of the fun they'll have, all those lovely slobs who get their basic subsistence and their dignity and their honor as a free gift from the State. The kids, especially. They'll *love* it. It's so fine it can be hidden inside an ordinary thread—or woven into the hair—or . . ." He spread his hands. "A million places.''

Fergus was gaping. Tarnhorst was concentrating on Morgan's words.

"And there's no possible way to leave fingerprints on anything that fine," Morgan continued. "You just hook it around a couple of nails or screws, across an open doorway or an alleyway—and wait."

"We wouldn't let it get into the people's hands," Tarnhorst said.

"You couldn't stop it," Morgan said flatly. "Manufacture the stuff and eventually one of the workers in the plant will figure out a way to steal some of it."

"Guards—" Fergus said faintly.

"Pfui. But even if you had a perfect guard system, I think I can guarantee that some of it would get into the hands of the—common people. Unless you want to cut off all imports from the Belt."

Tarnhorst's voice hardened. "You mean you'd deliberately—"

"I mean exactly what I said," Morgan cut in sharply. "Make of it what you want."

"I suppose you have that kind of trouble out in the Belt?" Tarnhorst asked.

"No. We don't have your kind of people out in the Belt, Mr. Tarnhorst. We have men who kill, yes. But we don't have the kind of juvenile and grown-up delinquents who will kill senselessly, just for kicks. That kind is too stupid to live long out there. We are in no danger from borazon-tungsten filaments. You are." He paused just for a moment, then said: "I'm ready to give you the details of the process now, Mr. Fergus."

"I don't think I—" Fergus began with a sickly sound in his voice. But Tarnhorst interrupted him.

"We don't want it, commodore. Forget it."

"Forget it?" Morgan's voice was as cutting as the filament he had been discussing. "Forget that Jack Latrobe was murdered?"

"We will pay indemnities, of course," Tarnhorst said, feeling that it was futile.

"Fergus will pay indemnities," Morgan said. "In money, the indemnities will come to the precise amount he was willing to pay for the cable secret. I suggest that your Government confiscate that amount from him and send it to us. That may be necessary in view of the second indemnity."

"Second indemnity?"

"Mr. Fergus' life."

Tarnhorst shook his head briskly. "No. We can't execute Fergus. Impossible."

"Of course not," Morgan said soothingly. "I don't suggest that you should. But I do suggest that Mr. Fergus be very careful about going through doorways— or any other kind of opening—from now on. I suggest that he refrain from passing between *any* pair of reasonably solid, well-anchored objects. I suggest that he stay away from bathtubs. I suggest that he be very careful about putting his legs under a table or desk. I suggest that he not look out of windows. I could make several suggestions. And he shouldn't go around feeling in front of him, either. He might lose something."

"I understand," said Edway Tarnhorst.

So did Sam Fergus. Morgan could tell by his face.

*   *   *

When the indemnity check arrived on Ceres some time later, a short, terse note came with it.

"I regret to inform you that Mr. Samuel Fergus, evidently in a state of extreme nervous and psychic tension, took his own life by means of a gunshot wound in the head on the 21st of this month.   The enclosed check will pay your indemnity in full.   Tarnhorst."

Morgan smiled grimly.   It was as he had expected.   He had certainly never had any intention of going to all the trouble of killing Sam Fergus.

DEAN McLAUGHLIN

The Permanent Implosion

The fire was out. It had taken two tries, but now it was out and the well was capped. Workmen were beginning to cut up the shoved-aside wreck of the heat-buckled drill rig. A bulldozer bumbled ponderously around, scraping up random debris.

Mick Candido sat on the truck's running board and worked on his pipe. It was always going out, or the tobacco was getting too tightly packed in the bowl to burn right—or something. His body was sticky with sweat under his clothes. He was tired. It had been a rough day.

Money in the bank, though.

A thump and then a scuffing rustle back in the truck's body told him Ken Storch had heaved another roll of hose aboard. One more to go, he thought—and then the pump. Then they'd be loaded, ready to go. The other trucks had already gone.

He gave up on his pipe. He leaned back and watched the helicopter coming over the wind-scalloped, treeless hills. It was down low to the horizon, no larger than a gnat. The sky was clean—the rich blue of the high plains, and a few white featherwisps of cirrus. He pulled out his tobacco pouch, zipped his pipe inside, and returned it to his pocket.

Another thump hit the truck bed. Ken Storch came around his side. His shirt was dark with sweat. He brushed hair back from his forehead with a grimy hand. "All done but the pump, Mr. Candido."

Candido stood up. He was a big man—not so much in height as in muscular mass: broad shoulders, thick body, and powerful legs and arms. He'd been first-string center on the football team at East Texas College for three years, and he hadn't done bad on the wrestling squad either.

"Right," he said, and they walked down the hill to the mud-plastered trench. It had been full a few hours ago; now a few puddles glistened slickly in the deeper hollows. They'd had to use almost all of it.

Together, they lifted the pump and carried it back up the slope. It weighed one hundred and sixty pounds; not much for a pump, but it could throw four hoses of water at once—hard. You could depend on it to keep on throwing water, too, which was a necessary thing when you were in your klansman's suit—asbestos hood and coverall—trying to get the dynamite in close enough to the torch that the blast would snuff it.   Times like those, Niagara itself couldn't be too much water; it steamed off your back like smoke.

They raised the pump over the tailgate and slid it into the truck until it pushed up against the wet rolls of hose.   Hardly out of breath at all, Candido folded the tailgate up and hooked it shut, then rattled it to make sure it was fast.

"Back to the motel?" Storch asked.

"Not yet," Candido said.   He was watching the helicopter again.   It was a lot closer now.   He could see the blurry sweep of its rotors, and he was thinking of the long, bumpy ride back to Sand Springs—three and a half hours on dirt tracks you could call roads only in the sense that jeeps and trucks with lug tires could struggle over them.   If the copter was going to land here—and it looked that way— and if it was going back almost right away, maybe he could cadge a ride aboard. If they had space for another passenger.

He thought about his room in the motel.   It was air-conditioned.   He needed a shower and fresh clothes.   He needed another treatment of salve on the burns he'd got in spite of his klansman's suit.   And maybe a big steak dinner, and then a good long sleep.

He always felt that way when a job was done.

The helicopter settled on its wheels with a blast of wind.   Dust and sand flew. Before the rotors had stopped turning, the door opened and a man stepped down. He wore a business suit, but the helicopter was an Army machine: painted ugly green, and a white serial number stenciled on its flank like the brand on a cow.

The man came toward the truck.   He walked carefully, watching the ground where he set his feet.   He wore ordinary street shoes with low sides.   The sand gave way under his feet.

"Hello ," he said.   "I'm looking for Michael Candido.   You work for him?" He nodded to the truck.   *Wellfire Blasting, Inc*. it said in flame-limned letters on the door.   *Fort Worth, Texas*.

"I *am* him," Mick Candido said.

"Good," the man said.   "We need you.   I just came from Denver."

He said it as if Denver meant something.

"I'm from Fort Worth, myself," Candido said.   "What did you say your name was?"

"Hugh Trask," the man said hurriedly, as if the business of names was a nuisance to be got out of the way as fast as possible.   "Civil Defense, Denver District." He was somewhere in his forties.   His jowls had a meaty, thick look.

"Pleased to meet," Candido said.   He stuck out his hand.   It was filthy. "Now, business?"

"You mean you haven't heard?   You don't know about the whirlwind?"

"Friend," Candido said, "when I'm out on a job, I don't hear nothing but job and I don't think anything but job."

"Well, we need a man with your experience," Trask said.   He nodded back toward the helicopter.   "Will you take the job?"

Candido frowned.   "Since when did they have a field near Denver?"

"Field?" Trask's face was blank.

"Oil field," Candido said. "Wells."

"Oh!" Trask understood now. "But it's not an oil field. It's not even a fire. What we want you for . . . well, it's complicated." He waved a hand to the helicopter. "I'll tell you about it on the way."

Candido got out his pipe. He made sure he could draw through it, then packed tobacco in the bowl. He took his time. "I'll accept a ride back to town," he said, making it sound like a major concession. "You've got me curious, all right. I'll listen." He turned to Ken Storch. "You take the truck in," he said.

"Then you'll take the job?" Hugh Trask asked anxiously.

"I said I'll listen," Candido said. He got his pipe lighted and broke the match and dropped the pieces in the pocket of his denim shirt. "If I like how it sounds, we'll talk business." He started upslope toward the helicopter. Trask tagged alongside. "You're authorized to sign a contract?" he asked Trask.

Trask was out of breath, though the climb wasn't steep. Behind them, Storch got the truck started. There was a grind of gears.

"I don't know," Trask said. "I think so. We have a disaster fund, and this . . . well, this is that, for sure. But surely business arrangements can wait. This . . . this is important."

The door in the helicopter's side was open. Candido grabbed the hand-hold inside, stuck his foot in the toe-step, climbed inside. Out of the bright sunlight, it was like suddenly going blind. He groped and found a seat and sat down. "It's always a good time to talk business," he said. The seat was much too small for him, but he was accustomed to that. Most seats were. "Business happens to be my game."

"Lift up, Mr. Trask?" someone asked from up forward.

"Yes. Take off," Trask said. He was buckling into the seat across the narrow aisle. Candido found his own seat belt. Its straps were just barely long enough to reach around him. The helicopter's idling engine roared up to power. A shutterlike shadow flicked across the forward window, then came again—then again and again. The helicopter vibrated, buzzed, surged, and the ground dropped away. After a moment, Candido could look out the window beside him and see, far below, the tiny fittings of the wellhead and the wrecked drill rig and the blackened earth in a circle around it like a blot of ink, and the men and the bulldozer swarming over the scene, like wonderfully perfect toys.

The low, rippling hills ridged the land like a lethargic, heaving sea. Candido watched them drift past underneath and listened to the engine's noise, and heard Trask tell of the thing that had happened near Denver.

No one would ever know exactly what had happened. The only men who might have known had vanished—devoured by the thing they'd created. There'd been a research laboratory on the plain northeast of Boulder; Civil Defense hadn't yet found what it had been doing. Anyway, it was gone now, and where it had been the center of a vast, powerful whirlwind wheeled and roared. Everything for miles around had been swept up by it—smashed, shredded, uprooted, and carried away.

"This is the significant point," Trask said. "Something in the center of that whirlwind . . . something is drawing air toward it, very forcefully. That's what's causing the whirlwind."

"Hm-m-m," Candido said. "Where's all this air going?"

"Huh?" Trask's brows squeezed together like rope twisted tight, beginning to bunch. "Why, I hadn't thought about that. However, I suppose our physicists know, and it makes no difference. The thing we want you for—you're experienced in the handling of explosives under . . . well, unusual conditions. Our physicists believe that the shock of an explosion close to the center of the whirlwind will destroy the . . . uh, the condition that is causing it."

Candido thought a minute. "How fast did you say the wind's going?"

Below them, the land opened into a deep, gully-carved valley. The kinked and twisting channel was white-crusted—dry as a skillet. Eye-glazing light shimmered on arid promontories. Then the land lifted again and the valley fell behind. Over the rolling plain, dust devils twisted.

"Understand," Trask said, "we haven't been able to get close to the center to measure the wind velocities there. And there's too much dust for us to estimate by observing things caught in it. But about five hundred yards out, it seems to be blowing steadily at a hundred and forty miles an hour."

Candido grunted as if he'd taken a fist in the gut. "Not what I call a breeze," he said. "Take something big to put a dent in it. What about these physicists of yours? How much of a blast do they figure it needs?"

"I don't handle technical details," Trask said. "I'm an administrator. I have no idea. I haven't discussed it with them."

"Maybe it'll make a difference whether I take the job or don't," Candido said. "Usually my price goes up five thousand for every hundredweight of Hercules over three hundred pounds. If it's over a ton, I don't even talk to you. I wave good-by. That's how it's sounding right now."

Far ahead now, they could see the town, Sand Springs. It was a patch of green on the scrub-dotted land, nestled among the naked hills, tiny with distance—too small, it seemed, for a town; but over it stood the toy-size water tower on spread legs. Ten-fifteen miles.

"They tell me it might not take a particularly large blast," Trask said. "They believe the thing that's causing it involves a delicate balance of forces, and only a small additional force would upset it."

"They think that, huh?" Candido said. He thought for a while, as the town came gradually nearer and nearer, hillcrest after hillcrest. He'd just finished a job, and it was money in the bank, and no new jobs were shaping up. This whirlwind wasn't his usual line of work, exactly, but it did have ginger in it—something different. Something new, a challenge, like the time he was a boy and a kid three years older had scratched a line in the dirt and said for him to cross it. He'd looked the kid up and down, taken his measure, and stepped across the line and smashed him flat. He began thinking about how to get to the center of that roaring wind.

"Naturally, you'll be given all the assistance we can," Trask said. He was talking quickly, anxious, trying to persuade him. "And all the equipment you need. This . . . this is a disaster. It's got to be stopped. Soon."

"Well," Candido said, and paused to read Trask's face. The man was frantic—maybe a little desperate, even—but that didn't help much when you were haggling with the government. Uncle Sam was a tough old skinflint when it came to bargaining, and even if you got it down in black and white on good crisp parchment, you still couldn't be sure the deal would stick. Just the same . . .

"I don't say I'll take the job," Candido said, "but I've got to admit I'm interested. Anyway, I'll go as far as Denver and look it over. Good enough?"

Trask called forward for the helicopter to change course and fly to Denver. Candido countermanded the instruction and obliged them to land at the edge of the town. It was a short walk to the motel. There he showered, shaved, and got a change of clothes. He packed, left word for his crew to bring the trucks down to Denver, caught a sandwich and coffee at the nearest cafe, and walked back to the helicopter.

The pilot already had the engine going when he climbed aboard. As soon as he was safety-belted in a seat the rotors began to turn and they were airborne. It was late afternoon. It was night before they arrived over Denver.

The helicopter had curved far east over the plains and approached the city on a westward course. The wind gusted roughly, jolting the craft. Thick cloud clotted the sky. The city's light filled the overcast with a glow like embering fire.

Trask had telephoned of their coming before they left Sand Springs, and in spite of the lateness of the hour there were men waiting in a conference room in the Centennial Hotel. The streets were wet with rain.

Candido glanced at the blank blackboard and the board next to it on which a topographic quadrangle map had been tacked. One of the men had a piece of chalk in his hand. He was almost bald and he wore rimless glasses and he was thin. His shirt was open at the throat. His tweed had leather patches at the elbows. A waiter arrived with a large pot of coffee and a half dozen cups. Candido remembered how long it had been since he'd been near a bed. He got out his pipe, stuffed the bowl, dabbed a match over it until the tobacco caught.

The man with the piece of chalk was Willard L'Heuroux, and he was a physicist from the university at Boulder. He rubbed the end of the chalk with his thumb. The palp of his thumb was white with the dust. He had only a few details to add to the information Trask had given already, but Candido listened carefully. Details could be important—even small ones.

The center of the whirlwind was over a rise of ground named Gunbarrel Hill. It showed clearly on the quadrangle map, even to someone who didn't know how to read contour lines. Candido knew how. He studied the few roads that gridded the area and thought about the wind that was strong even here, twenty or thirty miles away. He didn't like it.

L'Heuroux had some high altitude photographs of the whirlwind. It was a vast, round, doughnut-like cloud, like a hurricane but with almost no eye. Storm clouds surrounded the toroid, and the photoplane's pilot had reported a powerful downdraft even at sixty thousand feet.   Air was flowing toward the whirlwind's center from all directions—from above as well as from all points of the compass.

That was all the fact they had.   All the rest was theory, as unprovable as the noise an unseen tree makes in falling.   But one of the research problems being worked in the lab, which the whirlwind had smashed, had been a direct investigation of an aspect of Mach's principle—that in a universe with no material objects, all points are identical since there can be no reference points on which to base a system of co-ordinates.   No one really questioned this concept any more—at least, no one of the proper sophistication.

"Pardon me," Candido said.   "I always thought we've got a universe with a few material objects lying around."

"Quite true," L'Heuroux said.   "However, if we should choose to ignore that point—and mathematically I assure you it's very easy to do . . ."

Candido growled skeptically and rubbed his brows with the heels of his thumbs. "All right.   Go on."

Well now, if all locations in the universe were identical, it naturally followed that transfer of objects from one place to another should be ridiculously simple, since obviously they were in both positions—among others—all the time.   Of course, the real universe didn't precisely conform to the idealized scheme being utilized; some compensation had to be made.   This had been one of the problems the laboratory was investigating.   A secondary, more difficult problem had been to control selection of the non-different points which were being made congruent.

Maybe it was because he hadn't had a good night's sleep the last few days, but Candido couldn't grasp the concept.   Like trying to gnaw fog, he thought.   He added just enough cream to his coffee to lighten its blackness.   He drank half the cup in one draught.

Maybe the coffee helped.   At least he got the idea of the next part—that at the center of the whirlwind was a locus, a volume of space, which was simultaneously in two places.   One was a few yards above the surface of Gunbarrel Hill.   The other was . . . well, somewhere else.   And since something more than ninety-nine per cent of the universe is interstellar space, what could be more logical but that the somewhere else should be such a region?   And it was vacuum there—a vacuum more empty than any that could be made in any laboratory in the world.   Nothing could be done to prevent the air contained within the congruent volume from escaping into the emptiness around it.

Candido's pipe had gone out some time ago.   He opened his jackknife and pried the mess out of the bowl and dumped it in an ashtray.   He started over.

"You figure a hard blast of Hercules will knock this thing off?"

"That is our belief," L'Heuroux said.   "The whirlwind has destroyed all the equipment that created it.   Therefore, the condition of congruency must be one that is self-maintaining.   This would mean, we think, a moderately delicate balance of forces which an abrupt shock—such as a disturbance in the patterns of movement of the air molecules entering the sphere—would disrupt.   At least, that is our hope."

"And I'm the guy to set the charge," Candido said. It was like someone had pulled the plug, he thought, and air was draining out of the world like water from a bathtub. If it was in the southern hemisphere, he thought, the whirlwind would be wheeling in the other direction—clockwise instead of counterclockwise. He wondered how long before there wasn't any air left. He began to know how goldfish feel when their bowl is smashed.

"All right," he said. "You've got your man. You supply the equipment— I'm set up for fires, not wind—not a wind like this, anyway—and I'll do the job. Two hundred thousand."

Trask's face was like a papier-mâché mask, his eyes staring through the holes. "That's rather high," he said. His voice was a little unsteady.

"It's dangerous work," Candido said.

"But our budget isn't a tenth of that."

"Call Uncle," Candido said. "Two hundred thousand. I figure that's pretty cheap for all the air you can breathe."

The corners of Trask's mouth twitched as if he felt pain. He stood up. "If you'll excuse me," he said, and left the room.

Candido waited. Nobody spoke. Trask was gone ten minutes. He came back and stood in the doorway. "I'm instructed to offer fifty thousand," he said. "It will mean asking Congress for a special appropriation, but we can offer that much."

"As a taxpayer, I think that's a good offer," Candido said. "As a businessman, I say it's no good. Two hundred thousand."

Trask met his eyes for a moment, then turned and went out again.

Candido turned his attention to L'Heuroux. "How long's it been blowing?"

"Three days," L'Heuroux said. "Two and a half. It began in the afternoon, day before yesterday."

"How long before we don't have any air left?" Candido asked.

To judge by the look on the physicist's face, it was something he hadn't thought of. "Why, I really don't know," L'Heuroux said. "I'd have to compute. I don't think we have the data. I assume what you mean is, how long before the air pressure drops below the level at which it can support life."

"That's close enough," Candido said.

"Otherwise," L'Heuroux said, as if Candido hadn't spoken, "I would have to say we'll never have lost all our atmosphere. As the air pressure drops, there would be less pressure forcing air into the congruency. Therefore, since the pressure drop would be progressive, an infinite length of time would have to pass before all our atmosphere was gone."

"If I can't breathe, I don't call it air," Candido said. "How long do you figure?"

Trask came back then. He sat down. "All right," he said. "Two hundred thousand."

"In writing," Candido said.

"All right. In writing. Tomorrow morning."

"Good enough," Candido said, satisfied. "That'll just about pay my income tax."

*   *   *

The wind blew gale force at the edge of Boulder.   Houses had slashed roofs and trees lay uprooted.   The tank's Diesel was a growl above the whirlwind's blast.

They'd spent a day getting ready—moving the tank down from the Army camp near Cheyenne and learning how to drive it and waiting for his crew to make it down from the Gas Hills.   They'd come in last night.   The tank weighed sixty-four tons and it had a low silhouette.   Massive enough, Candido figured, that the wind wouldn't bother it too much.   Ken Storch rode in the gunner's seat beside him, and L'Heuroux rode in the turret.   Candido hoped the hatch lock would hold. He'd checked it and he thought it would, but if it didn't the wind would suck them out like marrow from a bone.   He was mildly curious what was on the other side of that congruency, but not so curious he wanted to go there.

Scraps of debris—some of them not small—skipped along the ground, sailed up into the air.   A tree branch went by.   A section of billboard touting Coors beer. Another advantage to the tank, it could move across country.   It didn't have to keep to the grid pattern of roads.   It could keep the wind at its back, if that was the only way it could move.

But here, still close to Boulder, he stayed on the road.   It was easier going, and the wind wasn't strong enough to bother him yet, and it was tricky to drive with just the narrow slit of the periscope to see through.   You could lose your bearings fast.   He gripped the brake levers, now and then tugging a little at one or the other, keeping the machine on an even course down the middle of the road.   There wasn't any traffic—just the tank and the empty road.   Rain squalls lashed the pavement and passed on.   The wind screeched like a mountain lion in rage.   Gusts made his ears pop, and he had to swallow to get his hearing right again.

The road turned, then turned again, and then they were grinding up the slope. Wind blasted on the tank's flank like a padded hammer, and the noise of it almost blotted out sound of the laboring Diesel.

"What's air pressure?" Candido asked.

"Twenty and six tenths," L'Heuroux said, behind him.

He felt vibration in his bucket seat.   He had to use the brakes a lot to keep the tank from drifting sidewise into the ditch.   The tank's treads clawed the pavement. Scrabbled.   Down to twenty and a half already, and still more than a mile to go. He could imagine the torn asphalt they were leaving behind them, even though he couldn't turn his periscope enough to see.

Then they were nearing the hillcrest, and here was the turn-off to where the research lab had been.   Candido hauled on the left brake lever and the left tread locked and the tank spun to the left and the wind hit the tank's side as if a shell had burst on the armor.   Candido let up on the brake and the tank stopped turning, and he upped the throttle and the Diesel's snarl raised its pitch a few notes and they ground forward into the drive.

The land was ripped bare like bones cleaned by carrion birds.   Not even grass grew in the earth.   Here and there, a wooden fencepost had held against the blast.

That was all.   Ahead, a little to the left of the road, the air was in violent turmoil. Debris and dust and cloud streamed inward from all directions.   Candido stopped the tank and studied the epicenter, but he was too far away to make out anything clearly.   He slacked the brakes and put in the clutch, and the tank lurched forward. "What's the pressure like?" he asked over his shoulder.

"Fifteen and seven tenths," L'Heuroux said.   The tank shuddered with the impact of wind.   Candido kept his eyes on the center of the converging winds, only now and then glancing at the road.   This road didn't have ditches at the verge; he didn't have to worry about getting caught in one of them.   He did some mental calculations.

"It should be up around twenty-five," he said.

"Within a point or two of that," L'Heuroux said.   "That's normal for this altitude."

Candido stopped the tank.   "We don't go any closer," he said.   The tank trembled in the wind's fury.   The wind was an unending scream.

"Is something wrong?" L'Heuroux asked.

Candido could just barely see what was left of the laboratory building's foundation.   He'd have liked to get closer, to study out the kind of ground he'd have to work over when they went in to plant the Hercules.   Not now, though.   Not with the pressure down there.   His shoulders felt like they were wearing plaster casts.   He felt a peculiar singing in his blood.

"Nothing's gone wrong yet," he said.   "It would if we kept on going."   He got the tank turned around.   He gave the Diesel full throttle.   It was like trying to probe bottom in quicksand.   The tank didn't move.   The Diesel didn't have any power.   The wind drove against the tank, striking from just off the starboard bow.   Its force was stronger than the Diesel.

"We don't go any closer without breathing equipment," Candido said.   "And a supercharger on the engine.   We're not getting enough air to breathe right, and if I'm any guess it's even thinner the closer you get to . . ."   He let a gesture complete the sentence.   "If we get much closer, we'd keel over.   And we'd have our engine stall."

He got the tank turned to the left, fed power to the Diesel.   They lumbered off the road.   The ground was uneven.   The tank bumped and jolted.   The engine still didn't have much power, but they were going crosswind now instead of fighting it.   He had to crab into it some, but that was possible.   They made headway.

"Why, I hadn't considered that," L'Heuroux said.

"Didn't think you had," Candido said.   "You're not in business.   Did you get a figure for wind velocity?"

"Not a very dependable one.   I think the equipment must be damaged."

"What's the figure you got?" Candido asked.

"Two hundred and ninety miles per hour," L'Heuroux said.

Candido twitched the right hand brake lever, quartering them into the wind a little more steeply.   He could feel the treads slip and jerk as they clawed for footing.   Ahead, the land sloped gently downward.   The wind sang its fury. Candido thought of all the air vanishing into that bottomless vacuum—air no man would ever breathe again.

*   *   *

The breathing equipment was no problem.   Face masks and air tanks and a compressor were part of Candido's stock of equipment.   A supercharger for the Diesel wasn't so easy.

Diesels weren't built for high-altitude work.   Superchargers didn't exist.   Candido catnapped most of the afternoon in his Boulder motel room while Trask and his subordinates telephoned everywhere, trying to locate something that would fill the need.   They had trouble, Trask said, because a lot of wires were blown down.

Finally—it was almost five—they found one in Dayton.   It was designed for a gasoline engine, but it could operate—not efficiently, but it could operate—at the tank Diesel's RMP.   It was loaded on a jet transport at Wright-Patterson and flown west.   Candido spent most of the night watching it being installed.   They had to cut away some of the armor to make room for it, and then they had to build a housing for it to protect it from the wind and flying objects.   It screamed like a devil with its tail being stepped on.   It was a jerry-rigged, makeshift assembly.   Candido made sure he could control it.   Finally, he was satisfied.

"All right," he said.   "Now, will it do the job where we're going?"

The engineer managing the job was a hairy, scrawny man named Henry Janiszewski.   "It's working as good as it ever will," he said, wiping his hands on a rag.   "If you want more than that, you'll have to ask someone else."   He rolled down his sleeves, exposing sergeant's stripes.

It was midmorning now, and nobody had got much sleep.   Trask didn't know.   L'Heuroux, when they woke him and got him to understand through his drowsiness what the question was, didn't know either.

"We don't go near the whirlwind till we've tested it," Candido said.

"Tested it?" Trask asked.   "How?"

"I want to know that engine works and gives power where the barometer says ten inches," Candido said.   "If it's going to quit, I want it to quit while we're testing it—not while I'm in it, looking that wind in the eye."

"But where in heaven is there a pressure chamber large enough to take that . . ."   L'Heuroux's hand flapped wildly in the direction of the tank, "that monster."

"Not heaven," Candido said.   "Here.   How should I know?   Don't you?"

So another search began.   It didn't take as long, this time.   Not many pressure chambers of size existed.   Someone in Washington dug out a list of them, and there was one big enough in a missile factory in the foothills southwest of Denver, less than fifty miles away.

Candido made the ride down in the cab of the tank's carrier rig.   He held his breathing equipment on his lap.   Rain fell most of the way—slashing, hurricane rain.   They were expected; the guard waved them through the gate without stopping, and pointed them the way to go.

For all its size, the pressure chamber was just barely big enough.   The tank fitted inside like a chick in its egg.   The pressure chamber and its massive vacuum pumps were part of the missile company's research equipment, and the whole rig-up had cost—Candido didn't catch how many hundred thousands.   They were proud how much it had cost.   Candido cracked a grin and said it was a lot of cash to spend for nothing.   They didn't get the joke.   They explained earnestly that a really solid vacuum was a hard thing to get, and to get a good one was worth a lot of money.   Candido shrugged and they got to business.

He breathed canned air through his mask and kept the Diesel running while they pumped the chamber down to ten inches.   They did it slowly, leaking some air back in to replenish the oxygen the Diesel burned.   As the air got thinner, the Diesel's growl changed note.   At just under fourteen inches, it began running rough.   Candido cut in the supercharger.   It smoothed out and stayed smooth the rest of the way down to ten.

He tried throttle settings all the way up the scale.   It was hard to tell much— the Diesel kept running all right, but its sound meant nothing in the thin air.   He cut the throttle back to idle, made sure the brakes were locked tight, and watched the few inches between the tank's foremost projection and the walls of the chamber while gingerly, fractions at a time, he let in the clutch.   The engine stalled.

It took several tries to get the Diesel started again, but finally it turned over. He advanced the throttle a little and tried the clutch again.   The brakes still held. He kept on trying.   He'd gone most of the way up the throttle settings before the tank even trembled when he let in the clutch.   The throttle was almost against the stops when, finally, the tank strained feebly against the brakes—lurched an inch or two forward before Candido hastily opened the clutch.

It wasn't much of a test, but it would have to do.   At least he could count on the Diesel to deliver power.   Not much, but some.   It was slushy, but not so bad he couldn't manage it.   He opened the hatch, poked his head out, and signed to the man watching through the window.   His ears felt the pressure change as they cracked the valves.   Air leaked back into the chamber.   A shrill whistle bit his ears.   The tank was good enough, now, to risk taking it up to the whirlwind's center.   It would still be a risk, but there were always risks.   You took a chance every time you crossed the street.

They drove north again through rain and the new-fallen night.   He slept in his motel room, woke early, and made sure all was ready for the day's work.

The explosive—a half-ton of high-nitro dynamite—was packed solidly in a lead container.   The canister's top was thin, but its sides and bottom were heavy.   The charge would be set down directly under the congruency.   The blast would be upwards, directly into it.   Under the lid, a radiodetonator nested among its wires like a spider in its web.   L'Heuroux had taken photographs, and enlargements showed the center of the whirlwind as a large globe suspended ten feet off the ground, in which the turbulent wind swirled in a different pattern than the inward driving winds surrounding it.   L'Heuroux had been disappointed that the various color sensitivities of the films and light filters he'd used had shown nothing to suggest the nature of the sphere.   Candido couldn't have cared less.   He made sure the rigging would hold the canister tightly in spite of the wind's force.   He checked the mechanism that would set it on the ground.   It would work all right.

Something clanged on the turret as he made the turn into the drive for the approach to the whirlwind's vortex.   A tree branch, or something else, caught in the wind.

He stopped the tank and locked the brakes.   He unwrapped another stick of gum and added it to the wad already in his mouth.   He slipped on his breather mask—made sure it fitted tight.   Glancing over his shoulder, he saw Ken Storch already wearing his mask.   L'Heuroux was fumbling with his.

He waited.   Finally, the physicist signed he was ready.   Candido turned forward again, slipped the brakes, and boosted the supercharger.   The Diesel snarled.   With a lurch, the tank advanced.   A sudden, brief slash of rain rattled like bullets on the tank's side.   Trickles of water dribbled in around the hatchways and around the turret.   Cold wet dripped on Candido's neck.   He had to yank the left brake handle constantly, to hold the tank on the road.   The tank boomed in the blast of the wind.

It got worse the nearer they came.   The pinwheeling wind swept more steeply across the road and its force was magnified.   The tank skidded and scuttled on the wind-polished earth; there'd been gravel on the road, once, but no more.   The parking lot, when they came to it, could be recognized only because it was flat and open while the land around it flowed unevenly.   Candido gave it hardly a glance.

Not much was left of the lab's foundations—some masses of concrete still bearing battered remnants of equipment they'd been poured to support, a few fragments of cinder block embedded at the edges of a level concrete floor that lifted perhaps half a foot above ground level, a few steel reinforcing bars jutting out of the floor—twisted, bent, and snapped off: ugly stubs.   Something carried in the wind caught momentarily against one of the longer bars.   The bar wrenched, gave way, and the object broke and its fragments whipped away so swiftly the eye couldn't follow.

The sphere was ten or eleven feet above the floor, suspended, motionless.   The wind drove into it, swirling everything trapped inside it into violent frenzy.   Surfaces, tendrils, wisps, and solid things whirled and gyrated crazily, and Candido thought of those part-transparent, part-opaque marbles he'd played with as a boy.   The globe was like one of those marbles, wildly spinning, shifting form inside endlessly—or like a picture he'd seen of the planet Jupiter, the planet's globe banded like a zebra and the whole monstrous thing whirling all the way around every nine and a fraction hours.   It dizzied the eye.

On the floor, a low, vaguely conical heap of rubbish had collected.   Candido stopped the tank—made sure the brakes would hold against the wind.   He studied the expanse of floor almost inch by inch, deciding how best to make the approach.   It wasn't going to be easy.   Those twisted steel rods and concrete piers could do nasty things to the tank's treads.   He had to cross at least fifty feet of that mess.

After a while, he moved the tank to a new point of vantage.   The floor looked just as bad from this angle.   The wind would make trouble, too.   It was like a maze game played with steel balls in a strong magnetic field, no mistakes allowed.   He took the tank around to the other side of the foundation, pausing for a good look every few yards.   There wasn't any good way to get in—just some that weren't as bad as others.   The wind forced jets in under the hatches.   It was like being stabbed with icicles.   The shrill whistlings were like red-hot needles in his ears.

He chose the best way he could find.   He hoped the treads would hold up.   It was all he could do.   Slowly, as if feeling his way, he got the tank up on the platform.   Moving only a few feet at a time, he advanced the machine across the concrete floor, twisting, backing and filling, crabbing carefully into the wind, and the wind was like something solid.   The wind tried to shoulder the tank—sidewise, cornerwise, or anywise except the way he wanted to go—toward the globe, and the globe hovered closer, ever closer as he picked his way toward it.   *Get thee behind me, Satan, and push!* he thought savagely.   That was what the wind was doing.   He fought it.

The rubbish under the sphere crunched and crushed under the treads like pith balls.   Here, miraculously, the wind did not blow.   Candido's ears popped.   His head rang and he had no strength and his blood pounded strongly.   He turned up the supercharger all the way, but still the Diesel's response to the throttle was soft. He knew what the trouble was, all right.   He glanced back at L'Heuroux; the physicist held up seven fingers.

He turned back to the periscope, shrugging.   Nothing he could do to change it. He maneuvered the tank forward and back until the debris had been flattened. He brought the tank inward once more, maneuvering until the tank's prow was as near to being directly under the sphere's center as his eye could gauge.   He opened the clutch—let the engine idle; no need to lock the brakes here.   He nodded to Storch.

The younger man had the controls of the explosives handling rig.   It was a makeshift: no manufacturer made a rig strong enough to hold against the wind, nor one that could be worked through the constricted ports intended for machine-gun muzzles.   It had been a job to build.   They'd had to make it flawless, perfect in operation.   There'd be no getting out to make repairs while the wind raged, nor here in this semivacuum.   It was all a man could do to hold to consciousness against the beating and the vagueness in his skull.

Storch handled the rig like he'd got a Doctorate in rig-handling from MIT.   Well, he should, Candido told himself.   He'd trained the man himself.   Through the periscope, he watched the heavy beams extend, proffering the massive canister forward, then down until the canister's butt touched ground.   The beams continued to droop lower and lower, until the long bolts slipped free of the flanges on the canister's sides.   Now the beams drew back, slowly, like arthritic arms that had made an offering to a tyrannical god.

"All right," Storch said.   His voice was muffled by his breathing mask.

Candido backed the tank away.   He gave Storch time to get the rig retracted. He turned the tank—began to trace the way back through the maze.   He couldn't go exactly the same way—some of the way he'd come was, going back, directly into the teeth of the wind.   It was like trying to push through a mountain.   Even if the Diesel had full power—it didn't, not here, the air pressure so low—in spite of the supercharger it hadn't the power to drive against the slamming wind.   He found another way.

A hundred yards off, he turned the tank back to face the sphere.   He looked at Storch—nodded.   Storch unlocked the radiodetonator box.   Candido didn't like using radio to set off a blast—you couldn't trust radio the way you could with wires—but with the wind the way it was, wire just wasn't possible.

The transmitter warmed. Storch looked to Candido. "Any time," Candido said, and turned to the periscope. After a moment, the canister exploded.

The canister's side burst, but the blast's main force was upward. They'd planned on that. It was a sudden belch of light—a jet of incandescence streaking up, stabbing into the sphere like a knife blade. A boll of smoke followed it upward, more slowly. The sphere swallowed them, one and then the other.

Candido watched. The sphere didn't change. The wind blew unslackened. Candido shrugged. If a blast had been going to do it, that blast would have done it. It hadn't. This is the way the world ends, he thought, and wondered where he'd heard the quote. He turned the tank broadside to the wind—started the long, gradual descent down the east slope of Gunbarrel Hill. After a while, he cut off the supercharger and ripped the breather mask from his face.

"Now what?" he asked.

All that came from L'Heuroux was silence. The wind roared and keened.

It was raining in Boulder again. The storm drains hadn't been built for such downpours. Streets in the lower sections were flooded. The creek was over its banks, and up in the canyon a lot of private bridges were gone. A house up there had been smashed by floodwaters, and three people were missing. The State Police had a six-year-old boy who'd been found, crying, climbing the canyon wall in the rain. No one knew where he came from. They couldn't get him to say much, and they couldn't make much sense out of what he did say.

"The more I think about it," Candido said, "the more I start wondering what made you think a blast would do it. What's different about a blast from the way the wind's tearing in there?"

Outside, through the window, he could see the trees writhe and sway in the rain like a modern dance group communicating agony. L'Heuroux cleaned his glasses with a rumpled handkerchief, not watching his hands.

"But remember," the physicist said, "we are dealing with a condition that is self-reinforcing. The wind that is entering the congruency is obviously part of the system. It seemed probable, therefore, that by disrupting the pattern of the winds, we could hope to destroy the condition."

"Well, it didn't work," Candido said.

L'Heuroux looked unhappy. "There was only one way we could find out."

At the end of the table, Trask harumphed. "I don't think that is advancing matters, gentlemen," he said. "I asked you here to discuss measures we will take now. All of us were disappointed when our attempt with explosives failed. We don't need to swell on this aspect. I presume, Dr. L'Heuroux, you have new measures to propose."

"Of course," L'Heuroux said. Candido smiled grimly. If you could look inside the man's head, you'd probably see the wheels spinning like a one-arm bandit's. Thirty seconds, mister, or back you go to chasing neutrinos, or whatever it is physicists chase these days.

"Our first attempt," L'Heuroux said, "was to disrupt the condition which maintains the congruency by creating a violent disturbance in the material passing through into the congruency.'' He sounded like he was lecturing in a classroom—only natural, Candido thought, this being a classroom generously loaned by the university. ''It was a logical thing to try first; however, it did not work. I think next we should try . . .'' He paused, as if for dramatic effect.

''Yeah?'' Candido asked.

''Next,'' L'Heuroux said, just as if Candido hadn't prompted him—except he bore down more heavily on the word than the word warranted—''we should test the condition's sensitivity to intense electromagnetic radiation. We have a laser which can supply the necessary output. And we have a million gauss magnet. We should try that, also.''

''Any special reason you think these'll do it?'' Candido asked.

''Certainly,'' L'Heuroux said, as if a question like that could come only from a mentally deficient five-year-old. ''We don't know enough about the congruency condition to be sure what type of external forces or fields it may be sensitive to. Therefore, what we must do is to investigate the condition's reaction to all the influences we can bring to bear.''

''Translated into English,'' Candido said, ''You're saying try anything, and if it doesn't work try something else.'' He tried to remember how many things Edison tried before he found something to make an electric light with. Two thousand? Four thousand? Fifteen? ''All right, you've got a couple of things you want to try. If they don't do the job, what's next on your list?''

''Have you an alternative to suggest?'' Trask asked.

''I'm not educated the way this guy is,'' Candido said. ''All I've got is a bachelor's in business administration. I don't know about this thing we're working on—I don't think he does, either, but I admit it. All I am, is an errand boy. Tell me the job and I'll do it, but now and then I like getting results from my work.''

''I think,'' Trask said, ''we'll try the laser and the magnet. Do you agree?'' Candido shrugged. ''It beats thumb twiddling.''

''We have to try everything possible,'' L'Heuroux said.

Candido wondered how you went about learning to breathe vacuum. It might come to that.

The wind still slammed across Gunbarrel Hill, and its cry was the cry of a slavering beast. The congruency's globe hovered like a ceaselessly spinning, pupilless eyeball over the foundations of the laboratory it had destroyed.

If the laser made a sound, it wasn't sound that could be heard above the sheeting of the wind. The thing was mounted in the turret, to beam its pulses of light through the aperture left when the cannon was removed. All through the drive from Boulder, L'Heuroux had been pouring liquid nitrogen from a DeWar flask into the laser's reservoir. It made the interior of the tank very cold. The laser looked like a large, old-fashioned slide projector—an unlovely, functional piece of hardware. L'Heuroux fumbled with it. A blast of wind shook the tank. Something vibrated. A flash of white light filled the tank's interior. L'Heuroux muttered something in annoyed tones. He poured more nitrogen into the reservoir.

There were several more of the white flashes. Then the laser was working. L'Heuroux uttered a satisfied sound. Through the periscope, Candido saw momentary flickerings of red in the streaked, swirling dust clouds. They seemed to be on target, but it was hard to be sure. The tank was a hundred yards from the congruency, halted, with brakes on, tail to the wind and turret turned to aim the laser into the sphere. If the laser was on target, it wasn't doing any good. The sphere didn't change. The wind kept on blowing.

"Want to move up closer?" Candido asked. It was hard to talk clearly through his breather mask. The laser began flashing white again.

"It's heated up," L'Heuroux said. His voice was muffled. He poured another jolt of nitrogen into the reservoir.

"We'll move closer," Candido said. It was possible—all that dust and cloud in the air—the laser's beams weren't getting through. He slipped the brakes, turned the tank toward the sphere, pushed up the throttle. He closed the distance to fifty yards, turned the tank butt to the wind. Ken Storch helped the physicist aim the turret again. The turret handled badly, pounded by the wind.

The laser flashed white only once this time, and then again Candido saw the flick of red in the airborne dust. This time, there wasn't any question about its reaching the sphere. He could see the momentary stab of red in the swirling clouds inside the sphere. After a dozen pulses, the laser started flashing white again.

"Well, now we know two things that don't work," Candido said. He made sure the Diesel was behaving. Its reply was a snarling roar. He let go the brakes and moved the tank carefully toward the sphere. The wrecked foundation didn't make as much trouble this time. He knew the way, and the tank had bent or snapped off some of the steel rods the last time it was here. He stopped the tank, as before, in the zone of calm over which the sphere hung suspended like shelter.

"All yours, Ken."

They'd rebuilt the handling rig for its new job. This time, instead of setting a massive canister down, it was to remove a small electromagnet from its supercooling bath and raise it close to the sphere. And this time—because it was a magnet—they couldn't use steel.

Storch manipulated the rig. The lid on the cold bath clattered aside and the magnet rose on the end of a double-jackknifed boom. The boom unfolded—extended to its full length like a scorpion's tail, stinger tipped. Then the boom lifted—floated upward as if it weighed less than nothing. It stopped with the stinger only inches from the whirling tumult inside the sphere. Wisps of frosty air trickled upward like smoke from the magnet into the sphere.

"Any time you want," Candido said over his shoulder. "It's ready."

"I can see for myself," L'Heuroux said, peering through his view slit. There was the sound of him fiddling with equipment. "Ready?" he asked.

"All your show," Candido said. He watched the end of the boom—they were all watching. L'Heuroux closed the switch.

The boom whipped like a fishing rod struck by a big one. It bent down as if a powerful weight suddenly was hung on its end; Candido hadn't thought the aluminum alloy could bend so far without snapping.   Then the current cut off automatically.   The boom sprung upward.   The tank jolted.   The end of the boom—magnet and all—went into the sphere and . . .

JEHOSAPHAT!

The boom recoiled, and the magnet and the end of the boom were gone.   None of the part that went into the sphere was left, as if jaws had chopped it off with the casual ease of a cow eating grass.   Beside him, Storch uttered a yelp of surprise.

That's the last time I stick my head in *that* lion's mouth.   It was a silly time to think of an old gag like that, but Candido thought of it.   For maybe thirty seconds he couldn't think of anything else.

"Now we know three things that don't work," he said finally, and he put the tank into gear.   "What do we try next?"

He got no answer all through the long descent down the eastern slope of the hill, nor during the long circle back westward, back to Boulder.

Two days later, the tank again snarled its way up the western slope of Gunbarrel Hill.   The asphalt was smashed and broken from the previous times the tank had used these roads.   Now and then, Candido noticed a chunk of rubble caught in a hollow where the wind couldn't sweep it away.   Except for such as those, the roadway was clean.

The original handling rig had been put back on, and the new load weighed approximately one and a quarter tons.   At first, Candido had balked at having anything to do with a chunk of condensed hell like this.   One of the problems when they were inventing thermonuclear weapons had been that even a sophisticated implosion-type A-bomb like the Alamogordo and Nagasaki blasts couldn't produce a temperature hot enough to make heavy hydrogen touch off in a fusion chain-reaction; so the ingenious and dedicated young men who are doing so much in this day and age to insure that men will all live as brothers—if they live at all—produced a special design of plutonium bomb that exploded, not as a simple, symmetrical fireball, but as a jet of plasma.   Thus, instead of dissipating its thermal energy in an expanding sphere which, within two or three seconds, has become more than half a mile across—so diffuse it can no longer maintain its chain reaction—this detonator type of bomb concentrates its energy in the jet, exactly like a shaped charge of a more conventional explosive.   The temperature thus obtained is on the order of ninety million degrees Centigrade—considerably hotter than the core of our sun—and quite sufficient to ignite an even more hellish chain-reaction in any deuterium that happens to be in its path.

Very earnestly and soberly, they'd emphasized to Candido that this was just the detonator part.   They'd cannibalized a Titan missile—one of the thirty or forty that crouched in silos in a circle around Denver—but they'd left off the lithium deuteride part from the thing they entrusted to the tank's handling rig.   They'd explained that the idea was to flood the entire volume occupied by the congruency with highly ionized nuclei of high kinetic energy.   The plutonium detonator was enough to do this.   They thought there was a good chance this would disrupt the condition that maintained the congruency.

Candido wasn't impressed.   They just wanted to try it because if they didn't they'd never be sure it wouldn't work.   When he was a kid, he'd learned not to play with matches.   They hadn't.

But the wind still blew.   The floods in Boulder got worse, and no one had a better idea.   They worked to convince him that the fail-safe mechanisms would prevent the bomb from going up until they were ready to set it off, and they promised him another hundred thousand.   They put it in writing.   He made sure his insurance was paid up, and said all right.   He still didn't like that thing from a nose cone on the tank's front end, but he liked the extra hundred thousand more.

"If this doesn't do it, I don't think anything will," he said.   The roads were roads he'd traveled before—familiar.   The force and the gusty blasting, and the abrasive, high-sustained yell of the wind were like an incredible symphony by a modern composer, but a thing he knew so well he paid it no attention.   He guided the tank and when they got close enough he put on his breather mask and gave the others time to get their masks on, and then he turned up the supercharger and they went on all the way to the heart of the whirlwind, into the zone of calm.   There was some new litter gathered under the sphere, but nothing of any great size or anything that would make any trouble.   Even the roundabout path across the pier- and bar-studded foundation was easier.   A beaten path.   And all the time he was thinking that the only men who could understand the congruency—what had created it and how it was maintained and how it could be erased—had vanished in the instant they made it, and L'Heuroux and all the other men who were trying to devise a weapon against it were fumbling children poking sticks into quicksand. Himself among them.

Ken Storch worked the handling rig with an expertise and care even greater than before—respect, Candido judged, for the power of the thing he was handling.   This was something you could understand only by knowing that no sane imagination can really encompass the concept of twenty thousand tons of TNT.   Storch was working the rig with the knowledge that its burden was a kind of death so blazing and immediate that even the fact of death would not have time to drive itself into his consciousness before his consciousness was shattered into its component atoms.

The arms of the handling rig withdrew from the bomb, and the bomb crouched squatly on a surface of crushed midden.   All of its essential structure was concealed by its casing: they'd insisted on that—even if he were cleared to obtain such knowledge, they said, he had no need to know how it was put together.   As if he could understand what he saw if he saw it.   As soon as the arms were clear, he backed the tank away.   In half an hour, the timing mechanism would arm the bomb—or if that failed, would at least release another mechanism so that a radio signal could arm it—and he intended to be far away from ground zero when it happened.

A tank didn't move very fast.

The bomb wasn't exploded until after they got back to Boulder.   Candido and L'Heuroux and Ken Storch were permitted to stand under the rooftop portico of an ornate building while a few yards away in the same shelter a half-dozen men worked to ready the detonating equipment.

It was a lot more sophisticated than the radio they'd used in the tank on their earlier try. This equipment transmitted a beamed, highly intricate, frequency-modulated signal; it was only to that exact signal—and no other—that the bomb would detonate. A small transmitter in the bomb itself had been announcing that it had armed itself—that it waited only for the signal to turn itself into a small, vest-pocket edition of doomsday. The men had been working all morning, preparing to transmit the signal that would do it. They weren't ready yet.

Then, finally, they were ready. In spite of the rain and clouds that made it impossible to see even a quarter mile, Trask passed each of them a pair of smoked glasses and advised them not to look in the direction of the whirlwind's center. Somebody with a parade-ground voice began announcing a countdown.

Candido held the glasses in his hand, then thought better of it and put them on. Always take the advice of someone who knows more about a thing than you do. The countdown paced off the seconds to zero, and someone at the transmitter did something—Candido didn't see because he was looking northwest, toward the center of the whirlwind, nine miles away. He knew someone did something because the sky's gray drabness, dimly seen through the glasses, brightened momentarily like a flashbulb silently bursting its light in a smoke-thickened room. Then it was dark again. After a long time, thunder came.

Candido took off his glasses. The wind was still blowing. Rain still drilled the rooftop in endless, spattering patterns. He cast a skeptical glance to L'Heuroux.

The physicist shook his head. "At this point, it's impossible to say. We have a powerful system here. It will take several hours, at least, to dissipate."

"Then we'll wait," Candido said.

An hour later, the rain was still falling. And two hours later. Three, and the wind blew gusts as strong as ever. All night it stormed. In the morning, the creek's floodwaters had spread to even higher ground. Still the rain came down, and the wind drove smashing waves against the walls of homes and buildings on the flooded land.

Candido lighted his pipe, bent the match double, and—not finding an ashtray in reach—stuck the match in his jacket pocket. They were back in the classroom again, and scrawled on the blackboard was a phrase: *Our daily life, which is all we have.* It was an annoying thing to have to look at, but his chair at the table was faced that way, so he couldn't turn aside. Nor could he change to another chair. Outside, as endlessly as a waterfall, the rain splashed down.

"Can you suggest anything at all?" Trask asked.

L'Heuroux rubbed a knuckle against his nose. "It's proving more refractory than we anticipated. Before we can recommend another approach, we'll have to study the data. I've gathered considerable information during our excursions. When we've analyzed this data, we'll know considerably more about this condition. Then we should be able to define a method of terminating it."

"What you're saying," Candido said, "is you don't know how to stop it."

L'Heuroux gave him an annoyed glance. "For the present, I must admit you are right. However, this is only a temporary state of affairs."

"Lasting," Candido said, "until we don't have any air left." There'd been a call last night.   A small well in Kansas had blown and gone torch.   He'd packed up his crew—all but Storch—and sent them east to fight it; they weren't needed here.   But it was bad business to send them on a job and not go himself; if he didn't at least show on the scene of a job, somebody might get the hunch any man could do that kind of work—well, they could, if they learned all the tricks and had the nerve and more than a man's share of luck.   If he let the crew go on too many jobs by themselves, some day there'd be three or a dozen guys in the business. One or two might even be rough competition, once they got themselves known. This job here was using up a lot of time.   More than he'd expected, and no end in sight.

"I've got work waiting, other places," he said.

"We have you on retainer, I believe," Trask said.

"Yeah, you do," Candido said.   "But I don't think you'll need me for the next forty-eight hours.   Unless you've got an operation planned, I'm taking off."

"I believe you don't realize," Trask said, "this is something more than just another job.   Unless this thing is stopped, no other work in the world will be worth doing.   It's . . . why, it's the air we breathe!"

Candido had other things to do than twiddle his thumbs.   "If you've got work for me, I'm here to do it.   If you don't, it doesn't matter where I am.   You'll know where to find me.   I've got your retainer, and I'm on call twenty-four hours a day."   He shoved his chair back, preparatory to leaving.

"Dr. L'Heuroux?" Trask asked.

"We'll have to study our data," the physicist said.

Candido rose, nodded to Trask, and turned to leave.   He wondered how far his three hundred thousand would go toward building him a home-size, self-sufficient pressure chamber.   Maybe he ought to set up a new business, too, selling air by the bottle—delivered to your door like a milkman—to the other people who built themselves pressure chambers.   Yeah, he thought sourly—and maybe sell cans of vacuum to companies that made radio tubes.   It made as much sense.   Maybe . . .

At the door, he turned and came back.   "How much is it worth if I stop this thing?"

Trask looked up, startled, like a deacon caught reading *Playboy*.   "You have your retainer," he said stiffly.

"That's for doing the work," Candido said.   "Pulling chestnuts and such. What I'm talking about now is figuring out how to do it."

Trask was suddenly quite interested.   "Do you know how?"

"He can't possibly," L'Heuroux said.   "He has absolutely no grasp of the principles involved."

"I know how," Candido said.   He went around to the window, glanced out at the rain, the wind-wracked trees, and turned and leaned a shoulder against the window's frame.   "It just came to me.   Your trouble, you've been going at it wrong—like the mathematician when they handed him the one about how many flies in a bottle."

"I don't know what you're talking about."

Candido shrugged.   "It's an old trick-type puzzle.   You've got a bottle—say

five-gallon size—with a fly in it.   And you put another fly in it, and then a second
later you put two more flies in, and another second later you put in four flies, and
then eight, and so on.''

L'Heuroux seized a stick of chalk—scrawled a formula on the blackboard under
the phrase about our daily life.   "Geometric progression.   Yes, go on.''

"Well, you keep at it," Candido said.   "And after three minutes the bottle's
exactly full.   None left over.   All right . . .''

L'Heuroux was scrawling hastily on the board.   "What volume does a fly take
up?''

"A third of a cubic centimeter," Candido said, and smiled as the physicist went
into a frenzy of conversion formulae.   "Now, what I want to know is, how full
is the bottle at two minutes and fifty-nine seconds?''

The physicist worked quickly.   His equations proliferated like ivy vines at east
coast universities.   Candido let him go on for almost a full minute.   "That's
enough," he said.

L'Heuroux turned.   "Either the flies take up less space," he said, "or the
bottle's larger.   Considerably larger.''

"I was just fudging the figures," Candido said.   "They don't matter.   You've
been going at it wrong, just like I said you were.   What the guy with the bottle's
been doing is doubling how many flies he's got every time.   Well, if that's what
you're doing, and if you don't have any flies left over after you add the last batch,
it figures the bottle was half full the time before.''

"Well, of course," L'Heuroux said.   "Why yes!   Of course!   But what does
this have to do with the congruency?''

"Not a thing," Candido said.   "I'm just saying that's how you've been going
at it—hind end frontwards, and we say down in Texas that's not the best way to
ride a horse.''   He shifted back to Trask.   "You haven't said.   What's it worth
if I stop this thing?''

"Dr. L'Heuroux has been advising us as a public service," Trask said.

"He's been getting paid in feeling important," Candido said.

"I deny that!" L'Heuroux spluttered.

He didn't even know better than to interrupt a man who was haggling.   Candido
ignored the interruption.   "You've been getting just about as much as you're
paying for," he said.   "I'll tell you what I want.   I want a clear deed to that
chunk of land.   I want to own what's left after I've stopped it.''

Trask looked like he'd been asked for an option on Brooklyn Bridge.   "Is that
all?''

"Any objections?" Candido asked.

"Oh no," Trask said quickly.   "Yes—I'm sure it can be arranged.   No trouble
at all.''   He was so eager to make the deal he didn't think to ask what Candido
wanted the property for.   He was no businessman, Candido thought.

"Shake," Candido said, and stuck out his hand.

Three days later, they were ready.   There was a steel mill and fabricating plant
in Denver—not an especially big one, but big enough for the job.   Mention that

it was to fight the whirlwind was all the plant manager needed to schedule the work right away, and as soon as machinery and men were cleared of other jobs they went to work.

Candido went east to Kansas.   He was gone only thirty-six hours.   It was a routine job, and the fire snuffed at the first blast.   He got back to Denver in time to catch four hours' sleep before the steel company phoned.   The rig he'd ordered was ready.

He inspected the product and pronounced himself satisfied.   It was fast, good work.   He shook the plant manager's hand.   This was a man who knew how to do business.   The new equipment was loaded and trucked north to Boulder.   They worked all night, and at ten in the morning the tank was ready to go.

It looked only a little like a tank now.   More closely, it resembled a beetle with a domelike shell steeply canted on its back, and paired grasshopper legs projecting their knees forward at about the angle flags are carried on parade.   The tank itself was small under all that.   He just hoped the wind wouldn't be too strong against it.   He'd have to hold tail to the wind all the way in.   He hoped the Diesel would have power enough to drive the rig when they got there.

"Might as well start," he told Storch.   He nodded to L'Heuroux.   "Come along. You'll see the way to do it."

Proudly, L'Heuroux declined.   Candido and Storch were alone in the tank when it left Boulder, groaning under its load.   It was hard going.   The wind drummed on the carapace, and though its round surface was like a shield to the wind, it was like a sail also, forcing the tank headlong forward.   He'd had to plan out the way they'd go, studying large scale topographic maps until his eyes burned.   He had to know that nowhere ahead was there too steep a slope, too sharp a declivity, nor any obstacle the tank couldn't clear—for once he began to move with this load, he was committed and could not turn aside.   To let the wind get its teeth around the edge of the carapace would be disaster.   The tank would be thrown like a tumbleweed, wrecked, and they'd be helpless in that hurricane wind.

The rain-sodden earth bogged under the treads, but the wind kept the tank moving. Candido kept an eye on the pennon he'd fixed to the tank's prow, showing him the bearing of the wind.   He kept the pennon whipping straight ahead.   He had a quadrangle map taped to the panel in front of him.   The route he'd planned was traced on it boldly.   He watched the landmarks.   The wind sang like a chorus in rage.   The tank rocked and lurched and jolted.   Blasts of wind shook it like a bone being gnawed.

The land was slopes and dells, and irrigation canals carved along the winding shoulders of low hills.   Most of the canals were hardly more than ditches, easily crossed.   One was a deep, slow river, full to its banks and flowing over.   The bridge was where the map showed it, and wonder of wonders it held the tank's weight.   He'd checked as much as he could, but the tank was a lot heavier than anything the bridge was built for.   Until he was over, he hadn't been sure.

He'd started from Boulder almost straight east.   The wind curved north and he turned with it.   The tank crossed the southernmost extreme of Gunbarrel Hill and descended again to the plain beyond.   Wire fences that had stood to the wind went down under the tank's weight.   A cornfield, cut to stubs by the wind, streamed dust like the smoke of a brushfire.   Wrecked foundations of barns and homes lay like open graves near the roads, now and then giving up another fragment to the tearing wind.   The tank turned north and then westward, and passed north of Gunbarrel Hill, and turned south again.   The spiral was tighter now.   Swinging east again, the tank mounted the Hill's slope.   The wind was like a powerful fist putting steady, driving pressure at the tank's rear.   He should have given the tank some kind of an upward projecting spine, Candido thought, like a sailboat's jib, to help hold the thing butt to the wind.   Too late to do it now.   The tank crossed a small watercourse—dry now—bumping on the rocks and creaking with internal stresses.

They came to the crest.   He could see the congruency's sphere off to his left, but he couldn't turn toward it.   Keeping the wind behind him, he circled it widely. Then again, more closely.   The foundation of the laboratory building was the final obstacle.   For this and all its hazards there could be no evasion.   The only way to go was straight in.   The best he could do was possibly to sidle past the most forbidding obstructions.   Candido studied the path ahead, trying to estimate the best possible path for the tank's treads.   Bent stubs of steel bar gleaned rubbish from the wind like fangs raking flesh; they could as easily slash the tank's treads— break them.   It was hard to make the brakes hold.   He could hardly slow the tank's ponderous, headlong drive.

A thump and a lurch, and the tank mounted onto the platform.   A crunch and a long, slowing grind as the tank straddled a pier and crumbled it under its belly. Candido felt something break.   He wondered if it was part of the tank or the pier. The tank barged onward, bumping and lurching, and he had to work on the brakes to keep the tank square to the wind.   Suddenly he felt something else give.

But the tank was in the dead zone now, under the sphere.   The wind's seethe was like sawteeth, snarling, but now it was without force.   Candido realized he hadn't put on his breather mask, and his ears felt plugged by the low pressure. With numb, fumbling, trembling fingers he got his mask on.   He breathed deeply, only now aware how badly he needed it.   His blood seemed to vibrate and burn.

He signaled to Storch, and the younger man unlocked and opened the turret-top hatch.   Leaning far back, Candido could look up through the opening and see the sphere overhead, whirling like a model of the planet Jupiter.   He shifted the tank back and forth, hitching it around until, finally, he was satisfied.   The tank had to be in just the right position.   Everything had to be just right.   When he was satisfied, he put a hand on Storch's shoulder.   He nodded.

"Ready," he said.   The mask changed the word to a mumble, but Storch understood.   The younger man checked the handling rig—modified again for this job—as carefully as if it were a supersonic aircraft.   Only when he was satisfied did he put it in gear, to take power from the engine.   Candido swung his periscope around to watch.

The hoodlike carapace separated into two hemispheres, like a beetle putting back its wing covers to fly.   Fingertip-held between paired booms, the bowl turned upward and extended like ladles, one to each side, as the booms straightened out from their original hairpin bend.   With a hard snap, the booms locked straight and the hemispheres—until now swinging free—locked level.   Rigid, Candido thought, and let himself breathe again.

Storch shifted to another gear.   Slowly, for the hemispheres were heavy and the gears had been rigged to account for that, the booms hinged upward.   Candido revved the Diesel.   It changed the speed of the hemispheres' rising hardly at all. Minutes—it seemed like days—passed.   Candido thought grimly of the joke about you'll never get it off the ground, and all he could hear was the Diesel's growl and the cry of the wind and the creak of metal joints under strain.   The wind touched the lips of the hemispheres.   The tank vibrated.   Something buzzed resonantly.

Candido cracked the throttle full open.   The engine erupted.   The hemispheres lifted like the wings of a startled bird, and suddenly the wind caught them and swung them upward in arcs on the ends of their booms.   The clang as they met overhead was like the gong of doom.   It burned the ears like dentists' drills.

Abruptly, wind battered the tank.   Thunder drummed.   Candido's ears popped with a sudden jump of pressure.   The thunder boomed on and on, as if they were sealed in a room with giants pounding on the walls.   He could feel the impact of the sound on his body.   It was like being shaken like a child's rag doll.   Slowly, by degrees, the thunder melted away.

Candido took off his breather mask.   Not needed now.   The air was full of dust. It smelled musty.   Through the open hatchway, he could see the steel globe enclosing the space where the congruency had been—where it might still be, for that matter, inside that steel container.   He breathed deeply.   Not until now had he been sure the two hemispheres would meet and fit together without smashing each other, or without one or the other overshooting and passing into the congruency. But the engineers who'd worked on the thing had designed well.   Neither had happened.

He climbed out of the tank.   The wind still blew, but now it was only a gentle, warm wind.   In all directions, storm clouds grayed the sky.   As he stood there on the tank's superstructure, it began to rain.   He got back inside.   He closed the hatch against the torrent.

"We stopped it, Ken," he said.   He opened the lunch pail he'd packed and handed a sandwich to Storch, took one himself, and poured himself a cup of coffee from the thermos.   "The wind's still blowing out there," he said.   "We'll have to stay here a while."

The jeep came, at last, in the last dim vestige of twilight.   Its headlamps glistened on the wet concrete of the foundation, but the rain had stopped, finally, more than an hour ago.

By that time, Candido had been able to look the tank over.   The treads had lost a total of seven shoes.   Several more were badly torn.   In two places, the linkage of the left tread was partly broken.   A few more yards and likely the tank would have been immobilized.   He felt numb and tight-skinned, thinking about that.

The congruency was still there, inside the steel shell.   The hemispheres hadn't sealed perfectly, and a trickle of air was leaking in through the crack. Trask and L'Heuroux climbed out of the jeep and approached. Candido leaned against the tank and let them come. They picked their way across the hazards of the wrecked foundation with a flashlight, even so stumbling from time to time. When they got there, at first they said nothing. Trask beamed the flashlight upward and played it over the steel globe's surface.

"I checked," Candido said. "No fractures. It'll hold, at least till we make a tighter one."

"Of course you realize," L'Heuroux said, "the congruency is still there, inside. This doesn't solve the problem."

"Doesn't it?" Candido asked. "Gentle breeze, we've got now." Actually, it was blowing a stiff twenty miles an hour, but the point was made. "When I've got a boat that leaks, I plug the hole."

The flashlight beam fixed on something that protruded from the globe's underside. It was a short length of pipe, with a valve wheel beside it. "What's that?" Trask asked.

"Just what it looks like," Candido said. "A storage tank's no good without an outlet."

"Outlet? Storage? I'm afraid I don't . . ."

"I'm starting a new business," Candido said. "That's why I wanted this chunk of land. I'm going to sell vacuums—the emptiest vacuums anywhere in the world. How much do you think they'll pay for a gallon of real nothing—no impurities?"

Another thought came. He smiled. Maybe he'd lay a pipeline—maybe all the way to the east coast. Plenty of people would pay for a vacuum you get just from turning a faucet, and he had an unlimited supply. Should be a real good business.

RANDALL GARRETT

A Case of Identity

T he pair of Men-at-Arms strolled along the Rue King John II, near the waterfront of Cherbourg, and a hundred yards south of the sea. In this district, the Keepers of the King's Peace always traveled in pairs, each keeping one hand near the truncheon at his belt and the other near the hilt of his small-sword. The average commoner was not a swordsman, but sailors are not common commoners. A man armed only with a truncheon would be at a disadvantage with a man armed with a cutlass.

The frigid wind from the North Sea whipped the edges of the Men-at-Arms' cloaks, and the light from the mantled gas lamps glowed yellowly, casting multiple shadows that shifted queerly as the Armsmen walked.

There were not many people on the streets. Most of them were in the bistros, where there were coal fires to warm the outer man and fiery bottled goods to warm the inner. There had been crowds in the street on the Vigil of the Feast of the Circumcision, nine days before, but now the Twelfth Day of Christmas had passed and the Year of Our Lord 1964 was in its second week. Money had run short and few could still afford to drink.

The taller of the two officers stopped and pointed ahead. "Ey, Robert. Old Jean hasn't got his light on."

"Hm-m-m. Third time since Christmas. Hate to give the old man a summons."

"Aye. Let's just go in and scare the Hell out of him."

"Aye," said the shorter man. "But we'll promise him a summons next time and keep our promise, Jack."

The sign above the door was a weatherbeaten dolphin-shaped piece of wood, painted blue. The Blue Dolphin.

Armsman Robert pushed open the door and went in, his eyes alert for trouble. There was none. Four men were sitting around one end of the long table at the left, and Old Jean was talking to a fifth man at the bar. They all looked up as the Armsmen came in. Then the men at the table went on with their conversation. The fifth customer's eyes went to his drink. The barkeep smiled ingratiatingly and came toward the two Armsmen.

"Evening, Armsmen," he said with a snaggle-toothed smile. "A little something to warm the blood?" But he knew it was no social call.

Robert already had out his summons book, pencil poised. "Jean, we have warned you twice before,'' he said frigidly. "The law plainly states that every place of business must maintain a standard gas lamp and keep it lit from sunset to sunrise. You know this.''

"Perhaps the wind—'' the barkeep said defensively.

"The wind? I will go up with you and we will see if perhaps the wind has turned the gas cock, ey?''

Old Jean swallowed. "Perhaps I did forget. My memory—''

"Perhaps explaining your memory to my lord the Marquis next court day will help you to improve it, ey?''

"No, no! Please, Armsman! The fine would ruin me!''

Armsman Robert made motions with his pencil as though he were about to write. "I will say it is first offense and the fine will be only half as much.''

Old Jean closed his eyes helplessly. "Please, Armsman. It will not happen again. It is just that I have been so used to Paul—he did everything, all the hard work. I have no one to help me now.''

"Paul Sarto has been gone for two weeks now,'' Robert said. "This is the third time you have given me that same excuse.''

"Armsman,'' said the old man earnestly, "I will not forget again. I promise you.''

Robert closed his summons book. "Very well. I have your word? Then you have my word that there will be no excuses next time. I will hand you the summons instantly. Understood?''

"Understood, Armsman! Yes, of course. Many thanks! I will not forget again!''

"See that you don't. Go and light it.''

Old Jean scurried up the stairway and was back within minutes. "It's lit now, Armsman.''

"Excellent. I expect it to be lit from now on. At sunset. Good night, Jean.''

"Perhaps a little—?''

"No Jean. Another time. Come, Jack.''

The Armsmen left without taking the offered drink. It would be ungentlemanly to take it after threatening the man with the law. The Armsman's Manual said that, because of the sword he is privileged to wear, an Armsman must be a gentleman at all times.

"Wonder why Paul left?'' Jack asked when they were on the street again. "He was well paid, and he was too simple to work elsewhere.''

Robert shrugged. "You know how it is. Wharf rats come and go. No need to worry about him. A man with a strong back and a weak mind can always find a bistro that will take care of him. He'll get along.''

Nothing further was said for the moment. The two Armsmen walked on to the corner, where the Quai Sainte Marie turned off to the south.

Robert glanced southwards and said: "Here's a happy one.''

"Too happy, if you ask me,'' said Jack.

Down the Quai Sainte Marie came a man. He was hugging the side of the building, stumbling toward them, propping himself up by putting the flat of his palms on the brick wall one after the other as he moved his feet.   He wore no hat, and, as the wind caught his cloak, the two Men-at-Arms saw something they had not expected.   He was naked.

"Blind drunk and freezing," Jack said.   "Better take him in."

They never got the chance.   As they came toward him, the stumbling man stumbled for the last time.   He dropped to his knees, looked up at them with blind eyes that stared past them into the darkness of the sky, then toppled to one side, his eyes still open, unblinking.

Robert knelt down.   "Sound your whistle!   I think he's dead!"

Jack took out his whistle and keened a note into the frigid air.

"Speak of the Devil," Robert said softly.   "It's Paul!   He doesn't smell drunk. I think . . .   *God!*"   He had tried to lift the head of the fallen man and found his palm covered with blood.   "It's soft," he said wonderingly.   "The whole side of his skull is crushed."

In the distance, they heard the clatter of hoofs as a mounted Sergeant-at-Arms came at a gallop toward the sound of the whistle.

Lord Darcy, tall, lean-faced, and handsome, strode down the hall to the door bearing the arms of Normandy and opened it.

"Your Highness sent for me?"   He spoke Anglo-French with a definite English accent.

There were three men in the room.   The youngest, tall, blond Richard, Duke of Normandy and brother to His Imperial Majesty, John IV, turned as the door opened.   "Ah.   Lord Darcy.   Come in."   He gestured toward the portly man wearing episcopal purple.   "My Lord Bishop, may I present my Chief Investigator, Lord Darcy.   Lord Darcy, this is his lordship, the Bishop of Guernsey and Sark."

"A pleasure, Lord Darcy," said the Bishop, extending his right hand.

Lord Darcy took the hand, bowed, kissed the ring.   "My Lord Bishop."   Then he turned and bowed to the third man, the lean, graying Marquis of Rouen.   "My Lord Marquis."

Then Lord Darcy faced the Royal Duke again and waited expectantly.

The Duke of Normandy frowned slightly.   "There appears to be some trouble with my lord the Marquis of Cherbourg.   As you know, My Lord Bishop is the elder brother of the Marquis."

Lord Darcy knew the family history.   The previous Marquis of Cherbourg had had three sons.   At his death, the eldest had inherited the title and government. The second had taken Holy Orders, and the third had taken a commission in the Royal Navy.   When the eldest had died without heirs, the Bishop could not succeed to the title, so the Marquisate went to the youngest son, Hugh, the present Marquis.

"Perhaps you had better explain, My Lord Bishop," said the Duke.   "I would rather Lord Darcy had the information first-hand."

"Certainly, Your Highness," said the Bishop.   He looked worried, and his right hand kept fiddling with the pectoral cross at his breast.

The Duke gestured toward the chairs.   "Please, my lords—sit down."

The four men settled themselves, and the Bishop began his story.

"My brother the Marquis," he said after a deep breath, "is missing."

Lord Darcy raised an eyebrow.   Normally, if one of His Majesty's Governors turned up missing, there would be a hue and cry from one end of the Empire to the other—from John O'Groat in Scotland to the southernmost tip of Gascony—from the German border on the east to New England and New France, across the Atlantic.   If my lord the Bishop of Guernsey and Sark wanted it kept quiet, then there was—there had *better* be!—a good reason.

"Have you met my brother, Lord Darcy?" the Bishop asked.

"Only briefly, my lord.   Once, about a year ago.   I hardly know him."

"I see."

The Bishop fiddled a bit more with his pectoral cross, then plunged into his story.   Three days before, on the tenth of January, the Bishop's sister-in-law, Elaine, Marquise de Cherbourg, had sent a servant by boat to St. Peter Port, Guernsey, the site of the Cathedral Church of the Diocese of Guernsey and Sark. The sealed message which he was handed informed My Lord Bishop that his brother the Marquis had been missing since the evening of the eighth.   Contrary to his custom, My Lord Marquis had not notified My Lady Marquise of any intention to leave the castle.   Indeed, he implied that he had intended to retire when he had finished with certain Government papers.   No one had seen him since he entered his study.   My lady of Cherbourg had not missed him until next morning, when she found that his bed had not been slept in.

"This was on the morning of Thursday the ninth, my lord?" Lord Darcy asked.

"That is correct, my lord," said the Bishop.

"May I ask why we were not notified until now?" Lord Darcy asked gently.

My Lord Bishop fidgeted.   "Well, my lord . . . you see . . . well, My Lady Elaine believes that . . . er . . . that his lordship, my brother, is not . . . er . . . *may* not be . . . er . . . quite right in his mind."

There! thought Lord Darcy.   *He got it out!   My Lord of Cherbourg is off his chump!   Or, at least, his lady thinks so.*

"What behavior did he display?" Lord Darcy asked quietly.

The Bishop spoke rapidly and concisely.   My lord of Cherbourg had had his first attack on the eve of St. Stephen's Day, the 26th of December, 1963.   His face had suddenly taken on a look of utter idiocy; it had gone slack, and the intelligence seemed to fade from his eyes.   He had babbled meaninglessly and seemed not to know where he was—and, indeed, to be somewhat terrified of his surroundings.

"Was he violent in any way?" asked Lord Darcy.

"No.   Quite the contrary.   He was quite docile and easily led to bed.   Lady Elaine called in a Healer immediately, suspecting that my brother may have had an apoplectic stroke.   As you know, the Marquisate supports a chapter of the Benedictines within the walls of Castle Cherbourg, and Father Patrique saw my brother within minutes.

"But by that time the attack had passed.   Father Patrique could detect nothing wrong, and my brother simply said it was a slight dizzy spell, nothing more.

However, since then there have been three more attacks—on the evenings of the second, the fifth, and the seventh of this month.   And now he is gone.''

"You feel, then, My Lord Bishop, that his lordship has had another of these attacks and may be wandering around somewhere . . . ah . . . *non compos mentis,* as it were?''

"That's exactly what I'm afraid of,'' the Bishop said firmly.

Lord Darcy looked thoughtful for a moment, then glanced silently at His Royal Highness, the Duke.

"I want you to make a thorough investigation, Lord Darcy,'' said the Duke. "Be as discreet as possible.   We want no scandal.   If there is anything wrong with my lord of Cherbourg's mind, we will have the best care taken, of course. But we must find him first.''   He glanced at the clock on the wall.   "There is a train for Cherbourg in forty-one minutes.   You will accompany My Lord Bishop.''

Lord Darcy rose smoothly from his chair.   "I'll just have time to pack, Your Highness.''   He bowed to the Bishop.   "Your servant, my lord.''   He turned and walked out the door, closing it behind him.

But instead of heading immediately for his own apartments, he waited quietly outside the door, just to one side.   He had caught Duke Richard's look.

Within, he heard voices.

"My Lord Marquis,'' said the Duke, "would you see that My Lord Bishop gets some refreshment?   If your lordship will excuse me I have some urgent work to attend to.   A report on this matter must be dispatched immediately to the King my brother.''

"Of course, Your Highness; of course.''

"I will have a carriage waiting for you and Lord Darcy.   I will see you again before you leave, my lord.   And now, excuse me.''

He came out of the room, saw Lord Darcy waiting, and motioned toward another room nearby.   Lord Darcy followed him in.   The Duke closed the door firmly and then said, in a low voice:

"This may be worse than it appears at first glance, Darcy.   De Cherbourg was working with one of His Majesty's personal agents trying to trace down the ring of Polish *agents provocateurs* operating in Cherbourg.   If he's actually had a mental breakdown and they've got hold of him, there will be Hell to pay.''

Lord Darcy knew the seriousness of the affair.   The Kings of Poland had been ambitious for the past half century.   Having annexed all of the Russian territory they could—as far as Minsk to the north and Kiev to the south—the Poles now sought to work their way westwards, toward the borders of the Empire.   For several centuries, the Germanic states had acted as buffers between the powerful Kingdom of Poland and the even more powerful Empire.   In theory, the Germanic states, as part of the old Holy Roman Empire, owed fealty to the Emperor—but no Anglo-French King had tried to enforce that fealty for centuries.   The Germanic states were, in fact, holding their independence because of the tug-of-war between Poland and the Empire.   If the troops of King Casimir IX tried to march into Bavaria, for instance, Bavaria would scream for Imperial help and would get it.   On the other hand, if King John IV tried to tax so much as a single sovereign out of Bavaria, and sent troops in to collect it, Bavaria would scream just as loudly for Polish aid. As long as the balance of power remained, the Germanies were safe.

Actually, King John had no desire to bring the Germanies into the Empire forcibly. That kind of aggression hadn't been Imperial policy for a good long time.   With hardly any trouble at all, an Imperial army could take over Lombardy or northern Spain.   But with the whole New World as Imperial domain, there was no need to add more of Europe.   Aggression against her peaceful neighbors was unthinkable in this day and age.

As long as Poland had been moving eastward, Imperial policy had been to allow her to go her way while the Empire expanded into the New World.   But that eastward expansion had ground to a halt.   King Casimir was now having trouble with those Russians he had already conquered.   To hold his quasi-empire together, he had to keep the threat of external enemies always before the eyes of his subjects, but he dared not push any farther into Russia.   The Russian states had formed a loose coalition during the last generation, and the King of Poland, Sigismund III, had backed down.   If the Russians ever really united, they would be a formidable enemy.

That left the Germanic states to the west and the Turks to the south.   Casimir had no desire to tangle with the Turks, but he had plans for the Germanic states.

The wealth of the Empire, the basis of its smoothly expanding economy, was the New World.   The importation of cotton, tobacco, and sugar—to say nothing of the gold that had been found in the southern continent—was the backbone of Imperial economy.   The King's subjects were well-fed, well-clothed, well-housed, and happy.   But if the shipping were to be blocked for any considerable length of time, there would be trouble.

The Polish Navy didn't stand a chance against the Imperial Navy.   No Polish fleet could get through the North Sea without running into trouble with either the Imperial Navy or that of the Empire's Scandinavian allies.   The North Sea was Imperial-Scandinavian property, jointly patrolled, and no armed ship was allowed to pass.   Polish merchantmen were allowed to come and go freely—after they had been boarded to make sure that they carried no guns.   Bottled up in the Baltic, the Polish Navy was helpless, and it wasn't big enough or good enough to fight its way out.   They'd tried it once, back in '39, and had been blasted out of the water.   King Casimir wouldn't try that again.

He had managed to buy a few Spanish and Italian ships and have them outfitted as privateers, but they were merely annoying, not menacing.   If caught, they were treated as pirates—either sunk or captured and their crews hanged—and the Imperial Government didn't even bother to protest to the King of Poland.

But King Casimir evidently had something else up his royal sleeve.   Something was happening that had both the Lords of the Admiralty and the Maritime Lords on edge.   Ships leaving Imperial ports—Le Havre, Cherbourg, Liverpool, London, and so on—occasionally disappeared.   They were simply never heard from again.

They never got to New England at all.   And the number was more than could be accounted for either by weather or piracy.

That was bad enough, but to make things worse, rumors had been spreading around the waterfronts of the Empire.   Primarily the rumors exaggerated the dangers of sailing the Atlantic.   The word was beginning to spread that the mid-Atlantic was a dangerous area—far more dangerous than the waters around Europe.   A sailor worth his salt cared very little for the threats of weather; give a British or a French sailor a seaworthy ship and a skipper he trusted, and he'd head into the teeth of any storm.   But the threat of evil spirits and black magic was something else again.

Do what they would, scientific researchers simply could not educate the common man to understand the intricacies and limitations of modern scientific sorcery.   The superstitions of a hundred thousand years still clung to the minds of ninety-nine per cent of the human race, even in a modern, advanced civilization like the Empire. How does one explain that only a small percentage of the population is capable of performing magic?   How to explain that all the incantations in the official grimoires won't help a person who doesn't have the Talent?   How to explain that, even with the Talent, years of training are normally required before it can be used efficiently, predictably, and with power?   People had been told again and again, but deep in their hearts they believed otherwise.

Not one person in ten who was suspected of having the Evil Eye really had it, but sorcerers and priests were continually being asked for counteragents.   And only God knew how many people wore utterly useless medallions, charms, and anti-hex shields prepared by quacks who hadn't the Talent to make the spells effective.   There is an odd quirk in the human mind that makes a fearful man prefer to go quietly to a wicked-looking, gnarled "witch" for a countercharm than to a respectable licensed sorcerer or an accredited priest of the Church.   Deep inside, the majority of people had the sneaking suspicion that evil was more powerful than good and that evil could be counteracted only by more evil.   Almost none of them would believe what scientific magical research had shown—that the practice of black magic was, in the long run, more destructive to the mind of the practitioner than to his victims.

So it wasn't difficult to spread the rumor that there was Something Evil in the Atlantic—and, as a result, more and more sailors were becoming leery of shipping aboard a vessel that was bound for the New World.

And the Imperial Government was absolutely certain that the story was being deliberately spread by agents of King Casimir IX.

Two things had to be done: The disappearances must cease, and the rumors must be stopped.   And my lord the Marquis of Cherbourg had been working toward those ends when he had disappeared.   The question of how deeply Polish agents were involved in that disappearance was an important one.

"You will contact His Majesty's agent as soon as possible," said Duke Richard. "Since there may be black magic involved, take Master Sean along—incognito. If a sorcerer suddenly shows up, they—whoever they may be—might take over. They might even do something drastic to de Cherbourg."

"I will exercise the utmost care, Your Highness," said Lord Darcy.

The train pulled into Cherbourg Station with a hiss and a blast of steam that made a great cloud of fog in the chill air. Then the wind picked up the cloud and blew it to wisps before anyone had stepped from the carriages. The passengers hugged their coats and cloaks closely about them as they came out. There was a light dusting of snow on the ground and on the platform, but the air was clear and the low winter sun shone brightly, if coldly, in the sky.

The Bishop had made a call on the teleson to Cherbourg Castle before leaving Rouen, and there was a carriage waiting for the three men—one of the newer models with pneumatic tires and spring suspension, bearing the Cherbourg arms on the doors, and drawn by two pairs of fine greys. The footman opened the near door and the Bishop climbed in, followed by Lord Darcy and a short, chubby man who wore the clothing of a gentleman's gentleman. Lord Darcy's luggage was put on the rack atop the carriage, but a small bag carried by the "gentleman's gentleman" remained firmly in the grasp of his broad fist.

Master Sean O Lochlainn, Sorcerer, had no intention of letting go of his professional equipment. He had grumbled enough about not being permitted to carry his symbol-decorated carpet bag, and had spent nearly twenty minutes casting protective spells around the black leather suitcase that Lord Darcy had insisted he carry.

The footman closed the door of the carriage and swung himself aboard. The four greys started off at a brisk trot through the streets of Cherbourg toward the Castle, which lay across the city, near the sea.

Partly to keep My Lord Bishop's mind off his brother's troubles and partly to keep from being overheard while they were on the train, Lord Darcy and the Bishop had tacitly agreed to keep their conversation on subjects other than the investigation at hand. Master Sean had merely sat quietly by, trying to look like a valet—at which he succeeded very well.

Once inside the carriage, however, the conversation seemed to die away. My lord the Bishop settled himself into the cushions and gazed silently out of the window. Master Sean leaned back, folded his hands over his paunch and closed his eyes. Lord Darcy, like my lord the Bishop, looked out the window. He had only been in Cherbourg twice before, and was not as familiar with the city as he would like to be. It would be worth his time to study the route the carriage was taking.

It was not until they came to the waterfront itself, turned, and moved down the Rue de Mer toward the towers of Castle Cherbourg in the distance, that Lord Darcy saw anything that particularly interested him.

There were, he thought, entirely too many ships tied up at the docks, and there seemed to be a great deal of goods waiting on the wharves to be loaded. On the other hand, there did not seem to be as many men working as the apparent volume of shipping would warrant.

Crews scared off by the "Atlantic Curse," Lord Darcy thought. He looked at the men loafing around in clumps, talking softly but, he thought, rather angrily. *Obviously sailors; out of work by their own choice and resenting their own fears.*

Probably trying to get jobs as longshoremen and being shut out by the Longshore-men's Guild.

Normally, he knew, sailors were considered as an auxiliary of the Longshore-men's Guild, just as longshoremen were considered as an auxiliary of the Seamen's Guild.   If a sailor decided to spend a little time on land, he could usually get work as a longshoreman; if a longshoreman decided to go to sea, he could usually find a berth somewhere.   But with ships unable to find crews, there were fewer long-shoremen finding work loading vessels.   With regular members of the Longshore-men's Guild unable to find work, it was hardly odd that the Guild would be unable to find work for the frightened seamen who had caused that very shortage.

The unemployment, in turn, threw an added burden on the Privy Purse of the Marquis of Cherbourg, since, by ancient law, it was obligatory upon the lord to take care of his men and their families in times of trouble.   Thus far, the drain was not too great, since it was spread out evenly over the Empire; my lord of Cherbourg could apply to the Duke of Normandy for aid under the same law, and His Royal Highness could, in turn, apply to His Imperial Majesty, John IV, King and Emperor of England, France, Scotland, Ireland, New England and New France, Defender of the Faith, et cetera.

And the funds of the Imperial Privy Purse came from all over the Empire.

Still, if the thing became widespread, the economy of the Empire stood in danger of complete collapse.

There had not been a complete cessation of activity on the waterfront, Lord Darcy was relieved to notice.   Aside from those ships that were making the Mediterranean and African runs, there were still ships that had apparently found crews for the Atlantic run to the northern continent of New England and the southern continent of New France.

One great ship, the *Pride of Calais,* showed quite a bit of activity; bales of goods were being loaded over the side amid much shouting of orders.   Close by, Lord Darcy could see a sling full of wine casks being lifted aboard, each cask bearing the words: *Ordwin Vayne, Vintner,* and a sorcerer's symbol burnt into the wood, showing that the wine was protected against souring for the duration of the trip. Most of the wine, Lord Darcy knew, was for the crew; by law each sailor was allowed the equivalent of a bottle a day, and, besides, the excellence of the New World wines was such that it did not pay to import the beverage from Europe.

Further on, Lord Darcy saw other ships that he knew were making the Atlantic run loading goods aboard.   Evidently the "Atlantic Curse" had not yet frightened the guts out of all of the Empire's seamen.

We'll come through, Lord Darcy thought.   *In spite of everything the King of Poland can do, we'll come through.   We always have.*

He did not think: *We always will.*   Empires and societies, he knew, died and were replaced by others.   The Roman Empire had died to be replaced by hordes of barbarians who had gradually evolved the feudal society, which had, in turn, evolved the modern system.   It was certainly possible that the eight-hundred-year-old Empire that had been established by Henry II in the Twelfth Century might some day collapse as the Roman Empire had—but it had already existed nearly twice as long, and there were no threatening hordes of barbarians to overrun it nor were there any signs of internal dissent strong enough to disrupt it.   The Empire was still stable and still evolving.

Most of that stability and evolution was due to the House of Plantagenet, the House which had been founded by Henry II after the death of King Stephen.   Old Henry had brought the greater part of France under the sway of the King of England. His son, Richard the Lion-Hearted, had neglected England during the first ten years of his reign, but, after his narrow escape from death from the bolt of a crossbowman at the Siege of Chaluz, he had settled down to controlling the Empire with a firm hand and a wise brain.   He had no children, but his nephew, Arthur, the son of King Richard's dead brother, Geoffrey, had become like a son to him.   Arthur had fought with the King against the treacheries of Prince John, Richard's younger brother and the only other claimant to the throne.   Prince John's death in 1216 left Arthur as the only heir, and, upon old Richard's death in 1219, Arthur, at thirty-two, had succeeded to the Throne of England.   In popular legend, King Arthur was often confused with the earlier King Arthur of Camelot—and for good reason. The monarch who was known even today as Good King Arthur had resolved to rule his realm in the same chivalric manner—partly inspired by the legends of the ancient Brittanic leader, and partly because of his own inherent abilities.

Since then, the Plantagenet line had gone through nearly eight centuries of trial and tribulation; of blood, sweat, toil, and tears; of resisting the enemies of the Empire by sword, fire, and consummate diplomacy to hold the realm together and to expand it.

The Empire had endured.   And the Empire would continue to endure only so long as every subject realized that it could *not* endure if the entire burden were left to the King alone.   *The Empire expects every man to do his duty*.

And Lord Darcy's duty, at this moment, was greater than the simple duty of finding out what had happened to my lord the Marquis of Cherbourg.   The problem ran much deeper than that.

His thoughts were interrupted by the voice of the Bishop.

"There's the tower of the Great Keep ahead, Lord Darcy.   We'll be there soon."

It was actually several more minutes before the carriage-and-four drew up before the main entrance of Castle Cherbourg.   The door was opened by a footman, and three men climbed out, Master Sean still clutching his suitcase.

My Lady Elaine, Marquise de Cherbourg, stood in her salon above the Great Hall, staring out the window at the Channel.   She could see the icy waves splashing and dancing and rolling with almost hypnotic effect, but she saw them without thinking about them.

Where are you, Hugh? she thought.   *Come back to me, Hugh.   I need you. I never knew how much I'd need you.*   Then there seemed to be a blank as her mind rested.   Nothing came through but the roll of the waves.

Then there was the noise of an opening door behind her.   She turned quickly, her long velvet skirts swirling around her like thick syrup. "Yes?" Her voice seemed oddly far away in her ears.

"You rang, my lady." It was Sir Gwiliam, the seneschal.

My Lady Elaine tried to focus her thoughts. "Oh," she said after a moment. "Oh, yes." She waved toward the refreshment table, upon which stood a decanter of Oporto, a decanter of Xerez, and an empty decanter. "Brandy. The brandy hasn't been refilled. Bring some of the Saint Coeurlandt Michele '46."

"The Saint Coeurlandt Michele '46, my lady?" Sir Gwiliam blinked slightly. "But my lord de Cherbourg would not—"

She turned to face him directly. "My lord of Cherbourg would most certainly not deny his lady his best Champagne brandy at a time like this, *Sieur* Gwiliam!" she snapped, using the local pronunciation instead of standard Anglo-French, thus employing a mild and unanswerable epithet. "Must I fetch it myself?"

Sir Gwiliam's face paled a little, but his expression did not change. "No my lady. Your wish is my command."

"Very well. I thank you, Sir Gwiliam." She turned back to the window. Behind her, she heard the door open and close.

Then she turned, walked over to the refreshment table, and looked at the glass she had emptied only a few minutes before.

Empty, she thought. *Like my life. Can I refill it?*

She lifted the decanter of Xerez, took out the stopple, and, with exaggerated care, refilled her glass. Brandy was better, but until Sir Gwiliam brought the brandy there was nothing to drink but the sweet wines. She wondered vaguely why she had insisted on the best and finest brandy in Hugh's cellar. There was no need for it. Any brandy would have done, even the *Aqua Sancta '60,* a foul distillate. She knew that by now her palate was so anesthetized that she could not tell the difference.

But where *was* the brandy? Somewhere. Yes. Sir Gwiliam.

Angrily, almost without thinking, she began to jerk at the bell-pull. Once. Pause. Once. Pause. Once . . .

She was still ringing when the door opened.

"Yes, my lady?"

She turned angrily—then froze.

Lord Seiger frightened her. He always had.

"I rang for Sir Gwiliam, my lord," she said, with as much dignity as she could summon.

Lord Seiger was a big man who had about him the icy coldness of the Norse home from which his ancestors had come. His hair was so blond as to be almost silver, and his eyes were a pale iceberg blue. The Marquise could not recall ever having seen him smile. His handsome face was always placid and expressionless. She realized with a small chill that she would be more afraid of Lord Seiger's smile than of his normal calm expression.

"I rang for Sir Gwiliam," my lady repeated.

"Indeed, my lady," said Lord Seiger, "but since Sir Gwiliam seemed not to answer, I felt it my duty to respond.   You rang for him a few minutes ago.   Now you are ringing again.   May I help?''

"No . . .   No . . .''   What could she say?

He came into the room, closing the door behind him.   Even twenty-five feet away, My Lady Elaine fancied she could feel the chill from him.   She could do nothing as he approached.   She couldn't find her voice.   He was tall and cold and blondly handsome—and had no more sexuality than a toad.   Less—for a toad must at least have attraction for another toad—and a toad was at least a living thing. My lady was not attracted to the man, and he hardly seemed living.

He came toward her like a battleship—twenty feet—fifteen . . .

She gasped and gestured toward the refreshment table.   "Would you pour some wine, my lord?   I'd like a glass of . . . the Xerez.''

It was as though the battleship had been turned in its course, she thought.   His course toward her veered by thirty degrees as he angled toward the table.

"Xerez, my lady?   Indeed.   I shall be most happy.''

With precise, strong hands, he emptied the last of the decanter into a goblet. "There is less than a glassful, my lady,'' he said, looking at her with expressionless blue eyes.   "Would my lady care for the Oporto instead?''

"No . . .   No, just the Xerez, my lord, just the Xerez.''   She swallowed. "Would you care for anything yourself?''

"I never drink, my lady.''   He handed her the partially filled glass.

It was all she could do to take the glass from his hand, and it struck her as odd that his fingers, when she touched them, seemed as warm as anyone else's.

"Does my lady really feel that it is necessary to drink so much?'' Lord Seiger asked.   "For the last four days . . .''

My lady's hand shook, but all she could say was: "My nerves, my lord.   My nerves.''   She handed back the glass, empty.

Since she had not asked for more, Lord Seiger merely held the glass and looked at her.   "I am here to protect you, my lady.   It is my duty.   Only your enemies have anything to fear from me.''

Somehow, she knew that what he said was true, but—

"Please.   A glass of Oporto, my lord.''

"Yes, my lady.''

He was refilling her glass when the door opened.

It was Sir Gwiliam, bearing a bottle of brandy.   "My lady, my lord, the carriage has arrived.''

Lord Seiger looked at him expressionlessly, then turned the same face on My Lady Elaine.   "The Duke's Investigators.   Shall we meet them here, my lady?''

"Yes.   Yes, my lord, of course.   Yes.''   Her eyes were on the brandy.

The meeting between Lord Darcy and My Lady Elaine was brief and meaningless. Lord Darcy had no objection to the aroma of fine brandy, but he preferred it fresh rather than secondhand.   Her recital of what had happened during the days immediately preceding the disappearance of the Marquis was not significantly different from that of the Bishop.

The coldly handsome Lord Seiger, who had been introduced as secretary to the Marquis, knew nothing. He had not been present during any of the alleged attacks.

Mr Lady the Marquise finally excused herself, pleading a headache. Lord Darcy noted that the brandy bottle went with her.

"My Lord Seiger," he said, "her ladyship seems indisposed. Whom does that leave in charge of the castle for the moment?"

"The servants and household are in charge of Sir Gwiliam de Bracy, the seneschal. The guard is in the charge of Captain Sir Androu Duglasse. I am not My Lord Marquis' Privy Secretary; I am merely aiding him in cataloguing some books."

"I see. Very well. I should like to speak to Sir Gwiliam and Sir Androu."

Lord Seiger stood up, walked over to the bell-pull and signaled. "Sir Gwiliam will be here shortly," he said. "I shall fetch Sir Androu myself." He bowed. "If you will excuse me, my lords."

When he had gone, Lord Darcy said: "An impressive looking man. Dangerous, too, I should say—in the right circumstances."

Seems a decent sort," said My Lord Bishop. "A bit restrained . . . er . . . stuffy, one might say. Not much sense of humor, but sense of humor isn't everything." He cleared his throat and then went on. "I must apologize for my sister-in-law's behavior. She's overwrought. You won't be needing me for these interrogations, and I really ought to see after her."

"Of course, my lord; I quite understand." Lord Darcy said smoothly.

My Lord Bishop had hardly gone when the door opened again and Sir Gwiliam came in. "Your lordship rang?"

"Will you be seated, Sir Gwiliam?" Lord Darcy gestured toward a chair. "We are here, as you know, to investigate the disappearance of my lord of Cherbourg. This is my man, Sean, who assists me. All you say here will be treated as confidential."

"I shall be happy to cooperate, your lordship," said Sir Gwiliam, seating himself.

"I am well aware, Sir Gwiliam," Lord Darcy began, "that you have told what you know to My Lord Bishop, but, tiresome as it may be, I shall have to hear the whole thing again. If you will be so good as to begin at the beginning, Sir Gwiliam . . ."

The seneschal dutifully began his story. Lord Darcy and Master Sean listened to it for the third time and found that it differed only in viewpoint, not in essentials. But the difference in viewpoint was important. Like My Lord Bishop, Sir Gwiliam told his story as though he were not directly involved.

"Did you actually ever see one of these attacks?" Lord Darcy asked.

Sir Gwiliam blinked. "Why . . . no. No, your lordship, I did not. But they were reported to me in detail by several of the servants."

"I see. What about the night of the disappearance? When did you last see My Lord Marquis?"

"Fairly early in the evening, your lordship. With my lord's permission, I went into the city about five o'clock for an evening of cards with friends. We played until rather late—two or two-thirty in the morning. My host, Master Ordwin Vayne, a well-to-do wine merchant in the city, of course insisted that I spend the night.   That is not unusual, since the castle gates are locked at ten and it is rather troublesome to have a guard unlock them.   I returned to the castle, then, at about ten in the morning, at which time my lady informed me of the disappearance of My Lord Marquis.''

Lord Darcy nodded.   That checked with what Lady Elaine had said.   Shortly after Sir Gwiliam had left, she had retired early, pleading a slight cold.   She had been the last to see the Marquis of Cherbourg.

"Thank you, sir seneschal,'' Lord Darcy said.   "I should like to speak to the servants later.   There is—''

He was interrupted by the opening of the door.   It was Lord Seiger, followed by a large, heavy-set, mustached man with dark hair and a scowling look.

As Sir Gwiliam rose, Lord Darcy said: "Thank you for your help, Sir Gwiliam. That will be all for now.''

"Thank you, your lordship; I am most anxious to help.''

As the seneschal left, Lord Seiger brought the mustached man into the room. "My lord, this is Sir Androu Duglasse, Captain of the Marquis' Own Guard. Captain, Lord Darcy, Chief Investigator for His Highness the Duke.''

The fierce-looking soldier bowed.   "I am at your service, m' lord.''

"Thank you.   Sit down, captain.''

Lord Seiger retreated through the door, leaving the captain with Lord Darcy and Master Sean.

"I hope I can be of some help, y' lordship,'' the captain said.

"I think you can, captain,'' Lord Darcy said.   "No one saw my lord the Marquis leave the castle, I understand.   I presume you have questioned your guards.''

"I have, y' lordship.   We didn't know m' lord was missing until next morning, when m' lady spoke to me.   I checked with the men who were on duty that night. The only one to leave after five was Sir Gwiliam, at five oh two, according to the book.''

"And the secret passage?'' Lord Darcy asked.   He had made it a point to study the plans of every castle in the Empire by going over the drawings in the Royal Archives.

The captain nodded.   "There is one.   Used during times of siege in the old days.   It's kept locked and barred nowadays.''

"And guarded?'' Lord Darcy asked.

Captain Sir Androu chuckled.   "Yes, y' lordship.   Most hated post in the Guard.   Tunnel ends up in a sewer, d'ye see.   We send a man out there for mild infractions of the rules.   Straightens him out to spend a few nights with the smell and the rats, guarding an iron door that hasn't been opened for years and couldn't be opened from the outside without a bomb—or from the inside, either, since it's rusted shut.   We inspect at irregular intervals to make sure the man's on his toes.''

"I see.   You made a thorough search of the castle?''

"Yes.   I was afraid he might have come down with another of those fainting spells he's had lately.   We looked everywhere he could have been.   He was nowhere to be found, y' lordship.   Nowhere.   He must have got out somewhere.''

"Well, we shall have to—'' Lord Darcy was interrupted by a rap on the door.

Master Sean, dutifully playing his part, opened it. "Yes, your lordship?"

It was Lord Seiger at the door. "Would you tell Lord Darcy that Henri Vert, Chief Master-at-Arms of the City of Cherbourg, would like to speak to him?"

For a fraction of a second, Lord Darcy was both surprised and irritated. How had the Chief Master-at-Arms known he was here? Then he saw what the answer must be.

"Tell him to come in, Sean," said Lord Darcy.

Chief Henri was a heavy-set, tough-looking man in his early fifties who had the air and bearing of a stolid fighter. He bowed. "Lord Darcy. May I speak to your lordship alone?" He spoke Anglo-French with a punctilious precision that showed it was not his natural way of speaking. He had done his best to remove the accent of the local *patois,* but his effort to speak properly was noticeable. "Certainly, Chief Henri. Will you excuse us, captain? I will discuss this problem with you later."

"Of course, your lordship."

Lord Darcy and Master Sean were left alone with Chief Henri.

"I *am* sorry to have interrupted, your lordship," said the Chief, "but His Royal Highness gave strict instructions."

"I had assumed as much, Chief Henri. Be so good as to sit down. Now— what has happened?"

"Well, your lordship," he said, glancing at Master Sean, "His Highness in-structed me over the teleson to speak to no one but you." Then the Chief took a good look and did a double take. "By the Blue! Master Sean O Lochlainn! I didn't recognize you in that livery!"

The sorcerer grinned. "I make a very good valet, eh, Henri?"

"Indeed you do! Well, then, I may speak freely?"

"Certainly," said Lord Darcy. "Proceed."

"Well, then." The Chief leaned forward and spoke in a low voice. "When this thing came up, I thought of you first off. I must admit that it's beyond me. On the night of the eighth, two of my men were patrolling the waterfront district. At the corner of Rue King John II and Quai Sainte Marie, they saw a man fall. Except for a cloak, he was naked—and if your lordship remember, that was a very cold night. By the time they got to him, he was dead."

Lord Darcy narrowed his eyes. "How had he died?"

"Skull fracture, your lordship. Somebody'd smashed in the right side of his skull. It's a wonder he could walk at all."

"I see. Proceed."

"Well, he was brought to the morgue. My men both identified him as one Paul Sarto, a man who worked around the bistros for small wages. He was also identified by the owner of the bistro where he had last worked. He seems to have been feeble-minded, willing to do manual labor for bed, board, and spending money. Needed taking care of a bit."

"Hm-m-m. We must trace him and find out why his baron had not provided for him," said Lord Darcy. "Proceed."

"Well, your lordship . . . er . . . there's more to it than that. I didn't look into the case immediately.   After all, another killing on the waterfront—''   He shrugged and spread his hands, palms up.   ''My sorcerer and my chirurgeon looked him over, made the usual tests.   He was killed by a blow from a piece of oak with a square corner—perhaps a two-by-two or something like that.   He was struck about ten minutes before the Armsmen found him.   My chirurgeon says that only a man of tremendous vitality could have survived that long—to say nothing of the fact that he was able to walk.''

''Excuse me, Henri,'' Master Sean interrupted.   ''Did your sorcerer make the FitzGibbon test for post-mortem activation?''

''Of course.   First test he made, considering the wound.   No, the body had not been activated after death and made to walk away from the scene of the crime. He actually died as the Armsmen watched.''

''Just checking,'' said Master Sean.

''Well, anyway, the affair might have been dismissed as another waterfront brawl, but there were some odd things about the corpse.   The cloak he was wearing was of aristocratic cut—not that of a commoner.   Expensive cloth, expensive tailoring. Also, he had bathed recently—and, apparently, frequently.   His toe- and fingernails were decently manicured and cut.''

Lord Darcy's eyes narrowed with interest.   ''Hardly the condition one would expect of a common laborer, eh?''

''Exactly, my lord.   So when I read the reports this morning, I went to take a look.   This time of year, the weather permits keeping a body without putting a preservation spell on it.''

He leaned forward, and his voice became lower and hoarser.   ''I only had to take one look, my lord.   Then I had to take action and call Rouen.   My lord, it is the Marquis of Cherbourg himself!''

Lord Darcy rode through the chilling wintry night on a borrowed horse, his dark cloak whipping around the palfrey's rump in the icy breeze.   The chill was more apparent than real.   A relatively warm wind had come in from the sea, bringing with it a slushy rain; the temperature of the air was above the freezing point—but not much above it.   Lord Darcy had endured worse cold than this, but the damp chill seemed to creep inside his clothing, through his skin, and into his bones.   He would have preferred a dry cold, even if it was much colder; at least, a dry cold didn't try to crawl into a man's cloak with him.

He had borrowed the horse from Chief Henri.   It was a serviceable hack, well-trained to police work and used to the cobbled streets of Cherbourg.

The scene at the morgue, Lord Darcy thought, had been an odd one.   He and Sean and Henri had stood by while the morgue attendant had rolled out the corpse. At first glance, Lord Darcy had been able to understand the consternation of the Chief Master-at-Arms.

He had only met Hugh of Cherbourg once and could hardly be called upon to make a positive identification, but if the corpse was not the Marquis to the life, the face was his in death.

The two Armsmen who had seen the man die had been asked separately, and without being told of the new identification, still said that the body was that of Paul Sarto, although they admitted he looked cleaner and better cared for than Paul ever had.

It was easy to see how the conflict of opinion came about. The Armsmen had seen the Marquis only rarely—probably only on state occasions, when he had been magnificently dressed. They could hardly be expected to identify a wandering, nearly nude man on the waterfront as their liege lord. If, in addition, that man was immediately identified in their minds with the man they had known as Paul Sarto, the identification of him as my lord the Marquis would be positively forced from their minds. On the other hand, Henri Vert, Chief Master-at-Arms of the City of Cherbourg, knew My Lord Marquis well and had never seen nor heard of Paul Sarto until after the death.

Master Sean had decided that further thaumaturgical tests could be performed upon the deceased. The local sorcerer—a mere journeyman of the Sorcerer's Guild—had explained all the tests he had performed, valiantly trying to impress a Master of the Art with his proficiency and ability.

"The weapon used was a fairly long piece of oak, Master. According to the Kaplan-Sheinwold test, a short club could not have been used. On the other hand, oddly enough, I could find no trace of evil or malicious intent, and—"

"Precisely why I intend to perform further tests, me boy," Master Sean had said. "We haven't enough information."

"Yes, Master," the journeyman sorcerer had said, properly humbled.

Lord Darcy made the observation— which he kept to himself—that if the blow had been dealt from the front, which it appeared to have been, then the killer was either left-handed or had a vicious right-hand backswing. Which, he had to admit to himself, told him very little. The cold chill of the unheated morgue had begun to depress him unduly in the presence of the dead, so he had left that part of the investigation to Master Sean and set out on his own, borrowing a palfrey from Chief Henri for the purpose.

The winters he had spent in London had convinced him thoroughly that no man of intelligence would stay anywhere near a cold seacoast. Inland cold was fine; seacoast warmth was all right. But this—!

Although he did not know Cherbourg well, Lord Darcy had the kind of mind that could carry a map in its memory and translate that map easily into the real world that surrounded him. Even a slight inaccuracy of the map didn't bother him.

He turned his mount round a corner and saw before him a gas lamp shielded with blue glass—the sign of an outstation of the Armsmen of Cherbourg. An Armsman stood at attention outside.

As soon as he saw that he was confronted by a mounted nobleman, the Man-at-Arms came to attention. "Yes, my lord! Can I aid you, my lord?"

"Yes, Armsman, you can," Lord Darcy said as he vaulted from the saddle. He handed the reins of the horse to the Armsman. "This mount belongs to Chief Henri at headquarters." He showed his card with the ducal arms upon it. "I am Lord Darcy, Chief Investigator for His Royal Highness the Duke. Take care of the horse. I have business in this neighborhood and will return for the animal. I should like to speak to your Sergeant-at-Arms.''

"Very good, my lord. The sergeant is within, my lord.''

After speaking to the sergeant, Lord Darcy went out again into the chill night.

It was still several blocks to his destination, but it would have been unwise to ride a horse all the way. He walked two blocks through the dingy streets of the neighborhood. Then, glancing about to make fairly certain he had not been followed or observed, he turned into a dark alley. Once inside, he took off his cloak and reversed it. The lining, instead of being the silk that a nobleman ordinarily wore, or the fur that would be worn in really cold weather, was drab, worn, brown, carefully patched in one place. From a pocket, he drew a battered slouch hat of the kind normally worn by commoners in this area and adjusted it to his head after carefully mussing his hair. His boots were plain and already covered with mud. Excellent!

He relaxed his spine—normally his carriage was one of military erectness—and slowly strolled out of the other end of the alley.

He paused to light a cheap cigar and then moved on toward his destination.

"Aaiiy?" The blowsy-looking woman in her mid-fifties looked through the opening in the heavy door. "What might you be wanting at this hour?''

Lord Darcy gave the face his friendliest smile and answered in the *patois* she had used. "Excuse me, Lady-of-the-House, but I'm looking for my brother, Vincent Coudé. Hate to call on him so late, but—''

As he had expected, he was interrupted.

"We don't allow no one in after dark unless they's identified by one of our people.''

"As you shouldn't, Lady-of-the-House,'' Lord Darcy agreed politely. "But I'm sure my brother Vincent will identify me. Just tell him his brother Richard is here. Ey?''

She shook her head. "He ain't here. Ain't been here since last Wednesday. My girl checks the rooms every day, and he ain't been here since last Wednesday.''

Wednesday! thought Lord Darcy. *Wednesday the eighth! The night the Marquis disappeared! The night the body was found only a few blocks from here!*

Lord Darcy took a silver coin from his belt pouch and held it out between the fingers of his right hand. "Would you mind going up and taking a look? He might've come in during the day. Might be asleep up there.''

She took the coin and smiled. "Glad to; glad to. You might be right; he might've come in. Be right back.''

But she left the door locked and closed the panel.

Lord Darcy didn't care about that. He listened carefully to her footsteps. Up the stairs. Down the hall. A knock. Another knock.

Quickly, Lord Darcy ran to the right side of the house and looked up. Sure enough, he saw the flicker of a lantern in one window. The Lady-of-the-House had unlocked the door and looked in to make sure that her roomer was not in. He ran back to the door and was waiting for her when she came down.

She opened the door panel and said sadly: "He still ain't here, Richard.''

Lord Darcy handed her another sixth-sovereign piece. "That's all right, Lady-of-the-House.   Just tell him I was here.   I suppose he's out on business."   He paused.   "When is his rent next due?"

She looked at him through suddenly narrowed eyes, wondering whether it would be possible to cheat her roomer's brother out of an extra week's rent.   She saw his cold eyes and decided it wouldn't.

"He's paid up to the twenty-fourth," she admitted reluctantly.   "But if he ain't back by then, I'll be turning his stuff out and getting another roomer."

"Naturally," Lord Darcy agreed.   "But he'll be back.   Tell him I was here. Nothing urgent.   I'll be back in a day or so."

She smiled.   "All right.   Come in the daytime, if y' can, Friend Richard. Thank y' much."

"Thank y' yourself, Lady-of-the-House," said Lord Darcy.   "A good and safe night to y'."   He turned and walked away.

He walked half a block and then dodged into a dark doorway.

So!   Sir James LeLein, agent of His Majesty's Secret Service, had not been seen since the night of the eighth.   That evening was beginning to take on a more and more sinister complexion.

He knew full well that he could have bribed the woman to let him into Sir James' room, but the amount he would have had to offer would have aroused suspicion. There was a better way.

It took him better than twenty minutes to find that way, but eventually he found himself on the roof of the two-story rooming house where Sir James had lived under the alias of Vincent Coudé.

The house was an old one, but the construction had been strong.   Lord Darcy eased himself down the slope of the shingled roof to the rain gutters at the edge. He had to lie flat, his feet uphill toward the point of the roof, his hands braced against the rain gutter to look down over the edge toward the wall below.   The room in which he had seen the glimmer of light from the woman's lantern was just below him.   The window was blank and dark, but the shutters were not drawn, which was a mercy.

The question was: Was the window locked?   Holding tight to the rain gutter, he eased himself down to the very edge of the roof.   His body was at a thirty-degree angle, and he could feel the increased pressure of blood in his head.   Cautiously, he reached down to see if he could touch the window.   He could!

Just barely, but he could!

Gently, carefully, working with the tips of the fingers of one hand, he teased the window open.   As was usual with these old houses, the glass panes were in two hinged panels that swung inward.   He got both of them open.

So far, the rain gutter had held him.   It seemed strong enough to hold plenty of weight.   He slowly moved himself around until his body was parallel with the edge of the roof.   Then he took a good grasp of the edge of the rain gutter and swung himself out into empty air.   As he swung round, he shot his feet out toward the lower sill of the window.

Then he let go and tumbled into the room.

He crouched motionlessly for a moment.   Had he been heard?   The sound had seemed tremendous when his feet had struck the floor.   But it was still early, and there were others moving about in the rooming house.   Still, he remained unmoving for a good two minutes to make sure there would be no alarm.   He was quite certain that if the Lady-of-the-House had heard anything that disturbed her, she would have rushed up the stairs.   No sound.   Nothing.

Then he rose to his feet and took a special device from the pocket of his cloak.

It was a fantastic device, a secret of His Majesty's Government.   Powered by the little zinc-copper couples that were the only known source of such magical power, they heated a steel wire to tremendously high temperature.   The thin wire glowed white-hot, shedding a yellow-white light that was almost as bright as a gas-mantle lamp.   The secret lay in the magical treatment of the steel filament.   Under ordinary circumstances, the wire would burn up in a blue-white flash of fire.   But, properly treated by a special spell, the wire was passivated and merely glowed with heat and light instead of burning.   The hot wire was centered at the focus of a parabolic reflector, and merely by shoving forward a button with his thumb, Lord Darcy had at hand a light source equal to—and indeed far superior to—an ordinary dark lantern.   It was a personal instrument, since the passivation was tuned to Lord Darcy and no one else.

He thumbed the button and a beam of light sprang into existence.

The search of Sir James LeLein's room was quick and thorough.   There was absolutely nothing of any interest to Lord Darcy anywhere in the room.

Naturally Sir James would have taken pains to assure that there would not be. The mere fact that the housekeeper had a key would have made Sir James wary of leaving anything about that would have looked out of place.   There was nothing here that would have identified the inhabitant of the room as anyone but a common laborer.

Lord Darcy switched off his lamp and brooded for a moment in the darkness. Sir James was on a secret and dangerous mission for His Imperial Majesty, John IV.   Surely there were reports, papers, and so on.   Where had Sir James kept the data he collected?   In his head?   That was possible, but Lord Darcy didn't think it was true.

Sir James had been working with Lord Cherbourg.   Both of them had vanished on the night of the eighth.   That the mutual vanishing was coincidental was possible— but highly improbable.   There were too many things unexplained as yet.   Lord Darcy had three tentative hypotheses, all of which explained the facts as he knew them thus far, and none of which satisfied him.

It was then that his eyes fell on the flowerpot silhouetted against the dim light that filtered in from outside the darkened room.   If it had been in the middle of the window sill, he undoubtedly would have smashed it when he came in; his feet had just barely cleared the sill.   But it was over to one side, in a corner of the window.   He walked over and looked at it carefully in the dimness.   Why, he asked himself, would an agent of the King be growing an African violet?

He picked up the little flowerpot, brought it away from the window, and shone his light on it.   It looked utterly usual.

With a grim smile, Lord Darcy put the pot, flower and all, into one of the capacious pockets of his cloak. Then he opened the window, eased himself over the sill, lowered himself until he was hanging only by his fingertips, and dropped the remaining ten feet to the ground, taking up the jar of landing with his knees.

Five minutes later, he had recovered his horse from the Armsman and was on his way to Castle Cherbourg.

The monastery of the Order of Saint Benedict in Cherbourg was a gloomy-looking pile of masonry occupying one corner of the great courtyard that surrounded the castle. Lord Darcy and Master Sean rang the bell at the entrance gate early on the morning of Tuesday, January 14th. They identified themselves to the doorkeeper and were invited into the Guests' Common Room to wait while Father Patrique was summoned. The monk would have to get the permission of the Lord Abbot to speak to outsiders, but that was a mere formality.

It was a relief to find that the interior of the monastery did not share the feeling of gloom with its exterior. The Common Room was quite cheerful and the winter sun shone brightly through the high windows.

After a minute or so, the inner door opened and a tall, rather pale man in Benedictine habit entered the room. He smiled pleasantly as he strode briskly across the room to take Lord Darcy's hand. "Lord Darcy, I am Father Patrique. Your servant, my lord."

"And I yours, your reverence. This is my man, Sean."

The priest turned to accept the introduction, then he paused and a gleam of humor came into his eyes. "Master Sean, the clothing you wear is not your own. A sorcerer cannot hide his calling by donning a valet's outfit."

Master Sean smiled back. "I hadn't hoped to conceal myself from a perceptive of your Order, Reverend Sir."

Lord Darcy, too, smiled. He had rather hoped that Father Patrique would be a perceptive. The Benedictines were quite good in bringing out that particular phase of Talent if a member of their Order had it, and they prided themselves on the fact that Holy Father Benedict, their Founder in the early part of the Sixth Century, had showed that ability to a remarkable degree long before the Laws of Magic had been formulated or investigated scientifically. To such a perceptive, identity cannot be concealed without a radical change in the personality itself. Such a man is capable of perceiving, *in toto,* the personality of another; such men are invaluable as Healers, especially in cases of demonic possession and other mental diseases.

"And now, how may I help you, my lord?" the Benedictine asked pleasantly.

Lord Darcy produced his credentials and identified himself as Duke Richard's Chief Investigator.

"Quite so," said the priest. "Concerning the fact that my lord the Marquis is missing, I have no doubt."

"The walls of a monastery are not totally impenetrable, are they, Father?" Lord Darcy asked with a wry smile.

Father Patrique chuckled. "We are wide open to the sight of God and the rumors of man. Please be seated; we will not be disturbed here."

"Thank you, Father," Lord Darcy said, taking a chair. "I understand you were called to attend my lord of Cherbourg several times since last Christmas. My lady of Cherbourg and my lord the Bishop of Guernsey and Sark have told me of the nature of these attacks—that, incidentally, is why this whole affair is being kept as quiet as possible—but I would like your opinion as a Healer.''

The priest shrugged his shoulders and spread his hands a little. ''I should be glad to tell you what I can, my lord, but I am afraid I know almost nothing. The attacks lasted only a few minutes each time and they had vanished by the time I was able to see My Lord Marquis. By then, he was normal—if a little puzzled. He told me he had no memory of such behavior as my lady reported. He simply blanked out and then came out of it, feeling slightly disoriented and a little dizzy.''

''Have you formed no diagnosis, Father?'' Lord Darcy asked.

The Benedictine frowned. ''There are several possible diagnoses, my lord. From my own observation, and from the symptoms reported by My Lord Marquis, I would have put it down as a mild form of epilepsy—what we call the *petit mal* type, the 'little sickness'. Contrary to popular opinion, epilepsy is not caused by demonic possession, but by some kind of organic malfunction that we know very little about.

''In *grand mal*, or 'great sickness' epilepsy, we find the seizures one normally thinks of as being connected with the disease—the convulsive 'fits' that cause the victim to completely lose control of his muscles and collapse with jerking limbs and so on. But the 'little sickness' merely causes brief loss of consciousness—sometimes so short that the victim does not even realize it. There is no collapse or convulsion; merely a blank daze lasting a few seconds or minutes.''

''But you are not certain of that?'' Lord Darcy asked.

The priest frowned. ''No. If my lady the Marquise is telling the truth—and I see no reason why she should not—his behavior during the . . . well, call them seizures . . . his behavior during the seizures was atypical. During a typical seizure of the *petit mal* type, the victim is totally blank—staring at nothing, unable to speak or move, unable to be roused. But my lord was not that way, according to my lady. He seemed confused, bewildered, and very stupid, but he was *not* unconscious.'' He paused and frowned.

''Therefore you have other diagnoses, Father?'' Lord Darcy prompted.

Father Patrique nodded thoughtfully. ''Yes. Always assuming that my lady the Marquise has reported accurately, there are other possible diagnoses. But none of them quite fits, any more than the first one does.''

''Such as?''

''Such as attack by psychic induction.''

Master Sean nodded slowly, but there was a frown in his eyes.

''The wax-and-doll sort of thing,'' said Lord Darcy.

Father Patrique nodded an affirmative. ''Exactly, my lord—although, as you undoubtedly know, there are far better methods than that—in practice.''

''Of course,'' Lord Darcy said brusquely. In theory, he knew, the simulacrum method *was* the best method. Nothing could be more powerful than an exact duplicate, according to the Laws of Similarity. The size of the simulacrum made little difference, but the accuracy of detail did—including internal organs.

But the construction of a wax simulacrum—aside from the artistry required—entailed complications which bordered on the shadowy area of the unknown.   Beeswax was more effective than mineral wax for the purpose because it was an animal product instead of a mineral one, thus increasing the similarity.   But why did the addition of sal ammoniac increase the potency?   Magicians simply said that sal ammoniac, saltpeter, and a few other minerals increased the similarity in some unknown way and let it go at that; sorcerers had better things to do than grub around in mineralogy.

"The trouble is," said Father Patrique, "that the psychic induction method nearly always involves physical pain or physical illness—intestinal disorders, heart trouble, or other glandular disturbances.   There are no traces of such things here unless one considers the malfunction of the brain as a glandular disorder—and even so, it should be accompanied by pain."

"Then you discount that diagnosis, too?" asked Lord Darcy.

Father Patrique shook his head firmly.   "I discount none of the diagnoses I have made thus far.   My data are far from complete."

"You have other theories, then."

"I do, my lord.   Actual demonic possession."

Lord Darcy narrowed his eyes and looked straight into the eyes of the priest. "You don't really believe that, Reverend Sir."

"No," Father Patrique admitted candidly, "I do not.   As a perceptive, I have a certain amount of faith in my own ability.   If more than one personality were inhabiting my lord's body, I am certain I would have perceived the . . . er . . . other personality."

Lord Darcy did not move his eyes from those of the Benedictine.   "I had assumed as much, your reverence," he said.   "If it were a case of multiple personality, you would have detected it, eh?"

"I am certain I would have, my lord," Father Patrique stated positively.   "If my lord of Cherbourg had been inhabited by another personality, I would have detected it, even if that other personality had been under cover."   He paused, then waved a hand slightly.   "You understand, Lord Darcy?   Alternate personalities in a single human body, a single human brain, can hide themselves.   The personality dominant at any given time conceals to the casual observer the fact that other—different—personalities are present.   But the . . . the *alter egos* cannot conceal themselves from a true perceptive."

"I understand," Lord Darcy said.

"There was only one personality in the . . . the *person*, the *brain*, of the Marquis of Cherbourg at the time I examined him.   And that personality was the personality of the Marquis himself."

"I see," Lord Darcy said thoughtfully.   He did not doubt the priest's statement. He knew the reputation Father Patrique had among Healers.   "How about drugs, Father?" he asked after a moment.   "I understand that there are drugs which can alter a man's personality."

The Benedictine Healer smiled.   "Certainly.   Alcohol—the essence of wines and beers—will do it.   There are others.   Some have a temporary effect; others have no effect in single dosages—or, at least, no detectable effect—but have an accumulative effect if the drug is taken regularly.   Oil of wormwood, for instance, is found in several of the more expensive liqueurs—in small quantity, of course. If you get drunk on such a liqueur, the effect is temporary and hardly distinguishable from that of alcohol alone.   But if taken steadily, over a period of time, a definite personality change occurs.''

Lord Darcy nodded thoughtfully, then looked at his sorcerer.   "Master Sean, the phial, if you please.''

The tubby little Irish sorcerer fished in a pocket with thumb and forefinger and brought forth a small stoppered glass phial a little over an inch long and half an inch in diameter.   He handed it to the priest, who looked at it with curiosity.   It was nearly filled with a dark amber fluid.   In the fluid were little pieces of dark matter, rather like coarse-cut tobacco, which had settled to the bottom of the phial and filled perhaps a third of it.

"What is it?'' Father Patrique asked.

Master Sean frowned.   "That's what I'm not rightly sure of, Reverend Sir.   I checked it to make certain there were no spells on it before I opened it.   There weren't.   So I unstoppered it and took a little whiff.   Smells like brandy, with just faint overtones of something else.   Naturally, I couldn't analyze it without having some notion of what it was.   Without a specimen standard, I couldn't use Similarity analysis.   Oh, I checked the brandy part, and that came out all right. The liquid is brandy.   But I can't identify the little crumbs of stuff.   His lordship had an idea that it might be a drug of some kind, and, since a Healer has all kinds of *materia medica* around, I thought perhaps we might be able to identify it.''

"Certainly," the priest agreed.   "I have a couple of ideas we might check right away.   The fact that the material is steeped in brandy indicates either that the material decays easily or that the essence desired is soluble in brandy.   That suggests several possibilities to my mind.''   He looked at Lord Darcy.   "May I ask where you got it, my lord?''

Lord Darcy smiled.   "I found it buried in a flowerpot.''

Father Patrique, realizing that he had been burdened with all the information he was going to get, accepted Lord Darcy's statement with a slight shrug.   "Very well, my lord; Master Sean and I will see if we can discover what this mysterious substance may be.''

"Thank you, Father.''   Lord Darcy rose from his seat.   "Oh—one more thing. What do you know about Lord Seiger?''

"Very little.   His lordship comes from Yorkshire . . . North Riding, if I'm not mistaken.   He's been working with my lord of Cherbourg for the past several months—something to do with books, I believe.   I know nothing of his family or anything like that, if that is what you mean.''

"Not exactly," said Lord Darcy.   "Are you his Confessor, Father?   Or have you treated him as a Healer?''

The Benedictine raised his eyebrows.   "No.   Neither.   Why?''

"Then I can ask you a question about his soul.   What kind of man is he?   What is the oddness I detect in him?   What is it about him that frightens my lady the Marquise in spite of his impeccable behavior?''   He noticed the hesitation in the priest's manner and went on before Father Patrique could answer.   ''This is not idle curiosity, your reverence.   I am investigating a homicide.''

The priest's eyes widened.   ''Not . . . ?''   He stopped himself.   ''I see.   Well, then.   Granted, as a perceptive, I know certain things about Lord Seiger.   He suffers from a grave illness of the soul.   How these things come about, we do not know, but occasionally a person utterly lacks that part of the soul we call 'conscience', at least insofar as it applies to certain acts.   We cannot think that God would fail to provide such a thing; therefore theologists ascribe the lack to an act of the Devil at some time in the early life of the child—probably prenatally and, therefore, before baptism can protect the child.   Lord Seiger is such a person.   A psychopathic personality.   Lord Seiger was born without an ability to distinguish between 'right' and 'wrong' as we know the terms.   Such a person performs a given act or refrains from performing it only according to the expediency of the moment.   Certain acts which you or I would look upon with abhorrence he may even look upon as pleasurable.   Lord Seiger is—basically—a homicidal psychopath.''

Lord Darcy said, ''I thought as much.''   Then he added dryly, ''He is, I presume, under restraint?''

''Oh, of course; of course!''   The priest looked aghast that anyone should suggest otherwise.   ''Naturally such a person cannot be condemned because of a congenital deficiency, but neither can he be allowed to become a danger to society.''   He looked at Master Sean.   ''You know something of Geas Theory, Master Sean?''

''Something,'' Master Sean agreed.   ''Not my field, of course, but I've studied a little of the theory.   The symbol manipulation's a little involved for me, I'm afraid.   Psychic Algebra's as far as I ever got.''

''Of course.   Well, Lord Darcy, to put it in layman's terms, a powerful spell is placed upon the affected person—a *geas*, it's called—which forces them to limit their activities to those which are not dangerous to his fellow man.   We cannot limit him too much, of course, for it would be sinful to deprive him entirely of his free will.   His sexual morals, for instance, are his own—but he cannot use force. The extent of the *geas* depends upon the condition of the individual and the treatment given by the Healer who performed the work.''

''It takes an extensive and powerful knowledge of sorcery, I take it?''   Lord Darcy asked.

''Oh, yes.   No Healer would even attempt it until he had taken his Th.D. and then specialized under an expert for a time.   And there are not many Doctors of Thaumaturgy.   Since Lord Seiger is a Yorkshireman, I would venture to guess that the work was done by His Grace the Archbishop of York—a most pious and powerful Healer.   I, myself, would not think of attempting such an operation.''

''You can, however, tell that such an operation has been performed?''

Father Patrique smiled.   ''As easily as a chirurgeon can tell if an abdominal operation has been performed.''

"Can a *geas* be removed?   or partially removed?"

"Of course—by one equally as skilled and powerful.   But I could detect that, too.   It has not been done in Lord Seiger's case."

"Can you tell what channels of freedom he has been allowed?"

"No," said the priest.   "That sort of thing depends upon the fine structure of the *geas*, which is difficult to observe without extensive analysis."

"Then," said Lord Darcy, "you cannot tell me whether or not there are circumstances in which his *geas* would permit him to kill?   Such as, for instance . . . er . . . self-defense?"

"No," the priest admitted.   "But I will say that it is rare indeed for even such a channel as self-defense to be left open for a psychopathic killer.   The *geas* in such a case would necessarily leave the decision as to what constituted 'self-defense' up to the patient.   A normal person knows when 'self-defense' requires killing one's enemy, rendering him unconscious, fleeing from him, giving him a sharp retort, or merely keeping quiet.   But to a psychopathic killer, a simple insult may be construed as an attack which requires 'self-defense'—which would give him permission to kill.   No Healer would leave such a decision in the hands of the patient." His face grew somber.   "Certainly no sane man would leave that decision to the mind of a man like Lord Seiger."

"Then you consider him safe, Father?"

The Benedictine hesitated only a moment.   "Yes.   Yes, I do.   I do not believe him capable of committing an antisocial act such as that.   The Healer took pains to make sure that Lord Seiger would be protected from most of his fellow men, too.   He is almost incapable of committing any offense against propriety; his behavior is impeccable at all times; he cannot insult anyone; he is almost incapable of defending himself physically except under the greatest provocation.

"I once watched him in a fencing bout with my lord the Marquis.   Lord Seiger is an expert swordsman—much better than my lord the Marquis.   The Marquis was utterly unable to score a touch upon Lord Seiger's person; Lord Seiger's defense was far too good.   *But*—neither could Lord Seiger score a touch upon my lord. He couldn't even try.   His brilliant swordsmanship is purely and completely defensive."   He paused.   "You are a swordsman yourself, my lord?"   It was only half a question; the priest was fairly certain that a Duke's Investigator would be able to handle any and all weapons with confidence.

He was perfectly correct.   Lord Darcy nodded without answering.   To be able to wield a totally defensive sword required not only excellent—superlative—swordsmanship, but the kind of iron self-control that few men possessed.   In Lord Seiger's case, of course, it could hardly be called *self*-control.   The control had been imposed by another.

"Then you can understand," the priest continued, "why I say that I believe he can be trusted.   If his Healer found it necessary to impose so many restrictions and protections, he would most certainly not have left any channel open for Lord Seiger to make any decision for himself as to when it would be proper to kill another."

"I understand, Father.   Thank you for your information.   I assure you it will remain confidential."

"Thank you, my lord.   If there is nothing else . . . ?"

"Nothing for the moment, Reverend Father.   Thank you again."

"A pleasure, Lord Darcy.   And now, Master Sean, shall we go to my laboratory?"

An hour later, Lord Darcy was sitting in the guest room which Sir Gwiliam had shown him to the day before.   He was puffing at his Bavarian pipe, filled with a blend of tobacco grown in the Southern Duchies of New England, his mind working at high speed, when Master Sean entered.

"My lord," said the tubby little sorcerer with a smile, "the good Father and I have identified the substance."

"Good!"   Lord Darcy gestured toward a chair.   "What was it?"

Master Sean sat down.   "We were lucky, my lord.   His Reverence *did* have a sample of the drug.   As soon as we were able to establish a similarity between our sample and his, we identified it as a mushroom known as the Devil's Throne. The fungus is dried, minced, and steeped in brandy or other spirit.   The liquid is then decanted off and the minced bits are thrown away—or, sometimes, steeped a second time.   In large doses, the drugged spirit results in insanity, convulsions, and rapid death.   In small doses, the preliminary stages are simply mild euphoria and light intoxication.   But if taken regularly, the effect is cumulative—first, a manic, hallucinatory state, then delusions of persecution and violence."

Lord Darcy's eyes narrowed.   "That fits.   Thank you.   Now there is one more problem.   I want positive identification of that corpse.   My Lord Bishop is not certain that it is his brother; that may just be wishful thinking.   My Lady Marquise refuses to view the body, saying that it could not possibly be her husband—and that is *definitely* wishful thinking.   But *I* must know for certain.   Can you make a test?"

"I can take blood from the heart of the dead man and compare it with blood from My Lord Bishop's veins, my lord."

"Ah, yes.   The Jacoby transfer method," said Lord Darcy.

"Not quite, my lord.   The Jacoby transfer requires at least two hearts.   It is dangerous to take blood from a living heart.   But the test I have in mind is equally as valid."

" I thought blood tests were unreliable between siblings."

"Well, now, as to that, my lord," Master Sean said, "in theory there is a certain very low probability that brother and sister, children of the same parents, would show completely negative results.   In other words, they would have zero similarity in that test.

"Blood similarity runs in a series of steps from zero to forty-six.   In a parent-child relationship, the similarity is always exactly twenty-three—in other words, the child is always related half to one parent and half to the other.

"With siblings, though, we find variations.   Identical twins, for instance, register a full forty-six point similarity.   Most siblings run much less, averaging twenty-three.   There *is* a possibility of two brothers or two sisters having only one-point similarity, and, as I said, my lord, of a brother and sister having zero similarity. But the odds are on the order of one point seven nine million million to one against it.   Considering the facial similarity of My Lord Bishop and My Lord Marquis, I would be willing to stake my reputation that the similarity would be sustantially greater than zero—perhaps greater than twenty-three.''

"Very well, Master Sean.   You have not failed me yet; I do not anticipate that you ever will.   Get me that data.''

"Yes, my lord.   I shall endeavor to give satisfaction.''   Master Sean left suffused with a glow of mixed determination and pride.

Lord Darcy finished his pipe and headed for the offices of Captain Sir Androu Duglasse.

The captain looked faintly indignant at Lord Darcy's question.   "I searched the castle quite thoroughly, y' lordship.   We looked everywhere that M' Lord Marquis could possibly have gone.''

"Come, captain,'' Lord Darcy said mildly, "I don't mean to impugn your ability, but I dare say there are places you didn't search simply because there was no reason to think my lord of Cherbourg would have gone there.''

Captain Sir Androu frowned.   "Such as, my lord?''

"Such as the secret tunnel.''

The captain looked suddenly blank.   "Oh,'' he said after a moment.   Then his expression changed.   "But surely, y' lordship, you don't think . . .''

"I don't *know*, that's the point.   My lord *did* have keys to every lock in the castle, didn't he?''

"All except to the monastery, yes.   My Lord Abbot has those.''

"Naturally.   I think we can dismiss the monastery.   Where else did you not look?''

"Well . . .''   The captain hesitated thoughtfully.   "I didn't bother with the strongroom, the wine cellar, or the icehouse.   I don't have the keys.   Sir Gwiliam would have told me if anything was amiss.''

"Sir Gwiliam has the keys, you say?   Then we must find Sir Gwiliam.''

Sir Gwiliam, as it turned out, was in the wine cellar.   Lord Seiger informed them that, at Lady Elaine's request, he had sent the seneschal down for another bottle of brandy.   Lord Darcy followed Captain Sir Androu down the winding stone steps to the cellars.

"Most of this is used as storage space,'' the captain said, waving a hand to indicate the vast, dim rooms around them.   "All searched very carefully.   The wine cellar's this way, y' lordship.''

The wine-cellar door, of heavy, reinforced oak, stood slightly ajar.   Sir Gwiliam, who had evidently heard their footsteps, opened it a little more and put his head out.   "Who is it?   Oh.   Good afternoon, my lord.   Good afternoon, captain. May I be of service?''

He stepped back, opening the door to let them in.

"I thank you, Sir Gwiliam," said Lord Darcy. "We come partly on business and partly on pleasure. I have noticed that my lord the Marquis keeps an excellent cellar; the wines are of the finest and the brandy is extraordinary. Saint Coeurlandt Michele '46 is difficult to come by these days."

Sir Gwiliam looked rather sad. "Yes, your lordship, it is. I fear the last two cases in existence are right here. I now have the painful duty of opening one of them." He sighed and gestured toward the table, where stood a wooden case that had been partially pried open. A glance told Lord Darcy that there was nothing in the bottles but brandy and that the leaden seals were intact.

"Don't let us disturb you, Sir Gwiliam," Lord Darcy said. "May we look around?"

"Certainly, your lordship. A pleasure." He went back to work on opening the brandy case with a pry bar.

Lord Darcy ran a practiced eye over the racks, noting labels and seals. He had not really expected that anyone would attempt to put drugs or poison into bottles; My Lady Elaine was not the only one who drank, and wholesale poisoning would be too unselective.

The wine cellar was not large, but it was well stocked with excellent vintages. There were a couple of empty shelves in one corner, but the rest of the shelves were filled with bottles of all shapes and sizes. Over them lay patinas of dust of various thicknesses. Sir Gwiliam was careful not to bruise his wines.

"His lordship's choices, or yours, Sir Gwiliam?" Lord Darcy asked, indicating the rows of bottles.

"I am proud to say that My Lord Marquis has always entrusted the selection of wines and spirits to me, your lordship."

"I compliment both of you," Lord Darcy said. "You for your excellent taste, and his lordship for recognizing that ability in you." He paused. "However, there is more pressing business."

"How may I help you, my lord?" Having finished opening the case, he dusted off his hands and looked with a mixture of pride and sadness at the Saint Coeurlandt Michele '46. Distilled in 1846 and aged in the wood for thirty years before it was bottled, it was considered possibly the finest brandy ever made.

Quietly, Lord Darcy explained that there had been several places where Captain Sir Androu had been unable to search. "There is the possibility, you see, that he might have had a heart attack—or some sort of attack—and collapsed to the floor."

Sir Gwiliam's eyes opened wide. "And he might be there yet? God in Heaven! Come, your lordship! This way! I have been in the icehouse, and so has the chef, but no one has opened the strongroom!"

He took the lead, running, with Lord Darcy right behind him and Sir Androu in the rear. It was not far, but the cellar corridors twisted oddly and branched frequently.

The strongroom was more modern than the wine cellar; the door was of heavy steel, swung on gimbaled hinges. The walls were of stone and concrete, many feet thick.

"It's a good thing the captain is here, your lordship," the seneschal said breathlessly as the three men stopped in front of the great vault door. "It takes two keys to open it. I have one, the captain has the other. My Lord Marquis, of course, has both. Captain?"

"Yes, yes, Gwiliam; I have mine here."

There were four keyholes on each side of the wide door. Lord Darcy recognized the type of construction. Only one of the four keyholes on each side worked. A key put into the wrong hole would ring alarms. The captain would know which hole to put his own key in, and so would Sir Gwiliam—but neither knew the other's proper keyhole. The shields around the locks prevented either man from seeing which keyhole the other used. Lord Darcy could not tell, even though he watched. The shields coverd the hands too well.

"Ready, captain?" Sir Gwiliam asked.

"Ready."

"Turn."

Both men turned their keys at once. The six-foot wide door clicked inside itself and swung open when Sir Gwiliam turned a handle on his side of the door.

There was a great deal worthy of notice inside—gold and silver utensils; the jeweled coronets of the Marquis and Marquise; the great Robes of State, embroidered with gold and glittering with gems—in short, all the paraphernalia for great occasions of state. In theory, all this belonged to the Marquis; actually, it was no more his than the Imperial Crown Jewels belonged to King John IV. Like the castle, it was a part of the office; it could be neither pawned nor sold.

But nowhere in the vault was there any body, dead or alive, nor any sign that there had ever been one.

"Well!" said Sir Gwiliam with a sharp exhalation. "I'm certainly glad of that! You had me worried, your lordship." There was a touch of reproach in his voice.

"I am as happy to find nothing as you are. Now let's check the icehouse."

The icehouse was in another part of the cellars and was unlocked. One of the cooks was selecting a roast. Sir Gwiliam explained that he unlocked the icehouse each morning and left the care of it with the Chief of the Kitchen, locking it again each night. A careful search of the insulated, ice-chilled room assured Lord Darcy that there was no one there who shouldn't be.

"Now we'll take a look in the tunnel," Lord Darcy said. "Have you the key, Sir Gwiliam?"

"Why . . . why, yes. But it hasn't been opened for years! Decades! Never since I've been here, at any rate."

"I have a key, myself, y' lordship," said the captain. "I just never thought of looking. Why would he go there?"

"Why, indeed? But we must look, nevertheless."

A bell rang insistently in the distance, echoing through the cellars.

"Dear me!" said Sir Gwiliam. "My lady's brandy! I quite forgot about it! Sir Androu has a key to the tunnel, my lord; would you excuse me?"

"Certainly, Sir Gwiliam. Thank you for your help."

"A pleasure, my lord." He hurried off to answer the bell.

"Did you actually expect to find My Lord Marquis in any of those places, your lordship?" asked Sir Androu. "Even if my lord had gone into one of them, would he have locked the door behind him?"

"I did not expect to find him in the wine cellar or the icehouse," Lord Darcy said, "but the strongroom presented a strong possibility. I merely wanted to see if there were any indications that he had been there. I must confess that I found none."

"To the tunnel, then," said the captain.

The entrance was concealed behind a shabby, unused cabinet. But the cabinet swung away from the steel door behind it with oiled smoothness. And when the captain took out a dull, patinaed key and opened the door, the lock turned smoothly and effortlessly.

The captain looked at his key, now brightened by abrasion where it had forced the wards, as though it were imbued with magic. "Well, I'll be cursed!" he said softly.

The door swung silently open to reveal a tunnel six feet wide and eight high. Its depths receded into utter blackness.

"A moment, m' lord," said the captain. "I'll get a lamp." He walked back down the corridor and took an oil lamp from a wall bracket.

The two of them walked down the tunnel together. On either side, the niter-stained walls gleamed whitely. The captain pointed down at the floor. "Somebody's been using this lately," he said softly.

"I had already noticed the disturbed dust and crushed crystals of niter," Lord Darcy said. "I agree with you."

"Who's been using the tunnel, then, y' lordship?"

"I am confident that my lord the Marquis of Cherbourg was one of them. His . . . er . . . confederates were here, too."

"But why? And how? No one could have got out without my guard seeing them."

"I am afraid you are right, my good captain." He smiled. "But that doesn't mean that the guard would have reported to you if his liege lord told him not to . . . eh?"

Sir Androu stopped suddenly and looked at Lord Darcy. "Great God in Heaven! And I thought—!" He brought himself up short.

"You thought *what?* Quickly, man!"

"Y' lordship, a new man enlisted in the Guard two months ago. Came in on m' lord's recommendation. Then m' lord reported that he misbehaved and had me put him on the sewer detail at night. The man's been on that detail ever since."

"Of course!" Lord Darcy said with a smile of triumph. "He would put one of his own men on. Come, captain; I must speak to this man."

"I . . . I'm afraid that's impossible, y' lordship. He's down as a deserter. Disappeared from post last night. Hasn't been seen since."

Lord Darcy said nothing. He took the lantern from the captain and knelt down to peer closely at the footprints on the tunnel floor.

"I should have looked more closely," he muttered, as if to himself. "I've taken too much for granted.   Ha!   Two men—carrying something heavy.   And followed by a third.''   He stood up.   "This puts an entirely different complexion on the matter.   We must act at once.   Come!''   He turned and strode back toward the castle cellar.

"But—   What of the rest of the tunnel?"

"There is no need to search it," Lord Darcy said firmly.   "I can assure you that there is no one in it but ourselves.   Come along."

In the shadows of a dingy dockside warehouse a block from the pier where the Danzig-bound vessel, *Esprit de Mer,* was tied up, Lord Darcy stood, muffled in a long cloak.   Beside him, equally muffled in a black naval cloak, his blond hair covered by a pulled-up cowl, stood Lord Seiger, his quite handsome face expressionless in the dimness.

"There she is," Lord Darcy said softly.   "She's the only vessel bound for a North Sea port from Cherbourg.   The Rouen office confirms that she was sold last October to a Captain Olsen.   He claims to be a Northman, but I will be willing to wager against odds that he's Polish.   If not, then he is certainly in the pay of the King of Poland.   The ship is still sailing under Imperial registry and flying the Imperial flag.   She carries no armament, of course, but she's a fast little craft for a merchant vessel."

"And you think we will find the evidence we need aboard her?" Lord Seiger asked.

"I am almost certain of it.   It will be either here or at the warehouse, and the man would be a fool to leave the stuff here now—especially when it can be shipped out aboard the *Esprit de Mer.*"

It had taken time to convince Lord Seiger that it was necessary to make this raid.   But once Lord Darcy had convinced him of how much was already known and verified everything by a teleson call to Rouen, Lord Seiger was both willing and eager.   There was a suppressed excitement in the man that showed only slightly in the pale blue eyes, leaving the rest of his face as placid as ever.

Other orders had had to be given.   Captain Sir Androu Duglasse had sealed Castle Cherbourg; no one—*no one*—was to be allowed out for any reason whatever. The guard had been doubled during the emergency.   Not even My Lord Bishop, My Lord Abbot, or My Lady Marquise could leave the castle.   Those orders came, not from Lord Darcy, but from His Royal Highness the Duke of Normandy himself.

Lord Darcy looked at his wrist watch.   "It's time, my lord," he said to Lord Seiger.   "Let's move in."

"Very well, my lord," Lord Seiger agreed.

The two of them walked openly toward the pier.

At the gate that led to the pier itself, two burly-looking seamen stood lounging against the closed gate.   When they saw the two cloaked men approaching, they became more alert, stepping away from the gate, toward the oncoming figures. Their hands went to the hilts of the scabbarded cutlasses at their belts.

Lord Seiger and Lord Darcy walked along the pier until they were within fifteen feet of the advancing guards, then stopped.

"What business have ye here?" asked one of the seamen.

It was Lord Darcy who spoke.   His voice was low and cold.   "Don't address me in that manner if you want to keep your tongue," he said in excellent Polish. "I wish to speak to your captain."

The first seaman looked blank at being addressed in a language he did not understand, but the second blanched visibly.   "Let me handle this," he whispered in Anglo-French to the other.   Then, in Polish: "Your pardon, lord.   My messmate here don't understand Polish.   What was it you wanted, lord?"

Lord Darcy sighed in annoyance.   "I thought I made myself perfectly clear. We desire to see Captain Olsen."

"Well, now, lord, he's given orders that he don't want to see no one.   Strict orders, lord."

Neither of the two sailors noticed that, having moved away from the gate, they had left their rear unguarded.   From the skiff that had managed to slip in under the pier under cover of darkness, four of the Marquis' Own silently lifted themselves to the deck of the pier.   Neither Lord Darcy nor Lord Seiger looked at them.

"Strict orders?" Lord Darcy's voice was heavy with scorn.   "I dare say your orders do not apply to Crown Prince Sigismund himself, do they?"

On cue, Lord Seiger swept the hood back from his handsome blond head.

It was extremely unlikely that either of the two sailors had ever seen Sigismund, Crown Prince of Poland—nor, if they had, that they would have recognized him when he was not dressed for a state occasion.   But certainly they had heard that Prince Sigismund was blond and handsome, and that was all Lord Darcy needed. In actuality, Lord Seiger bore no other resemblance, being a good head taller than the Polish prince.

While they stood momentarily dumfounded by this shattering revelation, arms silently encircled them, and they ceased to wonder about Crown Princes of any kind for several hours.   They were rolled quietly into the shadows behind a pile of heavy bags of ballast.

"Everyone else all set?" Lord Darcy whispered to one of the Guardsmen.

"Yes, my lord."

"All right.   Hold this gate.   Lord Seiger, let's go on."

"I'm right with you, my lord," said Lord Seiger.

Some little distance away, at the rear door of a warehouse just off the waterfront, a heavily armed company of the Men-at-Arms of Cherbourg listened to the instructions of Chief Master-at-Arms Henri Vert.

"All right.   Take your places.   Seal every door.   Arrest and detain anyone who tries to leave.   Move out."   With a rather self-important feeling, he touched the Duke's Warrant, signed by Lord Darcy as Agent of His Highness, that lay folded in his jacket pocket.

The Men-at-Arms faded into the dimness, moving silently to their assigned posts.

With Chief Henri remained six Sergeants-at-Arms and Master Sean O Lochlainn, Sorcerer.

"All right, Sean," said Chief Henri, "go ahead."

"Give us a little light from your dark lantern, Henri," said Master Sean, kneeling to peer at the lock of the door. He set his black suitcase on the stone pavement and quietly set his corthainn-wood magician's staff against the wall beside the door. The Sergeants-at-Arms watched the tubby little sorcerer with respect.

"Ho*ho*," Master Sean said, peering at the lock. "A simple lock. But there's a heavy bar across it on the inside. Take a little work, but not much time." He opened his suitcase to take out two small phials of powder and a thin laurel-wood wand.

The Armsmen watched in silence as the sorcerer muttered his spells and blew tiny puffs of powder into the lock. Then Master Sean pointed his wand at the lock and twirled it counterclockwise slowly. There was a faint sliding noise and a *snick!* of metal as the lock unlocked itself.

Then he drew the wand across the door a foot above the lock. This time, something heavy slid quietly on the other side of the door.

With an almost inaudible sigh, the door swung open an inch or so.

Master Sean stepped aside and allowed the sergeants and their chief to enter the door. Meanwhile, he took a small device from his pocket and checked it again. It was a cylinder of glass two inches in diameter and half an inch high, half full of liquid. On the surface of the liquid floated a tiny sliver of oak that would have been difficult to see if the top of the glass box had not been a powerful magnifying lens. The whole thing looked a little like a pocket compass—which, in a sense, it was.

The tiny sliver of oak had been recovered from the scalp of the slain man in the morgue, and now, thanks to Master Sean's thaumaturgical art, the little sliver pointed unerringly toward the piece of wood whence it had come.

Master Sean nodded in satisfaction. As Lord Darcy had surmised, the weapon was still in the warehouse. He glanced up at the lights in the windows of the top floor of the warehouse. Not only the weapon, but some of the plotters were still here.

He smiled grimly and followed the Armsmen in, his corthainn-wood staff grasped firmly in one hand and his suitcase in the other.

Lord Darcy stood with Lord Seiger on one of the lower decks of the *Esprit de Mer* and looked around. "So far, so good," he said in a low voice. "Piracy has its advantages, my lord."

"Indeed it does, my lord," Lord Seiger replied in the same tone.

Down a nearby ladder, his feet clad in soft-soled boots, came Captain Sir Androu, commander of the Marquis' Own. "So far, so good, m' lords," he whispered, not realizing that he was repeating Lord Darcy's sentiments. "We have the crew. All sleeping like children."

"*All* the crew?" Lord Darcy asked.

"Well, m' lord, all we could find so far. Some of 'em are still on shore leave.

Not due back 'til dawn. Otherwise, I fancy this ship would have pulled out long before this. No way to get word to the men, though, eh?"

"I have been hoping so," Lord Darcy agreed. "But the fact remains that we really don't know how many are left aboard. How about the bridge?"

"The second officer was on duty, m' lord. We have him."

"Captain's cabin?"

"Empty, m' lord."

"First officer's?"

"Also empty, m' lord. Might be both ashore."

"Possibly." There was a distinct possibility, Lord Darcy knew, that both the captain and the first officer were still at the warehouse—in which case, they would be picked up by Chief Henri and his men. "Very well. Let's keep moving down. We still haven't found what we're looking for." *And there will be one Hell of an international incident if we don't find it,* Lord Darcy told himself. *His Slavic Majesty's Government will demand all sorts of indemnities, and Lady Darcy's little boy will find himself fighting the aborigines in the jungles of New France.*

But he wasn't really terribly worried; his intuition backed up his logic in telling him that he was right.

Nevertheless, he mentally breathed a deep sigh of relief when he and Lord Seiger found what they were looking for some five or six minutes later.

There were four iron-barred cells on the deck just above the lowest cargo hold. They faced each other, two and two, across a narrow passageway. Two bosuns blocked the passageway.

Lord Darcy looked down the tweendecks hatch and saw them. He had gone down the ladders silently, peeking carefully below before attempting to descend, and his caution had paid off. Neither of the bosuns saw him. They were leaning casually against the opposite bulkheads of the passageway, talking in very low voices.

There was no way to come upon them by stealth, but neither had a weapon in hand, and there was nothing to retreat behind for either of them.

Should he, Lord Darcy wondered, wait for reinforcements? Sir Androu already had his hands full for the moment, and Lord Seiger would not, of course, be of any use. The man was utterly incapable of physical violence.

He lifted himself from the prone position from which he had been peeking over the hatch edge to look below, and whispered to Lord Seiger. "They have cutlasses. Can you hold your own against one of them if trouble comes?"

For answer, Lord Seiger smoothly and silently drew his rapier. "Against both of them if necessary, my lord," he whispered back.

"I don't think it will be necessary, but there's no need taking chances at this stage of the game." He paused. Then he drew a five-shot .42 caliber handgun from his belt holster. "I'll cover them with this."

Lord Seiger nodded and said nothing.

"Stay here," he whispered to Lord Seiger. "Don't come down the stairs . . . sorry, the *ladder* . . . until I call."

"Very well, my lord."

Lord Darcy walked silently up the ladder that led to the deck above. Then he came down again, letting his footfalls be heard.

He even whistled softly but audibly as he did so—an old Polish air he happened to know.

Then, without breaking his stride, he went on down the second ladder. He held his handgun in his right hand, concealed beneath his cloak.

His tactics paid off beautifully. The bosuns heard him coming and assumed that he must be someone who was authorized to be aboard the ship. They stopped their conversation and assumed an attitude of attention. They put their hands on the hilts of their cutlasses, but only as a matter of form. They saw the boots, then the legs, then the lower torso of the man coming down the ladder. And still they suspected nothing. An enemy would have tried to take them by surprise, wouldn't he?

Yes.

And he did.

Halfway down the steps, Lord Darcy dropped to a crouch and his pistol was suddenly staring both of them in the face.

"If either of you moves," said Lord Darcy calmly, "I will shoot him through the brain. Get your hands off those blade hilts and don't move otherwise. Fine. Now turn around. *V-e-r-r-ry slowly.*"

The men obeyed wordlessly. Lord Darcy's powerful hand came down twice in a deft neck-chop, and both men dropped to the floor unconscious.

"Come on down, my lord," said Lord Darcy. "There will be no need for swordplay."

Lord Seiger descended the ladder in silence, his sword sheathed.

There were two cell doors on either side of the passageway; the cells themselves had been built to discipline crewmen or to imprison sailors or passengers who were accused of crime on the high seas while the ship was in passage. The first cell on the right had a dim light glowing within it. The yellowish light gleamed through the small barred window in the door.

Both Lord Darcy and Lord Seiger walked over to the door and looked inside.

"That's what I was looking for," Lord Darcy breathed.

Within, strapped to a bunk, was a still, white-faced figure. The face was exactly similar to that of the corpse Lord Darcy had seen in the morgue.

"Are you sure it's the Marquis of Cherbourg?" Lord Seiger asked.

"I refuse to admit that there are *three* men who look that much alike," Lord Darcy whispered dryly. "Two are quite enough. Since Master Sean established that the body in the morgue was definitely *not* related to my lord of Guernsey and Sark, *this* must be the Marquis. Now, the problem will be getting the cell door open."

"*I vill open idt for you.*"

At the sound of the voice behind them, both Lord Darcy and Lord Seiger froze.

"To qvote you, Lord Darcy, 'If either of you moves, I vill shoodt him through the brain,' " said the voice. "Drop de gun, Lord Darcy."

As Lord Darcy let his pistol drop from his hand, his mind raced.

The shock of having been trapped, such as it had been, had passed even before the voice behind him had ceased. Shock of that kind could not hold him frozen long. Nor was his the kind of mind that grew angry with itself for making a mistake. There was no time for that.

He had been trapped. Someone had been hidden in the cell across the passageway, waiting for him. A neat trap. Very well; the problem was, how to get out of that trap.

"Bot' of you step to de left," said the voice. "Move avay from de cell port. Dat's it. Fine. Open de door, Ladislas."

There were two men, both holding guns. The shorter, darker of the two stepped forward and opened the door to the cell next to that in which the still figure of the Marquis of Cherbourg lay.

"Bot' of you step inside," said the taller of the two men who had trapped the Imperial agents.

There was nothing Lord Seiger and Lord Darcy could do but obey.

"Keep you de hands high in de air. Dat's fine. Now listen to me, and listen carefully. You t'ink you have taken dis ship. In a vay, you have. But not finally. I have you. I have de Marquis. You vill order your men off. Odervise, I vill kill all of you—vun adt a time. Understand? If I hang, I do not die alone."

Lord Darcy understood. "You want your crew back, eh, Captain Olsen? And how will you get by the Royal Navy?"

"De same vay I vill get out of Cherbourg harbor, Lord Darcy," the captain said complacently. "I vill promise release. You vill be able to go back home from Danzig. Vot goodt is any of you to us now?"

None, except as hostages, Lord Darcy thought. What had happened was quite clear. Somehow, someone had managed to signal to Captain Olsen that his ship was being taken. A signal from the bridge, perhaps. It didn't matter. Captain Olsen had not been expecting invaders, but when they had come, he had devised a neat trap. He had known where the invaders would be heading.

Up to that point, Lord Darcy knew, the Polish agents had planned to take the unconscious Marquis to Danzig. There, he would be operated on by a sorcerer and sent back to Cherbourg—apparently in good condition, but actually under the control of Polish agents. His absence would be explained by his "spells," which would no longer be in evidence. But now that Captain Olsen knew that the plot had been discovered, he had no further use for the Marquis. Nor had he any use for either Lord Darcy or Lord Seiger. Except that he could use them as hostages to get his ship to Danzig.

"What do you want, Captain Olsen?" Lord Darcy asked quietly.

"Very simply, dis: You vill order de soldiers to come below. Ve vill lock them up. Ven my men vake up, and de rest of de crew come aboard, ve vill sail at dawn. Ven ve are ready to sail, all may go ashore except you and Lord Seiger and de Marquis. Your men vill tell de officials in Cherbourg vhat has happened and vill tell dem dat ve vill sail to Danzig unmolested. Dere, you vill be set free and sent back to Imperial territory I give you my vord."

Oddly, Lord Darcy realized that the man meant it.   Lord Darcy knew that the man's word was good.   But was he responsible for the reactions of the Polish officials at Danzig?   Was he responsible for the reactions of Casimir IX?   No. Certainly not.

But, trapped as they were—

And then a hoarse voice came from across the passageway, from the fourth cell. "Seiger?   Seiger?"

Lord Seiger's eyes widened.   "Yes?"

Captain Olsen and First Officer Ladislas remained unmoved.   The captain smiled sardonically.   "Ah, yes.   I forgot to mention your so-brave Sir James LeLein. He vill make an excellent hostage, too."

The hoarse voice said: "They are traitors to the King, Seiger.   Do you hear me?"

"I hear you, Sir James," said Lord Seiger.

"Destroy them," said the hoarse voice.

Captain Olsen laughed.   "Shut up, LeLein.   You—"

But he never had time to finish.

Lord Darcy watched with unbelieving eyes as Lord Seiger's right hand darted out with blurring speed and slapped aside the captain's gun.   At the same time, his left hand drew his rapier and slashed out toward the first officer.

The first officer had been covering Lord Darcy.   When he saw Lord Seiger move, he swung his gun toward Lord Seiger and fired.   The slug tore into the Yorkshire nobleman's side as Captain Olsen spun away and tried to bring his own weapon to bear.

By that time, Lord Darcy himself was in action.   His powerful legs catapulted him toward First Officer Ladislas just as the point of Lord Seiger's rapier slashed across Ladislas' chest, making a deep cut over the ribs.   Then Ladislas was slammed out into the passageway by Lord Darcy's assault.

After that, Lord Darcy had too much to do to pay any attention to what went on between Lord Seiger and Captain Olsen.   Apparently oblivious to the blood gushing from the gash on his chest, Ladislas fought with steel muscles.   Darcy knew his own strength, but he also knew that this opponent was of nearly equal strength. Darcy held the man's right wrist in a vise grip to keep him from bringing the pistol around.   Then he smashed his head into Ladislas' jaw.   The gun dropped and spun away as both men fell to the deck.

Lord Darcy brought his right fist up in a smashing blow to the first officer's throat; gagging, the first officer collapsed.

Lord Darcy pushed himself to his knees and grabbed the unconscious man by the collar, pulling him half upright.

At that second, a tongue of steel flashed by Lord Darcy's shoulder, plunged itself into Ladislas' throat, and tore sideways.   The first officer died as his blood spurted fountainlike over Lord Darcy's arm.

After a moment, Lord Darcy realized that the fight was over.   He turned his head.

Lord Seiger stood nearby, his sword red.   Captain Olsen lay on the deck, his life's blood flowing from three wounds—two in the chest, and the third, like his first officer's, a slash across the throat.

"I had him," Lord Darcy said unevenly.   "There was no need to cut his throat."

For the first time, he saw a slight smile on Lord Seiger's face.

"I had my orders, my lord," said Lord Seiger, as his side dripped crimson.

With twelve sonorous, resounding strokes, the great Bell of the Benedictine Church of Saint Denys, in the courtyard of Castle Cherbourg, sounded the hour of midnight.   Lord Darcy, freshly bathed and shaved and clad in his evening wear, stood before the fireplace in the reception room above the Great Hall and waited patiently for the bell to finish its tally.   Then he turned and smiled at the young man standing beside him.   "As you were saying, Your Highness?"

Richard, Duke of Normandy, smiled back.   "Even royalty can't drown out a church bell, eh, my lord?"   Then his face became serious again.   "I was saying that we have made a clean sweep.   Dunkerque, Calais, Boulogne . . . all the way down to Hendaye.   By now, the English Armsmen will be picking them up in London, Liverpool, and so on.   By dawn, Ireland will be clear.   You've done a magnificent job, my lord, and you may rest assured that my brother the King will hear of it."

"Thank you, Your Highness, but I really—"

Lord Darcy was interrupted by the opening of the door.   Lord Seiger came in, then stopped as he saw Duke Richard.

The Duke reacted instantly.   "Don't bother to bow, my lord.   I have been told of your wound."

Lord Seiger nevertheless managed a slight bow.   "Your Highness is most gracious.   But the wound is a slight one, and Father Patrique has laid his hands on it.   The pain is negligible, Highness."

"I am happy to hear so."   The Duke looked at Lord Darcy.   "By the way . . . I am curious to know what made you suspect that Lord Seiger was a King's Agent. I didn't know, myself, until the King, my brother, sent me the information I requested."

"I must confess that I was not certain until Your Highness verified my suspicions on the teleson.   But it seemed odd to me that de Cherbourg would have wanted a man of Lord Seiger's . . . ah . . . peculiar talents merely as a librarian.   Then, too, Lady Elaine's attitude . . . er, your pardon, my lord—"

"Perfectly all right, my lord," said Lord Seiger expressionlessly.   "I am aware that many women find my presence distasteful—although I confess I do not know why."

"Who can account for the behavior of women?" Lord Darcy said.   "Your manners and behavior are impeccable.   Nonetheless, My Lady Marquise found, as you say, your presence distasteful.   She must have made this fact known to her husband the Marquis, eh?"

"I believe she did, my lord," said Lord Seiger.

"Very well," said Lord Darcy.   "Would My Lord Marquis, who is notoriously in love with his wife, have kept a *librarian* who frightened her?   No.   Therefore, either Lord Seiger's purpose here was much more important—or he was black-mailing the Marquis. I chose to believe the former.'' He did not add that Father Patrique's information showed that it was impossible for Lord Seiger to blackmail anyone.

"My trouble lay in not knowing who was working for whom. We knew only that Sir James was masquerading as a common working man, and that he was working with My Lord Marquis. But until Your Highness got in touch with His Majesty, we knew nothing more. I was working blind until I realized that Lord Seiger—''

He stopped as he heard the door open. From outside came Master Sean's voice: "After you, my lady, my lord, Sir Gwiliam.''

The Marquise de Cherbourg swept into the room, her fair face an expressionless mask. Behind her came My Lord Bishop and Sir Gwiliam, followed by Master Sean O Lochlainn.

Lady Elaine walked straight to Duke Richard. She made a small curtsy. "Your presence is an honor, Your Highness.'' She was quite sober.

"The honor is mine, my lady,'' replied the Duke.

"I have seen my lord husband. He is alive, as I knew he was. But his mind is gone. Father Patrique says he will never recover. I must know what has happened, Your Highness.''

"You will have to ask Lord Darcy that, my lady,'' the Duke said gently. "I should like to hear the complete story myself.''

My lady turned her steady gaze on the lean Englishman. "Begin at the beginning and tell me everything, my lord. I must know.''

The door opened again, and Sir Androu Duglasse came in. "Good morning, Y' Highness,'' he said with a low bow. "Good morning, m' lady, y' lordships, Sir Gwiliam, Master Sean.'' His eyes went back to Lady Elaine. "I've heard the news from Father Patrique, m' lady. I'm a soldier, m' lady, not a man who can speak well. I cannot tell you of the sorrow I feel.''

"I thank you, Sir Captain,'' said my lady, "I think you have expressed it very well.'' Her eyes went back to Lord Darcy. "If you please, my lord . . .''

"As you command, my lady,'' said Lord Darcy. "Er . . . captain, I don't think that what I have to say need be known by any others than those of us here. Would you watch the door? Explain to anyone else that this is a private conference. Thank you. Then I can begin.'' He leaned negligently against the fireplace, where he could see everyone in the room.

"To begin with, we had a hellish plot afoot—not against just one person, but against the Empire. The 'Atlantic Curse'. Ships sailing from Imperial ports to the New World were never heard from again. Shipping was dropping off badly, not only from ship losses, but because fear kept seamen off trans-Atlantic ships. They feared magic, although, as I shall show, pure magic had nothing to do with it.

"My lord the Marquis was working with Sir James LeLein, one of a large group of King's Agents with direct commissions to discover the cause of the 'Atlantic Curse'.   His Majesty had correctly deduced that the whole thing was a Polish plot to disrupt Imperial economy.

"The plot was devilish in its simplicity.   A drug, made by steeping a kind of mushroom in brandy, was being used to destroy the minds of the crews of trans-Atlantic ships.   Taken in small dosages, over a period of time, the drug causes violent insanity.   A ship with an insane crew cannot last long in the Atlantic.

"Sir James, working with My Lord Marquis and other agents, tried to get a lead on what was going on.   My Lord Marquis, not wanting anyone in the castle to know of his activities, used the old secret tunnel that leads to the city sewers in order to meet Sir James.

"Sir James obtained a sample of the drug after he had identified the ringleader of the Polish agents.   He reported to My Lord Marquis.   Then, on the evening of Wednesday, the eighth of January, Sir James set out to obtain more evidence. He went to the warehouse where the ringleader had his headquarters."

Lord Darcy paused and smiled slightly.   "By the by, I must say that the details of what happened in the warehouse were supplied to me by Sir James.   My own deductions only gave me a part of the story.

"At any rate, Sir James obtained entry to the second floor of the warehouse. He heard voices.   Silently, he went to the door of the room from which the voices came and looked in through the . . . er . . . the keyhole.   It was dark in the corridor, but well-lit in the room.

"What he saw was a shock to him.   Two men—a sorcerer and the ringleader himself—were there.   The sorcerer was standing by a bed, weaving a spell over a third man, who lay naked on the bed.   One look at the man in the bed convinced Sir James that the man was none other than the Marquis of Cherbourg himself!"

Lady Elaine touched her fingertips to her lips.   "Had he been poisoned by the drug, my lord?" she asked.   "Was that what had been affecting his mind?"

"The man was not your husband, my lady," Lord Darcy said gently.   "He was a double, a simple-minded man in the pay of these men.

"Sir James, of course, had no way of knowing that.   When he saw the Marquis in danger, he acted.   Weapon in hand, he burst open the door and demanded the release of the man whom he took to be the Marquis.   He told the man to get up. Seeing he was hypnotized, Sir James put his own cloak about the man's shoulders and the two of them began to back out of the room, his weapon covering the sorcerer and the ringleader.

"But there was another man in the warehouse.   Sir James never saw him.   This person struck him from behind as he backed out the door.

"Sir James was dazed.   He dropped his weapon.   The sorcerer and the ring-leader jumped him.   Sir James fought, but he was eventually rendered unconscious.

"In the meantime, the man whom Sir James attempted to rescue became fright-ened and fled.   In the darkness, he tumbled down a flight of oaken stairs and fractured his skull on one of the lower steps.   Hurt, dazed, and dying, he fled

from the warehouse toward the only other place in Cherbourg he could call home—
a bistro called the Blue Dolphin, a few blocks away. He very nearly made it.
He died a block from it, in the sight of two Armsmen."

"Did they intend to use the double for some sort of impersonation of my brother?"
asked the Bishop.

"In a way, my lord. I'll get to that in a moment."

"When I came here," Lord Darcy continued, "I of course knew nothing of all
this. I knew only that my lord of Cherbourg was missing and that he had been
working with His Majesty's Agents. Then a body was tentatively identified as
his. If it *were* the Marquis, who had killed him? If it were not, what was the
connection? I went to see Sir James and found that he had been missing since
that same night. Again, what was the connection?

"The next clue was the identification of the drug. How could such a drug be
introduced aboard ships so that almost every man would take a little each day?
The taste and aroma of the brandy would be apparent in the food or water. Obviously, then, the wine rations were drugged. And only the vintner who supplied
the wine could have regularly drugged the wine of ship after ship.

"A check of the Shipping Registry showed that new vintners had bought out old
wineries in shipping ports throughout the Empire in the past five years. All of
them, subsidized by the Poles, could underbid their competitors. They made good
wine and sold it cheaper than others could sell it. They got contracts. They
didn't try to poison every ship; only a few of those on the Atlantic run—just enough
to start a scare while keeping suspicion from themselves.

"There was still the problem of what had happened to My Lord Marquis. He
had *not* left the castle that night. And yet he had disappeared. But how? And
why?

"There were four places that the captain had not searched. I dismissed the
icehouse when I discovered that people went in and out of it all day. He could
not have gone to the strongroom because the door is too wide for one man to use
both keys simultaneously—which must be done to open it. Sir Gwiliam had been
in and out of the wine cellar. And there were indications that the tunnel had also
had visitors."

"Why should he have been in any of those places, my lord?" Sir Gwiliam asked.
"Mightn't he have simply left through the tunnel?"

"Hardly likely. The tunnel guard was a King's Agent. If the Marquis had
gone out that night and never returned, he would have reported the fact—not to
Captain Sir Androu, but to Lord Seiger. He did not so report. Ergo, the Marquis
did not leave the castle that night."

"Then what happened to him?" Sir Gwiliam asked.

"That brings us back to the double, Paul Sarto," said Lord Darcy. "Would
you explain, Master Sean?"

"Well, my lady, gentle sirs," the little sorcerer began, "My Lord Darcy deduced
the use of magic here. This Polish sorcerer—a piddling poor one, he is, too; when
I caught him in the warehouse, he tried to cast a few spells at me and they were

nothing.   He ended up docile as a lamb when I gave him a dose of good Irish sorcery.''

"Proceed, Master Sean,'' Lord Darcy said dryly.

"Beggin' your pardon, my lord.   Anyway, this Polish sorcerer saw that this Paul chap was a dead ringer for My Lord Marquis and decided to use him to control My Lord Marquis—Law of Similarity, d' ye see.   You know the business of sticking pins in wax dolls?   Crude method of psychic induction, but effective if the similarity is great enough.   And what could be more similar to a man than his double?''

"You mean they used this poor unfortunate man as a wax doll?'' asked the Marquise in a hushed voice.

"That's about it, your ladyship.   In order for the spells to work, though, the double would have to have very low mind power.   Well, he did.   So they hired him away from his old job and went to work on him.   They made him bathe and wear fine clothes, and slowly took control of his mind.   They told him that he *was* the Marquis.   With that sort of similarity achieved, they hoped to control the Marquis himself just as they controlled his simulacrum.''

My Lady Elaine looked horrified.   *"That* caused his terrible attacks?''

"Exactly, your ladyship.   When My Lord Marquis was tired or distracted, they were able to take over for a little while.   A vile business no proper sorcerer would stoop to, but workable.''

"But what did they do to my husband?'' asked the lady of Cherbourg.

"Well, now, your ladyship,'' said Master Sean, "what do you suppose would happen to his lordship when his simulacrum got his skull crushed so bad that it killed the simulacrum?   The shock to his lordship's mind was so great that it nearly killed him on the spot—*would* have killed him, too, if the similarity had been better established.   He fell into a coma, my lady.''

Lord Darcy took up the story again.   "The Marquis dropped where he was. He remained in the castle until last night, when the Polish agents came to get him. They killed the King's Agent on guard, disposed of the body, came in through the tunnel, got the Marquis, and took him to their ship.   When Captain Sir Androu told me that the guard had 'deserted', I knew fully what had happened.   I knew that My Lord Marquis was either in the vintner's warehouse or in a ship bound for Poland.   The two raids show that I was correct.''

"Do you mean,'' said Sir Gwiliam, "that my lord lay in that chilly tunnel all that time?   How horrible!''

Lord Darcy looked at the man for long seconds.   "No.   Not *all* that time, Sir Gwiliam.   No one—especially not the Polish agents—would have known he was there.   He was taken to the tunnel after he was found the next morning—in the wine cellar.''

"Ridiculous!'' said Sir Gwiliam, startled.   "I'd have seen him!''

"Most certainly you would have,'' Lord Darcy agreed.   "And most certainly you *did*.   It must have been quite a shock to return home after the fight in the warehouse to find the Marquis unconscious on the wine cellar floor. Once I knew you were the guilty man, I knew you had given away your employer. You told me that you had played cards with Ordwin Vayne that night; therefore I knew which vintner to raid.''

White-faced, Sir Gwiliam said, ''I have served my lord and lady faithfully for many years. I say you lie.''

''Oh?'' Lord Darcy's eyes were hard. ''Someone had to tell Ordwin Vayne where the Marquis was—someone who *knew* where he was. Only the Marquis, Sir Androu, and *you* had keys to the tunnel. I saw the captain's key; it was dull and filmed when I used it. The wards of the old lock left little bright scratches on it. He hadn't used it for a long time. Only *you* had a key that would let Ordwin Vayne and his men into that tunnel.''

''Pah! Your reasoning is illogical! If My Lord Marquis were unconscious, someone could have taken the key off him!''

''Not if he was in the tunnel. Why would anyone go there? The tunnel door was locked, so, even if he *were* there, a key would have to have been used to find him. But if he had fallen in the tunnel, he would still have been there when I looked. There was no reason for you or anyone else to unlock that tunnel—*until* you were looking for a place to conceal My Lord Marquis' unconscious body!''

''Why would he have gone to the wine cellar?'' Sir Gwiliam snapped. ''And why lock himself in?''

''He went down to check on some bottles you had in the wine cellar. Sir James' report led him to suspect you. Warehouses and wineries are subjected to rigorous inspection. Ordwin Vayne didn't want inspectors to find that he was steeping mushrooms in brandy. So the bottles were kept *here*—the safest place in Cherbourg. Who would suspect? The Marquis never went there. But he did suspect at last, and went down to check. He locked the door because he didn't want to be interrupted. No one but you could come in, and he would be warned if you put your key in the lock. While he was there, the simulacrumized Paul fell and struck his head on an oaken step. Paul died. The Marquis went comatose.

''When I arrived yesterday, you had to get rid of the evidence. So Vayne's men came and took the bottles of drug and the Marquis. If further proof is needed, I can tell you that we found the drug on the ship, in restoppered bottles containing cheap brandy and bits of mushroom. *But the bottles were labeled Saint Couerlandt Michele '46!* Who else in Cherbourg but you would have access to such empty bottles?''

Sir Gwiliam stepped back. ''Lies! All lies!''

''No!'' snapped a voice from the door. ''Truth! All truth!''

Lord Darcy had seen Captain Sir Androu silently open the door and let in three more men, but no one else had. Now the others turned at the sound of the voice.

Sitting in a wheelchair, looking pale but still strong, was Hugh, Marquis of Cherbourg. Behind him was Sir James LeLein. To one side stood Father Patrique.

''What Lord Darcy said is true in every particular,'' said my lord the Marquis in an icy voice.

Sir Gwiliam gasped and jerked his head around to look at my lady the Marquise. "You said his mind was gone!"

"A small lie—to trap a traitor." Her voice was icy.

"Sir Gwiliam de Bracy," said Sir James from behind the Marquis, "in the King's Name, I charge you with treason!"

Two things happened almost at once. Sir Gwiliam's hand started for his pocket. But by then, Lord Seiger's sword, with its curious offset hilt, was halfway from its sheath. By the time Sir Gwiliam had his pistol out, the sword had slashed through his jugular vein. Sir Gwiliam had just time to turn and fire once before he fell to the floor.

Lord Seiger stood there, looking down at Sir Gwiliam, an odd smile on his face.

For a second, no one spoke or moved. Then Father Patrique rushed over to the fallen seneschal. He was too late by far. With all his Healing power, there was nothing he could do now.

And then the Marquise walked over to Lord Seiger and took his free hand. "My lord, others may censure you for that act. I do not. That monster helped send hundreds of innocent men to insanity and death. He almost did the same for my beloved Hugh. If anything, he died too clean a death. I do not censure you, my lord. I thank you."

"I thank you, my lady. But I only did my duty." There was an odd thickness in his voice. "I had my orders, my lady."

And then, slowly, like a deflating balloon, Lord Seiger slumped to the floor.

Lord Darcy and Father Patrique realized at the same moment that Sir Gwiliam's bullet must have hit Lord Seiger, though he had shown no sign of it till then.

Lord Seiger had had no conscience, but he could not kill or even defend himself of his own accord. Sir James had been his decision-maker. Lord Seiger had been a King's Agent who would kill without qualm on order from Sir James—and was otherwise utterly harmless. The decision was never left up to him, only to Sir James.

Sir James, still staring at the fallen Lord Seiger, said: "But . . . how could he? I didn't tell him to."

"Yes, you did," Lord Darcy said wearily. "On the ship. You told him to destroy the traitors. When you called Sir Gwiliam a traitor, he acted. He had his sword halfway out before Sir Gwiliam drew that pistol. He would have killed Sir Gwiliam in cold blood if the seneschal had never moved at all. He was like a gas lamp, Sir James. You turned him on—and forgot to shut him off."

Richard, Duke of Normandy, looked down at the fallen man. Lord Seiger's face was oddly unchanged. It had rarely had any expression in life. It had none now.

"How is he, Reverend Father?" asked the Duke.

"He is dead, Your Highness."

"May the Lord have mercy on his soul," said Duke Richard.

Eight men and a woman made the Sign of the Cross in silence.

The following letter from Randall Garrett accompanied the manuscript of "A Case of Identity"—John W. Campbell

Dear John,

Herewith, "A Case of Identity." Lord Darcy and Master Sean ride again.

As you will see, I have carried the chronology of Lord Darcy's world one step further. In our own history, Henry of Anjou, in the right of his mother Matilda, who was the daughter of Henry I of England, became the first Plantagenet King of England under the title of Henry II. His father was Count Geoffrey of Anjou. He married Eleanor, Duchess of Aquitaine, thereby bringing Aquitaine under English rule. Besides being King of England, he was Duke of Normandy, Duke of Aquitaine, Duke of Brittany, and Count of Anjou, Maine, and Touraine. He ruled all of England and more than half of France.

He had four sons: Henry (known as the Young King), Richard (the Lion-Hearted), Geoffrey, and John (of Magna Carta fame).

Old Henry II died in 1189. He was predeceased by Young Henry (1183) and Geoffrey (1186), so the crown went to Richard.

When Richard died at the Siege of Chaluz, in France, the crown should have gone to Geoffrey under the law of primogeniture. But that law wasn't a law yet. It may have been a hypothesis or even a theory, but it wasn't a law. Besides, Geoffrey had been dead for thirteen years, leaving behind him a new-born son, Arthur. Geoffrey had been made Duke of Brittany, and, upon the death of Richard, the crown should have gone to the thirteen-year-old Arthur, now Duke of Brittany.

As Richard lay dying, he named his younger brother John as his heir. But, according to Duggan, "He had changed his mind so often that this carried little weight; had he lived another week he might have left all to Arthur."

The English barons did not want a child on the throne, so they declared for John. Normandy followed suit. Even Sir William Marshal, probably the closest to a true story-book knight of any who ever lived, said that even a bad king was better than a council of regency.

But the theory of primogeniture had been invented—or reinvented—by the Capets, the ruling house of France, and it was much more strongly imbedded in France than in England. Anjou, Maine, and Touraine went over to Arthur. Since he was Duke of Brittany, Brittany naturally backed him.

Old Queen Eleanor, meanwhile, now seventy-seven, had become Duchess of Aquitaine again. (Henry II had been Duke of Aquitaine; then it had gone to Richard. But only because the first was the husband and the second the son of the Duchess.) Eleanor was a tough-minded old biddy who was never one to forget a slight. She had wanted Geoffrey's son to be named Henry and she flew into a rage when she found that Geoffrey's wife, Constance, had, without even consulting Eleanor, given the boy the un-Norman name of Arthur. (The Arthurian romances were just coming into popularity at that time, and Lady Constance was somewhat of a romantic.) As a result, Eleanor of Aquitaine much preferred her son John to her grandson Arthur. Aquitaine, which included the Counties of Poitou and Gascony, became John's territory.

Naturally, the only way to settle the thing was to get all the armed knights into the field and battle it out. Duke Arthur didn't have a chance. He had Normandy to the north of him, Aquitaine to the south, and England across the Channel to the west.   Plus the fact that Philip of France was taking advantage of the civil war by sneaking in from the east.   Then, too, the people of Brittany hated anything French, so they couldn't co-operate with Anjou, Maine, and Touraine.

The upshot of it all was that, after three years of fighting, John captured Arthur. He disappeared into the castle at Rouen and was never seen again.   Historians agree that he was murdered by order of King John.   He was about sixteen.

Now, if Richard had lived another twenty years, Arthur would have been in a much better position.   Richard never really liked John, and if Arthur had stuck with Richard, John would never have had a chance.   Of course, we don't know what kind of man Arthur would have been if the neighbors had let him grow up, but I can make the assumption, for that very reason, that he would have been both a good Plantagenet and a good King.   If so, the history of the Angevin Empire would have been vastly different.

RANDALL GARRETT

JAMES H. SCHMITZ

Balanced Ecology

The diamondwood tree farm was restless this morning. Ilf Cholm had been aware of it for about an hour but had said nothing to Auris, thinking he might be getting a summer fever or a stomach upset and imagining things and that Auris would decide they should go back to the house so Ilf's grandmother could dose him. But the feeling continued to grow, and by now Ilf knew it was the farm.

Outwardly, everyone in the forest appeared to be going about their usual business. There had been a rainfall earlier in the day; and the tumbleweeds had uprooted themselves and were moving about in the bushes, lapping water off the leaves. Ilf had noticed a small one rolling straight towards a waiting slurp and stopped for a moment to watch the slurp catch it. The slurp was of average size, which gave it a tongue-reach of between twelve and fourteen feet, and the tumbleweed was already within range.

The tongue shot out suddenly, a thin, yellow flash. Its tip flicked twice around the tumbleweed, jerked it off the ground and back to the feed opening in the imitation tree stump within which the rest of the slurp was concealed. The tumbleweed said "Oof!" in the surprised way they always did when something caught them, and went in through the opening. After a moment, the slurp's tongue tip appeared in the opening again and waved gently around, ready for somebody else of the right size to come within reach.

Ilf, just turned eleven and rather small for his age, was the right size for this slurp, though barely. But, being a human boy, he was in no danger. The slurps of the diamondwood farms on Wrake didn't attack humans. For a moment, he was tempted to tease the creature into a brief fencing match. If he picked up a stick and banged on the stump with it a few times, the slurp would become annoyed and dart its tongue out and try to knock the stick from his hand.

But it wasn't the day for entertainment of that kind. Ilf couldn't shake off his crawly, uncomfortable feeling, and while he had been standing there, Auris and Sam had moved a couple of hundred feet farther uphill, in the direction of the Queen Grove, and home. He turned and sprinted after them, caught up with them as they came out into one of the stretches of grassland which lay between the individual groves of diamondwood trees.

Auris, who was two years, two months, and two days older than Ilf, stood on top of Sam's semiglobular shell, looking off to the right towards the valley where the diamondwood factory was.   Most of the world of Wrake was on the hot side, either rather dry or rather steamy; but this was cool mountain country.   Far to the south, below the valley and the foothills behind it, lay the continental plain, shimmering like a flat, green-brown sea.   To the north and east were higher plateaus, above the level where the diamondwood liked to grow.   Ilf ran past Sam's steadily moving bulk to the point where the forward rim of the shell made a flat upward curve, close enough to the ground so he could reach it.

Sam rolled a somber brown eye back for an instant as Ilf caught the shell and swung up on it, but his huge beaked head didn't turn.   He was a mossback, Wrake's version of the turtle pattern, and, except for the full-grown trees and perhaps some members of the clean-up squad, the biggest thing on the farm.   His corrugated shell was overgrown with a plant which had the appearance of long green fur; and occasionally when Sam fed, he would extend and use a pair of heavy arms with three-fingered hands, normally held folded up against the lower rim of the shell.

Auris had paid no attention to Ilf's arrival.   She still seemed to be watching the factory in the valley.   She and Ilf were cousins but didn't resemble each other. Ilf was small and wiry, with tight-curled red hair.   Auris was slim and blond, and stood a good head taller than he did.   He thought she looked as if she owned everything she could see from the top of Sam's shell; and she did, as a matter of fact, own a good deal of it—nine tenths of the diamondwood farm and nine tenths of the factory.   Ilf owned the remaining tenth of both.

He scrambled up the shell, grabbing the moss-fur to haul himself along, until he stood beside her.   Sam, awkward as he looked when walking, was moving at a good ten miles an hour, clearly headed for the Queen Grove.   Ilf didn't know whether it was Sam or Auris who had decided to go back to the house.   Whichever it had been, he could feel the purpose of going there.

"They're nervous about something," he told Auris, meaning the whole farm. "Think there's a big storm coming?"

"Doesn't look like a storm," Auris said.

Ilf glanced about the sky, agreed silently.   "Earthquake, maybe?"

Auris shook her head.   "It doesn't feel like earthquake."

She hadn't turned her gaze from the factory.   Ilf asked, "Something going on down there?"

Auris shrugged.   "They're cutting a lot today," she said.   "They got in a limit order."

Sam swayed on into the next grove while Ilf considered the information.   Limit orders were fairly unusual; but it hardly explained the general uneasiness.   He sighed, sat down, crossed his legs, and looked about.   This was a grove of young trees, fifteen years and less.   There was plenty of open space left between them. Ahead, a huge tumbleweed was dying, making happy, chuckling sounds as it pitched its scarlet seed pellets far out from its slowly unfolding leaves.   The pellets rolled hurriedly farther away from the old weed as soon as they touched the ground.   In a twelve-foot circle about their parent, the earth was being disturbed, churned, shifted steadily about.   The clean-up squad had arrived to dispose of the dying tumbleweed; as Ilf looked, it suddenly settled six or seven inches deeper into the softened dirt.   The pellets were hurrying to get beyond the reach of the clean-up squad so they wouldn't get hauled down, too.   But half-grown tumbleweeds, speckled yellow-green and ready to start their rooted period, were rolling through the grove towards the disturbed area.   They would wait around the edge of the circle until the clean-up squad finished, then move in and put down their roots. The ground where the squad had worked recently was always richer than any other spot in the forest.

Ilf wondered, as he had many times before, what the clean-up squad looked like. Nobody ever caught so much as a glimpse of them.   Riquol Cholm, his grandfather, had told him of attempts made by scientists to catch a member of the squad with digging machines.   Even the smallest ones could dig much faster than the machines could dig after them, so the scientists always gave up finally and went away.

"Ilf, come in for lunch!" called Ilf's grandmother's voice.

Ilf filled his lungs, shouted, "Coming, grand—"

He broke off, looked up at Auris.   She was smirking.

"Caught me again," Ilf admitted.   "Dumb humbugs!"   He yelled, "Come out, Lying Lou!   I know who it was."

Meldy Cholm laughed her low, sweet laugh, a silverbell called the giant greenweb of the Queen Grove sounded its deep harp note, more or less all together.   Then Lying Lou and Gabby darted into sight, leaped up on the mossback's hump.   The humbugs were small, brown, bobtailed animals, built with spider leanness and very quick.   They had round skulls, monkey faces, and the pointed teeth of animals who lived by catching and killing other animals.   Gabby sat down beside Ilf, inflating and deflating his voice pouch, while Lou burst into a series of rattling, clicking, spitting sounds.

"They've been down at the factory?" Ilf asked.

"Yes," Auris said.   "Hush now.   I'm listening."

Lou was jabbering along at the rate at which the humbugs chattered among themselves, but this sounded like, and was, a recording of human voices played back at high speed.   When Auris wanted to know what people somewhere were talking about, she sent the humbugs off to listen.   They remembered everything they heard, came back and repeated it to her at their own speed, which saved time. Ilf, if he tried hard, could understand scraps of it.   Auris understood it all.   She was hearing now what the people at the factory had been saying during the morning.

Gabby inflated his voice pouch part way, remarked in Grandfather Riquol's strong, rich voice, "My, my!   We're not being quite on our best behavior today, are we, Ilf?"

"Shut up," said Ilf.

"Hush now," Gabby said in Auris' voice.   "I'm listening."   He added in Ilf's voice, sounding crestfallen, "Caught me again!" then chuckled nastily.

Ilf made a fist of his left hand and swung fast.   Gabby became a momentary brown blur, and was sitting again on Ilf's other side.   He looked at Ilf with round, innocent eyes, said in a solemn tone, "We must pay more attention to details, men. Mistakes can be expensive!"

He'd probably picked that up at the factory. Ilf ignored him. Trying to hit a humbug was a waste of effort. So was talking back to them. He shifted his attention to catching what Lou was saying; but Lou had finished up at that moment. She and Gabby took off instantly in a leap from Sam's back and were gone in the bushes. Ilf thought they were a little jittery and erratic in their motions today, as if they, too, were keyed up even more than usual. Auris walked down to the front lip of the shell and sat on it, dangling her legs. Ilf joined her there.

"What were they talking about at the factory?" he asked.

"They did get in a limit order yesterday," Auris said. "And another one this morning. They're not taking any more orders until they've filled those two."

"That's good, isn't it?" Ilf asked.

"I guess so."

After a moment, Ilf asked, "Is that what *they're* worrying about?"

"I don't know," Auris said. But she frowned.

Sam came lumbering up to another stretch of open ground, stopped while he was still well back among the trees. Auris slipped down from the shell, said, "Come on but don't let them see you," and moved ahead through the trees until she could look into the open. Ilf followed her as quietly as he could.

"What's the matter?" he inquired. A hundred and fifty yards away, on the other side of the open area, towered the Queen Grove, its tops dancing gently like armies of slender green spears against the blue sky. The house wasn't visible from here; it was a big one-story bungalow built around the trunk of a number of trees deep within the grove. Ahead of them lay the road which came up from the valley and wound on through the mountains to the west.

Auris said, "An aircar came down here a while ago . . . There it is!"

They looked at the aircar parked at the side of the road on their left, a little distance away. Opposite the car was an opening in the Queen Grove where a path led to the house. Ilf couldn't see anything very interesting about the car. It was neither new nor old, looked like any ordinary aircar. The man sitting inside it was nobody they knew.

"Somebody's here on a visit," Ilf said.

"Yes," Auris said. "Uncle Kugus has come back."

Ilf had to reflect an instant to remember who Uncle Kugus was. Then it came to his mind in a flash. It had been some while ago, a year or so. Uncle Kugus was a big, handsome man with thick, black eyebrows, who always smiled. He wasn't Ilf's uncle but Auris'; but he'd had presents for both of them when he arrived. He had told Ilf a great many jokes. He and Grandfather Riquol had argued on one occasion for almost two hours about something or other; Ilf couldn't remember now what it had been. Uncle Kugus had come and gone in a tiny, beautiful, bright yellow aircar, had taken Ilf for a couple of rides in it, and told him about winning races with it. Ilf hadn't had too bad an impression of him.

"That isn't him," he said, "and that isn't his car."

"I know. He's in the house," Auris said. "He's got a couple of people with him. They're talking with Riquol and Meldy."

A sound rose slowly from the Queen Grove as she spoke, deep and resonant, like the stroke of a big, old clock or the hum of a harp. The man in the aircar turned his head towards the grove to listen. The sound was repeated twice. It came from the giant greenweb at the far end of the grove and could be heard all over the farm, even, faintly, down in the valley when the wind was favorable. Ilf said, "Lying Lou and Gabby were up here?"

"Yes. They went down to the factory first, then up to the house."

"What are they talking about in the house?" Ilf inquired.

"Oh, a lot of things." Auris frowned again. "We'll go and find out, but we won't let them see us right away."

Something stirred beside Ilf. He looked down and saw Lying Lou and Gabby had joined them again. The humbugs peered for a moment at the man in the aircar, then flicked out into the open, on across the road, and into the Queen Grove, like small, flying shadows, almost impossible to keep in sight. The man in the aircar looked about in a puzzled way, apparently uncertain whether he'd seen something move or not.

"Come on," Auris said.

Ilf followed her back to Sam. Sam lifted his head and extended his neck. Auris swung herself upon the edge of the undershell beside the neck, crept on hands and knees into the hollow between the upper and lower shells. Ilf climbed in after her. The shell-cave was a familiar place. He'd scuttled in there many times when they'd been caught outdoors in one of the violent electric storms which came down through the mountains from the north or when the ground began to shudder in an earthquake's first rumbling. With the massive curved shell above him and the equally massive flat shell below, the angle formed by the cool, leathery wall which was the side of Sam's neck and the front of his shoulder seemed like the safest place in the world to be on such occasions.

The undershell tilted and swayed beneath Ilf now as the mossback started forward. He squirmed around and looked out through the opening between the shells. They moved out of the grove, headed towards the road at Sam's steady walking pace. Ilf couldn't see the aircar and wondered why Auris didn't want the man in the car to see them. He wriggled uncomfortably. It was a strange, uneasy-making morning in every way.

They crossed the road, went swishing through high grass with Sam's ponderous side-to-side sway like a big ship sailing over dry land, and came to the Queen Grove. Sam moved on into the green-tinted shade under the Queen Trees. The air grew cooler. Presently he turned to the right, and Ilf saw a flash of blue ahead. That was the great thicket of flower bushes, in the center of which was Sam's sleeping pit.

Sam pushed through the thicket, stopped when he reached the open space in the center to let Ilf and Auris climb out of the shell-cave. Sam then lowered his forelegs, one after the other, into the pit, which was lined so solidly with tree roots that almost no earth showed between them, shaped like a mold to fit the lower half of his body, tilted forward, drawing neck and head back under his shell, slid slowly into the pit, straightened out and settled down. The edge of his upper shell was now level with the edge of the pit, and what still could be seen of him looked simply like a big, moss-grown boulder. If nobody came to disturb him, he might stay there unmoving the rest of the year. There were mossbacks in other groves of the farm which had never come out of their sleeping pits or given any indication of being awake since Ilf could remember. They lived an enormous length of time and a nap of half a dozen years apparently meant nothing to them.

Ilf looked questioningly at Auris. She said, "We'll go up to the house and listen to what Uncle Kugus is talking about."

They turned into a path which led from Sam's place to the house. It had been made by six generations of human children, all of whom had used Sam for transportation about the diamondwood farm. He was half again as big as any other mossback around and the only one whose sleeping pit was in the Queen Grove. Everything about the Queen Grove was special, from the trees themselves, which were never cut and twice as thick and almost twice as tall as the trees of other groves, to Sam and his blue flower thicket, the huge stump of the Grandfather Slurp not far away, and the giant greenweb at the other end of the grove. It was quieter here; there were fewer of the other animals. The Queen Grove, from what Riquol Cholm had told Ilf, was the point from which the whole diamondwood forest had started a long time ago.

Auris said, "We'll go around and come in from the back. They don't have to know right away that we're here . . ."

"Mr. Terokaw," said Riquol Cholm, "I'm sorry Kugus Ovin persuaded you and Mr. Bliman to accompany him to Wrake on this business. You've simply wasted your time. Kugus should have known better. I've discussed the situation quite thoroughly with him on other occasions."

"I'm afraid I don't follow you, Mr. Cholm," Mr. Terokaw said stiffly. "I'm making you a businesslike proposition in regard to this farm of diamondwood trees—a proposition which will be very much to your advantage as well as to that of the children whose property the Diamondwood is. Certainly you should at least be willing to listen to my terms!"

Riquol shook his head. It was clear that he was angry with Kugus but attempting to control his anger.

"Your terms, whatever they may be, are not a factor in this," he said. "The maintenance of a diamondwood forest is not entirely a business proposition. Let me explain that to you—as Kugus should have done.

"No doubt you're aware that there are less than forty such forests on the world of Wrake and that attempts to grow the trees elsewhere have been uniformly unsuccessful. That and the unique beauty of diamondwood products, which has never been duplicated by artificial means, is, of course, the reason that such products command a price which compares with that of precious stones and similar items."

Mr. Terokaw regarded Riquol with a bleak blue eye, nodded briefly. "Please continue, Mr. Cholm."

"A diamondwood forest," said Riquol, "is a great deal more than an assemblage of trees.   The trees are a basic factor, but still only a factor, of a closely integrated, balanced natural ecology.   The manner of independence of the plants and animals that make up a diamondwood forest is not clear in all details, but the interdependence is a very pronounced one.   None of the involved species seem able to survive in any other environment.   On the other hand, plants and animals not naturally a part of this ecology will not thrive if brought into it.   They move out or vanish quickly. Human beings appear to be the only exception to that rule.''

"Very interesting," Mr. Terokaw said dryly.

"It is," said Riquol.   "It is a very interesting natural situation and many people, including Mrs. Cholm and myself, feel it should be preserved.   The studied, limited cutting practiced on the diamondwood farms at present acts towards its preservation. That degree of harvesting actually is beneficial to the forests, keeps them moving through an optimum cycle of growth and maturity.   They are flourishing under the hand of man to an extent which was not usually attained in their natural, untouched state.   The people who are at present responsible for them—the farm owners and their associates—have been working for some time to have all diamondwood forests turned into Federation preserves, with the right to harvest them retained by the present owners and their heirs under the same carefully supervised conditions.   When Auris and Ilf come of age and can sign an agreement to that effect, the farms will in fact become Federation preserves.   All other steps to that end have been taken by now.

"That, Mr. Terokaw, is why we're not interested in your business proposition. You'll discover, if you wish to sound them out on it, that the other diamondwood farmers are not interested in it either.   We are all of one mind in that matter.   If we weren't, we would long since have accepted propositions essentially similar to yours.''

There was silence for a moment.   Then Kugus Ovin said pleasantly, "I know you're annoyed with me, Riquol, but I'm thinking of Auris and Ilf in this.   Perhaps in your concern for the preservation of a natural phenomenon, you aren't sufficiently considering their interests.''

Riquol looked at him, said, "When Auris reaches maturity, she'll be an extremely wealthy young woman, even if this farm never sells another cubic foot of diamondwood from this day on.   Ilf would be sufficiently well-to-do to make it unnecessary for him ever to work a stroke in his life—though I doubt very much he would make such a choice.''

Kugus smiled.   "There are degrees even to the state of being extremely wealthy," he remarked.   "What my niece can expect to gain in her lifetime from this careful harvesting you talk about can't begin to compare with what she would get at one stroke through Mr. Terokaw's offer.   The same, of course, holds true of Ilf.''

"Quite right," Mr. Terokaw said heavily.   "I'm generous in my business dealings, Mr. Cholm.   I have a reputation for it.   And I can afford to be generous because I profit well from my investments.   Let me bring another point to your attention.   Interest in diamondwood products throughout the Federation waxes and wanes, as you must be aware. It rises and falls. There are fashions and fads. At present, we are approaching the crest of a new wave of interest in these products. This interest can be properly stimulated and exploited, but in any event we must expect it will have passed its peak in another few months. The next interest peak might develop six years from now, or twelve years from now. Or it might never develop since there are very few natural products which cannot eventually be duplicated and usually surpassed by artificial methods, and there is no good reason to assume that diamondwood will remain an exception indefinitely.

"We should be prepared, therefore, to make the fullest use of this bonanza while it lasts. I am prepared to do just that, Mr. Cholm. A cargo ship full of cutting equipment is at present stationed a few hours' flight from Wrake. This machinery can be landed and in operation here within a day after the contract I am offering you is signed. Within a week, the forest can be leveled. We shall make no use of your factory here, which would be entirely inadequate for my purpose. The diamondwood will be shipped at express speeds to another world where I have adequate processing facilities set up. And we can hit the Federation's main markets with the finished products the following month."

Riquol Cholm said, icily polite now, "And what would be the reason for all that haste, Mr. Terokaw?"

Mr. Terokaw looked surprised. "To insure that we have no competition, Mr. Cholm. What else? When the other diamondwood farmers here discover what has happened, they may be tempted to follow our example. But we'll be so far ahead of them that the diamondwood boom will be almost entirely to our exclusive advantage. We have taken every precaution to see that. Mr. Bliman, Mr. Ovin and I arrived here in the utmost secrecy today. No one so much as suspects that we are on Wrake, much less what our purpose is. I make no mistakes in such matters, Mr. Cholm!"

He broke off and looked around as Meldy Cholm said in a troubled voice, "Come in, children. Sit down over there. We're discussing a matter which concerns you."

"Hello, Auris!" Kugus said heartily. "Hello, Ilf! Remember old Uncle Kugus?"

"Yes," Ilf said. He sat down on the bench by the wall beside Auris, feeling scared.

"Auris," Riquol Cholm said, "did you happen to overhear anything of what was being said before you came into the room?"

Auris nodded. "Yes." She glanced at Mr. Terokaw, looked at Riquol again. "He wants to cut down the forest."

"It's your forest and Ilf's, you know. Do you want him to do it?"

"Mr. Cholm, please!" Mr. Terokaw protested. "We must approach this properly. Kugas, show Mr. Cholm what I'm offering."

Riquol took the document Kugus held out to him, looked over it. After a moment, he gave it back to Kugus. "Auris," he said, "Mr. Terokaw, as he's indicated, is offering you more money than you would ever be able to spend in your life for the right to cut down your share of the forest. Now . . . do you want him to do it?''

"No," Auris said.

Riquol glanced at Ilf, who shook his head. Riquol turned back to Mr. Terokaw.

"Well, Mr. Terokaw," he said, "there's your answer. My wife and I don't want you to do it, and Auris and Ilf don't want you to do it. Now . . ."

"Oh, come now, Riquol!" Kugus said, smiling. "No one can expect either Auris or Ilf to really understand what's involved here. When they come of age—"

"When they come of age," Riquol said, "they'll again have the opportunity to decide what they wish to do." He made a gesture of distaste. "Gentlemen, let's conclude this discussion. Mr. Terokaw, we thank you for your offer, but it's been rejected."

Mr. Terokaw frowned, pursed his lips.

"Well, not so fast, Mr. Cholm," he said. "As I told you, I make no mistakes in business matters. You suggested a few minutes ago that I might contact the other diamondwood farmers on the planet on the subject but predicted that I would have no better luck with them."

"So I did," Riquol agreed. He looked puzzled.

"As a matter of fact," Mr. Terokaw went on, "I already have contacted a number of these people. Not in person, you understand, since I did not want to tip off certain possible competitors that I was interested in diamondwood at present. The offer was rejected, as you indicated it would be. In fact, I learned that the owners of the Wrake diamondwood farms are so involved in legally binding agreements with one another that it would be very difficult for them to accept such an offer even if they wished to do it."

Riquol nodded, smiled briefly. "We realized that the temptation to sell out to commercial interests who would not be willing to act in accordance with our accepted policies could be made very strong," he said. "So we've made it as nearly impossible as we could for any of us to yield to temptation."

"Well," Mr. Terokaw continued, "I am not a man who is easily put off. I ascertained that you and Mrs. Cholm are also bound by such an agreement to the other diamondwood owners of Wrake not to be the first to sell either the farm or its cutting rights to outside interests, or to exceed the established limits of cutting. But you are not the owners of this farm. These two children own it between them."

Riquol frowned. "What difference does that make?" he demanded. "Ilf is our grandson. Auris is related to us and our adopted daughter."

Mr. Terokaw rubbed his chin.

"Mr. Bliman," he said, "please explain to these people what the legal situation is."

Mr. Bliman cleared his throat. He was a tall, thin man with fierce dark eyes, like a bird of prey. "Mr. and Mrs. Cholm," he began, "I work for the Federation Government and am a specialist in adoptive procedures. I will make this short.

Some months ago, Mr. Kugus Ovin filed the necessary papers to adopt his niece, Auris Luteel, citizen of Wrake. I conducted the investigation which is standard in such cases and can assure you that no official record exists that you have at any time gone through the steps of adopting Auris.''

"*What?*" Riquol came half to his feet. Then he froze in position for a moment, settled slowly back in his chair. "What is this? Just what kind of trick are you trying to play?" he said. His face had gone white.

Ilf had lost sight of Mr. Terokaw for a few seconds, because Uncle Kugus had suddenly moved over in front of the bench on which he and Auris were sitting. But now he saw him again and he had a jolt of fright. There was a large blue and silver gun in Mr. Terokaw's hand, and the muzzle of it was pointed very steadily at Riquol Cholm.

"Mr. Cholm," Mr. Terokaw said, "before Mr. Bliman concludes his explanation, allow me to caution you! I do not wish to kill you. This gun, in fact, is not designed to kill. But if I pull the trigger, you will be in excruciating pain for some minutes. You are an elderly man and it is possible that you would not survive the experience. This would not inconvenience us very seriously. Therefore, stay seated and give up any thoughts of summoning help . . . Kugus, watch the children. Mr. Bliman, let me speak to Mr. Het before you resume."

He put his left hand up to his face, and Ilf saw he was wearing a wrist-talker. "Het," Mr. Terokaw said to the talker without taking his eyes off Riquol Cholm, "you are aware, I believe, that the children are with us in the house?"

The wrist-talker made murmuring sounds for a few seconds, then stopped.

"Yes," Mr. Terokaw said. "There should be no problem about it. But let me know if you see somebody approaching the area . . ." He put his hand back down on the table. "Mr. Bliman, please continue."

Mr. Bliman cleared his throat again.

"Mr. Kugus Ovin," he said, "is now officially recorded as the parent by adoption of his niece, Auris Luteel. Since Auris has not yet reached the age where her formal consent to this action would be required, the matter is settled."

"Meaning," Mr. Terokaw added, "that Kugus can act for Auris in such affairs as selling the cutting rights on this tree farm. Mr. Cholm, if you are thinking of taking legal action against us, forget it. You may have had certain papers purporting to show that the girl was your adopted child filed away in the deposit vault of a bank. If so, those papers have been destroyed. With enough money, many things become possible. Neither you nor Mrs. Cholm nor the two children will do or say anything that might cause trouble to me. Since you have made no rash moves, Mr. Bliman will now use an instrument to put you and Mrs. Cholm painlessly to sleep for the few hours required to get you off this planet. Later, if you should be questioned in connection with this situation, you will say about it only what certain psychological experts will have impressed on you to say, and within a few months, nobody will be taking any further interest whatever in what is happening here today.

"Please do not think that I am a cruel man. I am not. I merely take what steps are required to carry out my purpose. Mr. Bliman, please proceed!"

Ilf felt a quiver of terror. Uncle Kugus was holding his wrist with one hand and Auris' wrist with the other, smiling reassuringly down at them. Ilf darted a glance over to Auris' face. She looked as white as his grandparents but she was making no attempt to squirm away from Kugus, so Ilf stayed quiet, too. Mr. Bliman stood up, looking more like a fierce bird of prey than ever, and stalked over to Riquol Cholm, holding something in his hand that looked unpleasantly like another gun. Ilf shut his eyes. There was a moment of silence, then Mr. Terokaw said, "Catch him before he falls out of the chair. Mrs. Cholm, if you will just settle back comfortably . . ."

There was another moment of silence. Then, from beside him, Ilf heard Auris speak.

It wasn't regular speech but a quick burst of thin, rattling gabble, like human speech speeded up twenty times or so. It ended almost immediately.

"What's that? What's that?" Mr. Terokaw said, surprised.

Ilf's eyes flew open as something came in through the window with a whistling shriek. The two humbugs were in the room, brown blurs flicking here and there, screeching like demons. Mr. Terokaw exclaimed something in a loud voice and jumped up from the chair, his gun swinging this way and that. Something scuttled up Mr. Bliman's back like a big spider, and he yelled and spun away from Meldy Cholm lying slumped back in her chair. Something ran up Uncle Kugus' back. He yelled, letting go of Ilf and Auris, and pulled out a gun of his own. "Wide aperture!" roared Mr. Terokaw, whose gun was making loud, thumping noises. A brown shadow swirled suddenly about his knees. Uncle Kugus cursed, took aim at the shadow and fired.

"Stop that, you fool!" Mr. Terokaw shouted. "You nearly hit me."

"Come," whispered Auris, grabbing Ilf's arm. They sprang up from the bench and darted out the door behind Uncle Kugus' broad back.

"Het!" Mr. Terokaw's voice came bellowing down the hall behind them. "Up in the air and look out for those children! They're trying to get away. If you see them start to cross the road, knock 'em out. Kugus—after them! They may try to hide in the house."

Then he yowled angrily, and his gun began making the thumping noises again. The humbugs were too small to harm people, but their sharp little teeth could hurt and they seemed to be using them now.

"In here," Auris whispered, opening a door. Ilf ducked into the room with her, and she closed the door softly behind them. Ilf looked at her, his heart pounding wildly.

Auris nodded at the barred window. "Through there! Run and hide in the grove. I'll be right behind you . . ."

"Auris! Ilf!" Uncle Kugus called in the hall. "Wait—don't be afraid. Where are you?" His voice still seemed to be smiling. Ilf heard his footsteps hurrying along the hall as he squirmed quickly sideways between two of the thick wooden bars over the window, dropped to the ground. He turned, darted off towards the nearest bushes. He heard Auris gabble something to the humbugs again, high and shrill, looked back as he reached the bushes and saw her already outside, running towards the shrubbery on his right.   There was a shout from the window.   Uncle Kugus was peering out from behind the bars, pointing a gun at Auris.   He fired. Auris swerved to the side, was gone among the shrubs.   Ilf didn't think she had been hit.

"They're outside!" Uncle Kugus yelled.   He was too big to get through the bars himself.

Mr. Terokaw and Mr. Bliman were also shouting within the house.   Uncle Kugus turned around, disappeared from the window.

"Auris!" Ilf called, his voice shaking with fright.

"Run and hide, Ilf!"   Auris seemed to be on the far side of the shrubbery, deeper in the Queen Grove.

Ilf hesitated, started running along the path that led to Sam's sleeping pit, glancing up at the open patches of sky among the treetops.   He didn't see the aircar with the man Het in it.   Het would be circling around the Queen Grove now, waiting for the other men to chase them into sight so he could knock them out with something.   But they could hide inside Sam's shell and Sam would get them across the road.   "Auris, where are you?" Ilf cried.

Her voice came low and clear from behind him.   "Run and hide, Ilf!"

Ilf looked back.   Auris wasn't there but the two humbugs were loping up the path a dozen feet away.   They darted past Ilf without stopping, disappeared around the turn ahead.   He could hear the three men yelling for him and Auris to come back.   They were outside, looking around for them now, and they seemed to be coming closer.

Ilf ran on, reached Sam's sleeping place.   Sam lay there unmoving, like a great mossy boulder filling the pit.   Ilf picked up a stone and pounded on the front part of the shell.

"Wake up!" he said desperately.   "Sam, wake up!"

Sam didn't stir.   And the men were getting closer.   Ilf looked this way and that, trying to decide what to do.

"Don't let them see you," Auris called suddenly.

"That was the girl over there," Mr. Terokaw's voice shouted.   "Go after her, Bliman!"

"Auris, watch out!" Ilf screamed, terrified.

"Aha!   And here's the boy, Kugus.   This way!   Het," Mr. Terokaw yelled triumphantly, "come down and help us catch them!   We've got them spotted . . ."

Ilf dropped to hands and knees, crawled away quickly under the branches of the blue flower thicket and waited, crouched low.   He heard Mr. Terokaw crashing through the bushes towards him and Mr. Bliman braying, "Hurry up, Het!   Hurry up!"   Then he heard something else.   It was the sound the giant greenweb some-times made to trick a flock of silverbells into fluttering straight towards it, a deep drone which suddenly seemed to be pouring down from the trees and rising up from the ground.

Ilf shook his head dizzily.   The drone faded, grew up again.   For a moment, he thought he heard his own voice call "Auris, where are you?" from the other side of the blue flower thicket.   Mr. Terokaw veered off in that direction, yelling something to Mr. Bliman and Kugus.   Ilf backed farther away through the thicket, came out on the other side, climbed to his feet and turned.

He stopped.   For a stretch of twenty feet ahead of him, the forest floor was moving, shifting and churning with a slow, circular motion, turning lumps of deep brown mold over and over.

Mr. Terokaw came panting into Sam's sleeping place, redfaced, glaring about, the blue and silver gun in his hand.   He shook his head to clear the resonance of the humming air from his brain.   He saw a huge, moss-covered boulder tilted at a slant away from him but no sign of Ilf.

Then something shook the branches of the thicket behind the boulder.   "Auris!" Ilf's frightened voice called.

Mr. Terokaw ran around the boulder, leveling the gun.   The droning in the air suddenly swelled to a roar.   Two big gray, three-fingered hands came out from the boulder on either side of Mr. Terokaw and picked him up.

"Awk!" he gasped, then dropped the gun as the hands folded him, once, twice, and lifted him towards Sam's descending head.   Sam opened his large mouth, closed it, swallowed.   His neck and head drew back under his shell and he settled slowly into the sleeping pit again.

The greenweb's roar ebbed and rose continuously now, like a thousand harps being struck together in a bewildering, quickening beat.   Human voices danced and swirled through the din, crying, wailing, screeching.   Ilf stood at the edge of the twenty-foot circle of churning earth outside the blue flower thicket, half stunned by it all.   He heard Mr. Terokaw bellow to Mr. Bliman to go after Auris, and Mr. Bliman squalling to Het to hurry.   He heard his own voice nearby call Auris frantically and then Mr. Terokaw's triumphant yell: "This way!   Here's the boy, Kugus!"

Uncle Kugus bounded out of some bushes thirty feet away, eyes staring, mouth stretched in a wide grin.   He saw Ilf, shouted excitedly and ran towards him.   Ilf watched, suddenly unable to move.   Uncle Kugus took four long steps out over the shifting loam between them, sank ankle-deep, knee-deep.   Then the brown earth leaped in cascades about him, and he went sliding straight down into it as if it were water, still grinning, and disappeared.   In the distance, Mr. Terokaw roared, "This way!" and Mr. Bliman yelled to Het to hurry up.   A loud, slapping sound came from the direction of the stump of the Grandfather Slurp.   It was followed by a great commotion in the bushes around there; but that only lasted a moment. Then, a few seconds later, the greenweb's drone rose and thinned to the wild shriek it made when it had caught something big and faded slowly away . . .

Ilf came walking shakily through the opening in the thickets to Sam's sleeping place.   His head still seemed to hum inside with the greenweb's drone but the Queen Grove was quiet again; no voices called anywhere.   Sam was settled into his pit.   Ilf saw something gleam on the ground near the front end of the pit.   He went over and looked at it, then at the big, moss-grown dome of Sam's shell.

"Oh, Sam," he whispered, "I'm not sure we should have done it . . . ."

Sam didn't stir. Ilf picked up Mr. Terokaw's blue and silver gun gingerly by the barrel and went off with it to look for Auris. He found her at the edge of the grove, watching Het's aircar on the other side of the road. The aircar was turned on its side and about a third of it was sunk in the ground. At work around and below it was the biggest member of the clean-up squad Ilf had ever seen in action.

They went up to the side of the road together and looked on while the aircar continued to shudder and turn and sink deeper into the earth. Ilf suddenly remembered the gun he was holding and threw it over on the ground next to the aircar. It was swallowed up instantly there. Tumbleweeds came rolling up to join them and clustered around the edge of the circle, waiting. With a final jerk, the aircar disappeared. The disturbed section of earth began to smooth over. The tumbleweeds moved out into it.

There was a soft whistling in the air, and from a Queen Tree at the edge of the grove a hundred and fifty feet away, a diamondwood seedling came lancing down, struck at a slant into the center of the circle where the aircar had vanished, stood trembling a moment, then straightened up. The tumbleweeds nearest it moved respectfully aside to give it room. The seedling shuddered and unfolded its first five-fingered cluster of silver-green leaves. Then it stood still.

Ilf looked over at Auris. "Auris," he said, "should we have done it?"

Auris was silent a moment.

"Nobody did anything," she said then. "They've just gone away again." She took Ilf's hand. "Let's go back to the house and wait for Riquol and Meldy to wake up."

The organism that was the diamondwood forest grew quiet again. The quiet spread back to its central mind unit in the Queen Grove, and the unit began to relax towards somnolence. A crisis had been passed—perhaps the last of the many it had foreseen when human beings first arrived on the world of Wrake.

The only defense against Man was Man. Understanding that, it had laid its plans. On a world now owned by Man, it adopted Man, brought him into its ecology, and its ecology into a new and again successful balance.

This had been a final flurry. A dangerous attack by dangerous humans. But the period of danger was nearly over, would soon be for good a thing of the past.

It had planned well, the central mind unit told itself drowsily. But now, since there was no further need to think today, it would stop thinking . . .

Sam the mossback fell gratefully asleep.

LEE CORREY

The Easy Way Out

They came out of space armed and ready.

The alien ship skittered into the Earth's atmosphere in an easterly direction and landed surreptitiously about midnight in the Rocky Mountains of North America. The Master had chosen the approach trajectory and landing area after a long survey in far orbit.

"*Whew!*" Ulmnarrgh breathed with relief as the ship's sensors reported no great hubbub created by the silent landing in the meadow among the high peaks. "I don't think we were detected. There were no probing emissions in the electromagnetic spectrum and no phasing of the gravitoinertial field."

"Keep your guard detectors up," the Master directed. "We'll wait for daylight. In the meantime, run out the screens and keep all defenses on the alert."

Harmarrght fidgeted. "By the Great Overlord!" he snapped under his breath to his mentor, the exobiologist Norvallk. "The Old Boy acts as though he's scared to death."

Turning an eye toward the youngster, Norvallk gently replied, "Don't cover up your nervousness with bravado. All of us remember how we felt on our first landing as a cadet. A certain amount of caution is always indicated, particularly in the face of the fact that the previous probe ship didn't come back from this world."

"The only logical reason for that is a technical malfunction," the youngster shot back.

The exobiologist shook his head sadly. "Logical answers don't always hold true in exploration. This planet's inhabited by communicating beings. If you're going to insist on using logic, calculate the conclusion you get when you take into account the loss of a ship on a planet whose inhabitants have an unknown level of technology. Mukch on that for a while!"

Harmarrght didn't. He had an immediate answer. "I've studied the history of our conquests for the Great Overlord, and nowhere on a thousand worlds has our high technology been equalled. *That,* sir, is an established fact! So now we crawl in here with pseudopods rolled up like a frightened orh. Why should we be so cautious when our technology makes conquest so simple?"

"You're here to learn why," Norvallk told him. "So shut up and observe. You've been trained; now you're about to be educated . . ." These young cubs just out of the Institute were always impetuous, he reminded himself.   Such attitudes made excellent warriors for the Great Overlord, but when were the professional institutes going to learn to temper their indoctrination when training explorers?

The Master called for a confrontation in the control bay.   This was a welcome relief to Norvallk who, as the chief exobiologist aboard, had nothing to do but sit and shiver until he could get out and have a look at things.

"Our position here, while secure at the moment, may be perilous," the Master pointed out to his crew.   "I want to impress again on you the complete nature of the situation.   You have all seen the reconnaissance images from the first orbiting probes that revealed the unmistakable sign of intelligent life: deliberate conversion of natural resources into more orderly features such as artificial waterways and geometrical groupings of artificial dwellings.

"It's unusual to find a planet inhabited by intelligent life.   But this planet appears to be unique in that it seems to support more than one type of intelligent life.

"Communication is by means of electromagnetic radiation.   There is no way of knowing at this time whether this is a naturally evolved trait, such as we found on Vagarragh Four, or the technically developed artificial extension of pressure wave communication such as we have.   Rastharrh, tell us what you have discovered."

The information theory expert was somewhat hesitant.   "I don't quite know what to make of it.   There's more than one coding group involved.   I've even run onto a highly unusual code group consisting completely of periodic transmissions of a carrier, and this may be highly indicative of a life form here that communicates by electromagnetic means.   It's difficult to conceive of any planetwide intelligent life form that uses more than one type of communication symbol code.   Here, there are many.   It leads me to believe that this planet may have evolved several high life forms, each communicating differently."

"Norvallk, is this possible?" the Master asked.

Norvallk shrugged.   "Anything is possible when dealing with intelligent, communicating beings.   The physical arrangement of the planet's land areas suggests that Rastharrh's hypothesis may be correct.   I wouldn't discount it.   We have got to have a first-hand look."

"And that's what we're going to get."   The Master gave his orders.

There was barely enough time to accomplish anything before the sun rose.   The planet had a very short rotational period.

It was not a bad-looking world, Norvallk decided as he surveyed the landing site.   He pointed out several features to Harmarrght.   "Frozen water over there on those high peaks.   And note the abundant inverted life forms growing stationary on the hills.   If they are at all like the ones on Chinarrghk, they have their brains in the ground and their energy receptors above ground.   And probably immobile as well . . ."

"No problem to overcome them if they can't move," Harmarrght stated flatly.

"That depends upon their biological operation and natural defenses, youngster. They could exude poisonous gases when disturbed, for example."

"We can handle that."

"Once we know about it."

"There is no obvious reason why we can't take over this planet for the Great Overlord."

"There may be several reasons why we can't. It all depends on the native life forms, particularly with regard to their Intelligence Index, Adaptability Index, and, most important, Ferocity Index."

"Oh, come now! If they're incapable of defending themselves against our advanced technology, they don't stand a chance!"

Norvallk did not answer his protégé. Lecturing no longer was effective.

It was nearly midday by the time the ground party was organized to leave the ship. Norvallk led it, supported by Rastharrh, the morphologist Grahhgh, three well-trained and experienced recording specialists, the three warrior techs. The whole party was armed with both energy weapons and projectile hurlers. Harmarrght accompanied Norvallk as his direct assistant.

The ten aliens proceeded down the slope from the meadow into the valley. There was a stream on the valley floor and a chance of encountering advanced life forms.

"There are life forms everywhere!" Harmarrght remarked.

"And they take many shapes, but they don't bother us. We'll have to set automatic traps for those flying forms; they're much too fast," Norvallk observed.

They did not reach the stream until well after sunset, but the light shed by the world's natural satellite permitted the party to find its way and continue to record some data.

At sunrise, they found the grizzly bear.

"Let's take it back to the ship!" was Harmarrght's first excited comment.

"Not so fast!" Norvallk cautioned. "We watch first. Quietly. It's feeding. Look how it reaches down into the water and knocks those water-dwellers out onto the bank."

"By the Great Overlord! It's *fast!*"

"Let's see if the Master can find some counterpart from a known world." Norvallk instructed the date recorders to beam their images back to the ship. In a quick communication with the Master, Norvallk set up the search through the memory banks of the ship's computer. As he was waiting for the answer, he gave a little instruction to Harmarrght, "Notice the covering of organic filaments that may either be manipulators, sensors, or thermal insulation. And the grouping of sensory transducers around the food intake orifice."

"It carries no weapons," Harmarrght pointed out.

"It may not need them. But note the plurality of sharp artifacts on the end of each appendage. Are you willing to state unequivocally that they are not artificial?"

A message came from the ship. Zero readout from the memory bank. Plus the Master's direct order, "Bring the life form in for study, preferably functioning."

With obvious relish, Harmarrght hefted his energy projector and started forward. Norvallk tried to stop him, but it was too late.

Very few native life forms will bother a feeding grizzly bear. *Ursus horribilis* is not only strong, but easily provoked.   But Harmarrght didn't know this.   He found out quickly.

He fired an energy bolt at what should have been an area of vital control in the bear's midsection with the intent to paralyze the beast.   The shot singed white-tipped hair and burned a hole through the skin.   It hurt the bear and drew its attention to the young alien.

"Cover him!" Norvallk yelled to his party.   One of the warrior techs burst forward to get between Harmarrght and the bear.

The bear stopped fishing and let out a bellowing roar.   This panicked the warrior tech who fired a projectile toward the bear's head.   Another of the warrior techs got into position.   But the bear moved . . . fast.

The grizzly brought its huge forepaw down on the closest warrior alien.   Armor and all, the warrior splattered.

The next swipe of the huge paw demolished Grahhgh, who had the misfortune to get within range.   While trying to get to the second warrior, the bear stepped on Rastharrh, putting part of him out of commission.   The bear rose on its hind legs to its full height of eight feet and started to swing again, aiming toward Harmarrght, but the second warrior fired an explosive bolt that caught the grizzly in the roof of the mouth and congealed its brain.

It took a little time for Norvallk to get things straightened out again.   As the four transports came from the ship to pick up the dead and injured, he whirled on Harmarrght, managed to suppress his anger, and said sarcastically, "So.   It had no weapons, eh?   Evidence of a low technology, huh?   I thought that you had studied bio-engineering . . ."

The young cadet could only remark, "Its Ferocity Index must be unreasonably high . . ."

Three more transports had to be sent from the ship to lift the grizzly's carcass. The party then resumed its course down the stream, minus three of its members. "Standing orders," Norvallk told them.   "We take no further action against indigenous life forms except when attacked.   We'll merely observe and record data. It seems that most of the other life forms have a very low Ferocity Index, but I am not going to take the chance of losing the rest of this party."

Harmarrght said nothing; he was now reasonably subdued.

Two sunrises later, the party discovered another silvertip grizzly.   The aliens didn't repeat their first mistake; they stood well back and watched this bear carefully.

It was leisurely dining on the remains of a freshly-killed white-tail deer at the edge of a small clearing alongside the stream.   Apparently wanting a bit of variety in its diet, the bear had managed to find an easy mark in an unsuspecting young deer.

"I am beginning to suspect that the Ferocity Index of this life form is a little bit too high for comfort," Norvallk observed.

"But still nothing that we can't overcome with our existing weapons," Harmarrght added.

"There are many other things yet to consider," his mentor told him. "Observe and remember."

While they were watching the second grizzly dine, a report came in from the ship. "The dead beast has been given a preliminary examination. Its colloidal control network is very complex and contains a highly organized colloidal computer near its primary sensors. It has the capability of a very high Intelligence Index," the Master told them.

Norvallk hastily briefed the Master on their current find and added, "We see no signs of artifacts associated with the beast unless those sharp instruments on its appendages are tools."

"They aren't. They are natural."

"In that event, it isn't using tools. I don't know whether or not it's communicating right now. Too bad Rastharrh was injured; we could use him. A new life form has just arrived! It's smaller but covered with the same sort of organic filaments. Same configuration. It's going right up to the larger beast. We may be witnessing our first example of symbiosis on this world where the large beast does the hunting and shares the meal with a smaller communicating form."

The bear looked up from its meal and recognized the small bearlike form with its broad ribbon of light brown fur down each side. But the bear was still young and still hungry; it decided to put up a defense of its meal. It had yet to learn that there are few animals of any size willing to tangle with *Gulo luscus,* the wolverine.

The wolverine simply attacked the bear as though it did not know the meaning of fear. Its flashing teeth and slashing claws were smaller and less strong than the bear's, but sheer meanness was on its side. It ripped in to kill, giving no quarter. After the first encounter in which the bear's huge paw missed in a roundhouse swing, the battle was very short and very one-sided.

The grizzly took the easy way out. It retreated, ambling off into the pine forest as rapidly as it could move.

Norvallk was shaken, but Harmarrght was now petrified. "Let me kill it!" the youngster urged.

"No. You may not be able to," Norvallk stayed him.

"It will be easy!" He hefted his energy projector and patted it.

"We tried that once. Three of us for one of them. And the Ferocity Index on this little animal is going to be very difficult to compute. It's high. Let's see what the Master's computer says." Norvallk fed all of the available data back to the ship.

The computer chewed up the available data regarding size, probable body mass, and other related factors of the two different animals, bear and wolverine; it then compared this with data from other worlds, considered the possibility of reducing the high Ferocity Index of the bear, found that it could not logically do so, discovered that it could not handle the Ferocity Index of the wolverine, and ended up in a stoppage. The wolverine's Ferocity Index was off-scale.

In the meantime, Norvallk and his group kept observing and reporting.   "It's cleaning up what's left of the carcass, and it acts as though it hasn't eaten for days. It's simply glutting itself."

"Its Ferocity Index may diminish when its hunger drive is satiated," Harmarrght ventured to predict.

"In any case, it can't finish that carcass, and we'll be able to take it back to the ship for analysis."

"Ugh! I wonder," Harmarrght remarked, reeling from the odor that now wafted in their direction.

"It's fouling the remains of the carcass with musk!" Norvallk observed in amazement and almost gagged.

The wolverine, being unable to finish, had simply protected what was left so he could return to complete the meal at a later date.   It then sat up on its haunches, shaded its eyes with a forepaw, and looked around.

The alien party worked very hard at remaining unseen and unheard, although most of them were gasping as a result of the horrible smell.

"Did you say something about technology earlier?" Norvallk managed to ask his student between stifled coughs.

The wolverine found its direction again and ambled off.

"Do we follow?" Harmarrght asked.   "Or do we stay here and suffocate?"

"Let's go!   Keep it in sight, but *don't* let it detect you," Norvallk ordered his party.   He had no desire to tangle with this little beast.   But he had to find out more about it.

As they went along, Norvallk asked Harmarrght, "Do you still think that this world would be easy to conquer?"

"Well . . . Nothing so far that our weapons couldn't cope with.   It might be expensive and it might take time, but we could do it . . . if what we've seen is any indication.   They're tough, but we're just as tough and just as well-armed."

"Wouldn't you say that this being has a reasonably high Ferocity Index?"

"Yes," Harmarrght admitted.

"Which means we would have to kill them all or subdue them.   From the looks of them, we'd probably have to kill them.   But suppose we don't get them all. Would you like to live here knowing that one of those things was on the loose?"

"If I'm armed and expecting it, why not?"

"What did you learn at the Institute?"   Norvallk exploded.   "Didn't they teach you anything about the economics of conquest and exploitation?   Didn't they teach you how to evaluate the Indices?"

"Well, yes, but . . ."

"Did you ever stop to consider the difficulties of conquering a world whose inhabitants have low Intelligence Index, low Adaptability Index, low Technical Index, but high Ferocity Index?   Under those circumstances, a takeover becomes a disaster if the natives fight to the death with no quarter given!   *Successful* colonization requires that the native life not only be overcome, but also be re-trained and made suitable to work under the direction of the colonizers.   You can't spend all your time fighting.   Now that you're on a new planet for the first time, maybe you'll realize that a planet is a big chunk of real estate.   You can't wipe out every dangerous animal on it, but if they're too dangerous you *must* dispatch them lest they continue to breed and remain a constant threat.   Under a situation like that, you have to withdraw from the planet and write it off.''

"Retreat?   But we've never had to do that!   We've *never* written off a world!'' Harmarrght objected.

"We'd have written off a dozen of them if we'd known then what we know now.   Those worlds were very expensive acquisitions,'' Norvallk reminded him as they moved along, keeping the wolverine in sight but not permitting their conversation to betray their presence.   "You were filled with propaganda about the glorious exploits of those who did the dirty work.   It looks different when you've been on the scene.   Or it should.   What is your evaluation of this world thus far? Apply what you've been taught.   You can even use logic if you want.''

"Thus far, we've discovered two life forms with high Ferocity Index,'' Harmarrght said by way of review and lead-in.   "But they evidenced no obvious Communications Index, a moderate Intelligence Index, and a very low Technology Index . . .''

"I'm not willing to concede that point yet,'' Norvallk put in.   "But go on.''

"*Ergo,* the dominant species might not have a high Ferocity Index being dependent upon symbiosis with other species to acquire this factor.   I make the presumption that Ferocity Index would logically have to be lower in more intelligent, communicating beings than . . .''

"An assumption without adequate evidence,'' Norvallk pointed out.

"Well, on the other hand, the two forms already discovered might not be the dominant species on the planet.   They might simply co-exist with the dominant form.''

"Suppose the dominant form has a higher Ferocity Index,'' Norvallk said.

"Oh, quite unlikely!   We've *never* encountered anything before with the fantastic Ferocity Index that would be required!''

"Harmarrght, it's a big universe.''

"Yes, but very few planets exist with the physical characteristics of this one. It seems to me that the Overlord might be unhappy with a recommendation to abandon it now that . . .''

"Which means that we must gather as much data as we can.''   Norvallk indicated the wolverine.   "Watch!   The animal is hunting something new.''

By climbing a tree, the wolverine finished off a squirrel.   Very shortly thereafter, a porcupine managed to get out of its way.   The wolverine then proceeded to catch a rabbit and a chipmunk, but it befouled them and cached them instead of eating them.

"Well, we seem to have stumbled on the beast that probably has the highest Ferocity Index in this neighborhood,'' Norvallk commented, then stopped in his tracks as the wolverine emerged into a clearing.

"A dwelling!''   Harmarrght exclaimed.   "If it belongs to this beast, it indicates a much higher Intelligence Index than I expected for it.   Look: smoke comes from a vent on the roof, indicating a mastery of the chemical combustion process which . . .''

''Don't assume that it belongs to the animal,'' Norvallk cut in and pointed out the tools scattered here and there around the cabin and the plot of ground that was a garden.   ''It couldn't possibly handle tools of that size.   It's demonstrably a hunter, and I wouldn't expect it to be a farmer, too.''   He snapped orders to his exploring party.   Quietly, the various specialists ranged themselves in hiding around the clearing so that their recorders had a view of the cabin from several sides.   The warriors were given strict orders not to use their weapons except in defense of the party.

The wolverine prowled around the cabin for some time.   Norvallk waited patiently, but Harmarrght fidgeted nervously.   ''Let me go up and see what's inside that dwelling,'' he finally suggested.

''Not while I'm in charge of the party,'' Norvallk said.   ''This is an exploration crew, not a military group.   I equate such bravery to stupidity at this point.   I do not want to have to return your remains to the ship . . . providing that the animal left any remains or that we could get to you afterwards.''

''But one bolt from this projector . . .''

''How many others might be inside that dwelling?''   Norvallk posed the rhetorical question to his student.

There was a movement behind one of the windows.   Then, as Norvallk came up on the alert, two human children dashed out of the cabin with yells of delight.

With great consternation, Norvallk watched these two new life forms run fearlessly up to the wolverine.

''Glutton! You're back!'' one of them cried.

They dropped to the ground in front of the little animal and began to stroke its coat.   The wolverine responded playfully, for it had known these children all its life.   They had found it as a cub, half-frozen and starved, somehow separated from its mother.   Although these children had raised it as a pet, it often reverted to feral state and disappeared into the hills for days.   But it always came back.   Hunting was difficult and dangerous; it was far easier to be fed on schedule by the children.   And the humans were capable of giving it something very pleasurable and desirable: love.

Glutton, the wolverine, rolled on its back and permitted great indignities to be taken.   One of the children ran into the house and returned with some meat in a dish—and was disappointed when the wolverine refused it.   But Glutton did not befoul this meal as it had done with others it could not eat.

The young bipeds talked to it, played with it, and fondled it for some time.   The aliens recorded every movement and sound.   Norvallk was very busy trying to make things add up in his mind; he was quite unhappy with the conclusions he was reaching.   Harmarrght merely watched in great confusion; he was having great difficulty rationalizing what his own logic told him with what he had been taught.

A larger biped appeared in the cabin door.   ''Boys!   Lunch time!   Come in now!''

They started to go, but the wolverine wanted more play and love.   It growled and tried to nip at one boy's leg.

The human child turned around and cuffed the wolverine smartly, scolding it as he did so.

The wolverine shook its fur and followed the boys into the cabin.

Norvallk wasted no time regrouping his party and getting them back to the ship.

"You've done an excellent job under most hazardous conditions," the Master told Norvallk and the rest of the party. "Your data confirms the conclusion we've already reached here. Ulmnarrgh has received radiations from life forms that are orbiting this world as well as in transit to nearby planets. The varied inhabitants of this world are already out in space and expanding with explosive speed. I will be recommending rather drastic measures to the Overlord. In the meantime, we raise ship at once and try to get out of here without being destroyed."

As the ship boosted away under maximum drive, Norvallk sat reviewing the data with his student. "It should be perfectly obvious to you at this point that the standard method of evaluating Ferocity Index and integrating the various Indices are useless for this planet. Tell me, have you ever run an exercise with data like this?"

"Well . . . no," Harmarrght admitted. "But this is a very slim amount of data taken in restricted locality. I will admit that the planet is dangerous . . ."

"It's the most dangerous planet I know of."

"Well . . . yes. Even our most difficult conquests involved life forms with Ferocity Indices that we could at least measure. But the drastic measures the Master spoke of might certainly . . ."

"Forgive me for anticipating you," Norvallk broke in, "but those drastic recommendations are likely to involve re-routing of ship lanes away from this vicinity and perhaps even abandonment of nearby outposts."

"But we could certainly overcome . . ."

"Again, my apologies. Do you think we could fight the several life forms we saw on that planet without expending millions of warriors and a great deal of equipment? Remember the universal law of living organisms: the Law of Least Effort. This is a big galaxy, and there are more comfortable and less expensive parts of it in which to operate."

"I guess you're right," Harmarrght admitted. "There are easier things to do."

Back on the planet, the wolverine, although it didn't consciously know the Law of Least Effort, responded to it, too. It curled up on the rug in front of the fireplace and snoozed while beings with a higher Ferocity Index quietly ate their lunch around a table.

KEITH LAUMER

The Last Command

I come to awareness, sensing a residual oscillation traversing my hull from an arbitrarily designated heading of 035. From the damping rate I compute that the shock was of intensity 8.7, emanating from a source within the limits 72 meters/ 46 meters. I activate my primary screens, trigger a return salvo. There is no response. I engage reserve energy cells, bring my secondary battery to bear— futilely. It is apparent that I have been ranged by the Enemy and severely damaged.

My positional sensors indicate that I am resting at an angle of 13 degrees 14 seconds, deflected from a base line at 21 points from median. I attempt to right myself, but encounter massive resistance. I activate my forward scanners, shunt power to my IR microstrobes. Not a flicker illuminates my surroundings. I am encased in utter blackness.

Now a secondary shock wave approaches, rocks me with an intensity of 8.2. It is apparent that I must withdraw from my position—but my drive trains remain inert under full thrust. I shift to base emergency power, try again. Pressure mounts; I sense my awareness fading under the intolerable strain; then, abruptly, resistance falls off and I am in motion.

It is not the swift maneuvering of full drive, however, I inch forward, as if restrained by massive barriers. Again I attempt to penetrate the surrounding darkness, and this time perceive great irregular outlines shot through with fracture planes. I probe cautiously, then more vigorously, encountering incredible densities.

I channel all available power to a single ranging pulse, direct it upward. The indication is so at variance with all experience that I repeat the test at a new angle. Now I must accept the fact: I am buried under 207.6 meters of solid rock!

I direct my attention to an effort to orient myself to my uniquely desperate situation. I run through an action-status check list of thirty thousand items, feel dismay at the extent of power loss. My main cells are almost completely drained, my reserve units at no more than .4 charge. Thus my sluggishness is explained. I review the tactical situation, recall the triumphant announcement from my commander that the Enemy forces are annihilated, that all resistance has ceased. In memory, I review the formal procession; in company with my comrades of the Dinochrome Brigade, many of us deeply scarred by Enemy action, we parade before the Grand Commandant, then assemble on the depot ramp. At command,

515

we bring our music storage cells into phase and display our Battle Anthem.   The nearby star radiates over a full spectrum, unfiltered by atmospheric haze.   It is a moment of glorious triumph.   Then the final command is given—

The rest is darkness.   But it is apparent that the victory celebration was premature.   The Enemy has counterattacked with a force that has come near to immobilizing me.   The realization is shocking, but the .1 second of leisurely introspection has clarified my position.   At once, I broadcast a call on Brigade Action wavelength:

"Unit LNE to Command, requesting permission to file VSR."

I wait, sense no response, call again, using full power.   I sweep the enclosing volume of rock with an emergency alert warning.   I tune to the all-units band, await the replies of my comrades of the Brigade.   None answers.   Now I must face the reality: I alone have survived the assault.

I channel my remaining power to my drive and detect a channel of reduced density.   I press for it and the broken rock around me yields reluctantly.   Slowly, I move forward and upward.   My pain circuitry shocks my awareness center with emergency signals; I am doing irreparable damage to my overloaded neural systems, but my duty is clear: I must seek and engage the Enemy.

Emerging from behind the blast barrier, Chief Engineer Pete Reynolds of the New Devonshire Port Authority pulled off his rock mask and spat grit from his mouth.

"That's the last one; we've bottomed out at just over two hundred yards.   Must have hit a hard stratum down there."

"It's almost sundown," the paunchy man beside him said shortly.   "You're a day and a half behind schedule."

"We'll start backfilling now, Mr. Mayor.   I'll have pilings poured by oh-nine hundred tomorrow, and with any luck the first section of pad will be in place in time for the rally."

"I'm . . ."   The mayor broke off, looked startled.   "I thought you told me that was the last charge to be fired . . ."

Reynolds frowned.   A small but distinct tremor had shaken the ground underfoot. A few feet away, a small pebble balanced atop another toppled and fell with a faint clatter.

"Probably a big rock fragment falling," he said.   At that moment, a second vibration shook the earth, stronger this time.   Reynolds heard a rumble and a distant impact as rock fell from the side of the newly blasted excavation.   He whirled to the control shed as the door swung back and Second Engineer Mayfield appeared.

"Take a look at this, Pete!"   Reynolds went across to the hut, stepped inside. Mayfield was bending over the profiling table.

"What do you make of it?" he pointed.   Superimposed on the heavy red contour representing the detonation of the shaped charge of the tremor that completed the drilling of the final pile core were two other traces, weak but distinct.

"About .1 intensity."   Mayfield looked puzzled.   "What . . ."

The tracking needle dipped suddenly, swept up the screen to peak at .21, dropped back. The hut trembled. A stylus fell from the edge of the table. The red face of Mayor Daugherty burst through the door.

"Reynolds, have you lost your mind? What's the idea of blasting while I'm standing out in the open? I might have been killed!"

"I'm not blasting," Reynolds snapped. "Jim, get Eaton on the line, see if they know anything." He stepped to the door, shouted.

A heavyset man in sweat-darkened coveralls swung down from the seat of a cable-lift rig. "Boss, what goes on?" he called as he came up. "Damn near shook me out of my seat!"

"I don't know. You haven't set any trim charges?"

"No, Boss. I wouldn't set no charges without your say-so."

"Come on." Reynolds started out across the rubble-littered stretch of barren ground selected by the Authority as the site of the new spaceport. Halfway to the open mouth of the newly blasted pit, the ground under his feet rocked violently enough to make him stumble. A gout of dust rose from the excavation ahead. Loose rock danced on the ground. Beside him, the drilling chief grabbed his arm.

"Boss, we better get back!"

Reynolds shook him off, kept going. The drill chief swore and followed. The shaking of the ground went on, a sharp series of thumps interrupting a steady trembling.

"It's a quake!" Reynolds yelled over the low rumbling sound. He and the chief were at the rim of the core now.

"It can't be a quake, Boss," the latter shouted. "Not in these formations!"

"Tell it to the geologists . . ." The rock slab they were standing on rose a foot, dropped back. Both men fell. The slab bucked like a small boat in choppy water.

"Let's get out of here!" Reynolds was up and running. Ahead, a fissure opened, gaped a foot wide. He jumped it, caught a glimpse of black depths, a glint of wet clay twenty feet below—

A hoarse scream stopped him in his tracks. He spun, saw the drill chief down, a heavy splinter of rock across his legs. He jumped to him, heaved at the rock. There was blood on the man's shirt. The chief's hands beat the dusty rock before him. Then other men were there, grunting, sweaty hands gripping beside Reynolds'. The ground rocked. The roar from under the earth had risen to a deep, steady rumble. They lifted the rock aside, picked up the injured man and stumbled with him to the aid shack.

The mayor was there, white-faced.

"What is it, Reynolds? If you're responsible—"

"Shut up!" Reynolds brushed him aside, grabbed the phone, punched keys.

"Eaton! What have you got on this temblor?"

"Temblor, hell." The small face on the four-inch screen looked like a ruffled hen. "What in the name of Order are you doing out there? I'm reading a whole series of displacements originating from that last core of yours! What did you do, leave a pile of trim charges lying around?"

"It's a quake.   Trim charges, hell!   This thing's broken up two hundred yards of surface rock.   It seems to be traveling north-northeast—"

"I see that; a traveling earthquake!"   Eaton flapped his arms, a tiny and ridiculous figure against a background of wall charts and framed diplomas.   "Well . . . do something, Reynolds!   Where's Mayor Daugherty?"

"Underfoot!"   Reynolds snapped, and cut off.

Outside, a layer of sunset-stained dust obscured the sweep of level plain.   A rock-dozer rumbled up, ground to a halt by Reynolds.   A man jumped down.

"I got the boys moving equipment out," he panted.   "The thing's cutting a trail straight as a rule for the highway!"   He pointed to a raised roadbed a quarter-mile away.

"How fast is it moving?"

"She's done a hundred yards; it hasn't been ten minutes yet!"

"If it keeps up another twenty minutes, it'll be into the Intermix!"

"Scratch a few million cees and six months' work then, Pete!"

"And Southside Mall's a couple miles farther."

"Hell, it'll damp out before then!"

"Maybe.   Grab a field car, Dan."

"Pete!"   Mayfield came up at a trot.   "This thing's building!   The centroid's moving on a heading of 022—"

"How far sub-surface?"

"It's rising; started at two-twenty yards, and it's up to one-eighty!"

"What have we stirred up?"   Reynolds stared at Mayfield as the field car skidded to a stop beside them.

"Stay with it, Jim.   Give me anything new.   We're taking a closer look."   He climbed into the rugged vehicle.

"Take a blast truck—"

"No time!"   He waved and the car gunned away into the pall of dust.

The rock car pulled to a stop at the crest of the three-level Intermix on a lay-by designed to permit tourists to enjoy the view of the site of the proposed port, a hundred feet below.   Reynolds studied the progress of the quake through field glasses.   From this vantage point, the path of the phenomenon was a clearly defined trail of tilted and broken rock, some of the slabs twenty feet across.   As he watched, the fissure lengthened.

"It looks like a mole's trail."   Reynolds handed the glasses to his companion, thumbed the Send key on the car radio.

"Jim, get Eaton and tell him to divert all traffic from the Circular south of Zone Nine.   Cars are already clogging the right-of-way.   The dust is visible from a mile away, and when the word gets out there's something going on, we'll be swamped."

"I'll tell him, but he won't like it!"

"This isn't politics!   This thing will be into the outer pad area in another twenty minutes!"

"It won't last—"

"How deep does it read now?"

"One-five!" There was a moment's silence. "Pete, if it stays on course, it'll surface at about where you're parked!"

"Uh-huh. It looks like you can scratch one Intermix. Better tell Eaton to get a story ready for the press."

"Pete—talking about newshounds," Dan said beside him. Reynolds switched off, turned to see a man in a gay-colored driving outfit coming across from a battered Monojag sportster which had pulled up behind the rock car. A big camera case was slung across his shoulder.

"Say, what's going on down there?" he called.

"Rock slide," Reynolds said shortly. "I'll have to ask you to drive on. The road's closed . . ."

"Who're you?" The man looked belligerent.

"I'm the engineer in charge. Now pull out, brother." He turned back to the radio. "Jim, get every piece of heavy equipment we own over here, on the double." He paused, feeling a minute trembling in the car. "The Intermix is beginning to feel it," he went on. "I'm afraid we're in for it. Whatever that thing is, it acts like a solid body boring its way through the ground. Maybe we can barricade it."

"Barricade an earthquake?"

"Yeah . . . I know how it sounds . . . but it's the only idea I've got."

"Hey . . . what's that about an earthquake?" The man in the colored suit was still there. "By gosh, I can feel it—the whole bridge is shaking!"

"Off, Mister—now!" Reynolds jerked a thumb at the traffic lanes where a steady stream of cars was hurtling past. "Dan, take us over to the main track. We'll have to warn this traffic off . . ."

"Hold on, fellow," the man unlimbered his camera. "I represent the New Devon *Scope*. I have a few questions—"

"I don't have the answers," Pete cut him off as the car pulled away.

"Hah!" the man who had questioned Reynolds yelled after him. "Big shot! Think you can . . ." His voice was lost behind them.

In a modest retirees' apartment block in the coast town of Idlebreeze, forty miles from the scene of the freak quake, an old man sat in a reclining chair, half dozing before a yammering Tri-D tank.

". . . Grandpa," a sharp-voiced young woman was saying. "It's time for you to go to bed."

"Bed? Why do I want to go to bed? Can't sleep anyway . . ." He stirred, made a pretense of sitting up, showing an interest in the Tri-D. "I'm watching this show."

"It's not a show, it's the news," a fattish boy said disgustedly. "Ma, can I switch channels—"

"Leave it alone, Bennie," the old man said. On the screen, a panoramic scene spread out, a stretch of barren ground across which a furrow showed. As he watched, it lengthened.

". . . Up here at the Intermix we have a fine view of the whole curious business, lazangemmun," the announcer chattered. "And in our opinion it's some sort of publicity stunt staged by the Port Authority to publicize their controversial Port project—"

"Ma, can I change channels?"

"Go ahead, Bennie—"

"Don't touch it," the old man said. The fattish boy reached for the control, but something in the old man's eye stopped him.

"The traffic's still piling up here," Reynolds said into the phone.

"Damn it, Jim, we'll have a major jam on our hands—"

"He won't do it, Pete! You know the Circular was his baby—the super all-weather pike that nothing could shut down. He says you'll have to handle this in the field—"

"Handle, hell! I'm talking about preventing a major disaster! And in a matter of minutes, at that!"

"I'll try again—"

"If he says no, divert a couple of the big ten-yard graders and block it off yourself. Set up field 'arcs, and keep any cars from getting in from either direction."

"Pete, that's outside your authority!"

"You heard me!"

Ten minutes later, back at ground level, Reynolds watched the boom-mounted polyarcs swinging into position at the two roadblocks a quarter of a mile apart, cutting off the threatened section of the raised expressway. A hundred yards from where he stood on the rear cargo deck of a light grader rig, a section of rock fifty feet wide rose slowly, split, fell back with a ponderous impact. One corner of it struck the massive pier supporting the extended shelf of the lay-by above. A twenty-foot splinter fell away, exposing the reinforcing-rod core.

"How deep, Jim?" Reynolds spoke over the roaring sound coming from the disturbed area.

"Just subsurface now, Pete! It ought to break through—" His voice was drowned in a rumble as the damaged pier shivered, rose up, buckled at its midpoint and collapsed, bringing down with it a large chunk of pavement and guard rail, and a single still-glowing light pole. A small car that had been parked on the doomed section was visible for an instant just before the immense slab struck. Reynolds saw it bounce aside, then disappear under an avalanche of broken concrete.

"My God, Pete—" Dan blurted. "That damned fool newshound—!"

"Look!" As the two men watched, a second pier swayed, fell backward into the shadow of the span above. The roadway sagged, and two more piers snapped. With a bellow like a burst dam, a hundred-foot stretch of the road fell into the roiling dust cloud.

"Pete!" Mayfield's voice burst from the car radio. "Get out of there! I threw a reader on that thing and it's chattering . . . !"

Among the piled fragments, something stirred, heaved, rising up, lifting multiton pieces of the broken road, thrusting them aside like so many potato chips. A dull blue radiance broke through from the broached earth, threw an eerie light on the shattered structure above. A massive, ponderously irresistible shape thrust forward through the ruins. Reynolds saw a great blue-glowing profile emerge from the rubble like a surfacing submarine, shedding a burden of broken stone, saw immense treads ten feet wide claw for purchase, saw the mighty flank brush a still standing pier, send it crashing aside.

"Pete . . . what . . . what is it—?"

"I don't know." Reynolds broke the paralysis that had gripped him. "Get us out of here, Dan, fast! Whatever it is, it's headed straight for the city!"

I emerge at last from the trap into which I had fallen, and at once encounter defensive works of considerable strength. My scanners are dulled from lack of power, but I am able to perceive open ground beyond the barrier, and farther still, at a distance of 5.7 kilometers, massive walls. Once more I transmit the Brigade Rally signal; but as before, there is no reply. I am truly alone.

I scan the surrounding area for the emanations of Enemy drive units, monitor the EM spectrum for their communications. I detect nothing; either my circuitry is badly damaged, or their shielding is superb.

I must now make a decision as to possible courses of action. Since all my comrades of the Brigade have fallen, I compute that the walls before me must be held by Enemy forces. I direct probing signals at the defenses, discover them to be of unfamiliar construction, and less formidable than they appear. I am aware of the possibility that this may be a trick of the Enemy; but my course is clear.

I re-engage my driving engines and advance on the Enemy fortress.

"You're out of your mind, Father," the stout man said. "At your age—"

"At your age, I got my nose smashed in a brawl in a bar on Aldo," the old man cut him off. "But I won the fight."

"James, you can't go out at this time of night. . . ." an elderly woman wailed.

"Tell them to go home." The old man walked painfully toward his bedroom door. "I've seen enough of them for today."

"Mother, you won't let him do anything foolish?"

"He'll forget about it in a few minutes; but maybe you'd better go now and let him settle down."

"Mother . . . I really think a home is the best solution."

"Yes, Grandma," the young woman nodded agreement. "After all, he's past ninety—and he has his veteran's retirement . . ."

Inside his room, the old man listened as they departed. He went to the closet, took out clothes, began dressing.

City Engineer Eaton's face was chalk-white on the screen.

"No one can blame me," he said. "How could I have known—"

"Your office ran the surveys and gave the PA the green light," Mayor Daugherty yelled.

"All the old survey charts showed was 'Disposal Area.' "   Eaton threw out his hands.   "I assumed—"

"As City Engineer, you're not paid to make assumptions!   Ten minutes' research would have told you that was a 'Y' category area!"

"What's 'Y' category mean?" Mayfield asked Reynolds.   They were standing by the field Comm center, listening to the dispute.   Nearby, boom-mounted Tri-D cameras hummed, recording the progress of the immense machine, its upper turret rearing forty-five feet into the air, as it ground slowly forward across smooth ground toward the city, dragging behind it a trailing festoon of twisted reinforcing iron crusted with broken concrete.

"Half-life over one hundred years," Reynolds answered shortly.   "The last skirmish of the war was fought near here.   Apparently this is where they buried the radio-active equipment left over from the battle."

"But, that was more than seventy years ago—"

"There's still enough residual radiation to contaminate anything inside a quarter mile radius."

"They must have used some hellish stuff."   Mayfield stared at the dull shine half a mile distant.

"Reynolds, how are you going to stop this thing?"   The mayor had turned on the PA Engineer.

"Me stop it?   You saw what it did to my heaviest rigs: flattened them like pancakes.   You'll have to call out the military on this one, Mr. Mayor."

"Call in Federation forces?   Have them meddling in civic affairs?"

"The station's only sixty-five miles from here.   I think you'd better call them fast.   It's only moving at about three miles per hour but it will reach the south edge of the Mall in another forty-five minutes."

"Can't you mine it?   Blast a trap in its path?"

"You saw it claw its way up from six hundred feet down.   I checked the specs; it followed the old excavation tunnel out.   It was rubble-filled and capped with twenty-inch compressed concrete."

"It's incredible," Eaton said from the screen.   "The entire machine was encased in a ten-foot shell of reinforced armocrete.   It had to break out of that before it could move a foot!"

"That was just a radiation shield; it wasn't intended to restrain a Bolo Combat Unit."

"What *was*, may I inquire?"   The mayor glared.

"The units were deactivated before being buried," Eaton spoke up, as if he were eager to talk.   "Their circuits were fused.   It's all in the report—"

"The report you should have read somewhat sooner," the mayor snapped.

"What . . . what started it up?"   Mayfield looked bewildered.   "For seventy years it was down there, and nothing happened!"

"Our blasting must have jarred something," Reynolds said shortly.   "Maybe closed a relay that started up the old battle reflex circuit."

"You know something about these machines?" the mayor asked.

"I've read a little."

"Then speak up, man.   I'll call the station, if you feel I must.   What measures should I request?"

"I don't know, Mr. Mayor.   As far as I know, nothing on New Devon can stop that machine now."

The mayor's mouth opened and closed.   He whirled to the screen, blanked Eaton's agonized face, punched in the code for the Federation Station.

"Colonel Blane!" he blurted as a stern face came onto the screen.   "We have a major emergency on our hands!   I'll need everything you've got!   This is the situation—"

I encounter no resistance other than the flimsy barrier, but my progress is slow. Grievous damage has been done to my main-drive sector due to overload during my escape from the trap; and the failure of my sensing circuitry has deprived me of a major portion of my external receptivity.   Now my pain circuits project a continuous signal to my awareness center; but it is my duty to my commander and to my fallen comrades of the Brigade to press forward at my best speed; but my performance is a poor shadow of my former ability.

And now at last the Enemy comes into action!   I sense aerial units closing at supersonic velocities; I lock my lateral batteries to them and direct salvo fire; but I sense that the arming mechanisms clatter harmlessly.   The craft sweep over me, and my impotent guns elevate, track them as they release detonants that spread out in an envelopmental pattern which I, with my reduced capabilities, am powerless to avoid.   The missiles strike; I sense their detonations all about me; but I suffer only trivial damage.   The Enemy has blundered if he thought to neutralize a Mark XXVIII Combat Unit with mere chemical explosives!   But I weaken with each meter gained.

Now there is no doubt as to my course.   I must press the charge and carry the walls before my reserve cells are exhausted.

From a vantage point atop a bucket rig four hundred yards from the position the great fighting machine had now reached, Pete Reynolds studied it through night glasses.   A battery of beamed polyarcs pinned the giant hulk, scarred and rust-scaled, in a pool of blue-white light.   A mile and a half beyond it, the walls of the Mall rose sheer from the garden setting.

"The bombers slowed it some," he reported to Eaton via scope.   "But it's still making better than two miles per hour.   I'd say another twenty-five minutes before it hits the main ring-wall.   How's the evacuation going?"

"Badly!   I get no cooperation!   You'll be my witness, Reynolds, I did all I could—"

"How about the mobile batteries; how long before they'll be in position?" Reynolds cut him off.

"I've heard nothing from Federation Central—typical militaristic arrogance, not keeping me informed—but I have them on my screens.   They're two miles out—say three minutes."

"I hope you made your point about N-heads."

"That's outside my province!" Eaton said sharply.   "It's up to Brand to carry out this portion of the operation!"

"The HE Missiles didn't do much more than clear away the junk it was dragging," Reynolds' voice was sharp.

"I wash my hands of responsibility for civilian lives," Eaton was saying when Reynolds shut him off, changed channels.

"Jim, I'm going to try to divert it," he said crisply.   "Eaton's sitting on his political fence; the Feds are bringing artillery up, but I don't expect much from it. Technically, Brand needs Sector O.K. to use Nu-clear stuff, and he's not the boy to stick his neck out—"

"Divert it how?   Pete, don't take any chances—"

Reynolds laughed shortly.   "I'm going to get around it and drop a shaped drilling charge in its path.   Maybe I can knock a tread off.   With luck, I might get its attention on me, and draw it away from the Mall.   There are still a few thousand people over there, glued to their Tri-D's.   They think it's all a swell show."

"Pete, you can't walk up on that thing!   It's hot . . ."   He broke off.   "Pete— there's some kind of nut here—he claims he has to talk to you; says he knows something about that damned juggernaut.   Shall I send . . . ?"

Reynolds paused with his hand on the cut-off switch.   "Put him on," he snapped. Mayfield's face moved aside and an ancient, bleary-eyed visage stared out at him. The tip of the old man's tongue touched his dry lips.

"Son, I tried to tell this boy here, but he wouldn't listen—"

"What have you got, old-timer?" Pete cut in.   "Make it fast."

"My name's Sanders.   James Sanders.   I'm . . . I was with the Planetary Volunteer Scouts, back in '71—"

"Sure, Dad," Pete said gently.   "I'm sorry, I've got a little errand to run—"

"Wait . . ."   The old man's face worked.   "I'm old, Son—too damned old. I know.   But bear with me.   I'll try to say it straight.   I was with Hayle's squadron at Toledo.   Then afterwards, they shipped us . . . but hell, you don't care about that!   I keep wandering, Son; can't help it.   What I mean to say is—I was in on that last scrap, right here at New Devon—only we didn't call it New Devon then. Called it Hellport.   Nothing but bare rock and Enemy emplacements . . ."

"You were talking about the battle, Mr. Sanders," Pete said tensely.   "Go on with that part."

"Lieutenant Sanders," the oldster said.   "Sure, I was Acting Brigade Commander.   See, our major was hit at Toledo—and after Tommy Chee stopped a sidewinder . . ."

"Stick to the point, Lieutenant!"

"Yes, sir!" the old man pulled himself together with an obvious effort.   "I took the Brigade in; put out flankers, and ran the Enemy into the ground.   We mopped 'em up in a thirty-three hour running fight that took us from over by Crater Bay all the way down here to Hellport.   When it was over, I'd lost six units, but the Enemy was done.   They gave us Brigade Honors for that action.   And then . . ."

"Then what?"

"Then the triple-dyed yellow-bottoms at Headquarters put out the order the

Brigade was to be scrapped; said they were too hot to make decon practical.   Cost too much, they said!   So after the final review . . .''   He gulped, blinked.   ''They planted 'em deep, two hundred meters, and poured in special High-R concrete.''

''And packed rubble in behind them,'' Reynolds finished for him.   ''All right, Lieutenant, I believe you!   But what started that machine on a rampage?''

''Should have known they couldn't hold down a Bolo Mark XXVIII!''   The old man's eyes lit up.   ''Take more than a few million tons of rock to stop Lenny when his battle board was lit!''

''Lenny?''

''That's my old Command Unit out there, Son.   I saw the markings on the 3-D.   Unit LNE of the Dinochrome Brigade!''

''Listen!''   Reynolds snapped out.   ''Here's what I intend to try . . .''   He outlined his plan.

''Ha!''   Sanders snorted.   ''It's quite a notion, Mister, but Lenny won't give it a sneeze.''

''You didn't come here to tell me we were licked,'' Reynolds cut in.   ''How about Brand's batteries?''

''Hell, Son, Lenny stood up to point-blank Hellbore fire on Toledo, and—''

''Are you telling me there's nothing we can do?''

''What's that?   No, Son, that's not what I'm saying . . .''

''Then what!''

''Just tell these johnnies to get out of my way Mister.   I think I can handle him.''

At the field Comm hut, Pete Reynolds watched as the man who had been Lieutenant Sanders of the Volunteer Scouts pulled shiny black boots over his thin ankles, and stood.   The blouse and trousers of royal blue polyon hung on his spare frame like wash on a line.   He grinned, a skull's grin.

''It doesn't fit like it used to; but Lenny will recognize it.   It'll help.   Now, if you've got that power pack ready . . .''

Mayfield handed over the old-fashioned field instrument Sanders had brought in with him.

''It's operating, sir—but I've already tried everything I've got on that infernal machine; I didn't get a peep out of it.''

Sanders winked at him.   ''Maybe I know a couple of tricks you boys haven't heard about.''   He slung the strap over his bony shoulder and turned to Reynolds.

''Guess we better get going, Mister.   He's getting close.''

In the rock car Sanders leaned close to Reynolds' ear.   ''Told you those Federal guns wouldn't scratch Lenny.   They're wasting their time.''

Reynolds pulled the car to a stop at the crest of the road, from which point he had a view of the sweep of ground leading across to the city's edge.   Lights sparkled all across the towers of New Devon.   Close to the walls, the converging fire of the ranked batteries of infinite repeaters drove into the glowing bulk of the machine, which plowed on, undeterred.   As he watched, the firing ceased.

''Now, let's get in there, before they get some other scheme going,'' Sanders said.

The rock car crossed the rough ground, swung wide to come up on the Bolo from the left side.   Behind the hastily-rigged radiation cover, Reynolds watched the immense silhouette grow before him.

"I knew they were big," he said.   "But to see one up close like this—"   He pulled to a stop a hundred feet from the Bolo.

"Look at the side ports," Sanders said, his voice crisper now.   "He's firing anti-personnel charges—only his plates are flat.   If they weren't, we wouldn't have gotten within half a mile."   He unclipped the microphone and spoke into it:

"Unit LNE, break off action and retire to ten-mile line!"

Reynolds' head jerked around to stare at the old man.   His voice had rung with vigor and authority as he spoke the command.

The Bolo ground slowly ahead.   Sanders shook his head, tried again.

"No answer, like that fella said.   He must be running on nothing but memories now . . ."   He re-attached the microphone and before Reynolds could put out a hand, had lifted the anti-R cover and stepped off on the ground.

"Sanders—get back in here!" Reynolds yelled.

"Never mind, Son.   I've got to get in close.   Contact induction."   He started toward the giant machine.   Frantically, Reynolds started the car, slammed it into gear, pulled forward.

"Better stay back," Sanders' voice came from his field radio.   "This close, that screening won't do you much good."

"Get in the car!" Reynolds roared.   "That's hard radiation!"

"Sure; feels funny, like a sunburn, about an hour after you come in from the beach and start to think maybe you got a little too much."   He laughed.   "But I'll get to him . . ."

Reynolds braked to a stop, watched the shrunken figure in the baggy uniform as it slogged forward, leaning as against a sleetstorm.

"I'm up beside him," Sanders' voice came through faintly on the field radio. "I'm going to try to swing up on his side.   Don't feel like trying to chase him any farther."

Through the glasses, Reynolds watched the small figure, dwarfed by the immense bulk of the fighting machine as he tried, stumbled, tried again, swung up on the flange running across the rear quarter inside the churning bogie wheel.

"He's up," he reported.   "Damned wonder the track didn't get him before . . ."

Clinging to the side of the machine, Sanders lay for a moment, bent forward across the flange.   Then he pulled himself up, wormed his way forward to the base of the rear quarter turret, wedged himself against it.   He unslung the communicator, removed a small black unit, clipped it to the armor; it clung, held by a magnet.   He brought the microphone up to his face.

In the Comm shack Mayfield leaned toward the screen, his eyes squinted in tension.   Across the field Reynolds held the glasses fixed on the man lying across the flank of the Bolo.   They waited.

The walls are before me, and I ready myself for a final effort, but suddenly I am aware of trickle currents flowing over my outer surface.   Is this some new trick of the Enemy? I tune to the wave-energies, trace the source. They originate at a point in contact with my aft port armor. I sense modulation, match receptivity to a computed pattern. And I hear a voice:

"Unit LNE, break it off, Lenny. We're pulling back now, Boy! This is Command to LNE; pull back to ten miles. If you read me, Lenny, swing to port and halt."

I am not fooled by the deception. The order appears correct, but the voice is not that of my Commander. Briefly I regret that I cannot spare energy to direct a neutralizing power flow at the device the Enemy has attached to me. I continue my charge.

"Unit LNE! Listen to me, Boy; maybe you don't recognize my voice, but it's me! You see—some time has passed. I've gotten old. My voice has changed some, maybe. But it's me! Make a port turn, Lenny. Make it now!"

I am tempted to respond to the trick, for something in the false command seems to awaken secondary circuits which I sense have been long stilled. But I must not be swayed by cleverness of the Enemy. My sensing circuitry has faded further as my energy cells drain; but I know where the Enemy lies. I move forward, but I am filled with agony, and only the memory of my comrades drives me on.

"Lenny, answer me. Transmit on the old private band—the one we agreed on. Nobody but me knows it, remember?"

Thus the Enemy seeks to beguile me into diverting precious power. But I will not listen.

"Lenny—not much time left. Another minute and you'll be into the walls. People are going to die. Got to stop you, Lenny. Hot here. My God, I'm hot. Not breathing too well, now. I can feel it; cutting through me like knives. You took a load of Enemy power, Lenny; and now I'm getting my share. Answer me, Lenny. Over to you . . ."

It will require only a tiny allocation of power to activate a communication circuit. I realize that it is only an Enemy trick, but I compute that by pretending to be deceived, I may achieve some trivial advantage. I adjust circuitry accordingly, and transmit:

"Unit LNE to Command. Contact with Enemy defensive line imminent. Request supporting fire!"

"Lenny . . . you can hear me! Good boy, Lenny! Now make a turn, to port. Walls . . . close . . ."

"Unit LNE to Command. Request positive identification; transmit code 685749."

"Lenny—I can't . . . don't have code blanks. But it's me . . ."

"In absence of recognition code, your transmission disregarded." *I send. And now the walls loom high above me. There are many lights, but I see them only vaguely. I am nearly blind now.*

"Lenny—less'n two hundred feet to go. Listen, Lenny. I'm climbing down. I'm going to jump down, Lenny, and get around under your force scanner pickup. You'll see me, Lenny. You'll know me then."

The false transmission ceases. I sense a body moving across my side. The gap closes. I detect movement before me, and in automatic reflex fire anti-P charges before I recall that I am unarmed.

A small object has moved out before me, and taken up a position between me and the wall behind which the Enemy conceal themselves. It is dim, but appears to have the shape of a man. . . .

I am uncertain. My alert center attempts to engage inhibitory circuitry which will force me to halt, but it lacks power. I can override it. But still I am unsure. Now I must take a last risk, I must shunt power to my forward scanner to examime this obstacle more closely. I do so, and it leaps into greater clarity. It is indeed a man—and it is enclothed in regulation blues of the Volunteers. Now, closer, I see the face, and through the pain of my great effort, I study it . . .

"He's backed against the wall," Reynolds said hoarsely. "It's still coming. Fifty feet to go—"

"You were a fool, Reynolds!" the mayor barked. "A fool to stake everything on that old dotard's crazy ideas!"

"Hold it!" As Reynolds watched, the mighty machine slowed, halted, ten feet from the sheer wall before it. For a moment it sat, as though puzzled. Then it backed, halted again, pivoted ponderously to the left and came about.

On its side, a small figure crept up, fell across the lower gun deck. The Bolo surged into motion, retracing its route across the artillery-scarred gardens.

"He's turned it," Reynolds let his breath out with a shuddering sigh. "It's headed out for open desert. It might get twenty miles before it finally runs out of steam."

The strange voice that was the Bolo's came from the big panel before Mayfield:

"Command . . . Unit LNE reports main power cells drained, secondary cells drained; now operating at .037 percent efficiency, using Final Emergency Power. Request advice as to range to be covered before relief maintenance available."

"It's a long, long way, Lenny . . ." Sanders' voice was a bare whisper. *"But I'm coming with you . . ."*

Then there was only the crackle of static. Ponderously, like a great mortally stricken animal, the Bolo moved through the ruins of the fallen roadway, heading for the open desert.

"That damned machine," the mayor said in a hoarse voice. "You'd almost think it was alive."

"You would at that," Pete Reynolds said.

HARRY HARRISON

The Powers of Observation

It's just a matter of native ability. I've had the same training as a lot of other guys, and if I remember things better, or can jump faster, than most of them, maybe that's the reason why I'm out here in no-man's-land where East brushes West and why they're behind desks in Washington.

One of the first things I was ever taught by the Department was to look out for the unusual. I whispered a soft word of thanks to my instructors as I watched this big blond Apollo type walk down the beach.

His feet sank into the sand!

Yes they did, and don't go telling me that that doesn't mean anything. The sand on the Makarska beach is like the sand on any other beach on the Yugoslavian coast, firm and compact. You can make footsteps in it—but not *that* deep.

All right, go ahead and laugh if you want to, but don't forget what I told you about my training, so just for the moment take my word about this. These footprints were unusual. I was sitting up and looking out to sea when he went by, and I didn't move my head to look at him. But, since I was wearing sunglasses, I followed him with my eyes, head dead center all the time. He was an absolutely normal guy; blond, about six foot, wearing blue nylon bathing trunks and sporting an appendectomy scar and a scowl. You see a million like him on every beach in the world every summer. But not with those footprints.

Look, don't laugh, I asked you not to. I'll explain in a second. I let him walk on by and turn into the hotel and while he was doing it I was standing up and as soon as he was out of sight I was walking back the way he had come, towards this old woman who was selling *raznici* from a little stall. Sure I could have done it simpler, I was almost certain at the time that I wasn't under observation—but that's the point. I could have been. Unless people know better, if you act innocent you are innocent. Act innocent all the time and et cetera all the time. I went and had some *raznici*, my fourth portion for the day. Not that I like the things, but the stall made a good cover, an excuse for random action.

"*Jedan*," I said, and held up one finger in case my American accent obscured my tiny command of Serbo-Croatian. She bobbed her head and pulled a wood splint off the bed of charcoal and used her big carving knife to push the pieces of roasted meat from the splint onto the plate with the raw onion. Not a very complicated dish, but you get used to it after a while. To all appearances I was watching her carefully and digging out my money, but all I was really interested in were those footprints. I could see twelve of them from where I was standing, twelve that I was completely certain of, and while the food was being slowly dished out and the battered aluminum dinar coins counted two of them were obliterated by other bathers. I did a quick estimate of the elapsed time and footprints destroyed and came up with an extrapolated life of six minutes for the remaining footsteps. Or three minutes with a one hundred percent safety margin which is the way I like to operate when I can. Good enough. I took my change, chewed the last gristly bit, and strolled back down the beach counting the coins.

Was it chance my course paralleled the remaining three footprints? Was it chance I walked at the same speed as the blond stranger? Was it chance that built the atom bomb?

My right foot came down in line with—and a few inches away from—a right footprint, and as my foot came up I dropped the coins. It took me exactly 3.8 seconds to pick up the coins, and while picking them up I put my index finger into the blond man's heelprint and into my own. That's all. It was a risk to take, if anyone were watching, but calculated risks are part of this business.

I didn't smile and I didn't alter my walking pace, I just jiggled my change and went back and sat down on my towel again.

That was outside. Inside it was Mardi Gras, Fourth of July, rockets and cherry bombs and ticker tape from the windows.

It was childishly simple. I'm five ten and weigh one hundred eighty and I hit my foot into the sand in the same place and at the same speed and in the same way the blond had done. I could be off in my figure for the compressibility of the sand, but only by a few percent, and I assumed it was displaced at a predictable rate on a sine curve, and I wasn't off at all in my measurement of the depth of the two impressions so, plus or minus five percent for error, that six foot tall joker weighed in the neighborhood of four hundred and twelve pounds.

Jackpot!

Time for action. And thought. I could do both at the same time. He had gone into the hotel, I would go into the hotel. The Jadran was big, new and international and almost everyone on this chunk of beach was staying there. As I picked up my towel and trudged slowly towards it I put the brain box into gear and thought of the next step. Communication and report, the answer came back instantly. The Department would be very interested in what I had discovered, and once I had relieved myself of the information I would be a free agent again and could look into the matter further. It should not be hard to find the heavyweight blond if he were registered at the hotel.

After the hot sunlight the lobby was dim, and apparently empty except for a fat German couple who were either asleep or dead in the overstuffed chairs. As I passed I looked into the bar and it was empty too, except for the bartender, Petar, who was polishing glasses listlessly. I turned in without breaking step, as though I had been headed here all the time and had not just decided at that instant to go in. The opportunity was too good to miss since Petar was my eyes and ears in this hotel—and well paid for the service.

"Buon giorno," I said. *"Guten Tag,"* he sighed back. Petar comes from the island of Cres which belonged to the Austrians until 1918 and the Italians until 1945. He grew up with both languages as well as the native Serbo-Croatian. With this background he had picked up English and a little French and was in great demand as a bartender in the coastal hotels with their international clientele. He was also underpaid and undertipped and very happy to see my spanking-new greenbacks.

"Let me have a *pivo,"* I said, and he took a bottle of East German dark beer out of the freezer. I climbed onto a stool and when he poured it out our heads were close together. "For ten bucks," I said. "The name and room number of a man, blond, six feet tall who wears blue swim trunks and has an appendectomy scar."

"How much is six feet?"

"One hundred eighty-two centimeters," I flashed right back.

"Oh, him. A Russian by name of Alexei Svirsky. Room 146. He has a Bulgarian passport but he drives in a Tatra with Polish number plates. Who else but a Russian?"

"Who but." I knocked back the beer, and the tattered one thousand dinar bill I slipped him had a crisp sawbuck folded underneath it. The change came back, though the ten spot didn't, and I left a tip and headed for the door, but I wheeled around before I had gone two steps. I caught the trace of a vanishing smile on his hounddog chops.

"For ten bucks more," I said, letting the palmed bill project a bit from under my hand on the bar top, "how much is Alexei Svirsky paying you to report if anyone asks questions about him?"

"Five thousand dinar, cheapskate bum. Not him, his friends. He don't talk much."

"Here's ten thousand and another five when you tell me they asked and you told them there were no questions."

A slow nod, the bills shuffled and changed hands, and I left. My flanks guarded. I was very free with Uncle's money, but dinars aren't worth very much in any case. I went to my room, locked the door, tested to see if the place had been bugged since I left—it had not—then leaned out the open window. The pink concrete wall dropped six stories to a desolate patio floored with hard tramped dirt and a few patches of yellowed grass. A row of dead plants leaned against one wall and four empty beer kegs baked and drew flies in the sun. There was no one in sight, nor were there any bugs on the wall outside my room. I sat down in the chair facing my window and the row of windows in the other wing of the hotel.

"How do you read me?" I said in a low voice.

Across the way a curtain was closed, then opened again. It was next to an open window.

"I've spotted a suspect.   He may not be the one we were told to look out for, but there is strong evidence to believe that he is.   Bulgarian passport but could be Russian.   Name of Alexei Svirsky in Room 146, and he weighs four hundred twelve pounds—at a rough estimate."   The curtain twitched an interrogative, repeat.   "That's right.   Four hundred twelve pounds.   I'm going to investigate."

As soon as I finished talking I turned away so I couldn't see the frantic jiggle of the curtain.   I liked this setup: I didn't have to take any backtalk.   The agent over there had a parabolic dish and a directional microphone.   He could pick up a whisper in this room.   But he couldn't talk to me.

While I was showering the phone rang but I ignored it.   I could have been out, right?   Moving a little faster now I pulled on slacks and a sport shirt and put on my sneakers with the ridged soles.   There was no one around when I went out into the hall and down the stairs to the floor where I knew Room 146 was located. Since I had passed on my old information now it was time to gather some new. I found the room and knocked on the door.

Brash perhaps, but a way to get results.   I would mumble something about wrong room and get a closer look at Svirsky and the layout of his room.   If my visit worried him and he ran, we would find out things; if he stayed we would find some facts as well.

No one answered the door.   I knocked again and leaned against the panel to listen.   No shower, no voices, nothing.   A little calculated risk was in order. The tool steel picklock worked as fast as a key would in this primitive lock, perhaps faster.   I stepped in and closed the door behind me.   The room was empty.

My bird had flown.   There were still marks on the bedcover where a suitcase had lain while it was being packed.   The door of the big wooden wardrobe stood open, and if one of the coathangers had been swinging I would not have been surprised.   It had all happened very quickly and efficiently.   Nothing remained to mark Mr. Svirsky's visit.   I went into the bath.   The sink was dry, as was the shower, the towels folded neatly on the racks, threadbare but clean.   Everything *too* clean and spotless since I knew the chambermaids weren't that efficient.   And Svirsky had been staying here some days—so this was positive information.   There was even a trace of dust in the sink.   I rubbed at it with my finger just as the hall door opened.

Just a crack, a couple of inches, then it closed again.   But it was open long enough—and wide enough—to roll in a hand grenade.

As it bounced towards me I recognized the type (XII) place of manufacture (Plzn) and fuse time (three seconds).   Even before this last fact had impressed itself I had jumped backwards, slammed the door and collapsed inside the shower stall. Fast thinking and fast reflexes—that's a combination that can't be beat.   I hoped, as I hunkered down with my arms clasped over my head.

It made a good deal of noise when it exploded.

The bathroom door blew in, fragments of grenade thudded into the wall above me and the mirror crashed in bursting shards to the floor.   One steaming hunk of iron was imbedded in the tile about six inches in front of my nose.   This was the closest piece, and it was close enough, thank you.   I did not wait to examine it but was on my feet while the explosion still echoed, jumping over the remains of the destroyed bathroom door.   Speed was the most important thing now because I didn't want to be found in this room.   Diving through the still roiling cloud of smoke I pulled open the tottering door—it collapsed at my feet—and made it into the hall.   I could hear shouts and doors opening, but no one was in sight yet.   The stairwell was five paces away and I got there without being seen and started up. Fleury was waiting on the landing above.

"Svirsky has cleared out," I told him.   "He moved out fast and left someone behind to roll a grenade in on top of me."   There was the sound of running feet and shouts of multilingual amazement from the hall below.   "That means they were tipped off about me, so I am forced to admit that my informant, Petar the bartender, is a double agent."

"I know.   He was the one who threw the grenade into the room.   We have him in the truck and are going to question him under scopolamine before we send him home.   But I doubt if we'll learn anything, he's just small fry."

"What about Svirsky?"

"That's what I came to tell you.   Our road-watcher at Zadvarje, the next town, reports that a big Tatra with Polish plates just belted through there like a bomb, heading north towards Split.   Two men in the front and one in the back.   They were going too fast to make out anything more."

"Well that's more than enough.   I'll take the jeep and go after them.   Now that we have made contact we can't lose it."

Fleury chewed the inside of his lip worriedly.   "I really don't know, it's a risk . . ."

"Crossing the street is a risk these days.   Who do we have north of here that can head them off?"

"Just team Able Dog in Rijeka."

"That's pretty far away.   Tell them to head south on the coastal highway, and if the Tatra doesn't turn off we'll have it trapped between us.   We'll get a closer look at Alexei Svirsky yet."

Five minutes later I was on the road north, tooling the jeep around the tight turns of the twisting highway.   It wasn't really a jeep, but a Toyota land cruiser, with four-wheel drive, rugged and powerful.   A Japanese car with Austrian plates and an American driver.   We were about as international as the other side.   I put my foot to the floor and hoped the driver of the Tatra would remember what the roads inland were like.

Yugoslavia is shaped like a right hand, palm up, with the Adriatic Sea all along the bottom edge, running along the side of the hand and the little finger.   The coastal highway, what the locals call the *Magistrale,* runs all the way along the shore.   I was on this highway now, about the base of the pinky, heading north towards the fingertips—where I hoped the other car was heading.   That would be the fastest and easiest way to get out of the country, because Rijeka is up there at the end of the little finger and a good road turns east from here to Zagreb—on the top joint of the middle finger—and then on to Hungary at the tip of the index finger.

There was another way to get there that I hoped the comrades would not consider. The Velebit Mountains come right down to the coastline here, rugged and steep, and are crossed by the oldest and worst roads in the world. There are only a few of these goat tracks, all in terrible condition, and a car going this way could be easily followed and headed off. I'm sure the driver of the Tatra knew this as well as I did and would make the correct decision.

I drove. The Toyota whined up to over eighty in the straight and skidded broadside around the turns. I passed a loafing Alfa-Romeo with Milan plates, on a turn, and the driver shook his fist out the window and blared his highway horn at me. Split was right ahead and I worked my way through the traffic as fast as I could without attracting the attention of the milicija. There was no sign of a black Tatra, though I kept my eyes open. When I passed the turnoff to Sinj I tried to ignore it. Although it was a good road for about fifty miles it degenerated into a bumpy cow path in the hills. I knew that and I hoped that the Tatra driver did as well. Once past Split I opened her up again and hoped that I was following a car—not just a hunch.

At Zadar I saw them. The highway makes a long swing to the right here, bypassing the city, and there is a big Jugopetrol gas station right in the middle of the curve. When I spotted the station far ahead the Tatra was leaping out of it like a black bug. They had stopped to fill their tank, or wash their hands, and given me enough time to catch up and get them in sight. I whistled as I belted around the turn and into the straight stretch that led to the Maslenica Bridge. There were a number of alternative plans and I was musing over them, deciding which was best, when we came up to the bridge and my right front tire blew out.

Since I was doing seventy at the time it was just a matter of good reflexes, good brakes—and luck. I twisted and skidded all over the road, and if there had been any traffic I would have had it right then. But the vanishing Tatra was the only other car around and after some fancy work on the shoulder, two fence posts and a cloud of dust, I slid up to the guard rail at the bridge plaza and bucked to a stop.

Blow out? Now that I had a moment to think I ran the old memory reel back and thought about that puff of smoke from the rear window of the Tatra just before the tire blew. Either this was a remarkable coincidence—or they had a gunport back there and someone was a very good shot with a hand pistol. I don't believe in coincidences.

For just about two seconds I thought about this and admired the view of harsh stone running down to the blue water of the arm of the sea below, and the bright orange bridge leaping over to the limestone cliff on the far side. Very dramatic. I was completely alone and the only sounds were the vanishing hum of the Tatra and the click of my cooling engine. Then I unpried my fingers from the steering wheel and dug out the jack.

If they ever have a Toyota tire-changing championship, I'll place in the money. I threw the tools in the back, kicked her to life and went after the comrades, more anxious than ever to take a closer look at the frightened Svirsky.   The road along here is like nothing else on Earth—in fact the landscape looks like the moon.   Just rock, with sparse and deadlooking shrubs on it, falling straight to the sea, with the Adriatic Highway scratched along the face of the cliff.   I concentrated on the driving, not on the view.   I didn't see the Tatra again, though I did see Lukovo and Karlobag, jumbles of low, drab buildings, locked and tomblike under the heat of the afternoon sun.   About five miles beyond Karlobag I saw a tan Mercedes coming from the other direction and I slammed on my brakes as it whistled by, burning rubber as well.   Making a sharp U-turn I pulled up behind the Mercedes which was stopped on the narrow shoulder next to the guard rail.

"Hi Able, hi Dog," I said.   "Seen any black Tatras lately?"

Martins, who had never smiled since I met him, shook his head in a lugubrious no.   His partner, Baker, agreed.

"They have to have been here," I said, digging out my road map.   "They were only a few miles ahead of me."   I ran my finger along the map and sighed. "You're right.   They're not.   They turned off in Karlobag.   They knew they were being tailed and even the dimmest of them could have figured out that there was a reception party ahead.   Look."

I put my finger on the map and they looked.   "A side road goes off into the mountains here, then over the top where it joins up with a good road at Gospic. After that they have a straight run for the border.   Once they are past the first stretch."

"The first part is marked in yellow," Martins said.   "What does that mean?"

"I'm afraid to find out."   The map, issued by *Turisticki savez Jugoslavije,* was in Italian, and yellow roads were marked as being *Strada in macadam in cativo stato.* "In rough translation you could say unpaved and in lousy shape."

"That's bad," Martins said, looking like he was going to cry.   "In Yugoslavia that is very bad."

"I'll give you a complete description of it when I make my report . . ."

"No," Martins said.

"Orders," Baker added.   "We're supposed to take over the chase when we meet you.   That came right down from the top."

"Not fair!   I started this job and I should be left to finish it."

They shrugged, jumped into the Mercedes and charged off down the road.   I climbed into the Toyota and followed them.   So they could go first.   But no one had said I couldn't follow them.

In Karlobag a rusty sign labeled Gospic 41 pointed up a hill at a cloud of dust. I hit the road and my brakes at the same time, then lurched forward in compound low.   It was more of a quarry than a road, made up of rounded stones—some of them as big as tabletops.   I ground forward, dodging the worst ones, at five miles an hour.   There was a loud explosion around the turn ahead.   I hit the gas and bounced and skidded around it.

The Mercedes was off the road with its hood buried in the ditch.   Its front wheels were angled out as if they were very tired and both fenders were peeled back like a pair of open tin cans. Things were still happening. A man in a dark suit stood up from behind a boulder on the far side of the road and leveled a long-barreled pistol. Before he could shoot, Martins, who had been driving, had his gun resting on the window ledge and fired just once. It was very dramatic. Black suit screeched shrilly, threw his gun up in the air, spun about and fell.

"Look after Baker," I shouted. "I'll take care of your friend."

I circled, fast and quiet, and came up behind the man who was flat on the ground, trying to clamp his hand over his bleeding arm and wriggle over to his gun at the same time. "No seconds," I said, picking up the gun.

He rolled over and looked at me. *"Sveenyah . . ."* he growled.

"It is the same in every language," I told him, and pocketed the gun. "And who are you to call names? Do decent people travel around with land mines in their cars?" I left him that one to think about while I went back to help Martins. He had Baker laid out by the side of the road, the first-aid kit open, and was smearing antiseptic on a bloody gash on the younger agent's forehead.

"Out cold," he said. "Breathing regular and it doesn't seem too bad—but you never know."

"Carry him back to the road, it's only a hundred yards, and flag down a car. There must be a doctor in this town. If not, there's a big hospital in Zadar. And if you remember it, you could send someone back to look at your target over there in the weeds. I'm going on to talk to Svirsky about the kind of friends he has."

I didn't give him time to argue, just started the Toyota and bounced away up the road. This was going to be a stern chase where my four-wheel drive would finally come in handy. By missing the worst tombstones I could hold her on 20, even 25 on some stretches. I was pretty sure the Tatra couldn't do this well, rugged as it is. Particularly when I saw it two turns above me on the snake-bended road.

All things considered it was doing all right, bouncing and swaying and throwing up a cloud of dust at all of ten miles an hour. These cars, which are never seen in the West, are the pride of the Skoda works. They're big and round and solid, only for high party officials and types like that. They are built and sprung to take punishment, too. With a high fin down the middle of their backs like a Flash Gordon rocket ship and three headlights in the front they have more of a mad look than you would expect to find in this part of the world. Or maybe you would expect to. In any case, fin, headlights and shocks weren't helping him stay ahead. I was catching up slowly. We bounced and groaned and rattled around the bends and over the boulders and I was less than two hundred yards behind him when I saw, around the next turn, a spire and marker that might very well be the top of the hill. If he got there first, and onto a straight road, he might get away from me.

At this point the road headed away from the marker, went down and made a loop and came back on a higher level above the spot I was passing. A banked hillside separated the two stretches of road and I could see a beaten path where the pedestrians, goats and dogs took a shortcut to save walking the long loop of road. Where four legs go, four wheels go. I pulled the wheel hard right and bounced through the ditch and into the dirt.

In all truth it was smoother and better than the road, although just a bit more angled.   The engine growled, the tires spun and dug in, and we went straight up. I shouted *yippee* and held tight to the wheel.

When I came over the shoulder the Tatra had already rounded the turn and was bounding my way, its three eyes gleaming.   For a churning moment the Toyota hung up on the sharp lip, the front tires slipping on the smooth stones, until the back wheels dug in and shot us over the top.

Since the Tatra was about to pass me I did the only thing possible and ran full tilt into it.

I did manage to hit the hood so it jarred sideways.   There was a sound like an explosion in a garbage can factory when we collided—then the Tatra nosed off the road and crashed into a well-placed pile of rocks.   I braked, killed the engine and jumped out at the same time, but Svirsky was faster.   He had the back door open even before the crash and had bounced out like an overweight gazelle.   The driver was half-slumped over the wheel, mumbling to himself as he tried to drag out another of those long-barreled pistols.   I took it away from him and cracked him at the right spot in the back of the neck that would put him to sleep for a while and keep him out of mischief.   Then I followed Svirsky.

He had his head down and was pelting along the road like a runaway steam engine.   But I just happen to be faster.   When he reached the marker he turned off the road with me coming close behind him.   I reached the high marker, passed it—then jumped back.   The bullet tore a gouge from the stone just where I had been.   Svirsky must have been the backseat marksman who had taken out my tire, and his eye was still good.   Next to my head was an inscription, in German, something about this road dedicated to our noble Emperor, Franz-Josef.   I believed it.   And I bet it hadn't been touched since the Emperor watched them roll the last boulder into place.

Keeping low I ran around the other side of the commemoration plinth and saw Svirsky vanishing into a grove of pine trees.   Great!   If he had stayed on the road, he could have kept me away with his deadly popgun.   In the woods we were equal.

This was a northern forest, very much like the Alps.   We had climbed high enough to leave the baked, subtropical coast behind and enter this pleasant green highland.   Well me Leatherstocking, him the moose—or bear—I was going to do a little trapping.   I could hear my prey crashing through the underbrush ahead and I circled out to the side to swing around him, running low, silent and fast.

My friend Svirsky was no Indian scout—or even a boy scout.   He pushed those four hundred twelve pounds through the woods like a tank, and I kept him in sonar contact at all times.   When the crashing stopped I kept going until I had passed the spot where I had heard him last, then came silently back.

What a setup!   He was bent over behind a tree, looking back the way he had come, the gun pointed and ready.   I considered the best course, then decided that disarming him might be the wisest first step.   I came up silently behind him.

"Can I borrow that, Comrade?" I said as I reached over and—with a good tug— pulled the gun out of his hands.

For all of his weight he had good reflexes.   He swung at me and I had to jump aside to avoid getting slugged.

"Hands in the air, or *Hande hoch* or whatever."

Svirsky ignored both me and the gun and, scowling terribly, he kept coming on in a wrestler's crouch, arms extended.   I backed away.

"Someone can get hurt this way," I told him, "and the odds are that it's going to be you."

Still not a word, just that steady, machinelike advance.

"Don't say I didn't give fair warning.   Stop, stop, stop, that's three times."

He completely ignored me so I shot him in the leg.   The bullet ricocheted and screamed away and he kept coming.   I could see the hole in his pants leg so I knew that I hadn't missed.

"All right, iron man," I said, aiming carefully.   "Let's see how good your joints are."

This time I aimed at his knee cap, with the same results.   Nothing.   I was backed up to a tree.   I fired at the same spot once more before the bullets had any effect and the leg folded.   But he was right on top of me then, coming down like a falling mountain.   I couldn't get away in time and he hit me.   I threw the gun as far away as I could before he closed those big hands on me.

Talk about strong, this joker had muscles of steel.   I wriggled and twisted and kept moving, and I didn't try to hit him because I knew he had no nerves, no nerves at all.   I twisted and pushed away, tearing most of my shirt off at the same time, and managed to get out of that mechanical bearhug.

Now it was my turn.   I just climbed his back, locked my legs around his waist, and twisted his neck.   He still hadn't said anything, I doubt if he could talk, but he thrashed his arms something terrible and tried to pull me off.   He just couldn't reach me.   I turned and turned until he was glaring back at me over his right shoulder.   And then I turned some more.   He was facing straight backwards now, clicking his teeth at me.   And I kept twisting.   There was a sharp crack and his eyes closed and all the fight went out of him.   I just turned some more until his head came off.

Of course there was a lot of trailing wires and piping and that kind of thing, but I pulled it all loose and put the decapitated head on the ground.   Some of the wires sparked when they grounded.

Now I had to find out where the brain was.   Just because a robot looks like a man there is no reason to assume that its brain is in its head.   Svirsky may have thought with his stomach.   I had to find out.   Ever since we had heard the rumors that a humanoid robot was being field-tested in Yugoslavia we had all been planning for this moment.   Servo motors and power plants and hardware we knew about. But what kind of a brain were they using?   We were going to find out.   I pulled his shirt open and they hadn't even bothered to put the plastic flesh back completely the last time they had serviced him.   They must have been in a hurry to leave. A flap of skin was hanging loose just above his navel and I put my finger in and pulled.   He peeled open just like a banana, showing a broad, metallic chest under the soft plastic.   An access plate covered most of it, just like on an airplane's engine, with big slotted fasteners in the corners.   I bent a ten dinar coin twisting them open, then pulled the plate off and threw it away.

Well, well, I smiled to myself, and even went so far as to rub my hands together. Motors, junction boards, power pack, and so forth, all feeding into a bundle of wires in a realistic location where the spinal cord should have been and heading up through the neck.   Brain in head—and I had the head.

"Thank you, Comrade," I said, standing and dusting off my knees, "you have been very helpful.   I'm going to borrow your shirt, because you tore mine, and take some pictures of your innards to make our engineers happy."

I removed the shirt from the headless torso and propped him up so that the sun shone in through the access port.   Now camera.   I looked around carefully to be sure no one was in sight, then threw my torn shirt away.

"We have our secrets, too," I told him, but he didn't bother to answer.

I pushed with my thumbnail at the flesh over my sternum, then pulled with both hands until my skin stretched and parted.   The lens of my chest camera protruded through the opening.   "F2.5 at a 125th," I estimated, correctly of course, then shot the pictures, clicking them off with a neural impulse to the actuator.   I could easily hide the head in the Toyota and these pics would be all the detail we needed about the body.   Since there was no one else present I did not mind bragging aloud.

"Just like the space race, Comrade, neck and neck.   And you went to the robot race the same way.   Build strong, build for excess power, build double and treble in case of failure.   That makes for a mighty heavy robot.   Not even room left for speech circuits.   While we built with micro and micromicrominiaturization.   Sophisticated circuitry.   More goodies in the same size package.   And it works, too. When Washington heard you were going to be tested down here they couldn't resist field-testing me at the same time."

I started back to the Toyota, then turned and waved goodbye with my free hand.

"If you have any doubt about which approach works the best," I called out cheerily, "just notice who is carrying whose head under his arm."

FREDERIK POHL

The Gold at the Starbow's End

CONSTITUTION ONE

Log of Lt. Col. Sheffield N. Jackman, USAF, commanding U.S. Starship *Constitution,* Day 40.

All's well, friends.   Thanks to Mission Control for the batch of personal messages.   We enjoyed the concert you beamed us, in fact we recorded most of it so we can play it over again when communication gets hairy.

We are now approaching the six-week point in our expedition to Alpha Centauri, Planet Aleph, and now that we've passed the farthest previous manned distance from Earth we're really beginning to feel as if we're on our way.   Our latest navigation check confirms Mission Control's plot, and we estimate we should be crossing the orbit of Pluto at approximately 1631 hours, ship time, of Day 40, which is today.   Letski has been keeping track of the time dilation effect, which is beginning to be significant now that we are traveling about some six percent of the speed of light, and says this would make it approximately a quarter of two in the morning your time, Mission Control.   We voted to consider that the "coastal waters" mark.   From then on we will have left the solar system behind and thus will be the first human beings to enter upon the deeps of interstellar space.   We plan to have a ceremony.   Letski and Ann Becklund have made up an American flag for jettisoning at that point, which we will do through the Number Three survey port, along with the prepared stainless-steel plaque containing the President's commissioning speech.   We are also throwing in some private articles for each of us. I am contributing my Air Academy class ring.

Little change since previous reports.   We are settling down nicely to our routine. We finished up all our post-launch checks weeks ago, and as Dr. Knefhausen predicted we began to find time hanging heavy on our hands.   There won't be much to keep us busy between now and when we arrive at the planet Alpha-Aleph that is really essential to the operating of the spaceship.   So we went along with Kneffie's proposed recreational schedule, using the worksheets prepared by the NASA Division of Flight Training and Personnel Management.   At first—I think the boys back in Indianapolis are big enough to know this—it met with what you might call a cool reception.   The general consensus was that this business of learning number theory and the calculus of statement, which is what they handed us for openers, was for the birds.   We figured we weren't quite desperate enough for that yet, so we fooled around with other things.   Ann and Will Becklund played a lot of chess.   Dot Letski began writing a verse adaptation of "War and Peace." The rest of us hacked around with the equipment, and making astronomical observations and gabbing.   But all that began to get tiresome pretty fast, just as Kneffie said it would at the briefings.

We talked about his idea that the best way to pass time in a spaceship was learning to get interested in mathematical problems—no mass to transport, no competitive element to get tempers up and all that.   It began to make sense.   So now Letski is in his tenth day of trying to find a formula for primes, and my own dear Flo is trying to prove Goldbach's Conjecture by means of the theory of congruences. (This is the girl who two months ago couldn't add up a laundry list!)   It certainly passes the time.

Medically, we are all fit.   I will append the detailed data on our blood pressures, pulses, et cetera, as well as the tape from the rocket and navigating systems readouts. I'll report again as scheduled.   Take care of Earth for us—we're looking forward to seeing it again, in a few years!

WASHINGTON ONE

There was a lull in the urban guerrilla war in Washington that week.   The chopper was able to float right in to the South Lawn of the White House—no sniper fire, no heat-seeking missiles, not even rock-throwing.   Dr. Dieter von Knefhausen stared suspiciously at the knot of weary-looking pickets in their permitted fifty yards of space along the perimeter.   They didn't look militant, probably Gay Lib or, who knew what, maybe nature-food or single-tax; at any rate no rocks came from them, only a little disorganized booing as the helicopter landed.   Knefhausen bowed to *Herr Omnes* sardonically, hopped nimbly out of the chopper and got out of the way as it took off again, which it did at once.   He didn't trouble to run to the White House.   He strolled.   He did not fear these simple people, even if the helicopter pilot did.   Also he was not really eager to keep his appointment with the President.

The ADC who frisked him did not smile.   The orderly who conducted him to the West Terrace did not salute.   No one relieved him of the dispatch case with his slides and papers, although it was heavy.   You could tell right away when you were in the doghouse, he thought, ducking his head from the rotor blast as the pilot circled the White House to gain altitude before venturing back across the spread-out city.

It had been a lot different in the old days, he thought with some nostalgia.   He could remember every minute of those old days.   It was right here, this portico, where he had stood before the world's press and photographers to tell them about the Alpha-Aleph Project.   He had seen his picture next to the President's on all the front pages, watched himself on the TV newscasts, talking about the New Earth that would give America an entire colonizable planet four light-years away.   He remembered the launch at the Cape, with a million and a half invited guests from all over the world, foreign statesmen and scientists eating their hearts out with envy, American leaders jovial with pride.   The orderlies saluted then, all right.

His lecture fees had gone clear out of sight.   There was even talk of making him the Vice Presidential candidate in the next election—and it could have happened, too, if the election had been right then, and if there hadn't been the problem of his being born in another country.

Now it was all different.   He was taken up in the service elevator.   It wasn't so much that Knefhausen minded for his own sake, he told himself, but how did the word get out that there was trouble?   Was it only the newspaper stories?   Was there a leak?

The Marine orderly knocked once on the big door of the Cabinet room, and it was opened from inside.

Knefhausen entered.

"Come in, Dieter, boy, pull up a pew."   No Vice President jumping up to grab his arm and slap his back.   His greeting was thirty silent faces turned toward him, some reserved, some frankly hostile.   The full Cabinet was there, along with half a dozen department heads and the President's personal action staff, and the most hostile face around the big oval table was the President's own.

Knefhausen bowed.   An atavistic hankering for lyceum-cadet jokes made him think of clicking his heels and adjusting a monocle, but he didn't have a monocle and didn't yield to impulses like that.   He merely took his place standing at the foot of the table and, when the President nodded, said, "Good morning, gentlemen, and ladies.   I assume you want to see me about the stupid lies the Russians are spreading about the Alpha-Aleph program."

"Roobarooba," they muttered to each other.

The President said in his sharp tenor, "So you think they are just lies?"

"Lies or mistakes, Mr. President, what's the difference?   We are right and they are wrong, that's all."

"Roobaroobarooba."

The Secretary of State looked inquiringly at the President, got a nod and said: "Dr. Knefhausen, you know I've been on your team a long time and I don't want to disagree with any statement you care to make, but are you so sure about that? There are some mighty persuasive figures comin' out of the Russians."

"They are false, Mr. Secretary."

"Ah, well, Dr. Knefhausen.   I might be inclined to take your word for it, but others might not.   Not cranks or malcontents, Dr. Knefhausen, but good, decent people.   Do you have any evidence for them?"

"With your permission, Mr. President?"   The President nodded again. Knefhausen unlocked his dispatch case and drew out a slim sheaf of slides.   He handed them to a major of Marines, who looked to the President for approval and then did what Knefhausen told him.   The room lights went down and, after some fiddling with the focus, the first slide was projected over Knefhausen's head.   It showed a huge array of Y-shaped metal posts, stretching away into the distance of a bleak, powdery-looking landscape.

"This picture is our radio telescope on Farside, the Moon," he said.   "It is never visible from the Earth, because that portion of the Moon's surface is permanently turned away from us, for which reason we selected it for the site of the telescope.   There is no electrical interference of any kind.   The instrument is made up of thirty-three million separate dipole elements, aligned with an accuracy of one part in several million.   Its actual size is an approximate circle eighteen miles across, but by virtue of the careful positioning its performance is effectively equal to a telescope with a diameter of some twenty-six miles.   Next slide, please.''

Click. The picture of the huge RT display swept away and was replaced by another similar—but visibly smaller and shabbier—construction.

"This is the Russian instrument, gentlemen.   And ladies.   It is approximately one-quarter the size of ours in diameter.   It has less than one-tenth as many elements, and our reports—they are classified, but I am informed this gathering is cleared to receive this material?   Yes—our reports indicate the alignment is very crude.   Even terrible, you could say.

"The difference between the two instruments in information-gathering capacity is roughly a hundred to one, in our favor.   Lights, please.

"What this means," he went on smoothly, smiling at each of the persons around the table in turn as he spoke, "is that if the Russians say 'no' and we say 'yes,' bet on 'yes.'   Our radio telescope can be trusted.   Theirs cannot."

The meeting shifted uneasily in its chairs.   They were as anxious to believe Knefhausen as he was to convince them, but they were not sure.

Representative Belden, the Chairman of the House Ways and Means Committee, spoke for all of them.   "Nobody doubts the quality of your equipment.   Especially," he added, "since we still have bruises from the job of paying for it.   But the Russians made a flat statement.   They said that Alpha Centauri can't have a planet larger than one thousand miles in diameter, or nearer than half a billion miles to the star.   I have a copy of the Tass release here.   It admits that their equipment is inferior to our own, but they have a statement signed by twenty-two academicians that says their equipment could not miss on any object larger, or nearer, than what I have said, or on any body of any kind which would be large enough to afford a landing place for our astronauts.   Are you familiar with this statement?''

"Yes, of course, I have read it—"

"Then you know that they state positively that the planet you call 'Alpha-Aleph' does not exist."

"Yes, sir, that is what they state."

"Moreover, statements from authorities at the Paris Observatory and the UNESCO Astrophysical Center at Trieste, and from England's Astronomer Royal, all say that they have checked and confirmed their figures."

Knefhausen nodded cheerfully.   "That is correct, Representative Belden.   They confirm that if the observations are as stated, then the conclusions drawn by the Soviet installation at Novy Brezhnevgrad on Farside naturally follow.   I don't question the arithmetic.   I only say that the observations are made with inadequate equipment, and thus the Soviet astronomers have come to a false conclusion.   But I do not want to burden your patience with an unsupported statement," he added hastily as the Congressman opened his mouth to speak again, "so I will tell you all there is to tell. What the Russians say is theory. What I have to counter is not merely better theory, but also objective fact. I know Alpha-Aleph is there because I have seen it! Lights again, Major! And the next slide, if you please."

The screen lit up and showed glaring bare white with a sprinkling of black spots, like dust. A large one appeared in the exact center of the screen, with a dozen lesser ones sprinkled around it. Knefhausen picked up a flash pointer and aimed its little arrowhead of light at the central dot.

"This is a photographic negative," he said, "which is to say that it is black where the actual scene is white and vice versa. Those objects are astronomical. It was taken from our Briareus XII satellite near the orbit of Jupiter, on its way out to Neptune fourteen months ago. The central object is the star Alpha Centauri. It was photographed with a special instrument which filters out most of the light from the star itself, electronic in nature and something like the coronascope which is used for photographing prominences on our own Sun. We hoped that by this means we might be able to photograph the planet Alpha-Aleph. We were successful, as you can see." The flashpointer laid its little arrow next to the nearest small dot to the central star. "That, gentlemen, and ladies, is Alpha-Aleph. It is precisely where we predicted it from radio-telescope data."

There was another buzz from the table. In the dark it was louder than before. The Secretary of State cried sharply, "Mr. President! Can't we release this photograph?"

"We will release it immediately after this meeting," said the President.

"*Roobarooba.*"

Then the committee chairman: "Mr. President, I'm sure if you say that's the planet we want, then it's the planet. But others outside this country may wonder, for indeed all those dots look alike to me. Just to satisfy a layman's curiosity, *how* do you know that is Alpha-Aleph?"

"Slide Number Four, please—and keep Number Three in the carriage." The same scene, subtly different. "Note that in this picture, gentlemen, that one object, there, is in a different position. It has moved. You know that the stars show no discernible motion. It has moved because this photograph was taken eight months later, as Briareus XII was returning from the Neptune flyby, and the planet Alpha-Aleph has revolved in its orbit. This is not theory, it is evidence, and I add that the original tapes from which the photoprint was made are stored in Goldstone so there is no question that arises of foolishness."

"*Roobarooba,*" but in a higher and excited key.

Gratified, Knefhausen nailed down his point. "So, Major, if you will now return to Slide Three, yes—And if you will flip back and forth, between Three and Four, as fast as you can—Thank you." The little black dot called Alpha-Aleph bounced back and forth like a tennis ball, while all the other star points remained motionless.

"This is what is called the blank comparator process, you see. I point out that if what you are looking at is not a planet it is, Mr. President, the funniest star you ever saw. Also it is exactly at the distance and exactly with the orbital period we specified based on the RT data. Now, are there any more questions?''

"No, sir!" "That's great, Kneffie!" "I think that wraps it up." "That'll show the Commies."

The President's voice overrode them.

"I think we can have the lights on now, Major Merton," he said. "Dr. Knefhausen, thank you. I'd appreciate it if you would remain nearby for a few minutes, so you can join Murray and myself in the study to check over the text of our announcement before we release these pictures." He nodded sober dismissal to his chief science adviser and then, reminded by the happy faces of his cabinet, remembered to smile with pleasure.

CONSTITUTION TWO

Sheffield Jackman's log. Starship *Constitution*. Day 95.

According to Letski we are now traveling at just about fifteen percent of the speed of light, almost 30,000 miles per second. The fusion thrusters are chugging away handsomely; as predicted, the explosions sequence fast enough so that we feel them only as vibration. Fuel, power and life-support curves are sticking tight to optimum. No sweat of any kind with the ship, or, actually, with anything else.

Relativistic effects have begun to show up as predicted. Jim Barstow's spectral studies show the stars in front of us are shifting to the blue end, and the Sun and other stars behind us are shifting to the red. Without the spectroscope you can't see much, though. Beta Circini looks a little funny, maybe. As for the Sun, it's still very bright—Jim logged it as minus-six magnitude a few hours ago—and as I've never seen it in quite that way before, I can't tell whether the color looks bright or not. It certainly isn't the golden yellow I associate with type GO, but neither is Alpha Centauri ahead of us, and I don't really see a difference between them. I think the reason is simply that they are so bright that the color impressions are secondary to the brightness impressions, although the spectroscope, as I say, does show the differences. We've all taken turns at looking back. Naturally enough, I guess. We can still make out the Earth and even the Moon in the telescope, but it's chancy. Ski almost got an eyeful of the Sun at full light-gathering amplitude yesterday because the visual separation is only about twelve seconds of arc now. In a few more days they'll be too close to separate.

Let's see, what else?

We've been having a fine time with the recreational-math program. Ann has taken to binary arithmetic like a duck to water. She's involved in what I take to be some sort of statistical experimentation—we don't pry too much into what the others are doing until they're ready to talk about it—and, of all things, she demanded we produce coins to flip. Well, naturally none of us had taken any money with us! Except that it turns out two of us did. Ski had a Russian silver ruble that his mother's uncle had given him for luck, and I found an old Philadelphia transit token in my pocket. Ann rejected my transit token as too light to be reliable, but she now spends happy hours flipping the ruble, heads or tails, and writing down the results as a series of six-place binary numbers, heads for 1 and tails for 0.

After about a week my curiosity got too much so I began hinting to find out what she was doing. When I ask she says things like, "By means of the easy and the simple we grasp the laws of the whole world." When I say that's nice, but what does she hope to grasp by flipping the coin, she says, "When the laws of the whole world are grasped, therein lies perfection." So, as I say, we don't press each other and I leave it there. But it passes the time.

Kneffie would be proud of himself if he could see how our recreation keeps us busy. None of us has managed to prove Fermat's Last Theorem yet or anything like that, but of course that's the whole point. If we could *solve* the problems, we'd have used them up, and then what would we do for recreation? It does exactly what it was intended to. It keeps us mentally alert on this long and intrinsically rather dull boat ride.

Personal relations? Jes' fine, fellows, jes' fine. A lot better than any of us really hoped, back there at the personal-hygiene briefings in Mission Control. The girls take the stripey pills every day until three days before their periods, then they take the green pills for four days, then they lay off pills for four days, then back to the stripes. There was a little embarrassed joking about it at first, but now it's strictly routine, like brushing our teeth. We men take our red pills every day— Ski christened them "stop lights"—until the girls tell us they're about to lay off— you know what I mean, each girl tells her husband—then we take the Blue Devil— that's what we call the antidote—and have a hell of a time until the girls start on the stripes again. None of us thought any of this would work, you know. But it works fine. I don't even think sex until Flo kisses my ear and tells me she's getting ready to, excuse the expression, get in heat, and then like wow. Same with everybody. The aft chamber with the nice wide bunks we call Honeymoon Hotel. It belongs to whoever needs it, and never once have both bunks been used. The rest of the time we just sleep wherever is convenient, and nobody gets up tight about it.

Excuse my getting personal, but you told me you wanted to know everything, and there's not much else to tell. All systems remain optimum. We check them over now and again, but nothing has given any trouble, or even looked as though it might be thinking about giving trouble later on. And there's absolutely nothing worth looking at outside, but stars. We've all seen them about as much as we need to by now. The plasma jet thrums right along at our point-seven-five G. We don't even hear it any more.

We've got used to the recycling system. None of us really thought we'd get with the suction toilet, not to mention what happens to the contents, but it was only a little annoying the first few days. Now it's fine. The treated product goes into the algae tanks. The sludge from the algae goes into the hydroponic beds, but by then, of course, it's just greeny-brown vegetable matter. That's all handled semi-automatically anyway, of course, so our first real contact with the system comes in the kitchen.

The food we eat comes in the form of nice red tomatoes and nourishing rice pilaf and stuff like that. (We do miss animal protein a little; the frozen stores have to last a long time, so each hamburger is a special feast and we only have them once a week or so.)   The water we drink comes actually out of the air, condensed by the dehumidifiers into the reserve supply, where we get it to drink.   It's nicely aerated and chilled and tastes fine.   Of course, the way it gets into the air in the first place is by being sweated out of our pores or transpired from the plants—which are irrigated direct from the treated product of the reclamation tanks—and we all know, when we stop to think of it, that every molecule of it has passed through all our kidneys forty times by now.   But not directly.   That's the point. What we drink is clear sweet dew.   And if it once was something else, can't you say the same of Lake Erie?

Well, I think I've gone on long enough.   You've probably got the idea by now: We're happy in the service, and we all thank you for giving us this pleasure cruise!

WASHINGTON TWO

Waiting for his appointment with the President, Dr. Knefhausen reread the communique from the spaceship, chuckling happily to himself.   "Happy in the service." "Like wow."   "Kneffie would be proud of himself."   Indeed Kneffie was.   And proud of them, those little wonders, there!   So brave.   So strong.

He took as much pride in them as though they had been his own sons and daughters, all eight of them.   Everybody knew the Alpha-Aleph project was Knefhausen's baby, but he tried to conceal from the world that, in his own mind, he spread his fatherhood to include the crew.   They were the pick of the available world, and it was he who had put them where they were.   He lifted his head, listening to the distant chanting from the perimeter fence where today's disgusting exhibition of mob violence was doing its best to harass the people who were making the world go.   What great lumps they were out there, with their long hair and their dirty morals.   The heavens belonged only to angels, and it was Dieter von Knefhausen who had picked the angels.   It was he who had established the selection procedures—and if he had done some things that were better left unmentioned to make sure the procedures worked, what of it?   It was he who had conceived and adapted the highly important recreation schedule, and above all he who had conceived the entire project and persuaded the President to make it come true.   The hardware was nothing, only money.   The basic scientific concepts were known; most of the components were on the shelves; it took only will to put them together. The will would not have existed if it had not been for Knefhausen, who announced the discovery of Alpha-Aleph from his radio-observatory on Farside—gave it that name, although as everyone realized he could have called it by any name he chose, even his own—and carried on the fight for the project by every means until the President bought it.

It had been a hard, bitter struggle.   He reminded himself with courage that the worst was still ahead.   No matter.   Whatever it cost, it was done, and it was worthwhile.   These reports from *Constitution* proved it.   It was going exactly as planned, and—

"Excuse me, Dr. Knefhausen."

He looked up, catapulted back from almost half a light-year away.

"I said the President will see you now, Dr. Knefhausen," repeated the usher.

"Ah," said Knefhausen. "Oh, yes, to be sure. I was deep in thought."

"Yes, sir. This way, sir."

They passed a window and there was a quick glimpse of the turmoil at the gates, picket signs used like battleaxes, a thin blue cloud of tear gas, the sounds of shouting. "King Mob is busy today," said Knefhausen absently.

"There's no danger, sir. Through here, please."

The President was in his private study, but to Knefhausen's surprise he was not alone. There was Murray Amos, his personal secretary, which one could understand; but there were three other men in the room. Knefhausen recognized them as the Secretary of State, the Speaker of the House and, of all people, the Vice President. How strange, thought Knefhausen, for what was to have been a confidential briefing for the President alone! But he rallied quickly.

"Excuse me, Mr. President," he said cheerfully, "I must have understood wrong. I thought you were ready for our little talk."

"I am ready, Knefhausen," said the President. The cares of his years in the White House rested heavily on him today, Knefhausen thought critically. He looked very old and very tired. "You will tell these gentlemen what you would have told me."

"Ah, yes, I see," said Knefhausen, trying to conceal the fact that he did not see at all. Surely the President did not mean what his words said, therefore it was necessary to try to see what was his thought. "Yes, to be sure. Here is something, Mr. President. A new report from the *Constitution*! It was received by burst transmission from the Lunar Orbiter at Goldstone just an hour ago, and has just come from the decoding room. Let me read it to you. Our brave astronauts are getting along splendidly, just as we planned. They say—"

"Don't read us that just now," said the President harshly. "We'll hear it, but first there is something else. I want you to tell this group the full story of the Alpha-Aleph project."

"The full story, Mr. President?" Knefhausen hung on gamely. "I see. You wish me to begin with the very beginning, when first we realized at the observatory that we had located a planet—"

"No, Knefhausen. Not the cover story. The truth."

"Mr. President!" cried Knefhausen in sudden agony. "I must inform you that I protest this premature disclosure of vital—"

"The truth, Knefhausen!" shouted the President. It was the first time Knefhausen had ever heard him raise his voice. "It won't go out of this room, but you must tell them everything. Tell them why it is that the Russians were right and we lied! Tell them why we sent the astronauts on a suicide mission, ordered to land on a planet that we knew all along did not exist!"

CONSTITUTION THREE

Shef Jackman's journal, Day 130.

It's been a long time, hasn't it? I'm sorry for being such a lousy correspondent. I was in the middle of a thirteen-game chess series with Eve Barstow—she was playing the Bobby Fischer games and I was playing in the style of Reshevsky—

and Eve said something that made me think of old Kneffie, and that, of course, reminded me I owed you a transmission.   So here it is.

In my own defense, though, it isn't only that we've been busy with other things. It takes a lot of power for these chatty little letters.   Some of us aren't so sure they're worthwhile.   The farther we get the more power we need to accumulate for a transmission.   Right now it's not so bad, but, well, I might as well tell you the truth, right?   Kneffie made us promise that.   Always tell the truth, he said, because you're part of the experiment, and we need to know what you're doing, all of it.   Well, the truth in this case is that we were a little short of disposable power for a while because Jim Barstow needed quite a lot for research purposes. You will probably wonder what the research is, but we have a rule that we don't criticize, or even talk about, what anyone else is doing until they're ready, and he isn't ready yet.   I take the responsibility for the whole thing, not just the power drain but the damage to the ship.   I said he could go ahead with it.

We're going pretty fast now, and to the naked eye the stars fore and aft have blue-shifted and red-shifted nearly out of sight.   It's funny but we haven't been able to observe Alpha-Aleph yet, even with the disk obscuring the star.   Now, with the shift to the blue, we probably won't see it at all until we slow down.   We can still see the Sun, but I guess what we're seeing is ultraviolet when it's home. Of course the relativistic frequency shifts mean we need extra compensating power in our transmissions, which is another reason why, all in all, I don't think I'll be writing home every Sunday between breakfast and the baseball game, the way I ought to!

But the mission's going along fine.   The "personal relationships" keep on being just great.   We've done a little experimental research there, too, that wasn't on the program, but it's all O.K.   No problems.   Worked out great.   I think maybe I'll leave out some of the details, but we found some groovy ways to do things. Oh, hell, I'll give you one hint: Dot Letski says I should tell you to get the boys at Mission Control to crack open two of the stripey pills and one of the Blue Devils, mix them with a quarter-teaspoon of black pepper and about 2 cc of the conditioner fluid from the recycling system.   Serve over orange sherbet, and oh, boy.   After the first time we had it Flo made a crack about its being "seminal", which I thought was a private joke, but it broke everybody up.   Dot figured it out for herself weeks ago.   We wondered how she got so far so fast with "War and Peace" until she let us into the secret.   Then we found out what it could do for you, both emotionally and intellectually: the creative over the arousing, as they say.

Ann and Jerry Letski used up their own recreational programs early—real early. They were supposed to last the whole voyage!   They swapped microfiches, on the grounds that each was interested in an aspect of causality and they wanted to see what the other side had to offer.   Now Ann is deep into people like Kant and Carnap, and Ski is sore as a boil because there's no *Achillea millefolium* in the hydroponics garden.   Needs the stalks for his researches, he says.   He is making do with flipping his ruble to generate hexagrams; in fact we all borrow it now and then.   But it's not the right way.   Honestly, Mission Control, he's right.   Some thought should have been given to our other needs, besides sex and number theory.

We can't even use chop bones from the kitchen wastes, because there isn't any kitchen waste. I know you couldn't think of everything, but still—Anyway, we improvise as best we can, and mostly well enough.

Let's see, what else? Did I send you Jim Barstow's proof of Goldbach's Conjecture? Turned out to be very simple once he had devised his multiplex parity analysis idea. Mostly we don't fool with that sort of stuff any more, though. We got tired of number theory after we'd worked out all the fun parts, and if there is any one thing that we all work on—apart from our private interests—it is probably the calculus of statement. We don't do it systematically, only as time permits from our other activities, but we're all pretty well convinced that a universal grammar is feasible enough, and it's easy enough to see where that leads.

Flo has done more than most of us. She asked me to put in that Boole, Venn and all those old people were on the wrong track, but she thinks there might be something to Leibniz's "calculus ratiocinator" idea. There's a J. W. Swanson suggestion that she likes for multiplexing languages. (Jim took off from it to work out his parity analysis.) The idea is that you devise a double-vocabulary language. One set of meanings is conveyed, say, by phonemes, that is, the shape of the words themselves. Another set is conveyed by pitch. It's like singing a message, half of it conveyed by the words, the other half by the tune—like rock music. You get both sets of meanings at the same time. She's now working on third, fourth and nth dimensions so as to convey many kinds of meanings at once, but it's not very fruitful so far—except for using sex as one of the communications media. Most of the senses available are too limited to convey much.

By the way, we checked out all the existing "artificial languages" as best we could—put Will Becklund under hypnotic regression to recapture the Esperanto he'd learned as a kid, for instance. But they were all blind alleys. Didn't even convey as much as standard English or French.

Medical readouts follow. We're all healthy. Eve Barstow gave us a medical check to make sure. Ann and Ski had little rough spots in a couple of molars so she filled them for the practice more than because they needed it. I don't mean practice in filling teeth; she wanted to try acupuncture instead of procaine. Worked fine.

We all have this writing-to-Daddy-and-Mommy-from-Camp-Tanglewood feeling and we'd like to send you some samples of our home handicrafts. The trouble is there's so much of it. Everybody has something he's personally pretty pleased with, like Barstow's proof of most of the classic math problems and my multimedia adaptation of *"Sur le pont d'Avignon"*. It's hard to decide what to send you with the limited power available, and we don't want to waste it with junk. So we took a vote and decided the best thing was Ann's verse retelling of "War and Peace". It runs pretty long. I hope the power holds it. I'll transmit as much of it as I can. . . .

WASHINGTON THREE

Spring was well advanced in Washington. Along the Potomac the cherry blossoms were beginning to bud, and Rock Creek Park was the pale green of new leaves.   Even through the *whap, whap* of the helicopter rotor Knefhausen could hear an occasional rattle of small-arms fire from around Georgetown, and the Molotov cocktails and tear gas from the big Water Gate apartment development at the river's edge were steaming up the sky with smoke and fumes.   They never stopped, thought Knefhausen irritably.   What was the good of trying to save people like this?

It was distracting.   He found himself dividing his attention into three parts—the scarred, greening landscape below; the escort fireships that orbited around his own chopper; and the papers on his lap.   All of them annoyed him.   He couldn't keep his mind on any of them.   What he liked least was the report from the *Constitution.* He had had to get expert help in translating what it was all about, and he didn't like the need, and even less liked the results.   What had gone wrong? They were his kids, hand picked.   There had been no hint of, for instance, hippiness in any of them, at least not past the age of twenty, and only for Ann Becklund and Florence Jackman even then.   How had they got into this *I Ching* foolishness, and this stupid business with the *Achillea millefolium,* better known as the common yarrow?   What "experiments"?   Who started the disgustingly antiscientific acupuncture thing?   How dared they depart from their programmed power budget for "research purposes," and what were the purposes?   Above all, what was the "damage to the ship"?

He scribbled on a pad:

> With immediate effect, cut out the nonsense.   I have the impression you are all acting like irresponsible children.   You are letting down the ideals of our program.
>
> Knefhausen

After running the short distance from the chopper pad to the shelter of the guarded White House entrance, he gave the slip to a page from the Message Center for immediate encoding and transmission to the *Constitution* via Goldstone, Lunar Orbiter and Farside Base.   All they needed was a reminder, he persuaded himself, then they would settle down.   But he was still worried as he peered into a mirror, patted his hair down, smoothed his moustache with the tip of a finger and presented himself to the President's chief secretary.

This time they went down, not up.   Knefhausen was going to the basement chamber that had been successively Franklin Roosevelt's swimming pool, the White House press lounge, a TV studio for taping jolly little two-shots of the President with congressmen and senators for the folks back home to see and, now, the heavily armored bunker in which anyone trapped in the White House in the event of a successful attack from the city outside could hold out for several weeks, during which time the Fourth Armored would surely be able to retake the grounds from its bases in Maryland.   It was not a comfortable room, but it was a safe one. Besides being armored against attack, it was as thoroughly soundproof, spyproof and leak-proof as any chamber in the world, not excepting the Under-Kremlin, or the Colorado NOROM base.

Knefhausen was admitted and seated, while the President and a couple of others were in whispered conversation at one end of the room, and the several dozen other people present craned their necks to stare at Knefhausen.

After a moment the President raised his head. "All right," he said. He drank from a crystal goblet of water, looking wizened and weary, and disappointed at the way a boyhood dream had turned out: the presidency wasn't what it had seemed to be, from Muncie, Indiana. "We all know why we're here. The govermnent of the United States has given out information which was untrue. It did so knowingly and wittingly, and we've been caught at it. Now we want you to know the background, and so Dr. Knefhausen is going to explain the Alpha-Aleph project. Go ahead, Knefhausen."

Knefhausen stood up and walked unhurryingly to the little lectern set up for him, off to one side of the President. He opened his papers on the lectern, studied them thoughtfully for a moment with his lips pursed and said:

"As the President has said, the Alpha-Aleph project is a camouflage. A few of you learned this some months ago, and then you referred to it with other words. 'Fraud.' 'Fake.' Words like that. But if I may say it in French, it is not any of those words, it is a legitimate *ruse de guerre*. Not the *guerre* against our political enemies, or even against the dumb kids in the streets with their Molotov cocktails and bricks. I do not mean those wars, I mean the war against ignorance. For you see, there were certain signs—certain *things*—we had to know for the sake of science and progress. Alpha-Aleph was designed to find them out for us.

"I will tell you the worst parts first," he said. "Number one, there is no such planet as Alpha-Aleph. The Russians were right. Number two, we knew this all along. Even the photographs we produced were fakes, and in the long run the rest of the world will find this out and they will know of our *ruse de guerre*. I can only hope that they will not find out too soon, for if we are lucky and keep the secret for a while, then I hope we will be able to produce good results to justify what we have done. Number three, when the *Constitution* reaches Alpha Centauri there will be no place for them to land, no way to leave their spacecraft, no sources of raw materials which they might be able to use to make fuel to return—nothing but the star and empty space. This fact has certain consequences.

"The *Constitution* was designed with enough hydrogen fuel capacity for a one-way flight, plus maneuvering reserve. There will not be enough for them to come back, and the source they had hoped to tap, namely the planet Alpha-Aleph does not exist, so they will not come back. Consequently they will die there. Those are the bad things to which I must admit."

There was a sighing murmur from the audience. The President was frowning absently to himself. Knefhausen waited patiently for the medicine to be swallowed, then went on.

"You ask, then, why have we done this thing? Condemning eight young people to their death? The answer is simple: Knowledge. To put it in other words, we must have the basic scientific knowledge to protect the free world. You are all familiar, I si . . . I believe, with the known fact that basic scientific advances have been very few these past ten years and more. Much R&D. Much technology. Much applications. But in the years since Einstein, or better since Weizsäcker, very little basic.

"But without the new basic knowledge, the new technology must soon stop developing. It will run out of steam, you see.

"Now I must tell you a story. It is a true scientific story, not a joke; I know you do not want jokes from me at this time. There was a man named de Bono, a Maltese, who wished to investigate the process of creative thinking. There is not very much known about this process, but he had an idea how he could find something out. So he prepared for an experiment a room that was stripped of all furniture, with two doors, one across from the other. You go in one door, cross the room and then you walk out the other. He put at the door that was the entrance some material—two flat boards, some ropes. And he got as his subjects some young children. Now he said to the children: 'This is a game we will play. You must go through this room and out the other door, that is all. If you do that you win. But there is one rule. You must not touch the floor with your feet or your knees, or with any part of your body, or your clothing. We had here a boy,' he said, 'who was very athletic and walked across on his hands, but he was disqualified. You must not do that. Now go, and whoever does it fastest will win some chocolates.'

"So he took away all of the children but the first one and, one by one, they tried. There were ten or fifteen of them, and each of them did the same thing. Some it took longer to figure it out, some figured it out right away, but it always was the same trick: they sat down on the floor, they took the boards and the ropes, and they tied one board to each foot and they walked across the room like on skis. The fastest one thought of the trick right away and was across in a few seconds. The slowest took many minutes. But it was the same trick for all of them, and that was the first part of the experiment.

"Now this Maltese man, de Bono, performed the second part of the experiment. It was exactly like the first, with one difference. He did not give them two boards. He gave them only one board.

"And in the second part every child worked out the same trick, too, but it was, of course, a different trick. They tied the rope to the end of the single board and then they stood on it, and jumped up, tugging the rope to pull the board forward, hopping and tugging, moving a little bit at a time, and every one of them succeeded. But in the first experiment the average time to cross was maybe forty-five seconds. And in the second experiment the average time was maybe twenty seconds. With one board they did their job faster than with two.

"Perhaps now some of you see the point. Why did not any of the children in the first group think of this faster method of going across the room? It is simple. They looked at what they were given to use for materials and, they are like all of us, they wanted to use everything. But they did not need everything. They could do better with less, in a different way."

*   *   *

Knefhausen paused and looked around the room, savoring the moment. He had them now, he knew. It was just as it had been with the President himself, three years before. They were beginning to see the necessity of what had been done, and the pale, upturned faces were no longer as hostile, only perplexed and a little afraid.

He went on:

"So that is what Project Alpha-Aleph is about, gentlemen and ladies. We have selected eight of the most intelligent human beings we could find, healthy, young, very adventurous. Very creative. We played on them a nasty trick, to be sure. But we gave them an opportunity no one has ever had. The opportunity to think. To think for ten years. To think about basic questions. Out there they do not have the extra board to distract them. If they want to know something they cannot run to the library and look it up, and find that somebody has said that what they were thinking could not work. They must think it out for themselves.

"So in order to make this possible we have practiced a deception on them and it will cost them their lives. All right, that is tragic, yes. But if we take their lives we give them in exchange immortality.

"How do we do this? Trickery again, gentlemen and ladies. I do not say to them, 'Here, you must discover new basic approaches to science and tell them to us.' I camouflage the purpose, so that they will not be distracted even by that. We have told them that this is recreational, to help them pass the time. This, too, is a *ruse de guerre*. The 'recreation' is not to help them make the trip, it is the whole purpose of the trip.

"So we start them out with the basic tools of science. With numbers: That is, with magnitudes and quantification, with all that scientific observations are about. With grammar: This is not what you learned when you were thirteen years old. It is a technical term; it means with the calculus of statement and the basic rules of communication—that is so they can learn to think clearly by communicating fully and without fuzzy ambiguity. We give them very little else, only the opportunity to mix these two basic ingredients and come up with new forms of knowledge.

"What will come of these things? That is a fair question. Unfortunately there is no answer—not yet. If we knew the answer in advance, we would not have to perform the experiment. So we do not know what will be the end result of this, but already they have accomplished very much. Old questions that have puzzled the wisest of scientists for hundreds of years they have solved already. I will give you one example. You will say, yes, but what does it *mean?* I will answer, I do not know, I only know that it is so hard a question that no one else has ever been able to answer it. It is a proof of a thing which is called Goldbach's Conjecture. Only a conjecture; you could call it a guess. A guess by an eminent mathematician many, many years ago, that every even number can be written as the sum of two prime numbers. This is one of those simple problems in mathematics that everyone can understand and no one can solve. You can say, 'Certainly, sixteen is the sum of eleven and five, both of which are prime numbers, and thirty is the sum of twenty-three and seven, which also are both prime, and I can give you such numbers for any even number you care to name.'   Yes, you can; but can you prove that for *every* even number it will *always* be possible to do this? No.   You cannot.   No one has been able to, but our friends on the *Constitution* have done it, and this was in the first few months.   They have yet almost ten years. I cannot say what they will do in that time, but it is foolish to imagine that it will be anything less than very much indeed.   A new relativity, a new universal gravitation—I don't know, I am only saying words.   But much."

He paused again.   No one was making a sound.   Even the President was no longer staring straight ahead without expression, but was looking at him.

"It is not yet too late to spoil the experiment, and so it is necessary for us to keep the secret a bit longer.   But there you have it, gentlemen and ladies.   That is the truth about Alpha-Aleph."   He dreaded what would come next, postponed it for a second by consulting his papers, shrugged, faced them and said: "Now, are there any questions?"

Oh, yes, there were questions.   *Herr Omnes* was stunned a little, took a moment to overcome the spell of the simple and beautiful truths he had heard, but first one piped up, then another, then two or three shouting at once.   There were questions, to be sure.   Questions beyond answering.   Questions he did not have time to hear, much less answer, before the next question was on him.   Questions to which he did not know the answers.   Questions, worst of all, to which the answers were like pepper in the eyes, enraging, blinding the people to sense.   But he had to face them, and he tried to answer them.   Even when they shouted so that outside the thick double doors the Marine guards looked at each other uneasily, and wondered what made the dull rumble that penetrated the very good soundproofing of the room.   "What I want to know, who put you up to this?"   "Mr. Chairman, nobody; it is as I have said."   "But see now, Knefhausen, do you mean to tell us you're murderin' these good people for the sake of some Goldbach's theory?" "No, Senator, not for Goldbach's Conjecture, but for what great advances in science will mean in the struggle to keep the free world free."   "You're confessing you've dragged the United States into a palpable fraud?"   "A legitimate ruse of war, Mr. Secretary, because there was no other way."   "The photographs, Knefhausen?" "Faked, General, as I have told you.   I accept full responsibility." And on and on, the words "murder" and "fraud" and even "treason" coming faster and faster.

Until at last the President stood up and raised his hand.   Order was a long time coming, but at last they quieted down.

"Whether we like it or not, we're in it," he said simply.   "There is nothing else to say.   You have come to me, many of you, with rumors and asked for the truth.   Now you have the truth, and it is classified Top Secret and must not be divulged.   You all know what this means.   I will only add that I personally propose to see that any breach of this security is investigated with all the resources of the government, and punished with the full penalty of the law.   I declare this a matter of national emergency, and remind you that the penalty includes the death sentence when appropriate—and I say that in this case it is appropriate."   He looked very much older than his years, and he moved his lips as though something tasted bad in his mouth. He allowed no further discussion, and dismissed the meeting.

Half an hour later, in his private office, it was just Knefhausen and the President.

"All right," said the President, "it's all hit the fan. The next thing is the world will know it. I can postpone that a few weeks, maybe even months. I can't prevent it."

"I am grateful to you, Mr. President, for—"

"Shut up, Knefhausen. I don't want any speeches. There is one thing I want from you, and that is an explanation: What the hell is this about mixing up narcotics and free love and so on?"

"Ah," said Knefhausen, "you refer to the most recent communication from the *Constitution*. Yes. I have already dispatched, Mr. President, a strongly worded order. Because of the communications lag it wlll not be received for some months, but I assure you the matter will be corrected."

The President said bitterly, "I don't want any assurances, either. Do you watch television? I don't mean 'I Love Lucy' and ball games, I mean news. Do you know what sort of shape this country is in? The bonus marches in 1932, the race riots in 1967—they were nothing. Time was when we could call out the National Guard to put down disorder. Last week I had to call out the Army to use against three companies of the Guard. One more scandal and we're finished, Knefhausen, and this is a big one."

"The purposes are beyond reproach—"

"Your purposes may be. Mine may be, or I try to tell myself it is for the good of science I did this, and not so I will be in the history books as the president who contributed a major breakthrough. But what are the purposes of your friends on the *Constitution?* I agreed to eight martyrs, Knefhausen. I didn't agree to forty billion dollars out of the nation's pockets to give your eight young friends ten years of gangbangs and dope."

"Mr. President, I assure you this is only a temporary phase. I have instructed them to straighten out."

"And if they don't, what are you going to do about it?" The President, who never smoked, stripped a cigar, bit off the end and lit it. He said, "It's too late for me to say I shouldn't have let you talk me into this. So all I will say is you have to show results from this flimflam before the lid blows off, or I won't be President any more, and I doubt that you will be alive."

CONSTITUTION FOUR

This is Shef again and it's, oh, let me see, about Day 250. 300? No, I don't think so. Look, I'm sorry about the ship date, but I honestly don't think much in those terms any more. I've been thinking about other things. Also I'm a little upset. When I tossed the ruble the hexagram was K'an, which is danger, over Li, the Sun. That's a bad mood in which to be communicating with you. We aren't vengeful types, but the fact is that some of us were pretty sore when we found out what you'd done.   I don't *think* you need to worry, but I wish I'd got a much better hexagram.

Let me tell you the good parts first.   Our velocity is pushing point four oh C now.   The scenery is beginning to get interesting.   For several weeks the stars fore and aft have been drifting out of sight as the ones in front get up into the ultraviolet and the ones behind sink into the infrared.   You'd think that as the spectrum shifts the other parts of the EMF bands would come into the visible range. I guess they do, but stars peak in certain frequencies, and most of them seem to do it in the visible frequencies, so the effect is that they disappear.   The first thing was that there was a sort of round black spot ahead of us where we couldn't see anything at all, not Alpha Centauri, not Beta Centauri, not even the bright Circini stars.   Then we lost the Sun behind us, and a little later we saw the blackout spread to a growing circle of stars there.   Then the circles began to widen.

Of course, we know that the stars are really there.   We can detect them with phase-shift equipment, just as we can transmit and receive your messages by shifting the frequencies.   But we just can't see them any more.   The ones in direct line of flight, where we have a vector velocity of .34c or .37c—depending on whether they are in front of us or behind us—simply aren't radiating in the visible band any more.   The ones farther out to the side have been displaced visually because of the relativistic effects of our speed.   But what it looks like is that we're running the hell out of Nothing, in the direction of Nothing, and it is frankly a little scary.

Even the stars off to one side are showing relativistic color shifts.   It's almost like a rainbow, one of those full-circle rainbows that you see on the clouds beneath you from an airplane sometimes.   Only this circle is all around us.   Nearest the black hole in front the stars have frequency-shifted to a dull reddish color.   They go through orange and yellow and a sort of leaf green to the band nearest the black hole in back, which are bright blue shading to purple.   Jim Barstow has been practicing his farsight on them, and he can relate them to the actual sky map.   But I can't.   He sees something in the black hole in front of us that I can't see.   He says he thinks it's a bright radio source, probably Centaurus A, and he claims it is radiating strongly in the whole visible band now.   He means strongly for him, with his eyes.   I'm not sure I can see it at all.   There *may* be a sort of very faint, diffuse glow there, like the *gegenschein*, but I'm not sure.   Neither is anyone else.

But the starbow itself is beautiful.   It's worth the trip.   Flo has been learning oil painting so she can make a picture of it to send you for your wall, although when she found out what you'd been up to she got so sore she was thinking of booby-trapping it with a fusion bomb or something.   (But she's over that now. I think.)

So we're not so mad at you any more, although there was a time when if I'd been communicating with you at exactly that moment I would have said some bad things.

I just played this back, and it sounds pretty jumbled and confused.   I'm sorry about that.   It's hard for me to do this.   I don't mean hard like intellectually difficult—the way chess problems and tensor analysis used to be—but hard like shoveling sand with a teaspoon.   I'm just not used to constricting my thoughts in this straitjacket any more. I tried to get one of the others to communicate this time, but there were no takers. I did get a lot of free advice. Dot says I shouldn't waste my time remembering how we used to talk. She wanted to write an eidetic account in simplified notation for you, which she estimated a crash program could translate for you in reasonable time, a decade or two, and would give you an absolutely full account of everything. I objected that that involved practical difficulties. Not in preparing the account . . . shucks, we can all do that now. I don't forget anything, except irrelevant things like the standard-reckoning day that I don't want to remember in the first place, and neither does anyone else. But the length of transmission would be too much. We don't have the power to transmit the necessary number of groups, especially since the accident. Dot said we could Gödelize it. I said you were too dumb to de-Gödelize it. She said it would be very good practice for you.

Well, she's right about that, and it's time you all learned how to communicate in a sensible way, so if the power holds out I'll include Dot's eidetic account at the end—in Gödelized form. Lots of luck. I won't honestly be surprised if you miss a digit or something and it all turns into "Rebecca of Sunnybrook Farm" or some missing books of apocrypha or, more likely of course, gibberish. Ski says it won't do you any good in any case, because Henle was right. I pass that on without comment.

Sex. You always want to hear about sex. It's great. Now that we don't have to fool with the pills any more we've been having some marvelous times. Flo and Jim Barstow began making it as part of a multiplexed communications system that you have to see to believe. Sometimes when they're going to do it we all knock off and just sit around and watch them, cracking jokes and singing and helping with the auxiliary computations. When we had that little bit of minor surgery the other day—now we've got the bones seasoning—Ann and Ski decided to ball instead of using anesthesia, and they said it was better than acupuncture. It didn't block the sensation. They were aware of their little toes being lopped off, but they didn't perceive it as pain. So then Jim, when it was his turn, tried going through the amputation without anything at all in the expectation that he and Flo would go to bed together a little later, and that worked well too. He was all set up about it; claimed it showed a reverse causality that his theories predicted but that had not been demonstrated before. Said at last he was over the cause-preceding-the-effect hangup. It's like the Red Queen and the White Queen, and quite puzzling until you get the hang of it. (I'm not sure I've got the hang of it yet.) Suppose he hadn't balled Flo? Would his toe have hurt retroactively? I'm a little mixed up on this, Dot says because I simply don't understand phenomenology in general, and I think I'll have to take Ann's advice and work my way through Carnap, although the linguistics are so poor that it's hard to stay with it. Come to think of it, I don't have to. It's all in the Gödelized eidetic statement, after all. So I'll transmit the statement to you, and while I'm doing it that will be a sort of review for me and maybe I'll get my head right on causality.

Listen, let me give you a tip. The statement will also include Ski's trick of containing plasma for up to 500K milliseconds, so when you figure it out you'll know how to build those fusion power reactors you were talking about when we left. That's the carrot before your nose, so get busy on de-Gödelizing. The plasma dodge works fine, although, of course, we were sorry about what happened when we junked those dumb Rube Goldberg bombs you had going off and replaced them with a nice steady plasma flow. The explosion killed Will Becklund outright, and it looked hairy for all of us.

Well, anyway. I have to cut this short because the power's running a little low and I don't want to chance messing up the statement. It follows herewith:
$1973^{354} + 331^{852} + 17^{2008} + 5^{47} + 3^{9606} + 2^{88}$ take away 78.

Lots of luck, fellows!

WASHINGTON FOUR

Knefhausen lifted his head from the litter of papers on his desk. He rubbed his eyes, sighing. He had given up smoking the same time as the President, but, like the President, he was thinking of taking it up again. It could kill you, yes. But it was a tension-reducer, and he needed that. And what was wrong with something killing you. There were worse things than being killed, he thought dismally.

Looking at it any way you could, he thought objectively, the past two or three years had been hard on him. They had started so well and had gone so bad. Not as bad as those distant memories of childhood when everybody was so poor and Berlin was so cold and what warm clothes he had came from the *Winterhilfe*. By no means as hard as the end of the war. Nothing like as bad as those first years in South America and then in the Middle East, when even the lucky and famous ones, the Von Brauns and the Ehrickes, were having trouble getting what was due them and a young calf like Knefhausen had to peel potatoes and run elevators to live. But harder and worse than a man at the summit of his career had any reason to expect.

The Alpha-Aleph project, fundamentally, was sound! He ground his teeth, thinking about it. It would work—no, by God, it *was* working, and it would make the world a different place. Future generations would see.

But the future generations were not here yet, and in the present things were going badly.

Reminded, he picked up the phone and buzzed his secretary. "Have you got through to the President yet?" he demanded.

"I'm sorry, Dr. Knefhausen. I've tried every ten minutes, just as you said."

"Ah," he grunted. "No, wait. Let me see. What calls are there?"

Rustle of paper. "The news services, of course, asking about the rumors again. Jack Anderson's office. The man from CBS."

"No, no. I will not talk to the press. Anyone else."

"Senator Copley called, asking when you were going to answer the list of questions his committee sent you."

"I will give him an answer. I will give him the answer Götz von Berlichingen gave to the Bishop of Bamberg."

"I'm sorry, Dr. Knefhausen, I didn't quite catch—"

"No matter. Anything else?"

"Just a long-distance call, from a Mr. Hauptmann.   I have his number."

"Hauptmann?"   The name was puzzlingly familiar.   After a moment Knefhausen placed it: to be sure, the photo technician who had cooperated in the faked pictures from Briareus XII.   Well, he had his orders to stay out of sight and shut up.   "No, that's not important.   None of them are, and I do not wish to be disturbed with such nonsense.   Continue as you were, Mrs. Ambrose.   If the President is reached you are to put me on at once, but no other calls."

He hung up and turned to his desk.

He looked sadly and fondly at the papers.   He had them all out: the reports from the *Constitution,* his own drafts of interpretation and comment, and more than a hundred footnoted items compiled by his staff, to help untangle the meanings and implications of those ah, sometimes so cryptic reports from space:

"*Henle.* Apparently refers to Paul Henle (note appended); probably the citation intended is his statement, 'There are certain symbolisms in which certain things cannot be said.'   Conjecture that English language is one of those symbolisms."

"*Orange sherbet sundae.*   A classified experimental study was made of the material in Document Ref. No. CON-130, Para. 4.   Chemical analysis and experimental testing have indicated that the recommended mixture of pharmaceuticals and other ingredients produce a hallucinogen-related substance of considerable strength and not wholly known qualities.   One hundred subjects ingested the product or a placebo in a double-blind controlled test.   Subjects receiving the actual substance report reactions significantly different from the placebo.   Effects reported include feelings of immense competence and deepened understanding.   However, data is entirely subjective.   Attempts were made to verify claims by standard I.Q., manipulative and other tests, but the subjects did not cooperate well and several have since absented themselves without leave from the testing establishment."

"*Gödelized language.*   A system of encoding any message of any kind as a single very large number.   The message is first written out in clear language and then encoded as bases and exponents.   Each letter of the message is represented in order by the natural order of primes—that is, the first letter is represented by the base 2, the second by the base 3, the third by the base 5, then 7, 11, 13, 17, et cetera.   The identity of the letter occupying that position in the message is given by the exponent: simply, the exponent 1 meaning that the letter in that position is an A, the letter 2 meaning that it is a B, 3 a C, et cetera.   The message, as a whole, is then rendered as the product of all the bases and exponents.   *Example.* The word "cab" can thus be represented as 2^3 x 3^1 x 5^2, or 600.   (= 8x3x25.) The name 'Abe' would be represented by the number 56,250, or 2^1 x 3^2 x 5^5. (= 2x9x3125.)   A sentence like 'John lives' would be represented by the product of the following terms: $2^{10} \times 3^{15} \times 5^8 \times 7^{14} \times 11^0 \times 13^{12} \times 17^9 \times 19^{22} \times 23^5 \times 29^{19} \times 31^{27}$—in which the exponent '0' has been reserved for a space and the exponent '27' has been arbitrarily assigned to indicate a full stop.   As can be seen, the Gödelized form for even a short message involves a very large number, although such numbers may be transmitted quite compactly in the form of a sum of bases and exponents.   The example transmitted by the *Constitution* is estimated to equal the contents of a standard unabridged dictionary.

"*Farsight.* The subject James Madison Barstow is known to have suffered from some nearsightedness in his early school years, apparently brought on by excessive reading, which he attempted to cure through eye exercises similar to the 'Bates method'—note appended. His vision at time of testing for Alpha-Aleph project was optimal. Interviews with former associates indicate his continuing interest in increasing visual acuity. *Alternate explanation.* There is some indication that he was also interested in paranormal phenomena such as clairvoyance or prevision, and it is possible, though at present deemed unlikely, that his use of the term refers to 'looking ahead' in time."

And so on, and on.

Knefhausen gazed at the litter of papers lovingly and hopelessly, and passed his hand over his forehead. The kids! They were so marvelous . . . but so unruly . . . and so hard to understand. How unruly of them to have concealed their true accomplishments. The secret of hydrogen fusion! That alone would justify, more than justify, the entire project. But where was it? Locked in that number-jumber gibberish. Knefhausen was not without appreciation of the elegance of the method. He, too, was capable of taking seriously a device of such luminous simplicity. Once the number was written out you had only to start by dividing it by two as many times as possible, and the number of times would give you the first letter. Then divide by the next prime, three, and that number of times would give you the second letter. But the practical difficulties! You could not get even the first letter until you had the whole number, and IBM had refused even to bid on constructing a bank of computers to write that number out unless the development time was stretched to twenty-five years. *Twenty-five years.* And meanwhile in that number was hidden probably the secret of hydrogen fusion, possibly many greater secrets, most certainly the key to Knefhausen's own well being over the next few weeks . . .

His phone rang.

He grabbed it and shouted into it at once: "Yes, Mr. President!"

He had been too quick. It was only his secretary. Her voice was shaking but determined.

"It's not the President, Dr. Knefhausen, but Senator Copley is on the wire and he says it is urgent. He says—"

"No!" shouted Knefhausen and banged down the phone. He regretted it even as he was doing it. Copley was very high, chairman of the Armed Forces Committee; he was not a man Knefhausen wished to have as an enemy, and he had been very careful to make him a friend over years of patient fence-building. But he could not speak to him, or to anyone, while the President was not answering his calls. Copley's rank was high, but he was not in the direct hierarchical line over Knefhausen. When the top of that line refused to talk to him Knefhausen was cut off from the world.

He attempted to calm himself by examining the situation objectively. The pressures on the President just now: they were enormous. There was the continuing trouble in the cities, all the cities. There were the political conventions coming up. There was the need to get elected for a third term, and the need to get the law amended to make that possible. And yes, Knefhausen admitted to himself, the worst pressure of all was the rumors that were floating around about the *Constitution*. He had warned the President. It was unfortunate the President had not listened. He had said that a secret known to two people is compromised and a secret known to more than two is no secret. But the President had insisted on the disclosure to that ever-widening circle of high officials—sworn, of course, to secrecy, but what good was that? In spite of everything, there had been leaks. Fewer than one might have feared. More than one could stand.

He touched the reports from *Constitution* caressingly. Those beautiful kids, they could still make everything right, so wonderful . . .

Because it was he who had made them wonderful, he confessed to himself. He had invented the idea. He had selected them. He had done things which he did not quite even yet reconcile himself to to make sure that it was they and not some others who were on the crew. He had, above all, made doubly sure by insuring their loyalty in every way possible. Training. Discipline. Ties of affection and friendship. More reliable ties: loading their food supplies, their entertainment tapes, their programmed activities with every sort of advertising inducement, M/R compulsion, psychological reinforcement he could invent or find, so that whatever else they did they did not fail to report faithfully back to Earth. Whatever else happened, there was that. The data might be hard to untangle, but would be there. They could not help themselves; his commandments were stronger than God's; like Martin Luther they must say *Ich kann nicht anders,* and come Pope or Inquisition they must stand by it. They would learn, and tell what they learned, and thus the investment would be repaid . . .

The telephone!

He was talking before he had it even to his mouth. "Yes, yes! This is Dr. Knefhausen, yes!" he gabbled. Surely it must be the President now—

It was not.

"Knefhausen!" shouted the man on the other end. "Now, listen, I'll tell you what I told that bitch pig girl of yours, if I don't talk to you on the phone *right now* I'll have Fourth Armored in there to arrest you and bring you to me in twenty minutes. So listen!"

Knefhausen recognized both voice and style. He drew a deep breath and forced himself to be calm. "Very well, Senator Copley," he said, "what is it?"

"The game is blown, boy! That's what it is. That boy of yours in Huntsville, what's his name, the photo technician—"

"Hauptmann?"

"That's him! Would you like to know where he is, you dumb Kraut bastard?"

"Why, I suppose . . . I should think in Huntsville—"

"Wrong, boy! Your Kraut bastard friend claimed he didn't feel good and took some accrued sick time. Intelligence kept an eye on him up to a point, didn't stop him, wanted to see what he'd do. Well, they saw. They saw him leaving Orly Airport an hour ago in an Aeroflot plane. Put your brain to work on that

one, Knefhausen!   He's defected.   Now start figuring out what you're going to
do about it, and it better be good!''

Knefhausen said something, he did not know what, and hung up the phone, he
did not remember when.   He stared glassily into space for a time.

Then he flicked the switch for his secretary and said, not listening to her stammering apologies, ''That long-distance call that came from Hauptmann before, Mrs.
Ambrose.   You didn't say where it was from.''

''It was an overseas call, Dr. Knefhausen.   From Paris.   You didn't give me
a chance to—''

''Yes, yes.   I understand.   Thank you.   Never mind.''   He hung up and sat
back.   He felt almost relieved.   If Hauptmann had gone to Russia it could only
be to tell him that the picture was faked and not only was there no planet for the
astronauts to land on but it was not a mistake, even, actually a total fraud.   So
now it was all out of his hands.   History would judge him now.   The die was
cast.   The Rubicon was crossed.

So many literary allusions, he thought deprecatingly.   Actually it was not the
judgment of history that was immediately important but the judgment of certain
real people now alive and likely to respond badly.   And they would judge him not
so much by what might be or what should have been, as by what was.   He shivered
in the cold of that judgment, and reached for the telephone to try once more to call
the President.   But he was quite sure the President would not answer, then or ever
again.

CONSTITUTION FIVE

Old reliable P.O.'d Shef here.   Look, we got your message.   I don't want to
discuss it.   You've got a nerve.   You're in a bad mood, aren't you?   If you can't
say anything nice, don't say anything at all.   We do the best we can, and that's
not bad, and if we don't do exactly what you want us to maybe it's because we
know quite a lot more than you did when you fired us off at that blob of moonshine
you call Alpha-Aleph.   Well, thanks a lot for nothing.

On the other hand, thanks a little for what you did do, which at least worked
out to get us where we are, and I don't mean spatially.   So I'm not going to yell
at you.   I just don't want to talk to you at all.   I'll let the others talk for themselves.

Dot Letski speaking.   This is important.   Pass it on.   I have three things to
tell you that I do not want you to forget.   *One: Most problems have grammatical
solutions.*   The problem of transporting people from Earth to another planet does
not get solved by putting pieces of steel together one at a time at random, and
happening to find out you've built the *Constitution* by accident.   It gets solved by
constructing a model— = equation (= grammar)—which describes the necessary
circumstances under which the transportation occurs.   Once you have the grammatical
model, you just put the metal around it and it goes like gangbusters.

When you have understood this you will be ready for: *Two: There is no such
thing as causality.*   What a waste of time it has been, trying to assign ''causes''
to ''events''!   You say things like, ''Striking a match causes it to burn.''   True

statement? No, false statement. You find yourself in a whole waffle about whether the "act" of "striking" is "necessary" and/or "sufficient" and you get lost in words. Pragmatically useful grammars are without tenses. In a decent grammar—which this English-language one, of course, is not, but I'll do the best I can—you can make a statement like "There exists a conjunction of forms of matter—specified—which combine with the release of energy at a certain temperature—which may be the temperature associated with heat of friction." Where's the causality? "Cause" and "effect" are in the same timeless statement. So, *Three: There are no such things as empirical laws.* Ski came to understand that he was able to contain the plasma in our jet indefinitely, not by pushing particles around in brute-force magnetic squeezes, but by encouraging them to want to stay together. There are other ways of saying what he does— = "creates an environment in which centripetal exceed centrifugal forces"—, but the way I said it is better because it tells something about your characters. Bullies, all of you. Why can't you be nice to things if you want them to be nice to you? Be sure to pass this on to T'in Fa at Tientsin, Professor Morris at All Soul's and whoever holds the Carnap chair at UCLA.

Flo's turn. My mother would have loved my garden. I have drumsticks and daffodils growing side by side in the sludgy sand. They do so please us, and we them! I will probably transmit a full horticultural handbook at a future date, but meanwhile it is shameful to eat a radish. Carrots, on the other hand, enjoy it.

A statement of William Becklund, deceased. I emerged into the world, learned, grew, ate, worked, moved and died. Alternatively, I emerged from the hydrogen flare, shrank, disgorged and reentered the womb one misses so. You may approach it from either end, it makes no difference at all which way you look at it.

Observational datum, Letski. At time *t,* a Dirac number incommensurable with GMT, the following phenomenon is observed:

The radio source Centaurus A is identified as a positionally stable single collective object rather than two intersecting gas clouds and is observed to contract radially toward a center. Analysis and observation reveal it to be a Black Hole of which the fine detail is not detectable as yet. One infers all galaxies develop such central vortices, with implications of interest to astronomers and eschatologists. I, Seymour Letski, propose to take a closer look but the others prefer to continue programmed flight first. Harvard-Smithsonian notification service, please copy.

"Starbow," a preliminary study for a rendering into English of a poem by James Barstow:

> Gaggle of goslings but pick of our race
> We waddle through relativistic space.
> Dilated, discounted, despondent we scan:
> But vacant the Sign of the Horse and the Man.

Vacant the Sign of the Man and the Horse,
And now we conjecture the goal of our course.
Tricked, trapped and cozened, we ruefully run
After the child of the bachelor sun.
The trick is revealed and the trap is confessed
And we are the butts of the dim-witted jest.
O Gander who made us, O Goose who laid us,
How lewdly and twistedly you betrayed us!
We owe you a debt. We won't forget.
With fortune and firmness we'll pay you yet.
Give us some luck and we'll timely send
Your pot of gold from the starbow's end.

Ann Becklund:
I think it was Stanley Weinbaum who said that from three facts a truly superior mind should be able to deduce the whole universe. (Ski thinks it is possible with a finite number, but considerably larger than that.) We are so very far from being truly superior minds by those standards, or even by our own. Yet we have a much larger number of facts to work with than three, or even three thousand, and so we have deduced a good deal.

This is not as valuable to you as you might have hoped, dear old bastardly Kneffie and all you bastardly others, because one of the things that we have deduced is that we can't tell you everything, because you wouldn't understand. We could help you along, some of you, if you were here, and in time you would be able to do what we do easily enough, but not by remote control.

But all is not lost, folks! Cheer up! You don't deduce like we deduce, but on the other hand you have so very much more to work from. Try. Get smart. You can do it if you want to. Set your person at rest, compose your mind before you speak, make your relations firm before you ask for something. Try not to be loathsome about it. Don't be like the fellow in the Changes. "He brings increase to no one. Indeed, someone even strikes him."

We've all grown our toes back now, even Will, although it was particularly difficult for him since he had been killed, and we've inscribed the bones and used them with very good effect in generating the hexagrams. I hope you see the point of what we did. We could have gone on with tossing coins or throwing the yarrow stalks, or at least with the closest Flo could breed to yarrow stalks. We didn't want to do that because it's not the optimum way.

The person who doesn't keep his heart constantly steady might say, "Well, what's the difference?" That's a poor sort of question to ask. It implies a deterministic answer. A better question is, "Does it make a difference?", and the answer to that is, "Yes, probably, because in order to do something right you must do it right." That is the law of identity, in any language.

Another question you might ask is, "Well, what source of knowledge are you actually tapping when you consult the hexagrams?" That's a better kind of question in that it doesn't *force* a wrong answer, but the answer is, again, indeterminate. You might view the *I Ching* as a sort of Rorschach bundle of squiggles that has no innate meaning but is useful because your own mind interprets it and puts sense into it. Feel free! You might think of it as a sort of memory bank of encoded lore. Why not? You might skip it entirely and come to knowledge in some other tao, any tao you like. ("The superior man understands the transitory in the light of the eternity of the end.") That's fine, too!

But whatever way you do it, you should *do* it that way. We needed inscribed bones to generate hexagrams, because that was the right way, and so it was no particular sacrifice to lop off a toe each for the purpose. It's working out nicely, except for one thing. The big hangup now is that the translations are so degraded, Chinese to German, German to English and error seeping in at every step, but we're working on that now.

Perhaps I will tell you more at another time. Not now. Not very soon. Eve will tell you about that.

Eve Barstow, the Dummy, comes last and, I'm afraid, least.
When I was a little girl I used to play chess, badly, with very good players, and that's the story of my life. I'm a chronic over-achiever. I can't stand people who aren't smarter and better than I am, but the result is that I'm the runt of the litter every time. They are all very nice to me here, even Jim, but they know what the score is and so do I.

So I keep busy and applaud what I can't do. It isn't a bad life. I have everything I need, except pride.

Let me tell you what a typical day is like here between Sol and Centaurus. We wake up—if we have been sleeping, which some of us still do—and eat—if we are still eating, as all but Ski and, of course, Will Becklund do. The food is delicious and Florence has induced it to grow cooked and seasoned where that is desirable, so it's no trouble to go over and pick yourself a nice poached egg, or clutch of French fries. (I really prefer brioche in the mornings, but for sentimental reasons she can't manage it.) Sometimes we ball a little or sing old campfire songs. Ski comes down for that, but not for long, and then he goes back to looking at the universe. The starbow is magnificent and appalling. It is now a band about 40° across, completely surrounding us with colored light. One can always look in the other frequencies and see ghost stars before us and behind us, but in the birthright bands the view to the front and rear is now dead black and the only light is that beautiful banded ring of powdery stars.

Sometimes we write plays or have a little music. Shef had deduced four lost Bach piano concerti, very reminiscent of Corelli and Vivaldi, with everything going at once in the tuttis, and we've all adapted them for performance. I did mine on the Moog, but Ann and Shef synthesized whole orchestras. Shef's is particularly cute. You can tell that the flautist has early emphysema and two people in the violin section have been drinking, and he's got Toscanini conducting like a *risorgimento* metronome. Flo's oldest daughter made up words and now she sings a sort of nursery rhyme adaptation of some Buxtehude chorales; oh, I didn't tell you about the kids.   We have eleven of them now.   Ann, Dot and I have one apiece, and Florence has eight.   (But they're going to let me have quadruplets next week.) They let me take care of them pretty much for the first few weeks, while they're little, and they're *so* darling.

So mostly I spend my time taking care of the kids and working out tensor equations that Ski kindly gives me to do for him, and, I must confess it, feeling a little lonely. I *would* like to watch a TV quiz show over a cup of coffee with a friend!   They let me do over the interior of our mobile home now and then.   The other day I redid it in Pittsburgh suburban as a joke.   Would you believe French windows in inter-stellar space?   We never open them, of course, but they look real pretty with the chintz curtains and lace tiebacks.   And we've added several new rooms for the child-ren and their pets.   (Flo grew them the cutest little bunnies in the hydroponics plot.)

Well, I've enjoyed this chance to gossip, so will sign off now.   There is one thing I have to mention.   The others decided we don't want to get any more messages from you.   They don't like the way you try to work on our subconsciouses and all—not that you succeeed, of course, but you can see that it's still a little annoying—and so in future the dial will be set at six-six-oh, all right, but the switch will be in the "off" position.   It wasn't my idea, but I was glad to go along.   I *would* like some slightly less demanding company from time to time, although not, of course, yours.

WASHINGTON FIVE

Once upon a time the building that was now known as DoD Temp Restraining Quarters 7—you might as well call it with the right word, "jail", Knefhausen thought—had been a luxury hotel in the Hilton chain.   The maximum security cells were in the underground levels, in what had been meeting rooms.   There were no doors or windows to the outside.   If you did get out of your own cell you had a flight of stairs to get up before you were at ground level, and then the guards to break through to get to the open.   And then, even if there happened not to be an active siege going on at the moment, you took your chances with the roaming addicts and activists outside.

Knefhausen did not concern himself with these matters.   He did not think of escape, or at least didn't after the first few panicky moments, when he realized he was under arrest.   He stopped demanding to see the President after the first few days.   There was no point in appealing to the White House for help when it was the White House that had put him here.   He was still sure that if only he could talk to the President privately for a few moments he could clear everything up. But as a realist he had faced the fact that the President would never talk to him privately again.

So he counted his blessings.

First, it was comfortable here.   The bed was good, the rooms were warm.   The food still came from the banquet kitchens of the hotel, and it was remarkably good for jailhouse fare.

Second, the kids were still in space and still doing some things, great things, even if they did not report what.   His vindication was still a prospect.

Third, the jailers let him have newspapers and writing materials, although they would not bring him his books, or give him a television set.

He missed the books, but nothing else.   He didn't need TV to tell him what was going on outside.   He didn't even need the newspapers, ragged, thin and censored as they were.   He could hear for himself.   Every day there was the rattle of small-arms fire, mostly far-off and sporadic, but once or twice sustained and heavy and almost overhead, Brownings against AK-47s, it sounded like, and now and then the slap and smash of grenade launchers.   Sometimes he heard sirens hooting through the streets, punctuated by clanging bells, and wondered that there was still a civilian fire department left to bother.   (Or was it still civilian?)   Sometimes he heard the grinding of heavy motors that had to be tanks.   The newspapers did little to fill in the details, but Knefhausen was good at reading between the lines.   The Administration was holed up somewhere—Key Biscayne, or Camp David, or Southern California, no one was saying where.   The cities were all in red revolt.   *Herr Omnes* had taken over.

For these disasters Knefhausen felt unjustly blamed.   He composed endless letters to the President, pointing out that the serious troubles of the Administration had nothing to do with Alpha-Aleph; the cities had been in revolt for most of a generation, the dollar had become a laughingstock since the Indochinese wars. Some he destroyed, some he could get no one to take from him, a few he managed to dispatch—and got no answers.

Once or twice a week a man from the Justice Department came to ask him the same thousand pointless questions once again.   They were trying to build up a dossier to prove it was all his fault, Knefhausen suspected.   Well, let them.   He would defend himself when the time came.   Or history would defend him.   The record was clear.   With respect to moral issues, perhaps, not so clear, he conceded. No matter.   One could not speak of moral questions in an area so vital to the search for knowledge as this.   The dispatches from the *Constitution* had already produced so much—although, admittedly, some of the most significant parts were hard to understand.   The Gödel message had not been unscrambled, and the hints of its contents remained only hints.

Sometimes he dozed and dreamed of projecting himself to the *Constitution*.   It had been a year since the last message.   He tried to imagine what they had been doing.   They would be well past the midpoint now, decelerating.   The starbow would be broadening and diffusing every day.   The circles of blackness before and behind them would be shrinking.   Soon they would see Alpha Centauri as no man had ever seen it.   To be sure, they would then see that there was no planet called Aleph circling the primary, but they had guessed that somehow long since. Brave, wonderful kids!   Even so they had gone on.   This foolishness with drugs and sex, what of it?   One opposed such goings-on in the common run of humanity, but it had always been so that those who excelled and stood out from the herd could make their own rules.   As a child he had learned that the plump, proud air leader sniffed cocaine, that the great warriors took their sexual pleasure sometimes with each other.   And intelligent man did not concern himself with such questions, which was one more indication that the man from the Justice Department, with his constant hinting and prying into Knefhausen's own background, was not really very intelligent.

The good thing about the man from the Justice Department was that one could sometimes deduce things from his questions, and rarely, oh, very rarely, he would sometimes answer a question himself. "Has there been a message from the *Constitution?*" "No, of course not, Dr. Knefhausen. Now, tell me again, who suggested this fraudulent scheme to you in the first place?"

Those were the highlights of his days, but mostly the days just passed unmarked.

He did not even scratch them off on the wall of his cell, like the prisoner in the Chateau d'If. It would have been a pity to mar the hardwood paneling. Also he had other clocks and calendars. There was the ticking of the arriving meals, the turning of the seasons as the man from the Justice Department paid his visits. Each of these was like a holiday—a holy day, not joyous but solemn. First there would be a visit from the captain of the guards with two armed soldiers standing in the door. They would search his person and his cell on the chance that he had been able to smuggle in a . . . a what? A nuclear bomb, maybe. Or a pound of pepper to throw in the Justice man's eyes. They would find nothing, because there was nothing to find. And then they would go away and for a long time there would be nothing. Not even a meal, even if a meal time happened to be due. Nothing at all, until an hour or three hours later the Justice man would come in with his own guard at the door, equally vigilant inside and out, and his engineer manning the tape recorders, and his questions.

And then there was the day when the man from the Justice Department came and he was not alone. With him was the President's secretary, Murray Amos.

How treacherous is the human heart! When it has given up hope how little it takes to make it hope again!

"Murray!" cried Knefhausen, almost weeping, "it's so good to see you again! The President, is he well? What can I do for you? Have there been developments?"

Murray Amos paused in the doorway. He looked at Dieter von Knefhausen and said bitterly, "Oh, yes, there have been developments. Plenty of them. The Fourth Armored has just changed sides, so we are evacuating Washington. And the President wants you out of here at once."

"No, no! I mean . . . oh, yes, it is good that the President is concerned about my welfare, although it is bad about the Fourth Armored. But what I mean, Murray, is this: Has there been a message from the *Constitution?*"

Amos and the Justice Department man looked at each other. "Tell me, Dr. Knefhausen," said Amos silkily, "how did you manage to find that out?"

"Find it out? How could I find it out? No, I only asked because I hoped. There has been a message, yes? In spite of what they said? They have spoken again?"

"As a matter of fact, there has been," said Amos thoughtfully. The Justice Department man whispered piercingly in his ear, but Amos shook his head. "Don't worry, we'll be coming in a second.   The convoy won't go without us . . .   Yes, Knefhausen, the message came through to Goldstone two hours ago.   They have it at the decoding room now.''

"Good, very good!'' cried Knefhausen.   "You will see, they will justify all. But what do they say?   Have you good scientific men to interpret it?   Can you understand the contents?''

"Not exactly,'' said Amos, "because there's one little problem the code room hadn't expected and wasn't prepared for.   The message wasn't coded.   It came in clear, but the language was Chinese.''

CONSTITUTION SIX
   Ref.: CONSIX T51/11055/*7
   CLASSIFIED MOST SECRET
Subject: Transmission from U.S. Starship *Constitution*.

The following message was received and processed by the decrypt section according to standing directives.   Because of its special nature, an investigation was carried out to determine its provenance.   Radio-direction data received from Farside Base indicate its origin along a line of sight consistent with the present predicted location of the *Constitution*.   Strength of signal was high but within appropriate limits, and degradation of frequency separation was consistent with relativistic shifts and scattering due to impact with particle and gas clouds.

Although available data do not prove beyond doubt that this transmission originated with the starship, no contra-indications were found.

On examination, the text proved to be a phonetic transcription of what appears to be a dialect of Middle Kingdom Mandarin.   Only a partial translation has been completed.   (See note appended to text.)   The translation presented unusual difficulties for two reasons: One, the difficulty of finding a translator of sufficient skill who could be granted appropriate security status; two, because—conjecturally—the language used may not correspond exactly to any dialect but may be an artifact of the *Constitution*'s personnel.   (See PARA EIGHT.)

This text is PROVISIONAL AND NOT AUTHENTICATED and is furnished only as a first attempt to translate the contents of the message into English.   Efforts are being continued to translate the full message, and to produce a less corrupt text for the section herewith.   Later versions and emendations will be forwarded when available.

   TEXT FOLLOWS:

   PARA ONE.   The one who speaks for all—*Lt-Col Sheffield H Jackman*— rests.   With righteous action comes surcease from care.   I—*identity not certain, but probably Mrs. Annette Marin Becklund, less probably one of the other three female personnel aboard, or one of their descendants*— come in his place, moved by charity and love.
   PARA TWO.   It is not enough to study or to do deeds which make the people frown and bow their heads.   It is not enough to comprehend the

nature of the sky or the sea. Only through the understanding of all can one approach wisdom, and only through wisdom can one act rightly.

PARA THREE. These are the precepts as it is given us to see them:

PARA FOUR. The one who imposes his will by force lacks justice. Let him be thrust from a cliff.

PARA FIVE. The one who causes another to lust for a trifle of carved wood or a sweetmeat lacks courtesy. Let him be restrained from the carrying out of wrong practices.

PARA SIX. The one who ties a knot and says, "I do not care who must untie it," lacks foresight. Let him wash the ulcers of the poor and carry nightsoil for all until he learns to see the day to come as brother to the day that is.

PARA SEVEN. We who are in this here should not impose our wills on you who are in that here by force. Understanding comes late. We regret the incident of next week, for it was done in haste and in error. The one who speaks for all acted without thinking. We who are in this here were sorry for it afterward.

PARA EIGHT. You may wonder—*literally: ask thoughtless questions of the hexagrams*—why we are communicating in this language. The reason is in part recreational, in part heuristic—*literally: because on the staff hand one becomes able to strike a blow more ably when blows are struck repeatedly*—but the nature of the process is such that you must go through it before you can be told what it is. Our steps have trodden this path. In order to reconstruct the Chinese of the *I Ching* it was first necessary to reconstruct the German of the translation from which the English was made. Error lurks at every turn. [*Literally: false apparitions shout at one each time the path winds*.] Many flaws mark our carving. Observe it in silence for hours and days until the flaws become part of the work.

PARA NINE. It is said that you have eight days before the heavier particles arrive. The dead and broken will be few. It will be better if all airborne nuclear reactors are grounded until the incident is over.

PARA TEN. When you have completed rebuilding send us a message, directed to the planet Alpha-Aleph. Our home should be prepared by then. We will send a ferry to help colonists across the stream when we are ready:

The above text comprises the first 852 groups of the transmission. The remainder of the text, comprising approximately 7,500 groups, has not been satisfactorily translated. In the opinion of a consultant from the Oriental Languages Department at Johns Hopkins it may be a poem.

/s/Durward S. RICHTER

Durward S. RICHTER
Major General, USMC

Chief Cryptographer
Commanding

Distribution: X X X
BY HAND ONLY

WASHINGTON SIX

The President of the United States—Washington—opened the storm window of his study and leaned out to yell at his Chief Science Adviser. "Harry, get the lead out! We're waiting for you!"

Harry looked up and waved, then continued doggedly plowing through the dripping jungle that was the North Lawn. Between the overgrown weeds and the rain and the mud it was slow going, but the President had little sympathy. He slammed down the window and said, "That man, he just goes out of his way to aggravate me. How long am I supposed to wait for him so I can decide if we have to move the capital or not?"

The Vice President looked up from her knitting. "Jimbo, honey, why do you fuss yourself like that? Why don't we just move and get it over with?"

"Well, it looks so lousy." He threw himself into a chair despondently. "I was really looking forward to the Tenth Anniversary parade," he complained. "Ten years, that's really worth bragging about! I don't want to hold it out in the sticks, I want it right down Constitution Avenue, just like the old days, with the people cheering and the reporters and the cameras all over and everything. Then let that son of a bitch in Omaha say I'm not the real President."

His wife said placidly, "Don't fuss yourself about him, honey. You know what I've been thinking, though? The parade might look a little skimpy on Constitution Avenue anyway. It would be real nice on a kind of littler street."

"Oh, what do you know? Anyway, where would we go? If Washington's under water, what makes you think Bethesda would be any better?"

His Secretary of State put down his solitaire cards and looked interested. "Doesn't have to be Bethesda," he said. "I got some real nice land up near Dulles we could use. It's high there."

"Why, sure. Lots of nice land over to Virginia," the Vice President confirmed. "Remember when we went out on that picnic after your Second Inaugural? That was at Fairfax Station. There were hills all around. Just beautiful."

The President slammed his fist on the coffee table and yelled, "I'm not the President of Fairfax Station, I'm the President of the U. S. of A.! What's the capital of the U. S. of A.? Washington! My God, don't you see how those jokers in Houston and Omaha and Salt Lake and all would laugh if they heard I had to move out of my own capital?"

He broke off, because his Chief Science Adviser was coming in the door, shaking himself, dripping mud as he got out of his oilskin slicker. "Well?" demanded the President. "What did they say?"

Harry sat down. "It's terrible out there. Anybody got a dry cigarette?"

The President threw him a pack. Harry dried his fingers on his shirt front before he drew one out. "Well," he said, "I went to every boat captain I could find. They all said the same. Ships they talked to, places they'd been. All the same. Tides rising all up and down the coast."

He looked around for a match. The President's wife handed him a gold cigarette lighter with the Great Seal of the United States on it, which, after some effort, he managed to ignite. "It don't look good, Jimmy. Right now it's low tide and that's all right, but it's coming in. And tomorrow it'll come in a little higher. And there will be storms—not just rain like this. I mean, you got to figure on a tropical depression coming up from the Bahamas now and then."

"We're not in the tropics," said the Secretary of State suspiciously.

"It doesn't mean that," said the Science Adviser, who had once given the weather reports over the local ABC television station, when there was such a thing as a television network. "It means storms. Hurricanes. But they're not the worst things, it's the tide. If the ice is melting, then they're going to keep getting higher regardless."

The President drummed his fingers on the coffee table. Suddenly he shouted, "I don't *want* to move my capital!"

No one answered. His temper outbursts were famous. The Vice President became absorbed in her knitting, the Secretary of State picked up his cards and began to shuffle, the Science Adviser picked up his slicker and carefully hung it on the back of a door.

The President said, "You got to figure it this way. If we move out, then all those local yokels that claim to be the President of the United States are going to be just that much better off, and the eventual reunification of our country is going to be just that much more delayed." He moved his lips for a moment, then burst out, "I don't ask anything for myself! I never have. I only want to play the part I have to play in what's good for all of us, and that means keeping up my position as the *real* President, according to the U. S. of A. Constitution as amended. And that means I got to stay right here in the real White House, no matter what."

His wife said hesitantly, "Honey, how about this? The other Presidents had like a summer White House—Camp David and like that. Nobody fussed about it. Why couldn't you do the same as they did? There's the nicest old farmhouse out near Fairfax Station that we could fix up to be real pretty."

The President looked at her with surprise. "Now, that's good thinking," he declared. "Only we can't move permanently, and we have to keep this place garrisoned so nobody else will take it away from us, and we have to come back here once in a while. How about that, Harry?"

His Science Adviser said thoughtfully, "We could rent some boats, I guess. Depends. I don't know how high the water might get."

"No 'guess'! No 'depends'! That's a national priority. We have to do it that way to keep that bastard in Omaha paying attention to the real President."

"Well, Jimbo, honey," said the Vice President after a moment, emboldened by his recent praise, "you have to admit they don't pay a lot of attention to us right now. When was the last time they paid their taxes?"

The President looked at her foxily over his glasses. "Talking about that," he said, "I might have a little surprise for them anyway. What you might call a secret weapon."

"I hope it does better than we did in the last war," said his wife, "because if you remember, when we started to put down the uprising in Frederick, Maryland, we got the pee kicked out of us."

The President stood up, indicating the Cabinet meeting was over.

"Never mind," he said sunnily. "You go on out again, Harry, and see if you can find any good maps in the Library of Congress where they got the fires put out. Find us a nice high place within, um, twenty miles if you can. Then we'll get the Army to condemn us a Summer White House like Mae says, and maybe I can sleep in a bed that isn't moldy for a change."

His wife looked worried, "What are you going to do, Jim?"

He chuckled. "I'm going to check out my secret weapon."

He shooed them out of his study and, when they were gone, went to the kitchen and got himself a bottle of Fresca from the six-pack in the open refrigerator. It was warm, of course. The Marine guard company was still trying to get the gas generator back in operation, but they were having little success. The President didn't mind. They were his personal Praetorians and, if they lacked a little as appliance repairmen, they had proved their worth when the chips were down. The President was always aware that during the Troubles he had been no more than any other Congressman—appointed to fill a vacancy, at that—and his rapid rise to Speaker of the House and Heir Apparent, finally to the Presidency itself, was due not only to his political skills and knowhow but also to the fact that he was the only remotely legitimate heir to the Presidency who also happened to have a brother-in-law commanding the Marine garrison in Washington.

The President was, in fact, quite satisfied with the way the world was going. If he envied Presidents of the past—missiles, fleets of nuclear bombers, billions of dollars to play with—he certainly saw nothing, when he looked at the world around him, to compare with his own stature in the real world he lived in.

He finished the soda, opened his study door a crack and peered out. No one was nearby. He slipped out and down the back stairs. In what had once been the public parts of the White House you could see the extent of the damage more clearly. After the riots and the trashings and the burnings and the coups the will to repair and fix up had gradually dwindled away. The President didn't mind. He didn't even notice the charred walls and the fallen plaster. He was listening to the sound of a distant gasoline pump chugging away, and smiling to himself as he approached the underground level where his secret weapon was locked up.

The secret weapon, whose name was Dieter von Knefhausen, was trying to complete the total defense of every act of his life that he called his memoirs.

He was less satisfied with the world than the President.   He could have wished for many changes.   Better health, for one thing; he was well aware that his essential hypertension, his bronchitis and his gout were fighting the last stages of a total war to see which would have the honor of destroying their mutual battleground, which was himself.   He did not much mind his lack of freedom, but he did mind the senseless destruction of so many of his papers.

The original typescript of his autobiography was long lost, but he had wheedled the President—the pretender, that is, who called himself the President—into sending someone to find what could be found of them.   A few tattered and incomplete carbon copies had turned up.   He had restored some of the gaps as best his memory and available data permitted, telling again the story of how he had planned Project Alpha-Aleph and meticulously itemizing the details of how he had lied, forged and falsified to bring it about.

He was as honest as he could be.   He spared himself nothing.   He admitted his complicity in the "accidental" death of Ann Barstow's first husband in a car smash, thus leaving her free to marry the man he had chosen to go with the crew to Alpha Centauri.   He had confessed he had known the secret would not last out the duration of the trip, thus betraying the trust of the President who made it possible.   He put it all in, all he could remember, and boasted of his success.

For it was clear to him that his success was already proved.   What could be surer evidence of it than what had happened ten years ago?   The "incident of next week" was as dramatic and complete as anyone could wish.   If its details were still indecipherable, largely because of the demolition of the existing technology structure it had brought about, its main features were obvious.   The shower of heavy particles—baryon? perhaps even quarks?—had drenched the Earth.   The source had been traced to a point in the heavens identical with that plotted for the *Constitution*.

Also there were the messages received; taken together, there was no doubt that the astronauts had developed knowledge so far in advance of anything on Earth that, from two light-years out, they could impose their will on the human race.   They had done it.   In one downpour of particles, the entire military-industrial complex of the planet was put out of action.

How?   How?   Ah, thought Knefhausen, with envy and pride, that was the question.   One could not know.   All that was known was that every nuclear device—bomb, power plant, hospital radiation source or stockpile—had simultaneously soaked up the stream of particles and at that moment ceased to exist as a source of nuclear energy.   It was not rapid and catastrophic, like a bomb.   It was slow and long-lasting.   The uranium and the plutonium simply melted, in the long, continuous reaction that was still bubbling away in the seething lava lakes where the silo had stood and the nuclear power plants had generated electricity.   Little radiation was released, but a good deal of heat.

Knefhausen had long since stopped regretting what could not be helped, but wistfully he still wished he had the opportunity to measure the total heat flux properly.   Not less than 10^{16} watt-years, he was sure, just to judge by the effects on the Earth's atmosphere, the storms, the gradual raising of temperature all over, above all by the rumors about the upward trend of sea level that bespoke the melting of the polar ice caps.   There was no longer even a good weather net, but the fragmentary information he was able to piece together suggested a world increase of four, maybe as many as six or seven degrees Celsius already, and the reactions still seething away in Czechoslovakia, the Congo, Colorado and a hundred lesser infernos.

Rumors about the sea level?

Not rumors, no, he corrected himself, lifting his head and staring at the snake of hard rubber hose that began under the duckboards at the far end of the room and ended outside the barred window, where the gasoline pump did its best to keep the water level inside his cell below the boards.   Judging by the inflow, the grounds of the White House must be nearly awash.

The door opened.   The President of the United States (Washington) walked in, patting the shoulder of the thin, scared, hungry-looking kid who was guarding the door.

"How's it going, Knefhausen?" the President began sunnily.   "You ready to listen to a little reason yet?"

"I'll do whatever you say, Mr. President, but as I have told you there are certain limits.   Also I am not a young man, and my health—"

"Screw your health and your limits," shouted the President.   "Don't start up with me, Knefhausen!"

"I am sorry, Mr. President," whispered Knefhausen.

"Don't be sorry!   I judge by results.   You know what it takes to keep that pump going just so you won't drown?   Gas is rationed, Knefhausen!   Takes a high national priority to get it!   I don't know how long I'll be able to justify this continuous drain on our resources if you don't cooperate."

Sadly, but stubbornly, Knefhausen said: "As far as I am able, Mr. President, I cooperate."

"Yeah.   Sure."   But the President was in an unusually good mood today, Knefhausen observed, with the prisoner's paranoid attention to detail, and in a moment he said: "Listen, let's not get uptight about this.   I'm making you an offer.   Say the word and I'll fire that dumb son of a bitch Harry Stokes and make you my chief Science Adviser.   How would that be?   Right up at the top again. An apartment of your own.   Electric lights!   Servants—you can pick 'em out yourself, and there're some nice-looking little girls in the pool.   The best food you ever dreamed of.   A chance to perform a real service for the U. S. of A., helping to reunify this great country to become once again the great power it should and must be!"

"Mr. President," Knefhausen said, "naturally, I wish to help in any way I can, but we have been over all this before.   I'll do anything you like, but I don't know how to make the bombs work again.   You saw what happened, Mr. President. They're gone."

"I didn't say bombs, did I?   Look, Kneffie, I'm a reasonable man.   How about this: You promise to use your best scientific efforts *in any way you can*.   You say you can't make bombs; all right.   But there will be other things."

"What other things, Mr. President?"

"Don't push me, Knefhausen. Anything at all. Anything where you can perform a service for your country. You give me that promise and you're out of here today. Or would you rather I just turned off the pump?"

Knefhausen shook his head, not in negation but in despair. "You do not know what you are asking. What can a scientist do for you today? Ten years ago, yes—even five years ago. We could have worked something out maybe, I could have done something. But now the preconditions do not exist. When all the nuclear plants went out—when the factories that depended on them ran out of power—when the fertilizer plants couldn't fix nitrogen and the insecticide plants couldn't deliver—when the people began to die of hunger and the pestilences started—"

"I know all that, Knefhausen. Yes, or no?"

The scientist hesitated, looking thoughtfully at his adversary. A gleam of the old shrewdness appeared in his eyes.

"Mr. President," he said slowly. "You know something. Something has happened."

"Right," crowed the President. "You're smart. Now tell me, what is it I know?"

Knefhausen shook his head. After seven decades of vigorous life, and another decade of slowly dying, it was hard to hope again. This terrible little man, this upstart, this lump—he was not without a certain animal cunning, and he seemed very sure. "Please, Mr. President. Tell me."

The President put a finger to his lips, and then an ear to the door. When he was convinced no one could be listening, he came closer to Knefhausen and said softly:

"You know that I have trade representatives all over, Knefhausen. Some in Houston, some in Salt Lake, some even in Montreal. They are not always there just for trade. Sometimes they find things out, and tell me. Would you like to know what my man in Anaheim has just told me?"

Knefhausen did not answer, but his watery old eyes were imploring.

"A message," whispered the President.

"From the *Constitution?*" cried Knefhausen. "But, no, it is not possible! Far-side is gone, Goldstone is destroyed, the orbiting satellites are running down—"

"It wasn't a radio message," said the President. "It came from Mount Palomar. Not the big telescope, because it got ripped off, too, but what they call a Schmidt. Whatever that is. It still works. And they still have some old fogies who look through it now and then, for old times' sake. And they got a message, in laser light. Plain Morse code. From what they said was Alpha Centauri. From your little friends, Knefhausen."

He took a piece of paper from his pocket and held it up.

Knefhausen was racked by a fit of coughing, but he managed to croak: "Give it to me!"

The President held it away. "A deal, Knefhausen?"

"Yes, yes! Anything you say, but give me the message!"

"Why, certainly," smiled the President, and passed over the much-creased sheet of paper.   It said:

> PLEASE BE ADVISED.   WE HAVE CREATED THE PLANET ALPHA-ALEPH.   IT IS BEAUTIFUL AND GRAND.   WE WILL SEND OUR FERRIES TO BRING SUITABLE PERSONS AND OTHERS TO STOCK IT AND TO COMPLETE CERTAIN OTHER BUSINESS.   OUR SPECIAL REGARDS TO DR. DIETER VON KNEFHAUSEN, WHOM WE WANT TO TALK TO VERY MUCH.   EXPECT US WITHIN THREE WEEKS OF THIS MESSAGE.

Knefhausen read it over twice, stared at the President and read it again.   "I . . . I am very glad," he said inadequately.

The President snatched it back, folded it and put it in his pocket, as though the message itself was the key to power.   "So you see," he said, "it's simple.   You help me, I help you."

"Yes.   Yes, of course," said Knefhausen, staring past him.

"They're your friends.   They'll do what you say.   All those things you told me that they can do—"

"Yes, the particles, the ability to reproduce, the ability, God save us, to build a planet—"   Knefhausen might have gone on cataloguing the skills of the spacemen indefinitely, but the President was impatient:

"So it's only a matter of days now, and they'll be here.   You can imagine what they'll have!   Guns, tools, everything—and all you have to do is get them to join me in restoring the United States of America to its proper place.   I'll make it worth their while, Knefhausen!   And yours, too.   They—"

The President stopped, observing the scientist carefully.   Then he cried "Knefhausen!" and leaped forward to catch him.

He was too late.   The scientist had fallen limply to the duckboards.   The guard, when ordered, ran for the White House doctor, who limped as rapidly to the scene as his bad legs and brain soaked with beer would let him, but he was too late, too.   Everything was too late for Knefhausen, whose old heart had failed him . . . as it proved a few days later—when the great golden ships from Alpha-Aleph landed and disgorged their bright, terrible crewmen to clean up the Earth—just in time.

JOE W. HALDEMAN

Hero

"Tonight we're going to show you eight silent ways to kill a man." The guy who said that was a sergeant who didn't look five years older than I. Ergo, as they say, he couldn't possibly ever have killed a man, not in combat, silently or otherwise.

I already knew eighty ways to kill people, though most of them were pretty noisy. I sat up straight in my chair and assumed a look of polite attention and fell asleep with my eyes open. So did most everybody else. We'd learned that they never schedule anything important for these after-chop classes.

The projector woke me up and I sat through a short movie showing the "eight silent ways." Some of the actors must have been brainwipes, since they were actually killed.

After the movie a girl in the front row raised her hand. The sergeant nodded at her and she rose to parade rest. Not bad looking, but kind of chunky about the neck and shoulders. Everybody gets that way after carrying a heavy pack around for a couple of months.

"Sir"—we had to call sergeants "sir" until graduation—"most of those methods, really, they looked . . . kind of silly."

"For instance?"

"Like killing a man with a blow to the kidneys, from an entrenching tool. I mean, when would you *actually* just have an entrenching tool, and no gun or knife? And why not just bash him over the head with it?"

"He might have a helmet on," he said reasonably.

"Besides, Taurans probably don't even *have* kidneys!"

He shrugged. "Probably they don't." This was 1997, and we'd never seen a Tauran; hadn't even found any pieces of Taurans bigger than a scorched chromosome. "But their body chemistry is similar to ours, and we have to assume they're similarly complex creatures. They *must* have weaknesses, vulnerable spots. You have to find out where they are.

"That's the important thing." He stabbed a finger at the screen. "That's why those eight convicts got caulked for your benefit . . . you've got to find out how to kill Taurans, and be able to do it whether you have a megawatt laser or just an emery board."

She sat back down, not looking too convinced.

"Any more questions?"   Nobody raised a hand.

"OK.—tench-hut!"   We staggered upright and he looked at us expectantly.

"Screw you, sir," came the tired chorus.

"Louder!"

"SCREW YOU, SIR!"

One of the army's less-inspired morale devices.

"That's better.   Don't forget, predawn maneuvers tomorrow.   Chop at 0330, first formation, 0400.   Anybody sacked after 0340 gets one stripe.   Dismissed."

I zipped up my coverall and went across the snow to the lounge for a cup of soya and a joint.   I'd always been able to get by on five or six hours of sleep, and this was the only time I could be by myself, out of the army for a while. Looked at the newsfax for a few minutes.   Another ship got caulked, out by Aldebaran sector.   That was four years ago.   They were mounting a reprisal fleet, but it'll take four years more for them to get out there.   By then, the Taurans would have every portal planet sewed up tight.

Back at the billet, everybody else was sacked and the main lights were out.   The whole company'd been dragging ever since we got back from the two-week lunar training.   I dumped my clothes in the locker, checked the roster and found out I was in bunk 31.   Damn it, right under the heater.

I slipped through the curtain as quietly as possible so as not to wake up my bunkmate.   Couldn't see who it was, but I couldn't have cared less.   I slipped under the blanket.

"You're late, Mandella," a voice yawned.   It was Rogers.

"Sorry I woke you up," I whispered.

" 'Sallright."   She snuggled over and clasped me spoon-fashion.   She was warm and reasonably soft.   I patted her hip in what I hoped was a brotherly fashion. "Night, Rogers."

"G'night, Stallion."   She returned the gesture, a good deal more pointedly.

Why do you always get the tired ones when you're ready and the randy ones when you're tired?   I bowed to the inevitable.

II

"Awright, let's get some *back* inta that!   Stringer team!   Move it up—move up!"

A warm front had come in about midnight and the snow had turned to sleet. The permaplast stringer weighed five hundred pounds and was a bitch to handle, even when it wasn't covered with ice.   There were four of us, two at each end, carrying the plastic girder with frozen fingertips.   Rogers and I were partners.

"Steel!" the guy behind me yelled, meaning that he was losing his hold.   It wasn't steel, but it was heavy enough to break your foot.   Everybody let go and hopped away.   It splashed slush and mud all over us.

"Damn it, Petrov," Rogers said, "why didn't you go out for Star Fleet, or maybe the Red Cross?   This damn thing's not that damn heavy.''   Most of the girls were a little more circumspect in their speech.

"Awright, get a *move* on, stringers—Epoxy team!   Dog 'em!   Dog 'em!''

Our two epoxy people ran up, swinging their buckets.   "Let's go, Mandella. I'm freezin'.''

"Me, too,'' the girl said earnestly.

"One—two—heave!''   We got the thing up again and staggered toward the bridge.   It was about three-quarters completed.   Looked as if the Second Platoon was going to beat us.   I wouldn't give a damn, but the platoon that got their bridge built first got to fly home.   Four miles of muck for the rest of us, and no rest before chop.

We got the stringer in place, dropped it with a clank, and fitted the static clamps that held it to the rise-beams.   The female half of the epoxy team started slopping glue on it before we even had it secured.   Her partner was waiting for the stringer on the other side.   The floor team was waiting at the foot of the bridge, each one holding a piece of the light stressed permaplast over his head, like an umbrella. They were dry and clean.   I wondered aloud what they had done to deserve it, and Rogers suggested a couple of colorful, but unlikely possibilities.

We were going back to stand by the next stringer when the Field First—he was named Dougelstein, but we called him "Awright"—blew a whistle and bellowed, "Awright, soldier boys and girls, ten minutes.   Smoke 'em if you got 'em.''   He reached into his pocket and turned on the control that heated our coveralls.

Rogers and I sat down on our end of the stringer and I took out my weed box. I had lots of joints, but we weren't allowed to smoke them until after night-chop. The only tobacco I had was a cigarro butt about three inches long.   I lit it on the side of the box; it wasn't too bad after the first couple of puffs.   Rogers took a puff to be sociable, but made a face and gave it back.

"Were you in school when you got drafted?'' she asked.

"Yeah.   Just got a degree in Physics.   Was going after a teacher's certificate.'' She nodded soberly.   "I was in Biology . . .''

"Figures.''   I ducked a handful of slush.   "How far?''

"Six years, bachelor's and technical.''   She slid her boot along the ground, turning up a ridge of mud and slush the consistency of freezing ice milk.   "Why the hell did this have to happen?''

I shrugged.   It didn't call for an answer, least of all the answer that the UNEF kept giving us.   Intellectual and physical elite of the planet, going out to guard humanity against the Tauran menace.   It was all just a big experiment.   See whether we could goad the Taurans into ground action.

Awright blew the whistle two minutes early, as expected, but Rogers and I and the other two stringers got to sit for a minute while the epoxy and floor teams finished covering our stringer.   It got cold fast, sitting there with our suits turned off, but we remained inactive, on principle.

I really didn't see the sense of us having to train in the cold.   Typical army half-logic.   Sure, it was going to be cold where we were going; but not ice-cold or snow-cold.   Almost by definition, a portal planet remained within a degree or two of absolute zero all the time, since collapsars don't shine—and the first chill you felt would mean that you were a dead man.

Twelve years before, when I was ten years old, they had discovered the collapsar jump. Just fling an object at a collapsar with sufficient speed, and it pops out in some other part of the galaxy. It didn't take long to figure out the formula that predicted where it would come out: it just traveled along the same "line"—actually an Einsteinian geodesic—it would have followed if the collapsar hadn't been in the way—until it reaches another collapsar field, whereupon it reappears, repelled with the same speed it had approaching the original collapsar. Travel time between the two collapsars is exactly zero.

It made a lot of work for mathematical physicists, who had to redefine simultaneity, then tear down general relativity and build it back up again. And it made the politicians very happy, because now they could send a shipload of colonists to Fomalhaut for less than it once cost to put a brace of men on the Moon. There were a lot of people the politicians would just love to see on Fomalhaut, implementing a glorious adventure instead of stirring up trouble at home.

The ships were always accompanied by an automated probe that followed a couple of million miles behind. We knew about the portal planets, little bits of flotsam that whirled around the collapsars; the purpose of the drone was to come back and tell us in the event that a ship had smacked into a portal planet at .999 of the speed of light.

That particular catastrophe never happened, but one day a drone did come limping back alone. Its data were analyzed, and it turned out that the colonists' ship had been pursued by another vessel and destroyed. This happened near Aldebaran, in the constellation Taurus, but since "Aldebaranian" is a little hard to handle, they named the enemy Taurans.

Colonizing vessels thenceforth went out protected by an armed guard. Often the armed guard went out alone, and finally the colonization effort itself slowed to a token trickle. The United Nations Exploratory and Colonization Group got shortened to UNEF, United Nations Exploratory Force, emphasis on the "force".

Then some bright lad in the General Assembly decided that we ought to field an army of footsoldiers, to guard the portal planets of the nearer collapsars. This led to the Elite Conscription Act of 1996 and the most rigorously selected army in the history of warfare.

So here we are, fifty men and fifty women, with IQ's over 150 and bodies of unusual health and strength, slogging elitely through the mud and slush of central Missouri, reflecting on how useful our skill in building bridges will be, on worlds where the only fluid will be your occasional standing pool of liquid helium.

III

About a month later, we left for our final training exercise; maneuvers on the planet Charon. Though nearing perihelion it was still more than twice as far from the sun as Pluto.

The troopship was a converted "cattlewagon," made to carry two hundred colonists and assorted bushes and beasts. Don't think it was roomy, though, just because there were half that many of us. Most of the excess space was taken up with extra reaction mass and ordnance.

The whole trip took three weeks, accelerating at 2 Gs halfway; decelerating the other half. Our top speed, as we roared by the orbit of Pluto, was around one twentieth of the speed of light—not quite enough for relativity to rear its complicated head.

Three weeks of carrying around twice as much weight as normal . . . it's no picnic. We did some cautious exercises three times a day, and remained horizontal as much as possible. Still, we had several broken bones and serious dislocations. The men had to wear special supporters. It was almost impossible to sleep, what with nightmares of choking and being crushed, and the necessity of rolling over periodically to prevent blood pooling and bedsores. One girl got so fatigued that she almost slept through the experience of having a rib rub through to the open air.

I'd been in space several times before, so when we finally stopped decelerating and went into free fall, it was nothing but a relief. But some people had never been out, except for our training on the Moon, and succumbed to the sudden vertigo and disorientation. The rest of us cleaned up after them, floating through the quarters with sponges and inspirators to suck up globules of partly-digested "Concentrate, High-protein, Low-residue, Beef Flavor (Soya)."

A shuttle took us down to the surface in three trips. I waited for the last one, along with everybody else who wasn't bothered by free fall.

We had a good view of Charon, coming down from orbit. There wasn't much to see, though. It was just a dim, off-white sphere with a few smudges on it. We landed about two hundred meters from the base. A pressurized crawler came out and mated with the ferry, so we didn't have to suit up. We clanked and squeaked up to the main building, a featureless box of grayish plastic.

Inside, the walls were the same inspired color. The rest of the company was sitting at desks, chattering away. There was a seat next to Freeland.

"Jeff—feeling better?" He still looked a little pale.

"If the gods had meant for man to survive in free fall, they would have given him a cast-iron glottis. Somewhat better. Dying for a smoke."

"Yeah."

"*You* seemed to take it all right. Went up in school, didn't you?"

"Senior thesis in vacuum welding, yeah, three weeks in Earth orbit." I sat back and reached for my weed box, for the thousandth time. It still wasn't there, of course. The Life Support Unit didn't want to handle nicotine and THC.

"Training was bad enough," Jeff groused, "but *this* crap—"

"I don't know." I'd been thinking about it. "It might just all be worth it."

"Hell, no—this is a *space* war, let Star Fleet take care of it . . . they're just going to send us out and either we sit for fifty years on some damn ice cube of a portal planet, or we get—"

"Well, Jeff, you've got to look at it the other way, too. Even if there's only one chance in a thousand that we'll be doing some good, keeping the Taurans—"

"Tench-hut!" We stood up in a raggety-ass fashion, by twos and threes. The door opened and a full major came in. I stiffened a little. He was the highest-ranking officer I'd ever seen. He had a row of ribbons stitched into his coveralls, including a purple strip meaning he'd been wounded in combat, fighting in the old American army. Must have been that Indochina thing, but it had fizzled out before I was born. He didn't look that old.

"Sit, sit." He made a patting motion with his hand. Then he put his hands on his hips and scanned the company with a small smile on his face. "Welcome to Charon. You picked a lovely day to land; the temperature outside is a summery eight point one five degrees Absolute. We expect little change for the next two centuries or so." Some of us laughed half-heartedly.

"You'd best enjoy the tropical climate here at Miami Base, enjoy it while you can. We're on the center of sunside here, and most of your training will be on darkside. Over there, the temperature drops to a chilly two point zero eight.

"You might as well regard all the training you got on Earth and the Moon as just a warm-up exercise, to give you a fair chance of surviving Charon. You'll have to go through your whole repertory here: tools, weapons, maneuvers. And you'll find that, at these temperatures, tools don't work the way they should, weapons don't want to fire. And people move v-e-r-y cautiously."

He studied the clipboard in his hand. "Right now, you have forty-nine women and forty-eight men. Two deaths, one psychiatric release. Having read an outline of your training program, I'm frankly surprised that so many of you pulled through.

"But you might as well know that I won't be displeased if as few as fifty of you graduate from this final phase. And the only way not to graduate is to die. Here. The only way anybody gets back to Earth—including me—is after a combat tour.

"You will complete your training in one month. From here you go to Stargate collapsar, a little over two lights away. You will stay at the settlement on Stargate I, the largest portal planet, until replacements arrive. Hopefully, that will be no more than a month; another group is due here as soon as you leave.

"When you leave Stargate, you will be going to a strategically important collapsar, set up a military base there, and fight the enemy, if attacked. Otherwise, maintain the base until further orders.

"The last two weeks of your training will consist of constructing such a base, on darkside. There you will be totally isolated from Miami Base: no communication, no medical evacuation, no resupply. Sometime before the two weeks are up, your defense facilities will be evaluated in an attack by guided drones. They will be armed.

"All of the permanent personnel here on Charon are combat veterans. Thus, all of us are forty to fifty years of age, but I think we can keep up with you. Two of us will be with you at all times, and will accompany you at least as far as Stargate. They are Captain Sherman Stott, your company commander, and Sergeant Octavio Cortez, your first sergeant. Gentlemen?"

Two men in the front row stood easily and turned to face us. Captain Stott was a little smaller than the major, but cut from the same mold; face hard and smooth as porcelain, cynical half-smile, a precise centimeter of beard framing a large chin, looking thirty at the most.   He wore a large, gunpowder-type pistol on his hip.

Sergeant Cortez was another story.   His head was shaved and the wrong shape; flattened out on one side where a large piece of skull had obviously been taken out.   His face was very dark and seamed with wrinkles and scars.   Half his left ear was missing and his eyes were as expressive as buttons on a machine.   He had a moustache-and-beard combination that looked like a skinny white caterpillar taking a lap around his mouth.   On anybody else, his schoolboy smile might look pleasant, but he was about the ugliest, meanest-looking creature I'd ever seen. Still, if you didn't look at his head and considered the lower six feet or so, he could pose as the "after" advertisement for a body-building spa.   Neither Stott nor Cortez wore any ribbons.   Cortez had a small pocket-laser suspended in a magnetic rig, sideways, under his left armpit.   It had wooden grips that were worn very smooth.

"Now, before I turn you over to the tender mercies of these two gentlemen, let me caution you again:

"Two months ago there was not a living soul on this planet, just some leftover equipment from the expedition of 1991.   A working force of forty-five men struggled for a month to erect this base.   Twenty-four of them, more than half, died in the construction of it.   This is the most dangerous planet men have ever tried to live on, but the places you'll be going will be this bad and worse.   Your cadre will try to keep you alive for the next month.   Listen to them . . . and follow their example; all of them have survived here for longer than you'll have to. Captain?"   The captain stood up as the major went out the door.

"Tench-*hut!*"   The last syllable was like an explosion and we all jerked to our feet.

"Now I'm only gonna say this *once* so you better listen," he growled.   "We *are* in a combat situation here and in a combat situation there is only *one* penalty for disobedience and insubordination."   He jerked the pistol from his hip and held it by the barrel, like a club.   "This is an Army model 1911 automatic *pistol* caliber .45 and it is a primitive, but effective, weapon.   The sergeant and I are authorized to use our weapons to kill to enforce discipline, don't make us do it because we will.   We *will.*"   He put the pistol back.   The holster snap made a loud crack in the dead quiet.

"Sergeant Cortez and I between us have killed more people than are sitting in this room.   Both of us fought in Vietnam on the American side and both of us joined the United Nations International Guard more than ten years ago.   I took a break in grade from major for the privilege of commanding this company, and First Sergeant Cortez took a break from sub-major, because we are both *combat* soldiers and this is the first *combat* situation since 1974.

"Keep in mind what I've said while the First Sergeant instructs you more specifically in what your duties will be under this command.   Take over, Sergeant." He turned on his heel and strode out of the room, with the little smile on his face that hadn't changed one millimeter during the whole harangue.

The First Sergeant moved like a heavy machine with lots of ball bearings.   When the door hissed shut he swiveled ponderously to face us and said, "At ease, siddown," in a surprisingly gentle voice.   He sat on a table in the front of the room.   It creaked—but held.

"Now the captain talks scary and I look scary, but we both mean well.   You'll be working pretty closely with me, so you better get used to this thing I've got hanging in front of my brain.   You probably won't see the captain much, except on maneuvers."

He touched the flat part of his head.   "And speaking of brains, I still have just about all of mine, in spite of Chinese efforts to the contrary.   All of us old vets who mustered into UNEF had to pass the same criteria that got you drafted by the Elite Conscription Act.   So I suspect all of you are smart and tough—but just keep in mind that the captain and I are smart and tough *and* experienced."

He flipped through the roster without really looking at it.   "Now, as the captain said, there'll be only one kind of disciplinary action, on maneuvers.   Capital punishment.   But normally *we* won't have to kill you for disobeying; Charon'll save us the trouble.

"Back in the billeting area, it'll be another story.   We don't much care what you do inside, but once you suit up and go outside, you've gotta have discipline that would shame a Centurian.   There will be situations where one stupid act could kill us all.

"Anyhow, the first thing we've gotta do is get you fitted to your fighting suits. The armorer's waiting at your billet; he'll take you one at a time.   Let's go."

IV

"Now I know you got lectured and lectured on what a fighting suit can do, back on Earth."   The armorer was a small man, partially bald, with no insignia of rank on his coveralls.   Sergeant Cortez told us to call him "sir," since he was a lieutenant.

"But I'd like to reinforce a couple of points, maybe add some things your instructors Earthside weren't clear about, or couldn't know.   Your First Sergeant was kind enough to consent to being my visual aid.   Sergeant?"

Cortez slipped out of his coveralls and came up to the little raised platform where a fighting suit was standing, popped open like a man-shaped clam.   He backed into it and slipped his arms into the rigid sleeves.   There was a click and the thing swung shut with a sigh.   It was bright green with CORTEZ stenciled in white letters on the helmet.

"Camouflage, Sergeant."   The green faded to white, then dirty gray.   "This is good camouflage for Charon, and most of your portal planets," said Cortez, from a deep well.   "But there are several other combinations available."   The gray dappled and brightened to a combination of greens and browns: "Jungle." Then smoothed out to a hard light ochre: "Desert."   Dark brown, darker, to a deep flat black: "Night or space."

"Very good, Sergeant. To my knowledge, this is the only feature of the suit which was perfected after your training. The control is around your left wrist and is admittedly awkward. But once you find the right combination, it's easy to lock in.

"Now, you didn't get much in-suit training Earthside because we didn't want you to get used to using the thing in a friendly environment. The fighting suit is the deadliest personal weapon ever built, and with no weapon it is easier for the user to kill himself through carelessness. Turn around, Sergeant.

"Case in point." He tapped a square protuberance between the shoulders. "Exhaust fins. As you know the suit tries to keep you at a comfortable temperature no matter what the weather's like outside. The material of the suit is as near to a perfect insulator as we could get, consistent with mechanical demands. Therefore, these fins get *hot*—especially hot, compared to darkside temperatures—as they bleed off the body's heat.

"All you have to do is lean up against a boulder of frozen gas; there's lots of it around. The gas will sublime off faster than it can escape from the fins; in escaping, it will push against the surrounding 'ice' and fracture it . . . and in about one hundredth of a second, you have the equivalent of a hand grenade going off right below your neck. You'll never feel a thing.

"Variations on this theme have killed eleven people in the past two months. And they were just building a bunch of huts.

"I assume you know how easily the waldo capabilities can kill you or your companions. Anybody want to shake hands with the sergeant?" He stepped over and clasped his glove. "He's had lots of practice. Until *you* have, be extremely careful. You might scratch an itch and wind up bleeding to death. Remember, semi-logarithmic response: two pounds' pressure exerts five pounds' force; three pounds gives ten; four pounds' twenty-three; five pounds, forty-seven. Most of you can muster up a grip of well over a hundred pounds. Theoretically, you could rip a steel girder in two with that, amplified. Actually, you'd destroy the material of your gloves and, at least on Charon, die very quickly. It'd be a race between decompression and flash-freezing. You'd be the loser.

"The leg waldos are also dangerous, even though the amplification is less extreme. Until you're really skilled, don't try to run, or jump. You're likely to trip, and that means you're likely to die.

"Charon's gravity is three-fourths of Earth normal, so it's not too bad. But on a really small world, like Luna, you could take a running jump and not come down for twenty minutes, just keep sailing over the horizon. Maybe bash into a mountain at eighty meters per second. On a small asteroid, it'd be no trick at all to run up to escape velocity and be off on an informal tour of intergalactic space. It's a slow way to travel.

"Tomorrow morning, we'll start teaching you how to stay alive inside of this infernal machine. The rest of the afternoon and evening, I'll call you one at a time to be fitted. That's all, Sergeant."

Cortez went to the door and turned the stopcock that let air into the air lock. A bank of infrared lamps went on to keep the air from freezing inside it. When the pressures were equalized, he shut the stopcock, unclamped the door and stepped in, clamping it shut behind him.   A pump hummed for about a minute, evacuating the air lock, then he stepped out and sealed the outside door.   It was pretty much like the ones on Luna.

"First I want Private Omar Almizar.   The rest of you can go find your bunks. I'll call you over the squawker."

"Alphabetical order, sir?"

"Yep.   About ten minutes apiece.   If your name begins with Z, you might as well get sacked."

That was Rogers.   She probably *was* thinking about getting sacked.

V

The sun was a hard white point directly overhead.   It was a lot brighter than I had expected it to be; since we were eighty A. U.'s out, it was only 1/6400th as bright as it is on Earth.   Still, it was putting out about as much light as a powerful streetlamp.

"This is considerably more light than you'll have on a portal planet," Captain Stott's voice crackled in our collective ear.   "Be glad that you'll be able to watch your step."

We were lined up, single file, on a permaplast sidewalk connecting the billet and the supply hut.   We'd practiced walking inside, all morning, and this wasn't any different except for the exotic scenery.   Though the light was rather dim, you could see all the way to the horizon quite clearly, with no atmosphere in the way. A black cliff that looked too regular to be natural stretched from one horizon to the other, passing within a kilometer of us.   The ground was obsidian-black, mottled with patches of white, or bluish, ice.   Next to the supply hut was a small mountain of snow in a bin marked OXYGEN.

The suit was fairly comfortable, but it gave you the odd feeling of being simultaneously a marionette and a puppeteer.   You apply the impulse to move your leg and the suit picks it up and magnifies it and moves your leg for you.

"Today we're only going to walk around the company area and nobody will *leave* the company area."   The captain wasn't wearing his .45, but he had a laser-finger like the rest of us.   And his was probably hooked up.

Keeping an interval of at least two meters between each person, we stepped off the permaplast and followed the captain over the smooth rock.   We walked carefully for about an hour, spiraling out, and finally stopped at the far edge of the perimeter.

"Now everybody pay close attention.   I'm going out to that blue slab of ice"— it was a big one, about twenty meters away—"and show you something that you'd better know if you want to live."

He walked out a dozen confident steps.   "First I have to heat up a rock—filters down."   I slapped the stud under my armpit and the filter slid into place over my image converter.   The captain pointed his finger at a black rock the size of a basketball and gave it a short burst.   The glare rolled a long shadow of the captain over us and beyond.   The rock shattered into a pile of hazy splinters.

"It doesn't take long for these to cool down."   He stooped and picked up a piece.   "This one is probably twenty or twenty-five degrees.   Watch."   He tossed the "warm" rock on the ice slab.   It skittered around in a crazy pattern and shot off the side.   He tossed another one, and it did the same.

"As you know you are not quite *perfectly* insulated.   These rocks are about the temperature of the soles of your boots.   If you try to stand on a slab of hydrogen the same thing will happen to you.   Except that the rock is *already* dead.

"The reason for this behavior is that the rock makes a slick interface with the ice—a little puddle of liquid hydrogen—and rides a few molecules above the liquid on a cushion of hydrogen vapor.   This makes the rock, or *you,* a frictionless bearing as far as the ice is concerned and you *can't* stand up without any friction under your boots.

"After you have lived in your suit for a month or so you *should* be able to survive falling down, but right *now* you just don't know enough.   Watch."

The captain flexed and hopped up onto the slab.   His feet shot out from under him and he twisted around in midair, landing on hands and knees.   He slipped off and stood on the ground.

"The idea is to keep your exhaust fins from making contact with the frozen gas. Compared to the ice they are as hot as a blast furnace and contact with any weight behind it will result in an explosion."

After that demonstration, we walked around for another hour or so, and returned to the billet.   Once through the air lock, we had to mill around for a while, letting the suits get up to something like room temperature.   Somebody came up and touched helmets with me.

"William?"   She had MC COY stenciled above her faceplate.

"Hi, Sean.   Anything special?"

"I just wondered if you had anyone to sleep with tonight."

That's right; I'd forgotten, there wasn't any sleeping roster here.   Everybody just chose his own partner.   "Sure, I mean, uh, no . . . no, I haven't asked anybody, sure, if you want to . . ."

"Thanks, William.   See you later."   I watched her walk away and thought that if anybody could make a fighting suit look sexy, it'd be Sean.   But even Sean couldn't.

Cortez decided we were warm enough and led us to the suit room where we backed the things into place and hooked them up to the charging plates—each suit had a little chunk of plutonium that would power it for several years, but we were supposed to run on fuel cells as much as possible.   After a lot of shuffling around, everybody finally got plugged in and we were allowed to unsuit, ninety-seven naked chickens squirming out of bright green eggs.   It was *cold*—the air, the floor, and especially the suits—and we made a pretty disorderly exit toward the lockers.

I slipped on tunic, trousers and sandals and was still cold.   I took my cup and joined the line for soya, everybody jumping up and down to keep warm.

"How c-cold, do you think, it is, M-Mandella?" That was McCoy.

"I don't, even want, to think, about it." I stopped jumping and rubbed myself as briskly as possible, while holding a cup in one hand. "At least as cold as Missouri was."

"Ung . . . wish they'd, get some damn heat in, this place." It always affects the small girls more than anybody else. McCoy was the littlest one in the company, a waspwaist doll barely five feet high.

"They've got the airco going. It can't be long now."

"I wish I, was a big, slab of, meat like, you."

I was glad she wasn't.

VI

We had our first casualty on the third day, learning how to dig holes.

With such large amounts of energy stored in a soldier's weapons, it wouldn't be practical for him to hack out a hole in the frozen ground with the conventional pick and shovel. Still, you can launch grenades all day and get nothing but shallow depressions—so the usual method is to bore a hole in the ground with the hand laser, drop a timed charge in after it's cooled down and, ideally, fill the hole with stuff. Of course, there's not much loose rock on Charon, unless you've already blown a hole nearby.

The only difficult thing about the procedure is getting away. To be safe, we were told, you've got to either be behind something really solid, or be at least a hundred meters away. You've got about three minutes after setting the charge, but you can't just spring away. Not on Charon.

The accident happened when we were making a really deep hole, the kind you want for a large underground bunker. For this, we had to blow a hole, then climb down to the bottom of the crater and repeat the procedure again and again until the hole was deep enough. Inside the crater we used charges with a five-minute delay, but it hardly seemed enough time—you really had to go slow, picking your way up the crater's edge.

Just about everybody had blown a double hole; everybody but me and three others. I guess we were the only ones paying really close attention when Bovanovitch got into trouble. All of us were a good two hundred meters away. With my image converter tuned up to about forty power, I watched her disappear over the rim of the crater. After that, I could only listen in on her conversation with Cortez.

"I'm on the bottom, Sergeant." Normal radio procedure was suspended for these maneuvers; only the trainee and Cortez could broadcast.

"O.K., move to the center and clear out the rubble. Take your time. No rush until you pull the pin."

"Sure, Sergeant." We could hear small echoes of rocks clattering; sound conduction through her boots. She didn't say anything for several minutes.

"Found bottom." She sounded a little out of breath.

"Ice, or rock?"

"Oh, it's rock, Sergeant.   The greenish stuff."

"Use a low setting, then.   One point two, dispersion four."

"God darn it, Sergeant, that'll take forever."

"Yeah, but that stuff's got hydrated crystals in it—heat it up too fast and you might make it fracture.   And we'd just have to leave you there, girl."

"O.K, one point two dee four."   The inside edge of the crater flickered red with reflected laser light.

"When you get about half a meter deep, squeeze it up to dee two."

"Roger."   It took her exactly seventeen minutes, three of them at dispersion two.   I could imagine how tired her shooting arm was.

"Now rest for a few minutes.   When the bottom of the hole stops glowing, arm the charge and drop it in.   Then *walk* out.   Understand?   You'll have plenty of time."

"I understand, Sergeant.   Walk out."   She sounded nervous.   Well, you don't often have to tiptoe away from a twenty microton tachyon bomb.   We listened to her breathing for a few minutes.

"Here goes."   Faint slithering sound of the bomb sliding down.

"Slow and easy now, you've got five minutes."

"Y-yeah.   Five."   Her footsteps started out slow and regular.   Then, after she started climbing the side, the sounds were less regular; maybe a little frantic. And with four minutes to go—

"Crap!"   A loud scraping noise, then clatters and bumps.

"What's wrong, Private?"

"Oh, crap."   Silence.   "Crap!"

"Private, you don't wanna get shot, you *tell me what's wrong!*"

"I . . .   I'm stuck, damn rockslide . . .   DO SOMETHING I can't move.   I can't move I, I—"

"Shut up!   How deep?"

"Can't move my crap, my damn legs HELP ME—"

"Then damn it use your arms—push!—you can move a ton with each hand." Three minutes.

Then she stopped cussing and started to mumble, in Russian, I guess, a low monotone.   She was panting and you could hear rocks tumbling away.

"I'm free."   Two minutes.

"Go as fast as you can."   Cortez's voice was flat, emotionless.

At ninety seconds she appeared crawling over the rim.   "Run, girl . . . you better run."   She ran five or six steps and fell, skidded a few meters and got back up, running; fell again, got up again—

It looked like she was going pretty fast, but she had only covered about thirty meters when Cortez said, "All right, Bovanovitch, get down on your stomach and lie still."   Ten seconds, but she didn't hear him, or she wanted to get just a little more distance, and she kept running, careless leaping strides and at the high point of one leap there was a flash and a rumble and something big hit her below the neck and her headless body spun off end over end through space, trailing a red-black spiral of flash-frozen blood that settled gracefully to the ground, a path of crystal powder that nobody disturbed while we gathered rocks to cover the juiceless thing at the end of it.

That night Cortez didn't lecture us, didn't even show up for night-chop. We were all very polite to each other and nobody was afraid to talk about it.

I sacked with Rogers; everybody sacked with a good friend, but all she wanted to do was cry, and she cried so long and so hard that she got me doing it, too.

VII

"Fire team A—move out!" The twelve of us advanced in a ragged line toward the simulated bunker. It was about a kilometer away, across a carefully prepared obstacle course. We could move pretty fast, since all of the ice had been cleared from the field, but even with ten days' experience we weren't ready to do more than an easy jog.

I carried a grenade launcher, loaded with tenth-microton practice grenades. Everybody had their laser-fingers set at point oh eight dee one; not much more than a flashlight. This was a *simulated* attack—the bunker and its robot defender cost too much to be used once and thrown away.

"Team B follow. Team leaders, take over."

We approached a clump of boulders at about the halfway mark, and Potter, my team leader, said "Stop and cover." We clustered behind the rocks and waited for team B.

Barely visible in their blackened suits, the dozen men and women whispered by us. As soon as they were clear, they jogged left, out of our line of sight.

"Fire!" Red circles of light danced a half-click downrange, where the bunker was just visible. Five hundred meters was the limit for these practice grenades; but I might luck out, so I lined the launcher up on the image of the bunker, held it at a 45° angle and popped off a salvo of three.

Return fire from the bunker started before my grenades even landed. Its automatic lasers were no more powerful than the ones we were using, but a direct hit would deactivate your image converter, leaving you blind. It was setting down a random field of fire, not even coming close to the boulders we were hiding behind.

Three magnesium-bright flashes blinked simultaneously, about thirty meters short of the bunker. "Mandella! I thought you were supposed to be *good* with that thing."

"Damn it, Potter—it only throws half a click. Once we get closer, I'll lay 'em right on top, every time."

"*Sure* you will." I didn't say anything. She wouldn't be team leader forever. Besides, she hadn't been such a bad girl before the power went to her head.

Since the grenadier is the assistant team leader, I was slaved into Potter's radio and could hear B team talk to her.

"Potter, this is Freeman. Losses?"

"Potter here—no, looks like they were concentrating on you."

"Yeah, we lost three.   Right now we're in a depression about eighty, a hundred meters down from you.   We can give cover whenever you're ready."

"O.K., start."   Soft click: "A team, follow me."   She slid out from behind the rock and turned on the faint pink beacon beneath her powerpack.   I turned on mine and moved out to run alongside of her and the rest of the team fanned out in a trailing wedge.   Nobody fired while B team laid down a cover for us.

All I could hear was Potter's breathing and the soft *crunch-crunch* of my boots. Couldn't see much of anything, so I tongued the image converter up to a log two intensification.   That made the image kind of blurry but adequately bright.   Looked like the bunker had B team pretty well pinned down; they were getting quite a roasting.   All of their return fire was laser; they must have lost their grenadier.

"Potter, this is Mandella.   Shouldn't we take some of the heat off B team?"

"Soon as I can find us good enough cover.   Is that all right with you?   Private?" She'd been promoted to corporal for the duration of the exercise.

We angled to the right and laid down behind a slab of rock.   Most of the others found cover nearby, but a few had to just hug the ground.

"Freeman, this is Potter."

"Potter, this is Smithy.   Freeman's out; Samuels is out.   We only have five men left.   Give us some cover so we can get—"

"Roger, Smithy."—*click*—"Open up, A team.   The B's are really hurtin'."

I peeked out over the edge of the rock.   My rangefinder said that the bunker was about three hundred fifty meters away, still pretty far.   I aimed just a smidgeon high and popped three, then down a couple of degrees and three more.   The first ones overshot by about twenty meters, then the second salvo flared up directly in front of the bunker.   I tried to hold on that angle and popped fifteen, the rest of the magazine, in the same direction.

I should have ducked down behind the rock to reload, but I wanted to see where the fifteen would land, so I kept my eyes on the bunker while I reached back to unclip another magazine—

When the laser hit my image converter there was a red glare so intense it seemed to go right through my eyes and bounce off the back of my skull.   It must have been only a few milliseconds before the converter overloaded and went blind, but the bright green afterimage hurt my eyes for several minutes.

Since I was officially "dead," my radio automatically cut off and I had to remain where I was until the mock battle was over.   With no sensory input besides the feel of my own skin—and it ached where the image converter had shone on it— and the ringing in my ears, it seemed like an awfully long time.   Finally, a helmet clanked against mine:

"You O.K., Mandella?"   Potter's voice.

"Sorry, I died of boredom twenty minutes ago."

"Stand up and take my hand."   I did so and we shuffled back to the billet. It must have taken over an hour.   She didn't say anything more, all the way back— it's a pretty awkward way to communicate—but after we'd cycled through the air lock and warmed up, she helped me undog my suit.   I got ready for a mild tongue-lashing, but when the suit popped open, before I could even get my eyes adjusted to the light, she grabbed me around the neck and planted a wet kiss on my mouth.

"Nice shooting, Mandella."

"Huh?"

"The last salvo before you got hit—four direct hits; the bunker decided it was knocked out, and all we had to do was walk the rest of the way."

"Great."   I scratched my face under the eyes and some dry skin flaked off. She giggled.

"You should see yourself, you look like . . ."

"All personnel report to the assembly area."   That was the captain's voice. Bad news.

She handed me a tunic and sandals.   "Let's go."

The assembly area/chop hall was just down the corridor.   There was a row of roll-call buttons at the door; I pressed the one beside my name.   Four of the names were covered with black tape.   That was good, we hadn't lost anybody else during today's maneuvers.

The captain was sitting on the raised dais, which at least meant we didn't have to go through the tench-hut bullshit.   The place filled up in less than a minute; a soft chime indicated the roll was complete.

Captain Stott didn't stand up.   "You did *fairly* well today, nobody got killed and I expected some to.   In that respect you exceeded my expectations but in *every* other respect you did a poor job.

"I am glad you're taking good care of yourselves because each of you represents an investment of over a million dollars and one fourth of a human life.

"But in this simulated battle against a *very* stupid robot enemy, thirty-seven of you managed to walk into laser fire and be killed in a simulated way and since dead people require no food *you* will require no food, for the next three days. Each person who was a casualty in this battle will be allowed only two liters of water and a vitamin ration each day."

We knew enough not to groan or anything, but there were some pretty disgusted looks, especially on the faces that had singed eyebrows and a pink rectangle of sunburn framing their eyes.

"Mandella."

"Sir?"

"You are far and away the worst burned casualty.   Was your image converter set on normal?"

Oh, crap.   "No, sir.   Log two."

"I see.   Who was your team leader for the exercise?"

"Acting Corporal Potter, sir."

"Private Potter, did you order him to use image intensification?"

"Sir, I . . . I don't remember."

"You don't.   Well as a memory exercise you may join the dead people.   Is that satisfactory?"

"Yes, sir."

"Good. Dead people get one last meal tonight, and go on no rations starting tomorrow. Are there any questions?" He must have been kidding. "All right. Dismissed."

I selected the meal that looked as if it had the most calories and took my tray over to sit by Potter.

"That was a quixotic damn thing to do. But thanks."

"Nothing. I've been wanting to lose a few pounds anyway." I couldn't see where she was carrying any extra.

"I know a good exercise," I said. She smiled without looking up from her tray. "Have anybody for tonight?"

"Kind of thought I'd ask Jeff . . ."

"Better hurry, then. He's lusting after Uhuru." Well, that was mostly true. Everybody did.

"I don't know. Maybe we ought to save our strength. That third day . . ."

"Come on," I scratched the back of her hand lightly with a fingernail. "We haven't sacked since Missouri. Maybe I've learned something new."

"Maybe you have." She tilted her head up at me in a sly way. "O.K."

Actually, she was the one with the new trick. The French corkscrew, she called it. She wouldn't tell me who taught it to her, though. I'd like to shake his hand.

VIII

The two weeks' training around Miami Base eventually cost us eleven lives. Twelve, if you count Dahlquist. I guess having to spend the rest of your life on Charon, with a hand and both legs missing, is close enough to dying.

Little Foster was crushed in a landslide and Freeland had a suit malfunction that froze him solid before we could carry him inside. Most of the other deaders were people I didn't know all that well. But they all hurt. And they seemed to make us more scared rather than more cautious.

Now darkside. A flier brought us over in groups of twenty, and set us down beside a pile of building materials, thoughtfully immersed in a pool of helium II.

We used grapples to haul the stuff out of the pool. It's not safe to go wading, since the stuff crawls all over you and it's hard to tell what's underneath; you could walk out onto a slab of hydrogen and be out of luck.

I'd suggested that we try to boil away the pool with our lasers, but ten minutes of concentrated fire didn't drop the helium level appreciably. It didn't boil, either; helium II is a "superfluid," so what evaporation there was had to take place evenly, all over the surface. No hot spots, so no bubbling.

We weren't supposed to use lights, to "avoid detection." There was plenty of starlight with your image converter cranked up to log three or four, but each stage of amplification meant some loss of detail. By log four, the landscape looked like a crude monochrome painting, and you couldn't read the names on people's helmets unless they were right in front of you.

The landscape wasn't all that interesting, anyhow.   There were half a dozen medium-size meteor craters—all with exactly the same level of helium II in them— and the suggestion of some puny mountains just over the horizon.   The uneven ground was the consistency of frozen spiderwebs; every time you put your foot down, you'd sink half an inch with a squeaking crunch.   It could get on your nerves.

It took most of a day to pull all the stuff out of the pool.   We took shifts napping, which you could do either standing up, sitting, or lying on your stomach.   I didn't do well in any of those positions, so I was anxious to get the bunker built and pressurized.

We couldn't build the thing underground—it'd just fill up with helium II—so the first thing to do was to build an insulating platform, a permaplast-vacuum sandwich three layers tall.

I was an acting corporal, with a crew of ten people.   We were carrying the permaplast layers to the building site—two people can carry one easily—when one of ''my'' men slipped and fell on his back.

''Damn it, Singer, watch your step.''   We'd had a couple of deaders that way.

''Sorry, Corporal.   I'm bushed, just got my feet tangled up.''

''Yeah, just watch it.''   He got back up all right, and with his partner placed the sheet and went back to get another.

I kept my eye on him.   In a few minutes he was practically staggering, not easy to do in that suit of cybernetic armor.

''Singer!   After you set that plank, I want to see you.''

''O.K.''   He labored through the task and mooched over.

''Let me check your readout.''   I opened the door on his chest to expose the medical monitor.   His temperature was two degrees high; blood pressure and heart rate both elevated.   Not up to the red line, though.

''You sick or something?''

''Hell, Mandella, I feel O.K., just tired.   Since I fell I've been a little dizzy.''

I chinned the medic's combination.   ''Doc, this is Mandella.   You wanna come over here for a minute?''

Sure, where are you?''   I waved and he walked over from poolside.

''What's the problem?''   I showed him Singer's readout.

He knew what all the other little dials and things meant, so it took him a while. ''As far as I can tell, Mandella . . . he's just hot.''

''Hell, I coulda told you that,'' said Singer.

''Maybe you better have the armorer take a look at his suit.''   We had two people who'd taken a crash course in suit maintenance; they were our ''armorers.''

I chinned Sanchez and asked him to come over with his tool kit.

''Be a couple of minutes, Corporal.   Carryin' a plank.''

''Well, put it down and get on over here.''   I was getting an uneasy feeling. Waiting for him, the medic and I looked over Singer's suit.

"Uh-oh," Doc Jones said. "Look at this." I went around to the back and looked where he was pointing. Two of the fins on the heat exchanger were bent out of shape.

"What is wrong?" Singer asked.

"You fell on your heat exchanger, right?"

"Sure, Corporal—that's it, it must not be working right."

"I don't think it's working at *all*," said Doc.

Sanchez came over with his diagnostic kit and we told him what had happened. He looked at the heat exchanger, then plugged a couple of jacks into it and got a digital readout from a little monitor in his kit. I didn't know what it was measuring, but it came out zero to eight decimal places.

Heard a soft click, Sanchez chinning my private frequency. "Corporal, this guy's a deader."

"What? Can't you fix the damn thing?"

"Maybe . . . maybe I could, if I could take it apart. But there's no way—"

"Hey! Sanchez?" Singer was talking on the general freak. "Find out what's wrong?" He was panting.

Click. "Keep your pants on, man, we're working on it." *Click.* "He won't last long enough for us to get the bunker pressurized. And I can't work on the heat exchanger from outside of the suit."

"You've got a spare suit, haven't you?"

"Two of 'em, the fit-anybody kind. But there's no place . . . say . . ."

"Right. Go get one of the suits warmed up." I chinned the general freak. "Listen, Singer, we've gotta get you out of that thing. Sanchez has a spare suit, but to make the switch, we're gonna have to build a house around you. Understand?"

"Huh-uh."

"Look, we'll just make a box with you inside, and hook it up to the life-support unit. That way you can breathe while you make the switch."

"Soun's pretty compis . . . complicated t'me."

"Look, just come along—"

"I'll be all right, man, jus' lemme res' . . ."

I grabbed his arm and led him to the building site. He was really weaving. Doc took his other arm and between us, we kept him from falling over.

"Corporal Ho, this is Corporal Mandella." Ho was in charge of the life-support unit.

"Go away, Mandella, I'm busy."

"You're going to be busier." I outlined the problem to her. While her group hurried to adapt the LSU—for this purpose, it need only be an air hose and heater— I got my crew to bring around six slabs of permaplast, so we could build a big box around Singer and the extra suit. It would look like a huge coffin, a meter square and six meters long.

We set the suit down on the slab that would be the floor of the coffin. "O.K, Singer, let's go."

No answer.

"Singer!"   He was just standing there.   Doc Jones checked his readout.

"He's out, man, unconscious."

My mind raced.   There might just be room for another person in the box.   "Give me a hand here."   I took Singer's shoulders and Doc took his feet, and we carefully laid him out at the feet of the empty suit.

Then I laid down myself, above the suit.   O.K., close 'er up."

"Look, Mandella, if anybody goes in there, it oughta be me."

"No, Doc. *My* job.   My man."   That sounded all wrong.   William Mandella, boy hero.

They stood a slab up on edge—it had two openings for the LSU input and exhaust—and proceeded to weld it to the bottom plank with a narrow laser beam. On Earth, we'd just use glue, but here the only fluid was helium, which has lots of interesting properties, but is definitely not sticky.

After about ten minutes we were completely walled up.   I could feel the LSU humming.   I switched on my suit light—the first time since we landed on darkside— and the glare made purple blotches dance in front of my eyes.

"Mandella, this is Ho.   Stay in your suit at least two or three minutes.   We're putting hot air in, but it's coming back just this side of liquid."   I lay and watched the purple fade.

"O.K., it's still cold, but you can make it."   I popped my suit.   It wouldn't open all the way, but I didn't have too much trouble getting out.   The suit was still cold enough to take some skin off my fingers and butt as I wiggled out.

I had to crawl feet-first down the coffin to get to Singer.   It got darker fast, moving away from my light.   When I popped his suit a rush of hot stink hit me in the face.   In the dim light his skin was dark red and splotchy.   His breathing was very shallow and I could see his heart palpitating.

First I unhooked the relief tubes—an unpleasant business—then the bio sensors, and then I had the problem of getting his arms out of their sleeves.

It's pretty easy to do for yourself.   You twist this way and turn that way and the arm pops out.   Doing it from the outside is a different matter: I had to twist his arm and then reach under and move the suit's arm to match—and it takes muscle to move a suit around from the outside.

Once I had one arm out it was pretty easy: I just crawled forward, putting my feet on the suit's shoulders, and pulled on his free arm.   He slid out of the suit like an oyster slipping out of its shell.

I popped the spare suit and after a lot of pulling and pushing, managed to get his legs in.   Hooked up the bio sensors and the front relief tube.   He'd have to do the other one himself, it's too complicated.   For the nth time I was glad not to have been born female; they have to have two of those damned plumber's friends, instead of just one and a simple hose.

I left his arms out of the sleeves.   The suit would be useless for any kind of work, anyhow; waldos have to be tailored to the individual.

His eyelids fluttered."Man . . . della.   Where . . . the hell . . ."

I explained, slowly, and he seemed to get most of it.   "Now I'm gonna close you up and go get into my suit. I'll have the crew cut the end off this thing and I'll haul you out. Got it?''

He nodded. Strange to see that—when you nod or shrug in a suit, it doesn't communicate anything.

I crawled into my suit, hooked up the attachments and chinned the general freak. ''Doc, I think he's gonna be O.K. Get us out of here now.''

''Will do.'' Ho's voice. The LSU hum was replaced by a chatter, then a throb; evacuating the box to prevent an explosion.

One corner of the seam grew red, then white and a bright crimson beam lanced through, not a foot away from my head. I scrunched back as far as I could. The beam slid up the seam and around three corners, back to where it started. The end of the box fell away slowly, trailing filaments of melted 'plast.

''Wait for the stuff to harden, Mandella.''

''Sanchez, I'm not that stupid.''

''Here you go.'' Somebody tossed a line to me. That *would* be smarter than dragging him out by myself. I threaded a long bight under his arms and tied it behind his neck. Then I scrambled out to help them pull, which was silly—they had a dozen people already lined up to haul.

Singer got out all right and was actually sitting up while Doc Jones checked his readout. People were asking me about it and congratulating me when suddenly Ho said ''Look!'' and pointed toward the horizon.

It was a black ship, coming in fast. I just had time to think it wasn't fair, they weren't supposed to attack until the last few days, and then the ship was right on top of us.

IX

We all flopped to the ground instinctively, but the ship didn't attack. It blasted braking rockets and dropped to land on skids. Then it skied around to come to a rest beside the building site.

Everybody had it figured out and was standing around sheepishly when the two suited figures stepped out of the ship.

A familiar voice crackled over the general freak. ''Every *one* of you saw us coming in and not *one* of you responded with laser fire. It wouldn't have done any good but it would have indicated a certain amount of fighting spirit. You have a week or less before the real thing and since the sergeant and *I* will be here *I* will insist that you show a little more will to live. Acting Sergeant Potter.''

''Here, sir.''

''Get me a detail of twelve men to unload cargo. We brought a hundred small robot drones for *tar*get practice so that you might have at least a fighting chance, when a live target comes over.

''Move *now*. We only have thirty minutes before the ship returns to Miami.''

I checked, and it was actually more like forty minutes.

* * *

Having the captain and sergeant there didn't really make much difference; we were still on our own, they were just observing.

Once we got the floor down, it only took one day to complete the bunker. It was a gray oblong, featureless except for the air-lock blister and four windows. On top was a swivel-mounted bevawatt laser. The operator—you couldn't call him a "gunner"—sat in a chair holding dead-man switches in both hands. The laser wouldn't fire as long as he was holding one of those switches. If he let go, it would automatically aim for any moving aerial object and fire at will. Primary detection and aiming was by means of a kilometer-high antenna mounted beside the bunker.

It was the only arrangement that could really be expected to work, with the horizon so close and human reflexes so slow. You couldn't have the thing fully automatic, because in theory, friendly ships might also approach.

The aiming computer could choose up to twelve targets, appearing simultaneously—firing at the largest ones first. And it would get all twelve in the space of half a second.

The installation was partly protected from enemy fire by an efficient ablative layer that covered everything except the human operator. But then they *were* dead-man switches. One man above guarding eighty inside. The army's good at that kind of arithmetic.

Once the bunker was finished, half of us stayed inside at all times—feeling very much like targets—taking turns operating the laser, while the other half went on maneuvers.

About four clicks from the base was a large "lake" of frozen hydrogen; one of our most important maneuvers was to learn how to get around on the treacherous stuff.

It really wasn't too difficult. You couldn't stand up on it, so you had to belly down and slide.

If you had somebody to push you from the edge, getting started was no problem. Otherwise, you had to scrabble with your hands and feet, pushing down as hard as was practical, until you started moving, in a series of little jumps. Once started, you would keep going until you ran out of ice. You could steer a little bit by digging in, hand and foot, on the appropriate side, but you couldn't slow to a stop that way. So it was a good idea not to go too fast, and to be positioned in such a way that your helmet didn't absorb the shock of stopping.

We went through all the things we'd done on the Miami side; weapons practice, demolition, attack patterns. We also launched drones at irregular intervals, toward the bunker. Thus, ten or fifteen times a day, the operators got to demonstrate their skill in letting go of the handles as soon as the proximity light went on.

I had four hours of that, like everybody else. I was nervous until the first "attack," when I saw how little there was to it. The light went on, I let go, the gun aimed and when the drone peeped over the horizon—*zzt!* Nice touch of color, the molten metal spraying through space. Otherwise not too exciting.

So none of us were worried about the upcoming "graduation exercise," thinking it would be just more of the same.

*   *   *

Miami Base attacked on the thirteenth day with two simultaneous missiles streaking over opposite sides of the horizon at some forty kilometers per second.   The laser vaporized the first one with no trouble, but the second got within eight clicks of the bunker before it was hit.

We were coming back from maneuvers, about a click away from the bunker. I wouldn't have seen it happen if I hadn't been looking directly at the bunker the moment of the attack.

The second missile sent a shower of molten debris straight toward the bunker. Eleven pieces hit, and, as we later reconstructed it, this is what happened.

The first casualty was Uhuru, pretty Uhuru inside the bunker, who was hit in the back and head and died instantly.   With the drop in pressure, the LSU went into high gear.   Friedman was standing in front of the main airco outlet and was blown into the opposite wall hard enough to knock him unconscious; he died of decompression before the others could get him to his suit.

Everybody else managed to stagger through the gale and get into their suits, but Garcia's suit had been holed and didn't do him any good.

By the time we got there, they had turned off the LSU and were welding up the holes in the wall.   One man was trying to scrape up the unrecognizable mess that had been Uhuru.   I could hear him sobbing and retching.   They had already taken Garcia and Friedman outside for burial.   The captain took over the repair detail from Potter.   Sergeant Cortez led the sobbing man over to a corner and came back to work on cleaning up Uhuru's remains, alone.   He didn't order anybody to help and nobody volunteered.

X

As a graduation exercise, we were unceremoniously stuffed into a ship—*Earth's Hope*, the same one we rode to Charon—and bundled off to Stargate at a little more than 1 G.

The trip seemed endless, about six months subjective time, and boring, but not as hard on the carcass as going to Charon had been.   Captain Stott made us review our training orally, day by day, and we did exercises every day until we were worn to a collective frazzle.

Stargate I was like Charon's darkside, only more so.   The base on Stargate I was smaller than Miami Base—only a little bigger than the one we constructed on darkside—and we were due to lay over a week to help expand the facilities.   The crew there was very glad to see us; especially the two females, who looked a little worn around the edges.

We all crowded into the small dining hall, where Submajor Williamson, the man in charge of Stargate I, gave us some disconcerting news:

"Everybody get comfortable.   Get off the tables, though, there's plenty of floor.

"I have some idea of what you just went through, training on Charon.   I won't say it's all been wasted.   But where you're headed, things will be quite different. Warmer."

He paused to let that soak in.

"Aleph Aurigae, the first collapsar ever detected, revolves around the normal star Epsilon Aurigae, in a twenty-seven-year orbit.   The enemy has a base of operations, not on a regular portal planet of Aleph, but on a planet in orbit around Epsilon.   We don't know much about the planet: just that it goes around Epsilon once every seven hundred forty-five days, is about three fourth the size of Earth, and has an albedo of 0.8, meaning it's probably covered with clouds.   We can't say precisely how hot it will be, but judging from its distance from Epsilon, it's probably rather hotter than Earth.   Of course, we don't know whether you'll be working . . . fighting on lightside or darkside, equator or poles.   It's highly unlikely that the atmosphere will be breathable—at any rate, you'll stay inside your suits.

"Now you know exactly as much about where you're going as I do.   Questions?"

"Sir," Stein drawled, "now we know where we're goin' . . . anybody know what we're goin' to do when we get there?"

Williamson shrugged.   "That's up to your captain—and your sergeant, and the captain of *Earth's Hope*, and *Hope*'s logistic computer.   We just don't have enough data yet, to project a course of action for you.   It may be a long and bloody battle, it may be just a case of walking in to pick up the pieces.   Conceivably, the Taurans might want to make a peace offer"—Cortez snorted—"in which case you would simply be part of our muscle, our bargaining power."   He looked at Cortez mildly. "No one can say for sure."

The orgy that night was kind of amusing, but it was like trying to sleep in the middle of a raucous beach party.   The only area big enough to sleep all of us was the dining hall; they draped a few bedsheets here and there for privacy, then unleashed Stargate's eighteen sex-starved men on our women, compliant and promiscuous by military custom—and law—but desiring nothing so much as sleep on solid ground.

The eighteen men acted as if they were compelled to try as many permutations as possible, and their performance was impressive—in a strictly quantitative sense, that is.

The next morning—and every other morning we were on Stargate I—we staggered out of bed and into our suits, to go outside and work on the "new wing."   Eventually, Stargate would be tactical and logistic headquarters for the war, with thousands of permanent personnel, guarded by half-a-dozen heavy cruisers in *Hope*'s class.   When we started, it was two shacks and twenty people; when we left, it was four shacks and twenty people.   The work was a breeze, compared to darkside, since we had all the light we needed, and got sixteen hours inside for every eight hours' work.   And no drone attack for a final exam.

When we shuttled back up to the *Hope,* nobody was too happy about leaving— though some of the more popular females declared it'd be good to get some rest— Stargate was the last easy, safe assignment we'd have before taking up arms against the Taurans.   And as Williamson had pointed out the first day, there was no way of predicting what that would be like.

Most of us didn't feel too enthusiastic about making a collapsar jump, either. We'd been assured that we wouldn't even feel it happen, just free fall all the way.

I wasn't convinced.   As a physics student, I'd had the usual courses in general relativity and theories of gravitation.   We only had a little direct data at that time— Stargate was discovered when I was in grade school—but the mathematical model seemed clear enough.

The collapsar Stargate was a perfect sphere about three kilometers in radius.   It was suspended forever in a state of gravitational collapse that should have meant its surface was dropping toward its center at nearly the speed of light.   Relativity propped it up, at least gave it the illusion of being there . . . the way all reality becomes illusory and observer-oriented when you study general relativity, or Buddhism.

At any rate, there would be a theoretical point in spacetime when one end of our ship was just above the surface of the collapsar, and the other end was a kilometer away—in our frame of reference.   In any sane universe, this would set up tidal stresses and tear the ship apart, and we would be just another million kilograms of degenerate matter on the theoretical surface, rushing headlong to nowhere for the rest of eternity; or dropping to the center in the next trillionth of a second.   You pays your money and you takes your frame of reference.

But they were right.   We blasted away from Stargate I, made a few course corrections and then just dropped, for about an hour.

Then a bell rang and we sank into our cushions under a steady two gravities of deceleration.   We were in enemy territory.

XI

We'd been decelerating at two gravities for almost nine days when the battle began.   Lying on our couches being miserable, all we felt were two soft bumps, missiles being released.   Some eight hours later, the squawkbox crackled: "Attention, all crew.   This is the captain."   Quinsana, the pilot, was only a lieutenant, but was allowed to call himself captain aboard the vessel, where he outranked all of us, even Captain Stott.   "You grunts in the cargo hold can listen, too.

"We just engaged the enemy with two fifty-bevaton tachyon missiles, and have destroyed both the enemy vessel and another object which it had launched approximately three microseconds before.

"The enemy has been trying to overtake us for the past one hundred seventy-nine hours, ship time.   At the time of the engagement, the enemy was moving at a little over half the speed of light, relative to Aleph, and was only about thirty AU's from *Earth's Hope*. It was moving at .47c relative to us, and thus we would have been coincident in spacetime"—rammed!—"in a little more than nine hours. The missiles were launched at 0719 ship's time, and destroyed the enemy at 1540, both tachyon bombs detonating within a thousand clicks of the enemy objects."

The two missiles were a type whose propulsion system itself was only a barely-controlled tachyon bomb.   They accelerated at a constant rate of 100 Gs, and were traveling at a relativistic speed by the time the nearby mass of the enemy ship detonated them.

"We expect no further interference from enemy vessels.   Our velocity with respect to Aleph will be zero in another five hours; we will then begin to journey back.   The return will take twenty-seven days."   General moans and dejected cussing.   Everybody knew all that already, of course; but we didn't care to be reminded of it.

So after another month of logycalisthenics and drill, at a constant 2 Gs, we got our first look at the planet we were going to attack.   Invaders from outer space, yes, sir.

It was a blinding white crescent basking two AU's from Epsilon.   The captain had pinned down the location of the enemy base from fifty AU's out, and we had jockeyed in on a wide arc, keeping the bulk of the planet between them and us. That didn't mean we were sneaking up on them—quite the contrary; they launched three abortive attacks—but it put us in a stronger defensive position.   Until we had to go to the surface, that is.   Then only the ship and its Star Fleet crew would be reasonably safe.

Since the planet rotated rather slowly—once every ten and one half days—a "stationary" orbit for the ship had to be one hundred fifty thousand clicks out. This made the people in the ship feel quite secure, with six thousand miles of rock and ninety thousand miles of space between them and the enemy.   But it meant a whole second's time lag in communication between us on the ground and the ship's battle computer.   A person could get awful dead while that neutrino pulse crawled up and back.

Our vague orders were to attack the base and gain control while damaging a minimum of enemy equipment.   We were to take at least one enemy alive.   We were under no circumstances to allow *ourselves* to be taken alive, however.   And the decision wasn't up to us; one special pulse from the battle computer and that speck of plutonium in your power plant would fission with all of .01% efficiency, and you'd be nothing but a rapidly expanding, very hot plasma.

They strapped us into six scoutships—one platoon of twelve people in each— and we blasted away from *Earth's Hope* at 8 Gs.   Each scoutship was supposed to follow its own carefully random path to our rendezvous point, one hundred eight clicks from the base.   Fourteen drone ships were launched at the same time, to confound the enemy's anti-spacecraft system.

The landing went off almost perfectly.   One ship suffered minor damage, a near miss boiling away some of the ablative material on one side of the hull, but it'd still be able to make it and return, as long as it kept its speed down while in the atmosphere.

We zigged and zagged and wound up first ship at the rendezvous point.   There was only one trouble.   It was under four kilometers of water.

I could almost hear that machine, ninety thousand miles away, grinding its mental gears, adding this new bit of data.   We proceeded just as if we were landing on solid ground: braking rockets, falling, skids out, hit the water, skip, hit the water, skip, hit the water, sink.

It would have made sense to go ahead and land on the bottom—we were streamlined, after all, and water just another fluid—but the hull wasn't strong enough to hold up a four-kilometer column of water.   Sergeant Cortez was in the scoutship with us.

"Sarge, tell that computer to *do* something!   We're gonna get—"

"Oh, shut up, Mandella.   Trust in th' lord."   "Lord" was definitely lowercase when Cortez said it.

There was a loud bubbly sigh, then another and a slight increase in pressure on my back that meant the ship was rising.   "Flotation bags?"   Cortez didn't deign to answer, or didn't know.

That must have been it.   We rose to within ten or fifteen meters of the surface and stopped, suspended there.   Through the port I could see the surface above, shimmering like a mirror of hammered silver.   I wondered what it could be like, to be a fish and have a definite roof over your world.

I watched another ship splash in.   It made a great cloud of bubbles and turbulence, then fell—slightly tailfirst—for a short distance before large bags popped out under each delta wing.   Then it bobbed up to about our level and stayed.

Soon all of the ships were floating within a few hundred meters of us, like a school of ungainly fish.

"This is Captain Stott.   Now listen carefully.   There is a beach some twenty-eight clicks from your present position, in the direction of the enemy.   You will be proceeding to this beach by scoutship and from there will mount your assault on the Tauran position."   That was *some* improvement; we'd only have to walk eighty clicks.

We deflated the bags, blasted to the surface and flew in a slow, spread-out formation to the beach.   It took several minutes.   As the ship scraped to a halt I could hear pumps humming, making the cabin pressure equal to the air pressure outside.   Before it had quite stopped moving, the escape slot beside my couch slid open.   I rolled out onto the wing of the craft and jumped to the ground.   Ten seconds to find cover—I sprinted across loose gravel to the "treeline," a twisty bramble of tall sparse bluish-green shrubs.   I dove into the briar patch and turned to watch the ships leave.   The drones that were left rose slowly to about a hundred meters, then took off in all directions with a bone-jarring roar.   The real scoutships slid slowly back into the water.   Maybe that was a good idea.

It wasn't a terribly attractive world, but certainly would be easier to get around in than the cryogenic nightmare we were trained for.   The sky was a uniform dull silver brightness that merged with the mist over the ocean so completely as to make it impossible to tell where water ended and air began.   Small wavelets licked at the black gravel shore, much too slow and graceful in the three-quarters Earth normal gravity.   Even from fifty meters away, the rattle of billions of pebbles rolling with the tide was loud in my ears.

The air temperature was 79° Centigrade, not quite hot enough for the sea to boil, even though the air pressure was low compared to Earth's.   Wisps of steam drifted quickly upward from the line where water met land.   I wondered how long a man would survive, exposed here without a suit.   Would the heat or the low oxygen— partial pressure one-eighth Earth normal—kill him first?   Or was there some deadly microorganism that would beat them both . . .

"This is Cortez.   Everybody come over and assemble by me."   He was standing on the beach a little to the left of me, waving his hand in a circle over his head. I walked toward him through the shrubs.   They were brittle, unsubstantial, seemed paradoxically dried-out in the steamy air.   They wouldn't offer much in the way of cover.

"We'll be advancing on a heading .05 radians east of north.   I want Platoon One to take point.   Two and Three follow about twenty meters behind, to the left and right.   Seven, command platoon, is in the middle, twenty meters behind Two and Three.   Five and Six, bring up the rear, in a semicircular closed flank.   Everybody straight?"   Sure, we could do that "arrowhead" maneuver in our sleep. "O.K., let's move out."

I was in Platoon Seven, the "command group."   Captain Stott put me there not because I was expected to give any commands, but because of my training in physics.

The command group was supposedly the safest place, buffered by six platoons: people were assigned to it because there was some tactical reason for them to survive at least a little longer than the rest.   Cortez was there to give orders. Chavez was there to correct suit malfuncts.   The senior medic, Doc Wilson—the only medic who actually had an MD—was there and so was Theodopolis, the radio engineer: our link with the captain, who had elected to stay in orbit.

The rest of us were assigned to the command group by dint of special training or aptitude, that wouldn't normally be considered of a "tactical" nature.   Facing a totally unknown enemy, there was no way of tellng what might prove important. Thus I was there because I was the closest the company had to a physicist.   Rogers was biology.   Tate was chemistry.   Ho could crank out a perfect score on the Rhine extrasensory perception test, every time.   Bohrs was a polyglot, able to speak twenty-one languages fluently, idiomatically.   Petrov's talent was that he had tested out to have not one molecule of xenophobia in his psyche.   Keating was a skilled acrobat.   Debby Hollister—"Lucky" Hollister—showed a remarkable aptitude for making money, and also had a consistently high Rhine potential.

XII

When we first set out, we were using the "jungle" camouflage combination on our suits.   But what passed for jungle in these anemic tropics was too sparse; we looked like a band of conspicuous harlequins trooping through the woods.   Cortez had us switch to black, but that was just as bad, as the light from Epsilon came evenly from all parts of the sky, and there were no shadows except us.   We finally settled on the duncolored desert camouflage.

The nature of the countryside changed slowly as we walked north, away from the sea.   The throned stalks, I guess you could call them trees, came in fewer numbers but were bigger around and less brittle; at the base of each was a tangled mass of vine with the same blue-green color, which spread out in a flattened cone some ten meters in diameter.   There was a delicate green flower the size of a man's head near the top of each tree.

Grass began to appear some five clicks from the sea.   It seemed to respect the trees' "property rights"; leaving a strip of bare earth around each cone of vine. At the edge of such a clearing, it would grow as timid blue-green stubble; then, moving away from the tree, would get thicker and taller until it reached shoulder-high in some places, where the separation between two trees was unusually large. The grass was a lighter, greener shade than the trees and vines.   We changed the color of our suits to the bright green we had used for maximum visibility on Charon. Keeping to the thickest part of the grass, we were fairly inconspicuous.

I couldn't help thinking that one week of training in a South American jungle would have been worth a hell of a lot more than all those weeks on Charon.   We wouldn't be so understrength, either.

We covered over twenty clicks each day, buoyant after months under 2 Gs. Until the second day, the only form of animal life we saw was a kind of black worm, finger-sized with hundreds of cilium legs like the bristles of a stiff brush.   Rogers said that there obviously had to be some sort of larger creature around, or there would be no reason for the trees to have thorns.   So we were doubly on guard, expecting trouble both from the Taurans and the unidentified "large creatures."

Potter's Second Platoon was on point; the general freak was reserved for her, since point would likely be the First Platoon to spot any trouble.

"Sarge, this is Potter," we all heard.   "Movement ahead."

"Get down then!"

"We are.   Don't think they see us."

"First Platoon, go up to the right of point.   Keep down.   Fourth, get up to the left.   Tell me when you get in position.   Sixth Platoon, stay back and guard the rear.   Fifth and Third, close with the command group."

Two dozen people whispered out of the grass, to join us.   Cortez must have heard from the Fourth Platoon.

"Good.   How about you, First . . .   O.K., fine.   How many are there?"

"Eight we can see."   Potter's voice.

"Good.   When I give the word, open fire.   Shoot to kill."

"Sarge . . . they're just animals."

"Potter—if you've known all this time what a Tauran looks like, you should've told us.   Shoot to kill."

"But we need . . ."

"We need a prisoner, but we don't need to escort him forty clicks to his home base and keep an eye on him while we fight.   Clear?"

"Yes.   Sergeant."

"O.K.   Seventh, all you brains and weirds, we're going up and watch.   Fifth and Third, come along to guard."

We crawled through the meter-high grass to where the Second Platoon had stretched out in a firing line.

"I don't see anything," Cortez said.

"Ahead and just to the left.   Dark green."

They were only a shade darker than the grass.   But after you saw the first one, you could see them all, moving slowly around some thirty meters ahead.

"Fire!"   Cortez fired first, then twelve streaks of crimson leaped out and the grass wilted back, disappeared and the creatures convulsed and died trying to scatter.

"Hold fire, hold it!"   Cortez stood up.   "We want to have something left—Second Platoon, follow me."   He strode out toward the smoldering corpses, laser finger pointed out front, obscene divining rod pulling him toward the carnage . . . I felt my gorge rising and knew that all the lurid training tapes, all the horrible deaths in training accidents, hadn't prepared me for this sudden reality . . . that I had a magic wand that I could point at a life and make it a smoking piece of half-raw meat; I wasn't a soldier nor ever wanted to be one nor ever would want—

"O.K., Seventh, come on up."

While we were walking toward them, one of the creatures moved, a tiny shudder, and Cortez flicked the beam of his laser over it with an almost negligent gesture. It made a hand-deep gash across the creature's middle.   It died, like the others, without emitting a sound.

They were not quite as tall as humans, but wider in girth.   They were covered with dark green, almost black fur; white curls where the laser had singed.   They appeared to have three legs and an arm.   The only ornament to their shaggy heads was a mouth, wet black orifice filled with flat black teeth.   They were thoroughly repulsive but their worst feature was not a difference from human beings but a similarity . . . wherever the laser had opened a body cavity, milk-white glistening veined globes and coils of organs spilled out, and their blood was dark clotting red.

"Rogers, take a look.   Taurans or not?"

Rogers knelt by one of the disemboweled creatures and opened a flat plastic box, filled with glittering dissecting tools.   She selected a scalpel.   "One way we might be able to find out."   Doc Wilson watched over her shoulder as she methodically slit the membrane covering several organs.

"Here."   She held up a blackish fibrous mass between two fingers, parody of daintiness through all that armor.

"So?"

"It's grass, Sergeant.   If the Taurans can eat the grass and breathe the air, they certainly found a planet remarkably like their home."   She tossed it away.   "They're animals, Sergeant, just damn animals."

"I don't know," Doc Wilson said.   "Just because they walk around on all fours, threes maybe, and are able to eat grass . . ."

"Well, let's check out the brain."   She found one that had been hit in the head and scraped the superficial black char from the wound.   "Look at that."

It was almost solid bone.   She tugged and ruffled the hair all over the head of another one. "What the hell does it use for sensory organs? No eyes, or ears, or . . ." She stood up. "Nothing in that head but a mouth and ten centimeters of skull. To protect nothing, not a damn thing."

"If I could shrug, I'd shrug," the doctor said. "It doesn't prove anything—a brain doesn't have to look like a mushy walnut and it doesn't have to be in the head. Maybe that skull isn't bone, maybe *that's* the brain, some crystal lattice . . ."

"Yeah, but the stomach's in the right place, and if those aren't intestines I'll eat—"

"Look," Cortez said, "this is all real interesting, but all we need to know is whether that thing's dangerous, then we've gotta move on, we don't have all—"

"They aren't dangerous," Rogers began. "They don't—"

"Medic! DOC!" Somebody was waving his arms, back at the firing line. Doc sprinted back to him, the rest of us following.

"What's wrong?" He had reached back and unclipped his medical kit on the run.

"It's Ho, she's out."

Doc swung open the door on Ho's biomedical monitor. He didn't have to look far. "She's dead."

"Dead?" Cortez said. "What the hell—"

"Just a minute." Doc plugged a jack into the monitor and fiddled with some dials on his kit. "Everybody's biomed readout is stored for twelve hours. I'm running it backwards, should be able to—there!"

"What?"

"Four and a half minutes ago—must have been when you opened fire—"

"Well?"

"Massive cerebral hemorrhage. No . . ." he watched the dials. "No . . . warning, no indication of anything out of the ordinary; blood pressure up, pulse up, but normal under the circumstances . . . nothing to . . . indicate—" He reached down and popped her suit. Her fine oriental features were distorted in a horrible grimace, both gums showing. Sticky fluid ran from under her collapsed eyelids and a trickle of blood still dripped from each ear. Doc Wilson closed the suit back up.

"I've never seen anything like it. It's as if a bomb went off in her skull."

"Oh crap," Rogers said, "she was Rhine-sensitive, wasn't she."

"That's right." Cortez sounded thoughtful. "All right, everybody listen. Platoon leaders, check your platoons and see if anybody's missing, or hurt. Anybody else in Seventh?"

"I . . . I've got a splitting headache, Sarge," Lucky said.

Four others had bad headaches. One of them affirmed that he was slightly Rhine-sensitive. The others didn't know.

"Cortez, I think it's obvious," Doc Wilson said, "that we should give these . . . monsters wide berth, especially shouldn't harm any more of them. Not with five people susceptible to whatever apparently killed Ho."

"Of course, damn it, I don't need anybody to tell me that.   We'd better get moving.   I just filled the captain in on what happened; he agrees that we'd better get as far away from here as we can, before we stop for the night.

"Let's get back in formation and continue on the same bearing.   Fifth Platoon, take over point; Second, come back to the rear.   Everybody else, same as before."

"What about Ho?" Lucky asked.

"She'll be taken care of.   From the ship."

After we'd gone half a click, there was a flash and rolling thunder.   Where Ho had been, came a wispy luminous mushroom cloud boiling up to disappear against the gray sky.

XIII

We stopped for the "night"—actually, the sun wouldn't set for another seventy hours—atop a slight rise some ten clicks from where we had killed the aliens.   But they weren't aliens, I had to remind myself—*we* were.

Two platoons deployed in a ring around the rest of us, and we flopped down exhausted.   Everybody was allowed four hours' sleep and had two hours' guard duty.

Potter came over and sat next to me.   I chinned her frequency.

"Hi, Marygay."

"Oh, William," her voice over the radio was hoarse and cracking.   "God, it's so horrible."

"It's over now—"

"I killed one of them, the first instant, I shot it right in the, in the—"

I put my hand on her knee.   The contact made a plastic click and I jerked it back, visions of machines embracing, copulating.   "Don't feel singled out, Marygay, whatever guilt there is, belongs evenly to all of us . . . but a triple portion for Cor—"

"You privates quit jawin' and get some sleep.   You both pull guard in two hours."

"O.K., Sarge."   Her voice was so sad and tired I couldn't bear it, I felt if I could only touch her I could drain off the sadness like a ground wire draining current but we were each trapped in our own plastic world.

"G'night, William."

"Night."   It's almost impossible to get sexually excited inside a suit, with the relief tube and all the silver chloride sensors poking you, but somehow this was my body's response to the emotional impotence, maybe remembering more pleasant sleeps with Marygay, maybe feeling that in the midst of all this death, personal death could be soon, cranking up the procreative derrick for one last try . . . lovely thoughts like this and I fell asleep and dreamed that I was a machine, mimicking the functions of life, creaking and clanking my clumsy way through the world, people too polite to say anything but giggling behind my back, and the little man who sat inside my head pulling the levers and clutches and watching the dials, he was hopelessly mad and was storing up hurts for the day—

"Mandella—wake up, damn it, your shift!"

I shuffled over to my place on the perimeter to watch for God knows what . . . but I was so weary I couldn't keep my eyes open. Finally I tongued a stimtab, knowing I'd pay for it later.

For over an hour I sat there, scanning my sector left, right, near, far; the scene never changing, not even a breath of wind to stir the grass.

Then suddenly the grass parted and one of the three-legged creatures was right in front of me. I raised my finger but didn't squeeze.

"Movement!"

"Movement!"

"HOLD YOUR FIRE. Don't shoot!"

"Movement."

"Movement." I looked left and right and as far as I could see, every perimeter guard had one of the blind dumb creatures standing right in front of him.

Maybe the drug I'd taken to stay awake made me more sensitive to whatever they did. My scalp crawled and I felt a formless *thing* in my mind, the feeling you get when somebody has said something and you didn't quite hear it, want to respond but the opportunity to ask him to repeat it is gone.

The creature sat back on its haunches, leaning forward on the one front leg. Big green bear with a withered arm. Its power threaded through my mind, spiderwebs, echo of night terrors, trying to communicate, trying to destroy me, I couldn't know.

"All right, everybody on the perimeter, fall back, slow. Don't make any quick gestures . . . anybody got a headache or anything?"

"Sergeant, this is Hollister." Lucky.

"They're trying to say something . . . I can almost . . . no, just—"

"Well?"

"All I can get is that they think we're, . . . think we're . . . well, *funny*. They aren't afraid."

"You mean the one in front of you isn't—"

"No, the feeling comes from all of them, they're all thinking the same thing. Don't ask me how I know, I just do."

"Maybe they thought it was funny, what they did to Ho."

"Maybe. I don't feel like they're dangerous. Just curious about us."

"Sergeant, this is Bohrs."

"Yeah."

"The Taurans have been here at least a year—maybe they've learned how to communicate with these . . . overgrown teddybears. They might be spying on us, might be sending back—"

"I don't think they'd show themselves, if that were the case," Lucky said. "They can obviously hide from us pretty well when they want to."

"Anyhow," Cortez said, "if they're spies, the damage has been done. Don't think it'd be smart to take any action against them.   I know you'd all like to see 'em dead for what they did to Ho, so would I, but we'd better be careful.''

I didn't want to see them dead, but I'd just as soon not see them in any condition. I was walking backwards slowly, toward the middle of camp.   The creature didn't seem disposed to follow.   Maybe he just knew we were surrounded.   He was pulling up grass with his arm and munching.

"O.K., all of you platoon leaders, wake everybody up, get a roll count.   Let me know if anybody's been hurt.   Tell your people we're moving out in one minute.''

I don't know what Cortez expected, but of course the creatures just followed right along.   They didn't keep us surrounded; just had twenty or thirty following us all the time.   Not the same ones, either.   Individuals would saunter away, new ones would join the parade.   It was pretty obvious that *they* weren't going to tire out.

We were each allowed one stimtab.   Without it, no one could have marched an hour.   A second pill would have been welcome after the edge started to wear off, but the mathematics of the situation forbade it: we were still thirty clicks from the enemy base; fifteen hours' marching at the least.   And though one could stay awake and energetic for a hundred hours on the 'tabs, aberrations of judgment and perception snowballed after the second 'tab, until *in extremis* the most bizarre hallucinations would be taken at face value, and a person would fidget for hours, deciding whether to have breakfast.

Under artificial stimulation, the company traveled with great energy for the first six hours, was slowing by the seventh, and ground to an exhausted halt after nine hours and nineteen kilometers.   The teddybears had never lost sight of us and, according to Lucky, had never stopped "broadcasting.''   Cortez's decision was that we would stop for seven hours, each platoon taking one hour of perimeter guard.   I was never so glad to have been in the Seventh Platoon, as we stood guard the last shift and thus were the only ones to get six hours of uninterrupted sleep.

In the few moments I lay awake after finally lying down, the thought came to me that the next time I closed my eyes could well be the last.   And partly because of the drug hangover, mostly because of the past day's horrors, I found that I really just didn't give a damn.

XIV

Our first contact with the Taurans came during my shift.

The teddybears were still there when I woke up and replaced Doc Jones on guard. They'd gone back to their original formation, one in front of each guard position. The one who was waiting for me seemed a little larger than normal, but otherwise looked just like all the others.   All the grass had been cropped where he was sitting, so he occasionally made forays to the left or right.   But he always returned to sit right in front of me, you would say staring if he had had anything to stare with.

We had been facing each other for about fifteen minutes when Cortez's voice rumbled:

"Awright everybody wake up and get hid!"

I followed instinct and flopped to the ground and rolled into a tall stand of grass.

"Enemy vessel overhead." His voice was almost laconic.

Strictly speaking, it wasn't really overhead, but rather passing somewhat east of us. It was moving slowly, maybe a hundred clicks per hour, and looked like a broomstick surrounded by a dirty soap bubble. The creature riding it was a little more human-looking than the teddybears, but still no prize. I cranked my image amplifier up to forty log two for a closer look.

He had two arms and two legs, but his waist was so small you could encompass it with both hands. Under the tiny waist was a large horseshoe-shaped pelvic structure nearly a meter wide, from which dangled two long skinny legs with no apparent knee joint. Above that waist his body swelled out again, to a chest no smaller than the huge pelvis. His arms looked surprisingly human, except that they were too long and undermuscled. There were too many fingers on his hands. Shoulderless, neckless; his head was a nightmarish growth that swelled like a goiter from his massive chest. Two eyes that looked like clusters of fish eggs, a bundle of tassles instead of a nose, and a rigidly open hole that might have been a mouth sitting low down where his Adam's apple should have been. Evidently the soap bubble contained an amenable environment, as he was wearing absolutely nothing except a ridged hide that looked like skin submerged too long in hot water, then dyed a pale orange. "He" had no external genitalia, nor anything that might hint of mammary glands.

Obviously, he either didn't see us, or thought we were part of the herd of teddybears. He never looked back at us, but just continued in the same direction we were headed, .05 rad east of north.

"Might as well go back to sleep now, if you can sleep after looking at *that* thing. We move out at 0435." Forty minutes.

Because of the planet's opaque cloud cover, there had been no way to tell, from space, what the enemy base looked like or how big it was. We only knew its position, the same way we knew the position the scoutships were supposed to land on. So it could easily have been underwater too, or underground.

But some of the drones were reconnaissance ships as well as decoys; and in their mock attacks on the base, one managed to get close enough to take a picture. Captain Stott beamed down a diagram of the place to Cortez—the only one with a visor in his suit—when we were five clicks from the base's "radio" position. We stopped and he called all of the platoon leaders in with the Seventh Platoon to confer. Two teddybears loped in, too. We tried to ignore them.

"O.K., the captain sent down some pictures of our objective. I'm going to draw a map; you platoon leaders copy." They took pads and styli out of their leg pockets, while Cortez unrolled a large plastic mat. He gave it a shake to randomize any residual charge, and turned on his stylus.

"Now, we're coming from this direction." He put an arrow at the bottom of the sheet. "First thing we'll hit is this row of huts, probably billets, or bunkers, but who the hell knows . . . our initial objective is to destroy these buildings—the whole base is on a flat plain; there's no way we could really sneak by them."

"Potter here. Why can't we jump over them?"

"Yeah, we could do that, and wind up completely surrounded, cut to ribbons. We take the buildings.

"After we do that . . . all I can say is that we'll have to think on our feet. From the aerial reconnaissance, we can figure out the function of only a couple of buildings—and that stinks. We might wind up wasting a lot of time demolishing the equivalent of an enlisted man's bar, ignoring a huge logistic computer because it looks like . . . a garbage dump or something."

"Mandella here," I said. "Isn't there a spaceport of some kind—seems to me we ought to . . ."

"I'll *get* to that, damn it. There's a ring of these huts all around the camp, so we've got to break through somewhere. This place'll be closest, less chance of giving away our position before we attack.

"There's nothing in the whole place that actually looks like a weapon. That doesn't mean anything, though; you could hide a bevawatt laser in each of those huts.

"Now, about five hundred meters from the huts, in the middle of the base, we'll come to this big flower-shaped structure." Cortez drew a large symmetrical shape that looked like the outline of a flower with seven petals. "What the hell this is, your guess is as good as mine. There's only one of them, though, so we don't damage it any more than we have to. Which means . . . we blast it to splinters if I think it's dangerous.

"Now, as far as your spaceport, Mandella, is concerned—there just isn't one. Nothing.

"That cruiser the *Hope* caulked had probably been left in orbit, like ours has to be. If they have any equivalent of a scoutship, or drone missiles, they're either not kept here or they're well hidden."

"Bohrs here. Then what did they attack with, while we were coming down from orbit?"

"I wish we knew, Private.

"Obviously, we don't have any way of estimating their numbers, not directly. Recon pictures failed to show a single Tauran on the grounds of the base. Meaning nothing, because it *is* an alien environment. Indirectly, though . . . we can count the number of broomsticks.

"There are fifty-one huts, and each has at most one broomstick. Four don't have one parked outside, but we located three at various other parts of the base. Maybe this indicates that there are fifty-one Taurans, one of whom was outside the base when the picture was taken."

"Keating here. Or fifty-one officers."

"That's right—maybe fifty thousand infantrymen stacked in one of these buildings. No way to tell. Maybe ten Taurans, each with five broomsticks, to use according to his mood.

"We've got one thing in our favor, and that's communications. They evidently use a frequency modulation of megahertz electromagnetic radiation."

"Radio!"

"That's right, whoever you are. Identify yourself when you speak. So, it's quite possible that they can't detect our phased-neutrino communications. Also, just prior to the attack, the *Hope* is going to deliver a nice dirty fission bomb; detonate it in the upper atmosphere right over the base. That'll restrict them to line-of-sight communications for some time; even those will be full of static."

"Why don't . . . Tate here . . . why don't they just drop the bomb right in their laps? Would save us a lot of—"

"That doesn't even deserve an answer, Private. But the answer is, they might. And you better hope they don't. If they caulk the base, it'll be for the safety of the *Hope*. *After* we've attacked, and probably before we're far enough away for it to make much difference.

"We keep that from happening by doing a good job. We have to reduce the base to where it can no longer function; at the same time, leave as much intact as possible. And take one prisoner."

"Potter here. You mean, at least one prisoner."

"I mean what I say. One only. Potter . . . you're relieved of your platoon. Send Chavez up."

"All right, Sergeant." The relief in her voice was unmistakable.

Cortez continued with his map and instructions. There was one other building whose function was pretty obvious; it had a large steerable dish antenna on top. We were to destroy it as soon as the grenadiers got in range.

The attack plan was very loose. Our signal to begin would be the flash of the fission bomb. At the same time, several drones would converge on the base, so we could see what their antispacecraft defenses were. We would try to reduce the effectiveness of those defenses without destroying them completely.

Immediately after the bomb and the drones, the grenadiers would vaporize a line of seven huts. Everybody would break through the hole into the base . . . and what would happen after that was anybody's guess.

Ideally, we'd sweep from that end of the base to the other, destroying certain targets, caulking all but one Tauran. But that was unlikely to happen, as it depended on the Taurans' offering very little resistance.

On the other hand, if the Taurans showed obvious superiority from the beginning, Cortez would give the order to scatter: everybody had a different compass bearing for retreat—we'd blossom out in all directions, the survivors to rendezvous in a valley some forty clicks east of the base. Then we'd see about a return engagement, after the *Hope* softened the base up a bit.

"One last thing," Cortez rasped. "Maybe some of you feel the way Potter evidently does, maybe some of your men feel that way . . . that we ought to go easy, not make this so much of a bloodbath. Mercy is a luxury, a weakness we can't afford to indulge in at this stage of the war. *All* we know about the enemy is that they have killed seven hundred and ninety-eight humans. They haven't shown any restraint in attacking our cruisers, and it'd be foolish to expect any this time, this first ground action.

"*They* are responsible for the lives of all of your comrades who died in training, and for Ho, and for all the others who are surely going to die today.   I can't *understand* anybody who wants to spare them.   But that doesn't make any difference.   You have your orders, and what the hell, you might as well know, all of you have a post-hypnotic suggestion that I will trigger by a phrase, just before the battle.   It will make your job easier."

"Sergeant . . ."

"Shut up.   We're short on time; get back to your platoons and brief them.   We move out in five minutes."

The platoon leaders returned to their men, leaving Cortez and the ten of us, plus three teddybears, milling around, getting in the way.

XV

We took the last five clicks very carefully, sticking to the highest grass, running across occasional clearings.   When we were five hundred meters from where the base was supposed to be, Cortez took the Third Platoon forward to scout, while the rest of us laid low.

Cortez's voice came over the general freak: "Looks pretty much like we expected.   Advance in a file, crawling.   When you get to the Third Platoon, follow your squad leader to the left, or right."

We did that and wound up with a string of eighty-three people in a line roughly perpendicular to the direction of attack.   We were pretty well hidden, except for the dozen or so teddybears that mooched along the line munching grass.

There was no sign of life inside the base.   All of the buildings were windowless, and a uniform shiny white.   The huts that were our first objective were large featureless half-buried eggs, some sixty meters apart.   Cortez assigned one to each grenadier.

We were broken into three fire teams: Team A consisted of platoons Two, Four, and Six; Team B was One, Three, and Five; the command platoon was Team C.

"Less than a minute now—filters down!—when I say 'fire', grenadiers take out your targets.   God help you if you miss."

There was a sound like a giant's belch and a stream of five or six iridescent bubbles floated up from the flower-shaped building.   They rose with increasing speed to where they were almost out of sight, then shot off to the south, over our heads.   The ground was suddenly bright and for the first time in a long time, I saw my shadow, a long one pointed north.   The bomb had gone off prematurely. I just had time to think that it didn't make too much difference; it'd still make alphabet soup out of their communications—

"Drones!"   A ship came screaming in just above tree level, and a bubble was in the air to meet it.   When they contacted, the bubble popped and the drone exploded into a million tiny fragments.   Another one came from the opposite side and suffered the same fate.

"FIRE!"   Seven bright glares of 500-microton grenades and a sustained concussion that I'm sure would have killed an unprotected man.

"Filters up."   Gray haze of smoke and dust.   Clods of dirt falling with a sound like heavy raindrops.

"Listen up:

> " *'Scots, wha hae wi' Wallace bled;*
> *Scots, wham Bruce has aften led,*
> *Welcome to your gory bed,*
> *Or to victory!'* "

I hardly heard him, for trying to keep track of what was going on in my skull. I knew it was just post-hypnotic suggestion, even remembered the session in Missouri when they'd implanted it, but that didn't make it any less compelling.   My mind reeled under the strong pseudo-memories; shaggy hulks that were Taurans—not at all what we now knew they looked like—boarding a colonist's vessel, eating babies while mothers watched in screaming terror—the colonists never took babies; they wouldn't stand the acceleration—then raping the women to death with huge veined purple members—ridiculous that they would feel desire for humans—holding the men down while they plucked flesh from their living bodies and gobbled it . . . a hundred grisly details as sharply remembered as the events of a minute ago, ridiculously overdone and logically absurd; but while my conscious mind was reflecting the silliness, somewhere much deeper, down in that sleeping giant where we keep our real motives and morals, something was thirsting for alien blood, secure in the conviction that the noblest thing a man could do would be to die killing one of those horrible monsters . . .

I knew it was all purest soya, and I hated the men who had taken such obscene liberties with my mind, but still I could hear my teeth grinding, feel cheeks frozen in a spastic grin, bloodlust . . . a teddybear walked in front of me, looking dazed. I started to raise my laserfinger, but somebody beat me to it and the creature's head exploded in a cloud of gray splinters and blood.

Lucky groaned, half-whining, "Dirty . . . filthy bastards."   Lasers flared and crisscrossed and all of the teddybears fell dead.

"*Watch* it, damn it," Cortez screamed.   "*Aim* those things— they aren't toys! "Team A, move out—into the craters to cover B."

Somebody was laughing and sobbing.   "What the crap is wrong with *you*, Petrov?"   First time I could remember Cortez cussing.

I twisted around and saw Petrov, behind and to my left, lying in a shallow hole, digging frantically with both hands, crying and gurgling.

"Crap," Cortez said.   "Team B! past the craters ten meters, get down in a line.   Team C—into the craters with A."

I scrambled up and covered the hundred meters in twelve amplified strides.   The craters were practically large enough to hide a scoutship, some ten meters in diameter.   I jumped to the opposite side of the hole and landed next to a fellow named Chin.   He didn't even look around when I landed, just kept scanning the base for signs of life.

"Team A—past Team B ten meters, down in line."   Just as he finished, the building in front of us burped and a salvo of the bubbles fanned out toward our lines.   Most people saw it coming and got down, but Chin was just getting up to make his rush and stepped right into one.

It grazed the top of his helmet, and disappeared with a faint pop.   He took one step backwards and toppled over the edge of the crater, trailing an arc of blood and brains.   Lifeless, spreadeagled, he slid halfway to the bottom, shoveling dirt into the perfectly symmetrical hole where the bubble had chewed through plastic, hair, skin, bone and brain indiscriminately.

"Everybody hold it.   Platoon leaders, casualty report . . . check . . . check, check . . . check, check, check . . . check.   We have three deaders.   Wouldn't be *any* if you'd have kept low.   So everybody grab dirt when you hear that thing go off.   Team A, complete the rush."

They completed the maneuver without incident.   "O.K.   Team C, rush to where B . . . hold it!   Down!"

Everybody was already hugging the ground.   The bubbles slid by in a smooth arc about two meters off the ground.   They went serenely over our heads and, except for one that made toothpicks out of a tree, disappeared in the distance.

"B, rush past A ten meters.   C, take over B's place.   You B grenadiers see if you can reach the Flower."

Two grenades tore up the ground thirty or forty meters from the structure.   In a good imitation of panic, it started belching out a continuous stream of bubbles— still, none coming lower than two meters off the ground.   We kept hunched down and continued to advance.

Suddenly, a seam appeared in the building, widened to the size of a large door, and Taurans came swarming out.

"Grenadiers, hold your fire.   B team, laser fire to the left and right, keep'em bunched up.   A and C, rush down the center."

One Tauran died trying to run through a laser beam.   The others stayed where they were.

In a suit, it's pretty awkward to run and try to keep your head down, at the same time.   You have to go from side to side, like a skater getting started; otherwise you'll be airborne.   At least one person, somebody in A team, bounced too high and suffered the same fate as Chin.

I was feeling pretty fenced-in and trapped, with a wall of laser fire on each side and a low ceiling that meant death to touch.   But in spite of myself, I felt happy, euphoric at finally getting the chance to kill some of those villainous baby-eaters.

They weren't fighting back, except for the rather ineffective bubbles—obviously not designed as an anti-personnel weapon—and they didn't retreat back into the building, either.   They just milled around, about a hundred of them, and watched us get closer.   A couple of grenades would caulk them all, but I guess Cortez was thinking about the prisoner.

"O.K., when I say 'go', we're going to flank 'em. B team will hold fire . . . Second and Fourth to the right, Sixth and Seventh to the left. B team will move forward in line to box them in.

"Go!" We peeled off to the left. As soon as the lasers stopped, the Taurans bolted, running in a group on a collision course with our flank.

"A Team, down and fire! Don't shoot until you're sure of your aim—if you miss you might hit a friendly. And fer Chris'sake save me one!"

It was a horrifying sight, that herd of monsters bearing down on us. They were running in great leaps—the bubbles avoiding them—and they all looked like the one we saw earlier, riding the broomstick; naked except for an almost transparent sphere around their whole bodies, that moved along with them. The right flank started firing, picking off individuals in the rear of the pack.

Suddenly a laser flared through the Taurans from the other side, somebody missing his mark. There was a horrible scream and I looked down the line to see someone, I think it was Perry, writhing on the ground, right hand over the smoldering stump of his left arm, seared off just below the elbow. Blood sprayed through his fingers and the suit, its camouflage circuits scrambled, flickered black-white-jungle-desert-green-gray. I don't know how long I stared—long enough for the medic to run over and start giving aid—but when I looked up the Taurans were almost on top of me.

My first shot was wild and high, but it grazed the top of the leading Tauran's protective bubble. The bubble disappeared and the monster stumbled and fell to the ground, jerking spasmodically. Foam gushed out of his mouth-hole, first white, then streaked with red. With one last jerk he became rigid and twisted backwards, almost to the shape of a horseshoe. His long scream, a high-pitched whistle, stopped just as his comrades trampled over him and I hated myself for smiling.

It was slaughter, even though our flank was outnumbered five to one. They kept coming without faltering, even when they had to climb over the drift of bodies and parts of bodies that piled up high, parallel to our flank. The ground between us was slick red with Tauran blood—all God's children got hemoglobin—and, like the teddybears, their guts looked pretty much like guts to my untrained eye. My helmet reverberated with hysterical laughter while we cut them to gory chunks. I almost didn't hear Cortez.

"Hold your fire—I said HOLD IT damn it! *Catch* a couple of the bastards, they won't hurt you."

I stopped shooting and eventually so did everybody else. When the next Tauran jumped over the smoking pile of meat in front of me, I dove to try to tackle him around those spindly legs.

It was like hugging a big, slippery balloon. When I tried to drag him down, he just popped out of my arms and kept running.

We managed to stop one of them by the simple expedient of piling half-a-dozen people on top of him. By that time the others had run through our line and were headed for the row of large cylindrical tanks that Cortez had said were probably for storage. A little door had opened in the base of each one.

"We've *got* our prisoner," Cortez shouted. *"Kill!"*

They were fifty meters away and running hard, difficult targets. Lasers slashed around them, bobbing high and low. One fell, sliced in two, but the others, about ten of them, kept going and were almost to the doors when the grenadiers started firing.

They were still loaded with 500-mike bombs, but a near miss wasn't enough— the concussion would just send them flying, unhurt in their bubbles.

"The buildings! Get the damn buildings!" The grenadiers raised their aim and let fly, but the bombs only seemed to scorch the white outside of the structures until, by chance, one landed in a door. That split the building just as if it had a seam; the two halves popped away and a cloud of machinery flew into the air, accompanied by a huge pale flame that rolled up and disappeared in an instant. Then the others all concentrated on the doors, except for potshots at some of the Taurans; not so much to get them as to blow them away before they could get inside. They seemed awfully eager.

All this time, we were trying to get the Taurans with laser fire, while they weaved and bounced around trying to get into the structures. We moved in as close to them as we could without putting ourselves in danger from the grenade blasts— that was still too far away for good aim.

Still, we were getting them one by one, and managed to destroy four of the seven buildings. Then, when there were only two aliens left, a nearby grenade blast flung one of them to within a few meters of a door. He dove in and several grenadiers fired salvos after him, but they all fell short, or detonated harmlessly on the side. Bombs were falling all around, making an awful racket, but the sound was suddenly drowned out by a great sigh, like a giant's intake of breath, and where the building had been was a thick cylindrical cloud of smoke, solid-looking, dwindling away into the stratosphere, straight as if laid down by a ruler. The other Tauran had been right at the base of the cylinder; I could see pieces of him flying. A second later, a shock wave hit us and I rolled helplessly, pinwheeling, to smash into the pile of Tauran bodies and roll beyond.

I picked myself up and panicked for a second when I saw there was blood all over my suit—when I realized it was only alien blood, I relaxed but felt unclean.

"Catch the bastard! Catch him!" In the confusion, the Tauran—now the only one left alive—had got free and was running for the grass. One platoon was chasing after him, losing ground, but then all of B Team ran over and cut him off. I jogged over to join in the fun.

There were four people on top of him, and fifty people watching.

"Spread out, damn it! There might be a thousand more of them waiting to get us in one place." We dispersed, grumbling. By unspoken agreement we were all sure that there were no more live Taurans on the face of the planet.

Cortez was walking toward the prisoner while I backed away. Suddenly the four men collapsed in a pile on top of the creature . . . even from my distance I could see the foam spouting from his mouth-hole. His bubble had popped. Suicide.

"Damn!" Cortez was right there. "Get off that bastard." The four men got off and Cortez used his laser to slice the monster into a dozen quivering chunks. Heartwarming sight.

"That's all right, though, we'll find another one—everybody!   Back in the arrowhead formation.   Combat assault, on the Flower."

Well, we assaulted the Flower, which had evidently run out of ammunition—it was still belching, but no bubbles—and it was empty.   We just scurried up ramps and through corridors, fingers at the ready, like kids playing soldier.   There was nobody home.

The same lack of response at the antenna installation, the "Salami," and twenty other major buildings, as well as the forty-four perimeter huts still intact.   So we had "captured" dozens of buildings, mostly of incomprehensible purpose, but failed in our main mission; capturing a Tauran for the xenologists to experiment with. Oh well, they could have all the bits and pieces of the creatures they'd ever want. That was something.

After we'd combed every last square centimeter of the base, a scoutship came in with the real exploration crew, Star Fleet scientists.   Cortez said, "All right, snap out of it," and the hypnotic compulsion fell away.

At first it was pretty grim.   A lot of the people, like Lucky and Marygay, almost went crazy with the memories of bloody murder multiplied a hundred times.   Cortez ordered everybody to take a sed-tab, two for the ones most upset.   I took two without being specifically ordered to do so.

Because it *was* murder, unadorned butchery—once we had the anti-spacecraft weapon doped out, we weren't in any danger.   The Taurans didn't seem to have any conception of person-to-person fighting.   We just herded them up and slaughtered them, in the first encounter between mankind and another intelligent species. What might have happened if we had sat down and tried to communicate?   Maybe it was the second encounter, counting the teddybears.   But they got the same treatment.

I spent a long time after that, telling myself over and over that it hadn't been *me* who so gleefully carved up those frightened, stampeding creatures.   Back in the Twentieth Century, they established to everybody's satisfaction that "I was just following orders" was an inadequate excuse for inhuman conduct . . . but what can you do when the orders come from deep down in that puppet master of the unconscious?

Worst of all was the feeling that perhaps my actions weren't all that inhuman. Ancestors only a few generations back would have done the same thing, even to their fellowmen, without any hypnotic conditioning.

So I was disgusted with the human race, disgusted with the army, and horrified at the prospect of living with myself for another century or so . . . well, there was always brainwipe.

The ship that the lone Tauran survivor had escaped in had got away, clean, the bulk of the planet shielding it from *Earth's Hope* while it dropped into Aleph's collapsar field.   Escaped to home, I guessed, wherever that was, to report what twenty men with hand-weapons could do to a hundred fleeing on foot, unarmed.

I suspected that the next time humans met Taurans in ground combat, we would be more evenly matched.   And I was right.